big NATE

I CAN'T TAKE IT!

More

big NATE

adventures from

LINCOLN PEIRCE

Big Nate From the Top

Big Nate Out Loud

Big Nate and Friends

Big Nate Makes the Grade

Big Nate All Work and No Play

Big Nate: Game On!

Big Nate: Great Minds Think Alike

Big Nate: The Crowd Goes Wild!

Big Nate: Say Good-bye to Dork City

Big Nate's Greatest Hits

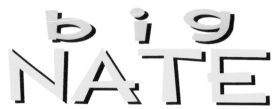

big NATE
I CAN'T TAKE IT!

by LINCOLN PEIRCE

**Andrews McMeel
Publishing**®

Kansas City • Sydney • London

Andrews McMeel Publishing, LLC
an Andrews McMeel Universal company
1130 Walnut Street, Kansas City, Missouri 64106

www.andrewsmcmeel.com

ISBN: 978-1-4494-7398-3

Library of Congress Control Number: 2013933500

Big Nate can be viewed on the Internet at
www.gocomics.com/big_nate

ATTENTION: SCHOOLS AND BUSINESSES

Andrews McMeel books are available at quantity discounts with bulk purchase for educational, business, or sales promotional use. For information, please e-mail the Andrews McMeel Publishing Special Sales Department:
specialsales@amuniversal.com.

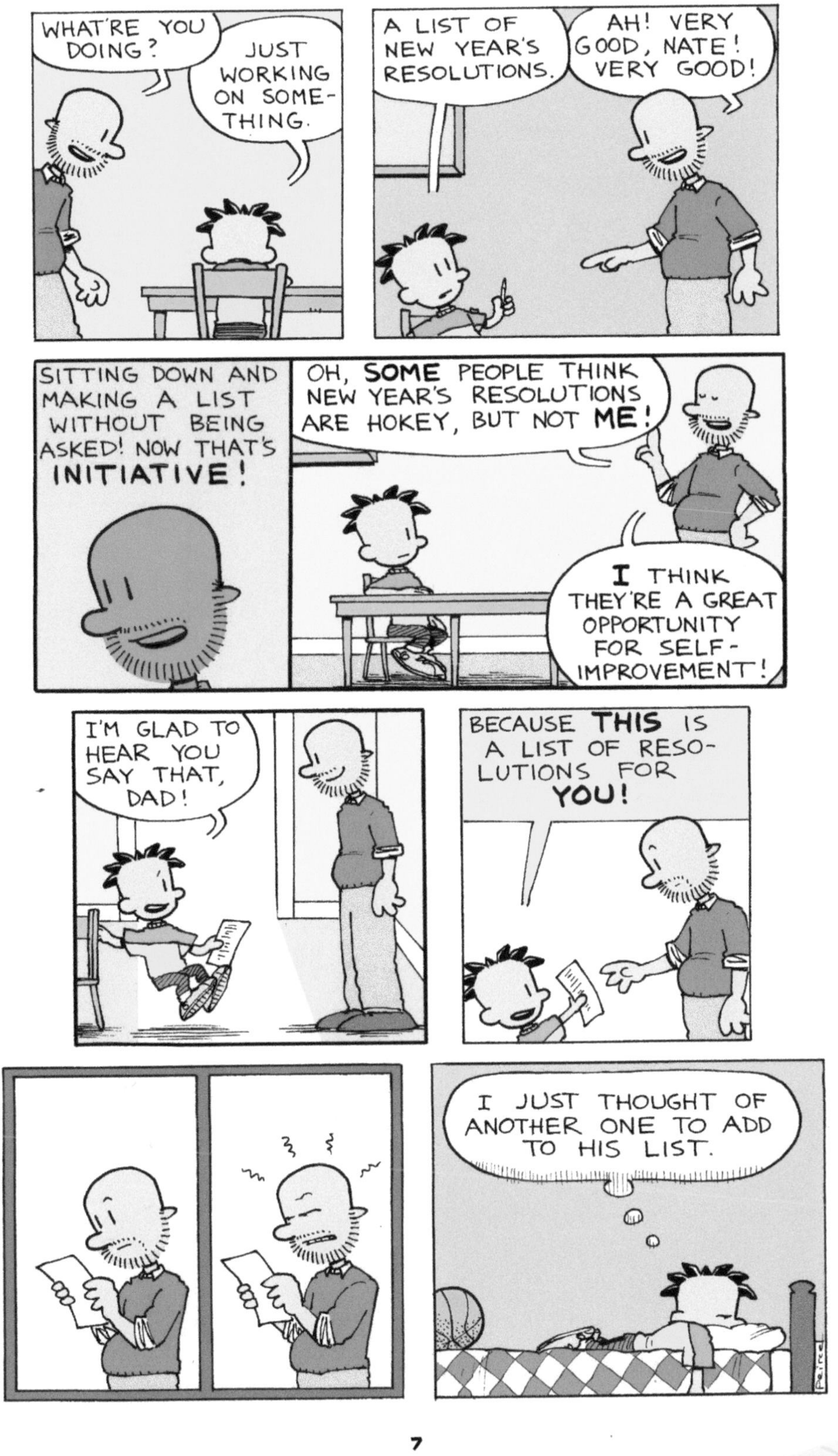
WHAT'RE YOU DOING?
JUST WORKING ON SOME-THING.
A LIST OF NEW YEAR'S RESOLUTIONS.
AH! VERY GOOD, NATE! VERY GOOD!
SITTING DOWN AND MAKING A LIST WITHOUT BEING ASKED! NOW THAT'S INITIATIVE!
OH, SOME PEOPLE THINK NEW YEAR'S RESOLUTIONS ARE HOKEY, BUT NOT ME!
I THINK THEY'RE A GREAT OPPORTUNITY FOR SELF-IMPROVEMENT!
I'M GLAD TO HEAR YOU SAY THAT, DAD!
BECAUSE THIS IS A LIST OF RESO-LUTIONS FOR YOU!
I JUST THOUGHT OF ANOTHER ONE TO ADD TO HIS LIST.

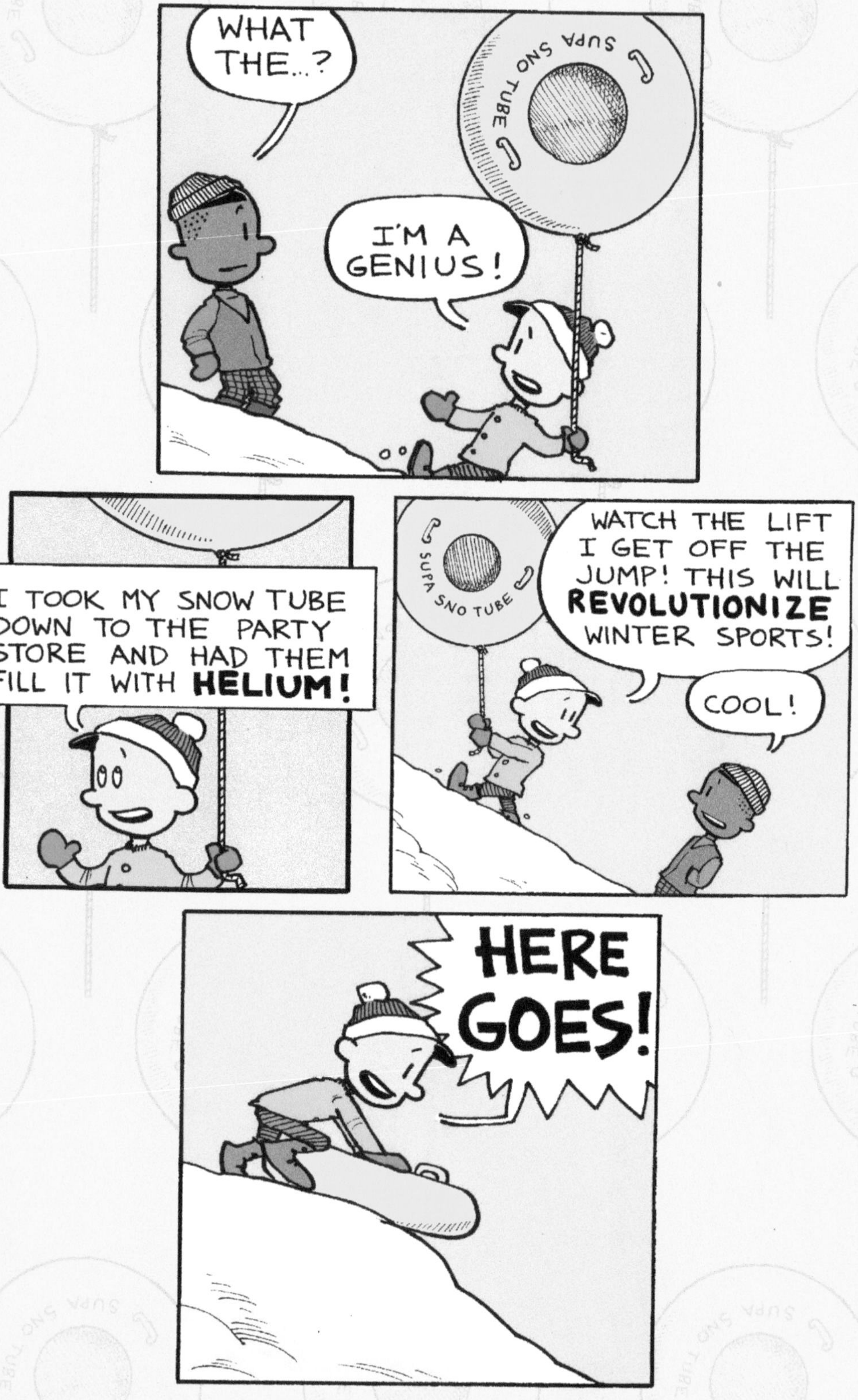
WHAT THE...?
SUPA SNO TUBE
I'M A GENIUS!
I TOOK MY SNOW TUBE DOWN TO THE PARTY STORE AND HAD THEM FILL IT WITH **HELIUM!**
SUPA SNO TUBE
WATCH THE LIFT I GET OFF THE JUMP! THIS WILL **REVOLUTIONIZE** WINTER SPORTS!
COOL!
HERE GOES!

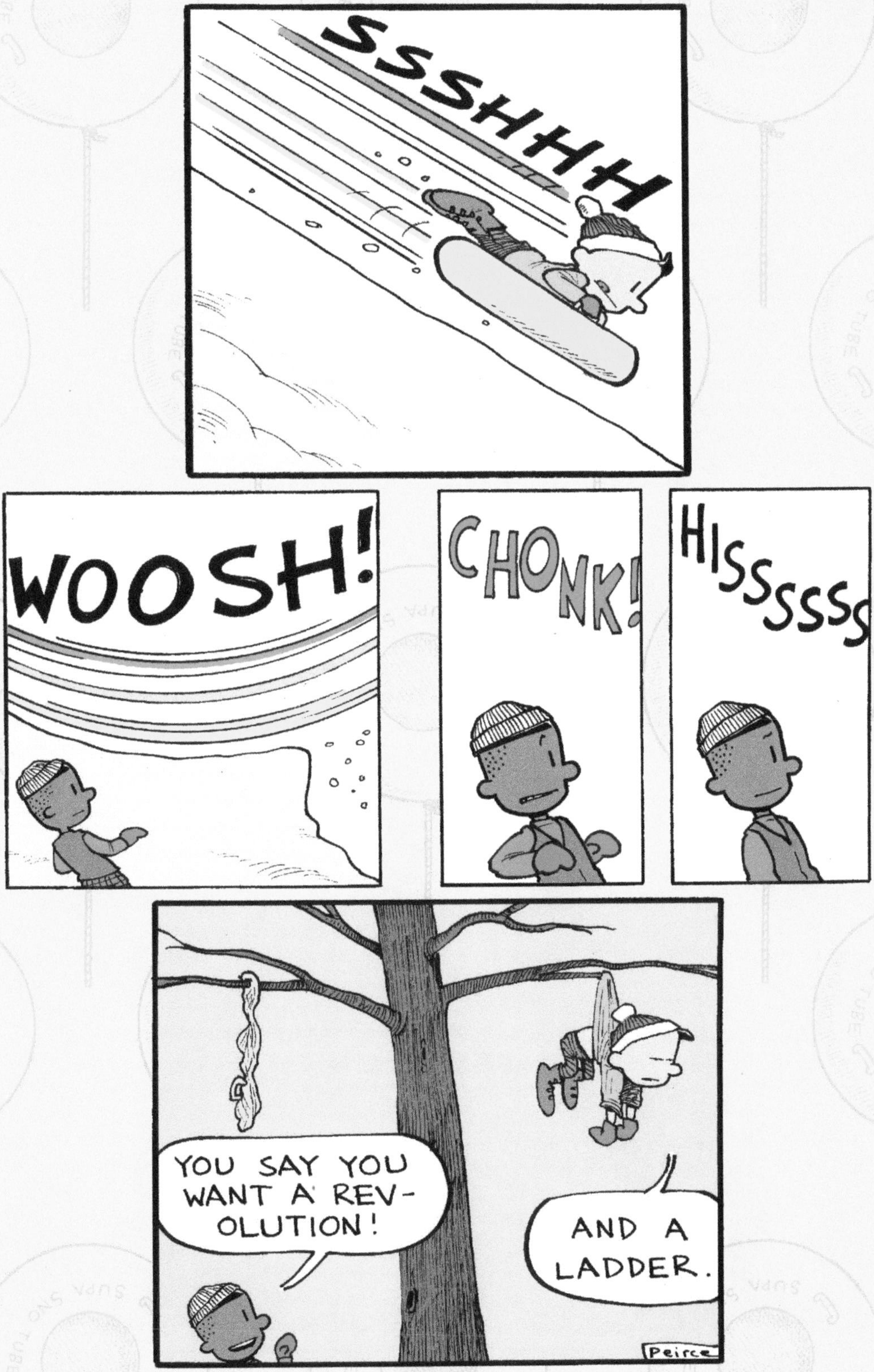
SSSHHH
WOOSH!
CHONK!
HISSSSSS
YOU SAY YOU WANT A REV-OLUTION!
AND A LADDER.
Peirce

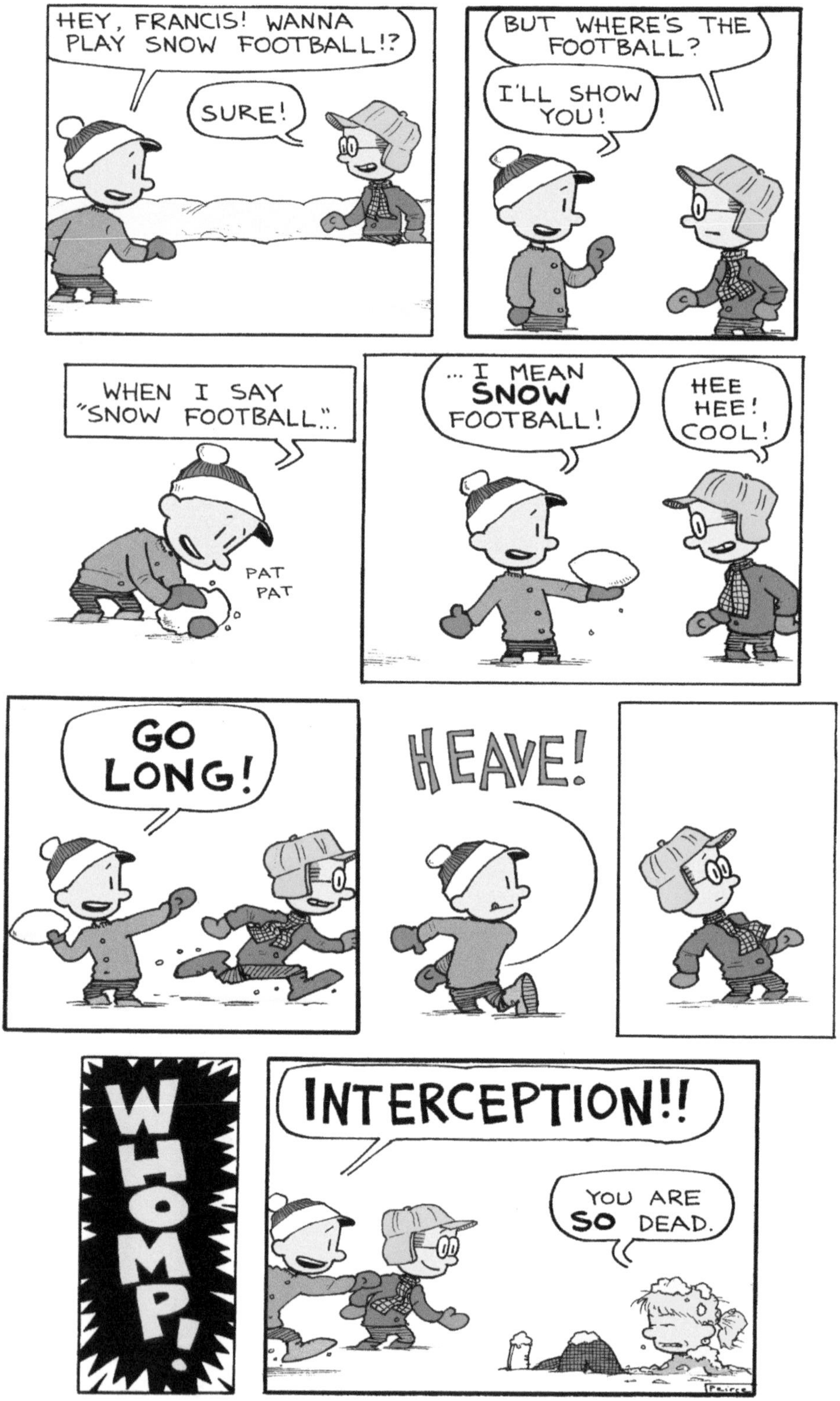
HEY, FRANCIS! WANNA PLAY SNOW FOOTBALL!?
SURE!
BUT WHERE'S THE FOOTBALL?
I'LL SHOW YOU!
WHEN I SAY "SNOW FOOTBALL"...
PAT PAT
... I MEAN **SNOW** FOOTBALL!
HEE HEE! COOL!
GO LONG!
HEAVE!
WHOMP!
INTERCEPTION!!
YOU ARE **SO** DEAD.

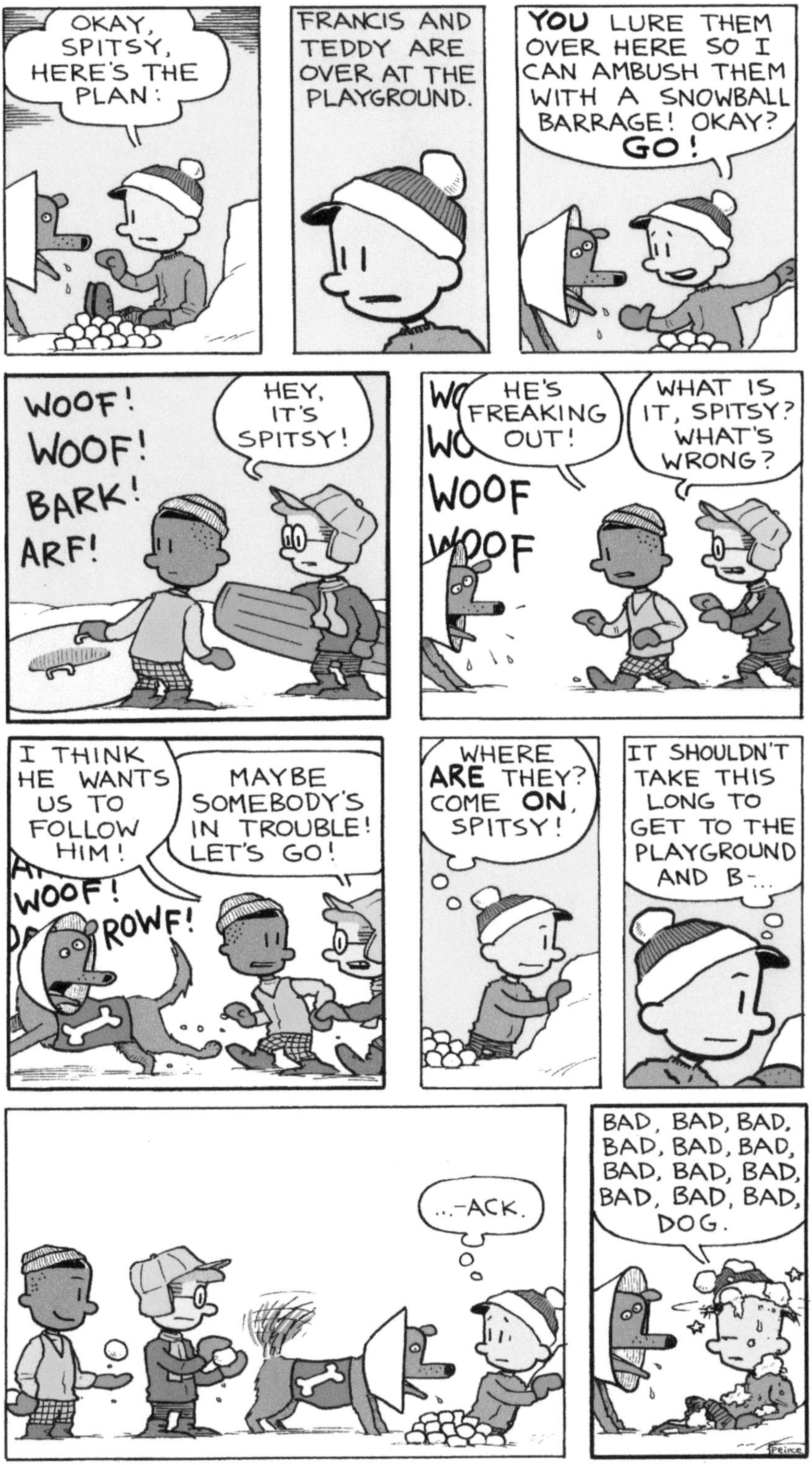
OKAY, SPITSY, HERE'S THE PLAN:
FRANCIS AND TEDDY ARE OVER AT THE PLAYGROUND.
YOU LURE THEM OVER HERE SO I CAN AMBUSH THEM WITH A SNOWBALL BARRAGE! OKAY? GO!
WOOF! WOOF! BARK! ARF!
HEY, IT'S SPITSY!
WOOF WOOF
HE'S FREAKING OUT!
WHAT IS IT, SPITSY? WHAT'S WRONG?
I THINK HE WANTS US TO FOLLOW HIM!
MAYBE SOMEBODY'S IN TROUBLE! LET'S GO!
WOOF!
ROWF!
WHERE ARE THEY? COME ON, SPITSY!
IT SHOULDN'T TAKE THIS LONG TO GET TO THE PLAYGROUND AND B-...
...-ACK.
BAD, BAD, BAD, BAD, BAD, BAD, BAD, BAD, BAD, BAD, BAD, BAD, DOG.
Peirce

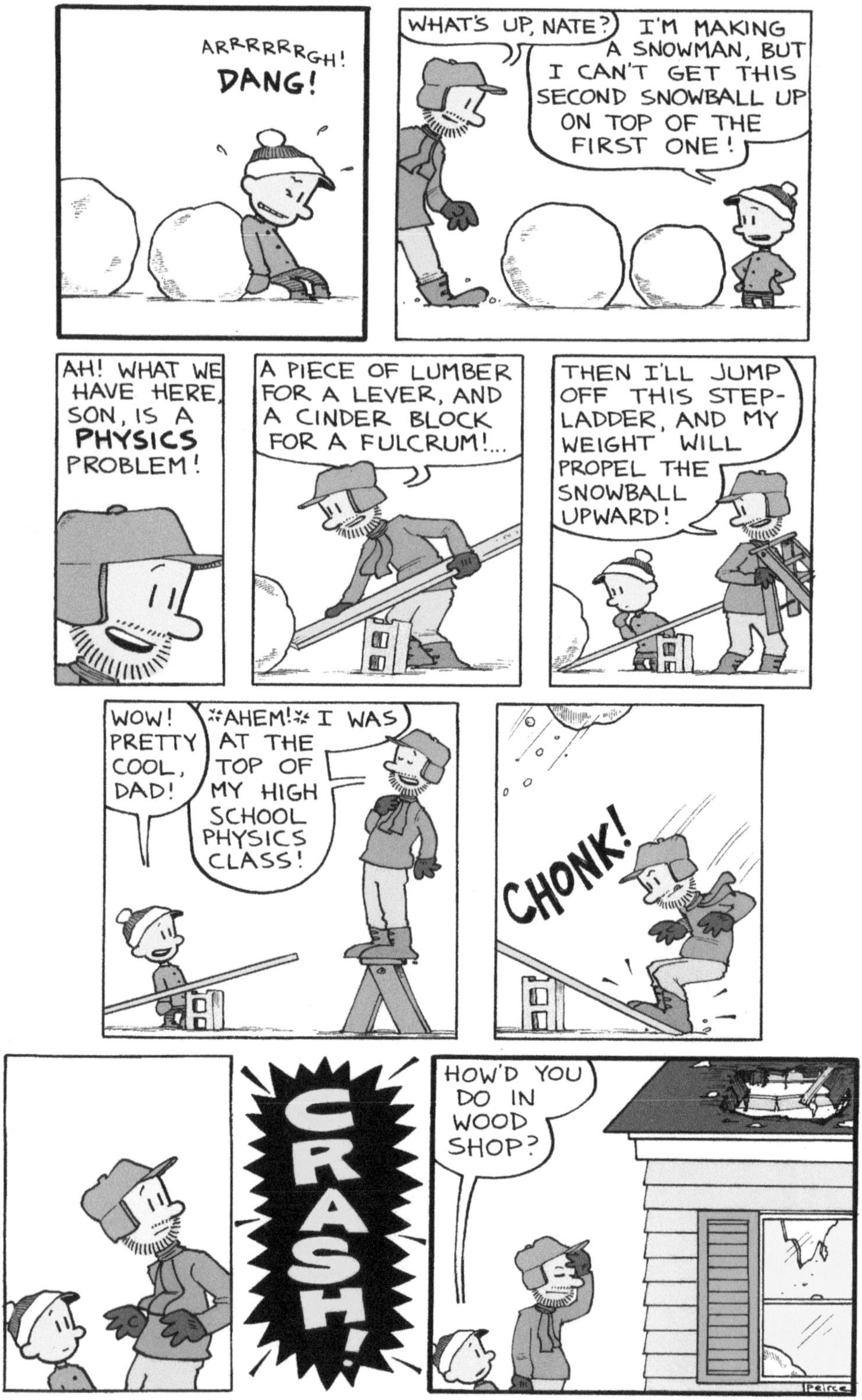
ARRRRRRGH!
DANG!
WHAT'S UP, NATE?
I'M MAKING A SNOWMAN, BUT I CAN'T GET THIS SECOND SNOWBALL UP ON TOP OF THE FIRST ONE!
AH! WHAT WE HAVE HERE, SON, IS A PHYSICS PROBLEM!
A PIECE OF LUMBER FOR A LEVER, AND A CINDER BLOCK FOR A FULCRUM!...
THEN I'LL JUMP OFF THIS STEP-LADDER, AND MY WEIGHT WILL PROPEL THE SNOWBALL UPWARD!
WOW! PRETTY COOL, DAD!
AHEM! I WAS AT THE TOP OF MY HIGH SCHOOL PHYSICS CLASS!
CHONK!
CRASH!
HOW'D YOU DO IN WOOD SHOP?
Peirce

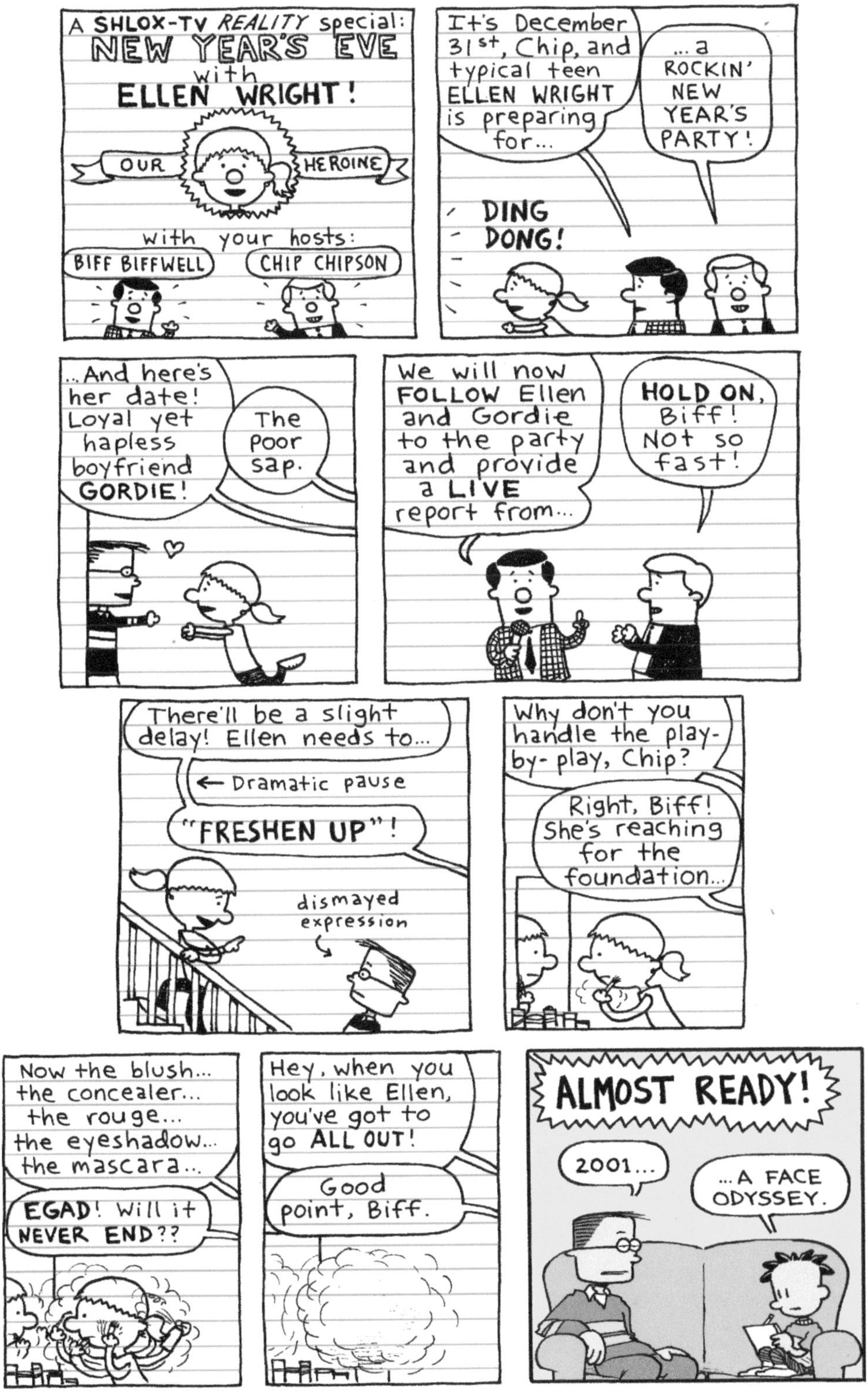
A SHLOX-TV REALITY special:
NEW YEAR'S EVE
with
ELLEN WRIGHT!
OUR
HEROINE
with your hosts:
BIFF BIFFWELL
CHIP CHIPSON
It's December 31st, Chip, and typical teen ELLEN WRIGHT is preparing for...
...a ROCKIN' NEW YEAR'S PARTY!
DING DONG!
...And here's her date! Loyal yet hapless boyfriend GORDIE!
The poor sap.
We will now FOLLOW Ellen and Gordie to the party and provide a LIVE report from...
HOLD ON, Biff! Not so fast!
There'll be a slight delay! Ellen needs to...
← Dramatic pause
"FRESHEN UP"!
dismayed expression
Why don't you handle the play-by-play, Chip?
Right, Biff! She's reaching for the foundation...
Now the blush... the concealer... the rouge... the eyeshadow... the mascara...
EGAD! Will it NEVER END??
Hey, when you look like Ellen, you've got to go ALL OUT!
Good point, Biff.
ALMOST READY!
2001...
...A FACE ODYSSEY.

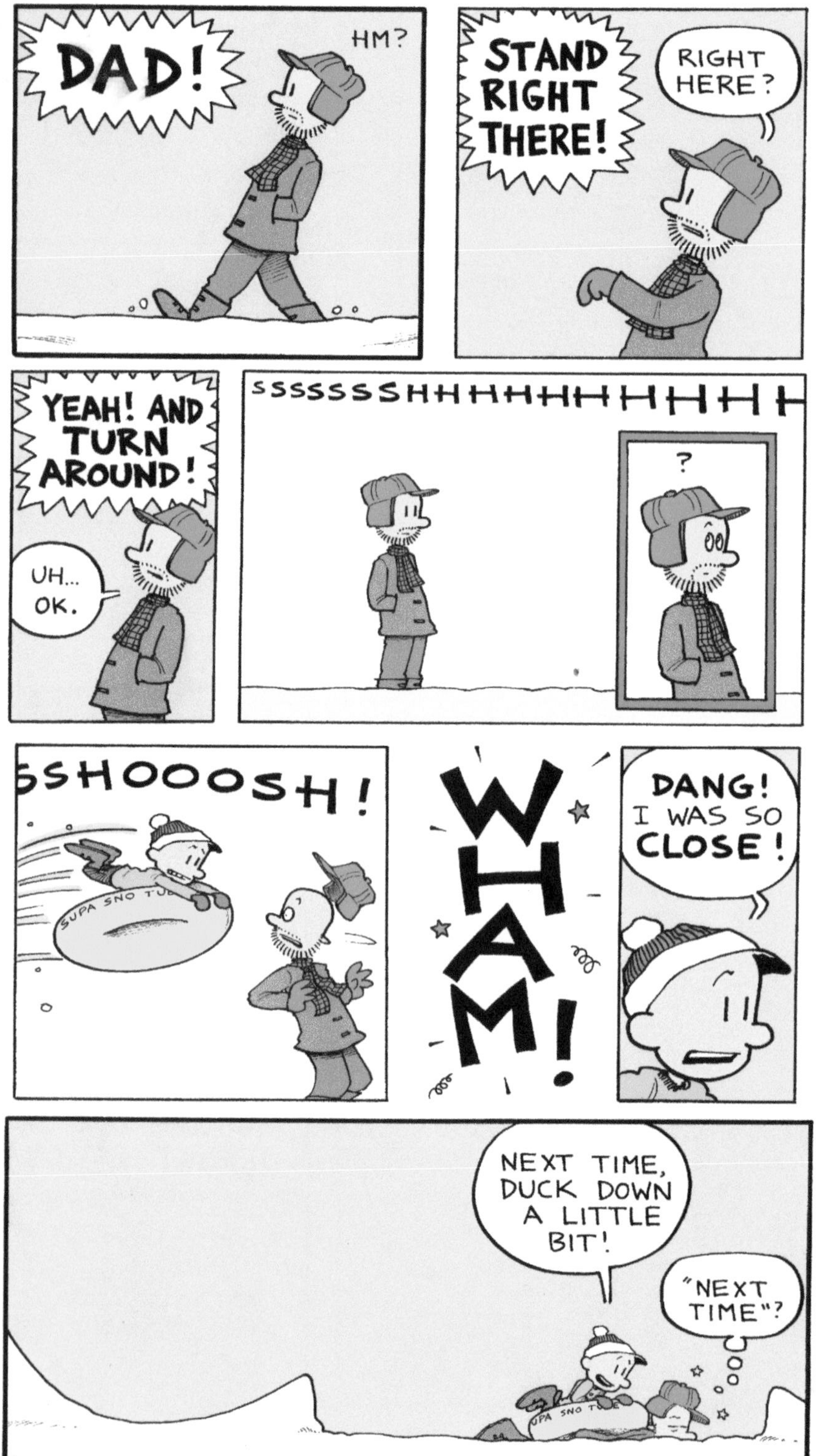
DAD!
HM?
STAND RIGHT THERE!
RIGHT HERE?
YEAH! AND TURN AROUND!
UH... OK.
SSSSSSSHHHHHHHHHHHH
?
SSHOOOOSH!
SUPA SNO TU
WHAM!
DANG! I WAS SO CLOSE!
NEXT TIME, DUCK DOWN A LITTLE BIT!
"NEXT TIME"?
SUPA SNO T

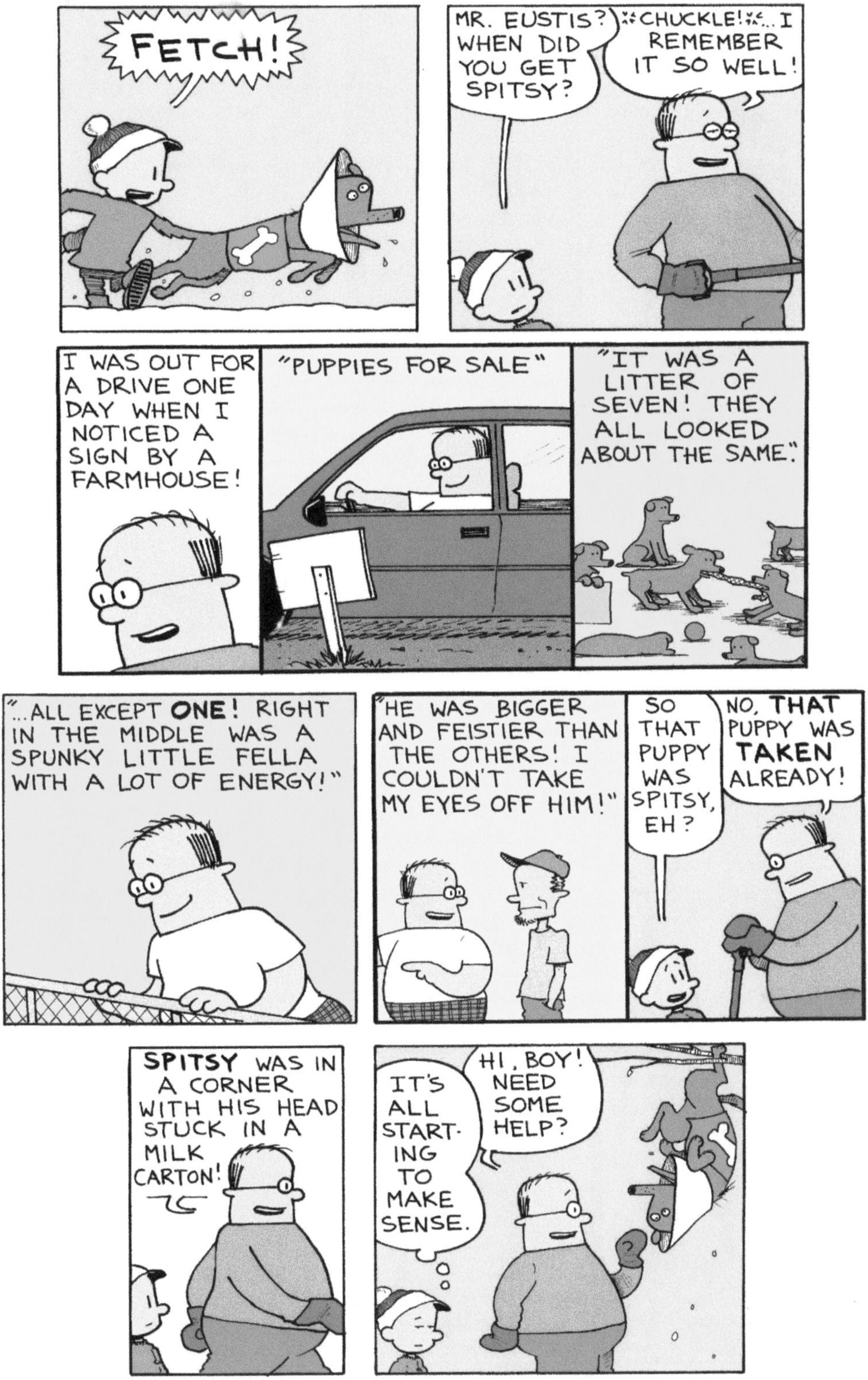
FETCH!
MR. EUSTIS? WHEN DID YOU GET SPITSY?
CHUCKLE!... I REMEMBER IT SO WELL!
I WAS OUT FOR A DRIVE ONE DAY WHEN I NOTICED A SIGN BY A FARMHOUSE!
"PUPPIES FOR SALE"
"IT WAS A LITTER OF SEVEN! THEY ALL LOOKED ABOUT THE SAME."
"...ALL EXCEPT ONE! RIGHT IN THE MIDDLE WAS A SPUNKY LITTLE FELLA WITH A LOT OF ENERGY!"
"HE WAS BIGGER AND FEISTIER THAN THE OTHERS! I COULDN'T TAKE MY EYES OFF HIM!"
SO THAT PUPPY WAS SPITSY, EH?
NO, THAT PUPPY WAS TAKEN ALREADY!
SPITSY WAS IN A CORNER WITH HIS HEAD STUCK IN A MILK CARTON!
IT'S ALL START-ING TO MAKE SENSE.
HI, BOY! NEED SOME HELP?

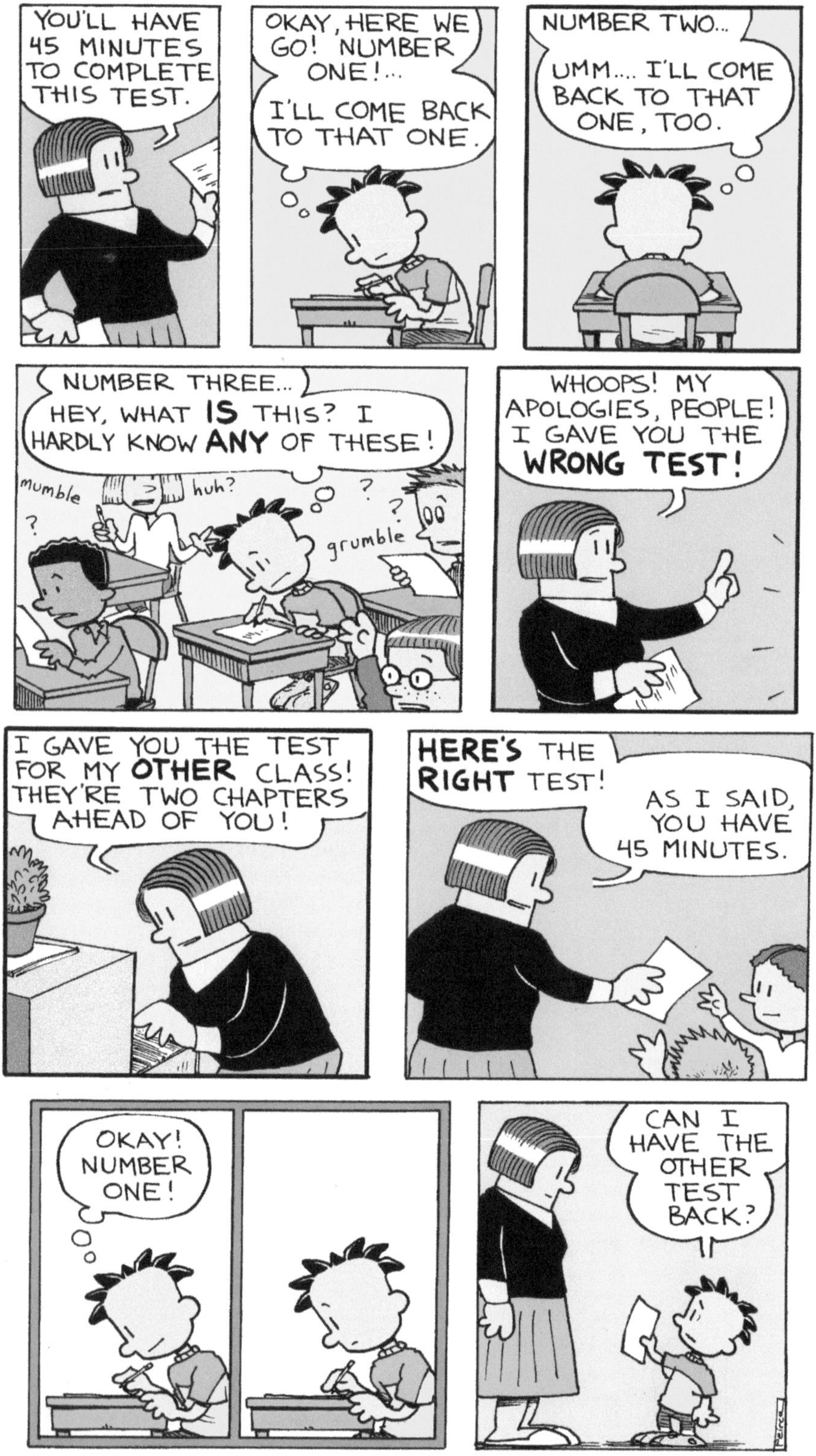
YOU'LL HAVE 45 MINUTES TO COMPLETE THIS TEST.
OKAY, HERE WE GO! NUMBER ONE!...
I'LL COME BACK TO THAT ONE.
NUMBER TWO...
UMM.... I'LL COME BACK TO THAT ONE, TOO.
NUMBER THREE...
HEY, WHAT IS THIS? I HARDLY KNOW ANY OF THESE!
mumble
huh?
?
?
?
grumble
WHOOPS! MY APOLOGIES, PEOPLE! I GAVE YOU THE WRONG TEST!
I GAVE YOU THE TEST FOR MY OTHER CLASS! THEY'RE TWO CHAPTERS AHEAD OF YOU!
HERE'S THE RIGHT TEST!
AS I SAID, YOU HAVE 45 MINUTES.
OKAY! NUMBER ONE!
CAN I HAVE THE OTHER TEST BACK?
Peirce

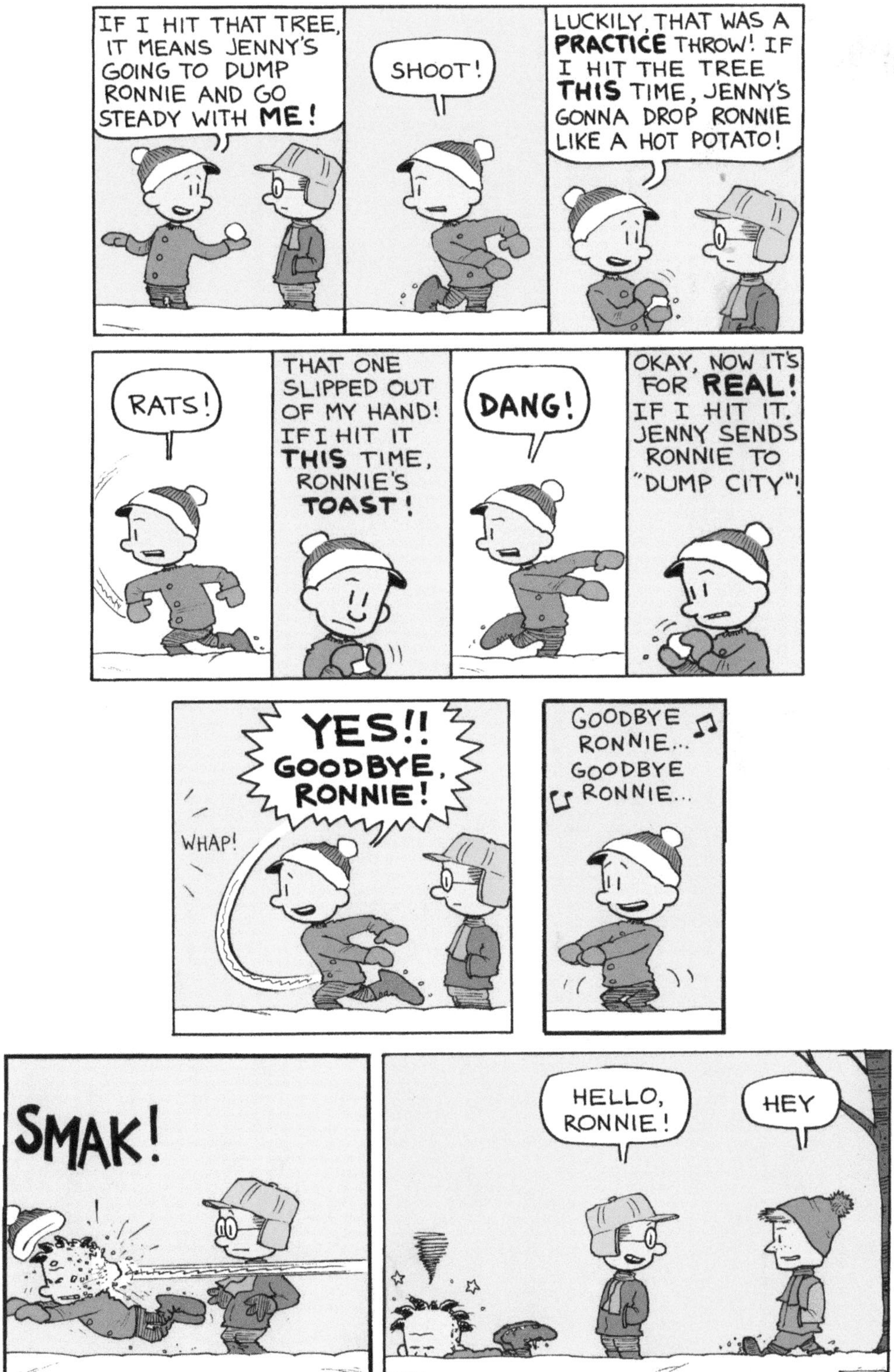
IF I HIT THAT TREE, IT MEANS JENNY'S GOING TO DUMP RONNIE AND GO STEADY WITH **ME**!
SHOOT!
LUCKILY, THAT WAS A **PRACTICE** THROW! IF I HIT THE TREE **THIS** TIME, JENNY'S GONNA DROP RONNIE LIKE A HOT POTATO!
RATS!
THAT ONE SLIPPED OUT OF MY HAND! IF I HIT IT **THIS** TIME, RONNIE'S **TOAST**!
DANG!
OKAY, NOW IT'S FOR **REAL**! IF I HIT IT, JENNY SENDS RONNIE TO "DUMP CITY"!
YES!! GOODBYE, RONNIE!
WHAP!
GOODBYE RONNIE... GOODBYE RONNIE...
SMAK!
HELLO, RONNIE!
HEY
Peirce

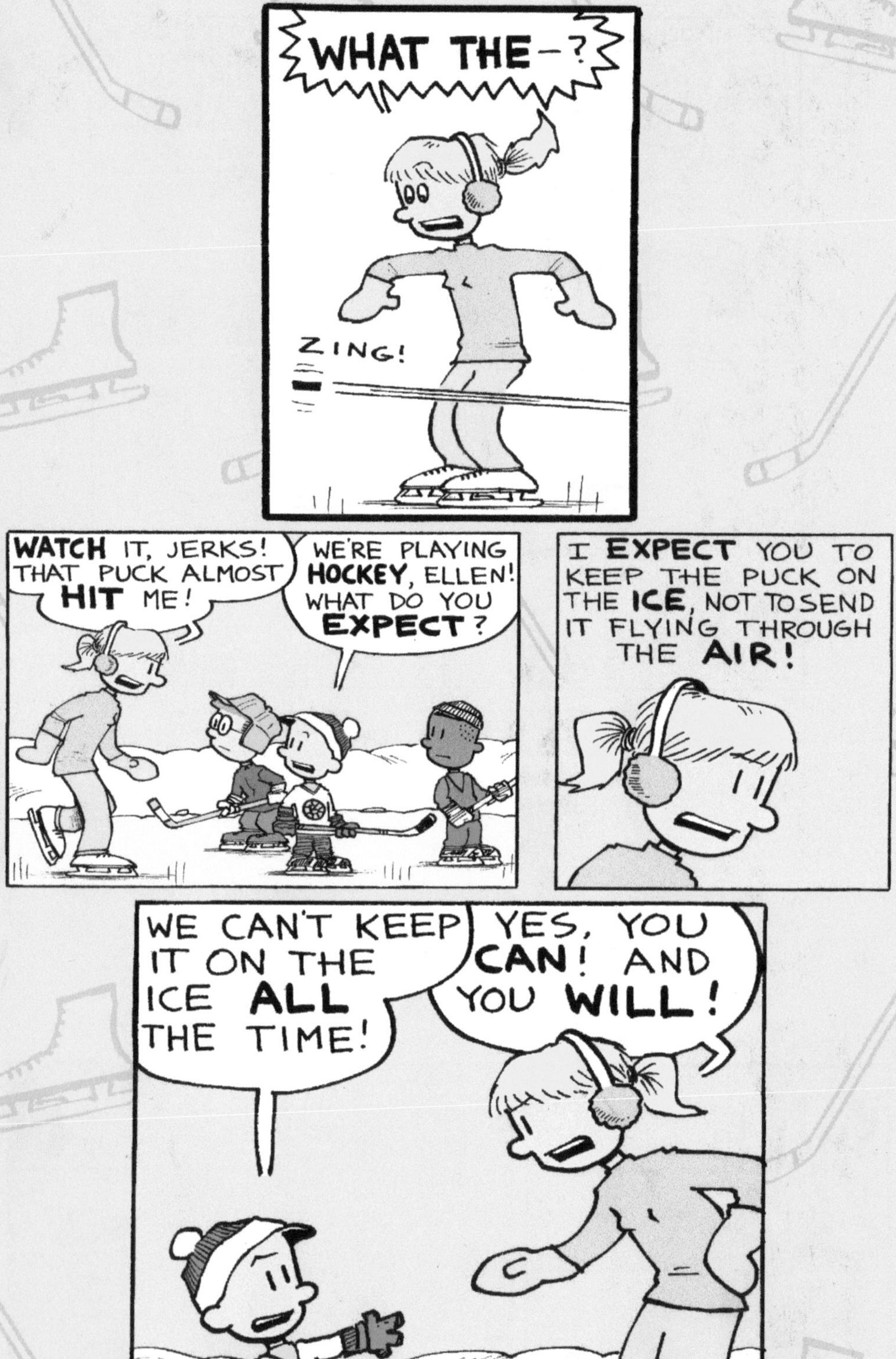
WHAT THE–?
ZING!
WATCH IT, JERKS! THAT PUCK ALMOST HIT ME!
WE'RE PLAYING HOCKEY, ELLEN! WHAT DO YOU EXPECT?
I EXPECT YOU TO KEEP THE PUCK ON THE ICE, NOT TO SEND IT FLYING THROUGH THE AIR!
WE CAN'T KEEP IT ON THE ICE ALL THE TIME!
YES, YOU CAN! AND YOU WILL!

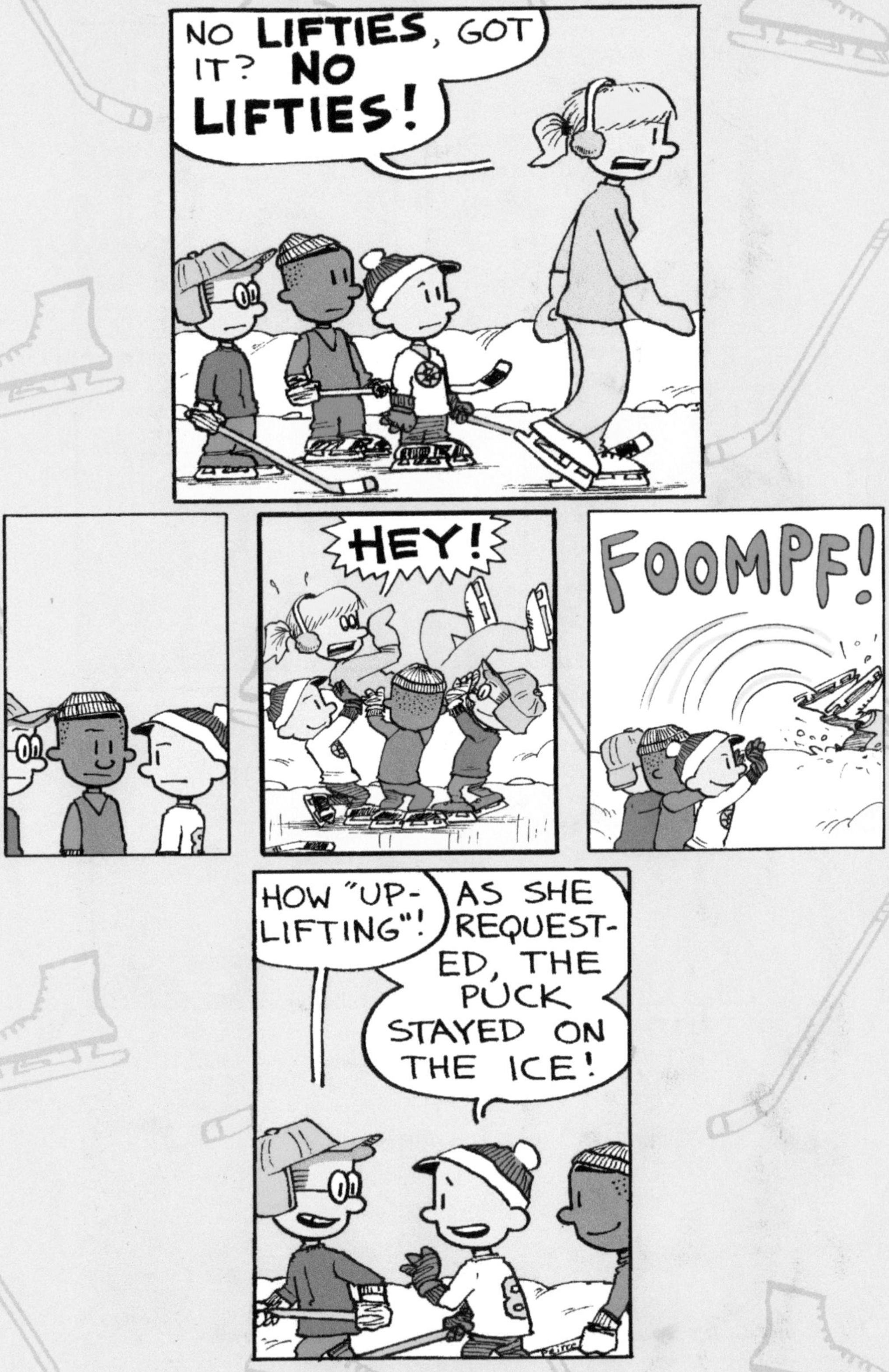
NO LIFTIES, GOT IT? NO LIFTIES!
HEY!
FOOMPF!
HOW "UP-LIFTING"!
AS SHE REQUEST-ED, THE PUCK STAYED ON THE ICE!

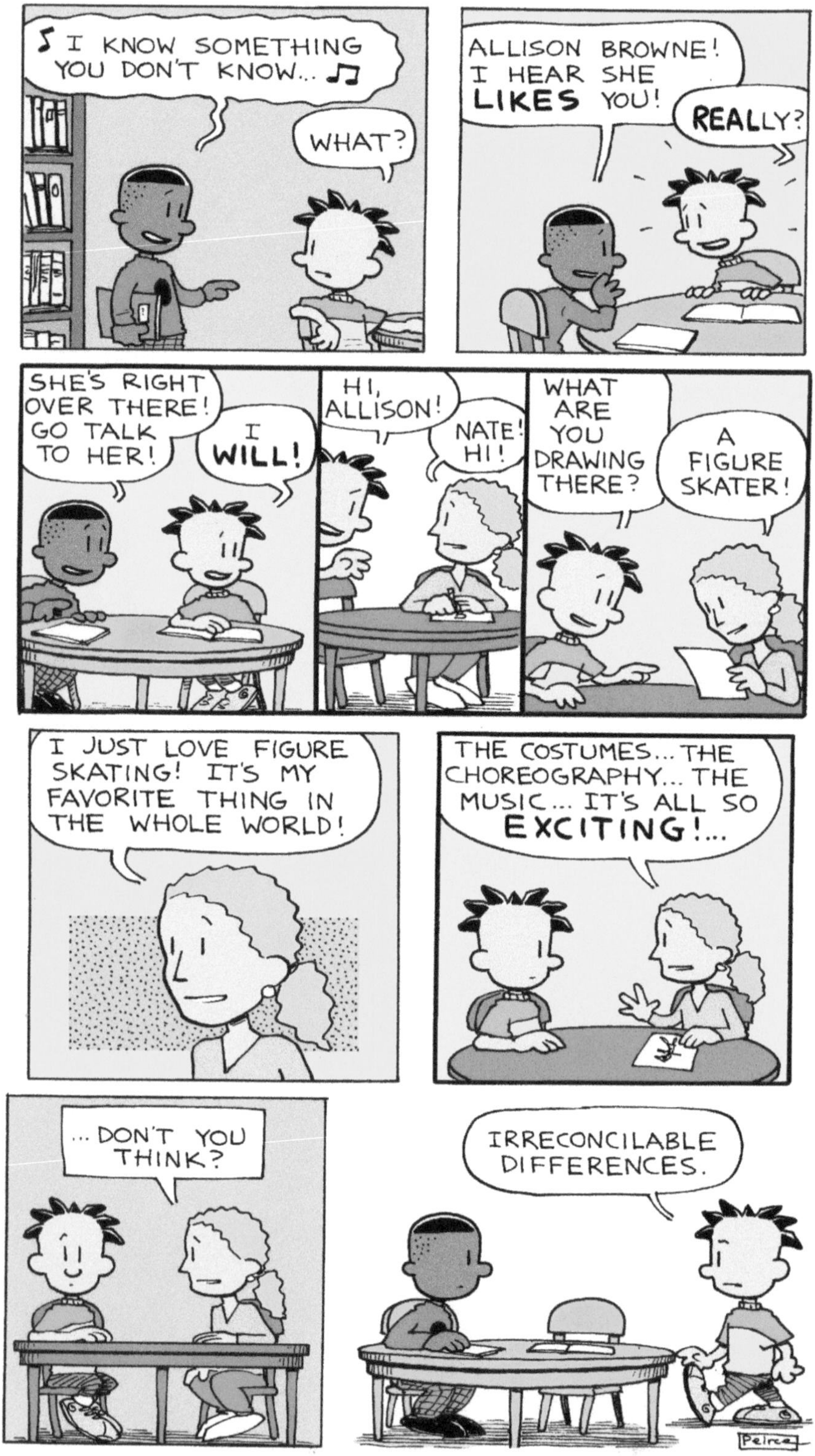
I KNOW SOMETHING YOU DON'T KNOW...
WHAT?
ALLISON BROWNE! I HEAR SHE LIKES YOU!
REALLY?
SHE'S RIGHT OVER THERE! GO TALK TO HER!
I WILL!
HI, ALLISON!
NATE! HI!
WHAT ARE YOU DRAWING THERE?
A FIGURE SKATER!
I JUST LOVE FIGURE SKATING! IT'S MY FAVORITE THING IN THE WHOLE WORLD!
THE COSTUMES... THE CHOREOGRAPHY... THE MUSIC... IT'S ALL SO EXCITING!...
...DON'T YOU THINK?
IRRECONCILABLE DIFFERENCES.
Peirce

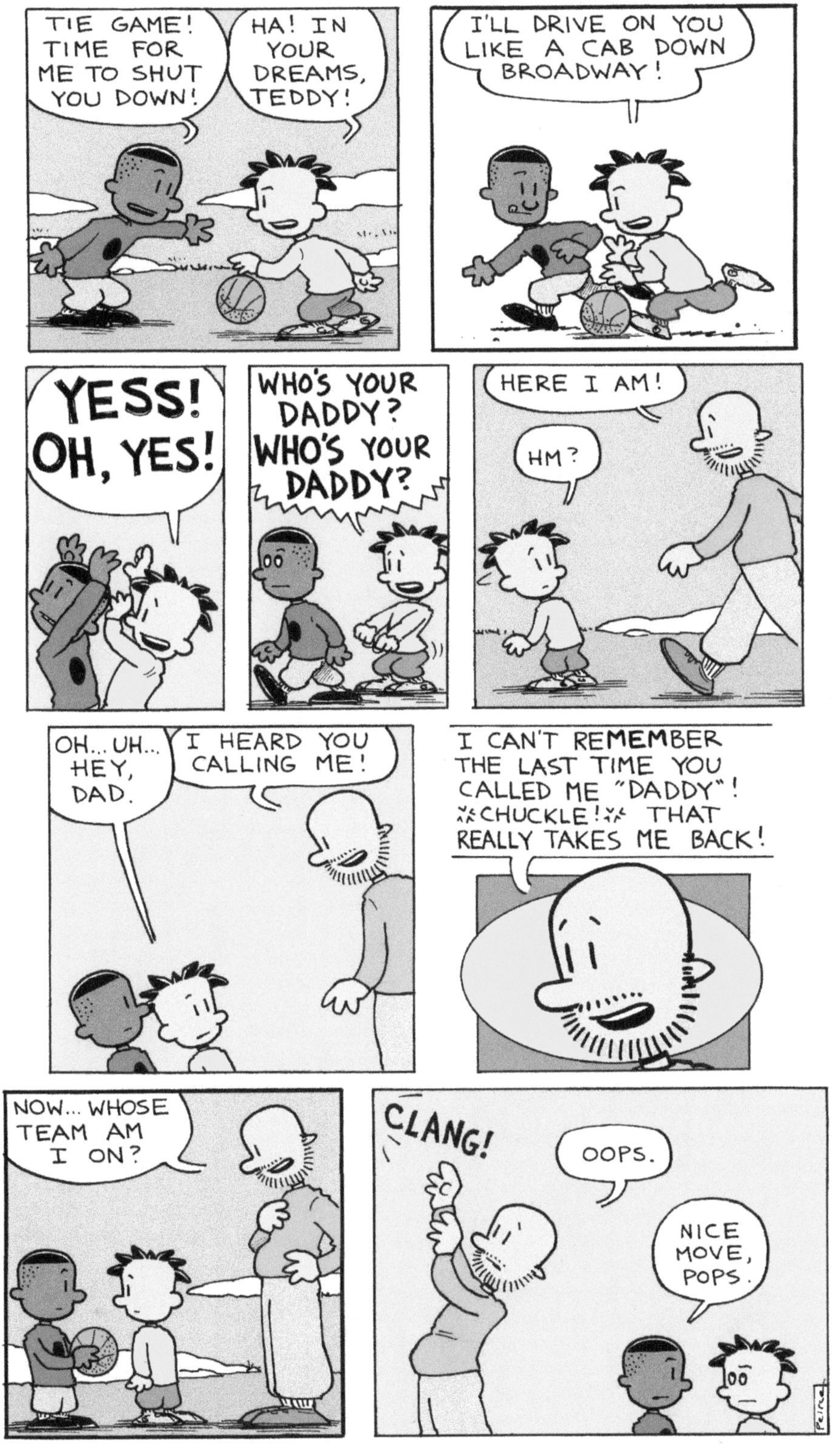
TIE GAME! TIME FOR ME TO SHUT YOU DOWN!
HA! IN YOUR DREAMS, TEDDY!
I'LL DRIVE ON YOU LIKE A CAB DOWN BROADWAY!
YESS! OH, YES!
WHO'S YOUR DADDY? WHO'S YOUR DADDY?
HERE I AM!
HM?
OH... UH... HEY, DAD.
I HEARD YOU CALLING ME!
I CAN'T REMEMBER THE LAST TIME YOU CALLED ME "DADDY"! *CHUCKLE!* THAT REALLY TAKES ME BACK!
NOW... WHOSE TEAM AM I ON?
CLANG!
OOPS.
NICE MOVE, POPS.

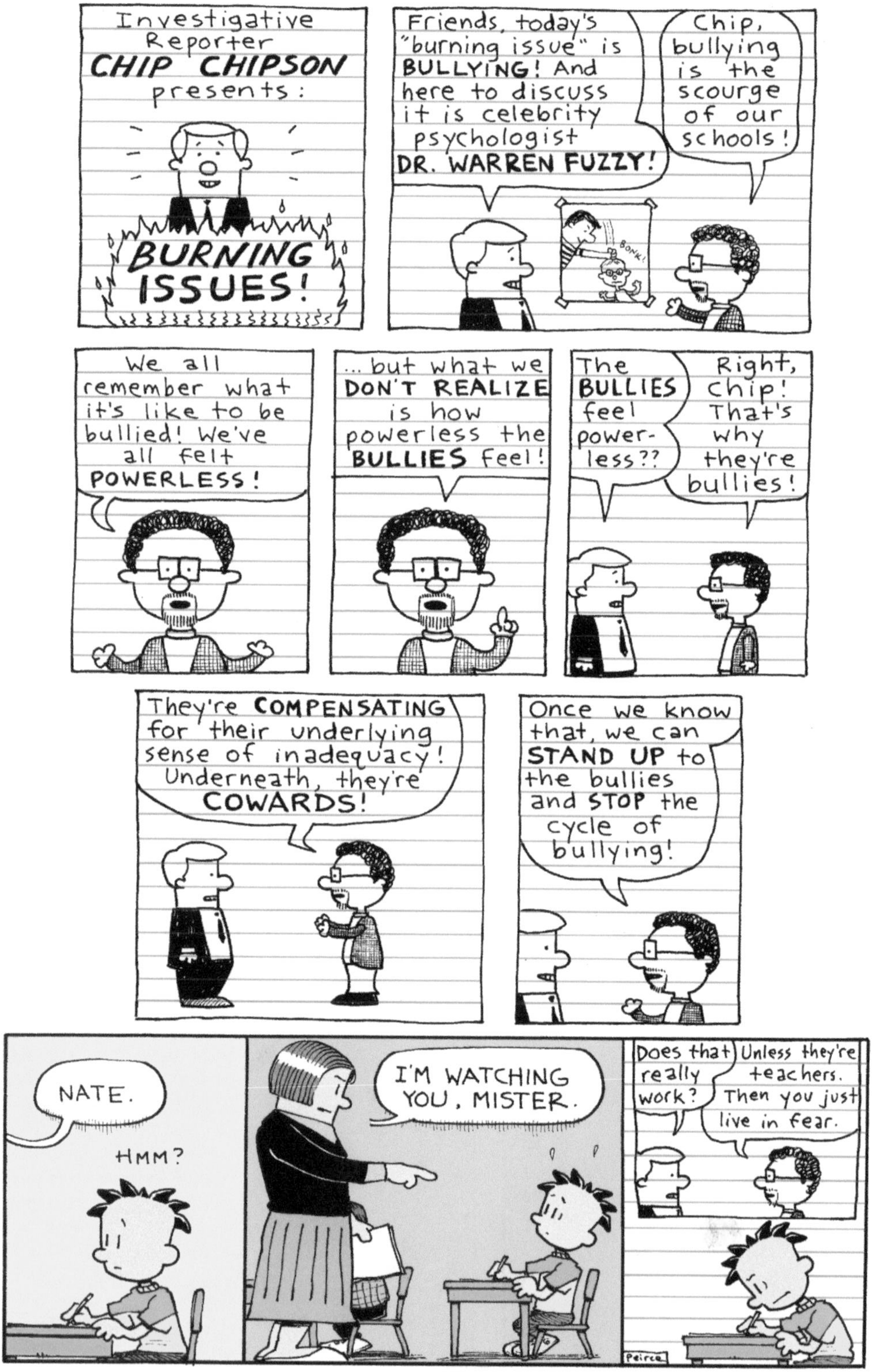

Investigative Reporter CHIP CHIPSON presents:
BURNING ISSUES!
Friends, today's "burning issue" is BULLYING! And here to discuss it is celebrity psychologist DR. WARREN FUZZY!
Chip, bullying is the scourge of our schools!
BONK!
We all remember what it's like to be bullied! We've all felt POWERLESS!
... but what we DON'T REALIZE is how powerless the BULLIES feel!
The BULLIES feel power-less??
Right, Chip! That's why they're bullies!
They're COMPENSATING for their underlying sense of inadequacy! Underneath, they're COWARDS!
Once we know that, we can STAND UP to the bullies and STOP the cycle of bullying!
NATE.
HMM?
I'M WATCHING YOU, MISTER.
Does that really work?
Unless they're teachers. Then you just live in fear.
Peirce

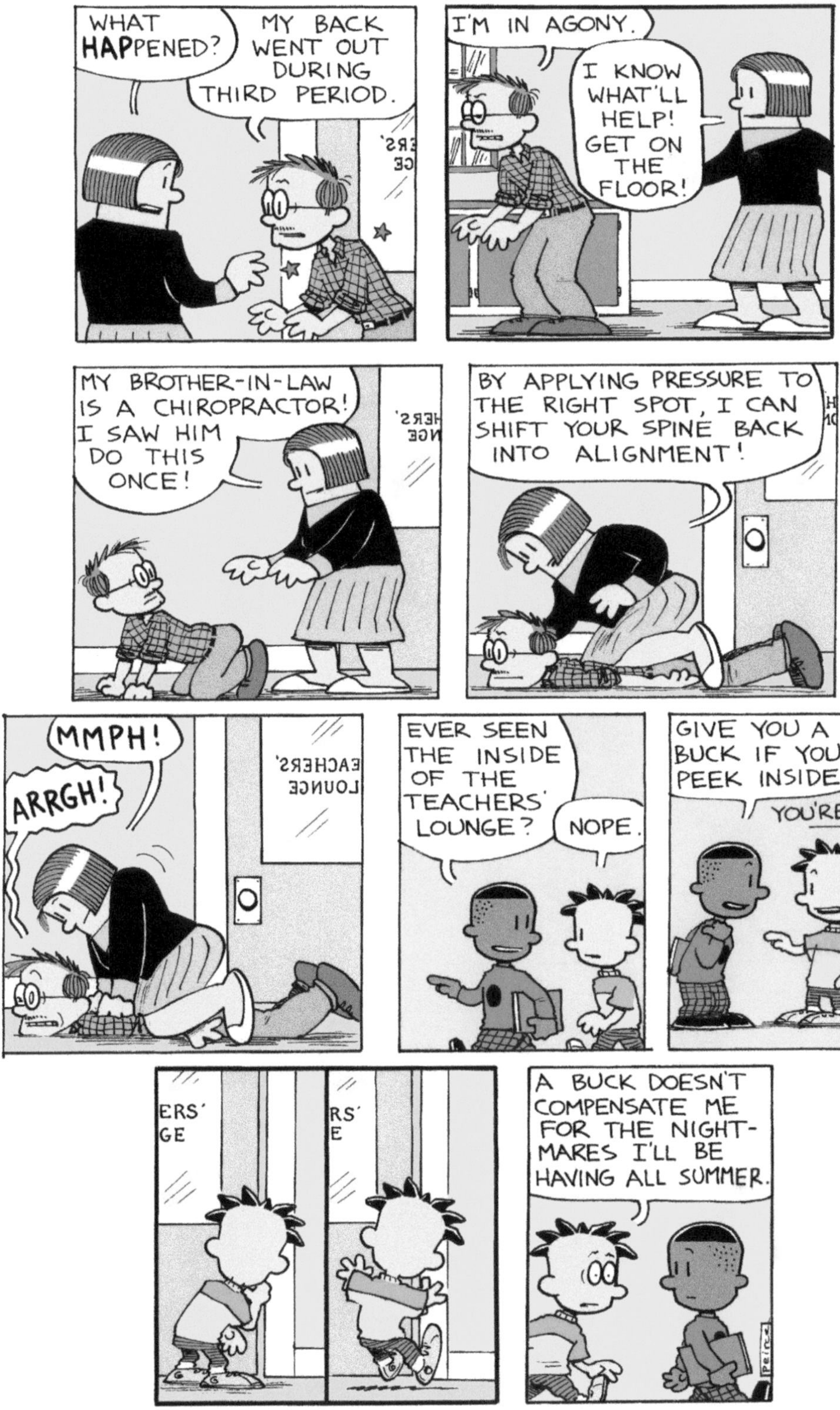
WHAT HAPPENED?
MY BACK WENT OUT DURING THIRD PERIOD.
I'M IN AGONY.
I KNOW WHAT'LL HELP! GET ON THE FLOOR!
MY BROTHER-IN-LAW IS A CHIROPRACTOR! I SAW HIM DO THIS ONCE!
BY APPLYING PRESSURE TO THE RIGHT SPOT, I CAN SHIFT YOUR SPINE BACK INTO ALIGNMENT!
MMPH!
ARRGH!
EVER SEEN THE INSIDE OF THE TEACHERS' LOUNGE?
NOPE.
GIVE YOU A BUCK IF YOU PEEK INSIDE!
YOU'RE ON!
A BUCK DOESN'T COMPENSATE ME FOR THE NIGHTMARES I'LL BE HAVING ALL SUMMER.

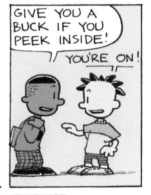

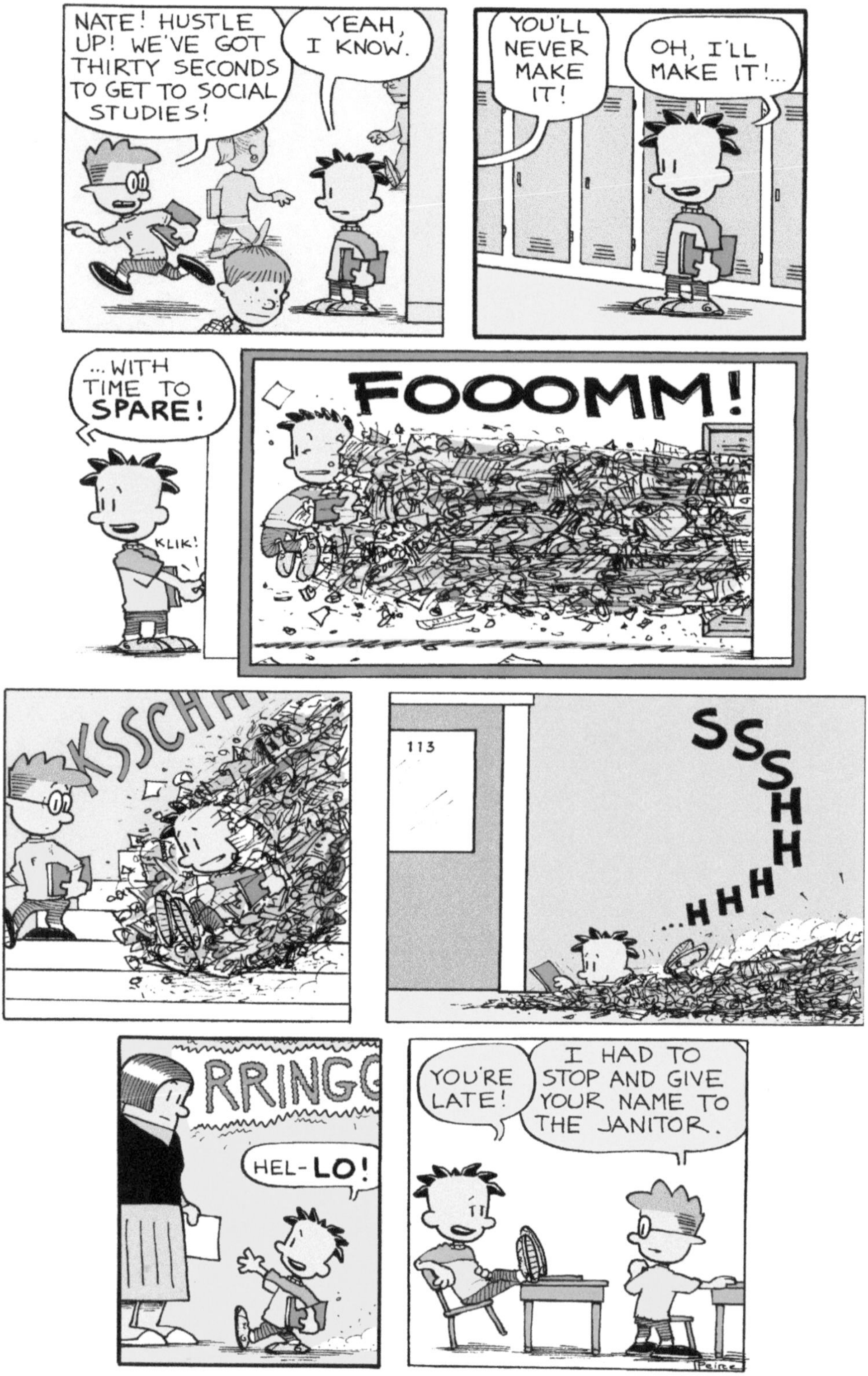
NATE! HUSTLE UP! WE'VE GOT THIRTY SECONDS TO GET TO SOCIAL STUDIES!
YEAH, I KNOW.
YOU'LL NEVER MAKE IT!
OH, I'LL MAKE IT!...
...WITH TIME TO SPARE!
KLIK!
FOOOMM!
KSSCHH
113
SSSHHHHHH
RRINGG
HEL-LO!
YOU'RE LATE!
I HAD TO STOP AND GIVE YOUR NAME TO THE JANITOR.
Peirce

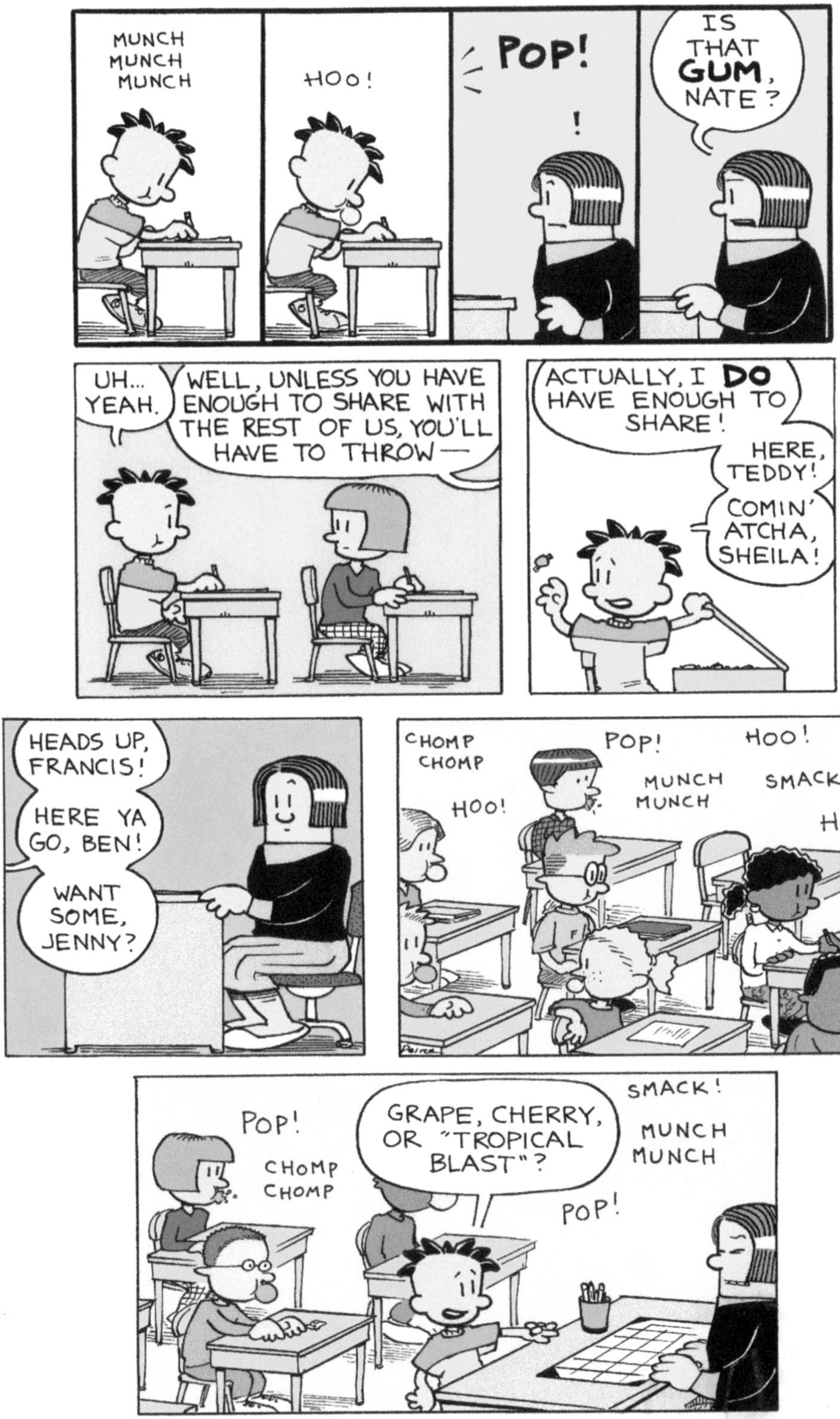
MUNCH MUNCH MUNCH
HOO!
POP!
!
IS THAT GUM, NATE?
UH... YEAH.
WELL, UNLESS YOU HAVE ENOUGH TO SHARE WITH THE REST OF US, YOU'LL HAVE TO THROW—
ACTUALLY, I DO HAVE ENOUGH TO SHARE!
HERE, TEDDY!
COMIN' ATCHA, SHEILA!
HEADS UP, FRANCIS!
HERE YA GO, BEN!
WANT SOME, JENNY?
CHOMP CHOMP
POP!
HOO!
HOO!
MUNCH MUNCH
SMACK!
HOOO!
POP!
CHOMP CHOMP
GRAPE, CHERRY, OR "TROPICAL BLAST"?
SMACK!
MUNCH MUNCH
POP!

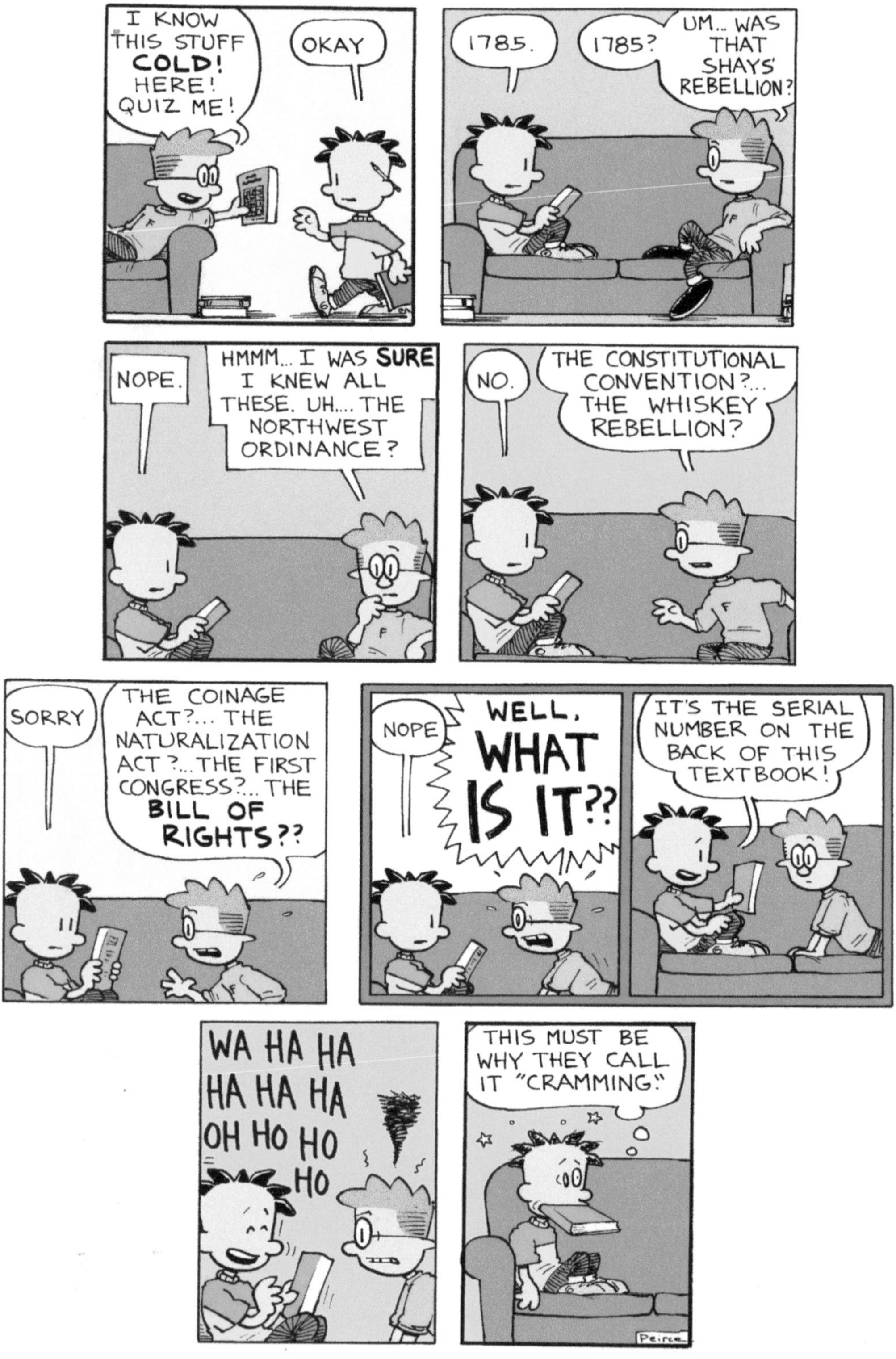
I KNOW THIS STUFF COLD! HERE! QUIZ ME!
OKAY
1785.
1785?
UM... WAS THAT SHAYS' REBELLION?
NOPE.
HMMM... I WAS SURE I KNEW ALL THESE. UH.... THE NORTHWEST ORDINANCE?
NO.
THE CONSTITUTIONAL CONVENTION?... THE WHISKEY REBELLION?
SORRY
THE COINAGE ACT?... THE NATURALIZATION ACT?... THE FIRST CONGRESS?... THE BILL OF RIGHTS??
NOPE
WELL, WHAT IS IT??
IT'S THE SERIAL NUMBER ON THE BACK OF THIS TEXTBOOK!
WA HA HA HA HA HA HA OH HO HO HO
THIS MUST BE WHY THEY CALL IT "CRAMMING."
Peirce

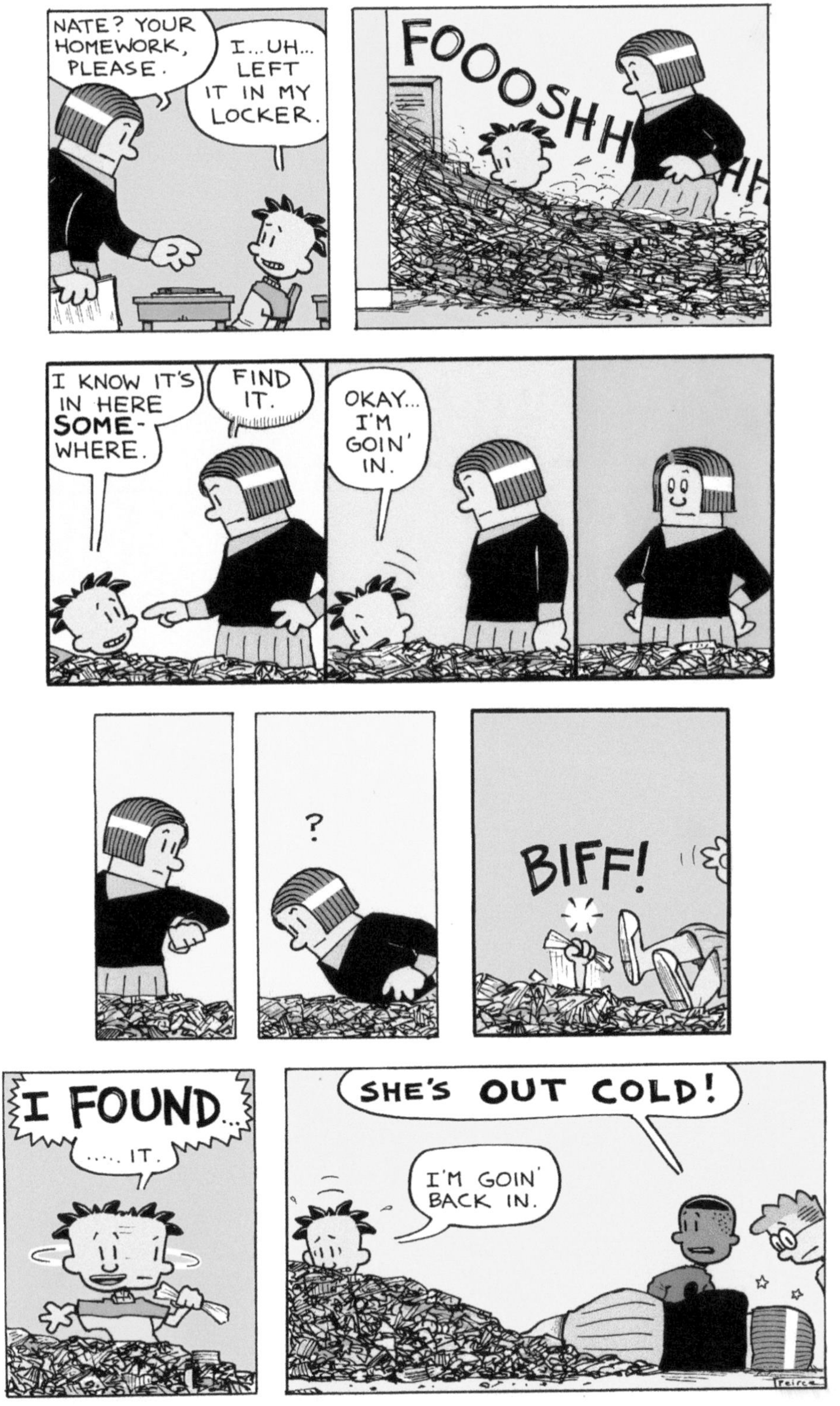
NATE? YOUR HOMEWORK, PLEASE.
I... UH... LEFT IT IN MY LOCKER.
FOOOSHHHH
I KNOW IT'S IN HERE **SOME**-WHERE.
FIND IT.
OKAY... I'M GOIN' IN.
?
BIFF!
I FOUND...
..... IT.
SHE'S OUT COLD!
I'M GOIN' BACK IN.
Peirce

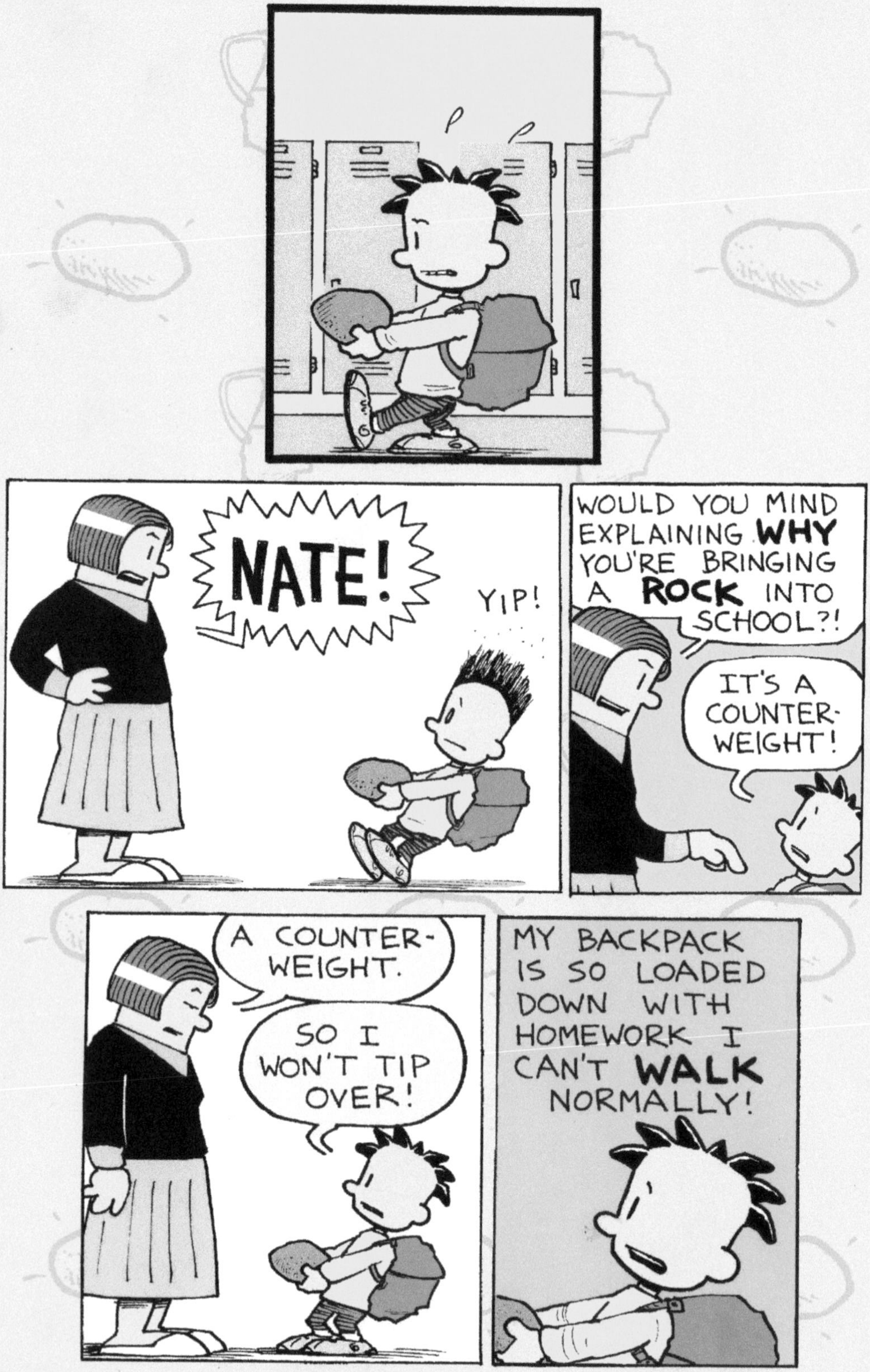
NATE!
YIP!
WOULD YOU MIND EXPLAINING WHY YOU'RE BRINGING A ROCK INTO SCHOOL?!
IT'S A COUNTER-WEIGHT!
A COUNTER-WEIGHT.
SO I WON'T TIP OVER!
MY BACKPACK IS SO LOADED DOWN WITH HOMEWORK I CAN'T WALK NORMALLY!

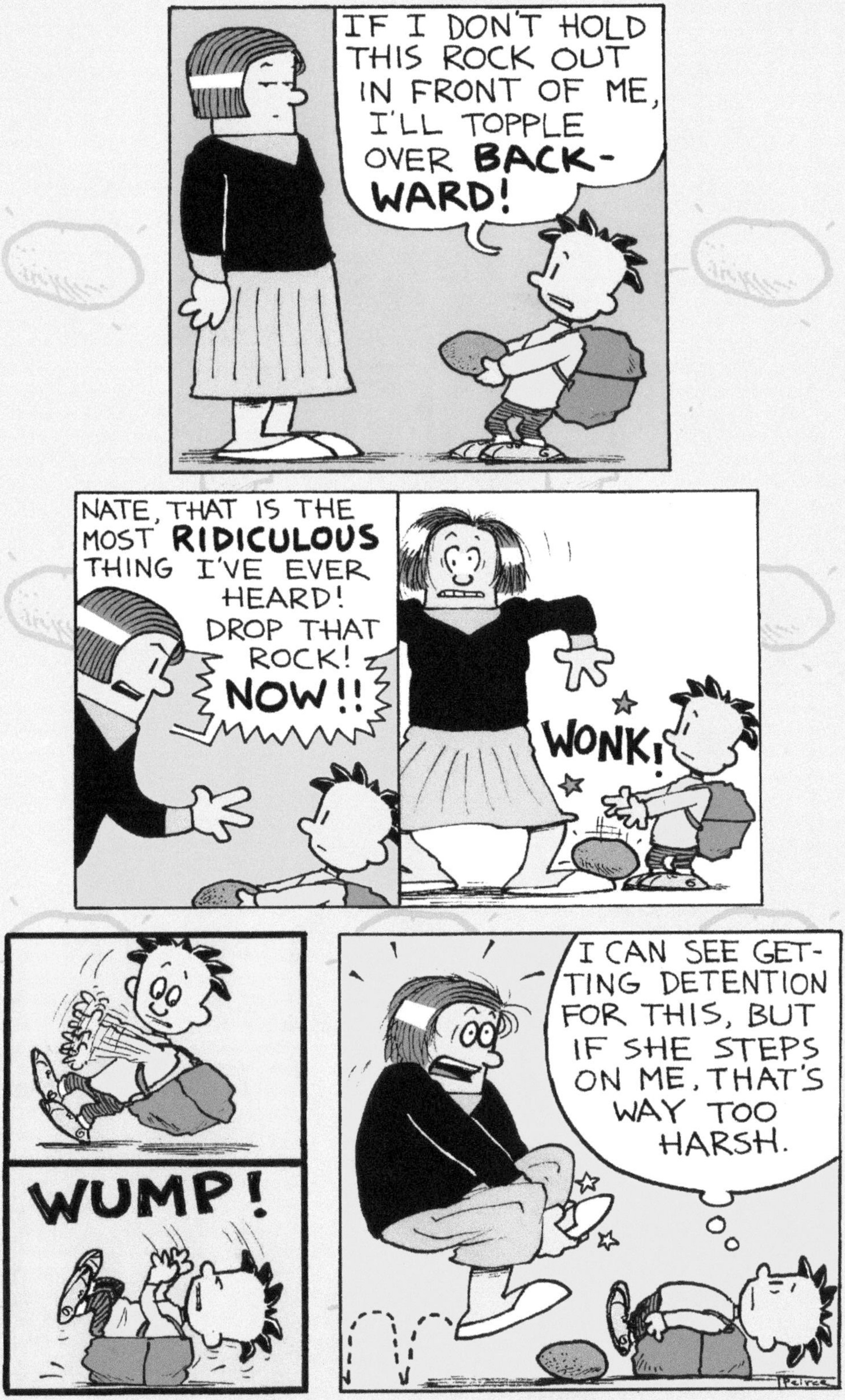
IF I DON'T HOLD THIS ROCK OUT IN FRONT OF ME, I'LL TOPPLE OVER **BACK-WARD!**
NATE, THAT IS THE MOST **RIDICULOUS** THING I'VE EVER HEARD! DROP THAT ROCK! **NOW!!**
WONK!
WUMP!
I CAN SEE GETTING DETENTION FOR THIS, BUT IF SHE STEPS ON ME, THAT'S WAY TOO HARSH.

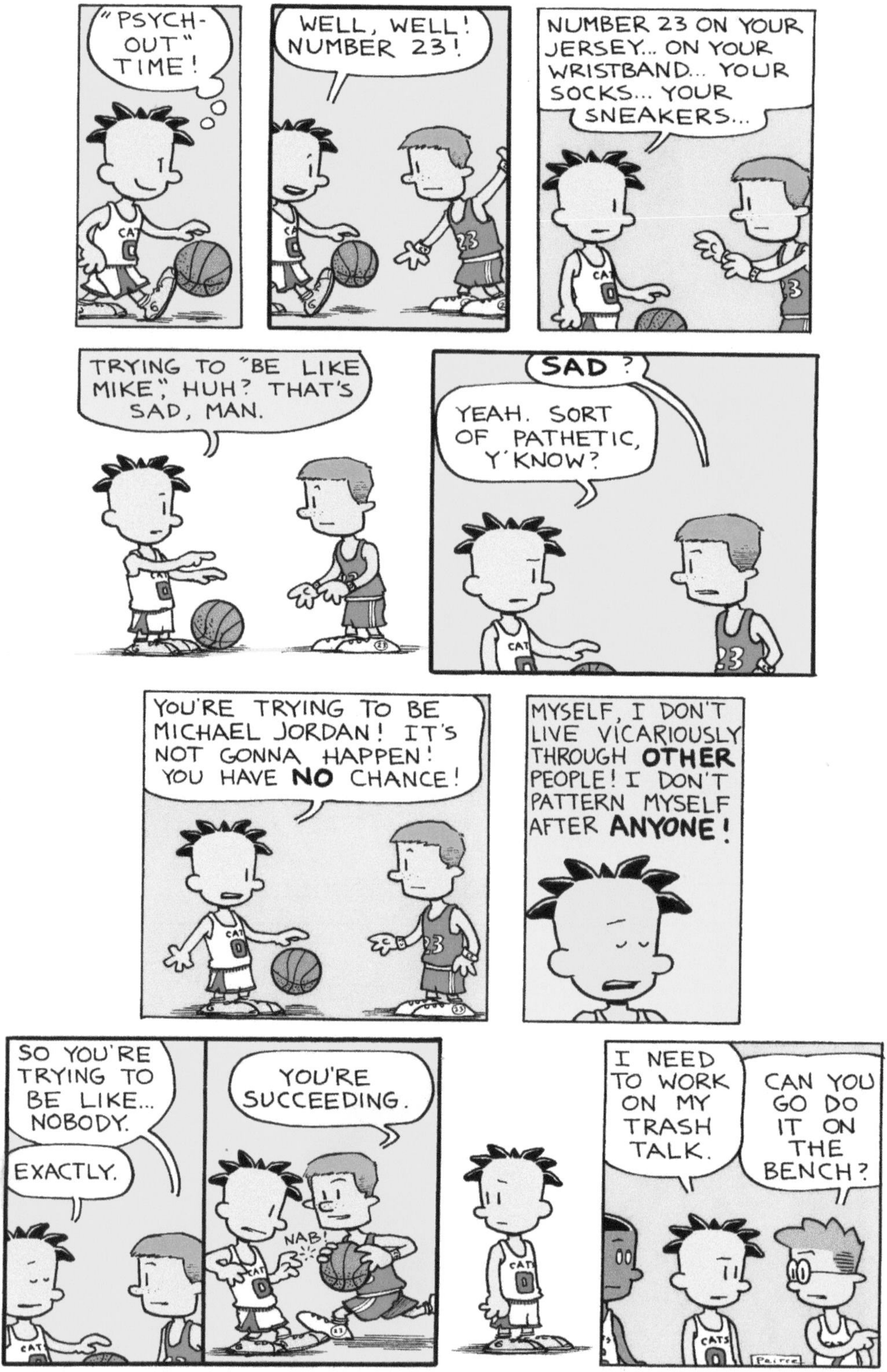
"PSYCH-OUT" TIME!
WELL, WELL! NUMBER 23!
NUMBER 23 ON YOUR JERSEY... ON YOUR WRISTBAND... YOUR SOCKS... YOUR SNEAKERS...
TRYING TO "BE LIKE MIKE", HUH? THAT'S SAD, MAN.
SAD?
YEAH. SORT OF PATHETIC, Y'KNOW?
YOU'RE TRYING TO BE MICHAEL JORDAN! IT'S NOT GONNA HAPPEN! YOU HAVE NO CHANCE!
MYSELF, I DON'T LIVE VICARIOUSLY THROUGH OTHER PEOPLE! I DON'T PATTERN MYSELF AFTER ANYONE!
SO YOU'RE TRYING TO BE LIKE... NOBODY.
EXACTLY.
YOU'RE SUCCEEDING.
NAB!
I NEED TO WORK ON MY TRASH TALK.
CAN YOU GO DO IT ON THE BENCH?
Peirce

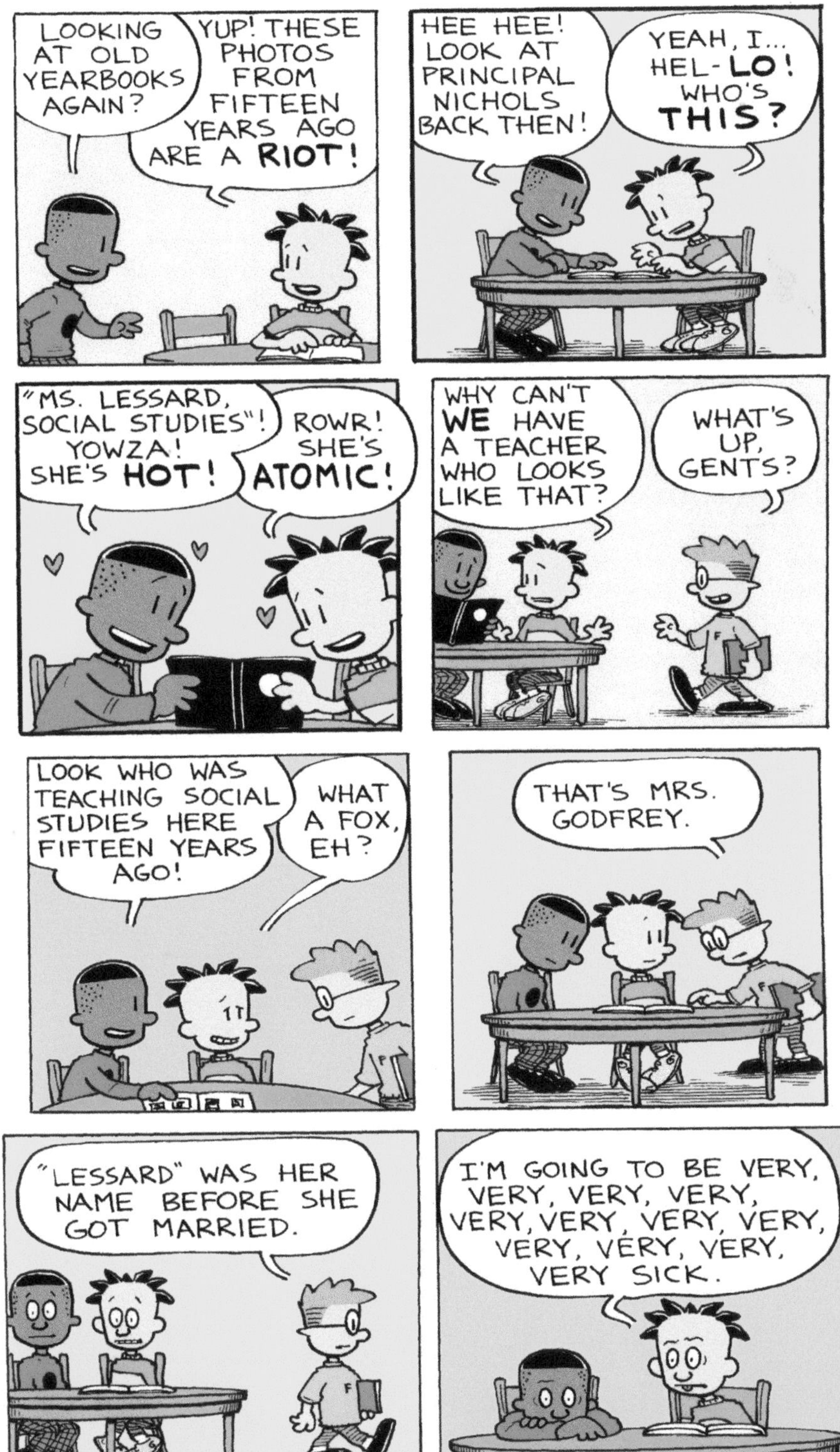
LOOKING AT OLD YEARBOOKS AGAIN?
YUP! THESE PHOTOS FROM FIFTEEN YEARS AGO ARE A RIOT!
HEE HEE! LOOK AT PRINCIPAL NICHOLS BACK THEN!
YEAH, I... HEL-LO! WHO'S THIS?
"MS. LESSARD, SOCIAL STUDIES"! YOWZA! SHE'S HOT!
ROWR! SHE'S ATOMIC!
WHY CAN'T WE HAVE A TEACHER WHO LOOKS LIKE THAT?
WHAT'S UP, GENTS?
LOOK WHO WAS TEACHING SOCIAL STUDIES HERE FIFTEEN YEARS AGO!
WHAT A FOX, EH?
THAT'S MRS. GODFREY.
"LESSARD" WAS HER NAME BEFORE SHE GOT MARRIED.
I'M GOING TO BE VERY, VERY, VERY, VERY, VERY, VERY, VERY, VERY, VERY, VERY, VERY, VERY SICK.
Peirce

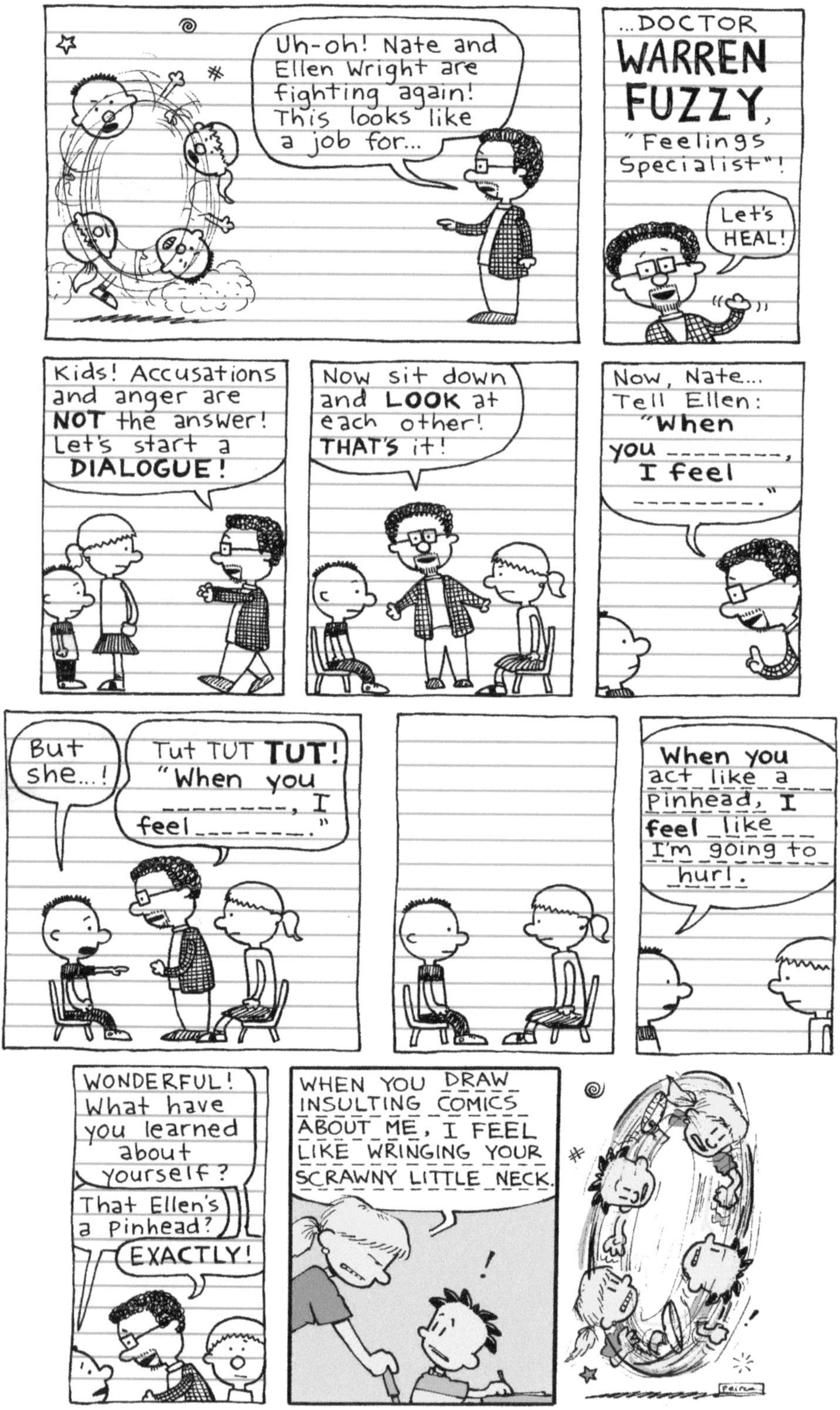
Uh-oh! Nate and Ellen Wright are fighting again! This looks like a job for...
...DOCTOR WARREN FUZZY, "Feelings Specialist"!
Let's HEAL!
Kids! Accusations and anger are **NOT** the answer! Let's start a **DIALOGUE**!
Now sit down and **LOOK** at each other! **THAT'S** it!
Now, Nate... Tell Ellen: "**When you** ________, **I feel** ________."
But she...!
Tut TUT **TUT**! "When you ________, I feel ________."
When you act like a Pinhead, I feel like I'm going to hurl.
WONDERFUL! What have you learned about yourself?
That Ellen's a Pinhead?
EXACTLY!
WHEN YOU DRAW INSULTING COMICS ABOUT ME, I FEEL LIKE WRINGING YOUR SCRAWNY LITTLE NECK.
!
!

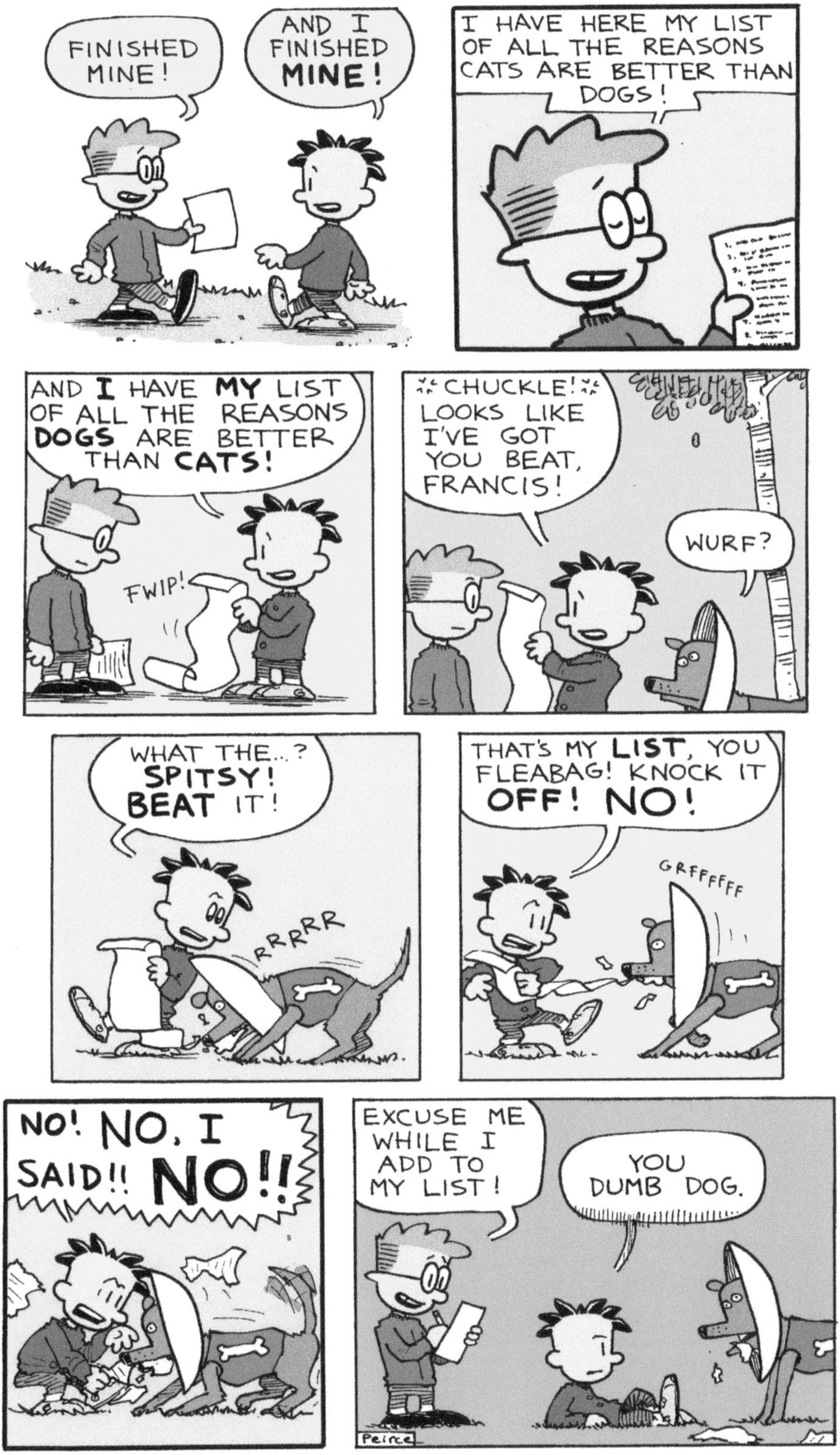
FINISHED MINE!
AND I FINISHED MINE!
I HAVE HERE MY LIST OF ALL THE REASONS CATS ARE BETTER THAN DOGS!
AND I HAVE MY LIST OF ALL THE REASONS DOGS ARE BETTER THAN CATS!
FWIP!
CHUCKLE! LOOKS LIKE I'VE GOT YOU BEAT, FRANCIS!
WURF?
WHAT THE...? SPITSY! BEAT IT!
RRRRR
THAT'S MY LIST, YOU FLEABAG! KNOCK IT OFF! NO!
GRFFFFFF
NO! NO, I SAID!! NO!!
EXCUSE ME WHILE I ADD TO MY LIST!
YOU DUMB DOG.
Peirce

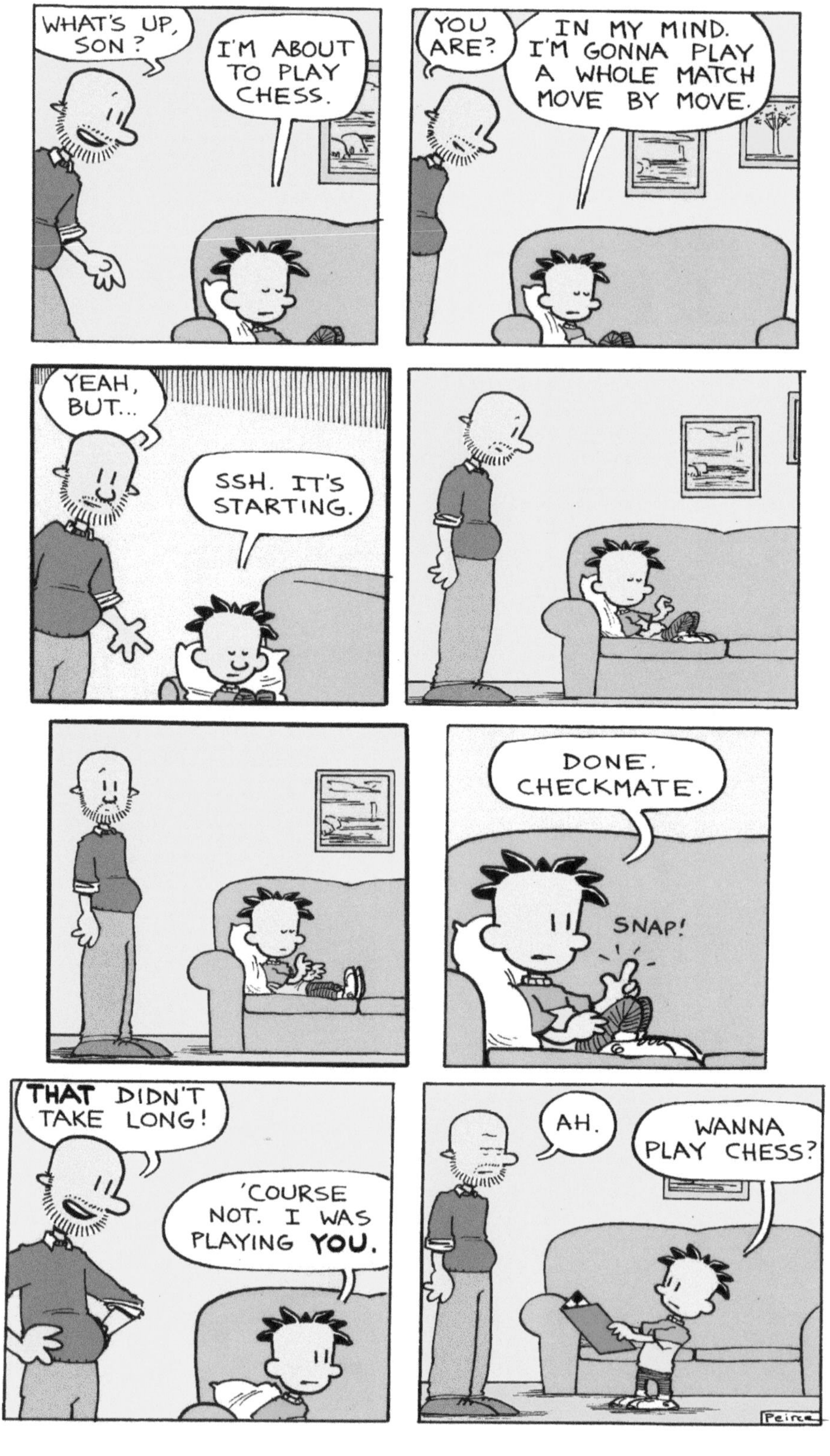
WHAT'S UP, SON?
I'M ABOUT TO PLAY CHESS.
YOU ARE?
IN MY MIND. I'M GONNA PLAY A WHOLE MATCH MOVE BY MOVE.
YEAH, BUT...
SSH. IT'S STARTING.
DONE. CHECKMATE.
SNAP!
THAT DIDN'T TAKE LONG!
'COURSE NOT. I WAS PLAYING YOU.
AH.
WANNA PLAY CHESS?
Peirce

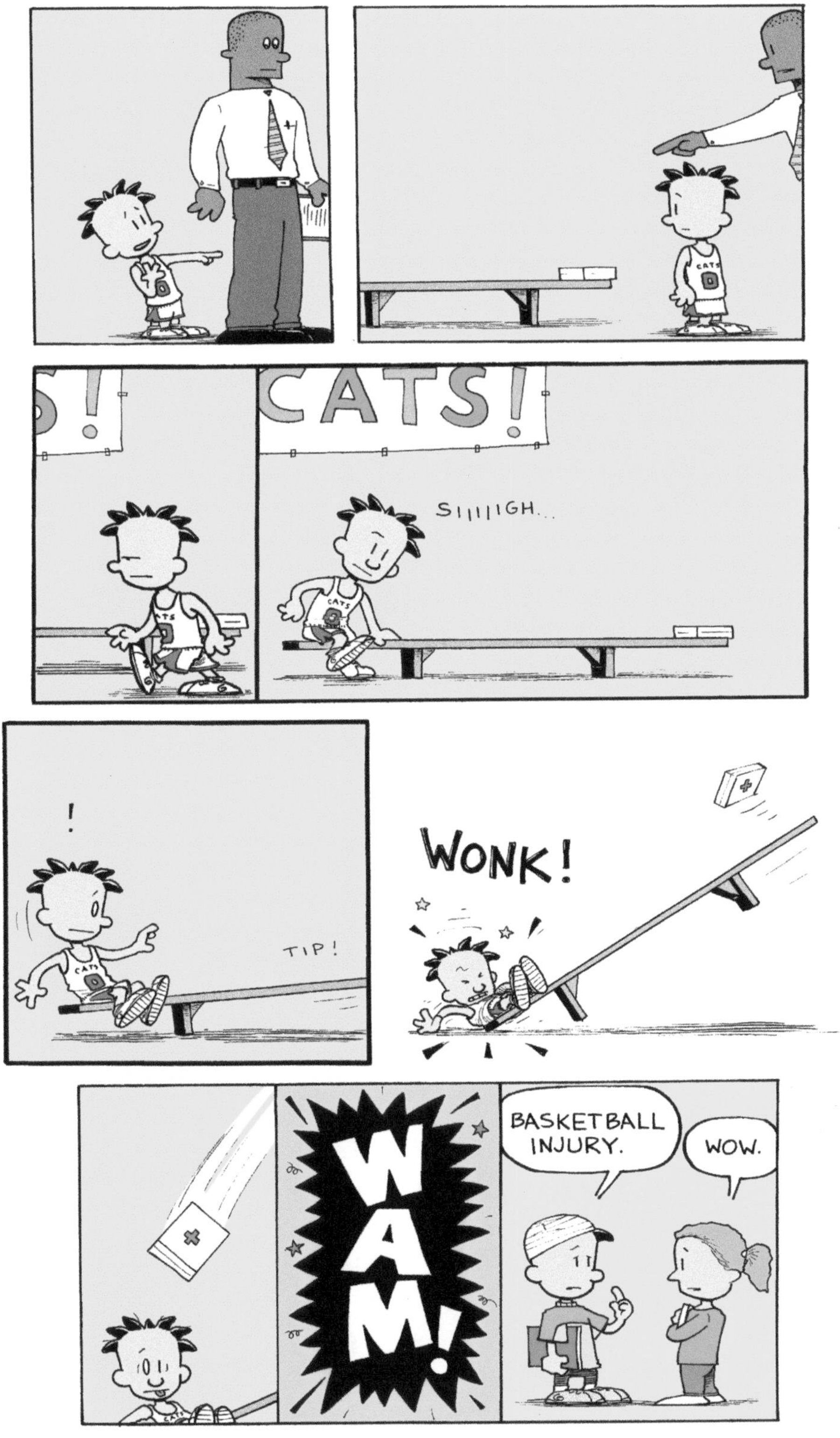
CATS!
SIIIIIGH...
!
TIP!
WONK!
WAM!
BASKETBALL INJURY.
WOW.

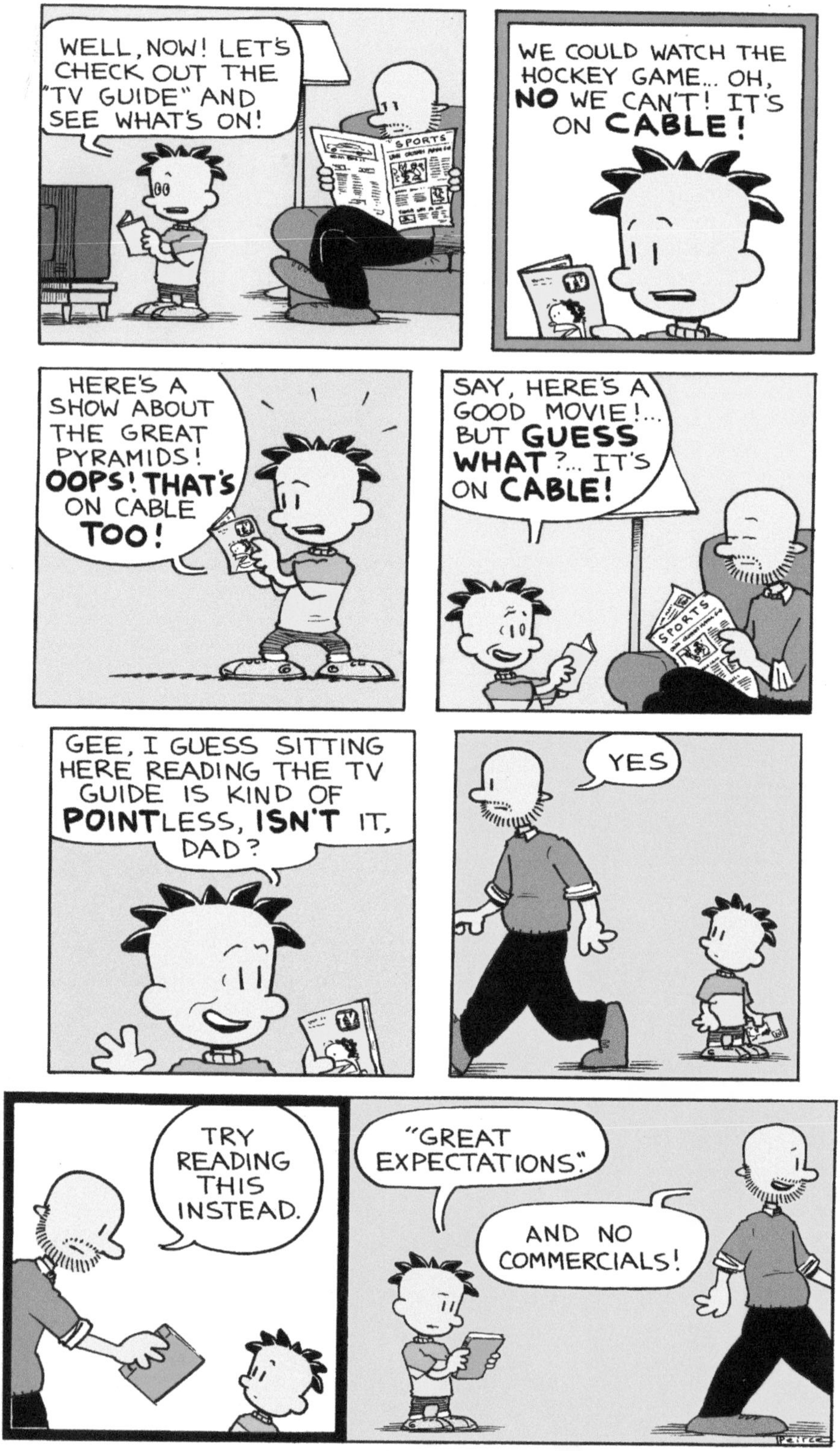
WELL, NOW! LET'S CHECK OUT THE "TV GUIDE" AND SEE WHAT'S ON!
SPORTS
WE COULD WATCH THE HOCKEY GAME... OH, NO WE CAN'T! IT'S ON CABLE!
HERE'S A SHOW ABOUT THE GREAT PYRAMIDS! OOPS! THAT'S ON CABLE TOO!
SAY, HERE'S A GOOD MOVIE!... BUT GUESS WHAT?... IT'S ON CABLE!
SPORTS
GEE, I GUESS SITTING HERE READING THE TV GUIDE IS KIND OF POINTLESS, ISN'T IT, DAD?
YES
TRY READING THIS INSTEAD.
"GREAT EXPECTATIONS."
AND NO COMMERCIALS!
Peirce

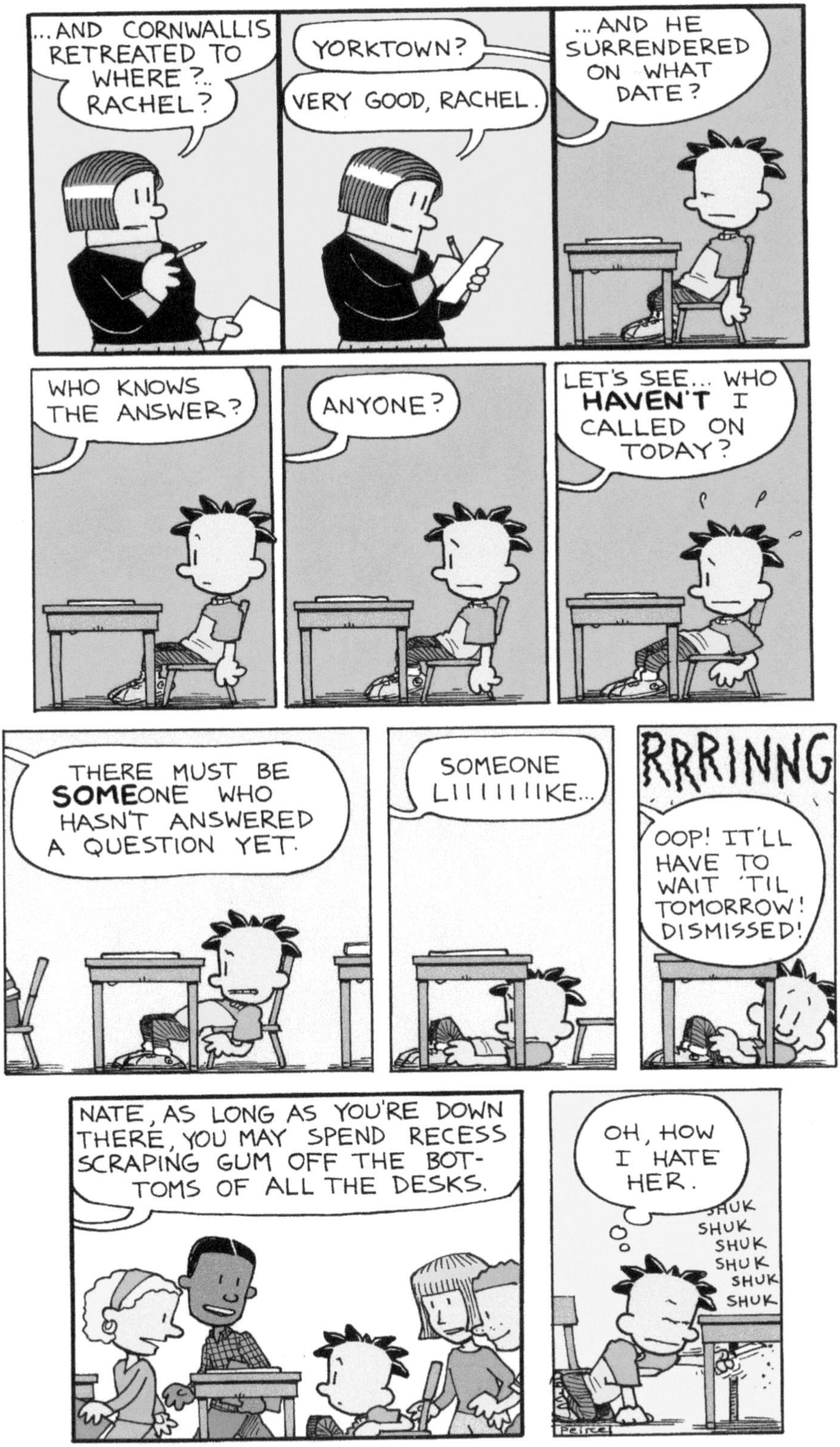
...AND CORNWALLIS RETREATED TO WHERE?.. RACHEL?
YORKTOWN?
VERY GOOD, RACHEL.
...AND HE SURRENDERED ON WHAT DATE?
WHO KNOWS THE ANSWER?
ANYONE?
LET'S SEE... WHO HAVEN'T I CALLED ON TODAY?
THERE MUST BE SOMEONE WHO HASN'T ANSWERED A QUESTION YET.
SOMEONE LIIIIIIIKE...
RRRINNG
OOP! IT'LL HAVE TO WAIT 'TIL TOMORROW! DISMISSED!
NATE, AS LONG AS YOU'RE DOWN THERE, YOU MAY SPEND RECESS SCRAPING GUM OFF THE BOTTOMS OF ALL THE DESKS.
OH, HOW I HATE HER.
SHUK SHUK SHUK SHUK SHUK SHUK
Peirce

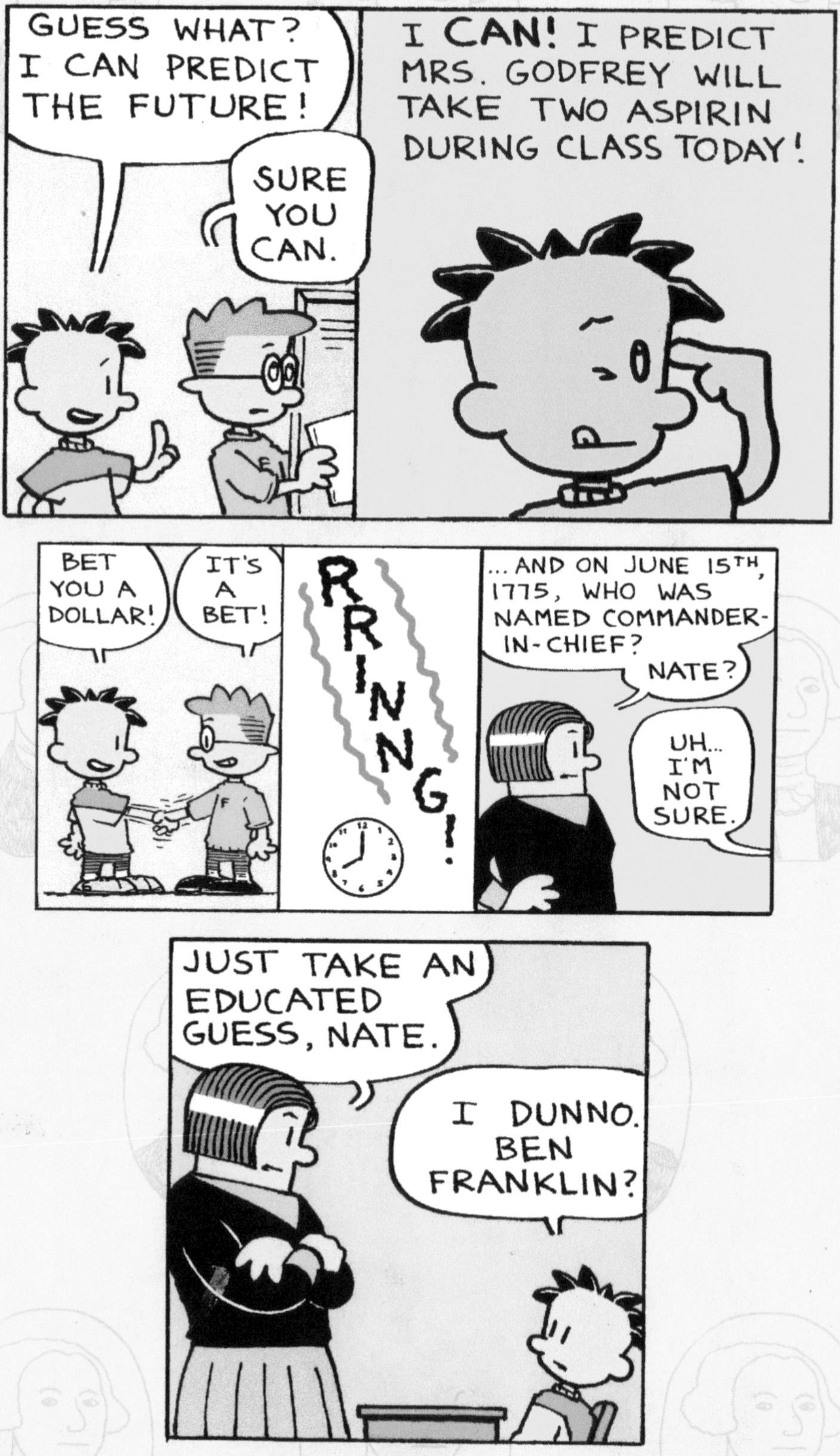
GUESS WHAT? I CAN PREDICT THE FUTURE!
SURE YOU CAN.
I CAN! I PREDICT MRS. GODFREY WILL TAKE TWO ASPIRIN DURING CLASS TODAY!
BET YOU A DOLLAR!
IT'S A BET!
RRINNG!
...AND ON JUNE 15TH, 1775, WHO WAS NAMED COMMANDER-IN-CHIEF?
NATE?
UH... I'M NOT SURE.
JUST TAKE AN EDUCATED GUESS, NATE.
I DUNNO. BEN FRANKLIN?

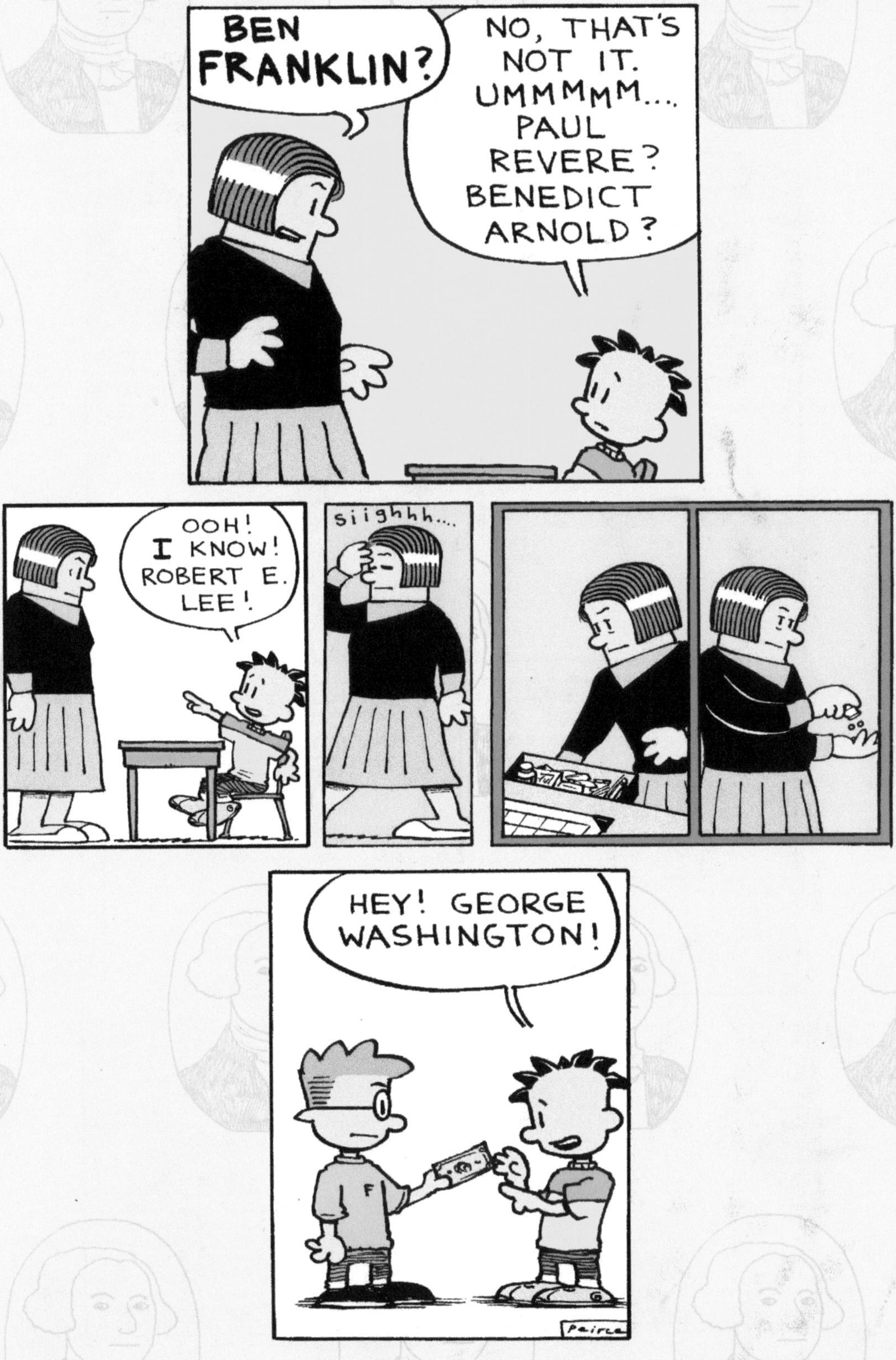
BEN FRANKLIN?
NO, THAT'S NOT IT. UMMMMM.... PAUL REVERE? BENEDICT ARNOLD?
OOH! I KNOW! ROBERT E. LEE!
siighhh....
HEY! GEORGE WASHINGTON!
Peirce

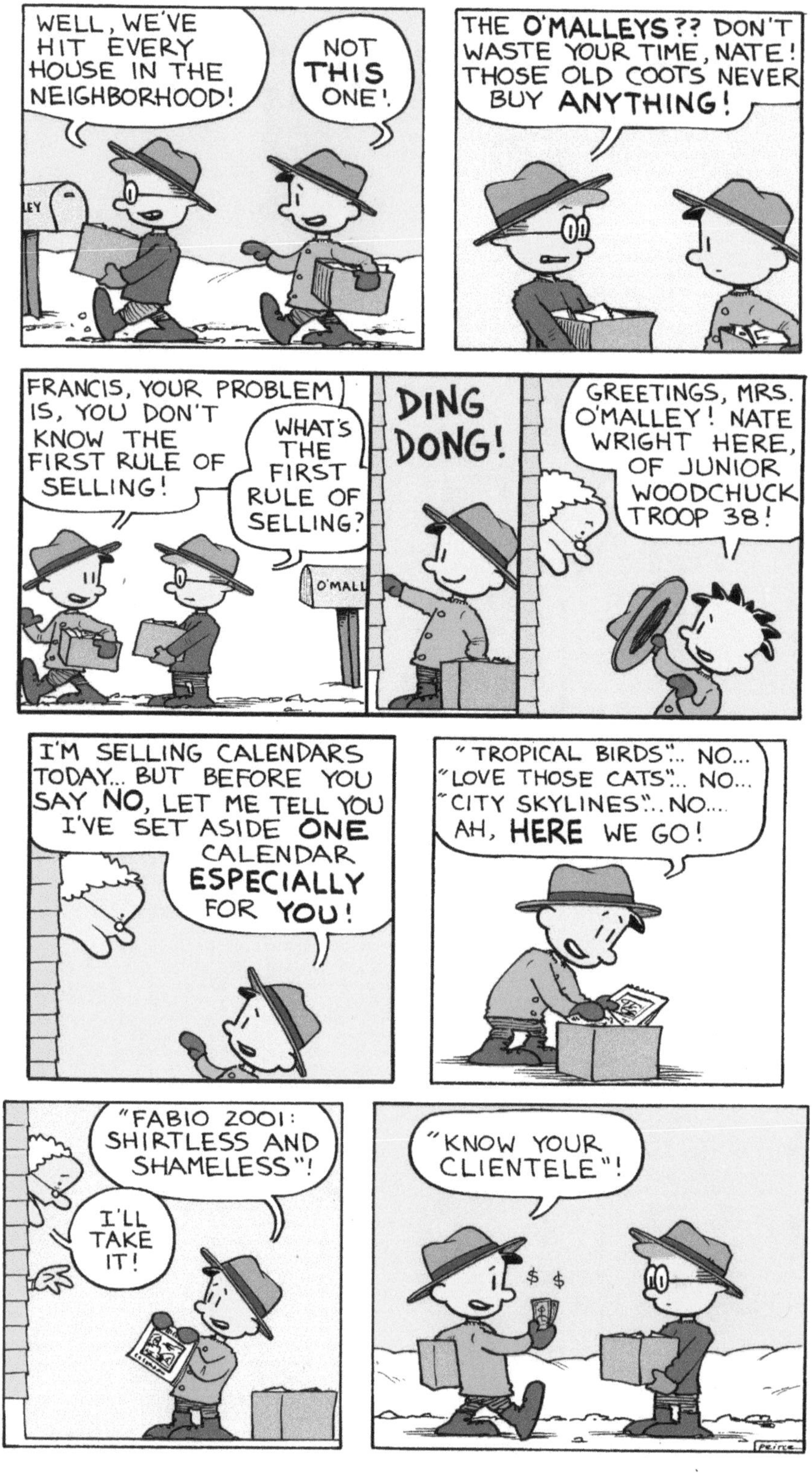
WELL, WE'VE HIT EVERY HOUSE IN THE NEIGHBORHOOD!
NOT THIS ONE!
THE O'MALLEYS?? DON'T WASTE YOUR TIME, NATE! THOSE OLD COOTS NEVER BUY ANYTHING!
FRANCIS, YOUR PROBLEM IS, YOU DON'T KNOW THE FIRST RULE OF SELLING!
WHAT'S THE FIRST RULE OF SELLING?
O'MALL
DING DONG!
GREETINGS, MRS. O'MALLEY! NATE WRIGHT HERE, OF JUNIOR WOODCHUCK TROOP 38!
I'M SELLING CALENDARS TODAY... BUT BEFORE YOU SAY NO, LET ME TELL YOU I'VE SET ASIDE ONE CALENDAR ESPECIALLY FOR YOU!
"TROPICAL BIRDS"... NO... "LOVE THOSE CATS"... NO... "CITY SKYLINES"... NO... AH, HERE WE GO!
"FABIO 2001: SHIRTLESS AND SHAMELESS"!
I'LL TAKE IT!
"KNOW YOUR CLIENTELE"!
$ $
peirce

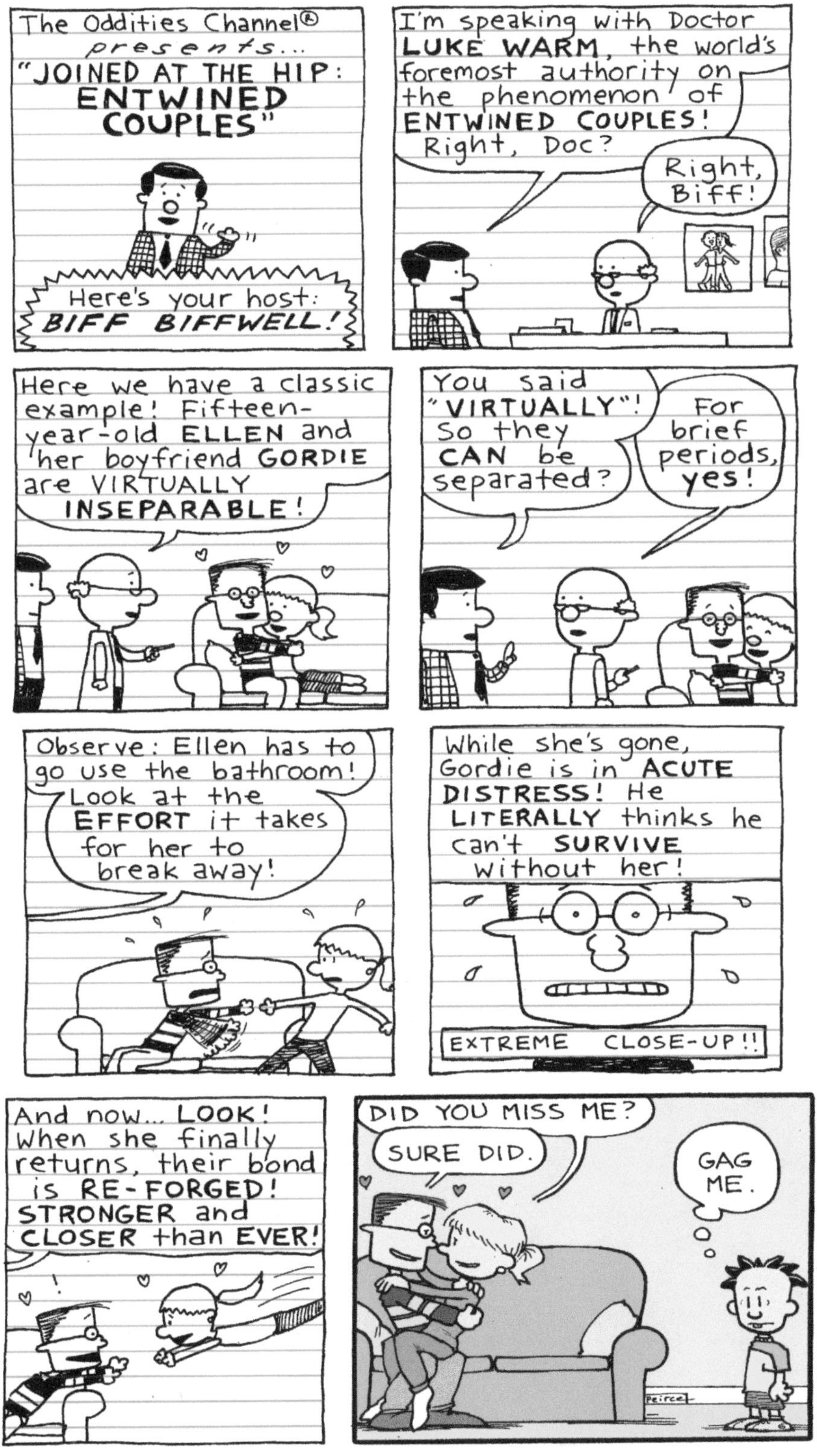
The Oddities Channel®
presents...
"JOINED AT THE HIP: ENTWINED COUPLES"
Here's your host: BIFF BIFFWELL!
I'm speaking with Doctor LUKE WARM, the world's foremost authority on the phenomenon of ENTWINED COUPLES! Right, Doc?
Right, Biff!
Here we have a classic example! Fifteen-year-old ELLEN and her boyfriend GORDIE are VIRTUALLY INSEPARABLE!
You said "VIRTUALLY"! So they CAN be separated?
For brief periods, yes!
Observe: Ellen has to go use the bathroom! Look at the EFFORT it takes for her to break away!
While she's gone, Gordie is in ACUTE DISTRESS! He LITERALLY thinks he can't SURVIVE without her!
EXTREME CLOSE-UP!!
And now... LOOK! When she finally returns, their bond is RE-FORGED! STRONGER and CLOSER than EVER!
DID YOU MISS ME?
SURE DID.
GAG ME.
Peirce

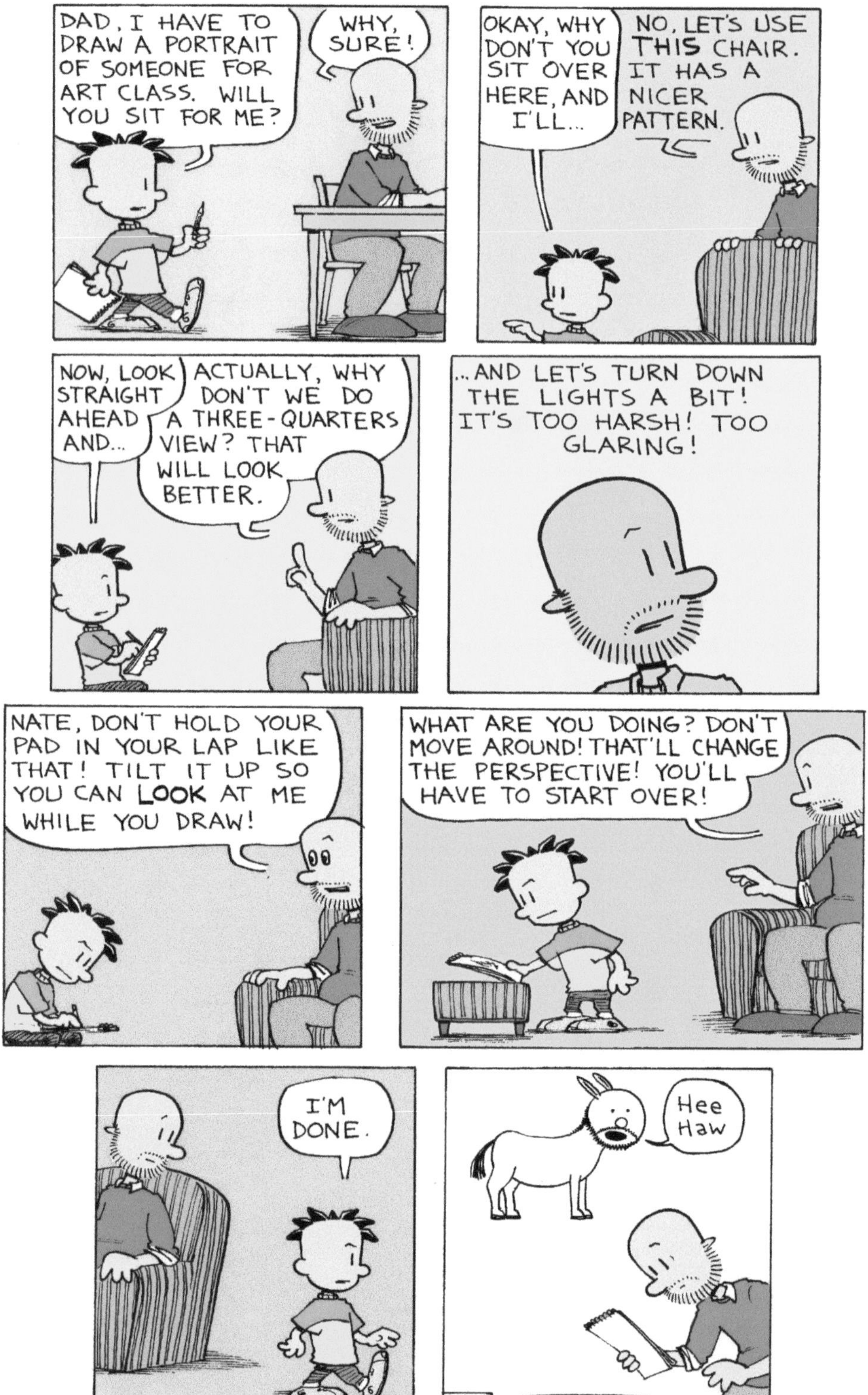
DAD, I HAVE TO DRAW A PORTRAIT OF SOMEONE FOR ART CLASS. WILL YOU SIT FOR ME?
WHY, SURE!
OKAY, WHY DON'T YOU SIT OVER HERE, AND I'LL...
NO, LET'S USE THIS CHAIR. IT HAS A NICER PATTERN.
NOW, LOOK STRAIGHT AHEAD AND...
ACTUALLY, WHY DON'T WE DO A THREE-QUARTERS VIEW? THAT WILL LOOK BETTER.
...AND LET'S TURN DOWN THE LIGHTS A BIT! IT'S TOO HARSH! TOO GLARING!
NATE, DON'T HOLD YOUR PAD IN YOUR LAP LIKE THAT! TILT IT UP SO YOU CAN LOOK AT ME WHILE YOU DRAW!
WHAT ARE YOU DOING? DON'T MOVE AROUND! THAT'LL CHANGE THE PERSPECTIVE! YOU'LL HAVE TO START OVER!
I'M DONE.
Hee Haw
Peirce

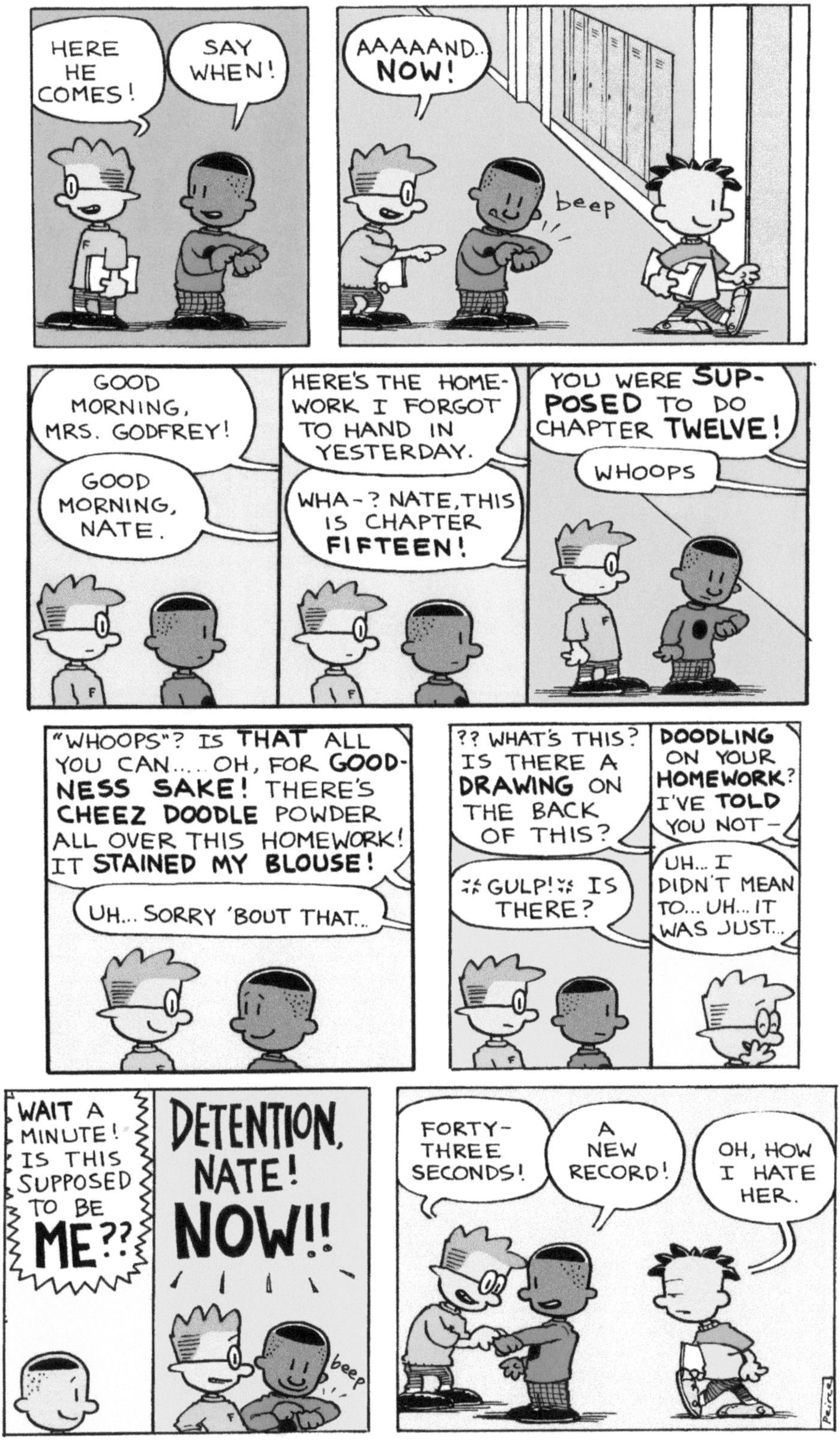
HERE HE COMES!
SAY WHEN!
AAAAAND.. NOW!
beep
GOOD MORNING, MRS. GODFREY!
GOOD MORNING, NATE.
HERE'S THE HOMEWORK I FORGOT TO HAND IN YESTERDAY.
WHA-? NATE, THIS IS CHAPTER FIFTEEN!
YOU WERE SUPPOSED TO DO CHAPTER TWELVE!
WHOOPS
"WHOOPS"? IS THAT ALL YOU CAN..... OH, FOR GOODNESS SAKE! THERE'S CHEEZ DOODLE POWDER ALL OVER THIS HOMEWORK! IT STAINED MY BLOUSE!
UH... SORRY 'BOUT THAT...
?? WHAT'S THIS? IS THERE A DRAWING ON THE BACK OF THIS?
GULP! IS THERE?
DOODLING ON YOUR HOMEWORK? I'VE TOLD YOU NOT-
UH... I DIDN'T MEAN TO... UH... IT WAS JUST...
WAIT A MINUTE! IS THIS SUPPOSED TO BE ME??
DETENTION, NATE! NOW!!
beep
FORTY-THREE SECONDS!
A NEW RECORD!
OH, HOW I HATE HER.
Peirce

FOR MY ASSIGNMENT, I WAS SUPPOSED TO DO A REPORT ON THE "LINCOLN-DOUGLAS DEBATES".

BUT I COULDN'T! **WHY?** BECAUSE THERE **IS** NOBODY NAMED "LINCOLN DOUGLAS"!

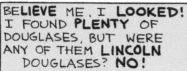

BE**LIEVE** ME, I **LOOKED!** I FOUND **PLENTY** OF DOUGLASES, BUT WERE ANY OF THEM **LINCOLN** DOUGLASES? **NO!**

...BUT HEY! LET'S SAY THERE **WAS** SOME TOTALLY OBSCURE GUY NAMED LINCOLN DOUGLAS! WHAT WERE THESE **DEBATES** ALL ABOUT? WHAT'S UP WITH **THAT?**

WHO WAS LINCOLN DOUGLAS DEBATING? WHEN DID IT HAPPEN? IF ANYBODY KNOWS, **TELL** ME, BECAUSE **I** CERTAINLY HAVE NO CLUE!

SO ANYWAY, YOU SEE MY PREDICAMENT! HOW CAN I WRITE A REPORT ON SOME CLOWN WHO NEVER **EXISTED?**

OBVIOUSLY, I **CAN'T!** SO INSTEAD, I DREW THIS GIANT QUESTION MARK TO FOREVER SYMBOLIZE THE UNKNOWABLE MYSTERY OF... LINCOLN DOUGLAS!

CLAP! CLAP! CLAP! CLAP! CLAP! CLAP! CLAP!

THANK YOU! THANK YOU!

CRIPES.

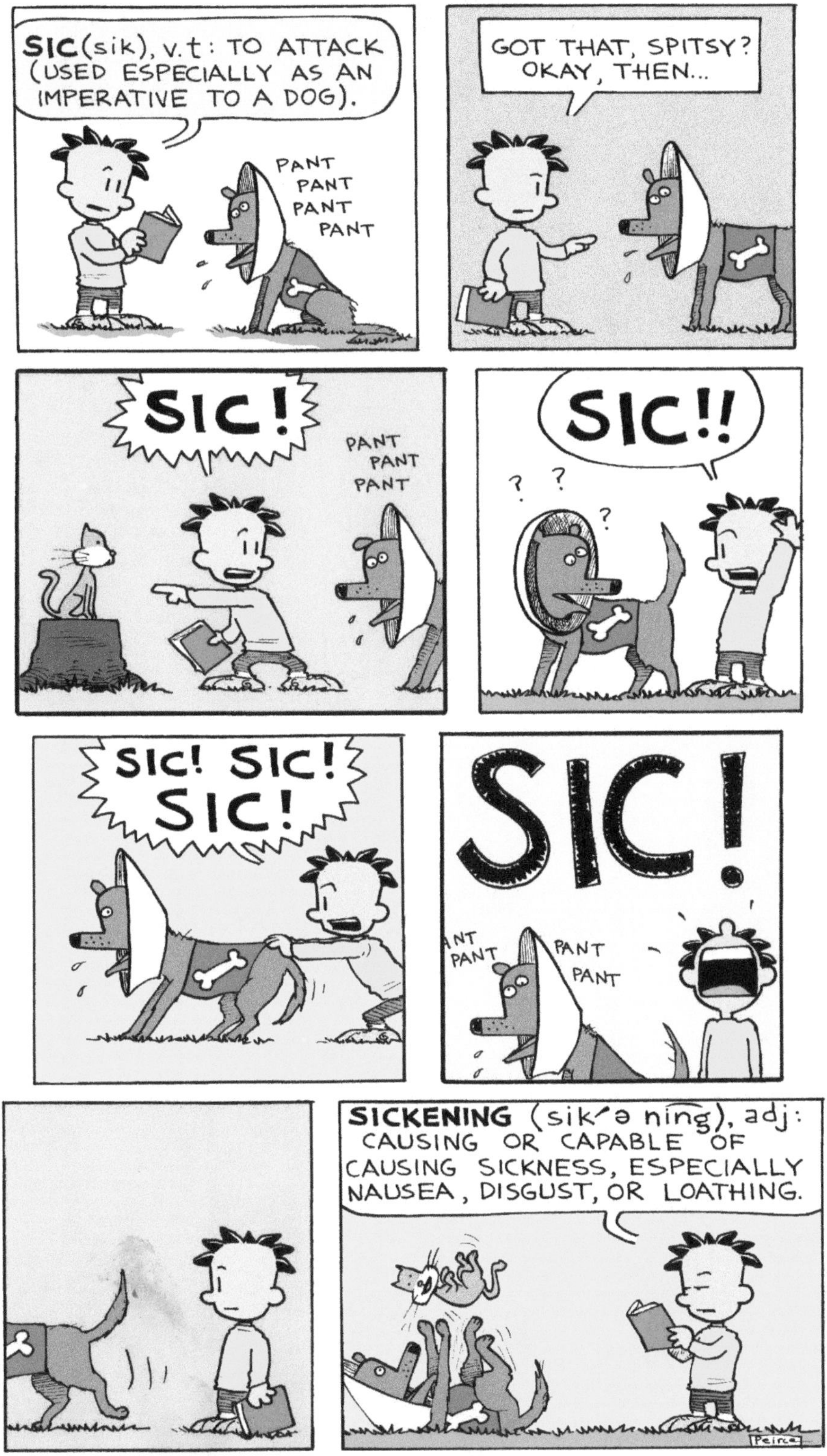
SIC (sik), v.t: TO ATTACK (USED ESPECIALLY AS AN IMPERATIVE TO A DOG).
PANT PANT PANT PANT
GOT THAT, SPITSY? OKAY, THEN...
SIC!
PANT PANT PANT
SIC!!
? ? ?
SIC! SIC! SIC!
SIC!
NT PANT
PANT PANT
SICKENING (sik'ə ning), adj: CAUSING OR CAPABLE OF CAUSING SICKNESS, ESPECIALLY NAUSEA, DISGUST, OR LOATHING.
Peirce

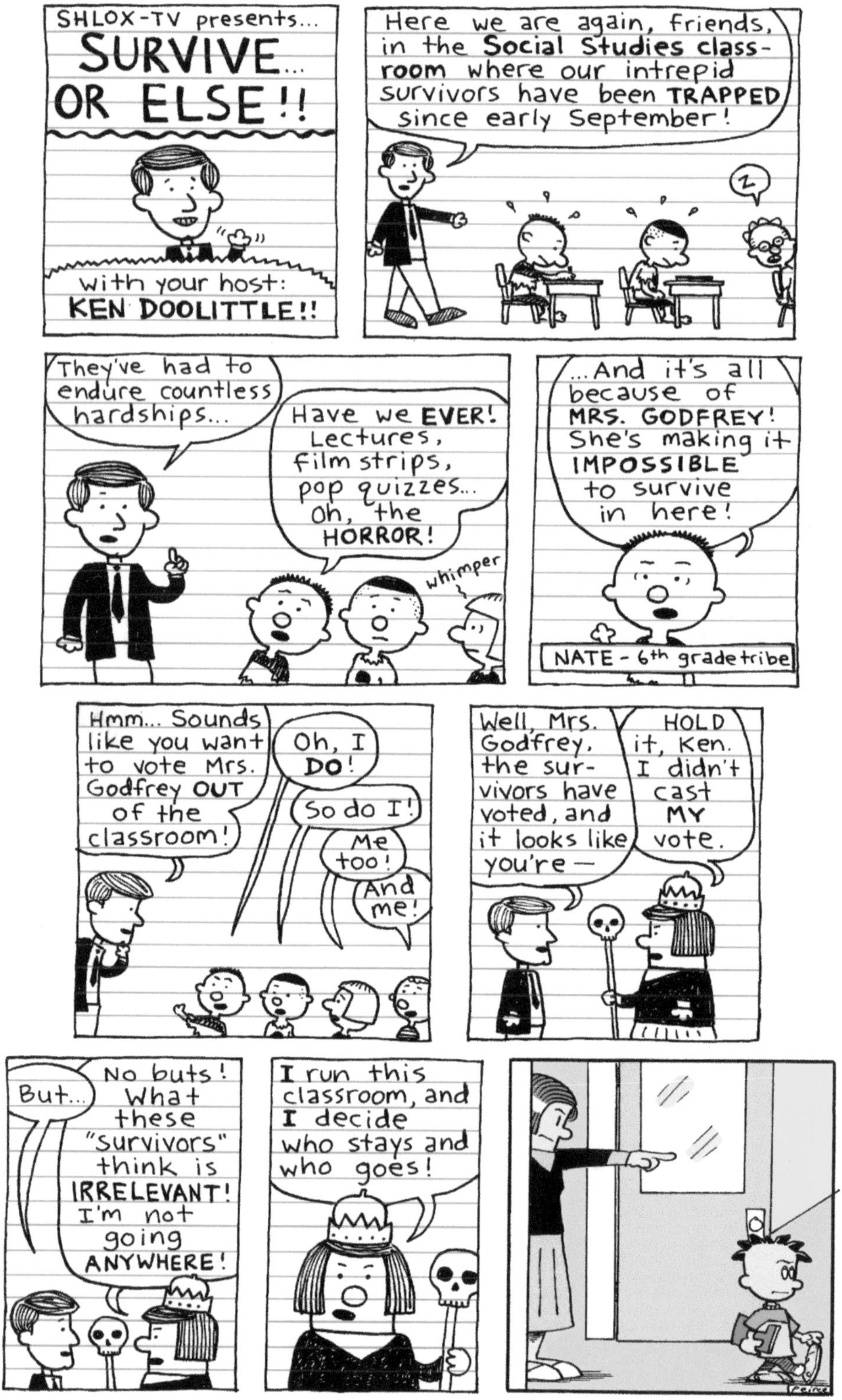

SHLOX-TV presents...
SURVIVE... OR ELSE!!
with your host: KEN DOOLITTLE!!
Here we are again, friends, in the Social Studies classroom where our intrepid survivors have been TRAPPED since early September!
z
They've had to endure countless hardships...
Have we EVER! Lectures, film strips, pop quizzes... Oh, the HORROR!
whimper
...And it's all because of MRS. GODFREY! She's making it IMPOSSIBLE to survive in here!
NATE - 6th grade tribe
Hmm... Sounds like you want to vote Mrs. Godfrey OUT of the classroom!
Oh, I DO!
So do I!
Me too!
And me!
Well, Mrs. Godfrey, the survivors have voted, and it looks like you're —
HOLD it, Ken. I didn't cast MY vote.
But...
No buts! What these "survivors" think is IRRELEVANT! I'm not going ANYWHERE!
I run this classroom, and I decide who stays and who goes!

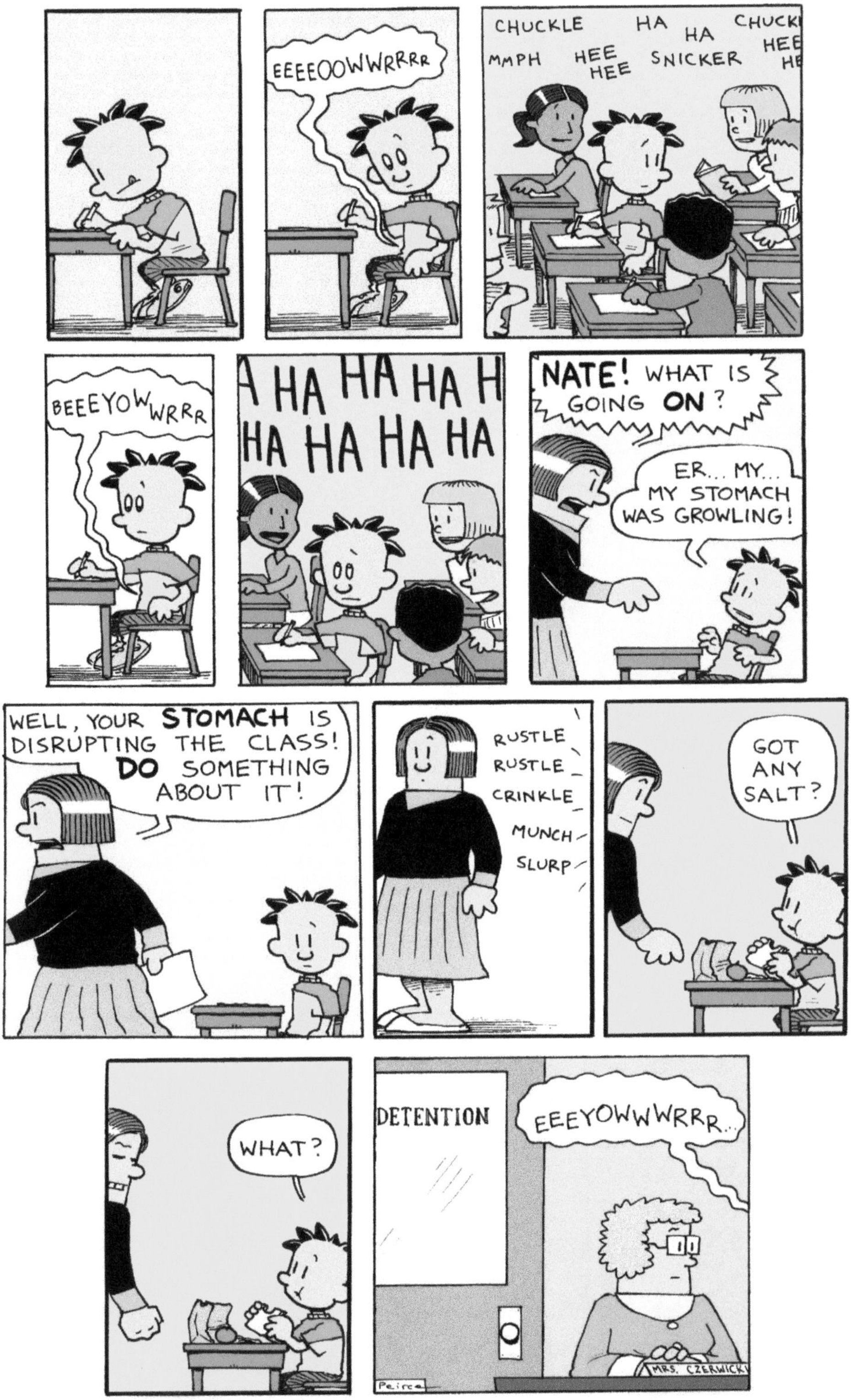
EEEEOOWWRRRR
CHUCKLE HA HA CHUCK
MMPH HEE HEE SNICKER HEE
BEEEYOWWRRRR
HA HA HA HA H
HA HA HA HA
NATE! WHAT IS GOING ON?
ER... MY... MY STOMACH WAS GROWLING!
WELL, YOUR STOMACH IS DISRUPTING THE CLASS! DO SOMETHING ABOUT IT!
RUSTLE
RUSTLE
CRINKLE
MUNCH
SLURP
GOT ANY SALT?
WHAT?
DETENTION
EEEYOWWWRRRR...
MRS. CZERWICKI
Peirce

SOUNDS of the GAME

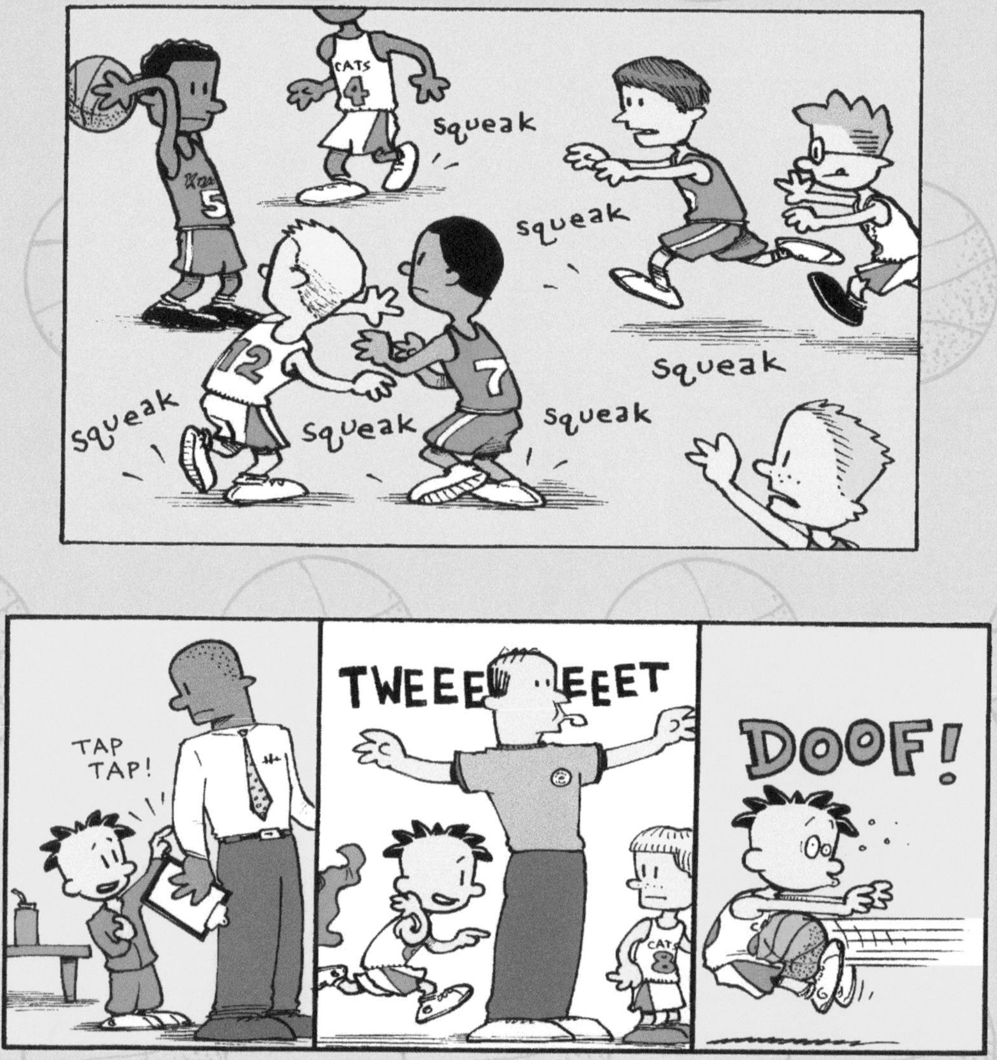

squeak
squeak
squeak
squeak
squeak
squeak
TAP TAP!
TWEEE EEET
DOOF!

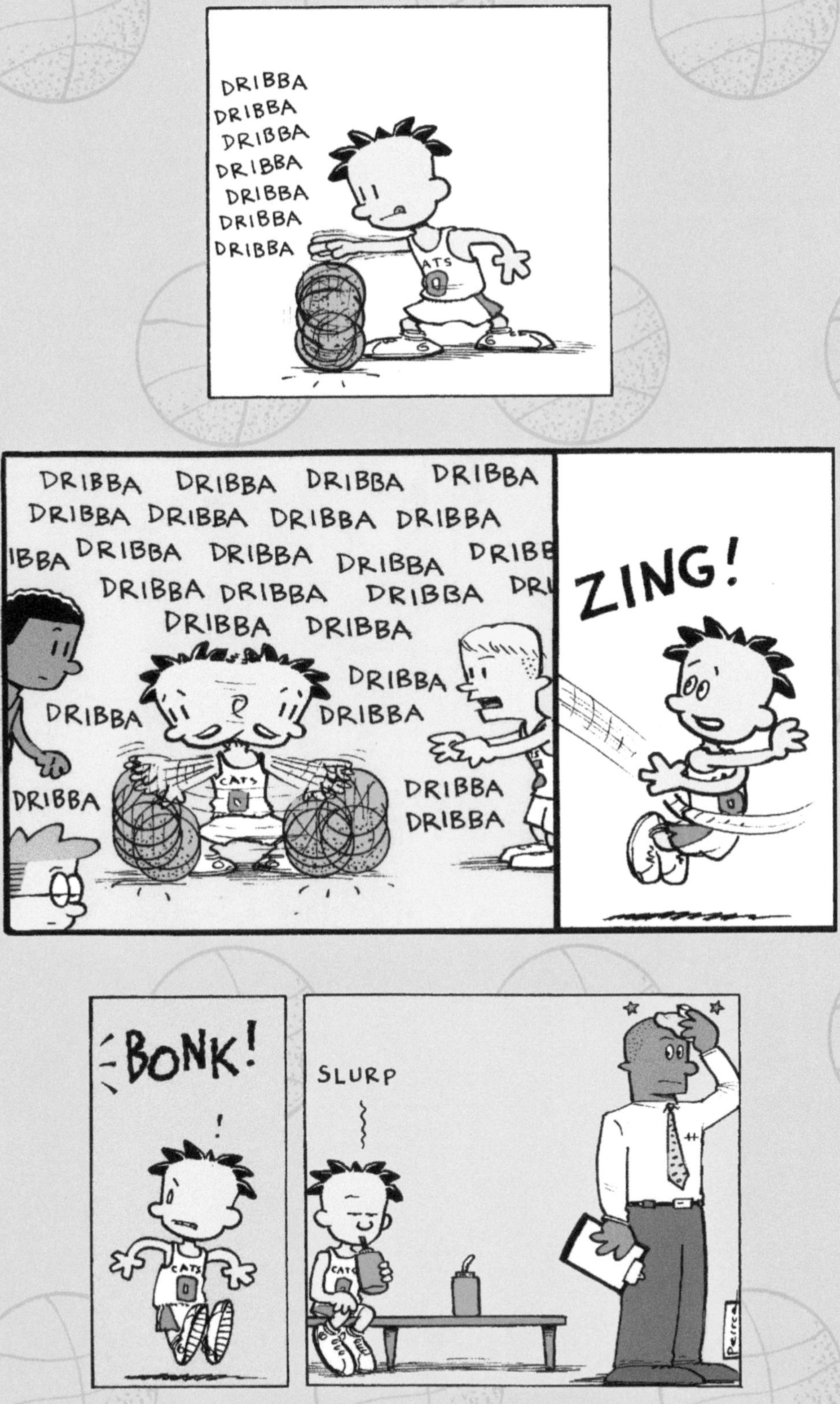
DRIBBA
DRIBBA
DRIBBA
DRIBBA
DRIBBA
DRIBBA
DRIBBA
DRIBBA DRIBBA DRIBBA DRIBBA
DRIBBA DRIBBA DRIBBA DRIBBA
DRIBBA DRIBBA DRIBBA
DRIBBA DRIBBA DRIBBA
DRIBBA DRIBBA
DRIBBA
DRIBBA
DRIBBA
DRIBBA
DRIBBA
DRIBBA
DRIBBA
ZING!
BONK!
!
SLURP

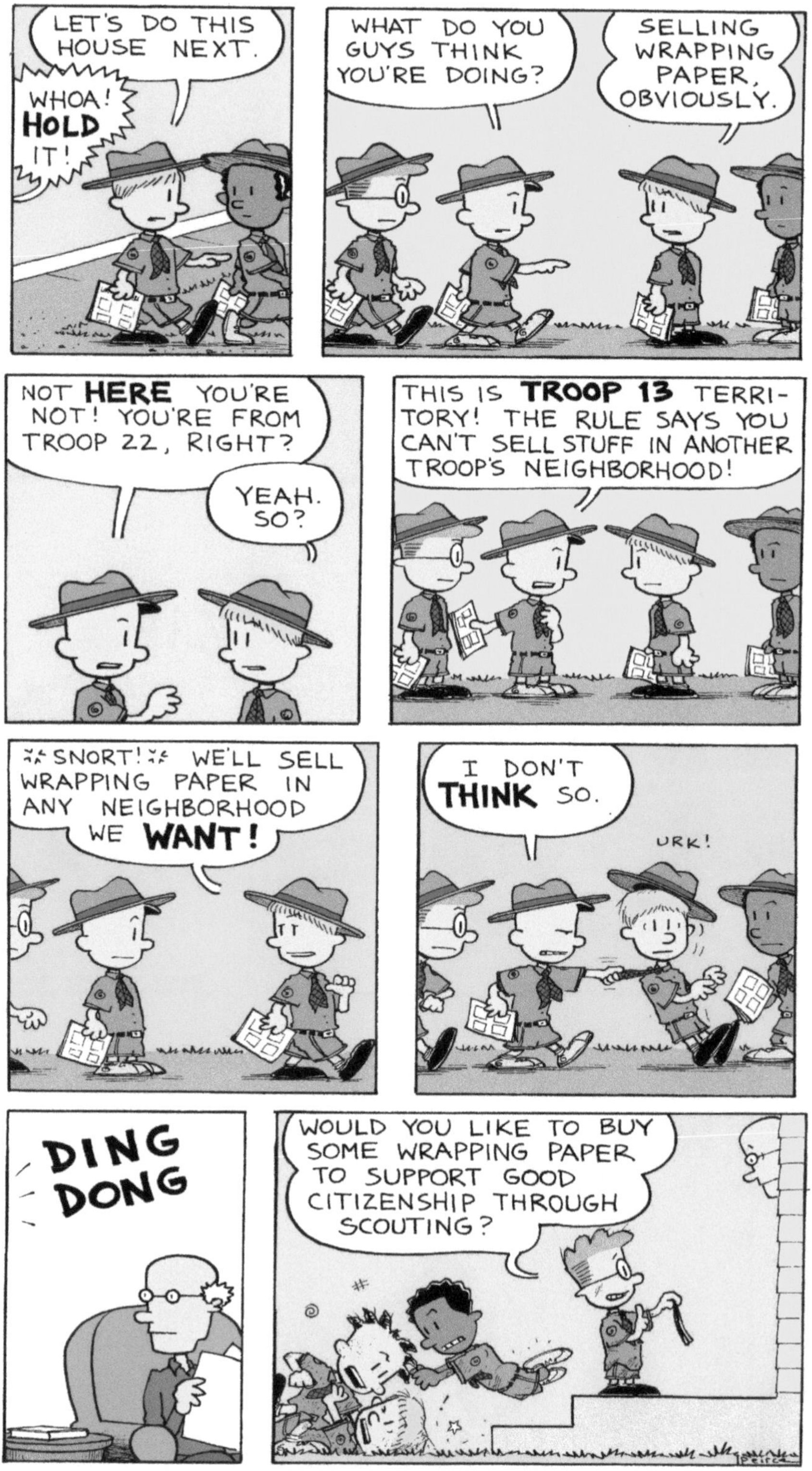

LET'S DO THIS HOUSE NEXT.
WHOA! HOLD IT!
WHAT DO YOU GUYS THINK YOU'RE DOING?
SELLING WRAPPING PAPER, OBVIOUSLY.
NOT HERE YOU'RE NOT! YOU'RE FROM TROOP 22, RIGHT?
YEAH. SO?
THIS IS TROOP 13 TERRITORY! THE RULE SAYS YOU CAN'T SELL STUFF IN ANOTHER TROOP'S NEIGHBORHOOD!
SNORT! WE'LL SELL WRAPPING PAPER IN ANY NEIGHBORHOOD WE WANT!
I DON'T THINK SO.
URK!
DING DONG
WOULD YOU LIKE TO BUY SOME WRAPPING PAPER TO SUPPORT GOOD CITIZENSHIP THROUGH SCOUTING?

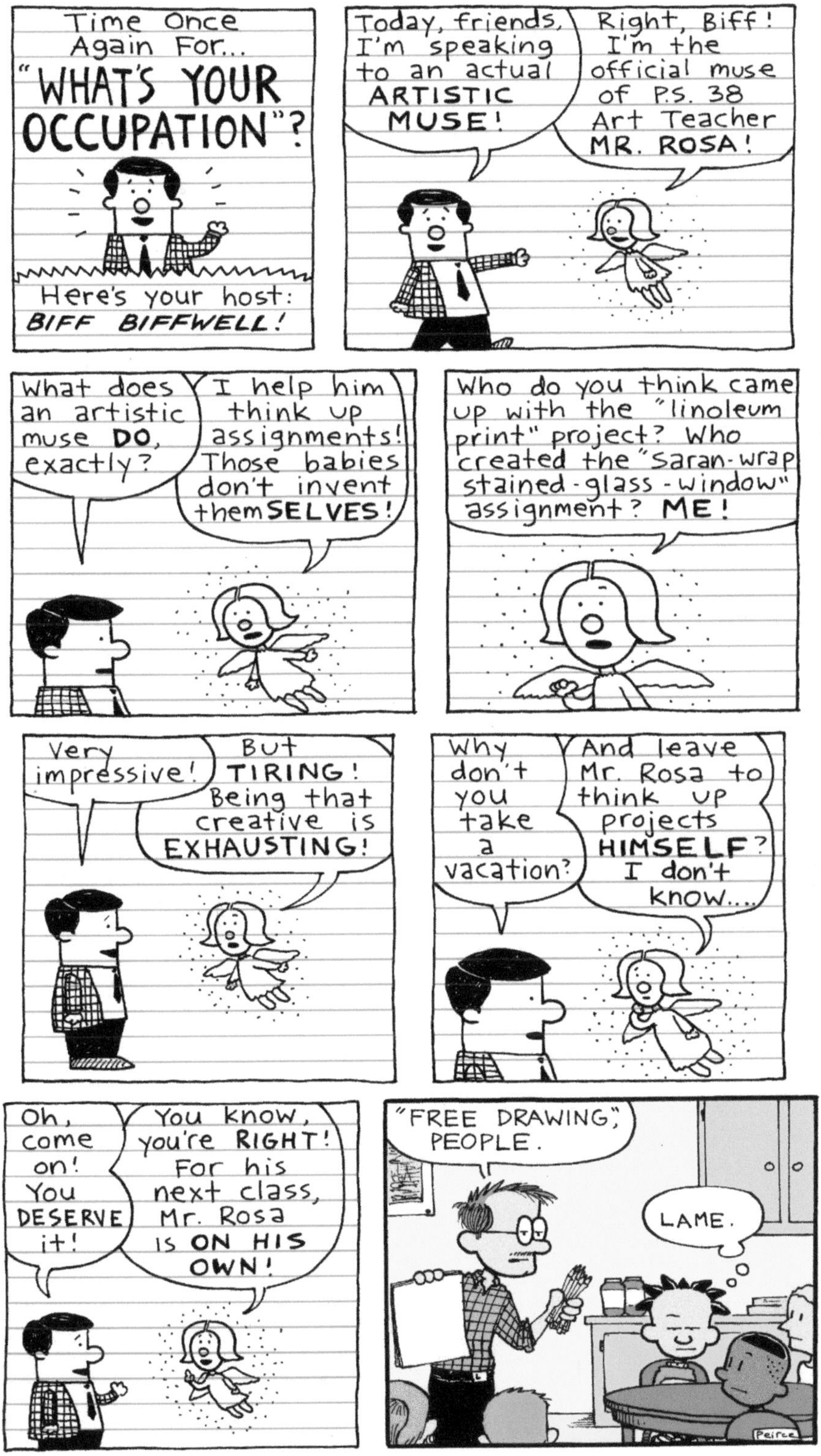
Time Once Again For... "WHAT'S YOUR OCCUPATION"?
Here's your host: BIFF BIFFWELL!
Today, friends, I'm speaking to an actual ARTISTIC MUSE!
Right, Biff! I'm the official muse of P.S. 38 Art Teacher MR. ROSA!
What does an artistic muse DO, exactly?
I help him think up assignments! Those babies don't invent themSELVES!
Who do you think came up with the "linoleum print" project? Who created the "Saran-wrap stained-glass-window" assignment? ME!
Very impressive!
But TIRING! Being that creative is EXHAUSTING!
Why don't you take a vacation?
And leave Mr. Rosa to think up projects HIMSELF? I don't know....
Oh, come on! You DESERVE it!
You know, you're RIGHT! For his next class, Mr. Rosa is ON HIS OWN!
"FREE DRAWING," PEOPLE.
LAME.
Peirce

★☆★☆★☆★☆★☆★
Time For Another
Scintillating Edition OF...
FACULTY
INTERVIEW!
with your host:
CHIP CHIPSON!

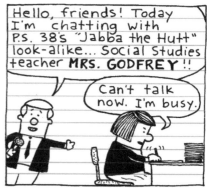

Hello, friends! Today I'm chatting with P.S. 38's "Jabba the Hutt" look-alike... Social Studies teacher MRS. GODFREY!!

Can't talk now. I'm busy.

Ah! I see you're correcting NATE WRIGHT's most recent test!

That's right, Chip, and he is FAILING miserably!

And yet... you seem HAPPY about that!

Of COURSE I'm happy about it! That's what I WANTED to happen!

I... I don't understand.

I told Nate to study Chapter Three! Then I tested him on Chapter TWELVE!

But... that's totally UNFAIR!

Exactly! That's how he'll LEARN: by absorbing DEFEAT after devastating DEFEAT!

You've got to BREAK kids' spirits while they're young, Chip! Sure, it may seem cruel... but deep down they LOVE you for it!

OH, HOW I LOATHE HER.

JUST AN OBSERVATION: THERE WERE NO MATADORS AT THE BATTLE OF BULL RUN.

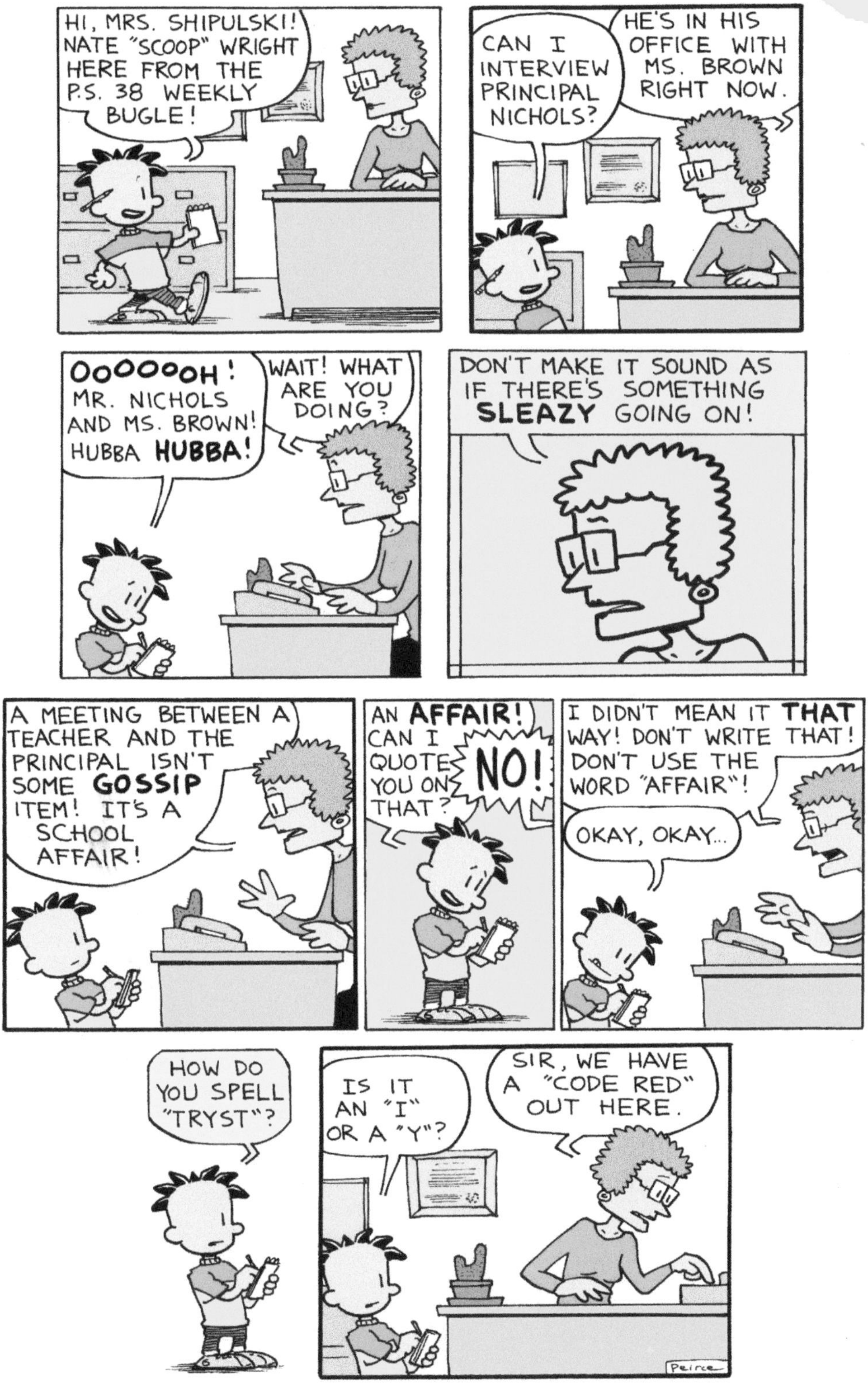

HI, MRS. SHIPULSKI! NATE "SCOOP" WRIGHT HERE FROM THE P.S. 38 WEEKLY BUGLE!
CAN I INTERVIEW PRINCIPAL NICHOLS?
HE'S IN HIS OFFICE WITH MS. BROWN RIGHT NOW.
OOOOOOH! MR. NICHOLS AND MS. BROWN! HUBBA **HUBBA**!
WAIT! WHAT ARE YOU DOING?
DON'T MAKE IT SOUND AS IF THERE'S SOMETHING **SLEAZY** GOING ON!
A MEETING BETWEEN A TEACHER AND THE PRINCIPAL ISN'T SOME **GOSSIP** ITEM! IT'S A SCHOOL AFFAIR!
AN **AFFAIR**! CAN I QUOTE YOU ON THAT?
NO!
I DIDN'T MEAN IT **THAT** WAY! DON'T WRITE THAT! DON'T USE THE WORD "AFFAIR"!
OKAY, OKAY...
HOW DO YOU SPELL "TRYST"?
IS IT AN "I" OR A "Y"?
SIR, WE HAVE A "CODE RED" OUT HERE.
Peirce

☆ ☆ ☆ ☆ ☆
CELEBRITY
INTER-
VIEW!

Here's your host: **CHIP CHIPSON!**

Friends, our guest today is "canine control specialist" **HERMAN SHEPHERD!**

Howdy, Chip.

Herman, isn't "canine control specialist" just a fancy-pants way of saying "**DOG CATCHER**"?

Not at all!

Of course, rounding up strays is **PART** of it, but the most **IMPORTANT** aspect of the job is **PROTECTING THE PUBLIC!**

For example: in 1997 I captured the infamous "**HYDRO PHOEBE**" and her rabid band of followers!

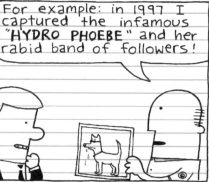

I also collared "Attila the Husky" in 1999...

...and, in 2001, "Notorious P.U.G!"

JL549712

KN753412

Impressive resumé!

Believe me, Chip, they're not **ALL** success stories. **MANY** dogs have slipped through my fingers!

Not **HARDENED CRIMINALS**, mind you, but dogs who nonetheless are **DANGEROUS!** Dogs who are a **MENACE** to everyone around them!

DID YOU HEAR SOMETHING?

HM?

Peirce

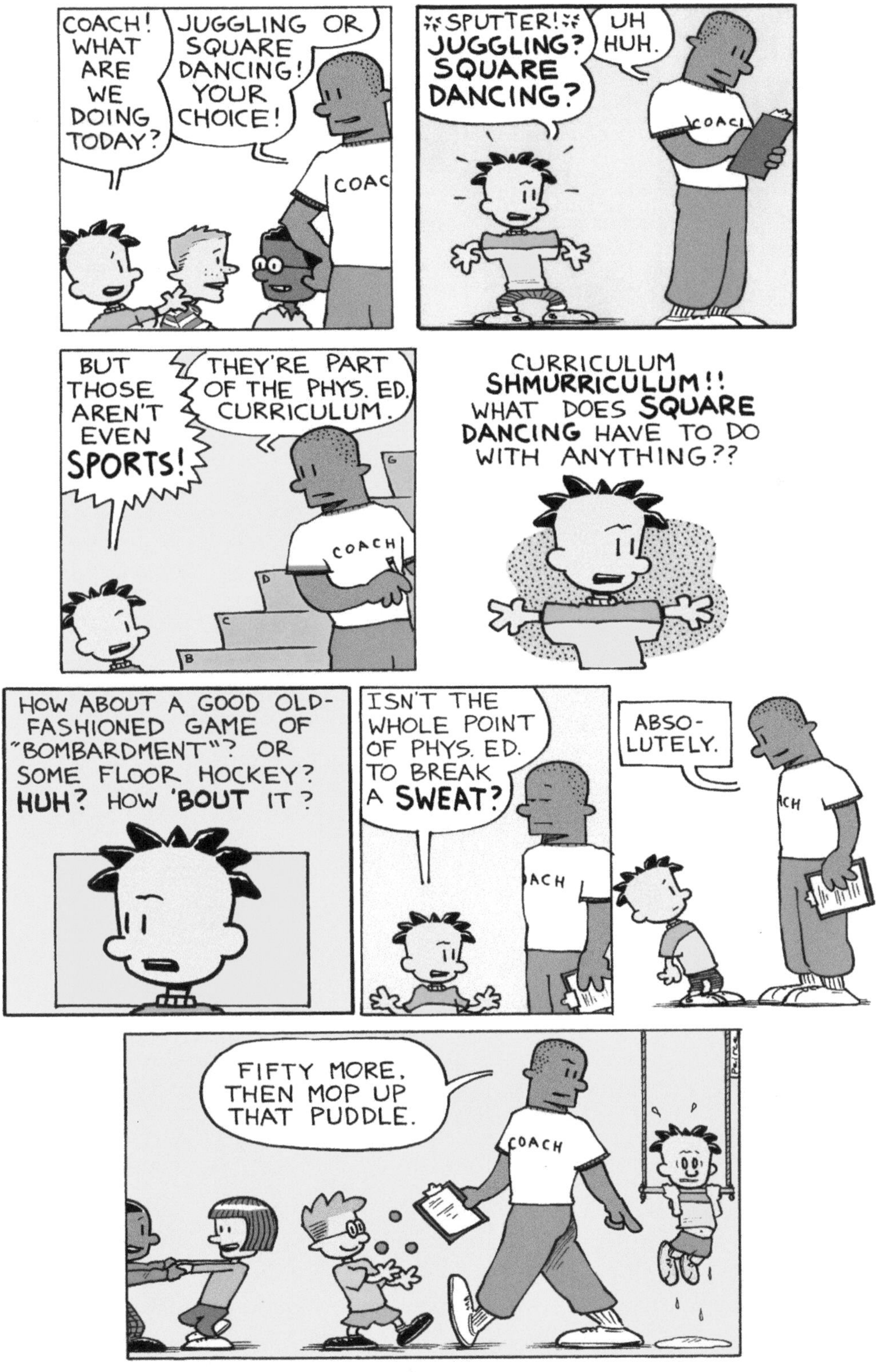
COACH! WHAT ARE WE DOING TODAY?
JUGGLING OR SQUARE DANCING! YOUR CHOICE!
SPUTTER! JUGGLING? SQUARE DANCING?
UH HUH.
BUT THOSE AREN'T EVEN SPORTS!
THEY'RE PART OF THE PHYS. ED. CURRICULUM.
CURRICULUM SHMURRICULUM!! WHAT DOES SQUARE DANCING HAVE TO DO WITH ANYTHING??
HOW ABOUT A GOOD OLD-FASHIONED GAME OF "BOMBARDMENT"? OR SOME FLOOR HOCKEY? HUH? HOW 'BOUT IT?
ISN'T THE WHOLE POINT OF PHYS. ED. TO BREAK A SWEAT?
ABSOLUTELY.
FIFTY MORE, THEN MOP UP THAT PUDDLE.

CELEBRITY
INTER-
VIEW!!
with your host: CHIP CHIPSON!

Folks, I'm coming to you live from HEAVEN where I'm chatting with legendary commander-in-chief... ABE LINCOLN!

So, Abe... excited about tomorrow?

Tomorrow?

PRESIDENTS' DAY! It's your birthday celebration!

Actually, Chip, my birthday was LAST week.

Tomorrow is simply an excuse to sell cars and have a three-day weekend.

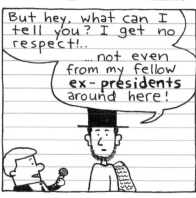

But hey, what can I tell you? I get no respect!.. ...not even from my fellow ex-presidents around here!

Like WASHINGTON over there! He's always busting my chops because HIS face is on the QUARTER and MY face is only on the...

HEY, ABE! "PENNY" FOR YOUR THOUGHTS!

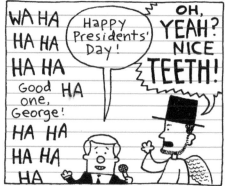

WA HA HA HA HA HA Good one, George! HA HA HA HA HA

Happy Presidents' Day!

OH, YEAH? NICE TEETH!

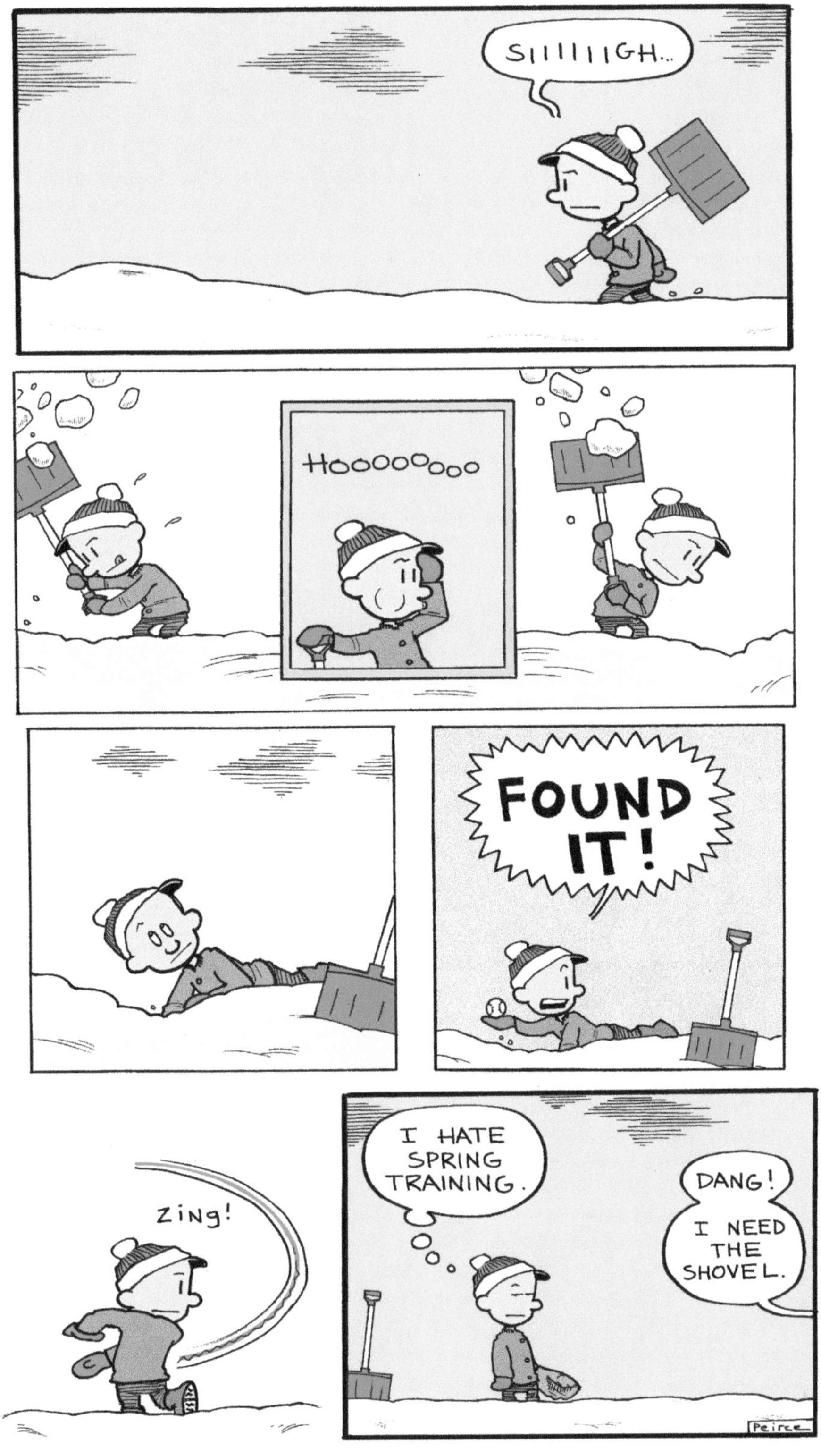
SIIIIIIGH...
HOOOOOOOO
FOUND IT!
ZING!
I HATE SPRING TRAINING.
DANG! I NEED THE SHOVEL.
Peirce

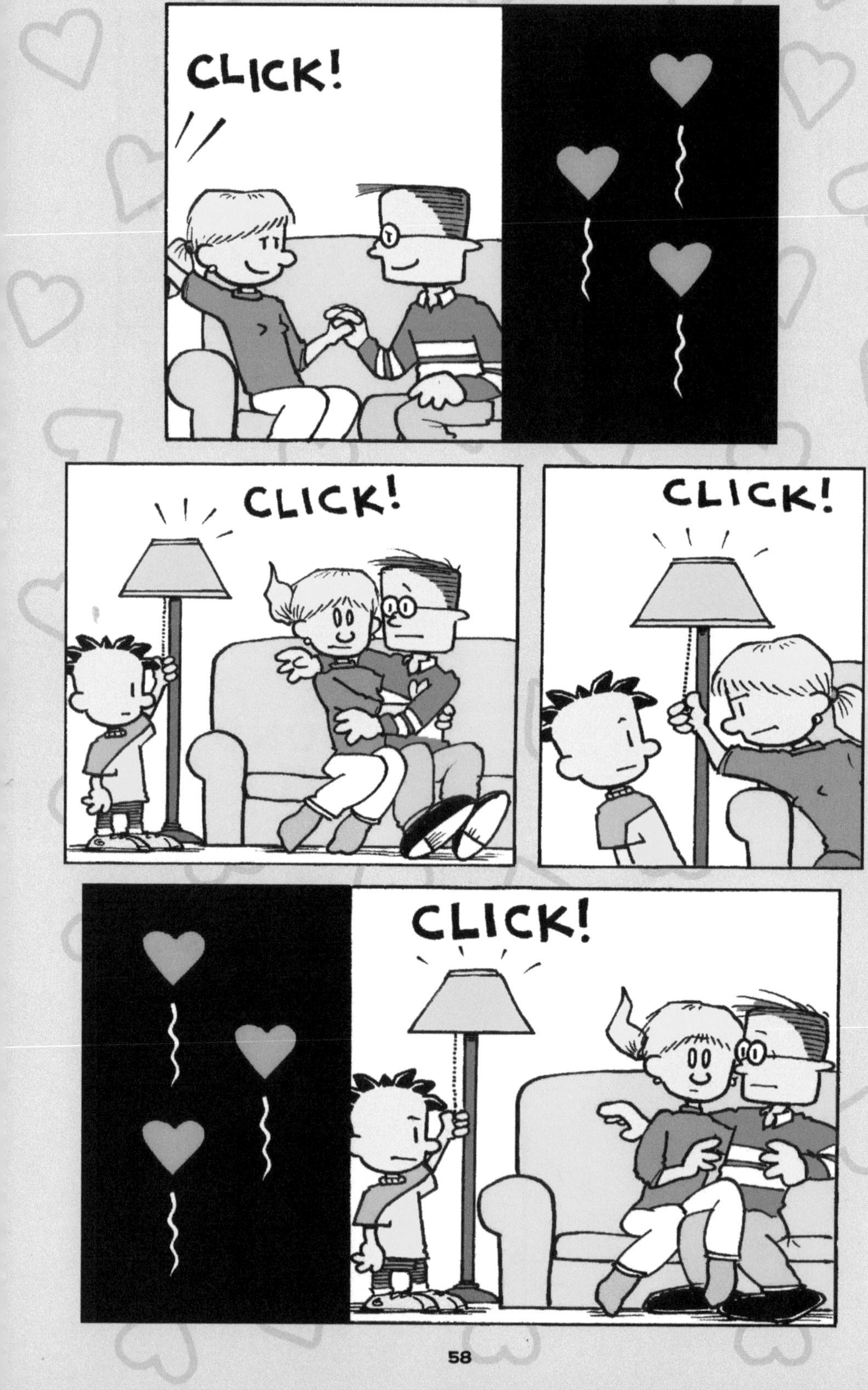
CLICK!
CLICK!
CLICK!
CLICK!

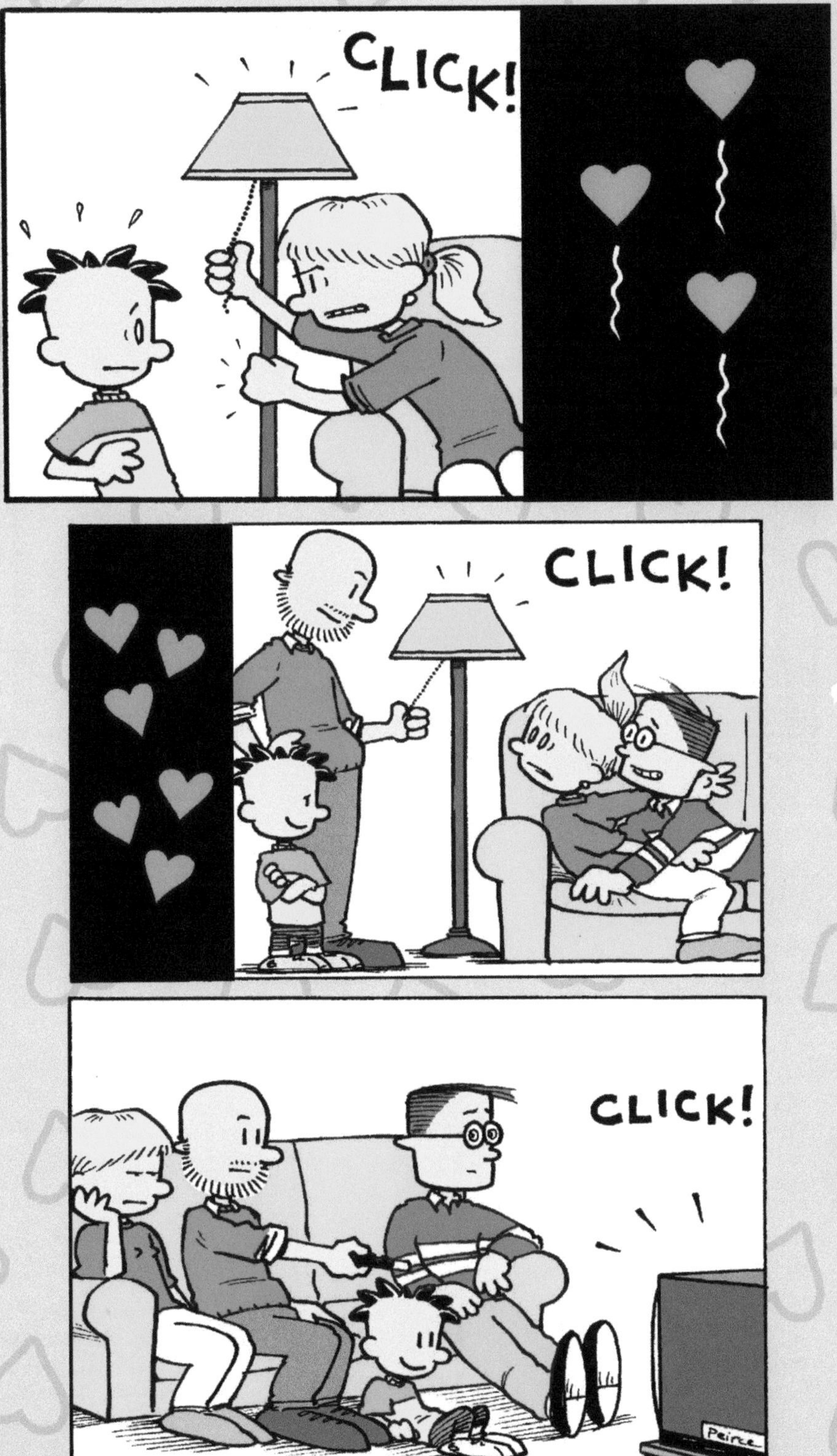
CLICK!
CLICK!
CLICK!
Peirce

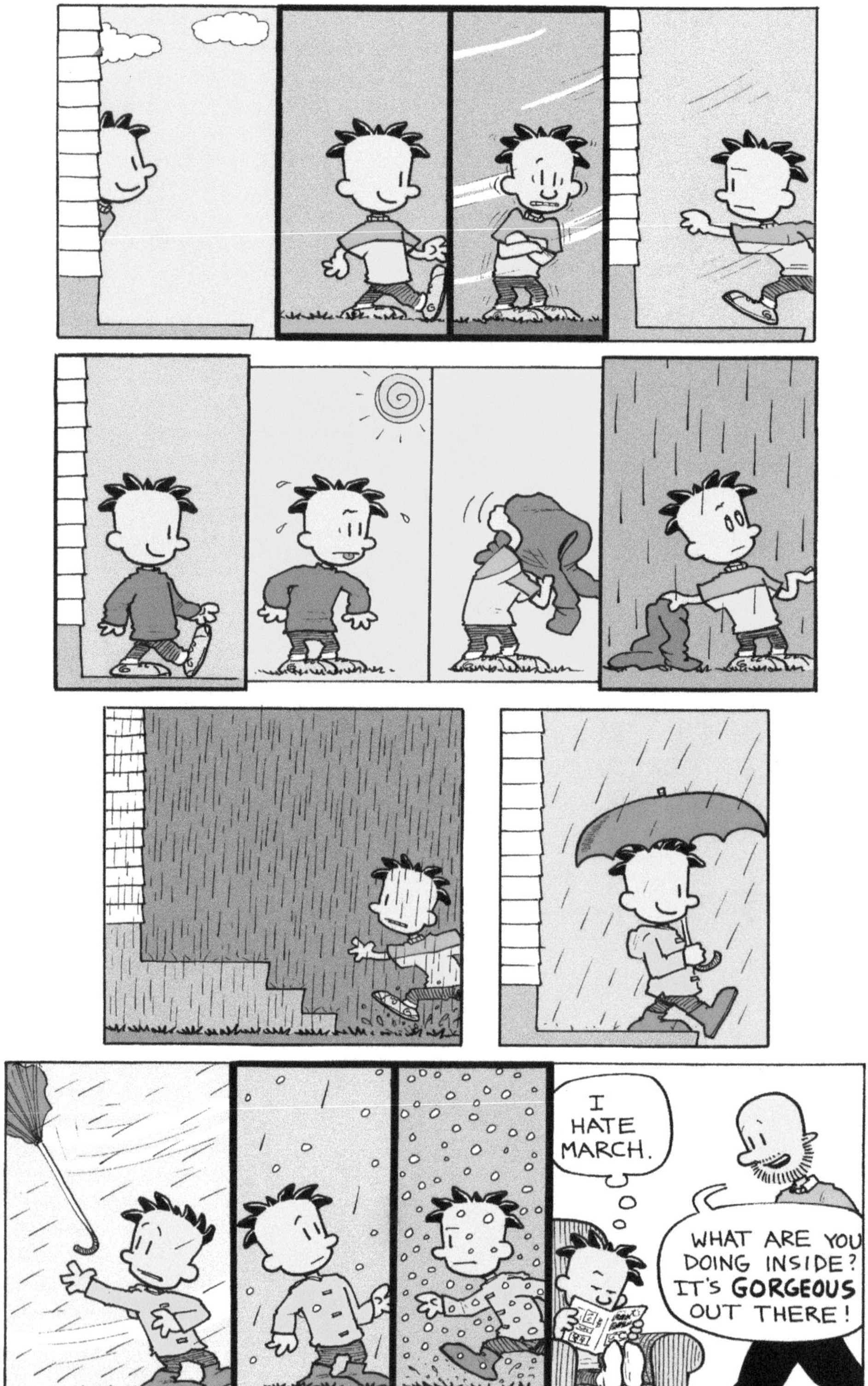
I HATE MARCH.
WHAT ARE YOU DOING INSIDE? IT'S **GORGEOUS** OUT THERE!

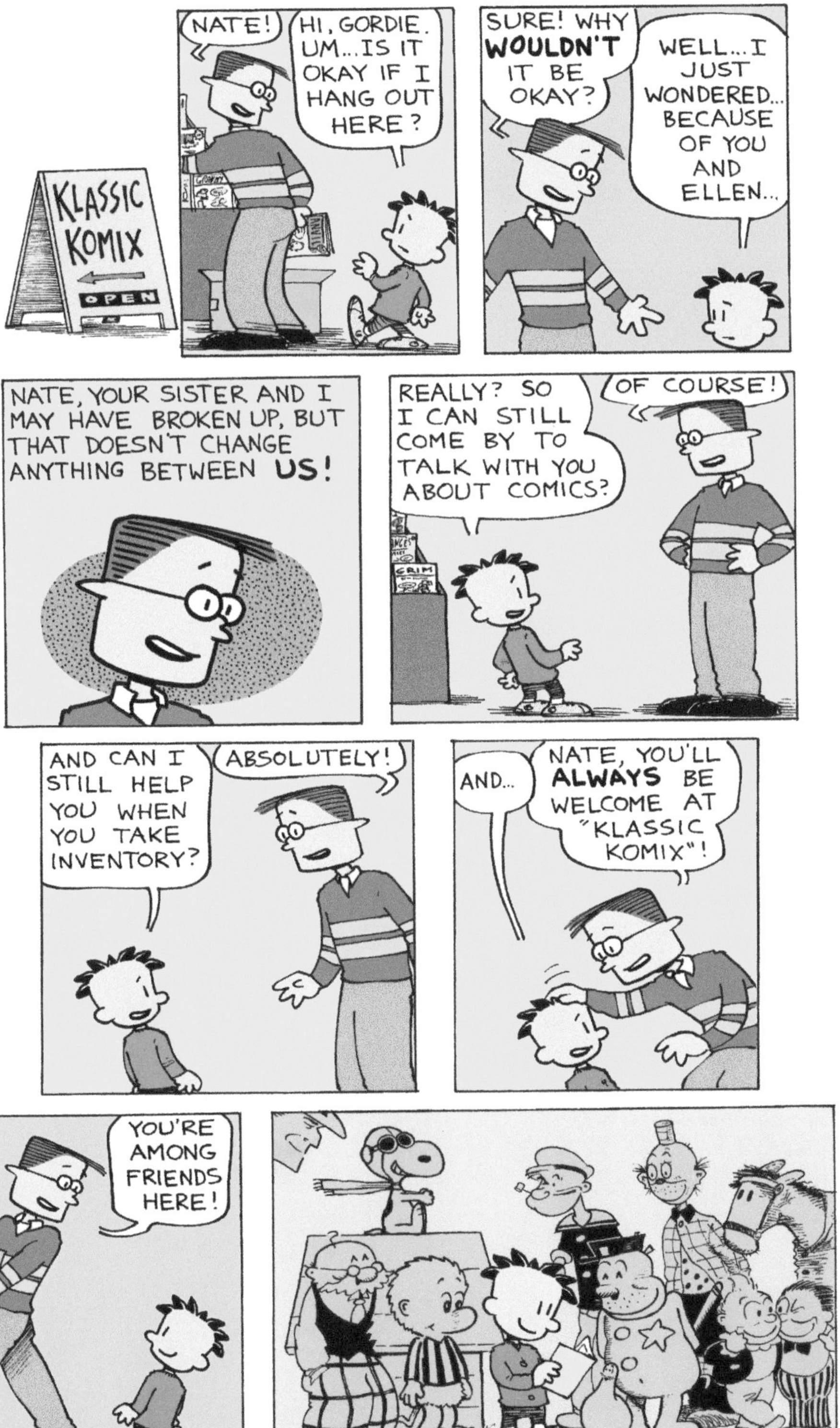
KLASSIC KOMIX
OPEN
NATE!
HI, GORDIE. UM... IS IT OKAY IF I HANG OUT HERE?
SURE! WHY **WOULDN'T** IT BE OKAY?
WELL... I JUST WONDERED... BECAUSE OF YOU AND ELLEN...
NATE, YOUR SISTER AND I MAY HAVE BROKEN UP, BUT THAT DOESN'T CHANGE ANYTHING BETWEEN **US**!
REALLY? SO I CAN STILL COME BY TO TALK WITH YOU ABOUT COMICS?
OF COURSE!
AND CAN I STILL HELP YOU WHEN YOU TAKE INVENTORY?
ABSOLUTELY!
AND...
NATE, YOU'LL **ALWAYS** BE WELCOME AT "KLASSIC KOMIX"!
YOU'RE AMONG FRIENDS HERE!
Peirce

WE NEED A TEACHER PROFILE FOR OUR NEXT EDITION. NATE, DO AN INTERVIEW WITH MR. GALVIN.
WHAT? WHOA!
HOW COME I'VE ALWAYS GOT TO DO THE LAME TEACHER INTERVIEWS?
JUST BECAUSE YOU'RE THE EDITOR, GINA, THAT DOESN'T MEAN YOU CAN MAKE ME DO ALL THE GRUNT WORK!
YOU INTERVIEW MR. GALVIN! GIVE ME SOMETHING ELSE TO DO!
SIGH...
OKAY! STOP WHINING! I'LL DO THE PIECE ON MR. GALVIN!
YOU CAN DO THE "UP CLOSE AND PERSONAL" WITH DEBBI DALTON.
WHO'S DEBBI DALTON?
SHE'S AN EIGHTH-GRADE GIRL WHO'S TRYING TO GET PERMISSION TO JOIN THE BOYS' WRESTLING TEAM.
...SO THEN I WROTE ANOTHER PETITION...
MY PENCIL JUST BROKE.
Peirce

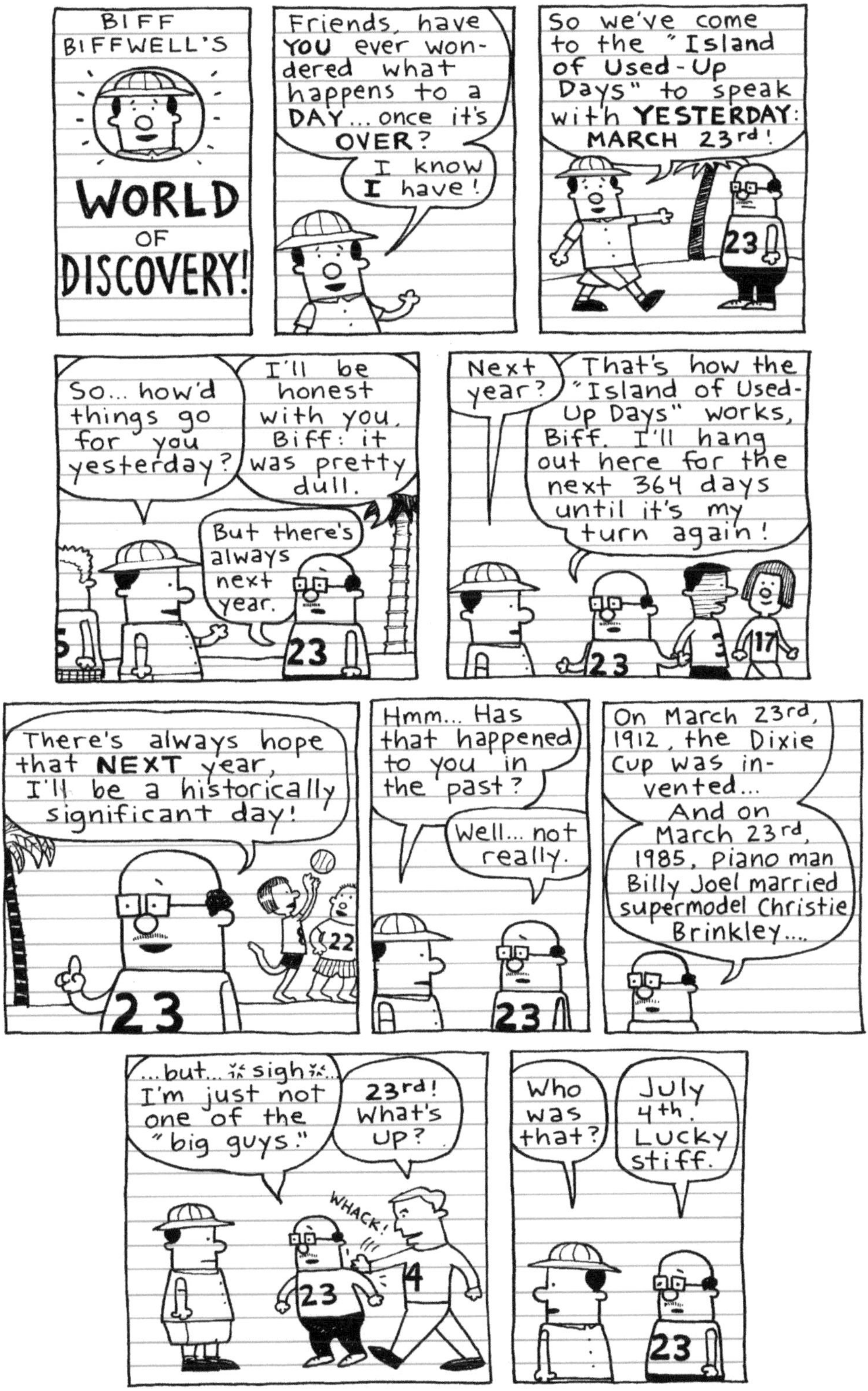
BIFF BIFFWELL'S WORLD OF DISCOVERY!
Friends, have YOU ever wondered what happens to a DAY... once it's OVER?
I know I have!
So we've come to the "Island of Used-Up Days" to speak with YESTERDAY: MARCH 23rd!
23
So... how'd things go for you yesterday?
I'll be honest with you, Biff: it was pretty dull.
But there's always next year.
Next year?
That's how the "Island of Used-Up Days" works, Biff. I'll hang out here for the next 364 days until it's my turn again!
17
There's always hope that NEXT year, I'll be a historically significant day!
22
Hmm... Has that happened to you in the past?
Well... not really.
On March 23rd, 1912, the Dixie Cup was invented... And on March 23rd, 1985, piano man Billy Joel married supermodel Christie Brinkley....
...but... sigh... I'm just not one of the "big guys."
23rd! What's up?
WHACK!
4
Who was that?
July 4th. Lucky stiff.

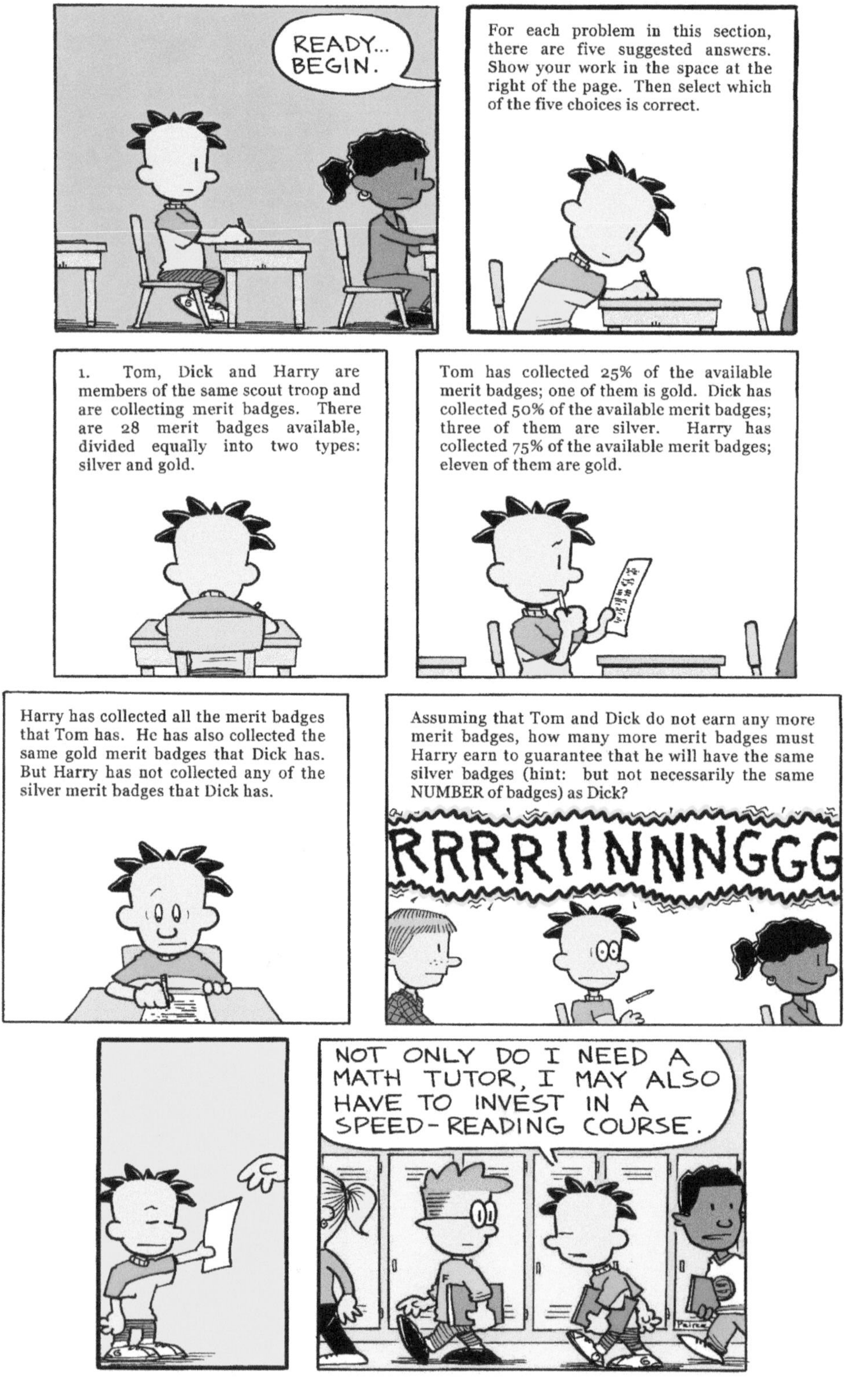

READY... BEGIN.
For each problem in this section, there are five suggested answers. Show your work in the space at the right of the page. Then select which of the five choices is correct.
1. Tom, Dick and Harry are members of the same scout troop and are collecting merit badges. There are 28 merit badges available, divided equally into two types: silver and gold.
Tom has collected 25% of the available merit badges; one of them is gold. Dick has collected 50% of the available merit badges; three of them are silver. Harry has collected 75% of the available merit badges; eleven of them are gold.
Harry has collected all the merit badges that Tom has. He has also collected the same gold merit badges that Dick has. But Harry has not collected any of the silver merit badges that Dick has.
Assuming that Tom and Dick do not earn any more merit badges, how many more merit badges must Harry earn to guarantee that he will have the same silver badges (hint: but not necessarily the same NUMBER of badges) as Dick?
RRRRIINNNGGG
NOT ONLY DO I NEED A MATH TUTOR, I MAY ALSO HAVE TO INVEST IN A SPEED-READING COURSE.

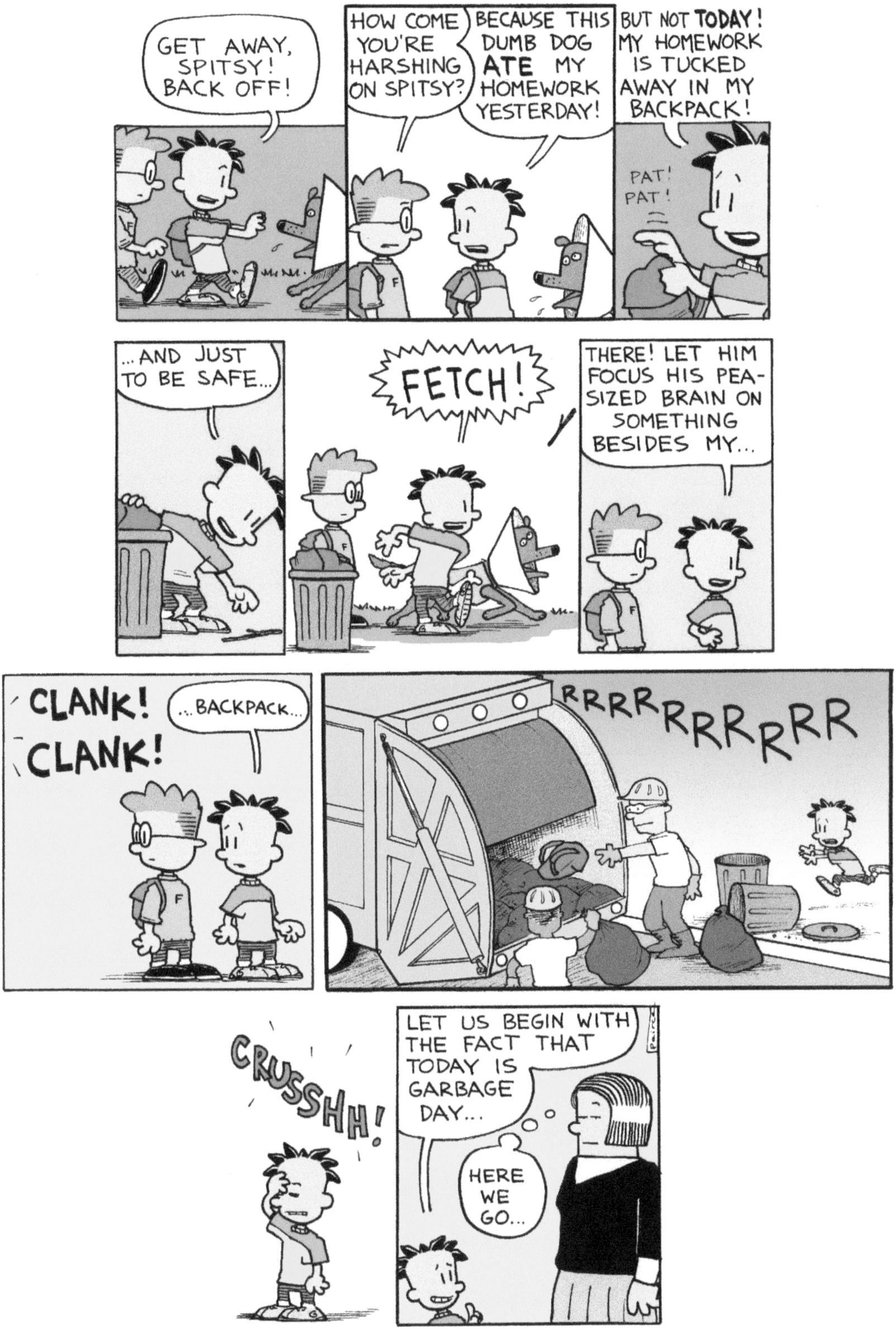
GET AWAY, SPITSY! BACK OFF!
HOW COME YOU'RE HARSHING ON SPITSY?
BECAUSE THIS DUMB DOG ATE MY HOMEWORK YESTERDAY!
BUT NOT TODAY! MY HOMEWORK IS TUCKED AWAY IN MY BACKPACK!
PAT! PAT!
...AND JUST TO BE SAFE...
FETCH!
THERE! LET HIM FOCUS HIS PEA-SIZED BRAIN ON SOMETHING BESIDES MY...
CLANK! CLANK!
...BACKPACK...
RRRRRRRRRRR
CRUSSHH!
LET US BEGIN WITH THE FACT THAT TODAY IS GARBAGE DAY...
HERE WE GO...

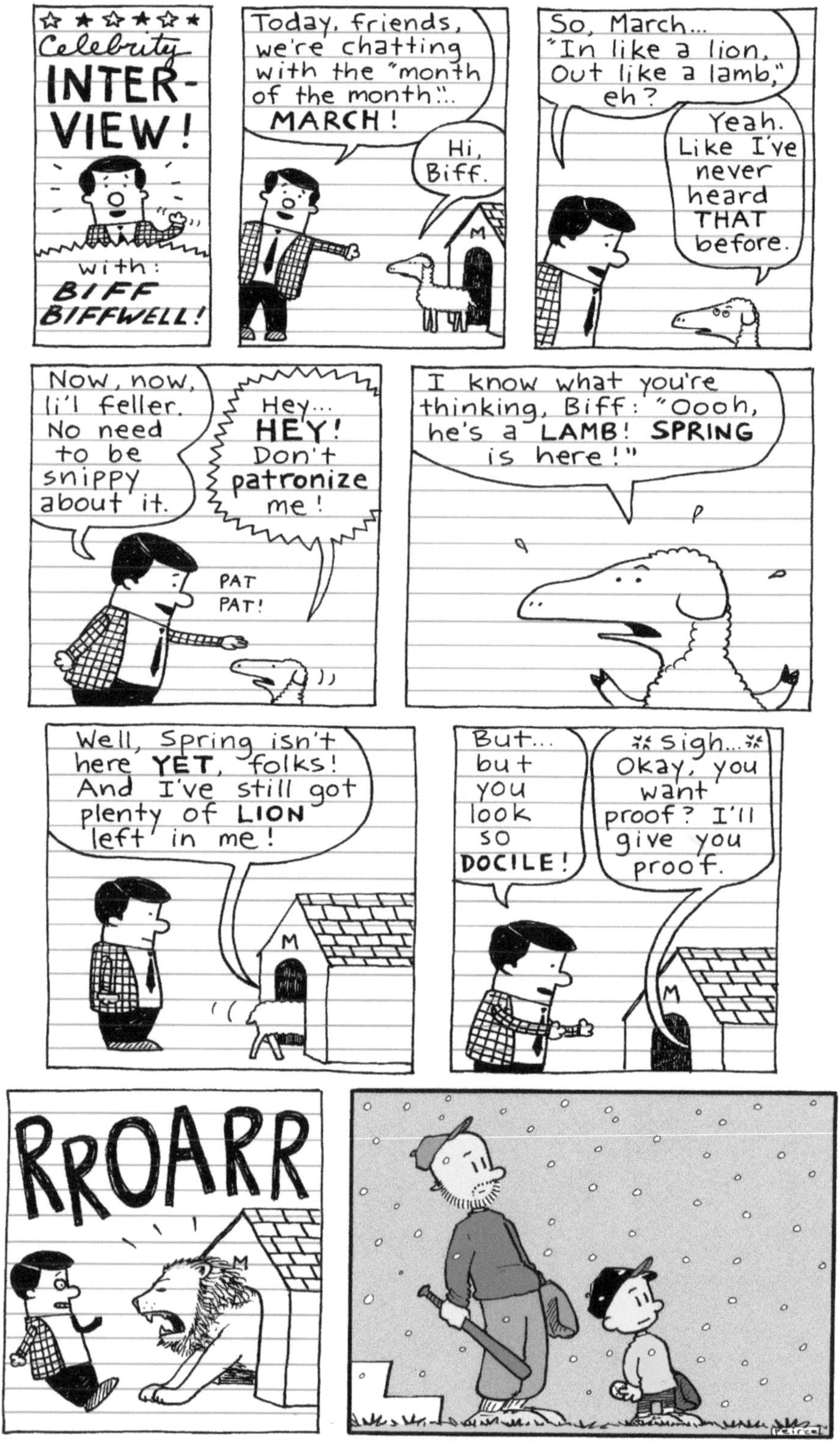
Celebrity INTERVIEW!
with: BIFF BIFFWELL!
Today, friends, we're chatting with the "month of the month"... MARCH!
Hi, Biff.
So, March... "In like a lion, Out like a lamb," eh?
Yeah. Like I've never heard THAT before.
Now, now, li'l feller. No need to be snippy about it.
PAT PAT!
Hey... HEY! Don't patronize me!
I know what you're thinking, Biff: "Oooh, he's a LAMB! SPRING is here!"
Well, Spring isn't here YET, folks! And I've still got plenty of LION left in me!
But... but you look so DOCILE!
sigh... Okay, you want proof? I'll give you proof.
RROARR
Peirce

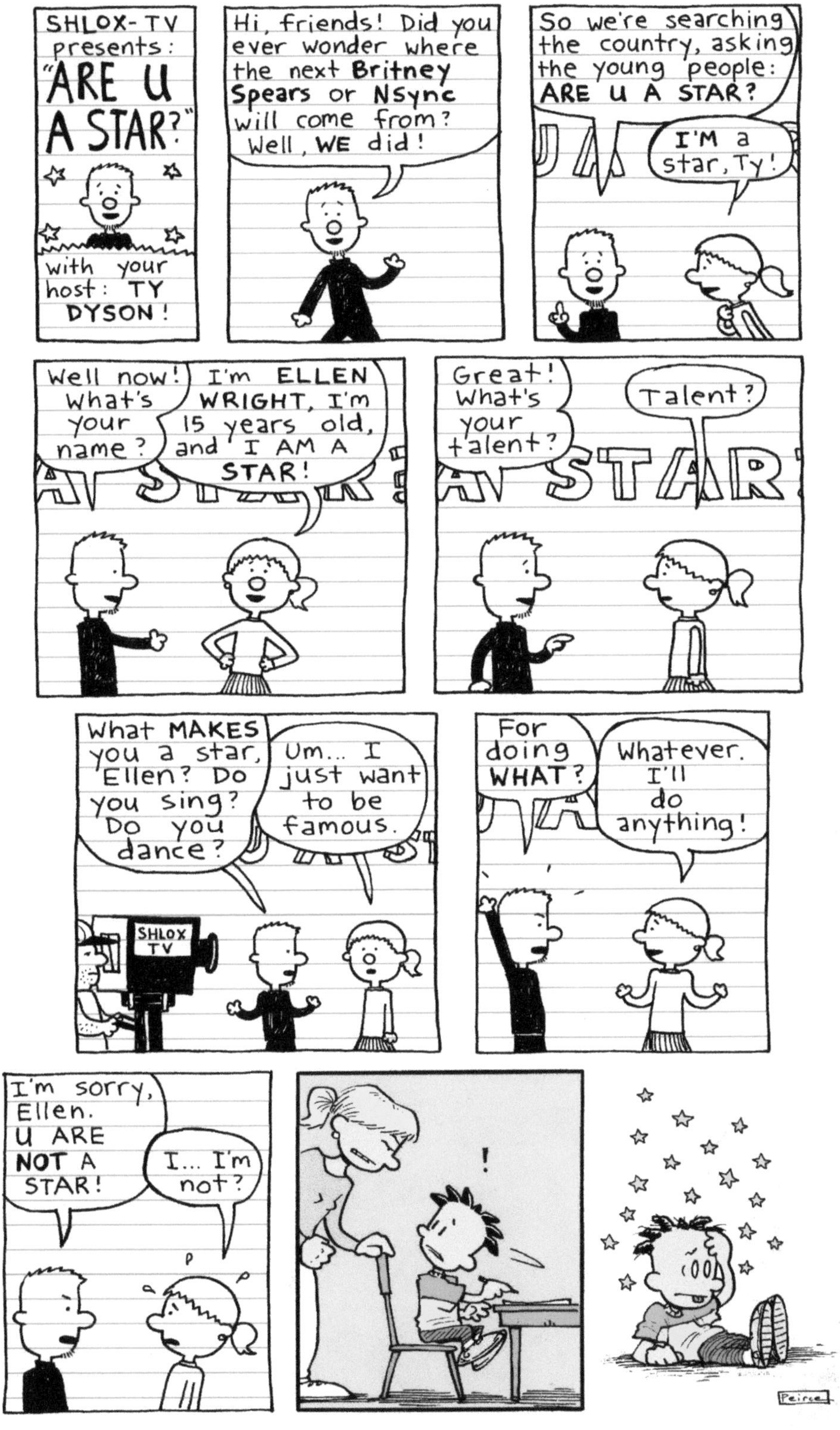
SHLOX-TV presents: "ARE U A STAR?"
with your host: TY DYSON!
Hi, friends! Did you ever wonder where the next Britney Spears or Nsync will come from? Well, WE did!
So we're searching the country, asking the young people: ARE U A STAR?
I'M a star, Ty!
Well now! What's your name?
I'm ELLEN WRIGHT, I'm 15 years old, and I AM A STAR!
Great! What's your talent?
Talent?
What MAKES you a star, Ellen? Do you sing? Do you dance?
Um... I just want to be famous.
SHLOX TV
For doing WHAT?
Whatever. I'll do anything!
I'm sorry, Ellen. U ARE NOT A STAR!
I... I'm not?
!
Peirce

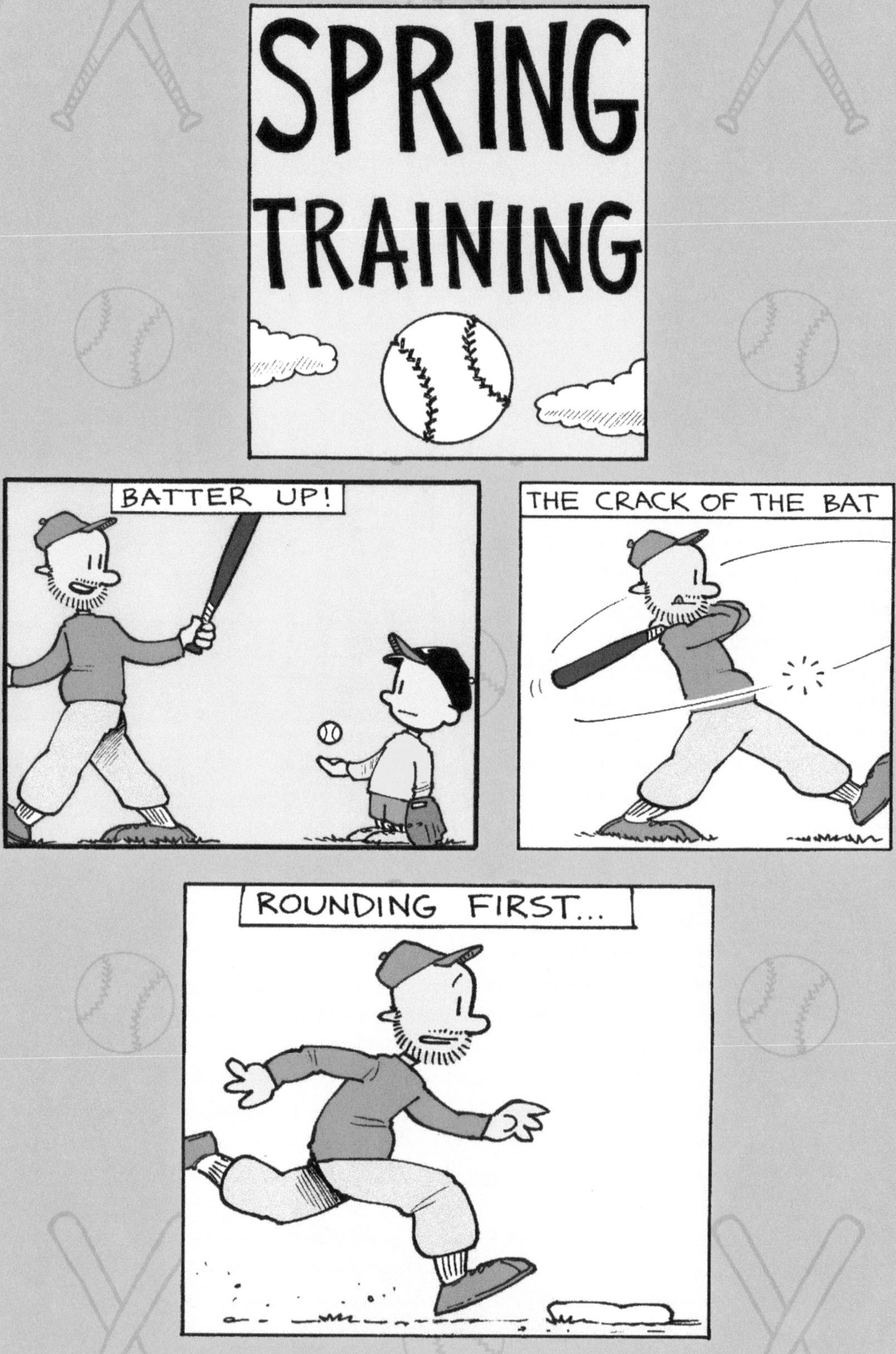
SPRING TRAINING
BATTER UP!
THE CRACK OF THE BAT
ROUNDING FIRST...

ROUNDING SECOND...

ROUNDING THIRD...

HEADING FOR HOME

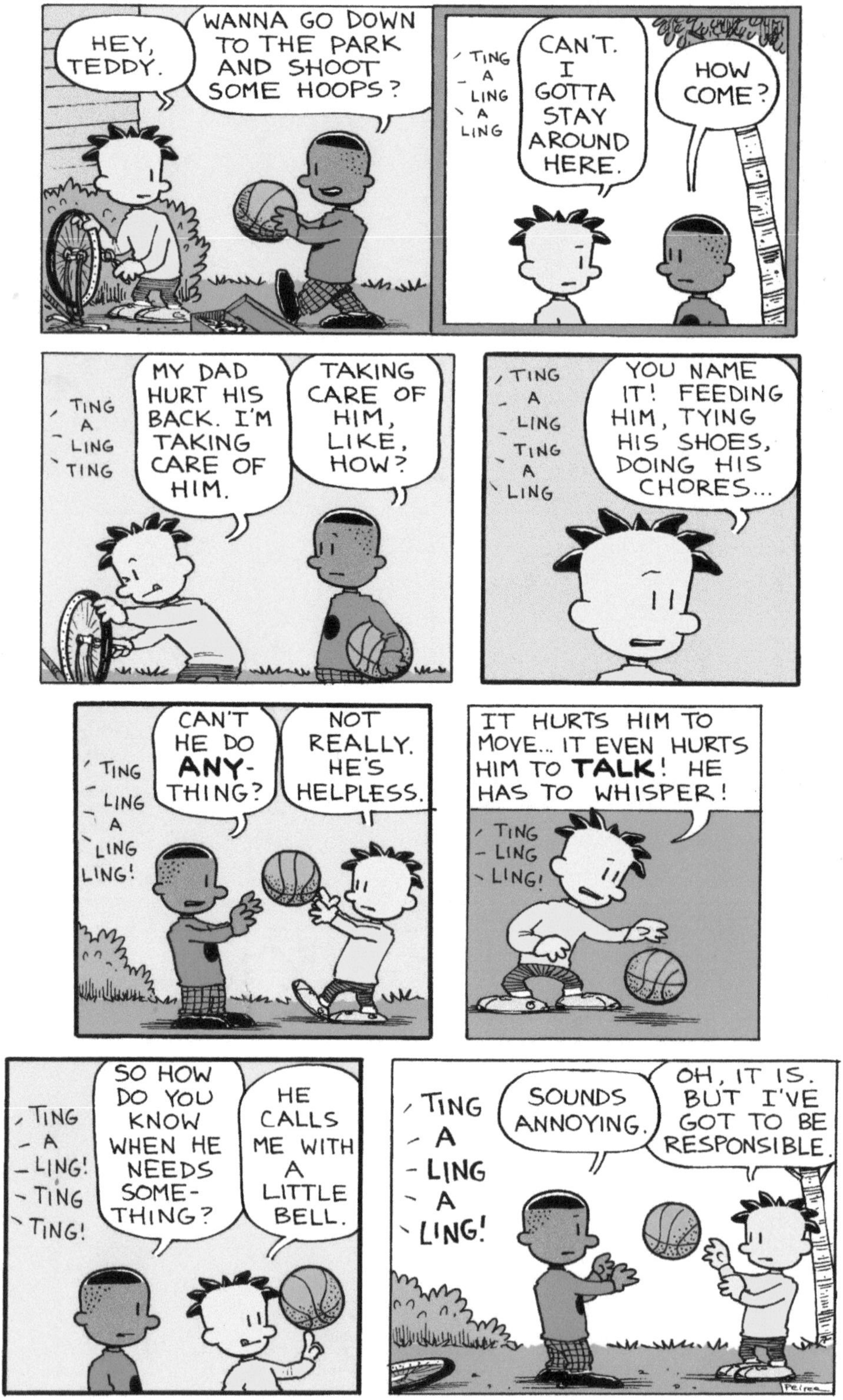
HEY, TEDDY.
WANNA GO DOWN TO THE PARK AND SHOOT SOME HOOPS?
TING A LING A LING
CAN'T. I GOTTA STAY AROUND HERE.
HOW COME?
TING A LING TING
MY DAD HURT HIS BACK. I'M TAKING CARE OF HIM.
TAKING CARE OF HIM, LIKE, HOW?
TING A LING TING A LING
YOU NAME IT! FEEDING HIM, TYING HIS SHOES, DOING HIS CHORES...
TING LING A LING LING!
CAN'T HE DO ANY-THING?
NOT REALLY. HE'S HELPLESS.
IT HURTS HIM TO MOVE... IT EVEN HURTS HIM TO TALK! HE HAS TO WHISPER!
TING LING LING!
TING A LING! TING TING!
SO HOW DO YOU KNOW WHEN HE NEEDS SOME-THING?
HE CALLS ME WITH A LITTLE BELL.
TING A LING A LING!
SOUNDS ANNOYING.
OH, IT IS. BUT I'VE GOT TO BE RESPONSIBLE.
Peirce

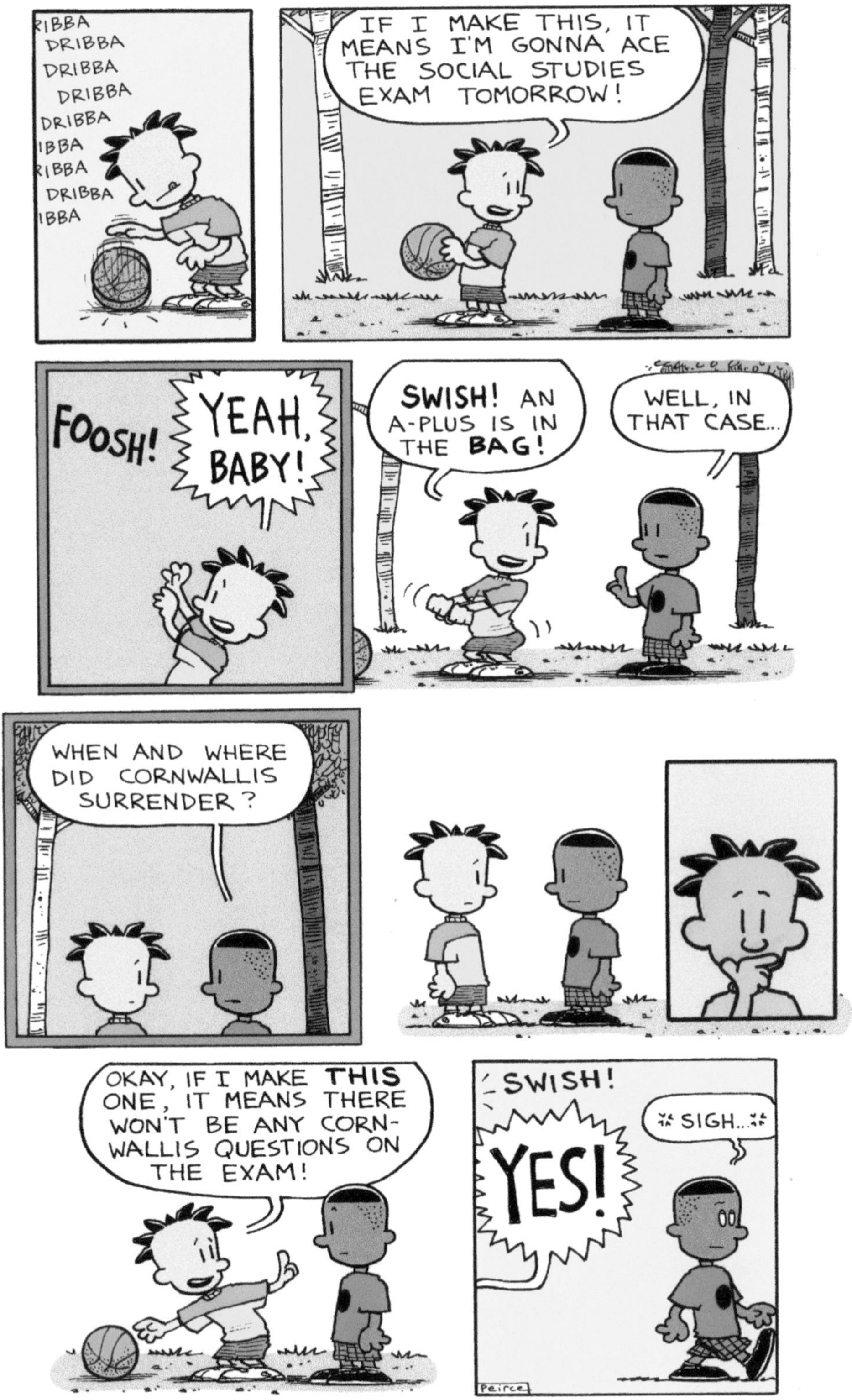

RIBBA DRIBBA DRIBBA DRIBBA DRIBBA IBBA RIBBA DRIBBA IBBA
IF I MAKE THIS, IT MEANS I'M GONNA ACE THE SOCIAL STUDIES EXAM TOMORROW!
FOOSH!
YEAH, BABY!
SWISH! AN A-PLUS IS IN THE BAG!
WELL, IN THAT CASE...
WHEN AND WHERE DID CORNWALLIS SURRENDER?
OKAY, IF I MAKE THIS ONE, IT MEANS THERE WON'T BE ANY CORN-WALLIS QUESTIONS ON THE EXAM!
SWISH!
YES!
SIGH...
Peirce

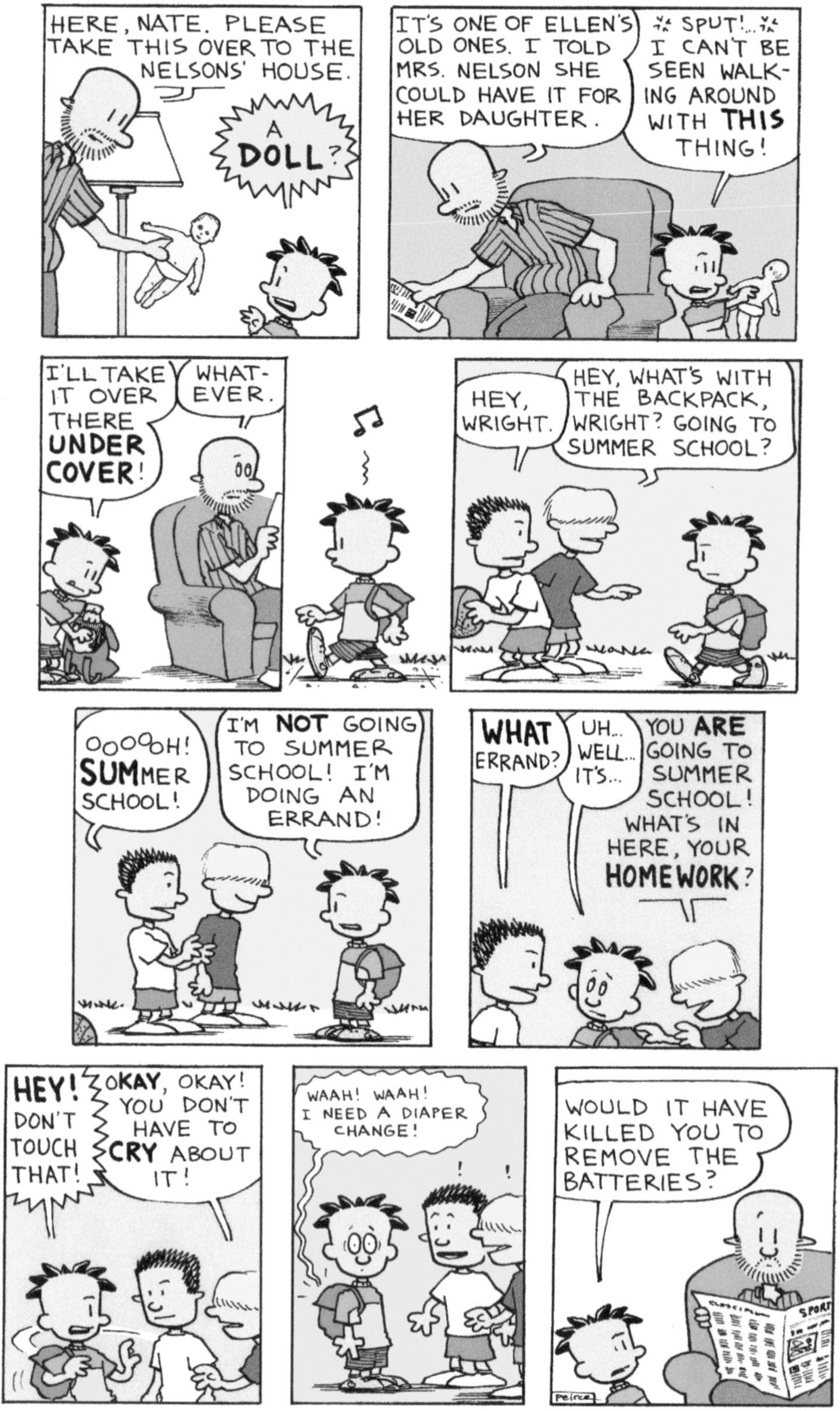
HERE, NATE. PLEASE TAKE THIS OVER TO THE NELSONS' HOUSE.
A **DOLL**?
IT'S ONE OF ELLEN'S OLD ONES. I TOLD MRS. NELSON SHE COULD HAVE IT FOR HER DAUGHTER.
SPUT!... I CAN'T BE SEEN WALKING AROUND WITH **THIS** THING!
I'LL TAKE IT OVER THERE **UNDER COVER**!
WHATEVER.
HEY, WRIGHT.
HEY, WHAT'S WITH THE BACKPACK, WRIGHT? GOING TO SUMMER SCHOOL?
OOOOOH! **SUM**MER SCHOOL!
I'M **NOT** GOING TO SUMMER SCHOOL! I'M DOING AN ERRAND!
WHAT ERRAND?
UH... WELL... IT'S...
YOU **ARE** GOING TO SUMMER SCHOOL! WHAT'S IN HERE, YOUR **HOMEWORK**?
HEY! DON'T TOUCH THAT!
OKAY, OKAY! YOU DON'T HAVE TO **CRY** ABOUT IT!
WAAH! WAAH! I NEED A DIAPER CHANGE!
! !
WOULD IT HAVE KILLED YOU TO REMOVE THE BATTERIES?
SPORTS
peirce

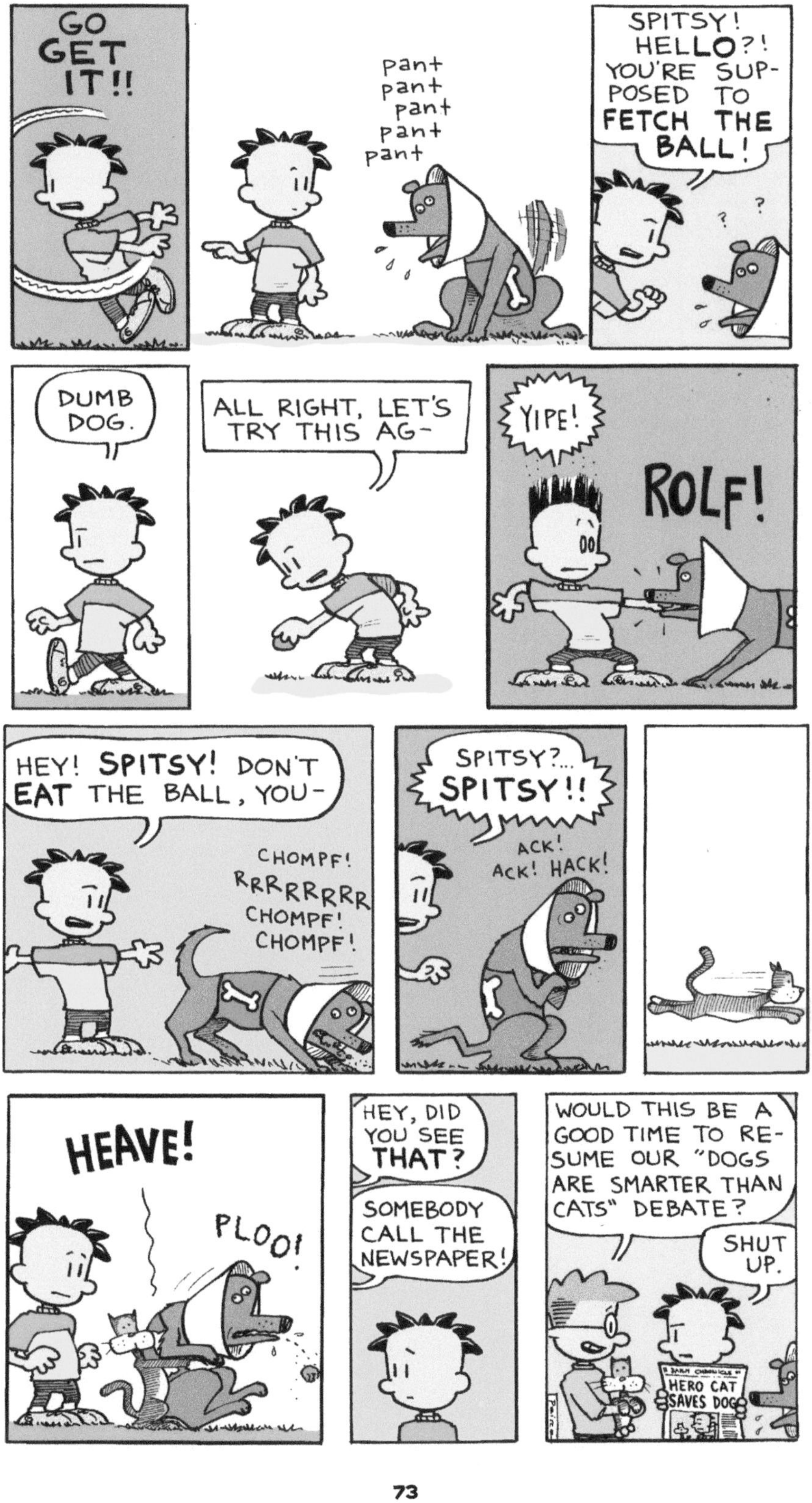
GO GET IT!!
pant pant pant pant pant
SPITSY! HELLO?! YOU'RE SUP- POSED TO FETCH THE BALL!
? ?
DUMB DOG.
ALL RIGHT, LET'S TRY THIS AG-
YIPE!
ROLF!
HEY! SPITSY! DON'T EAT THE BALL, YOU-
CHOMPF! RRRRRRRR CHOMPF! CHOMPF!
SPITSY?... SPITSY!!
ACK! ACK! HACK!
HEAVE!
PLOO!
HEY, DID YOU SEE THAT?
SOMEBODY CALL THE NEWSPAPER!
WOULD THIS BE A GOOD TIME TO RE- SUME OUR "DOGS ARE SMARTER THAN CATS" DEBATE?
SHUT UP.
HERO CAT SAVES DOG

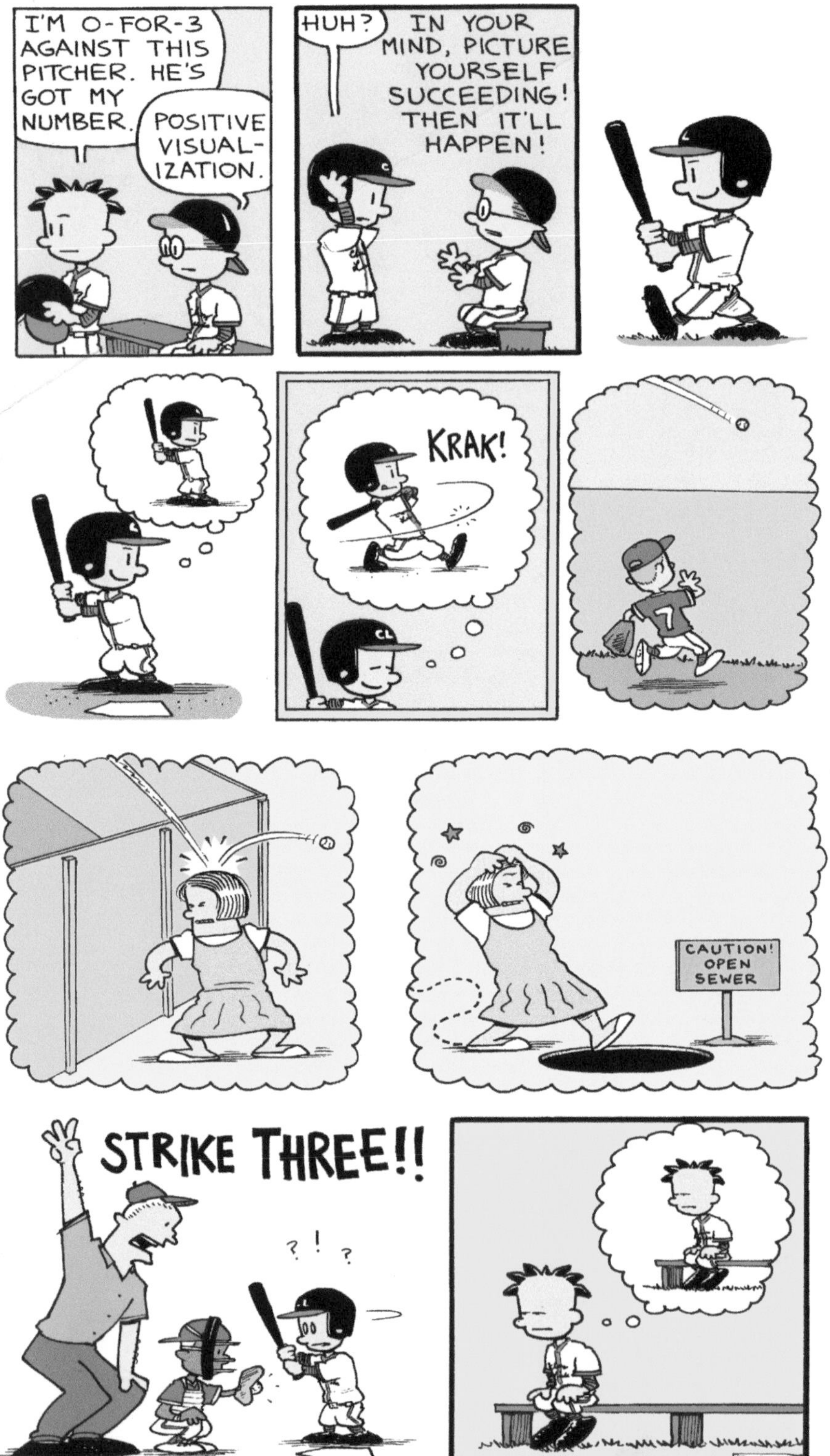
I'M O-FOR-3 AGAINST THIS PITCHER. HE'S GOT MY NUMBER.
POSITIVE VISUALIZATION.
HUH?
IN YOUR MIND, PICTURE YOURSELF SUCCEEDING! THEN IT'LL HAPPEN!
KRAK!
CAUTION! OPEN SEWER
STRIKE THREE!!
?!?
Peirce

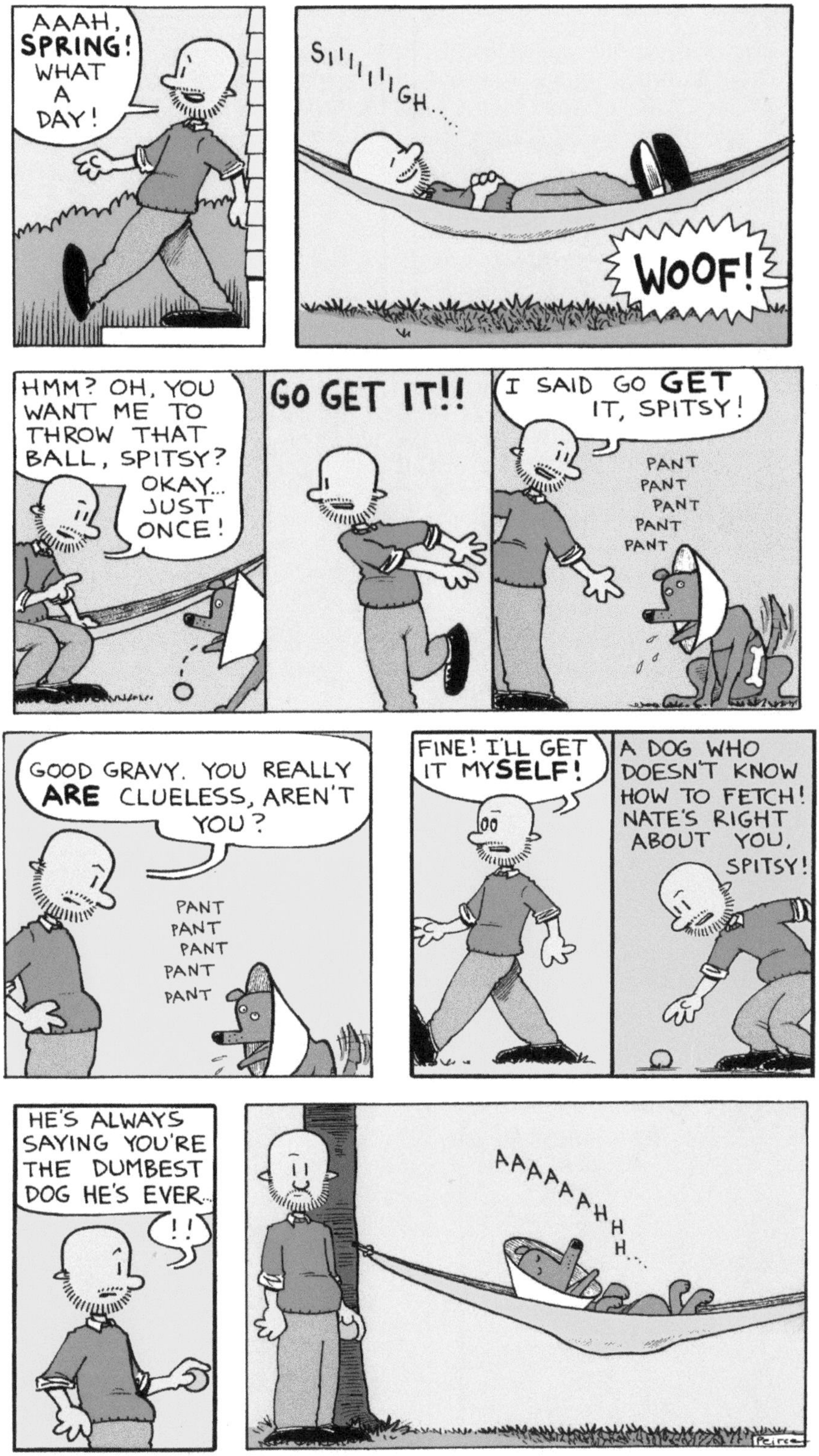
AAAH, **SPRING!** WHAT A DAY!
SIIIIIIGH....
WOOF!
HMM? OH, YOU WANT ME TO THROW THAT BALL, SPITSY? OKAY... JUST ONCE!
GO GET IT!!
I SAID GO **GET** IT, SPITSY!
PANT PANT PANT PANT PANT
GOOD GRAVY. YOU REALLY **ARE** CLUELESS, AREN'T YOU?
PANT PANT PANT PANT PANT
FINE! I'LL GET IT MY**SELF**!
A DOG WHO DOESN'T KNOW HOW TO FETCH! NATE'S RIGHT ABOUT YOU, SPITSY!
HE'S ALWAYS SAYING YOU'RE THE DUMBEST DOG HE'S EVER...
!!
AAAAAAHHH...
Peirce

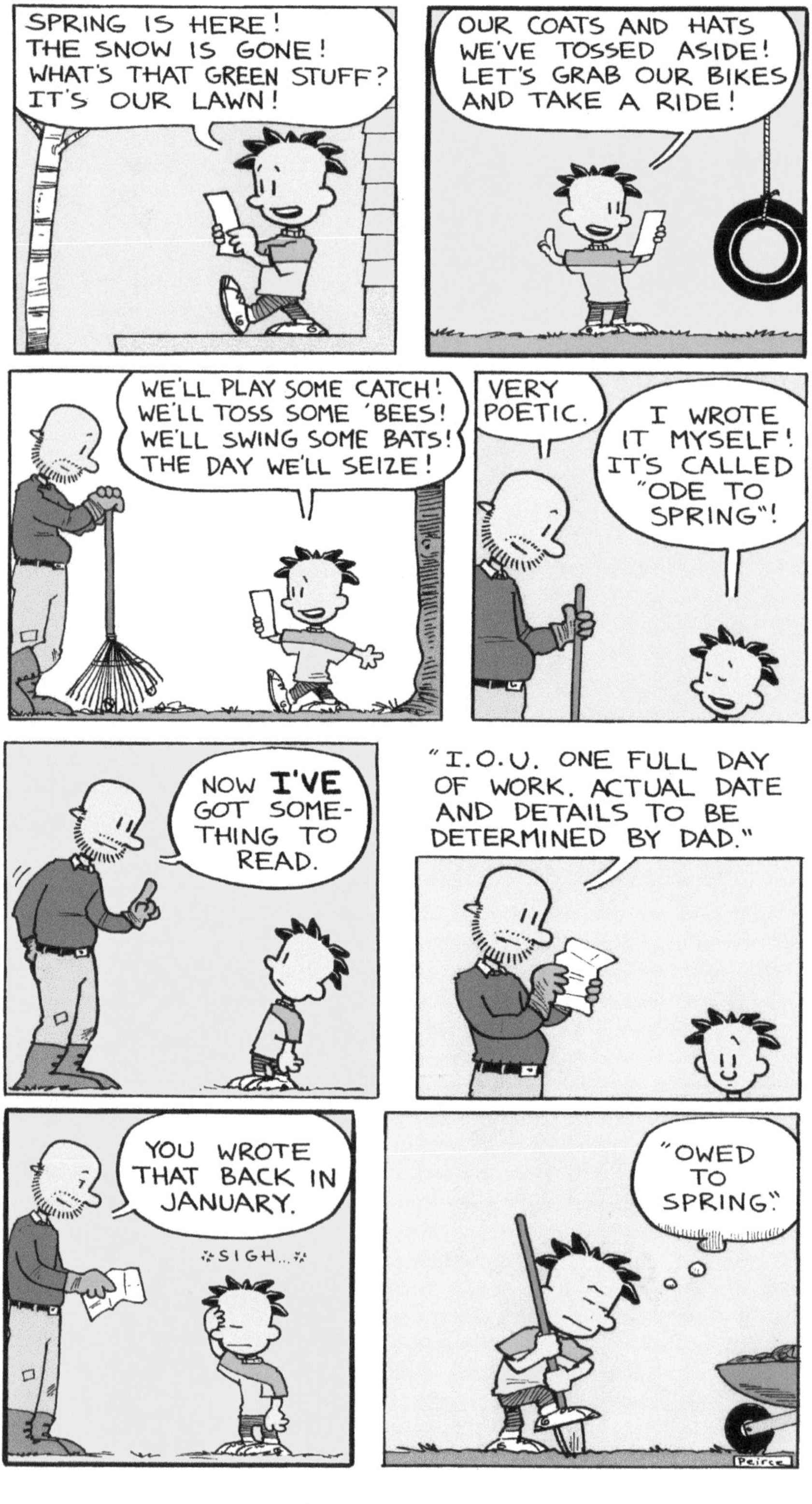
SPRING IS HERE! THE SNOW IS GONE! WHAT'S THAT GREEN STUFF? IT'S OUR LAWN!
OUR COATS AND HATS WE'VE TOSSED ASIDE! LET'S GRAB OUR BIKES AND TAKE A RIDE!
WE'LL PLAY SOME CATCH! WE'LL TOSS SOME 'BEES! WE'LL SWING SOME BATS! THE DAY WE'LL SEIZE!
VERY POETIC.
I WROTE IT MYSELF! IT'S CALLED "ODE TO SPRING"!
NOW I'VE GOT SOME-THING TO READ.
"I.O.U. ONE FULL DAY OF WORK. ACTUAL DATE AND DETAILS TO BE DETERMINED BY DAD."
YOU WROTE THAT BACK IN JANUARY.
SIGH...
"OWED TO SPRING."
Peirce

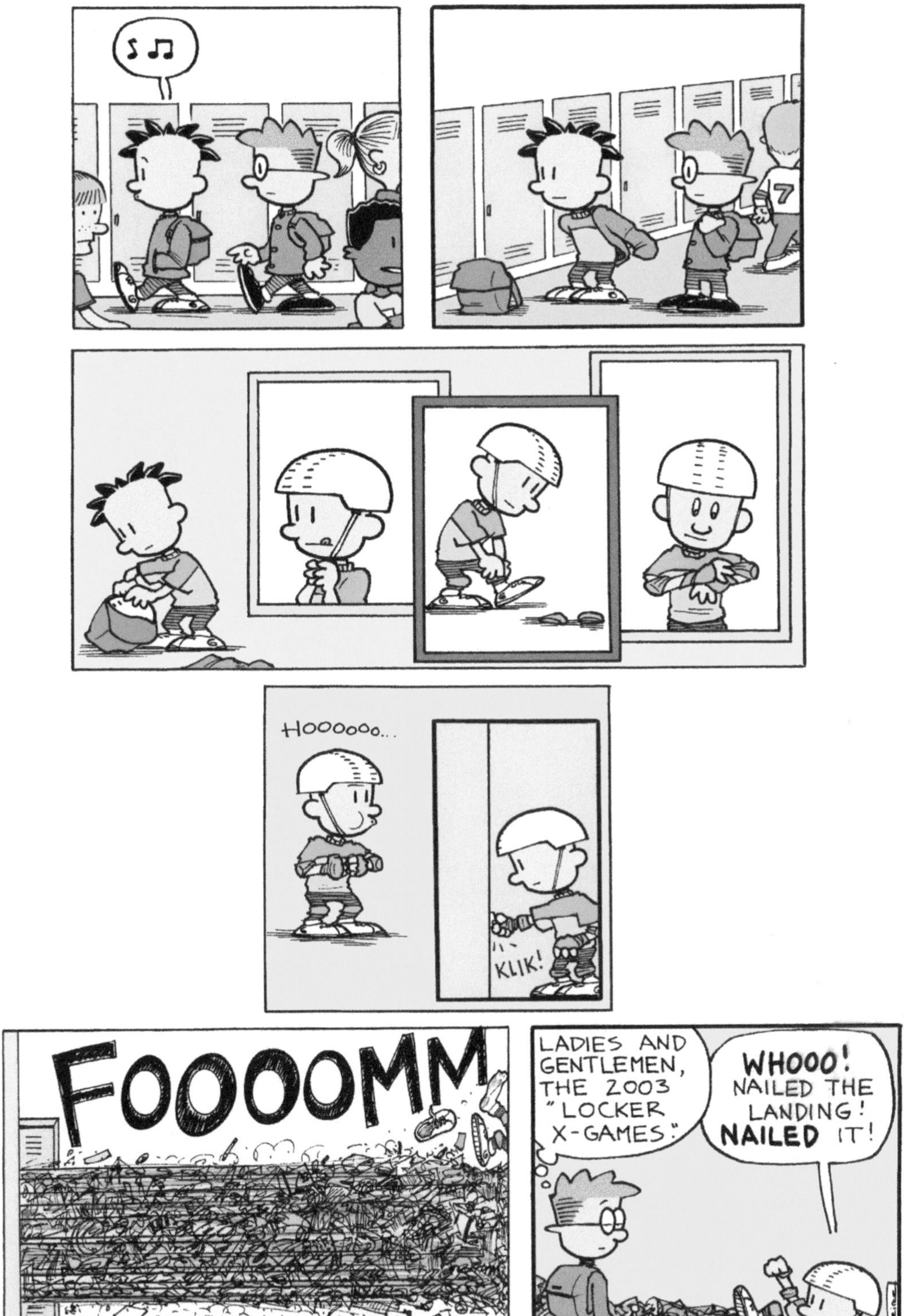
HOOOOOO...
KLIK!
FOOOOMM
LADIES AND GENTLEMEN, THE 2003 "LOCKER X-GAMES."
WHOOO! NAILED THE LANDING! NAILED IT!

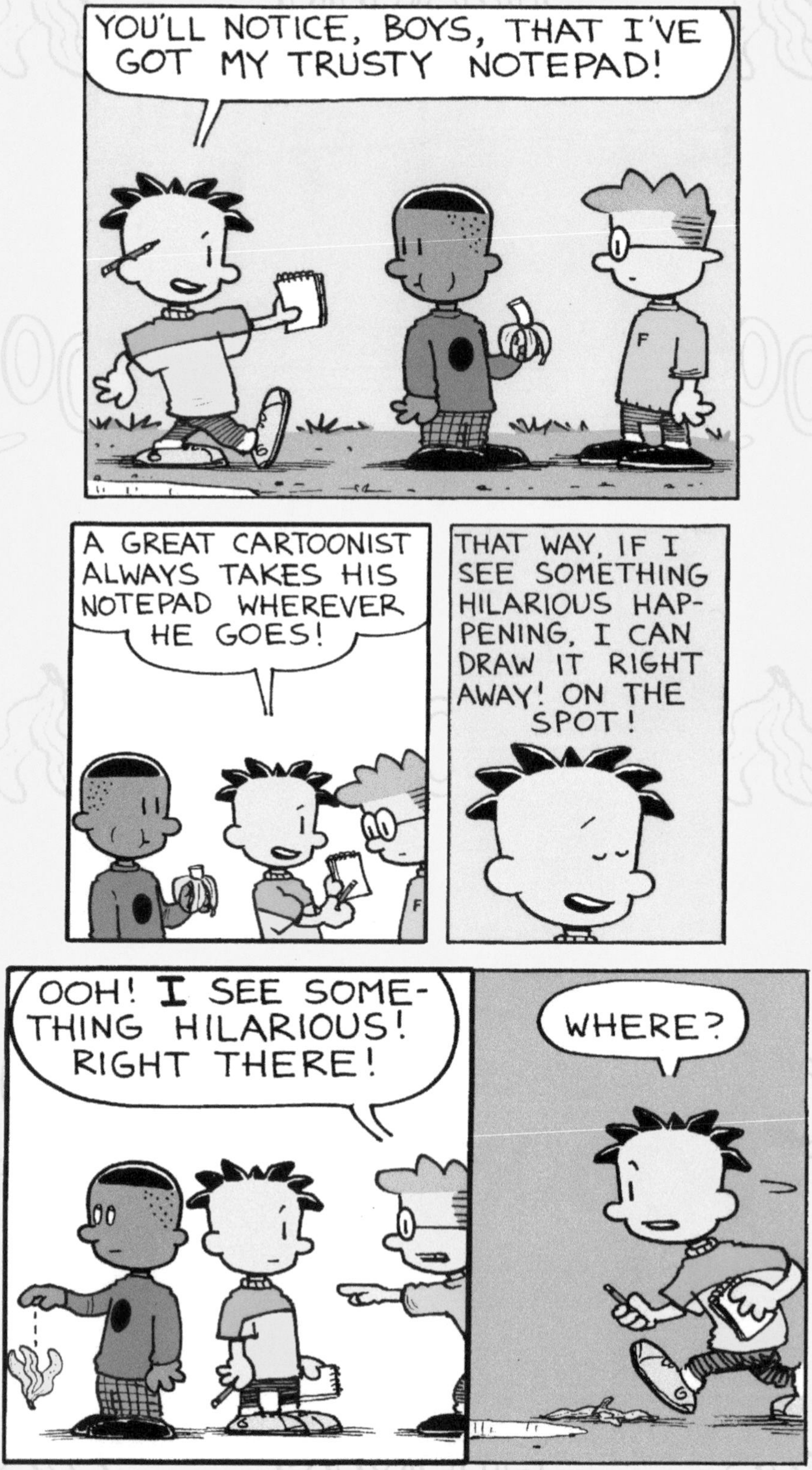
YOU'LL NOTICE, BOYS, THAT I'VE GOT MY TRUSTY NOTEPAD!
A GREAT CARTOONIST ALWAYS TAKES HIS NOTEPAD WHEREVER HE GOES!
THAT WAY, IF I SEE SOMETHING HILARIOUS HAP-PENING, I CAN DRAW IT RIGHT AWAY! ON THE SPOT!
OOH! I SEE SOME-THING HILARIOUS! RIGHT THERE!
WHERE?

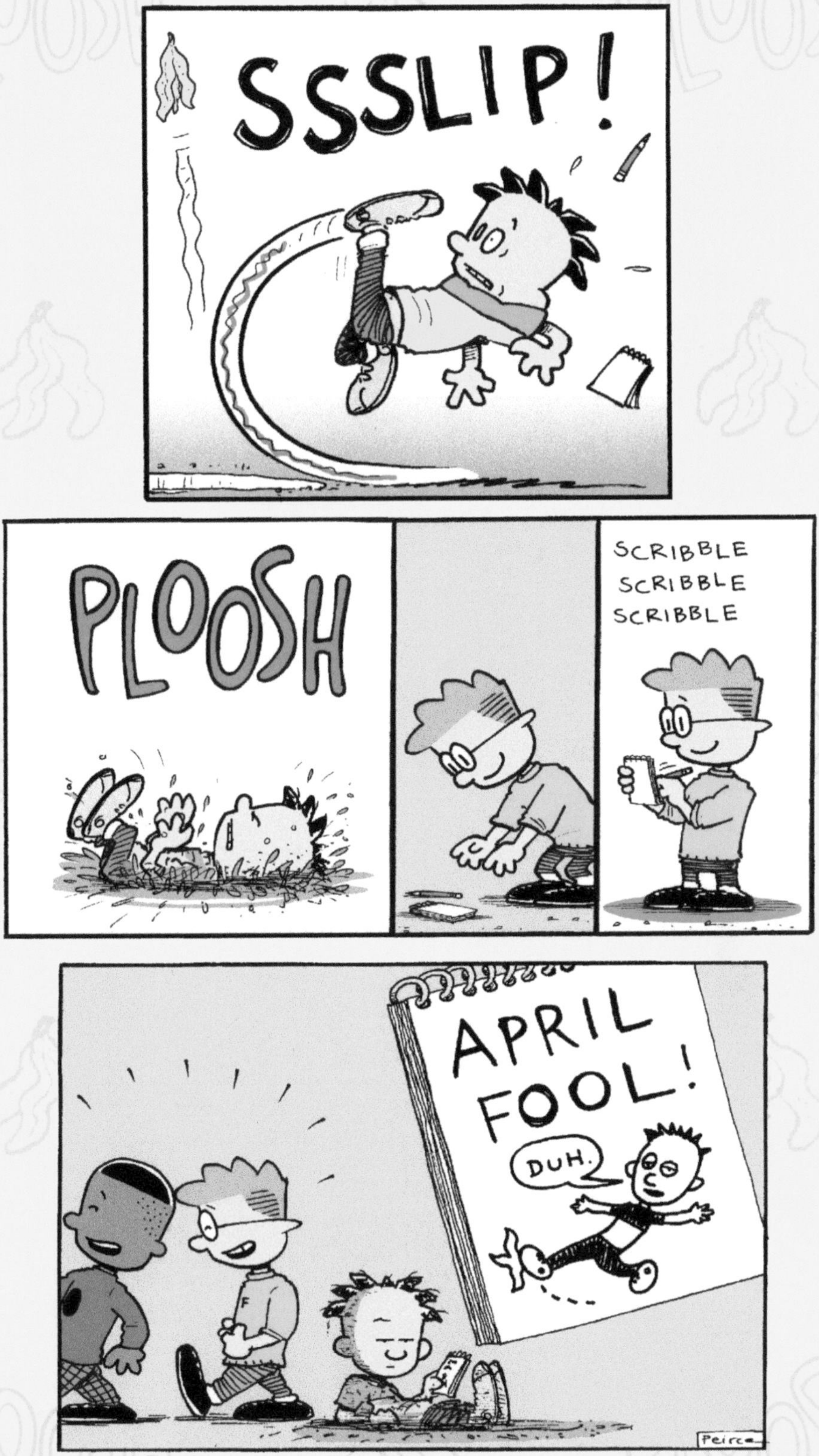
SSSLIP!
PLOOSH
SCRIBBLE
SCRIBBLE
SCRIBBLE
APRIL FOOL!
DUH.
Peirce

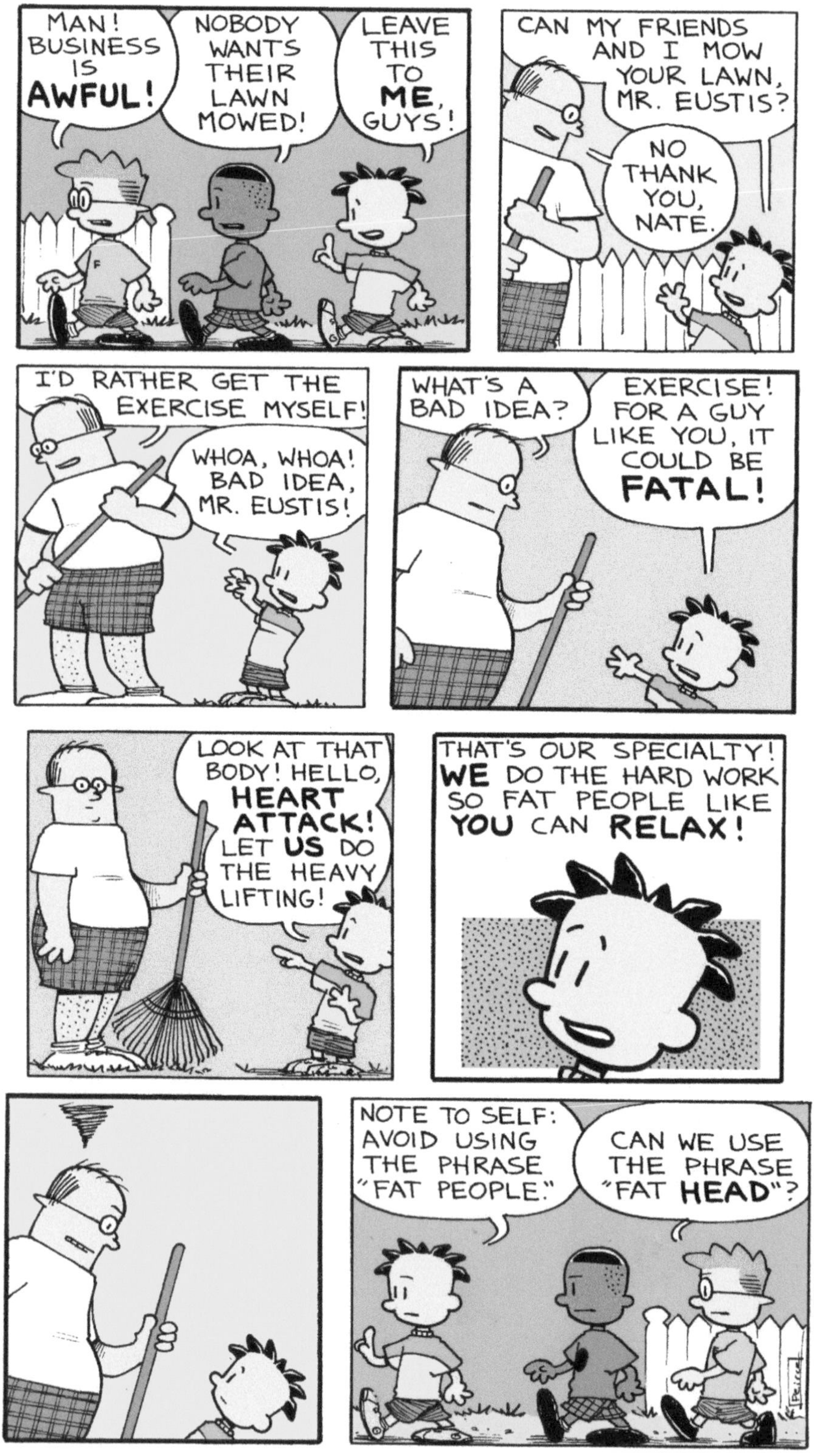
MAN! BUSINESS IS **AWFUL**!
NOBODY WANTS THEIR LAWN MOWED!
LEAVE THIS TO **ME**, GUYS!
CAN MY FRIENDS AND I MOW YOUR LAWN, MR. EUSTIS?
NO THANK YOU, NATE.
I'D RATHER GET THE EXERCISE MYSELF!
WHOA, WHOA! BAD IDEA, MR. EUSTIS!
WHAT'S A BAD IDEA?
EXERCISE! FOR A GUY LIKE YOU, IT COULD BE **FATAL**!
LOOK AT THAT BODY! HELLO, **HEART ATTACK**! LET **US** DO THE HEAVY LIFTING!
THAT'S OUR SPECIALTY! **WE** DO THE HARD WORK SO FAT PEOPLE LIKE **YOU** CAN **RELAX**!
NOTE TO SELF: AVOID USING THE PHRASE "FAT PEOPLE."
CAN WE USE THE PHRASE "FAT **HEAD**"?

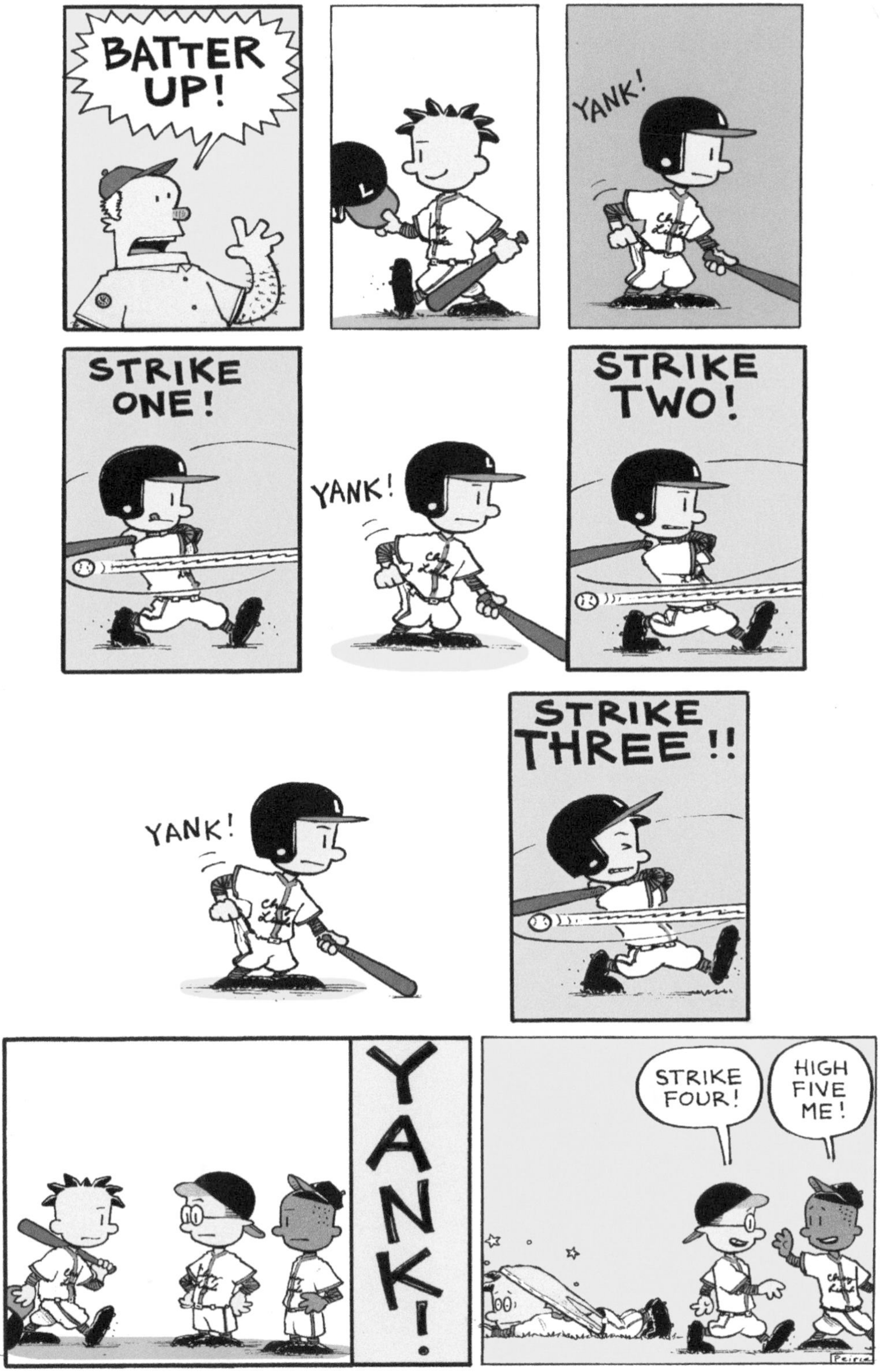
BATTER UP!
YANK!
STRIKE ONE!
YANK!
STRIKE TWO!
YANK!
STRIKE THREE!!
YANK!
STRIKE FOUR!
HIGH FIVE ME!
Peirce

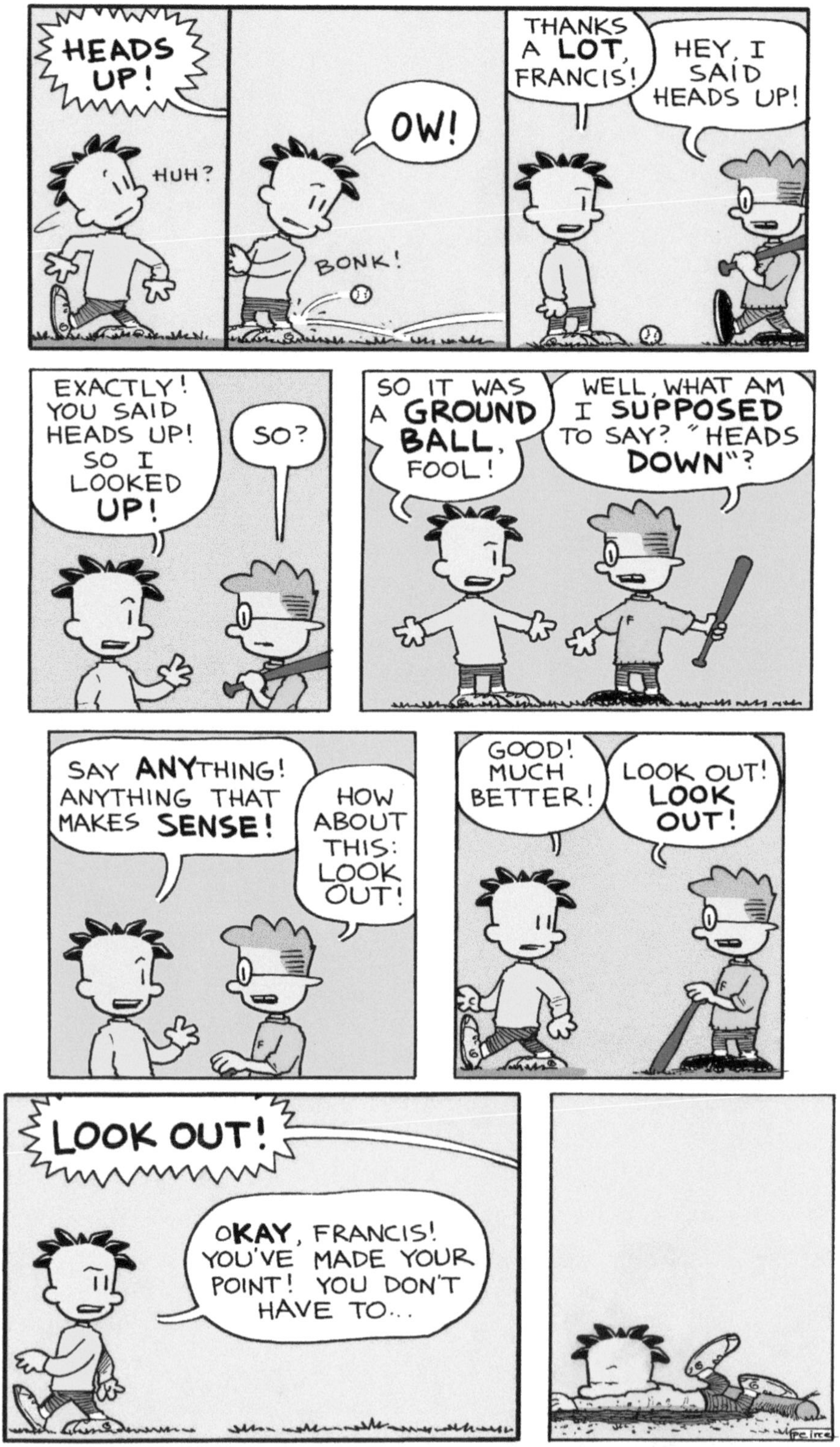
HEADS UP!
HUH?
OW!
BONK!
THANKS A LOT, FRANCIS!
HEY, I SAID HEADS UP!
EXACTLY! YOU SAID HEADS UP! SO I LOOKED UP!
SO?
SO IT WAS A GROUND BALL, FOOL!
WELL, WHAT AM I SUPPOSED TO SAY? "HEADS DOWN"?
SAY ANYTHING! ANYTHING THAT MAKES SENSE!
HOW ABOUT THIS: LOOK OUT!
GOOD! MUCH BETTER!
LOOK OUT! LOOK OUT!
LOOK OUT!
OKAY, FRANCIS! YOU'VE MADE YOUR POINT! YOU DON'T HAVE TO...
peirce

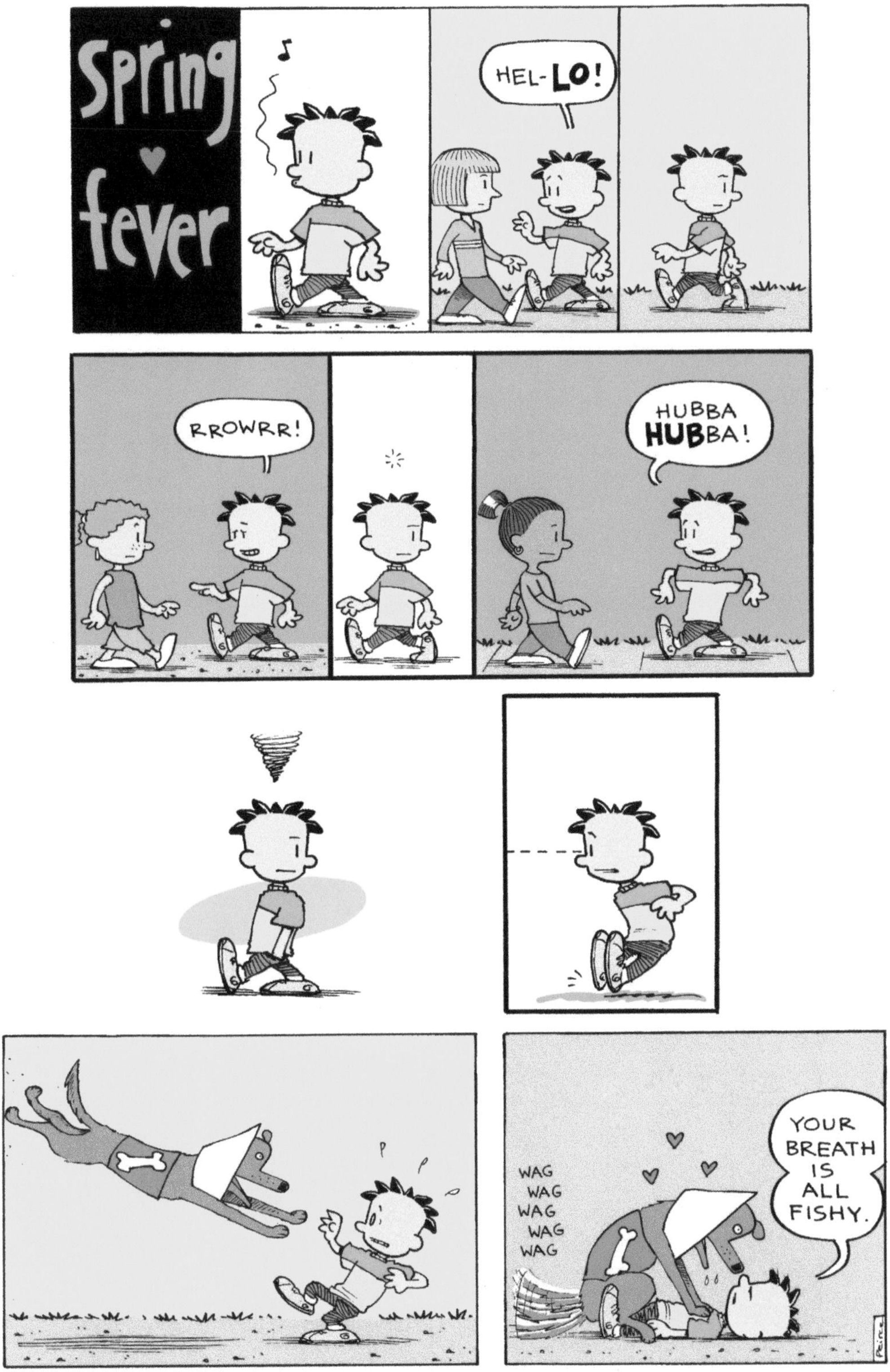
Spring fever
HEL-LO!
RROWRR!
HUBBA HUBBA!
WAG WAG WAG WAG WAG
YOUR BREATH IS ALL FISHY.

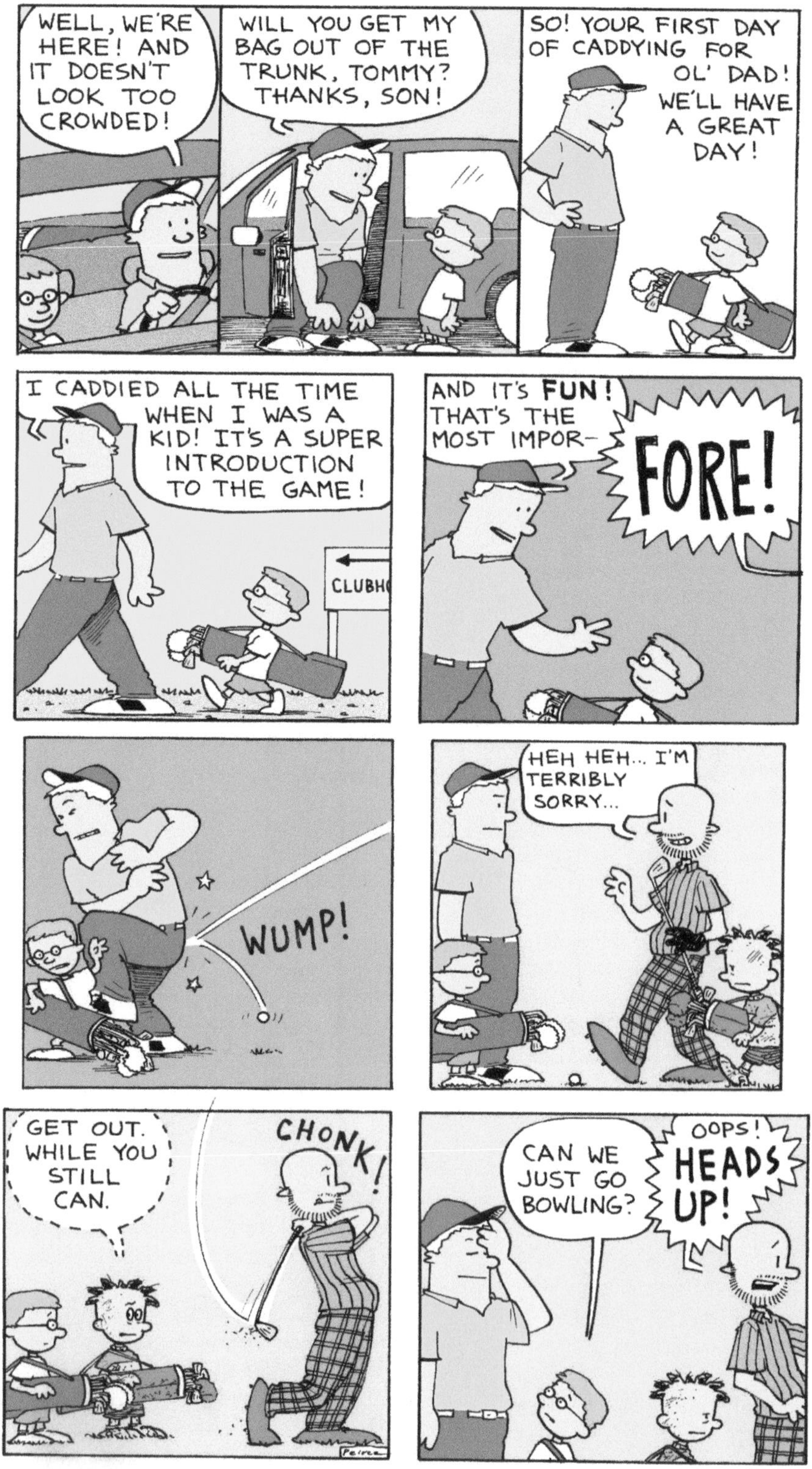
WELL, WE'RE HERE! AND IT DOESN'T LOOK TOO CROWDED!
WILL YOU GET MY BAG OUT OF THE TRUNK, TOMMY? THANKS, SON!
SO! YOUR FIRST DAY OF CADDYING FOR OL' DAD! WE'LL HAVE A GREAT DAY!
I CADDIED ALL THE TIME WHEN I WAS A KID! IT'S A SUPER INTRODUCTION TO THE GAME!
CLUBHO
AND IT'S FUN! THAT'S THE MOST IMPOR–
FORE!
WUMP!
HEH HEH... I'M TERRIBLY SORRY...
GET OUT. WHILE YOU STILL CAN.
CHONK!
CAN WE JUST GO BOWLING?
OOPS! HEADS UP!

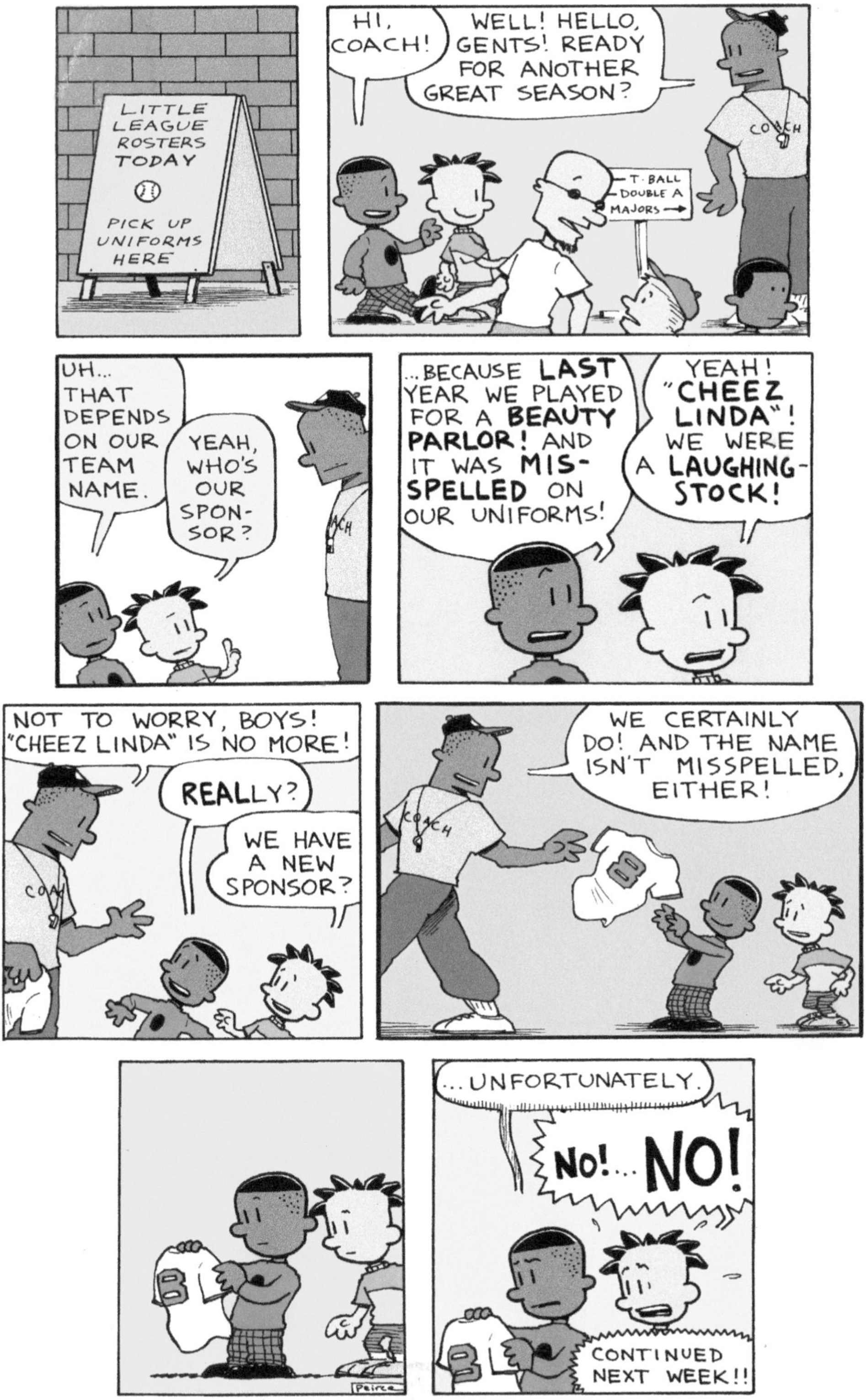
LITTLE LEAGUE ROSTERS TODAY
PICK UP UNIFORMS HERE
HI, COACH!
WELL! HELLO, GENTS! READY FOR ANOTHER GREAT SEASON?
COACH
T-BALL
DOUBLE A
MAJORS
UH... THAT DEPENDS ON OUR TEAM NAME.
YEAH, WHO'S OUR SPON-SOR?
...BECAUSE **LAST** YEAR WE PLAYED FOR A **BEAUTY PARLOR!** AND IT WAS **MIS-SPELLED** ON OUR UNIFORMS!
YEAH! "**CHEEZ LINDA**"! WE WERE A **LAUGHING-STOCK!**
NOT TO WORRY, BOYS! "CHEEZ LINDA" IS NO MORE!
REALLY?
WE HAVE A NEW SPONSOR?
WE CERTAINLY DO! AND THE NAME ISN'T MISSPELLED, EITHER!
COACH
Peirce
...UNFORTUNATELY.
NO!... NO!
CONTINUED NEXT WEEK!!

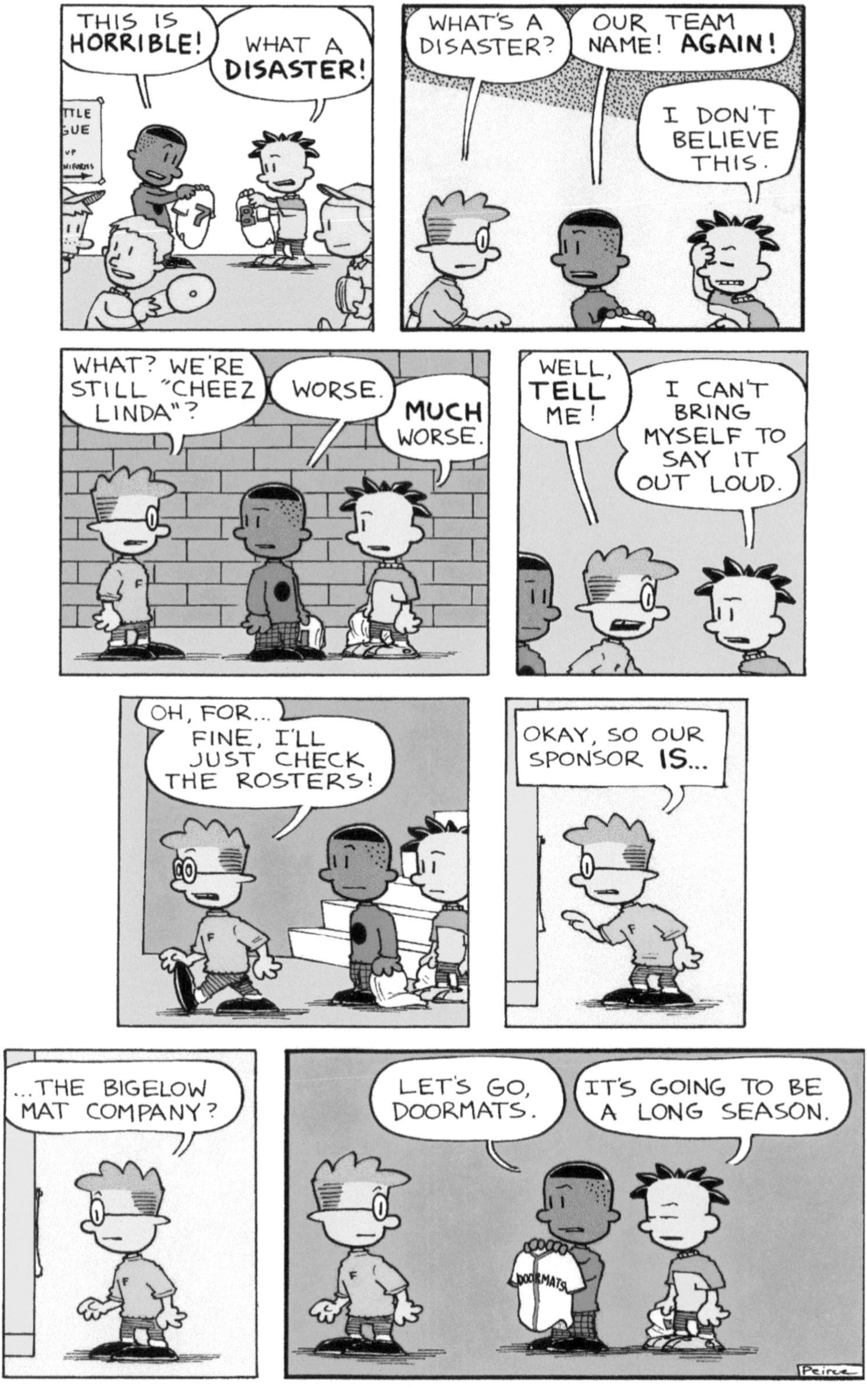
THIS IS HORRIBLE!
WHAT A DISASTER!
WHAT'S A DISASTER?
OUR TEAM NAME! AGAIN!
I DON'T BELIEVE THIS.
WHAT? WE'RE STILL "CHEEZ LINDA"?
WORSE.
MUCH WORSE.
WELL, TELL ME!
I CAN'T BRING MYSELF TO SAY IT OUT LOUD.
OH, FOR...
FINE, I'LL JUST CHECK THE ROSTERS!
OKAY, SO OUR SPONSOR IS...
...THE BIGELOW MAT COMPANY?
LET'S GO, DOORMATS.
IT'S GOING TO BE A LONG SEASON.
DOORMATS
Peirce

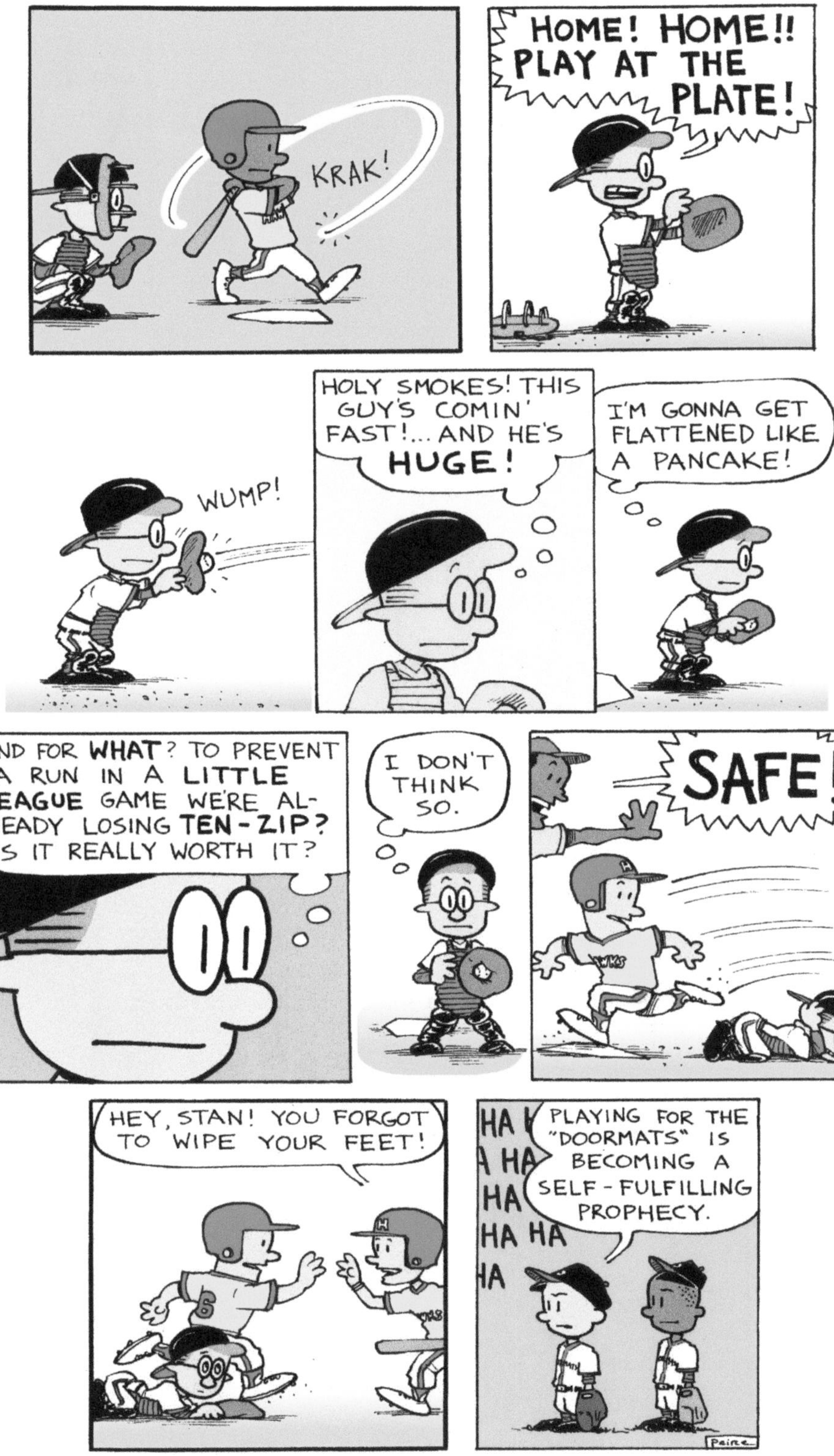
KRAK!
HOME! HOME!! PLAY AT THE PLATE!
WUMP!
HOLY SMOKES! THIS GUY'S COMIN' FAST!... AND HE'S HUGE!
I'M GONNA GET FLATTENED LIKE A PANCAKE!
AND FOR WHAT? TO PREVENT A RUN IN A LITTLE LEAGUE GAME WE'RE ALREADY LOSING TEN-ZIP? IS IT REALLY WORTH IT?
I DON'T THINK SO.
SAFE!
HEY, STAN! YOU FORGOT TO WIPE YOUR FEET!
HA HA HA HA HA HA HA HA
PLAYING FOR THE "DOORMATS" IS BECOMING A SELF-FULFILLING PROPHECY.
Peirce

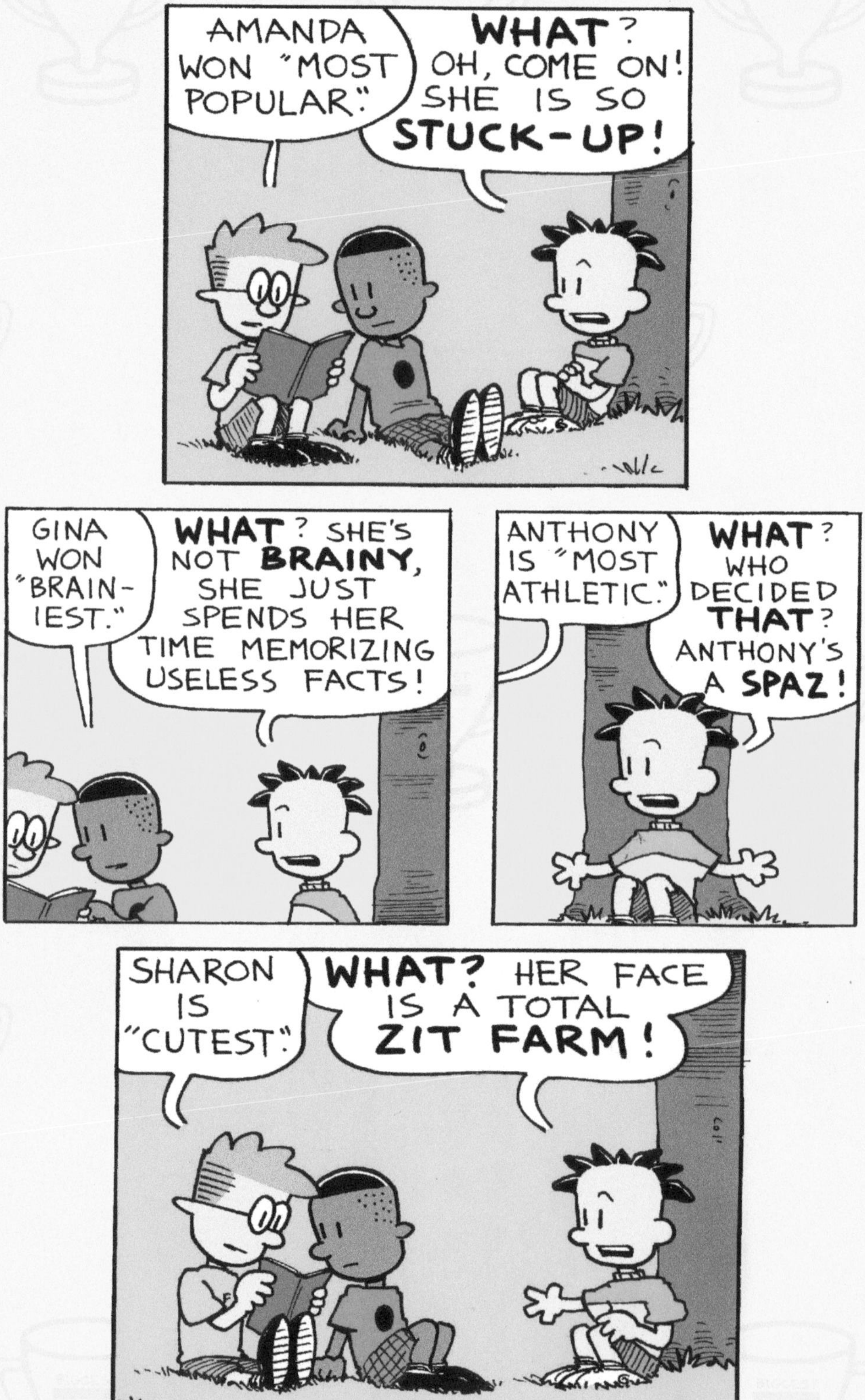
AMANDA WON "MOST POPULAR."
WHAT? OH, COME ON! SHE IS SO STUCK-UP!
GINA WON "BRAIN-IEST."
WHAT? SHE'S NOT BRAINY, SHE JUST SPENDS HER TIME MEMORIZING USELESS FACTS!
ANTHONY IS "MOST ATHLETIC."
WHAT? WHO DECIDED THAT? ANTHONY'S A SPAZ!
SHARON IS "CUTEST."
WHAT? HER FACE IS A TOTAL ZIT FARM!

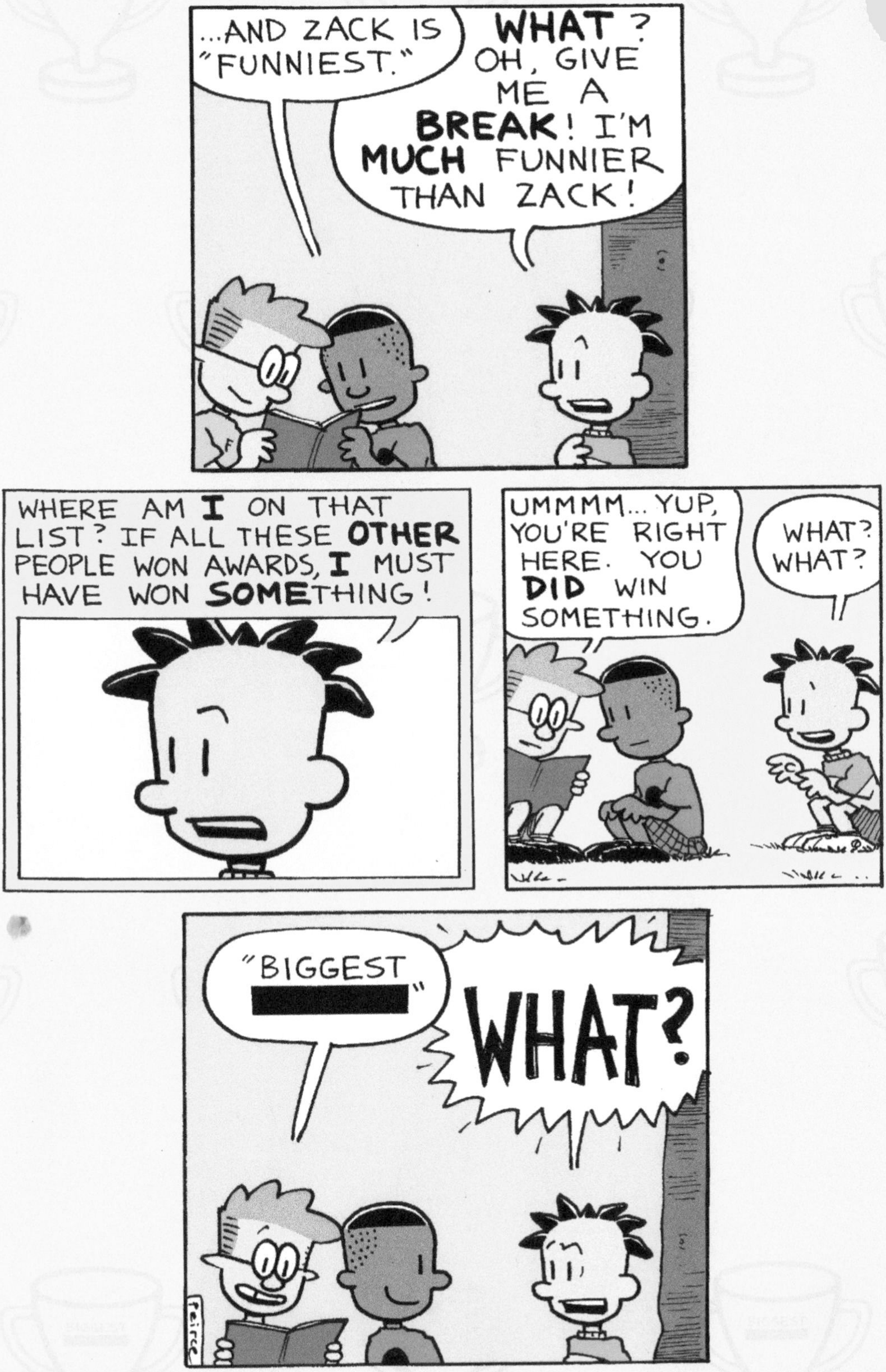
...AND ZACK IS "FUNNIEST."
WHAT? OH, GIVE ME A BREAK! I'M MUCH FUNNIER THAN ZACK!
WHERE AM I ON THAT LIST? IF ALL THESE OTHER PEOPLE WON AWARDS, I MUST HAVE WON SOMETHING!
UMMMM... YUP, YOU'RE RIGHT HERE. YOU DID WIN SOMETHING.
WHAT? WHAT?
"BIGGEST [redacted]"
WHAT?
peirce

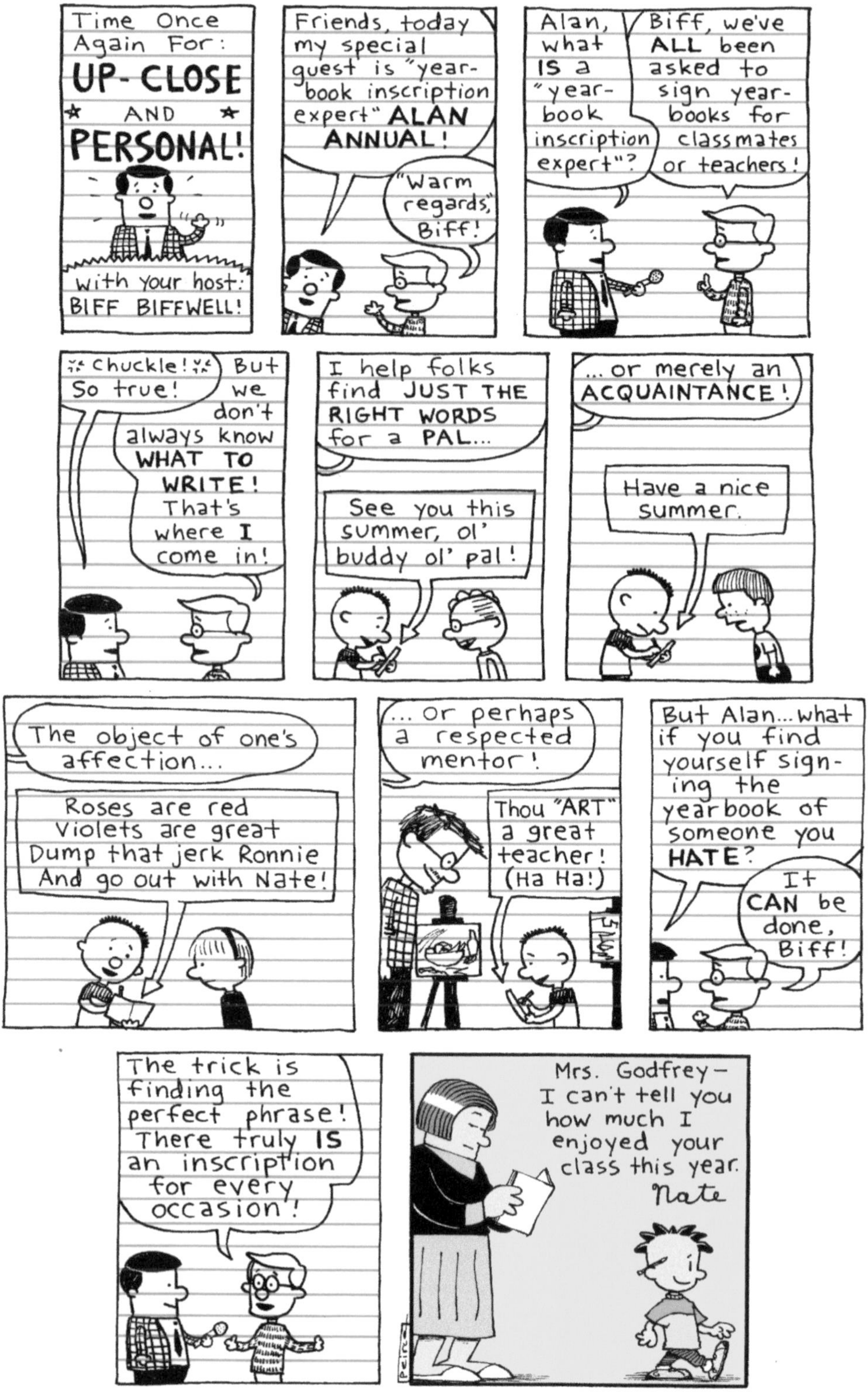
Time Once Again For: UP-CLOSE AND PERSONAL!
with your host: BIFF BIFFWELL!
Friends, today my special guest is "year-book inscription expert" ALAN ANNUAL!
"Warm regards," Biff!
Alan, what IS a "year-book inscription expert"?
Biff, we've ALL been asked to sign year-books for classmates or teachers!
Chuckle! So true!
But we don't always know WHAT TO WRITE! That's where I come in!
I help folks find JUST THE RIGHT WORDS for a PAL...
See you this summer, ol' buddy ol' pal!
... or merely an ACQUAINTANCE!
Have a nice summer.
The object of one's affection...
Roses are red
Violets are great
Dump that jerk Ronnie
And go out with Nate!
... Or perhaps a respected mentor!
Thou "ART" a great teacher! (Ha Ha!)
But Alan... what if you find yourself signing the yearbook of someone you HATE?
It CAN be done, Biff!
The trick is finding the perfect phrase! There truly IS an inscription for every occasion!
Mrs. Godfrey - I can't tell you how much I enjoyed your class this year. Nate

Biff & Chip **"ON SAFARI"**

Greetings, friends! We're here in the wilds of Suburbia...

...to observe one of nature's most LOATHSOME creatures:

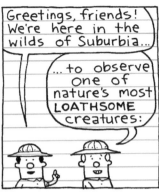

...the SIXTH-GRADE SOCIAL STUDIES TEACHER!

There she is, Biff! But... who's that WITH her?

That's a common schoolchild: "Academius Downtroddenus".

He looks EXHAUST-ED, Biff!

Oh, he IS! He's been her PRISONER since September!

SEPTEMBER? EGAD! Why doesn't she just EAT him and be DONE with it?

The schoolchild isn't FOOD for her, Chip! He's her AMUSEMENT! She screams at him, bosses him around, and brain-washes him with USELESS TRIVIA!

But... that's so CRUEL!

There IS hope, though, Chip. NATURE'S TIMETABLE is taking over!

See? She's going into SUMMER HIBER-NATION!

...And "Academius Downtroddenus" can ESCAPE! RUN! RUN!

RRRRIINNNGG

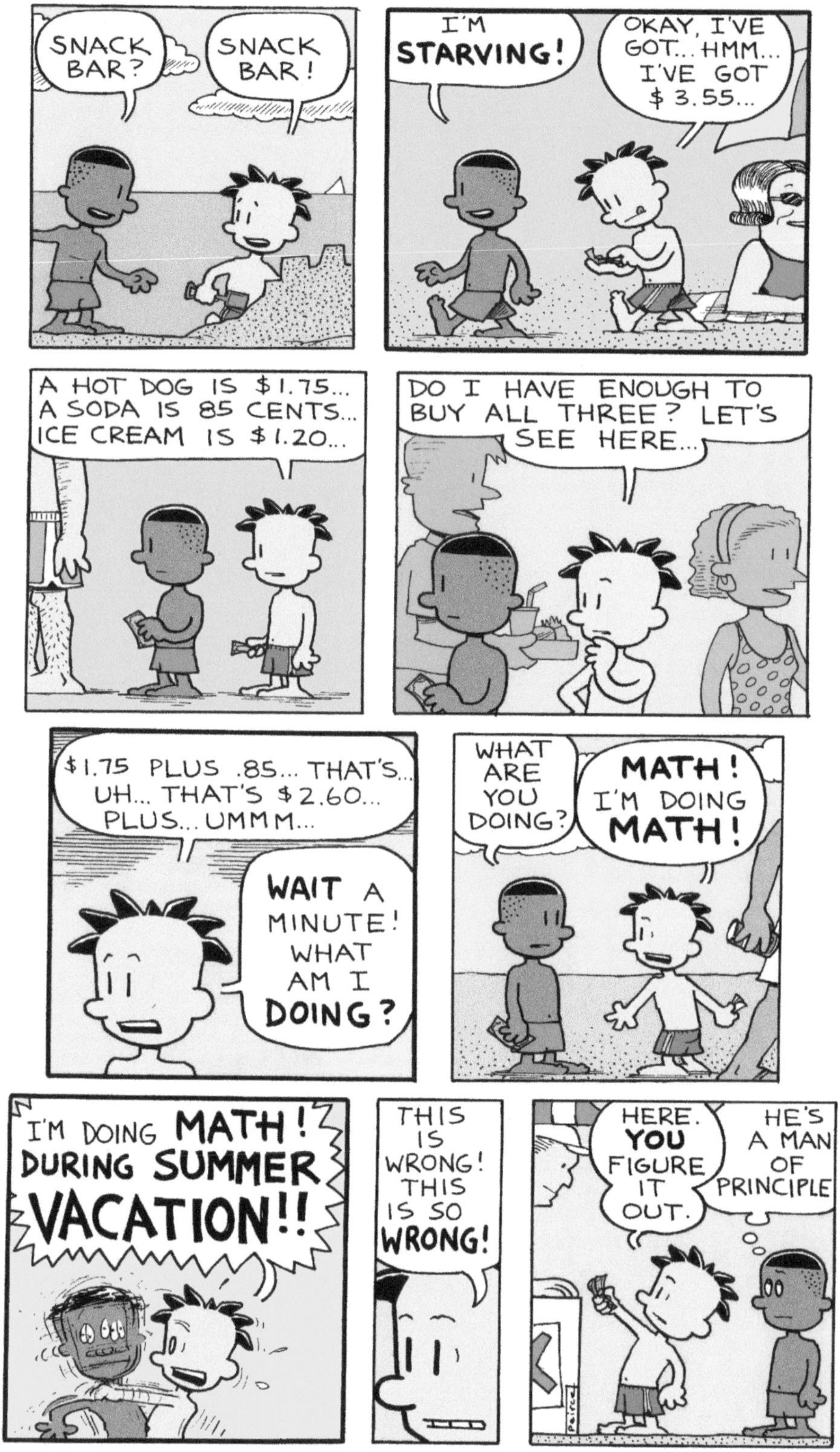
SNACK BAR?
SNACK BAR!
I'M STARVING!
OKAY, I'VE GOT... HMM... I'VE GOT $3.55...
A HOT DOG IS $1.75... A SODA IS 85 CENTS... ICE CREAM IS $1.20...
DO I HAVE ENOUGH TO BUY ALL THREE? LET'S SEE HERE...
$1.75 PLUS .85... THAT'S... UH... THAT'S $2.60... PLUS... UMMM...
WAIT A MINUTE! WHAT AM I DOING?
WHAT ARE YOU DOING?
MATH! I'M DOING MATH!
I'M DOING MATH! DURING SUMMER VACATION!!
THIS IS WRONG! THIS IS SO WRONG!
HERE. YOU FIGURE IT OUT.
HE'S A MAN OF PRINCIPLE
PEIRCE

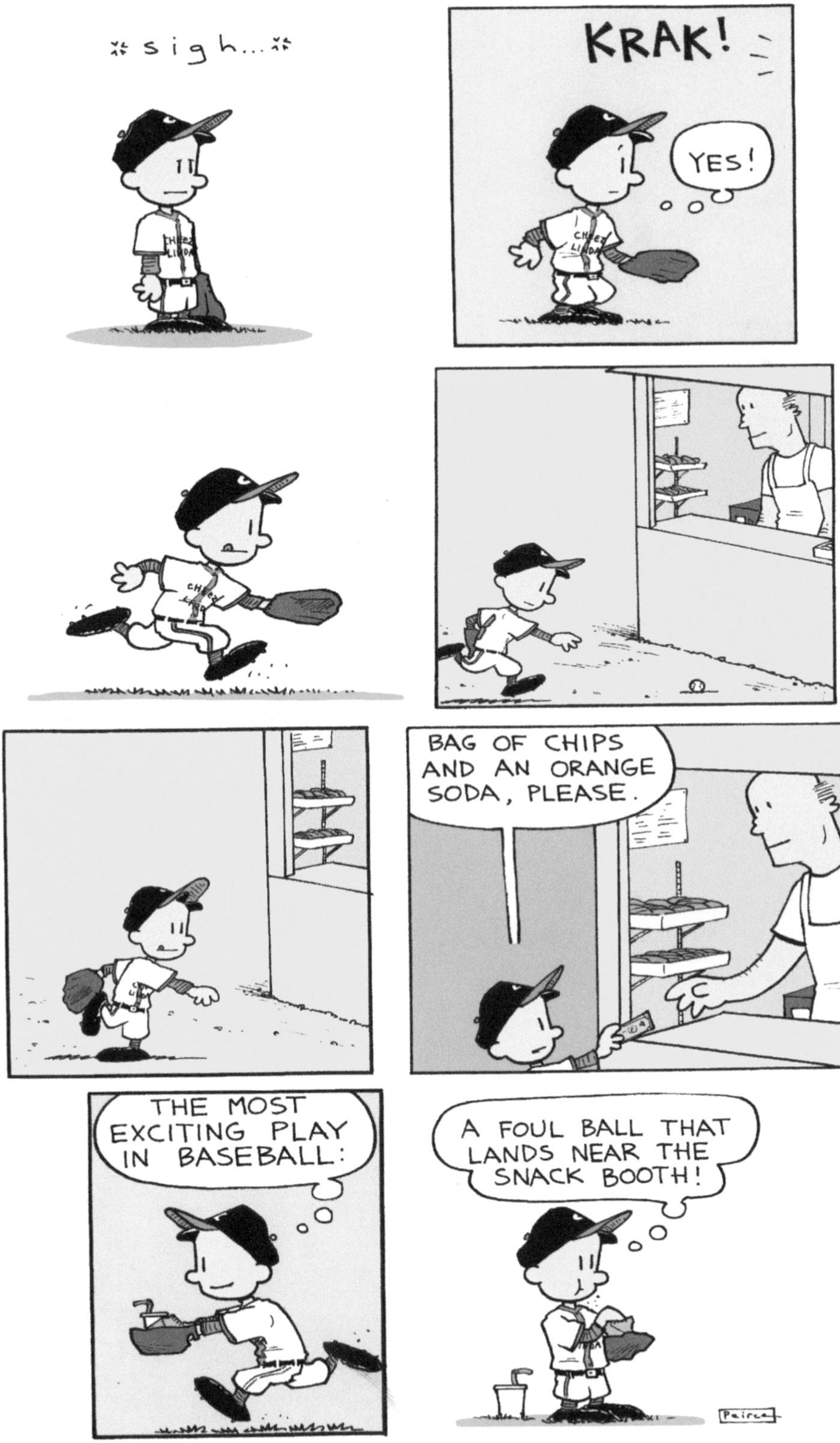
sigh...
KRAK!
YES!
BAG OF CHIPS AND AN ORANGE SODA, PLEASE.
THE MOST EXCITING PLAY IN BASEBALL:
A FOUL BALL THAT LANDS NEAR THE SNACK BOOTH!
Peirce

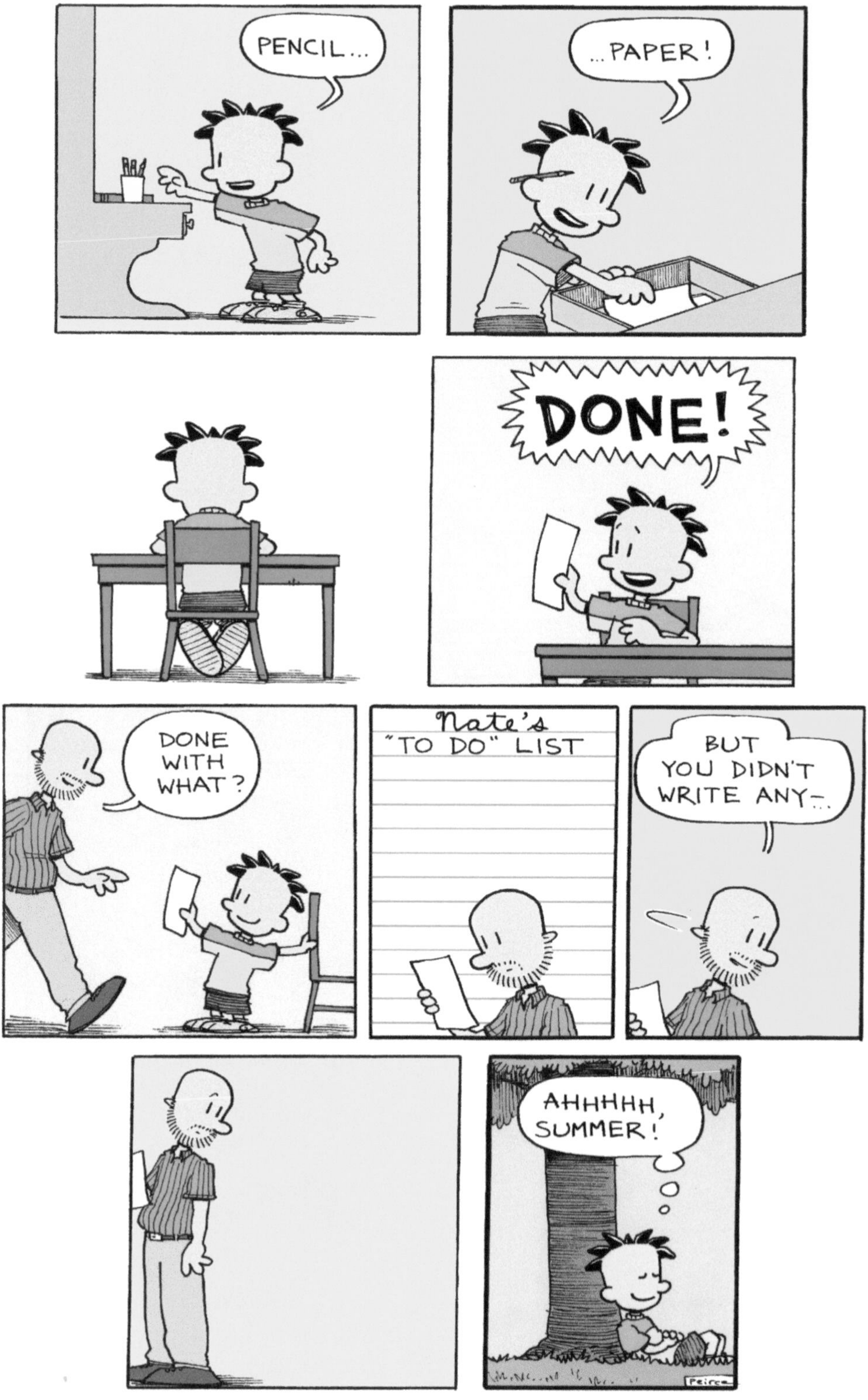
PENCIL...
...PAPER!
DONE!
DONE WITH WHAT?
Nate's "TO DO" LIST
BUT YOU DIDN'T WRITE ANY—...
AHHHHH, SUMMER!
Peirce

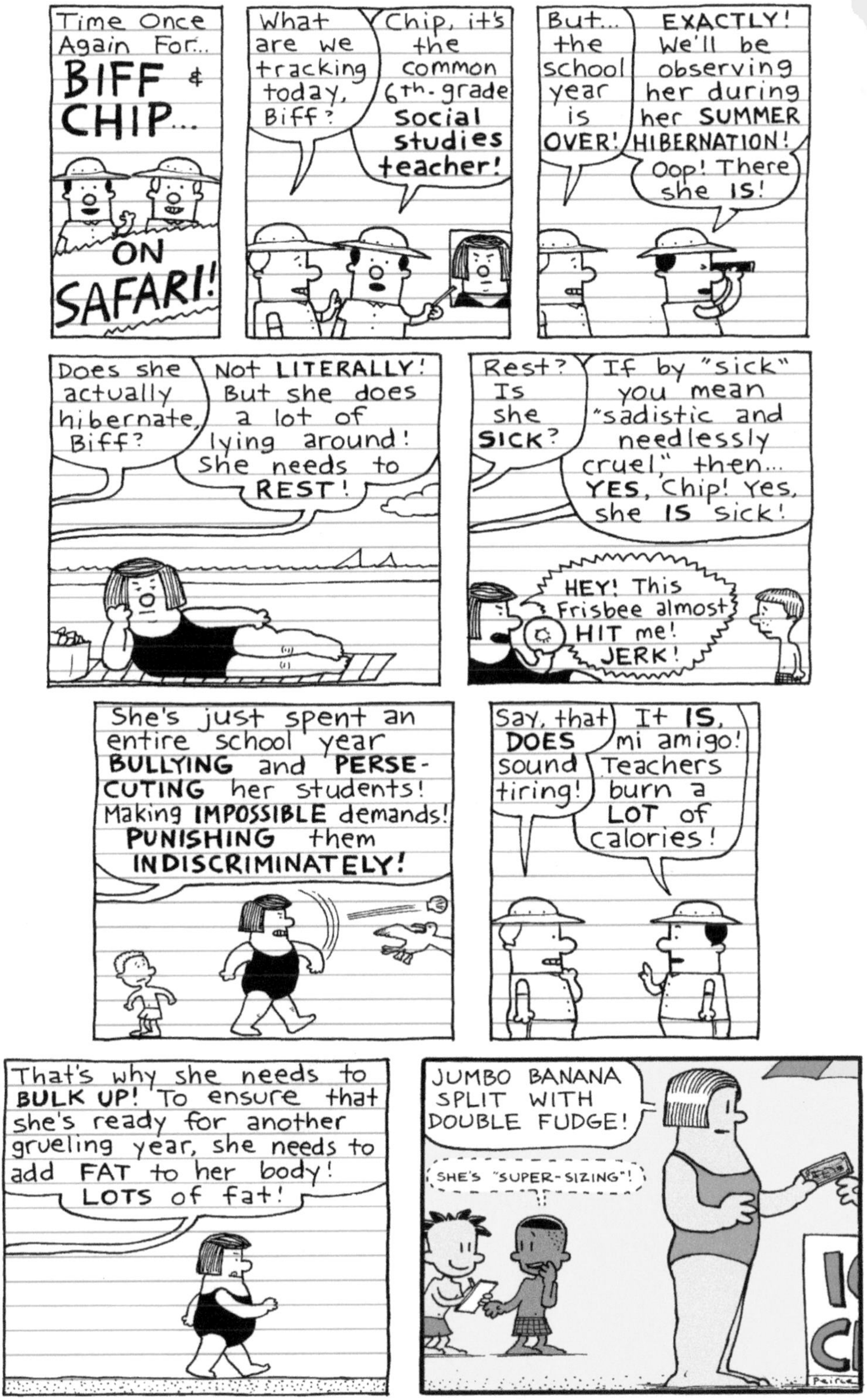

Time Once Again For...
BIFF & CHIP...
ON SAFARI!
What are we tracking today, Biff?
Chip, it's the common 6th-grade social studies teacher!
But... the school year is OVER!
EXACTLY! We'll be observing her during her SUMMER HIBERNATION!
Oop! There she IS!
Does she actually hibernate, Biff?
Not LITERALLY! But she does a lot of lying around! She needs to REST!
Rest? Is she SICK?
If by "sick" you mean "sadistic and needlessly cruel," then... YES, Chip! Yes, she IS sick!
HEY! This Frisbee almost HIT me! JERK!
She's just spent an entire school year BULLYING and PERSECUTING her students! Making IMPOSSIBLE demands! PUNISHING them INDISCRIMINATELY!
Say, that DOES sound tiring!
It IS, mi amigo! Teachers burn a LOT of calories!
That's why she needs to BULK UP! To ensure that she's ready for another grueling year, she needs to add FAT to her body! LOTS of fat!
JUMBO BANANA SPLIT WITH DOUBLE FUDGE!
SHE'S "SUPER-SIZING"!

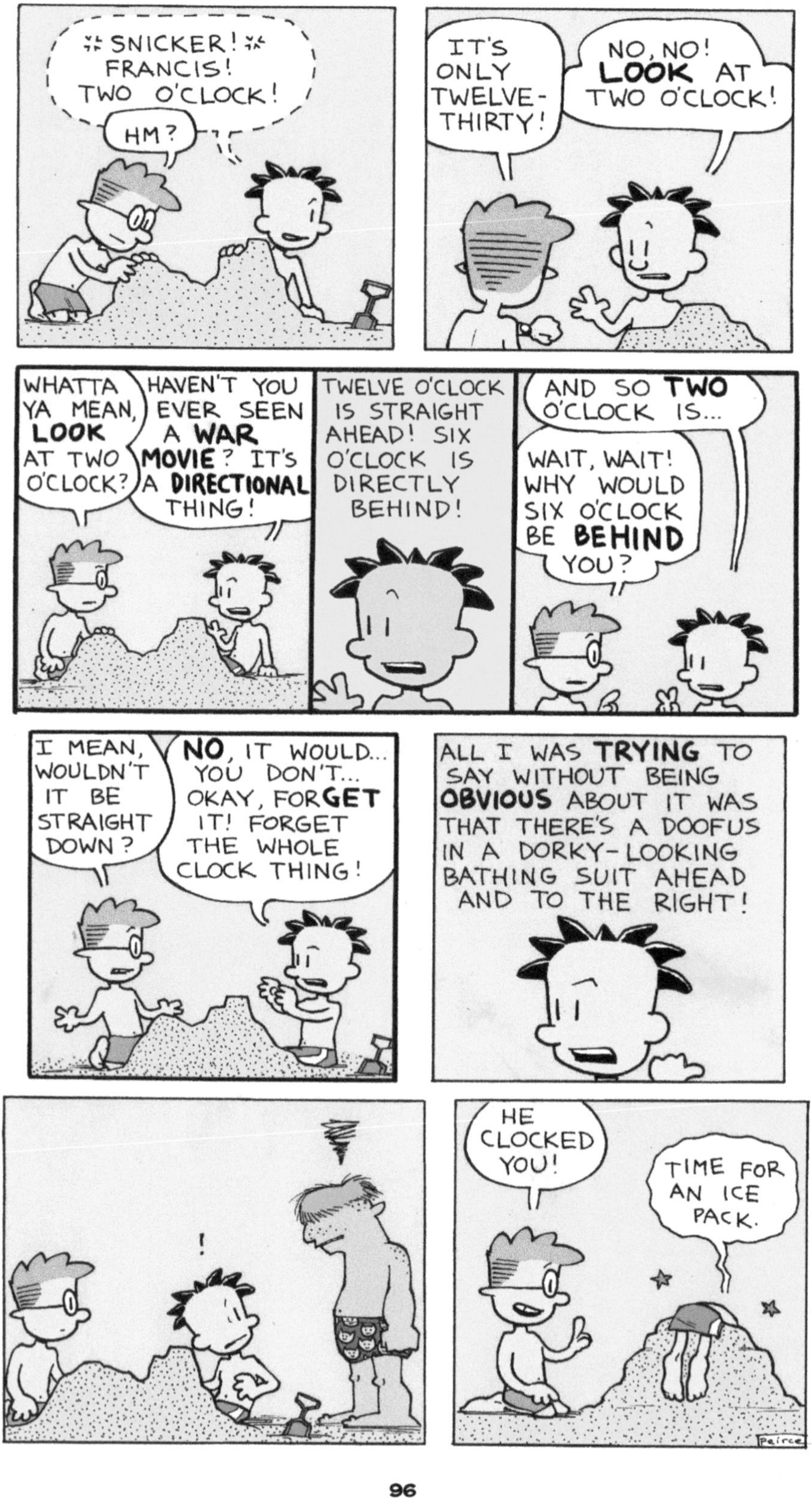

SNICKER!
FRANCIS! TWO O'CLOCK!
HM?
IT'S ONLY TWELVE-THIRTY!
NO, NO! **LOOK** AT TWO O'CLOCK!
WHATTA YA MEAN, **LOOK** AT TWO O'CLOCK?
HAVEN'T YOU EVER SEEN A **WAR MOVIE**? IT'S A **DIRECTIONAL** THING!
TWELVE O'CLOCK IS STRAIGHT AHEAD! SIX O'CLOCK IS DIRECTLY BEHIND!
AND SO **TWO** O'CLOCK IS...
WAIT, WAIT! WHY WOULD SIX O'CLOCK BE **BEHIND** YOU?
I MEAN, WOULDN'T IT BE STRAIGHT DOWN?
NO, IT WOULD... YOU DON'T... OKAY, FOR**GET** IT! FORGET THE WHOLE CLOCK THING!
ALL I WAS **TRYING** TO SAY WITHOUT BEING **OBVIOUS** ABOUT IT WAS THAT THERE'S A DOOFUS IN A DORKY-LOOKING BATHING SUIT AHEAD AND TO THE RIGHT!
!
HE CLOCKED YOU!
TIME FOR AN ICE PACK.
Peirce

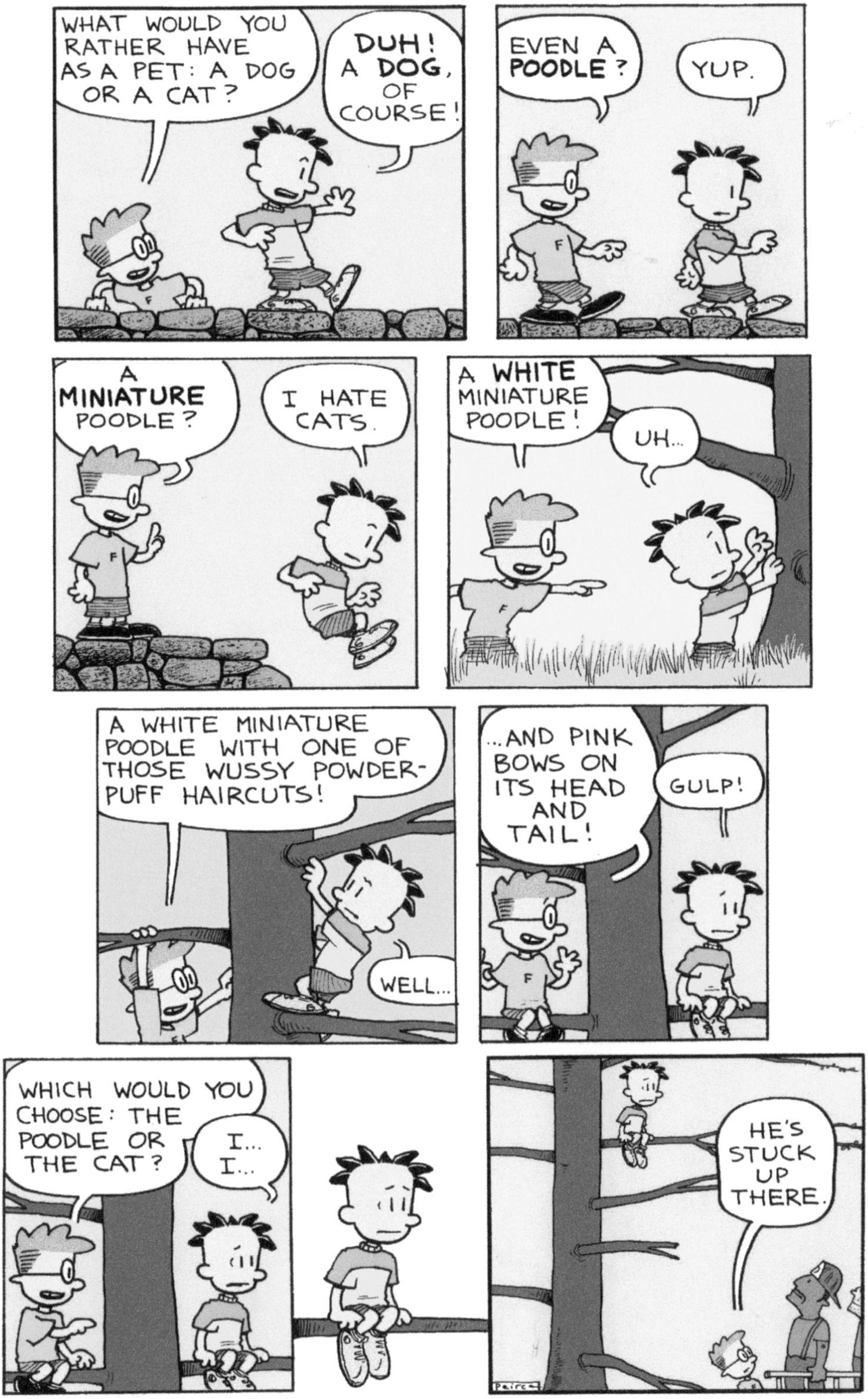
WHAT WOULD YOU RATHER HAVE AS A PET: A DOG OR A CAT?
DUH! A DOG, OF COURSE!
EVEN A POODLE?
YUP.
A MINIATURE POODLE?
I HATE CATS.
A WHITE MINIATURE POODLE!
UH...
A WHITE MINIATURE POODLE WITH ONE OF THOSE WUSSY POWDER-PUFF HAIRCUTS!
WELL...
...AND PINK BOWS ON ITS HEAD AND TAIL!
GULP!
WHICH WOULD YOU CHOOSE: THE POODLE OR THE CAT?
I... I...
HE'S STUCK UP THERE.
Peirce

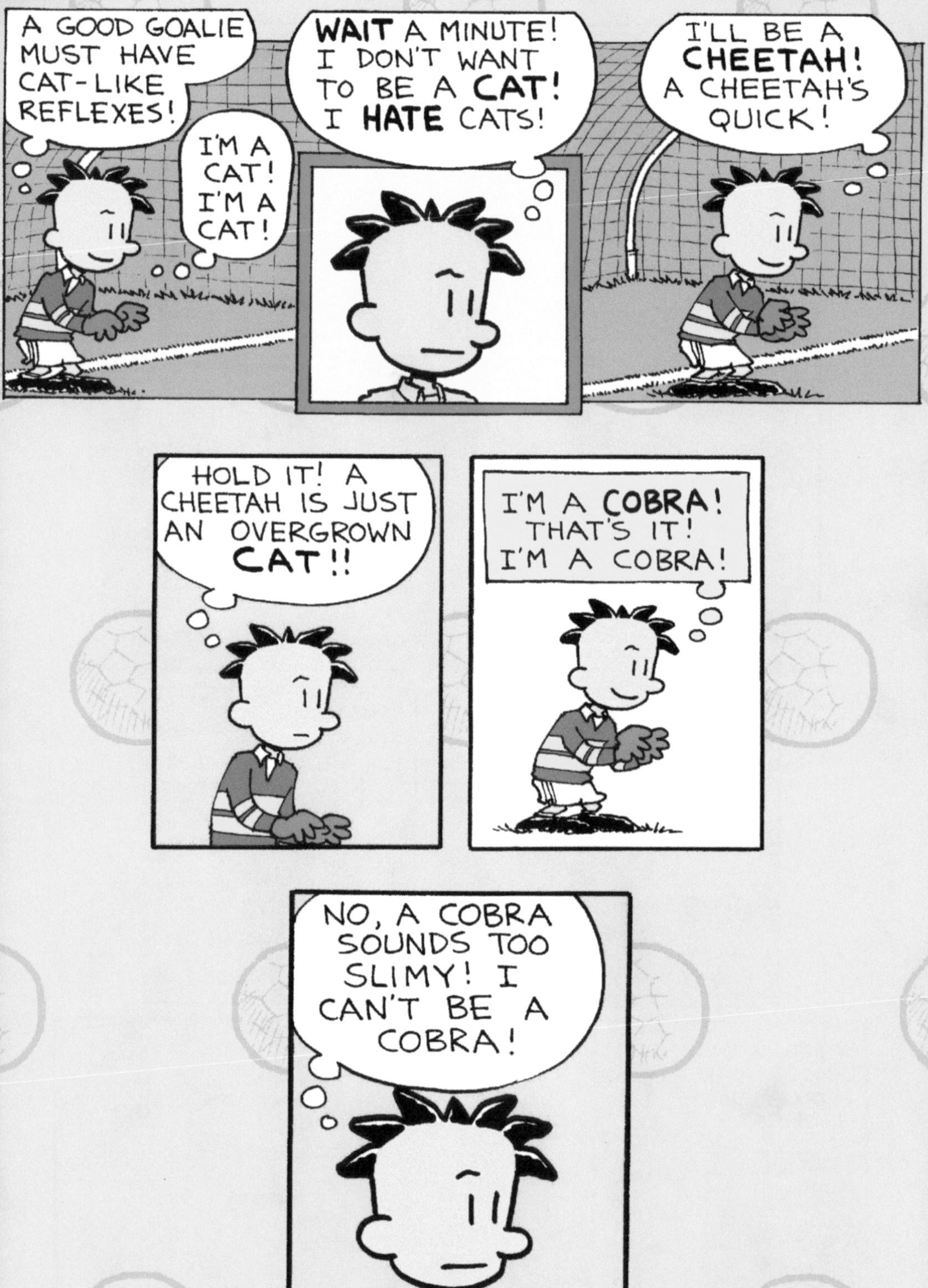
A GOOD GOALIE MUST HAVE CAT-LIKE REFLEXES!
I'M A CAT! I'M A CAT!
WAIT A MINUTE! I DON'T WANT TO BE A CAT! I HATE CATS!
I'LL BE A CHEETAH! A CHEETAH'S QUICK!
HOLD IT! A CHEETAH IS JUST AN OVERGROWN CAT!!
I'M A COBRA! THAT'S IT! I'M A COBRA!
NO, A COBRA SOUNDS TOO SLIMY! I CAN'T BE A COBRA!

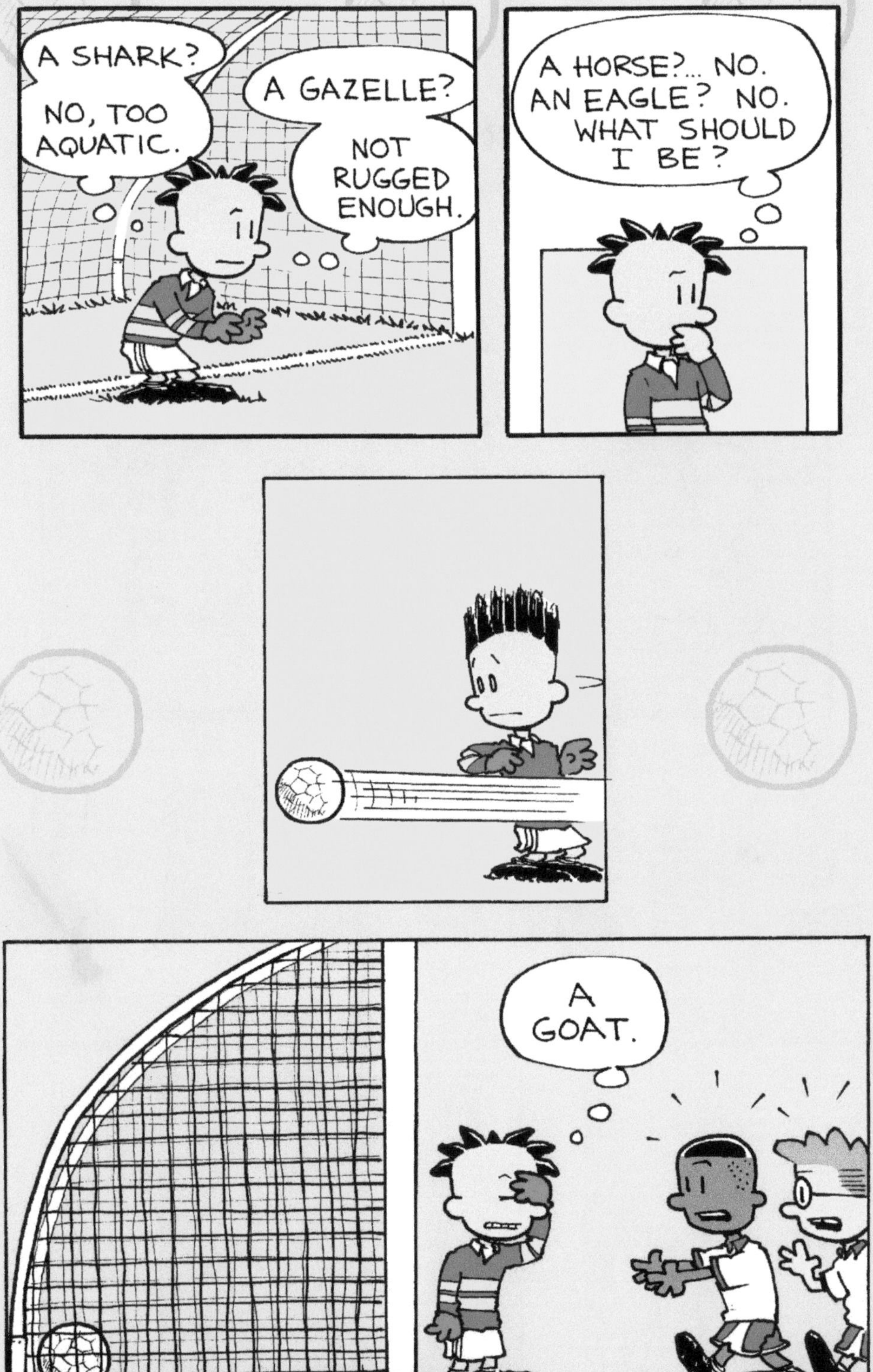
A SHARK?
NO, TOO AQUATIC.
A GAZELLE?
NOT RUGGED ENOUGH.
A HORSE?... NO. AN EAGLE? NO. WHAT SHOULD I BE?
A GOAT.
Peirce

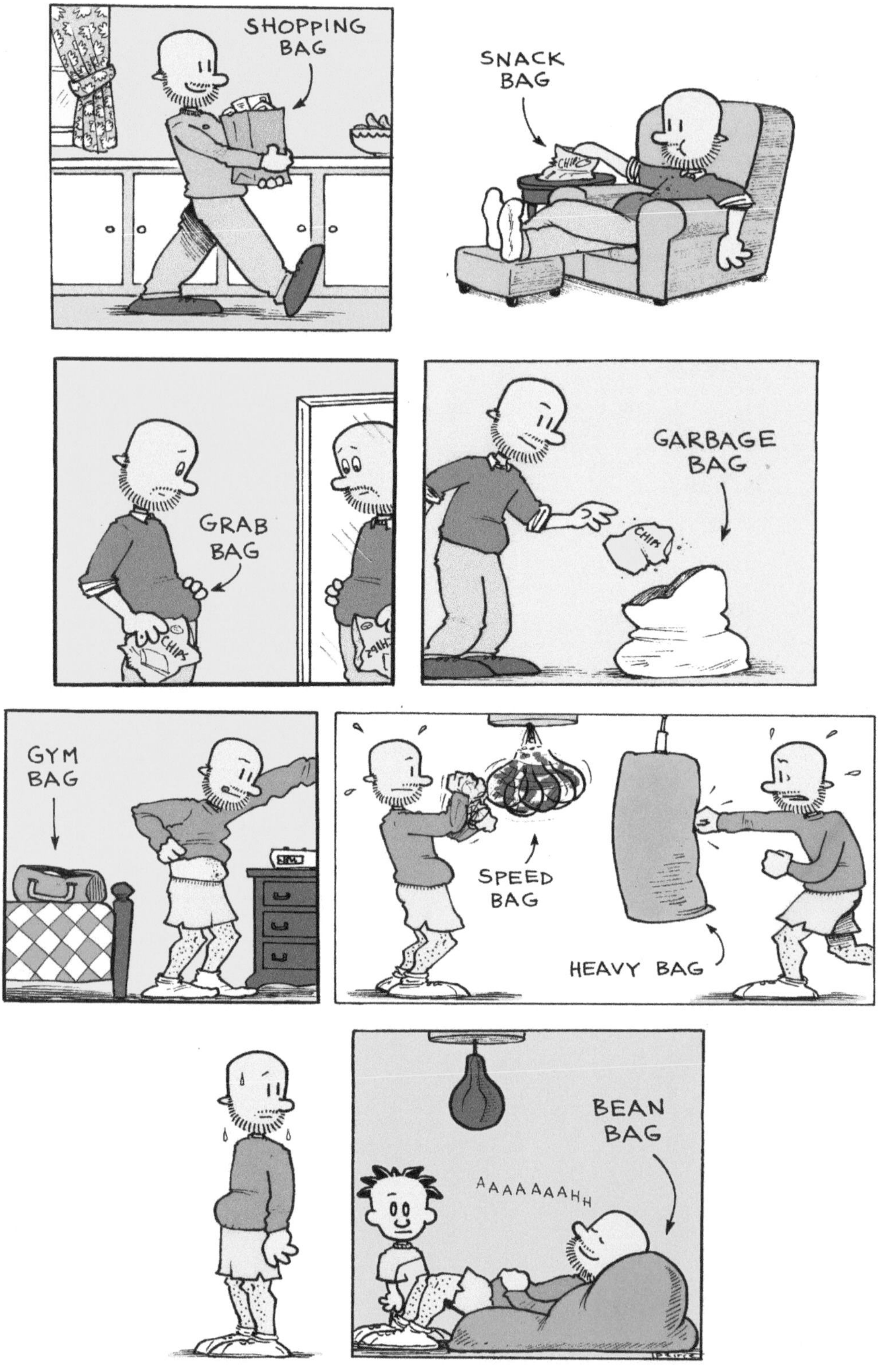
SHOPPING BAG
SNACK BAG
CHIPS
GRAB BAG
CHIPS
GARBAGE BAG
CHIPS
GYM BAG
SPEED BAG
HEAVY BAG
BEAN BAG
AAAAAAAHH

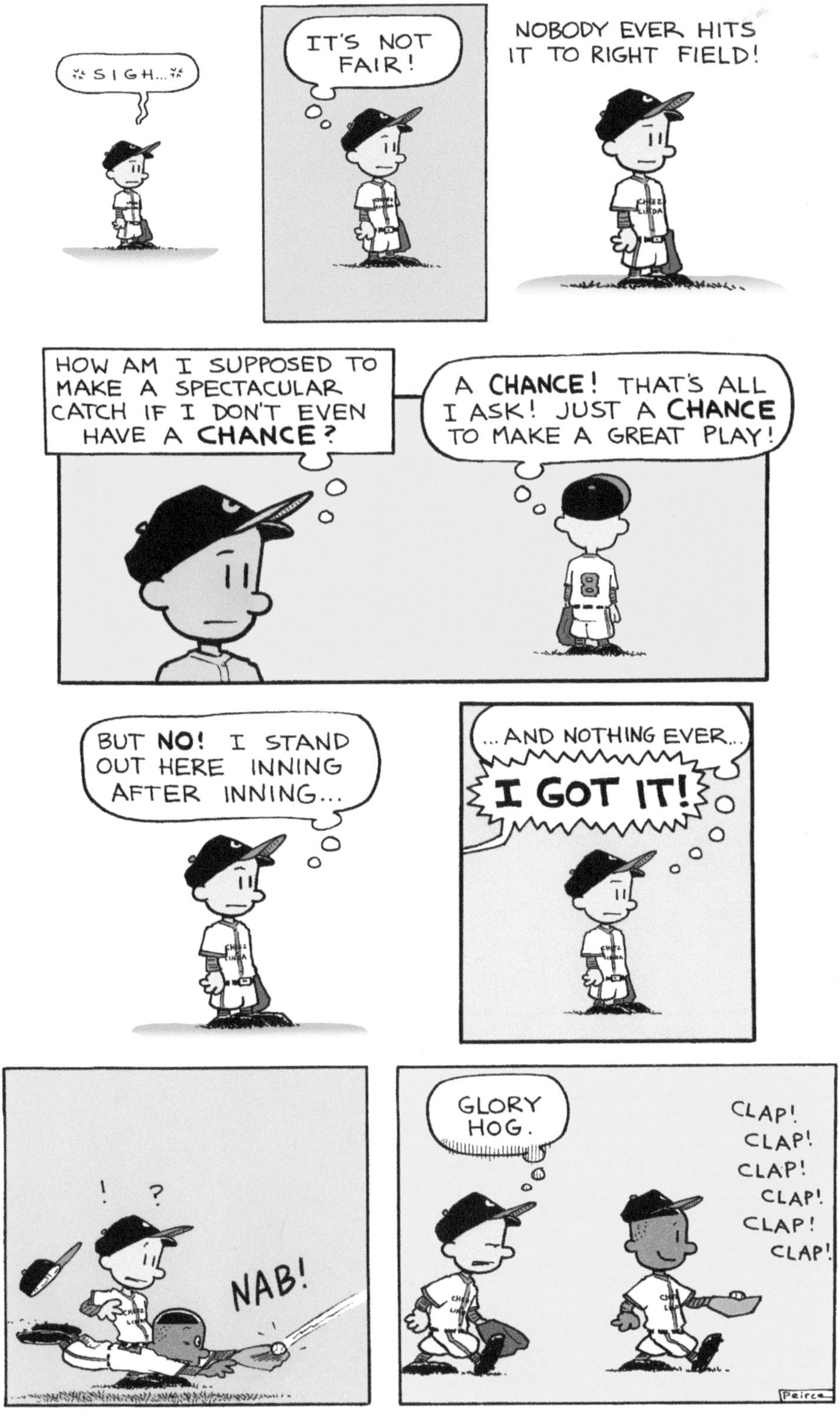
SIGH...
IT'S NOT FAIR!
NOBODY EVER HITS IT TO RIGHT FIELD!
HOW AM I SUPPOSED TO MAKE A SPECTACULAR CATCH IF I DON'T EVEN HAVE A CHANCE?
A CHANCE! THAT'S ALL I ASK! JUST A CHANCE TO MAKE A GREAT PLAY!
BUT NO! I STAND OUT HERE INNING AFTER INNING...
...AND NOTHING EVER...
I GOT IT!
! ?
NAB!
GLORY HOG.
CLAP! CLAP! CLAP! CLAP! CLAP! CLAP!
Peirce

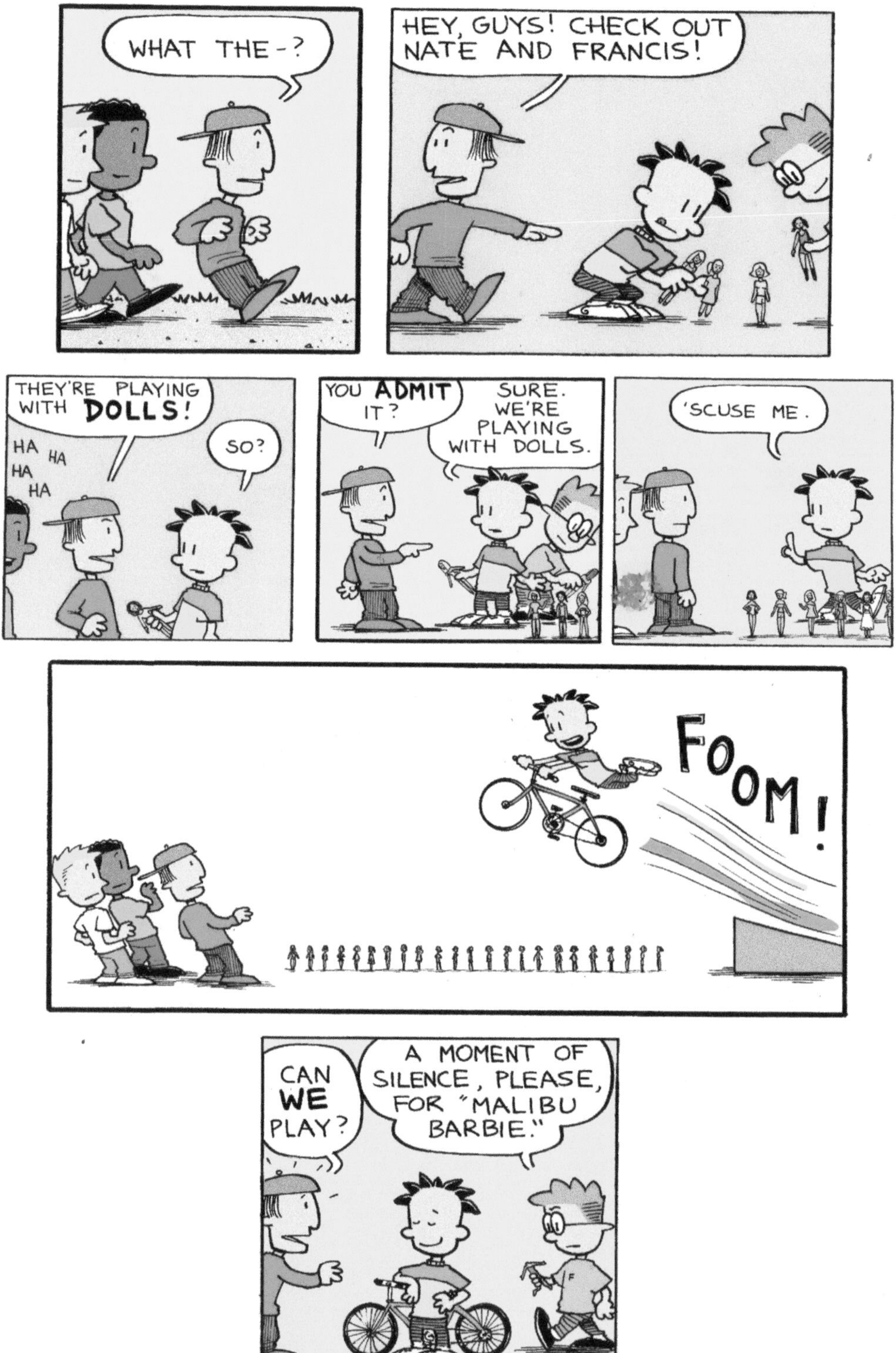
WHAT THE-?
HEY, GUYS! CHECK OUT NATE AND FRANCIS!
THEY'RE PLAYING WITH DOLLS!
HA HA HA HA
SO?
YOU ADMIT IT?
SURE. WE'RE PLAYING WITH DOLLS.
'SCUSE ME.
FOOM!
CAN WE PLAY?
A MOMENT OF SILENCE, PLEASE, FOR "MALIBU BARBIE."
Peirce

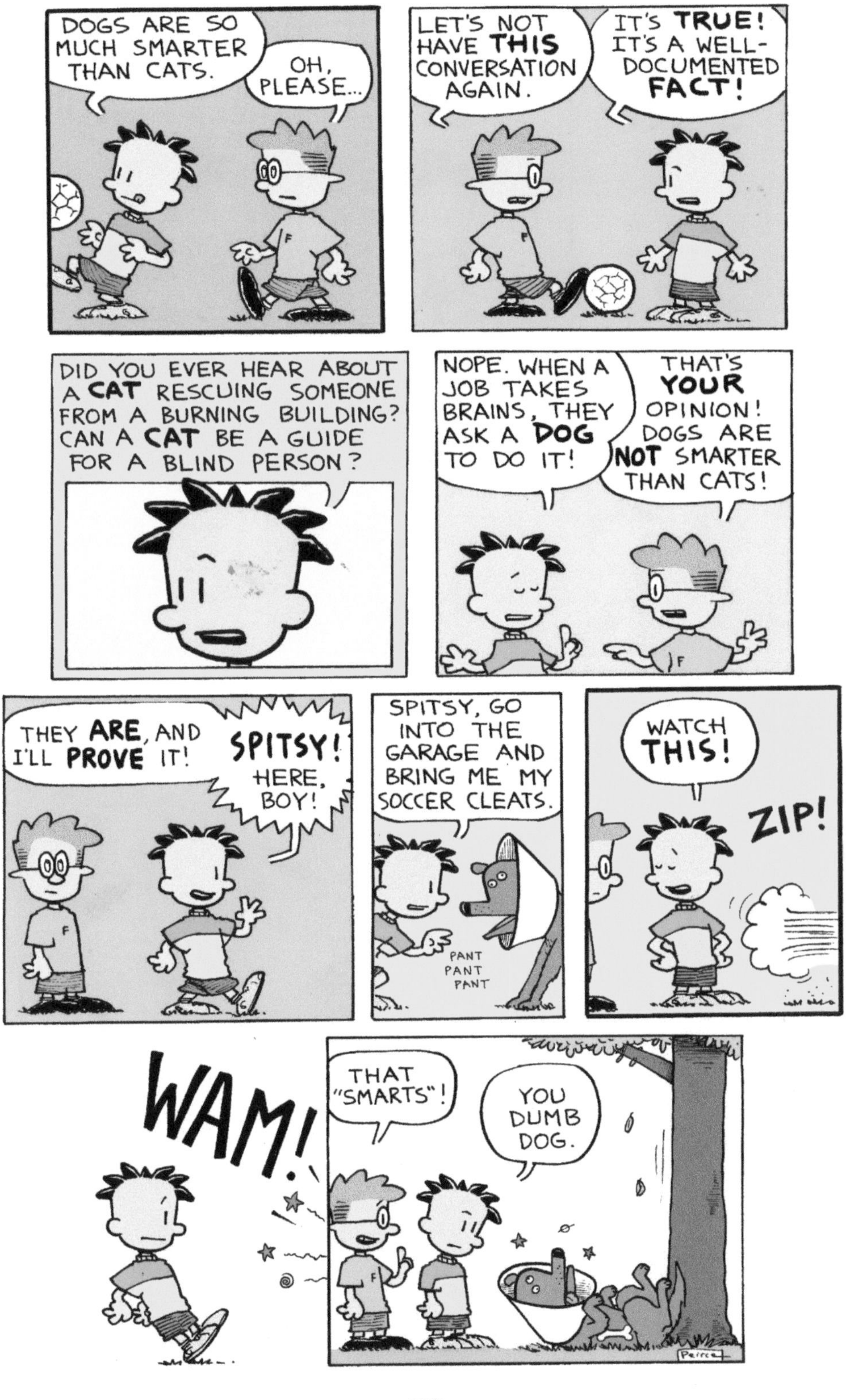

DOGS ARE SO MUCH SMARTER THAN CATS.
OH, PLEASE...
LET'S NOT HAVE THIS CONVERSATION AGAIN.
IT'S TRUE! IT'S A WELL-DOCUMENTED FACT!
DID YOU EVER HEAR ABOUT A CAT RESCUING SOMEONE FROM A BURNING BUILDING? CAN A CAT BE A GUIDE FOR A BLIND PERSON?
NOPE. WHEN A JOB TAKES BRAINS, THEY ASK A DOG TO DO IT!
THAT'S YOUR OPINION! DOGS ARE NOT SMARTER THAN CATS!
THEY ARE, AND I'LL PROVE IT!
SPITSY! HERE, BOY!
SPITSY, GO INTO THE GARAGE AND BRING ME MY SOCCER CLEATS.
PANT PANT PANT
WATCH THIS!
ZIP!
WAM!
THAT "SMARTS"!
YOU DUMB DOG.
Peirce

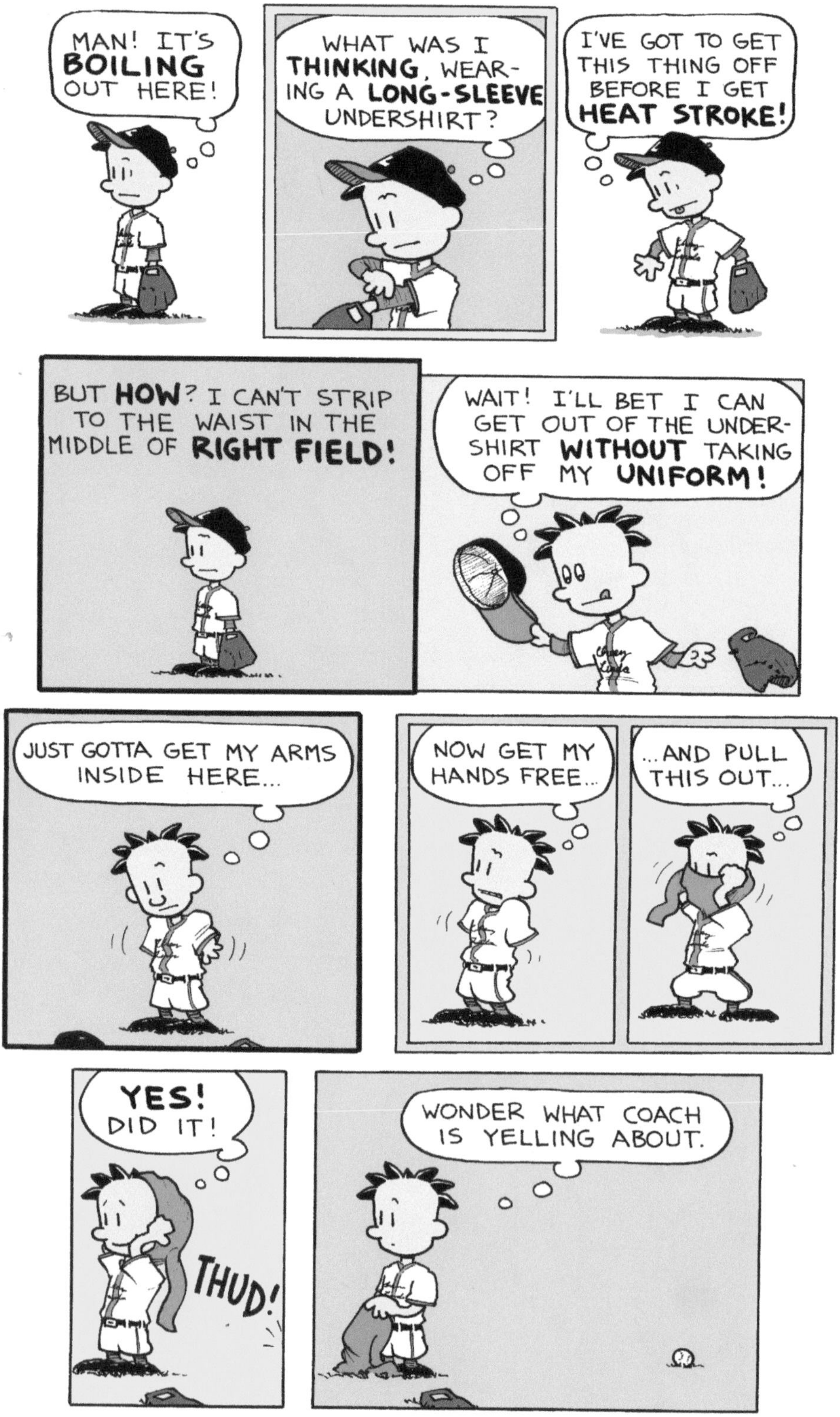
MAN! IT'S BOILING OUT HERE!
WHAT WAS I THINKING, WEARING A LONG-SLEEVE UNDERSHIRT?
I'VE GOT TO GET THIS THING OFF BEFORE I GET HEAT STROKE!
BUT HOW? I CAN'T STRIP TO THE WAIST IN THE MIDDLE OF RIGHT FIELD!
WAIT! I'LL BET I CAN GET OUT OF THE UNDERSHIRT WITHOUT TAKING OFF MY UNIFORM!
JUST GOTTA GET MY ARMS INSIDE HERE...
NOW GET MY HANDS FREE...
...AND PULL THIS OUT...
YES! DID IT!
THUD!
WONDER WHAT COACH IS YELLING ABOUT.

THERE!

PHYSICAL FITNESS MERIT BADGE, HERE I COME!

YOU'RE MY WITNESS, OKAY, FRANCIS? YOU'LL ATTEST TO THE FACT THAT I CLIMBED A FIFTEEN-FOOT ROPE!

YUP!

UP I GO!

YOU'RE HALFWAY!

OOF! GRUNT!

ALMOST THERE!

HM?

"FWIP! FWIP!

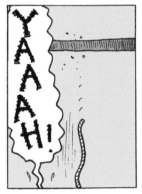

YAAH!

HOW'RE YOU DOING ON YOUR KNOT-TYING MERIT BADGE?

OW

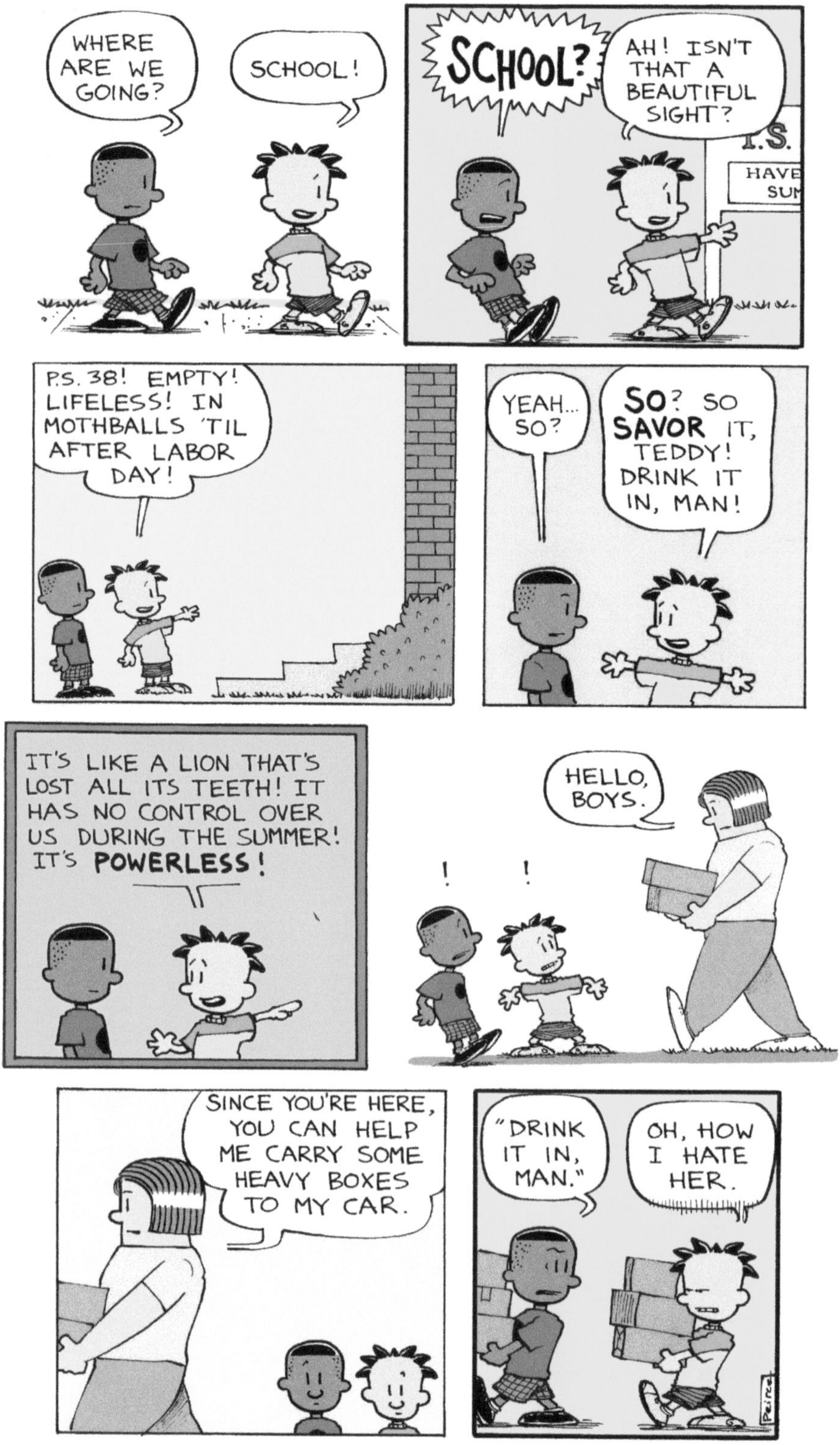
WHERE ARE WE GOING?
SCHOOL!
SCHOOL?
AH! ISN'T THAT A BEAUTIFUL SIGHT?
HAVE
SUM
P.S. 38! EMPTY! LIFELESS! IN MOTHBALLS 'TIL AFTER LABOR DAY!
YEAH... SO?
SO? SO SAVOR IT, TEDDY! DRINK IT IN, MAN!
IT'S LIKE A LION THAT'S LOST ALL ITS TEETH! IT HAS NO CONTROL OVER US DURING THE SUMMER! IT'S POWERLESS!
HELLO, BOYS.
!
!
SINCE YOU'RE HERE, YOU CAN HELP ME CARRY SOME HEAVY BOXES TO MY CAR.
"DRINK IT IN, MAN."
OH, HOW I HATE HER.
Peirce

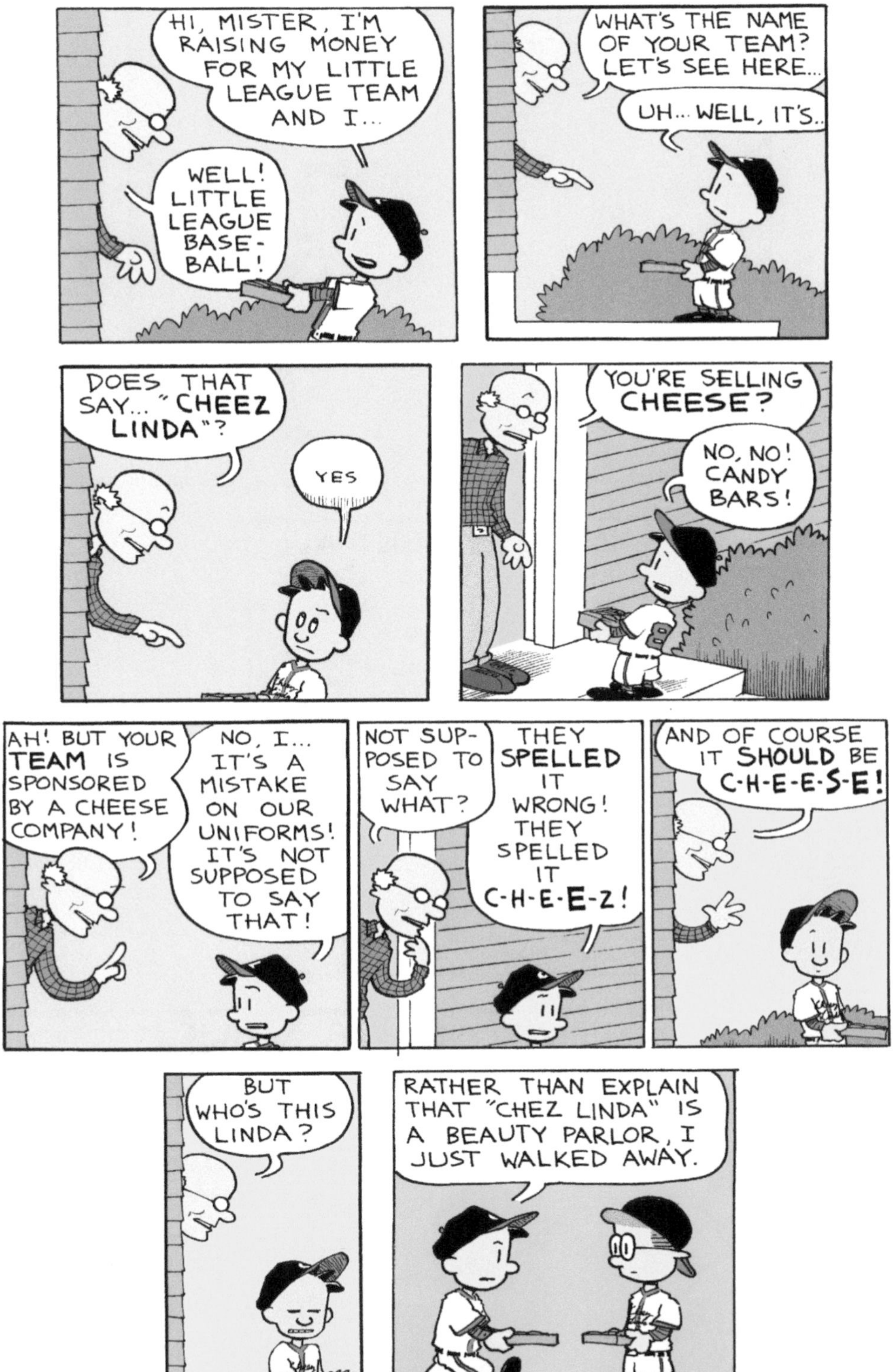
HI, MISTER, I'M RAISING MONEY FOR MY LITTLE LEAGUE TEAM AND I...
WELL! LITTLE LEAGUE BASE-BALL!
WHAT'S THE NAME OF YOUR TEAM? LET'S SEE HERE...
UH... WELL, IT'S...
DOES THAT SAY... "CHEEZ LINDA"?
YES
YOU'RE SELLING CHEESE?
NO, NO! CANDY BARS!
AH! BUT YOUR TEAM IS SPONSORED BY A CHEESE COMPANY!
NO, I... IT'S A MISTAKE ON OUR UNIFORMS! IT'S NOT SUPPOSED TO SAY THAT!
NOT SUPPOSED TO SAY WHAT?
THEY SPELLED IT WRONG! THEY SPELLED IT C-H-E-E-Z!
AND OF COURSE IT SHOULD BE C-H-E-E-S-E!
BUT WHO'S THIS LINDA?
RATHER THAN EXPLAIN THAT "CHEZ LINDA" IS A BEAUTY PARLOR, I JUST WALKED AWAY.

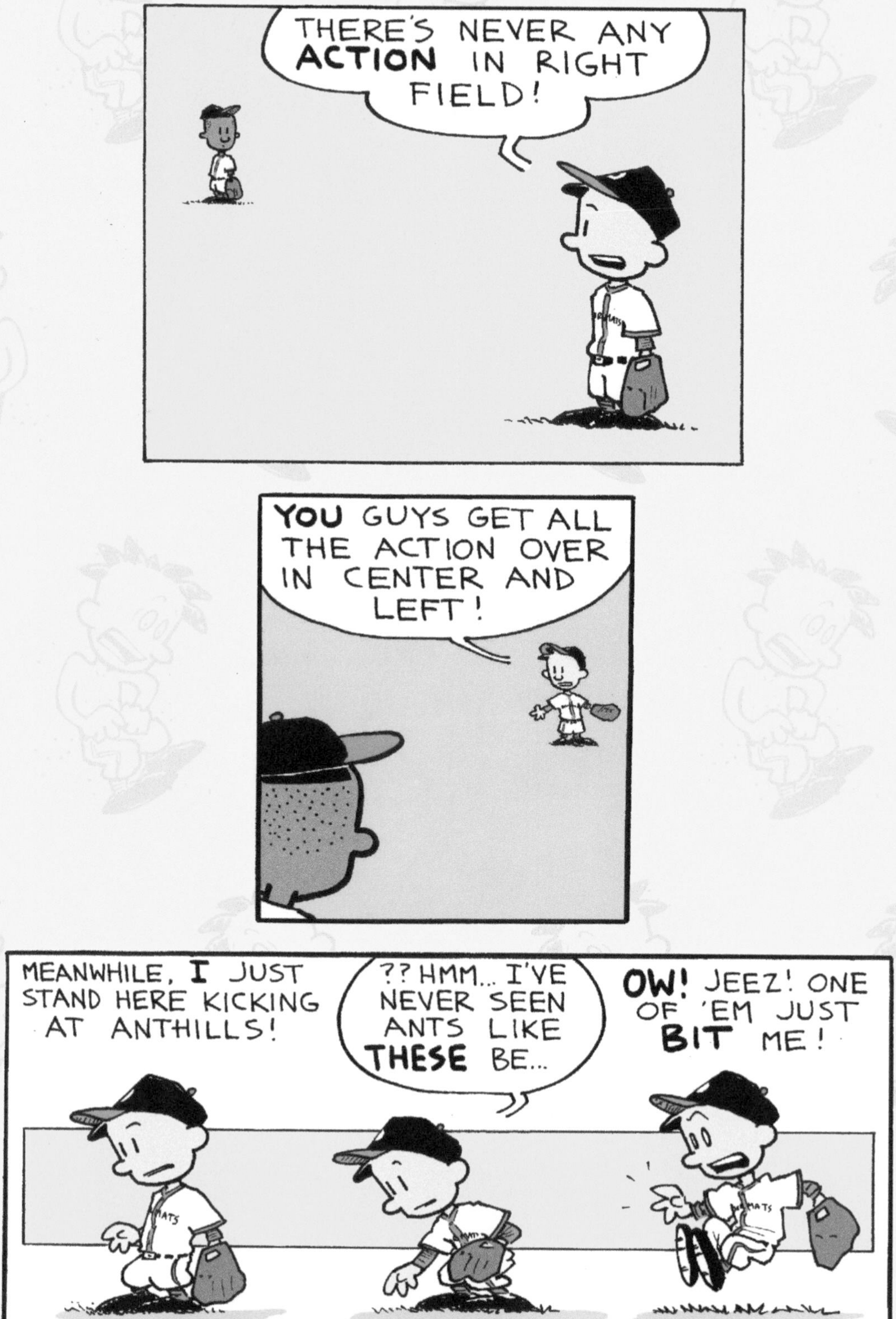
THERE'S NEVER ANY ACTION IN RIGHT FIELD!
YOU GUYS GET ALL THE ACTION OVER IN CENTER AND LEFT!
MEANWHILE, I JUST STAND HERE KICKING AT ANTHILLS!
??HMM... I'VE NEVER SEEN ANTS LIKE THESE BE...
OW! JEEZ! ONE OF 'EM JUST BIT ME!

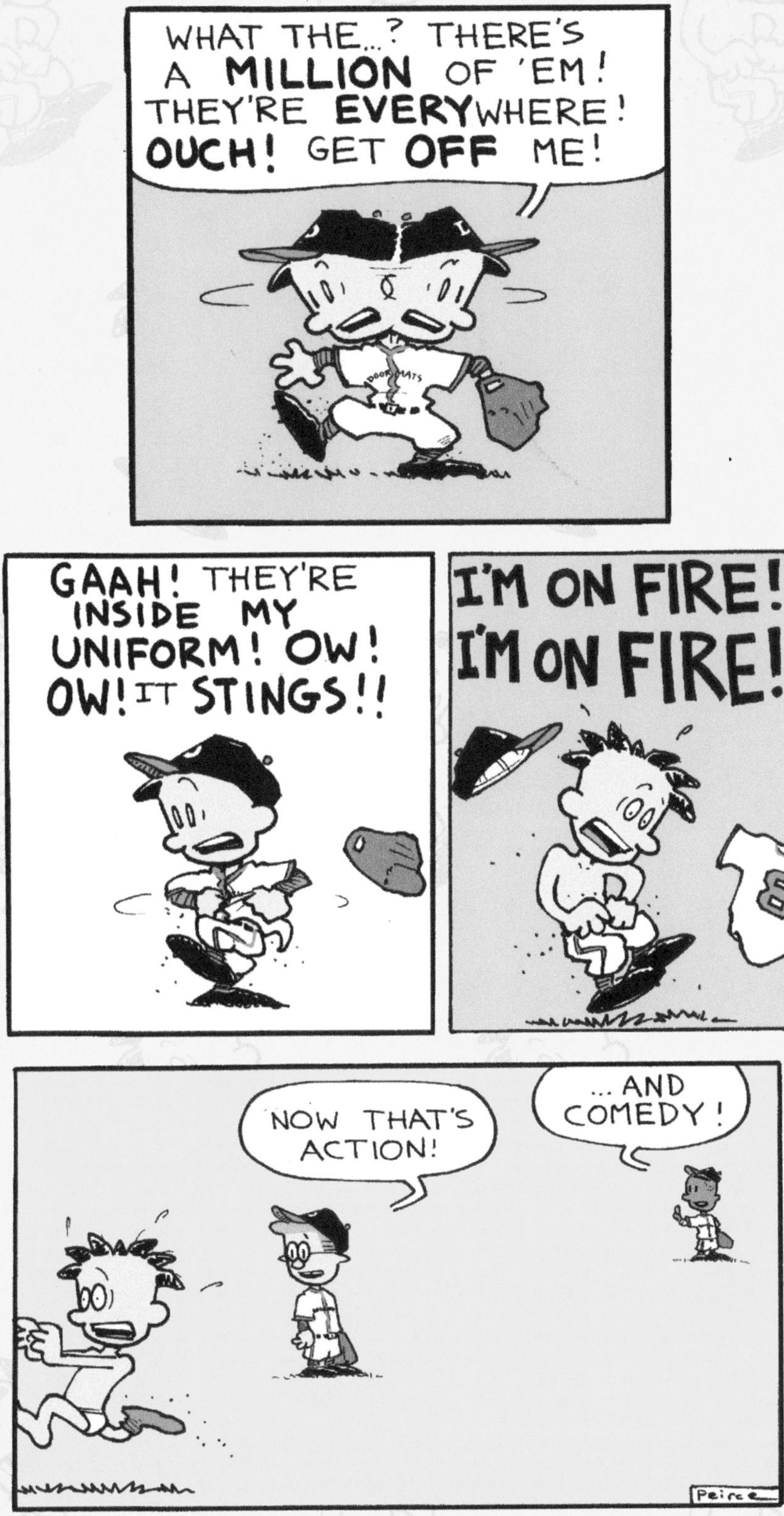
WHAT THE...? THERE'S A **MILLION** OF 'EM! THEY'RE **EVERY**WHERE! **OUCH!** GET **OFF** ME!
DOOR MATS
GAAH! THEY'RE INSIDE MY UNIFORM! OW! OW! IT STINGS!!
I'M ON FIRE! I'M ON FIRE!
NOW THAT'S ACTION!
...AND COMEDY!
Peirce

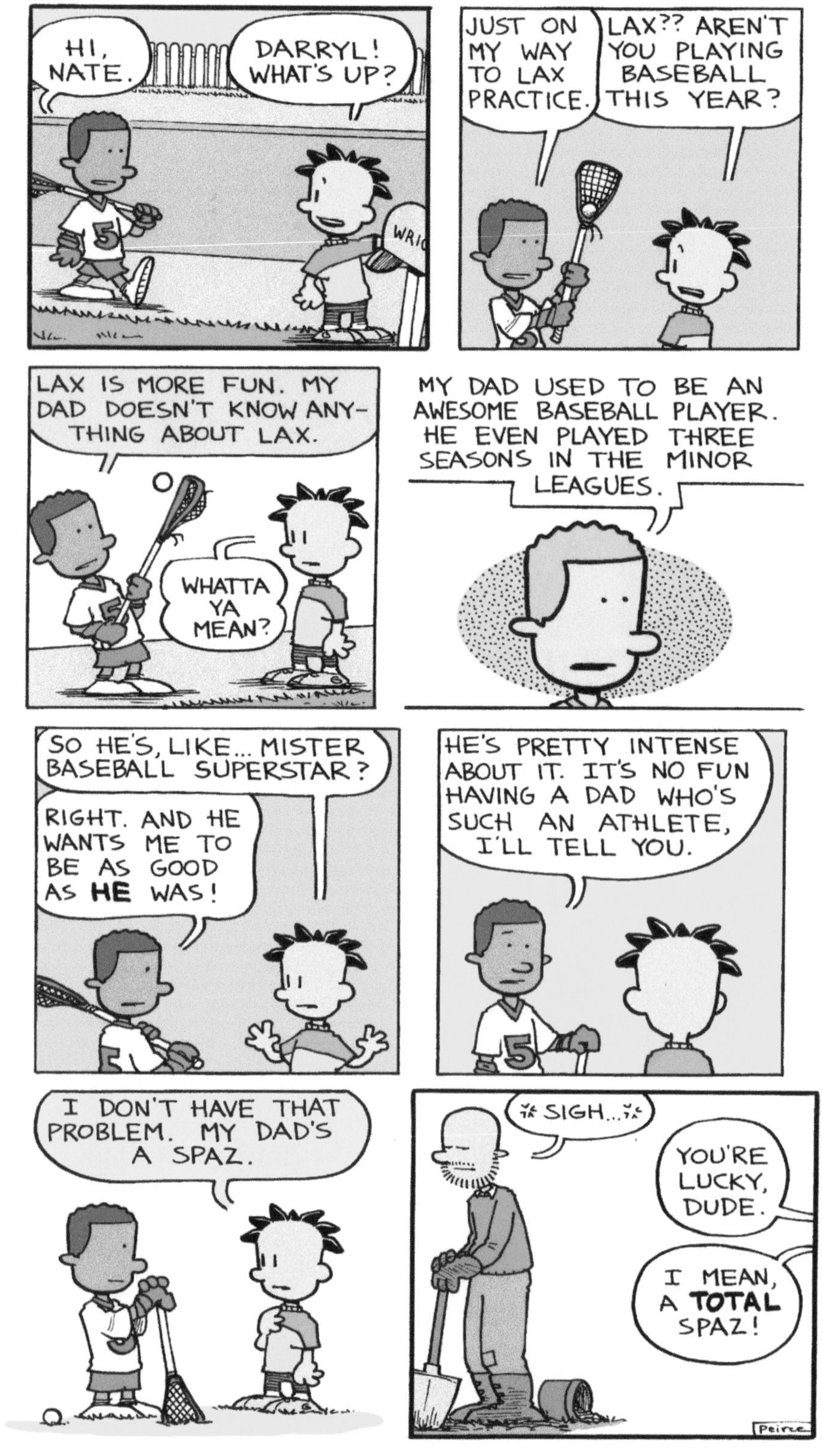
HI, NATE.
DARRYL! WHAT'S UP?
WRI
JUST ON MY WAY TO LAX PRACTICE.
LAX?? AREN'T YOU PLAYING BASEBALL THIS YEAR?
LAX IS MORE FUN. MY DAD DOESN'T KNOW ANYTHING ABOUT LAX.
WHATTA YA MEAN?
MY DAD USED TO BE AN AWESOME BASEBALL PLAYER. HE EVEN PLAYED THREE SEASONS IN THE MINOR LEAGUES.
SO HE'S, LIKE... MISTER BASEBALL SUPERSTAR?
RIGHT. AND HE WANTS ME TO BE AS GOOD AS **HE** WAS!
HE'S PRETTY INTENSE ABOUT IT. IT'S NO FUN HAVING A DAD WHO'S SUCH AN ATHLETE, I'LL TELL YOU.
I DON'T HAVE THAT PROBLEM. MY DAD'S A SPAZ.
SIGH...
YOU'RE LUCKY, DUDE.
I MEAN, A **TOTAL** SPAZ!
Peirce

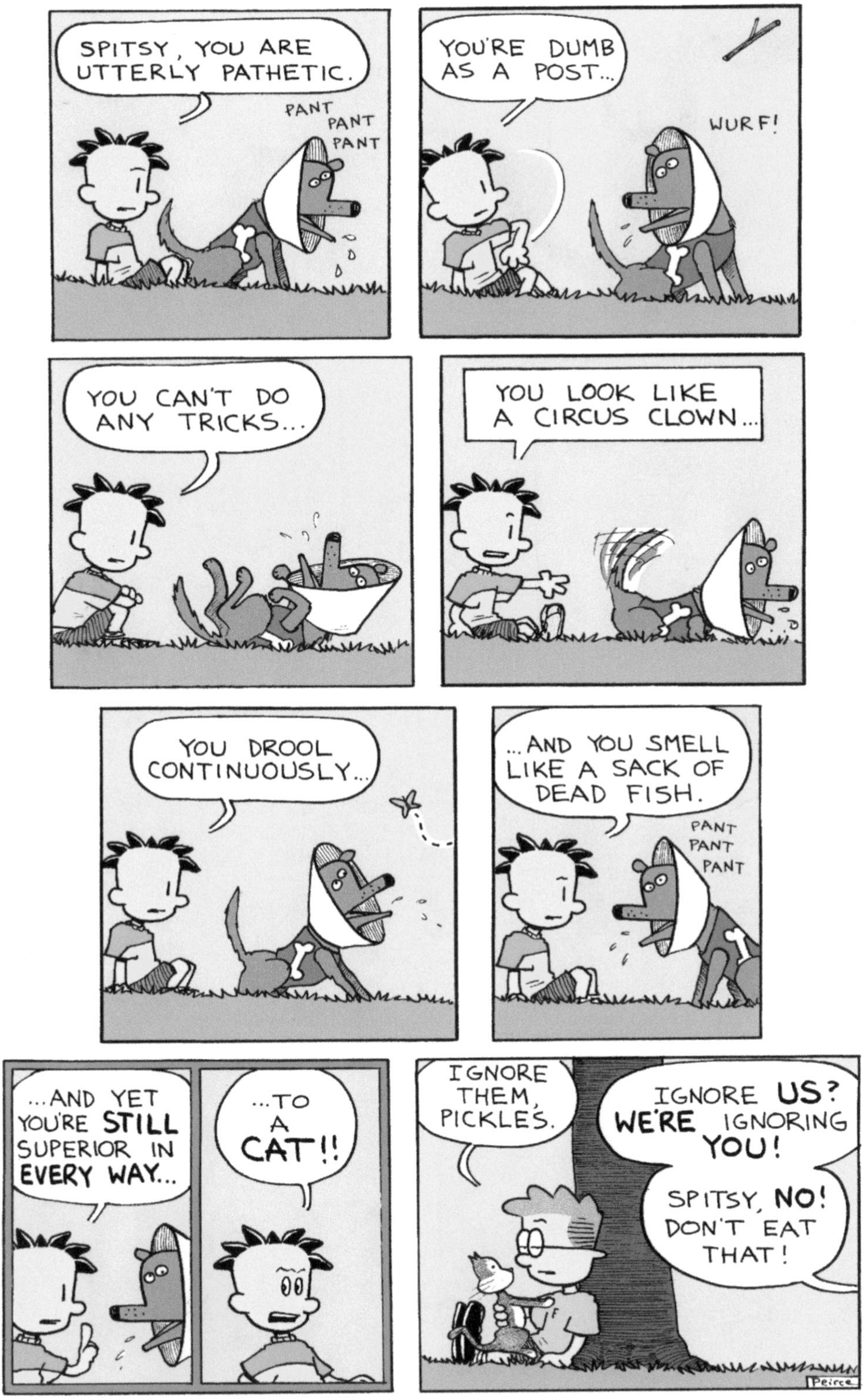
SPITSY, YOU ARE UTTERLY PATHETIC.
PANT PANT PANT
YOU'RE DUMB AS A POST...
WURF!
YOU CAN'T DO ANY TRICKS...
YOU LOOK LIKE A CIRCUS CLOWN...
YOU DROOL CONTINUOUSLY...
...AND YOU SMELL LIKE A SACK OF DEAD FISH.
PANT PANT PANT
...AND YET YOU'RE STILL SUPERIOR IN EVERY WAY...
...TO A CAT!!
IGNORE THEM, PICKLES.
IGNORE US? WE'RE IGNORING YOU!
SPITSY, NO! DON'T EAT THAT!
Peirce

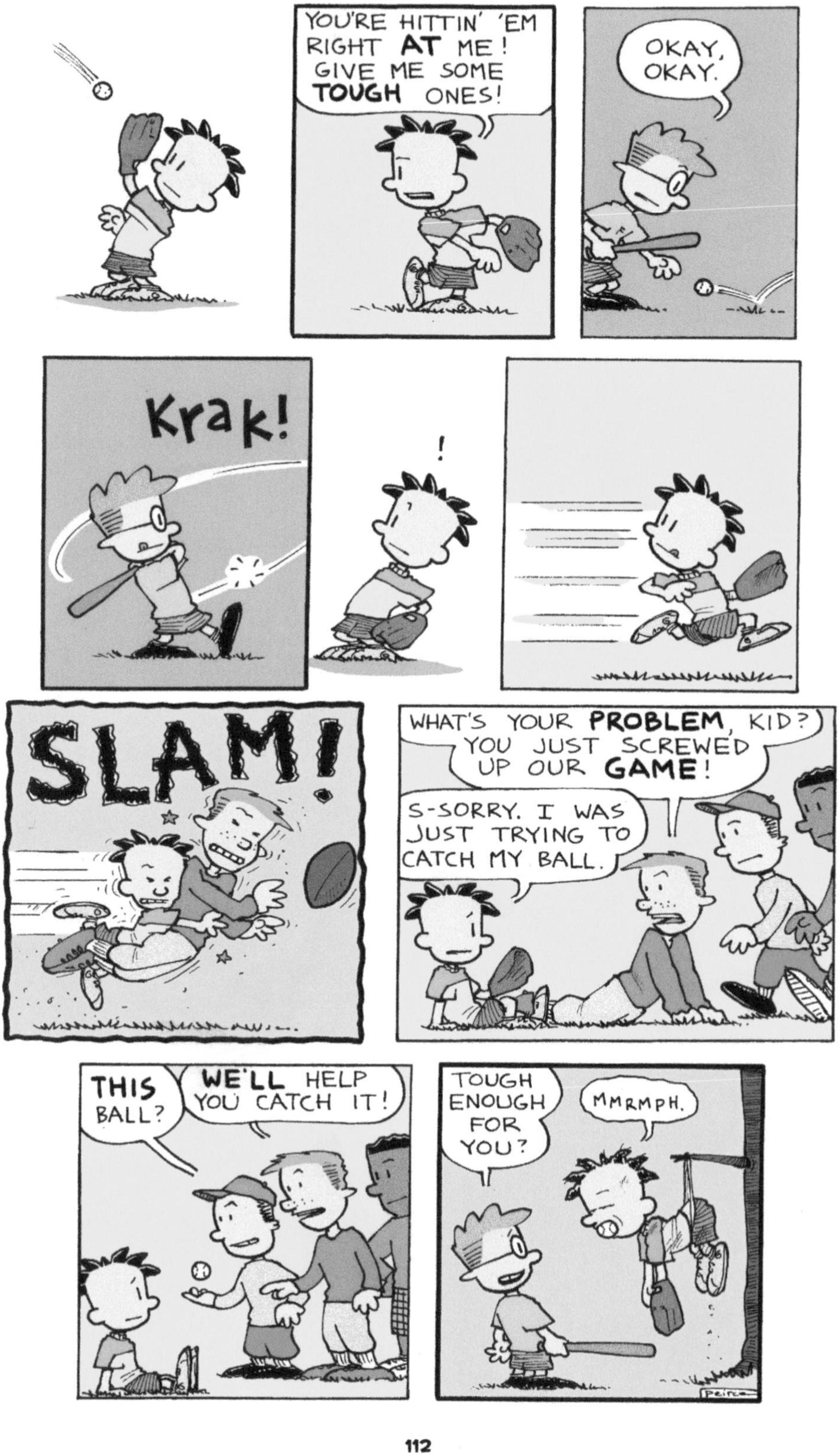
YOU'RE HITTIN' 'EM RIGHT AT ME! GIVE ME SOME TOUGH ONES!
OKAY, OKAY.
Krak!
!
SLAM!
WHAT'S YOUR PROBLEM, KID? YOU JUST SCREWED UP OUR GAME!
S-SORRY. I WAS JUST TRYING TO CATCH MY BALL.
THIS BALL?
WE'LL HELP YOU CATCH IT!
TOUGH ENOUGH FOR YOU?
MMRMPH.
Peirce

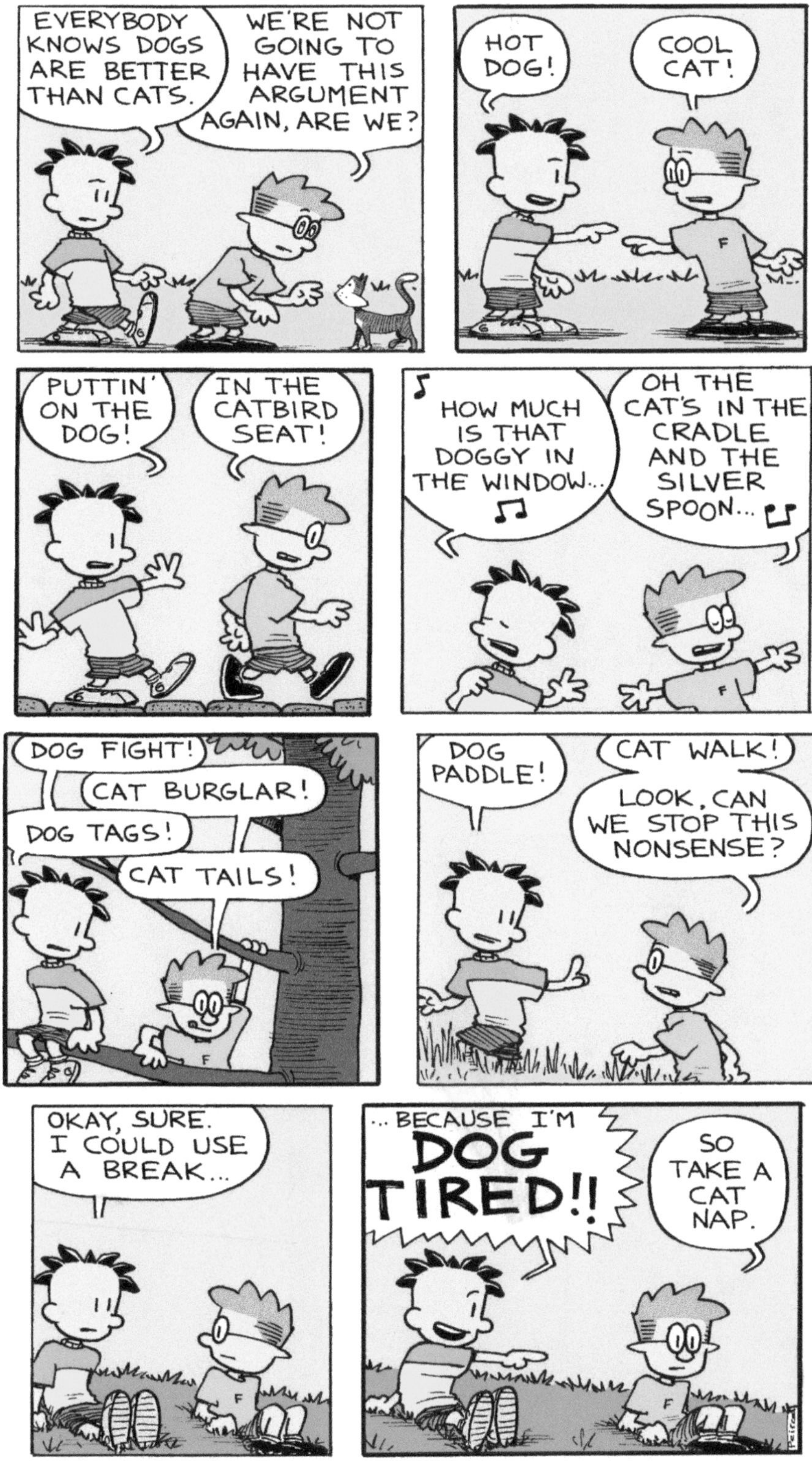
EVERYBODY KNOWS DOGS ARE BETTER THAN CATS.
WE'RE NOT GOING TO HAVE THIS ARGUMENT AGAIN, ARE WE?
HOT DOG!
COOL CAT!
PUTTIN' ON THE DOG!
IN THE CATBIRD SEAT!
HOW MUCH IS THAT DOGGY IN THE WINDOW...
OH THE CAT'S IN THE CRADLE AND THE SILVER SPOON...
DOG FIGHT!
CAT BURGLAR!
DOG TAGS!
CAT TAILS!
DOG PADDLE!
CAT WALK!
LOOK, CAN WE STOP THIS NONSENSE?
OKAY, SURE. I COULD USE A BREAK...
... BECAUSE I'M DOG TIRED!!
SO TAKE A CAT NAP.

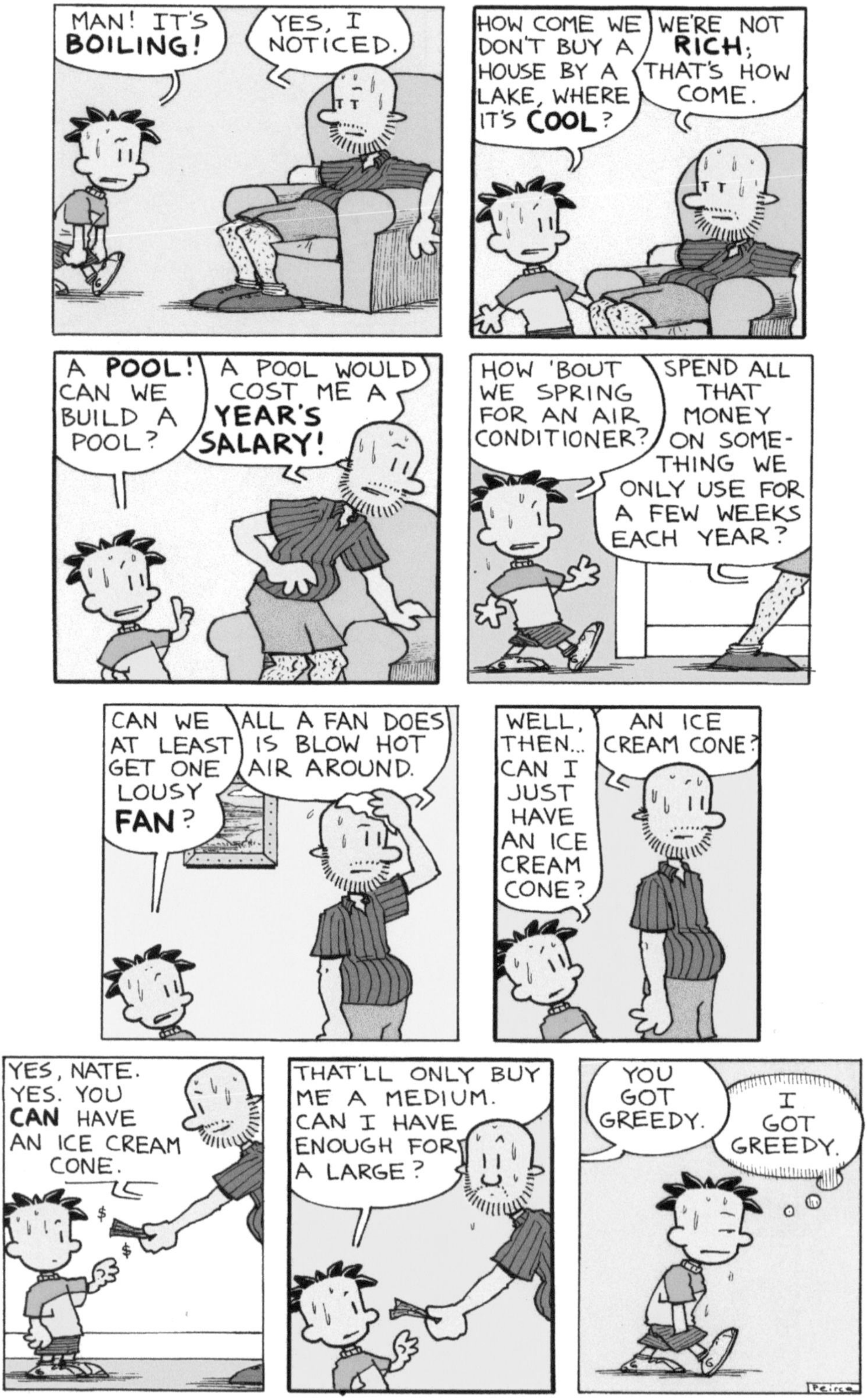
MAN! IT'S **BOILING**!
YES, I NOTICED.
HOW COME WE DON'T BUY A HOUSE BY A LAKE, WHERE IT'S **COOL**?
WE'RE NOT **RICH**; THAT'S HOW COME.
A **POOL**! CAN WE BUILD A POOL?
A POOL WOULD COST ME A **YEAR'S SALARY**!
HOW 'BOUT WE SPRING FOR AN AIR CONDITIONER?
SPEND ALL THAT MONEY ON SOME-THING WE ONLY USE FOR A FEW WEEKS EACH YEAR?
CAN WE AT LEAST GET ONE LOUSY **FAN**?
ALL A FAN DOES IS BLOW HOT AIR AROUND.
WELL, THEN... CAN I JUST HAVE AN ICE CREAM CONE?
AN ICE CREAM CONE?
YES, NATE. YES. YOU **CAN** HAVE AN ICE CREAM CONE.
THAT'LL ONLY BUY ME A MEDIUM. CAN I HAVE ENOUGH FOR A LARGE?
YOU GOT GREEDY.
I GOT GREEDY.
Peirce

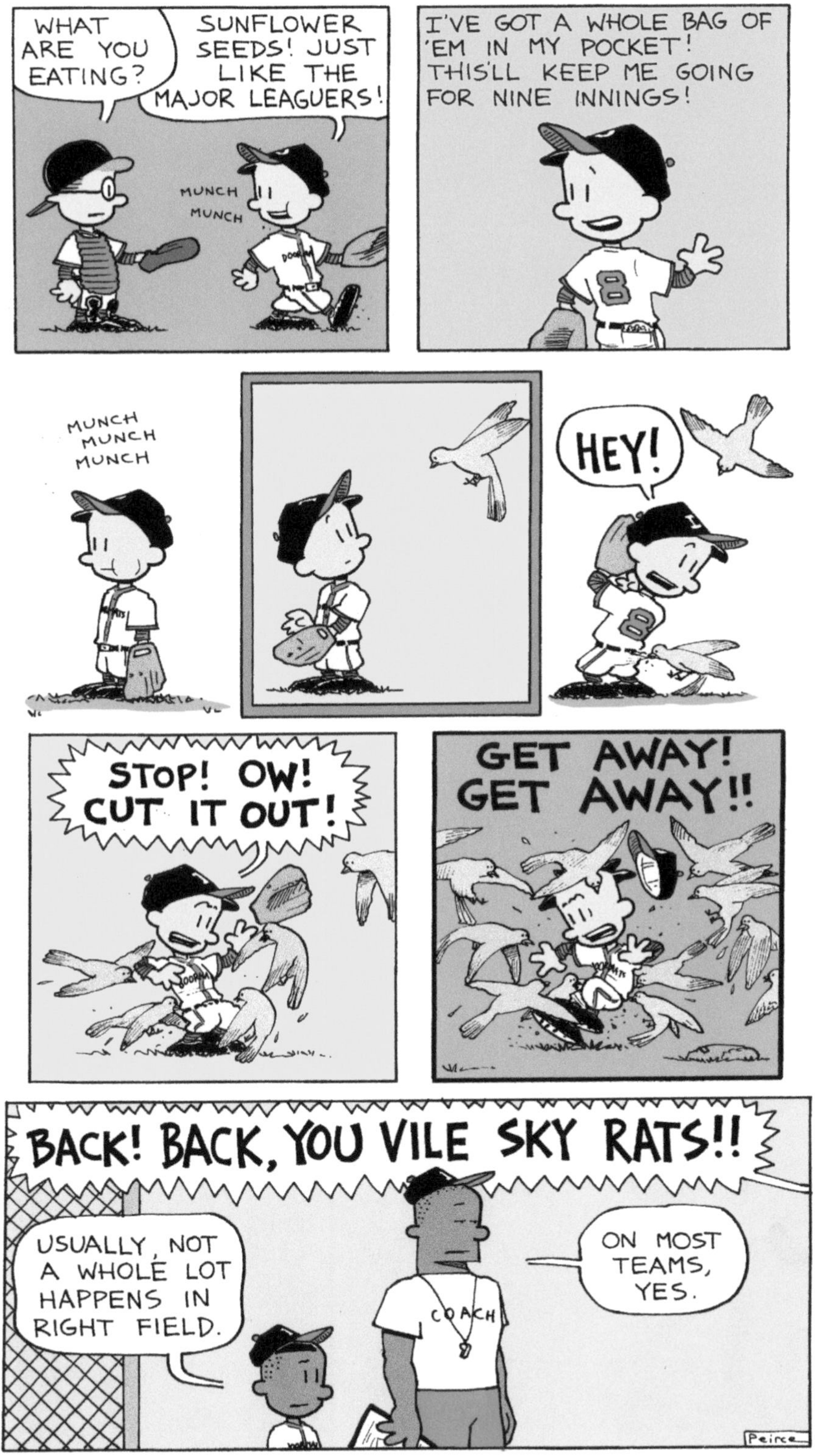
WHAT ARE YOU EATING?
SUNFLOWER SEEDS! JUST LIKE THE MAJOR LEAGUERS!
MUNCH MUNCH
I'VE GOT A WHOLE BAG OF 'EM IN MY POCKET! THIS'LL KEEP ME GOING FOR NINE INNINGS!
MUNCH MUNCH MUNCH
HEY!
STOP! OW! CUT IT OUT!
GET AWAY! GET AWAY!!
BACK! BACK, YOU VILE SKY RATS!!
USUALLY, NOT A WHOLE LOT HAPPENS IN RIGHT FIELD.
ON MOST TEAMS, YES.
COACH
Peirce

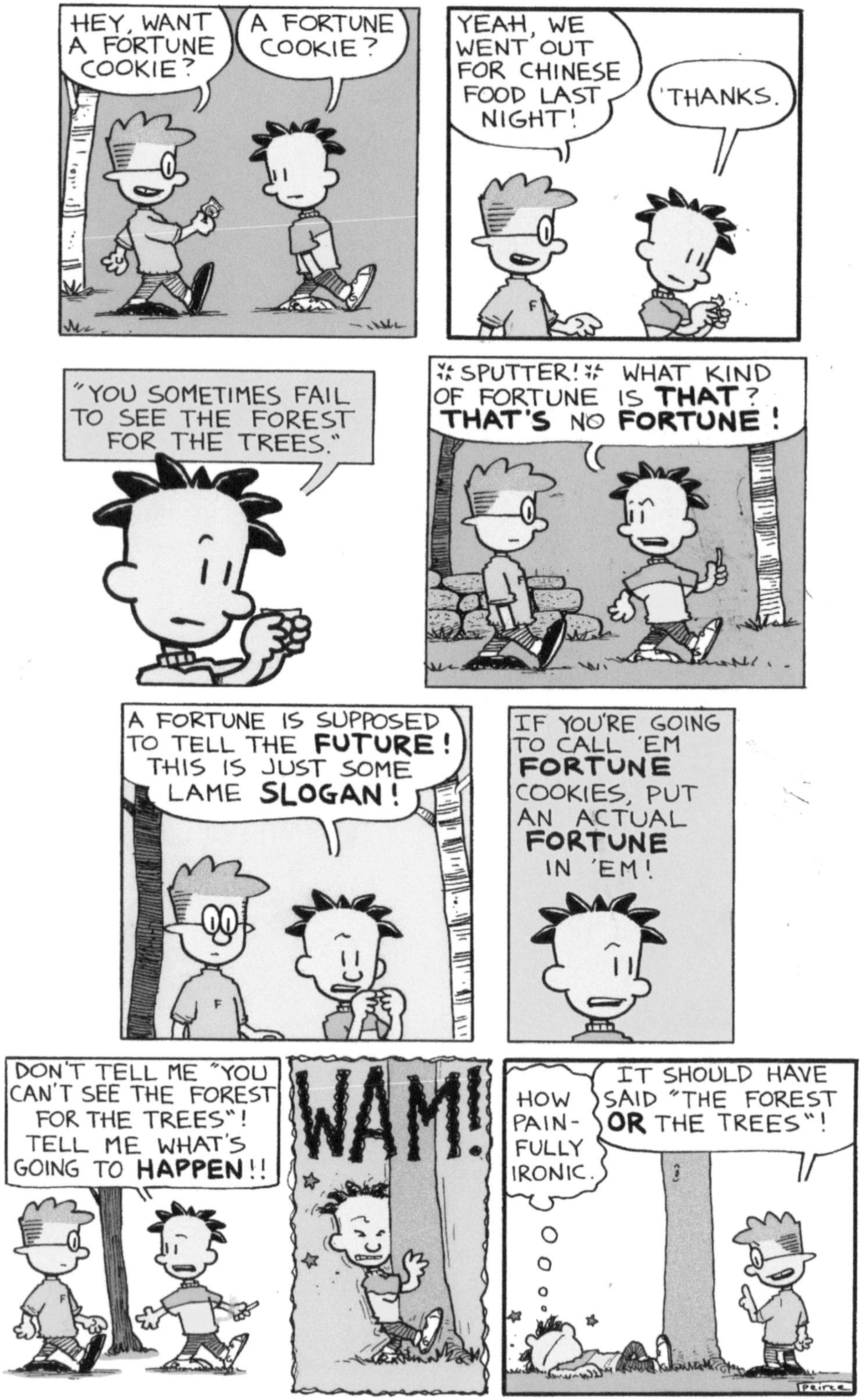
HEY, WANT A FORTUNE COOKIE?
A FORTUNE COOKIE?
YEAH, WE WENT OUT FOR CHINESE FOOD LAST NIGHT!
'THANKS.
"YOU SOMETIMES FAIL TO SEE THE FOREST FOR THE TREES."
SPUTTER! WHAT KIND OF FORTUNE IS THAT? THAT'S NO FORTUNE!
A FORTUNE IS SUPPOSED TO TELL THE FUTURE! THIS IS JUST SOME LAME SLOGAN!
IF YOU'RE GOING TO CALL 'EM FORTUNE COOKIES, PUT AN ACTUAL FORTUNE IN 'EM!
DON'T TELL ME "YOU CAN'T SEE THE FOREST FOR THE TREES"! TELL ME WHAT'S GOING TO HAPPEN!!
WAM!
HOW PAIN-FULLY IRONIC.
IT SHOULD HAVE SAID "THE FOREST OR THE TREES"!
PEIRCE

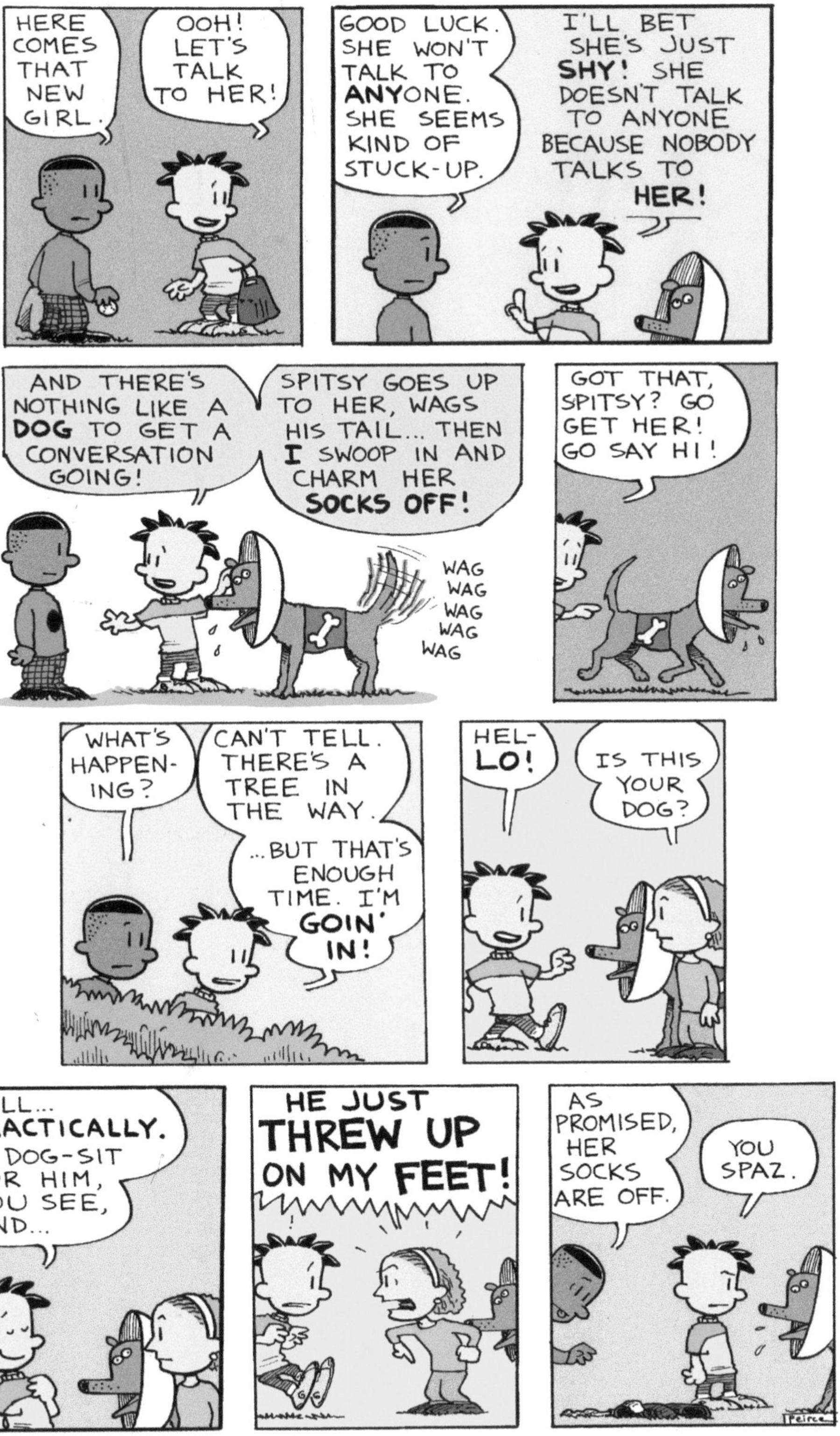
HERE COMES THAT NEW GIRL.
OOH! LET'S TALK TO HER!
GOOD LUCK. SHE WON'T TALK TO ANYONE. SHE SEEMS KIND OF STUCK-UP.
I'LL BET SHE'S JUST SHY! SHE DOESN'T TALK TO ANYONE BECAUSE NOBODY TALKS TO HER!
AND THERE'S NOTHING LIKE A DOG TO GET A CONVERSATION GOING!
SPITSY GOES UP TO HER, WAGS HIS TAIL... THEN I SWOOP IN AND CHARM HER SOCKS OFF!
WAG WAG WAG WAG WAG
GOT THAT, SPITSY? GO GET HER! GO SAY HI!
WHAT'S HAPPEN-ING?
CAN'T TELL. THERE'S A TREE IN THE WAY.
...BUT THAT'S ENOUGH TIME. I'M GOIN' IN!
HEL-LO!
IS THIS YOUR DOG?
WELL... PRACTICALLY. I DOG-SIT FOR HIM, YOU SEE, AND...
HE JUST THREW UP ON MY FEET!
AS PROMISED, HER SOCKS ARE OFF.
YOU SPAZ.
Peirce

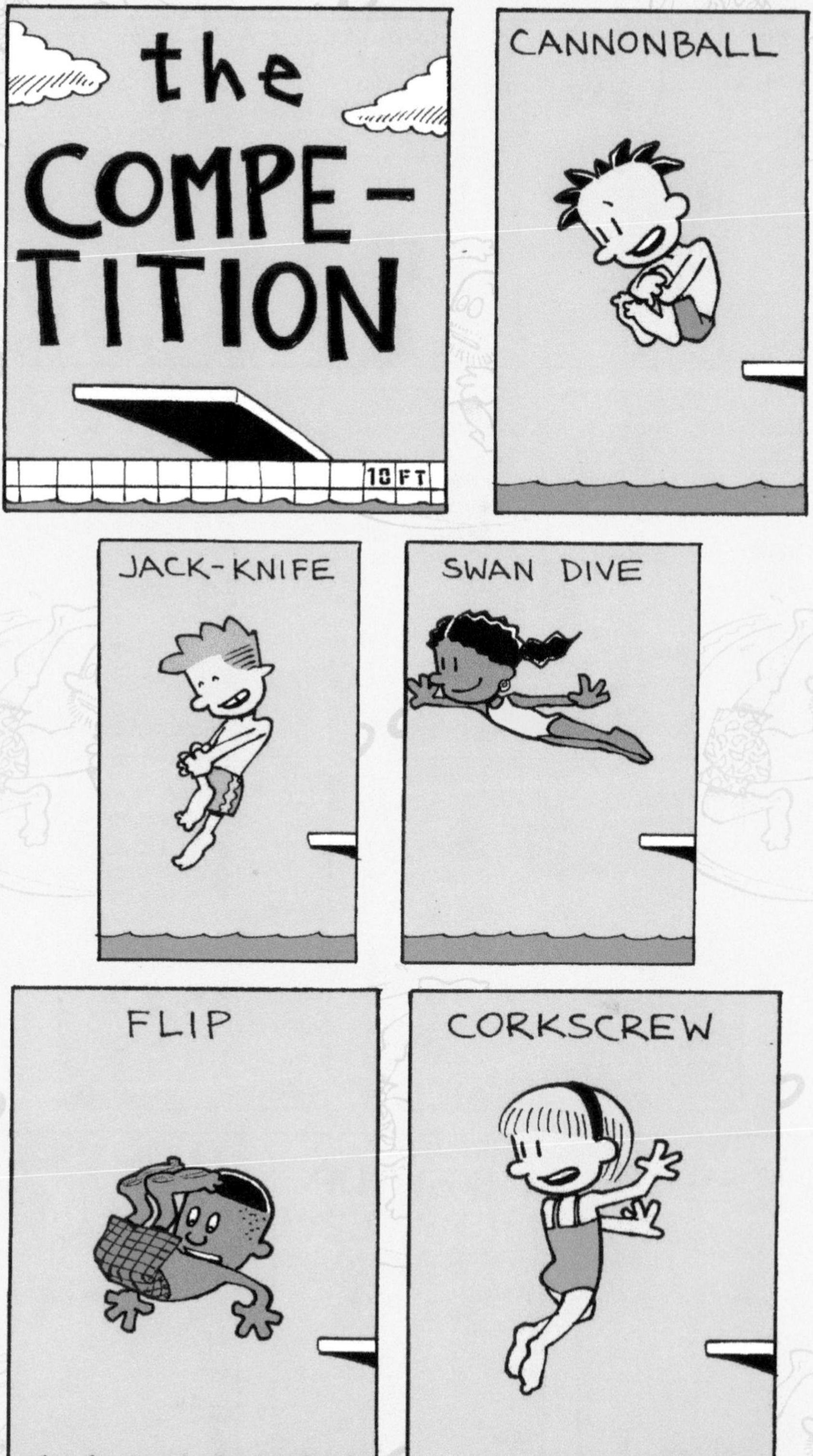
the COMPETITION
10 FT
CANNONBALL
JACK-KNIFE
SWAN DIVE
FLIP
CORKSCREW

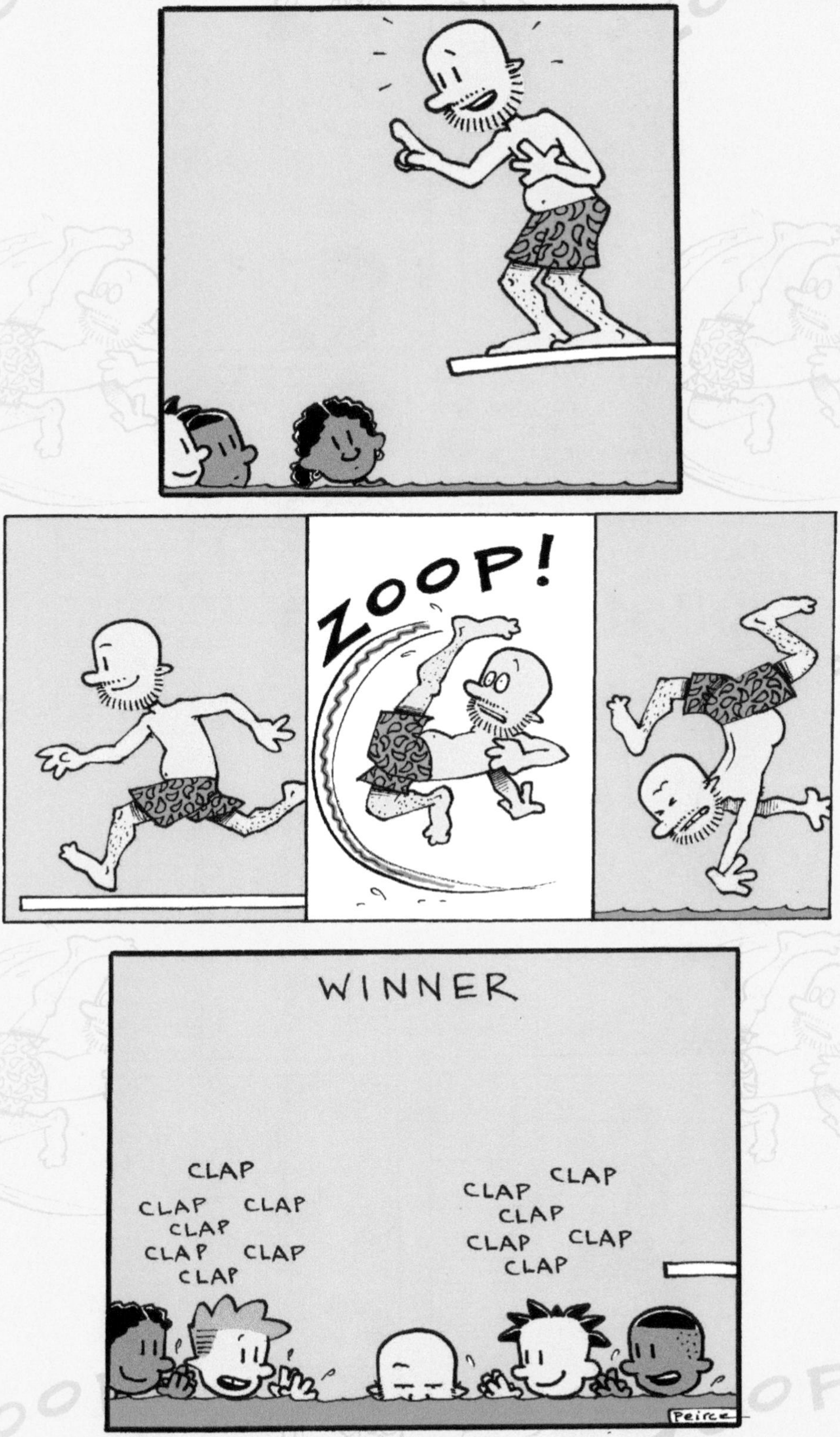
ZOOP!
WINNER
CLAP
CLAP CLAP
CLAP
CLAP CLAP
CLAP
CLAP
CLAP
CLAP
CLAP CLAP
CLAP
Peirce

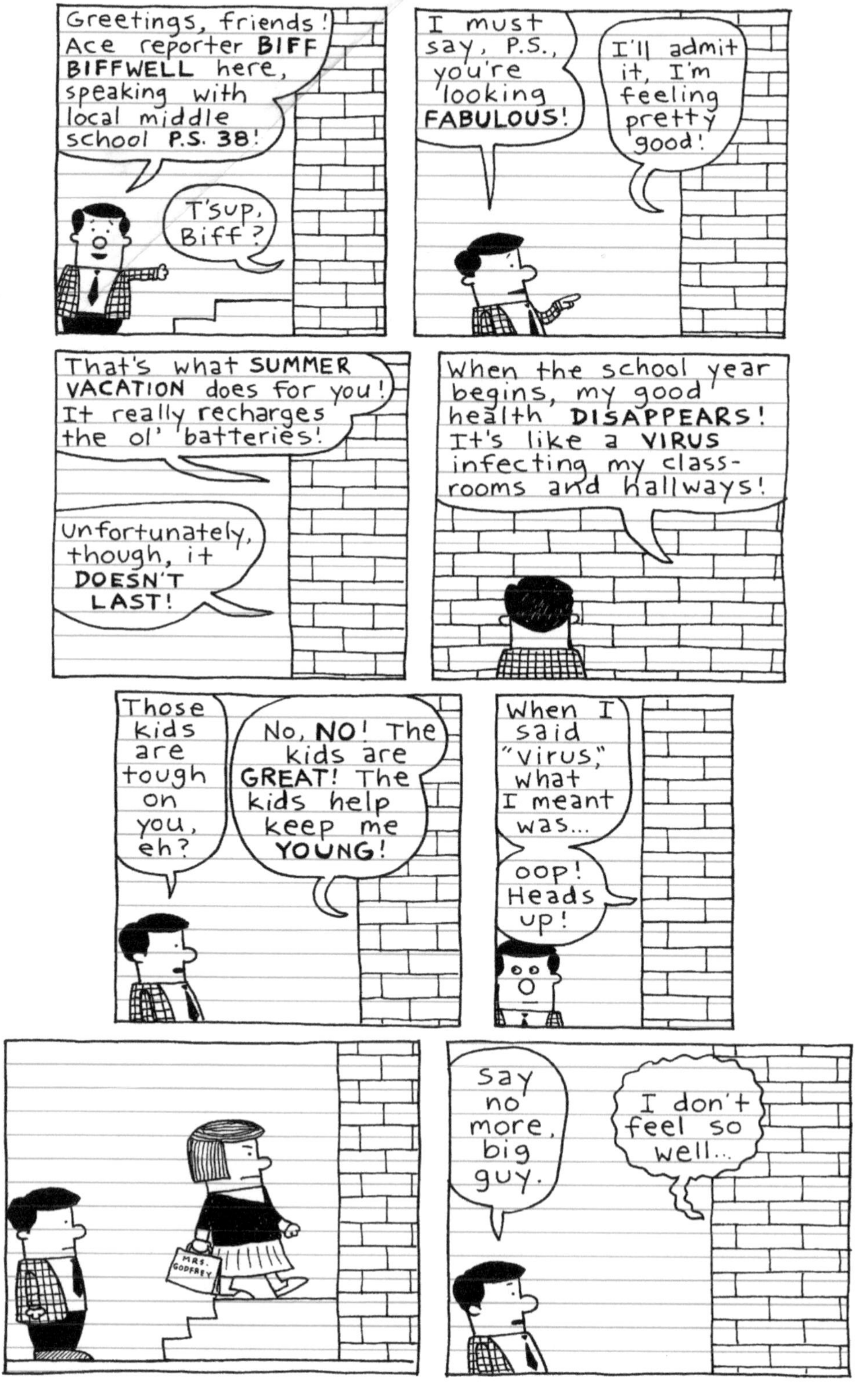
Greetings, friends! Ace reporter BIFF BIFFWELL here, speaking with local middle school P.S. 38!
T'sup, Biff?
I must say, P.S., you're looking FABULOUS!
I'll admit it, I'm feeling pretty good!
That's what SUMMER VACATION does for you! It really recharges the ol' batteries!
Unfortunately, though, it DOESN'T LAST!
When the school year begins, my good health DISAPPEARS! It's like a VIRUS infecting my classrooms and hallways!
Those kids are tough on you, eh?
No, NO! The kids are GREAT! The kids help keep me YOUNG!
When I said "virus," what I meant was...
oop! Heads up!
MRS. GODFREY
Say no more, big guy.
I don't feel so well...

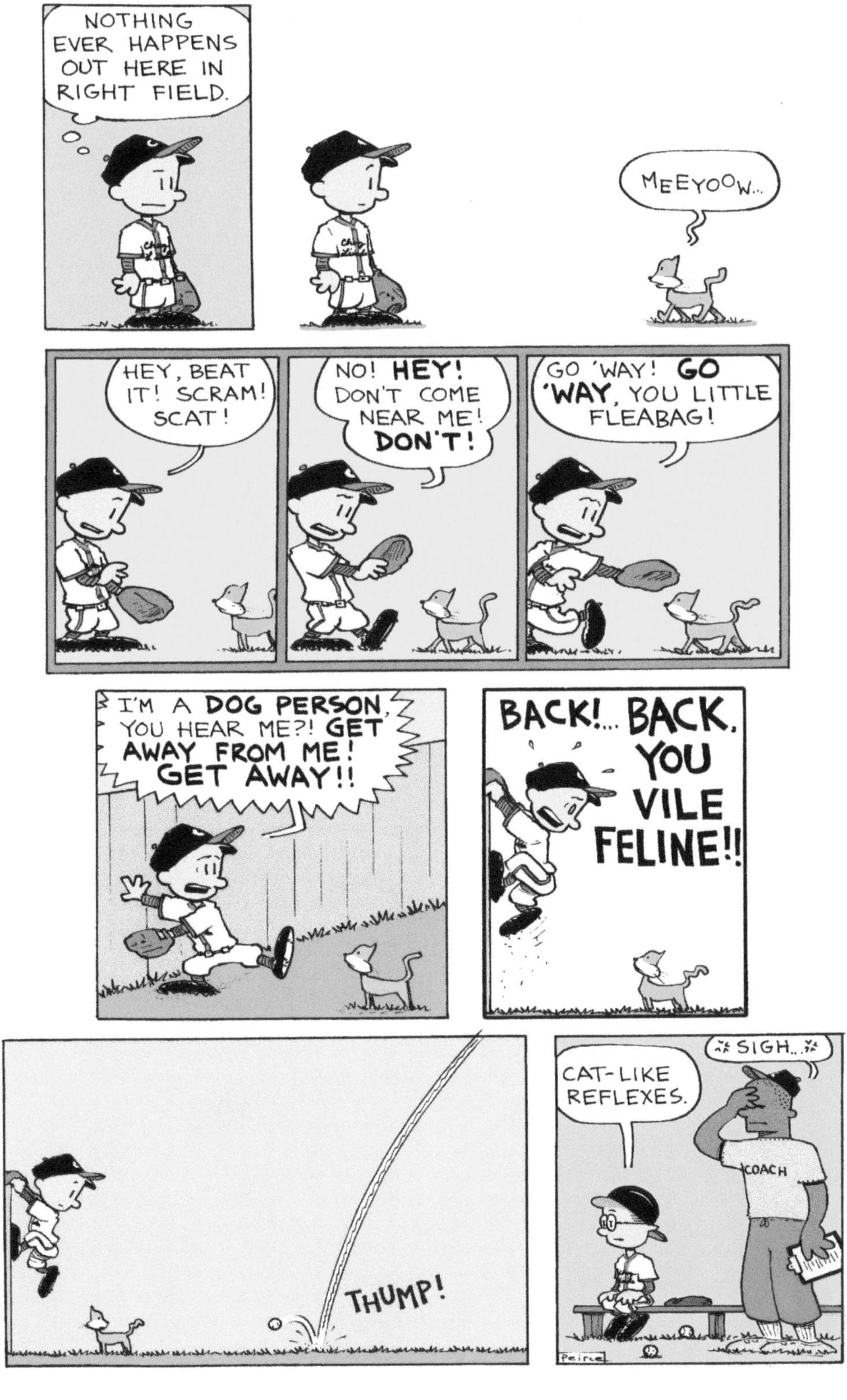
NOTHING EVER HAPPENS OUT HERE IN RIGHT FIELD.
MEEYOOW...
HEY, BEAT IT! SCRAM! SCAT!
NO! HEY! DON'T COME NEAR ME! DON'T!
GO 'WAY! GO 'WAY, YOU LITTLE FLEABAG!
I'M A DOG PERSON, YOU HEAR ME?! GET AWAY FROM ME! GET AWAY!!
BACK!... BACK, YOU VILE FELINE!!
THUMP!
CAT-LIKE REFLEXES.
SIGH...
COACH
Peirce

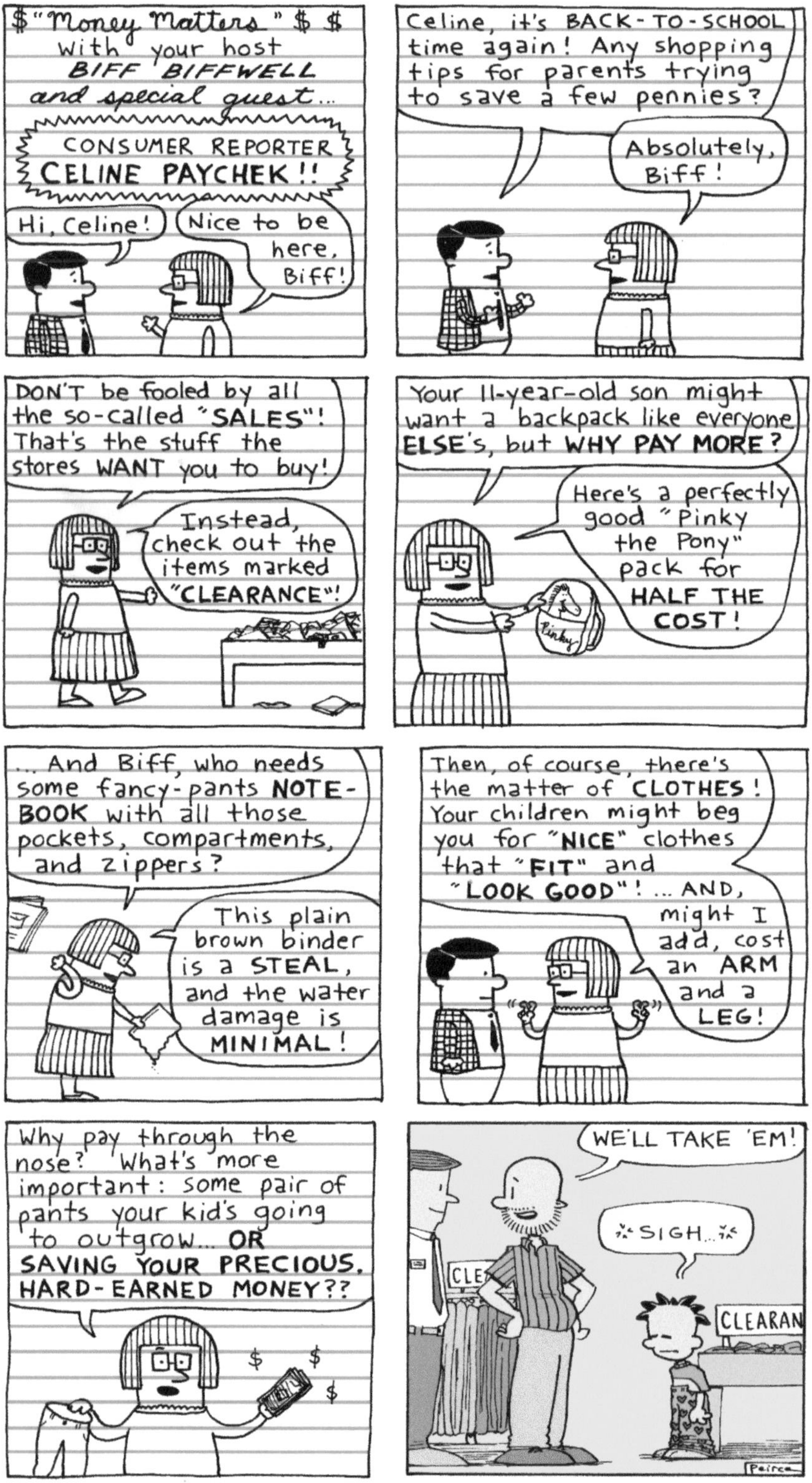
$ "Money Matters" $ $ with your host BIFF BIFFWELL and special guest...
CONSUMER REPORTER CELINE PAYCHEK!!
Hi, Celine!
Nice to be here, Biff!
Celine, it's BACK-TO-SCHOOL time again! Any shopping tips for parents trying to save a few pennies?
Absolutely, Biff!
DON'T be fooled by all the so-called "SALES"! That's the stuff the stores WANT you to buy!
Instead, check out the items marked "CLEARANCE"!
Your 11-year-old son might want a backpack like everyone ELSE's, but WHY PAY MORE?
Here's a perfectly good "Pinky the Pony" pack for HALF THE COST!
Pinky
...And Biff, who needs some fancy-pants NOTE-BOOK with all those pockets, compartments, and zippers?
This plain brown binder is a STEAL, and the water damage is MINIMAL!
Then, of course, there's the matter of CLOTHES! Your children might beg you for "NICE" clothes that "FIT" and "LOOK GOOD"! ...AND, might I add, cost an ARM and a LEG!
Why pay through the nose? What's more important: some pair of pants your kid's going to outgrow... OR SAVING YOUR PRECIOUS, HARD-EARNED MONEY??
$ $ $
WE'LL TAKE 'EM!
SIGH...
CLE
CLEARAN
Peirce

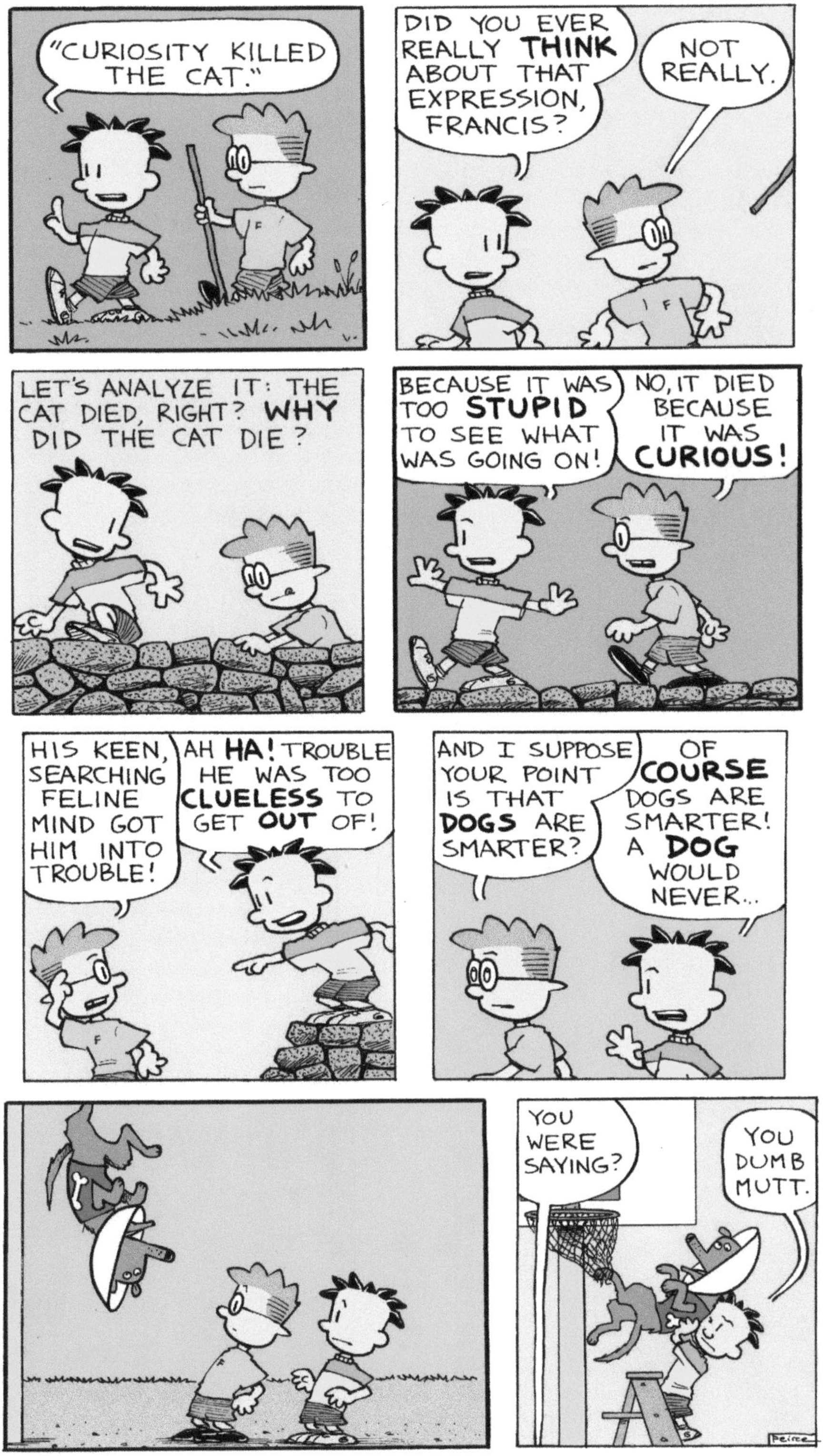
"CURIOSITY KILLED THE CAT."
DID YOU EVER REALLY THINK ABOUT THAT EXPRESSION, FRANCIS?
NOT REALLY.
LET'S ANALYZE IT: THE CAT DIED, RIGHT? WHY DID THE CAT DIE?
BECAUSE IT WAS TOO STUPID TO SEE WHAT WAS GOING ON!
NO, IT DIED BECAUSE IT WAS CURIOUS!
HIS KEEN, SEARCHING FELINE MIND GOT HIM INTO TROUBLE!
AH HA! TROUBLE HE WAS TOO CLUELESS TO GET OUT OF!
AND I SUPPOSE YOUR POINT IS THAT DOGS ARE SMARTER?
OF COURSE DOGS ARE SMARTER! A DOG WOULD NEVER...
YOU WERE SAYING?
YOU DUMB MUTT.
Peirce

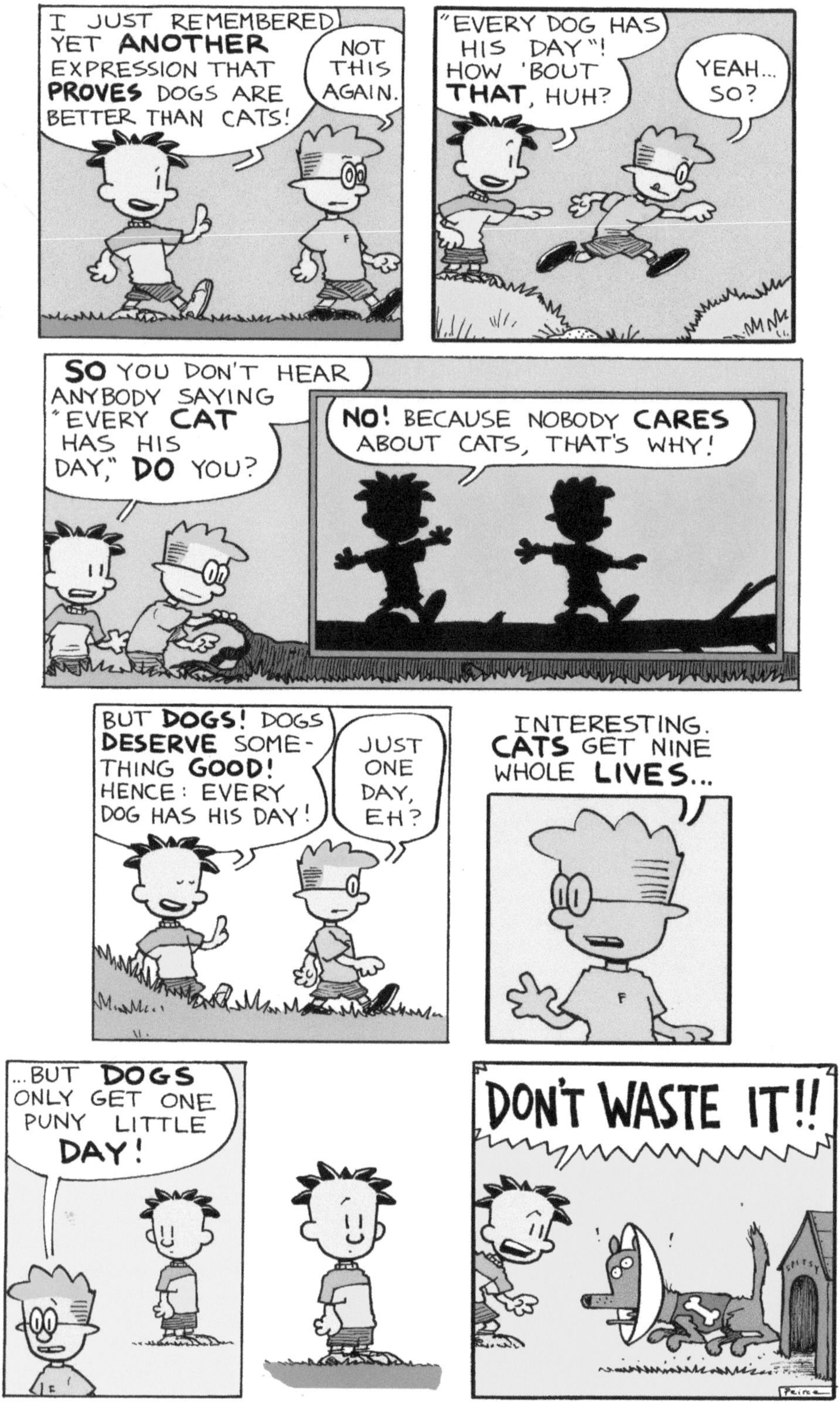
I JUST REMEMBERED YET ANOTHER EXPRESSION THAT PROVES DOGS ARE BETTER THAN CATS!
NOT THIS AGAIN.
"EVERY DOG HAS HIS DAY"! HOW 'BOUT THAT, HUH?
YEAH... SO?
SO YOU DON'T HEAR ANYBODY SAYING "EVERY CAT HAS HIS DAY," DO YOU?
NO! BECAUSE NOBODY CARES ABOUT CATS, THAT'S WHY!
BUT DOGS! DOGS DESERVE SOMETHING GOOD! HENCE: EVERY DOG HAS HIS DAY!
JUST ONE DAY, EH?
INTERESTING. CATS GET NINE WHOLE LIVES...
...BUT DOGS ONLY GET ONE PUNY LITTLE DAY!
DON'T WASTE IT!!
SPITSY

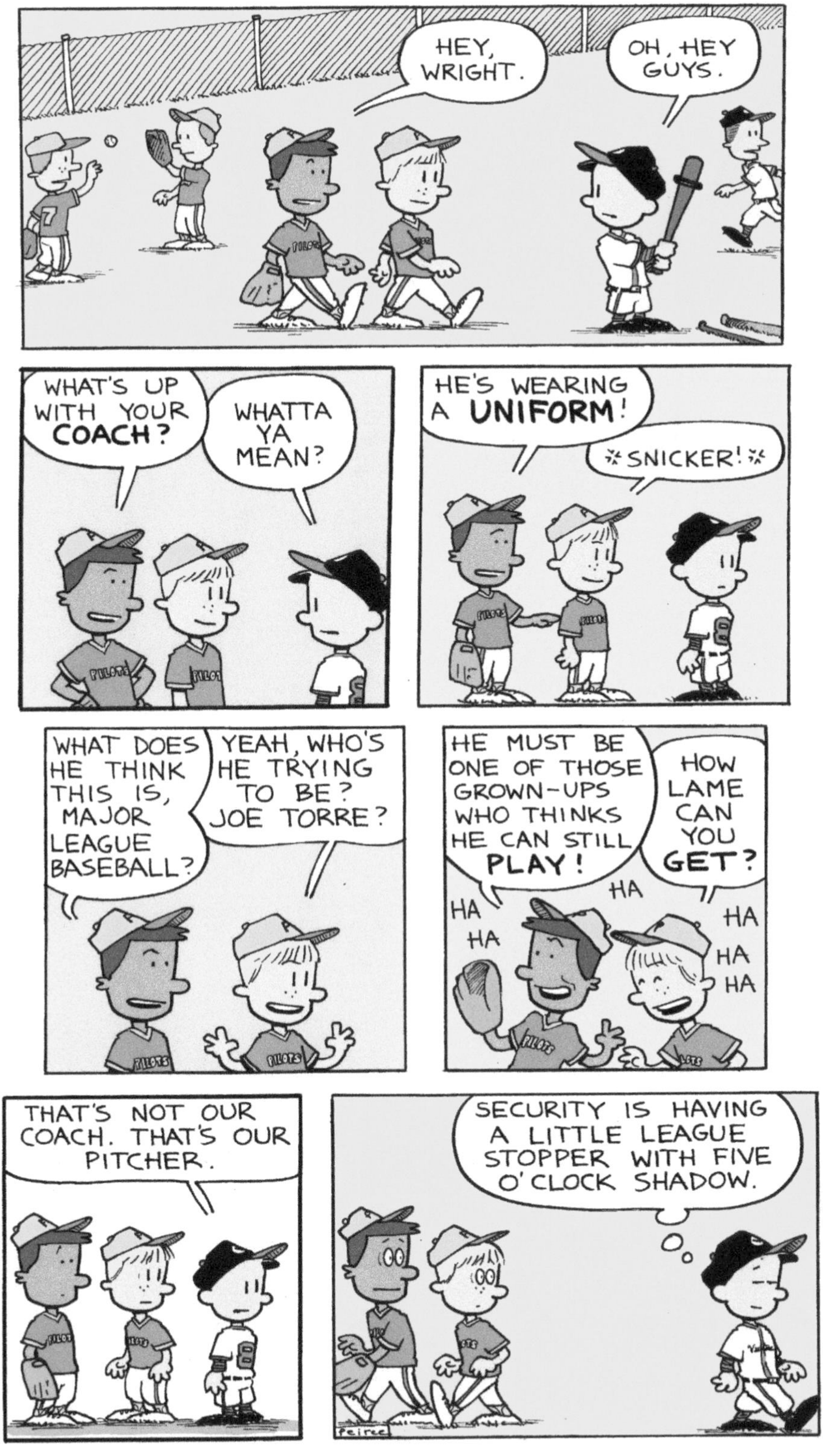
HEY, WRIGHT.
OH, HEY GUYS.
WHAT'S UP WITH YOUR **COACH?**
WHATTA YA MEAN?
HE'S WEARING A **UNIFORM!**
SNICKER!
WHAT DOES HE THINK THIS IS, MAJOR LEAGUE BASEBALL?
YEAH, WHO'S HE TRYING TO BE? JOE TORRE?
HE MUST BE ONE OF THOSE GROWN-UPS WHO THINKS HE CAN STILL **PLAY!**
HOW LAME CAN YOU **GET?**
HA HA HA HA HA HA
THAT'S NOT OUR COACH. THAT'S OUR PITCHER.
SECURITY IS HAVING A LITTLE LEAGUE STOPPER WITH FIVE O'CLOCK SHADOW.
Peirce

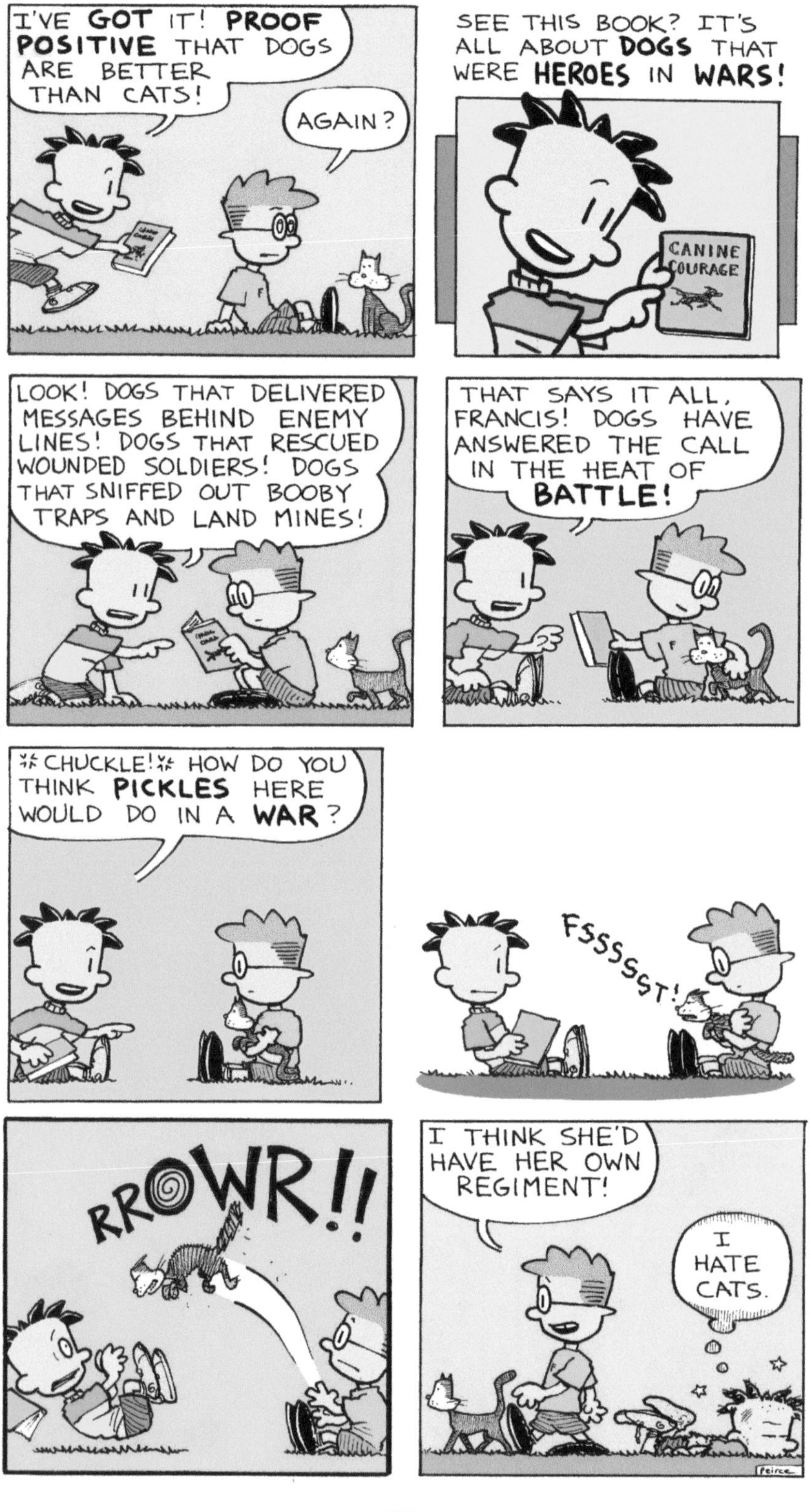
I'VE GOT IT! PROOF POSITIVE THAT DOGS ARE BETTER THAN CATS!
AGAIN?
SEE THIS BOOK? IT'S ALL ABOUT DOGS THAT WERE HEROES IN WARS!
CANINE COURAGE
LOOK! DOGS THAT DELIVERED MESSAGES BEHIND ENEMY LINES! DOGS THAT RESCUED WOUNDED SOLDIERS! DOGS THAT SNIFFED OUT BOOBY TRAPS AND LAND MINES!
THAT SAYS IT ALL, FRANCIS! DOGS HAVE ANSWERED THE CALL IN THE HEAT OF BATTLE!
CHUCKLE! HOW DO YOU THINK PICKLES HERE WOULD DO IN A WAR?
FSSSSST!
RROWR!!
I THINK SHE'D HAVE HER OWN REGIMENT!
I HATE CATS.
Peirce

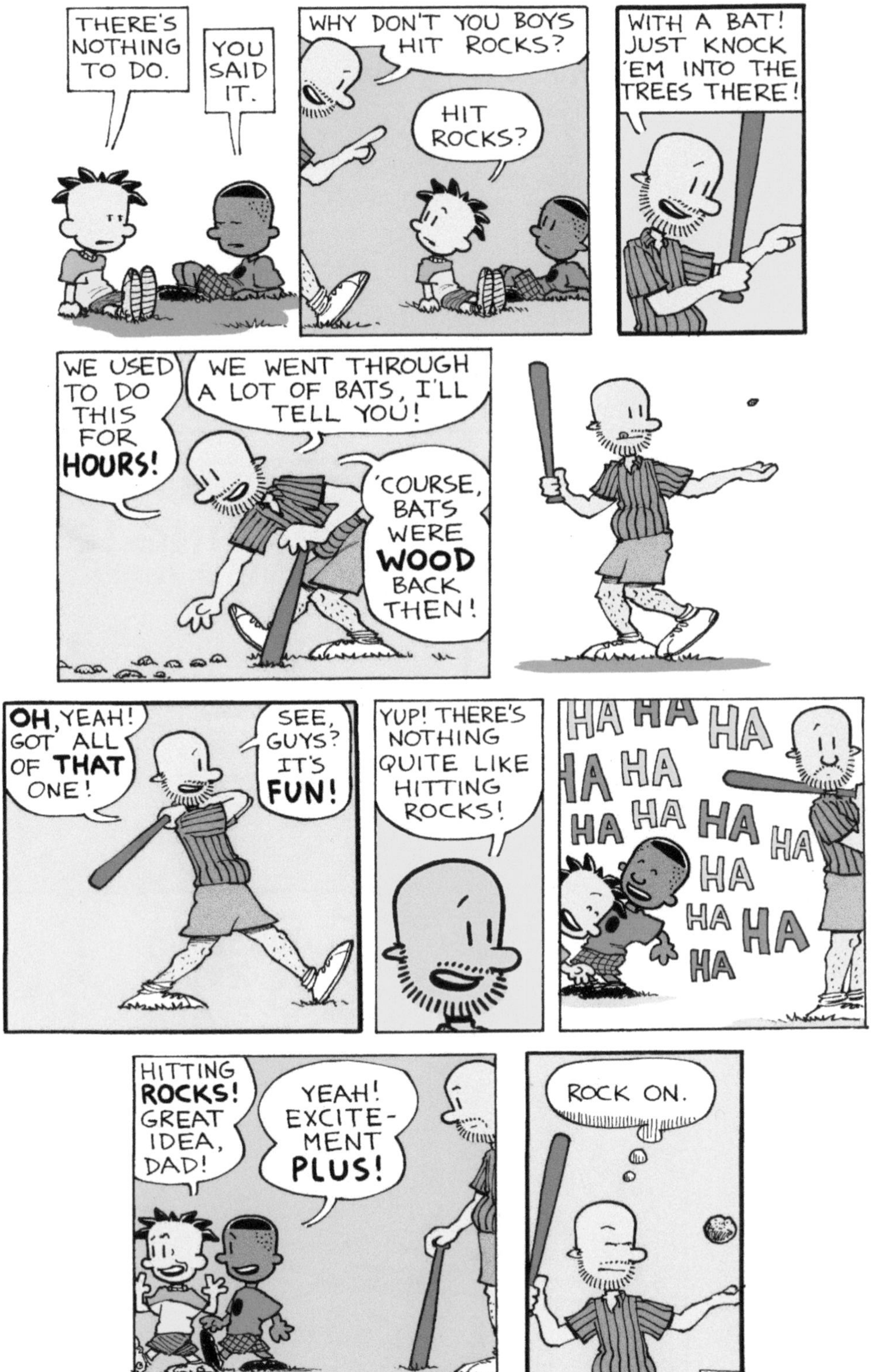
THERE'S NOTHING TO DO.
YOU SAID IT.
WHY DON'T YOU BOYS HIT ROCKS?
HIT ROCKS?
WITH A BAT! JUST KNOCK 'EM INTO THE TREES THERE!
WE USED TO DO THIS FOR HOURS!
WE WENT THROUGH A LOT OF BATS, I'LL TELL YOU!
'COURSE, BATS WERE WOOD BACK THEN!
OH, YEAH! GOT ALL OF THAT ONE!
SEE, GUYS? IT'S FUN!
YUP! THERE'S NOTHING QUITE LIKE HITTING ROCKS!
HA HA HA HA HA HA HA HA HA HA HA HA HA HA HA HA
HITTING ROCKS! GREAT IDEA, DAD!
YEAH! EXCITE-MENT PLUS!
ROCK ON.

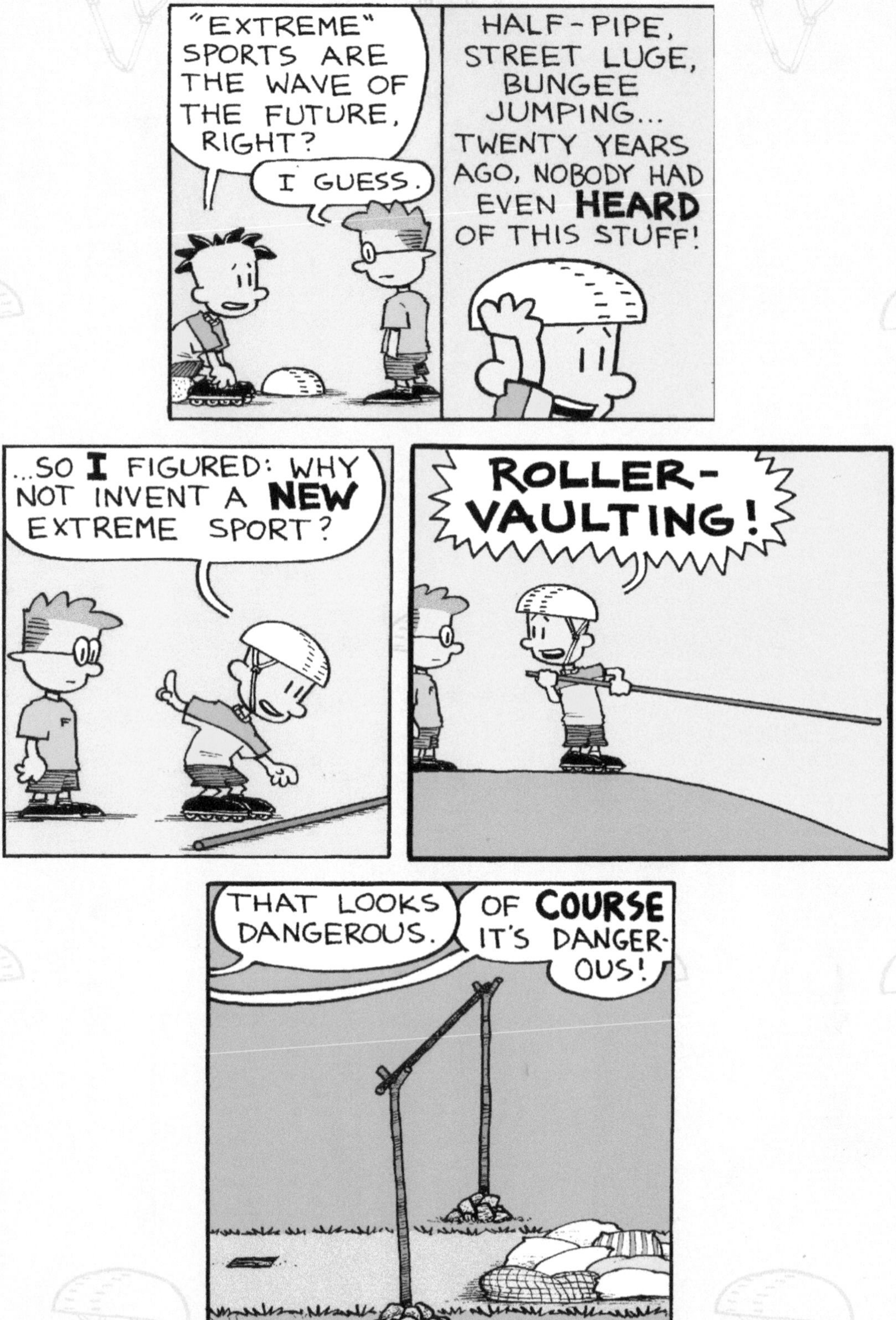
"EXTREME" SPORTS ARE THE WAVE OF THE FUTURE, RIGHT?
I GUESS.
HALF-PIPE, STREET LUGE, BUNGEE JUMPING... TWENTY YEARS AGO, NOBODY HAD EVEN HEARD OF THIS STUFF!
...SO I FIGURED: WHY NOT INVENT A NEW EXTREME SPORT?
ROLLER-VAULTING!
THAT LOOKS DANGEROUS.
OF COURSE IT'S DANGER-OUS!

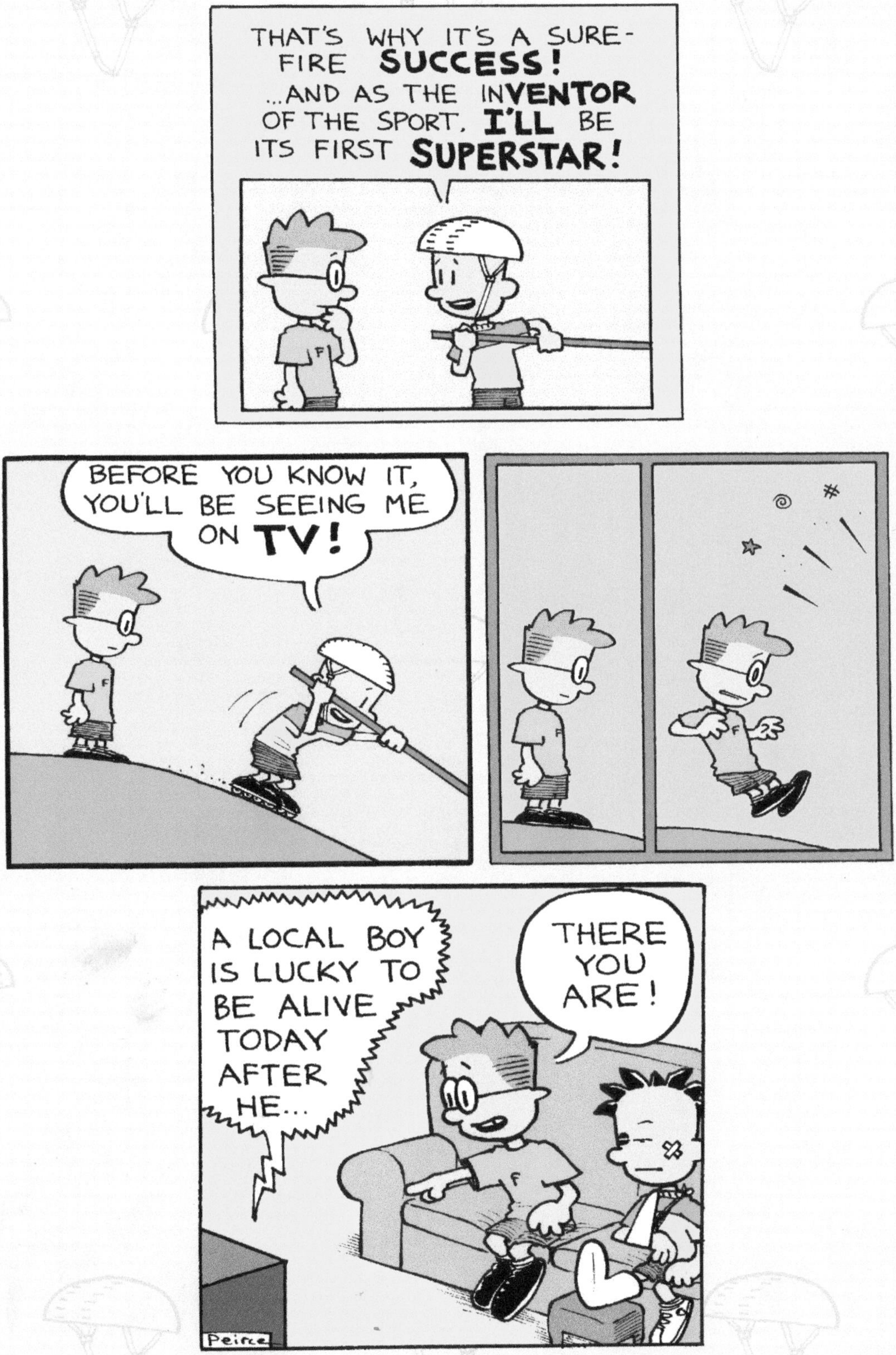
THAT'S WHY IT'S A SURE-FIRE SUCCESS! ...AND AS THE INVENTOR OF THE SPORT, I'LL BE ITS FIRST SUPERSTAR!
BEFORE YOU KNOW IT, YOU'LL BE SEEING ME ON TV!
#
A LOCAL BOY IS LUCKY TO BE ALIVE TODAY AFTER HE...
THERE YOU ARE!
Peirce

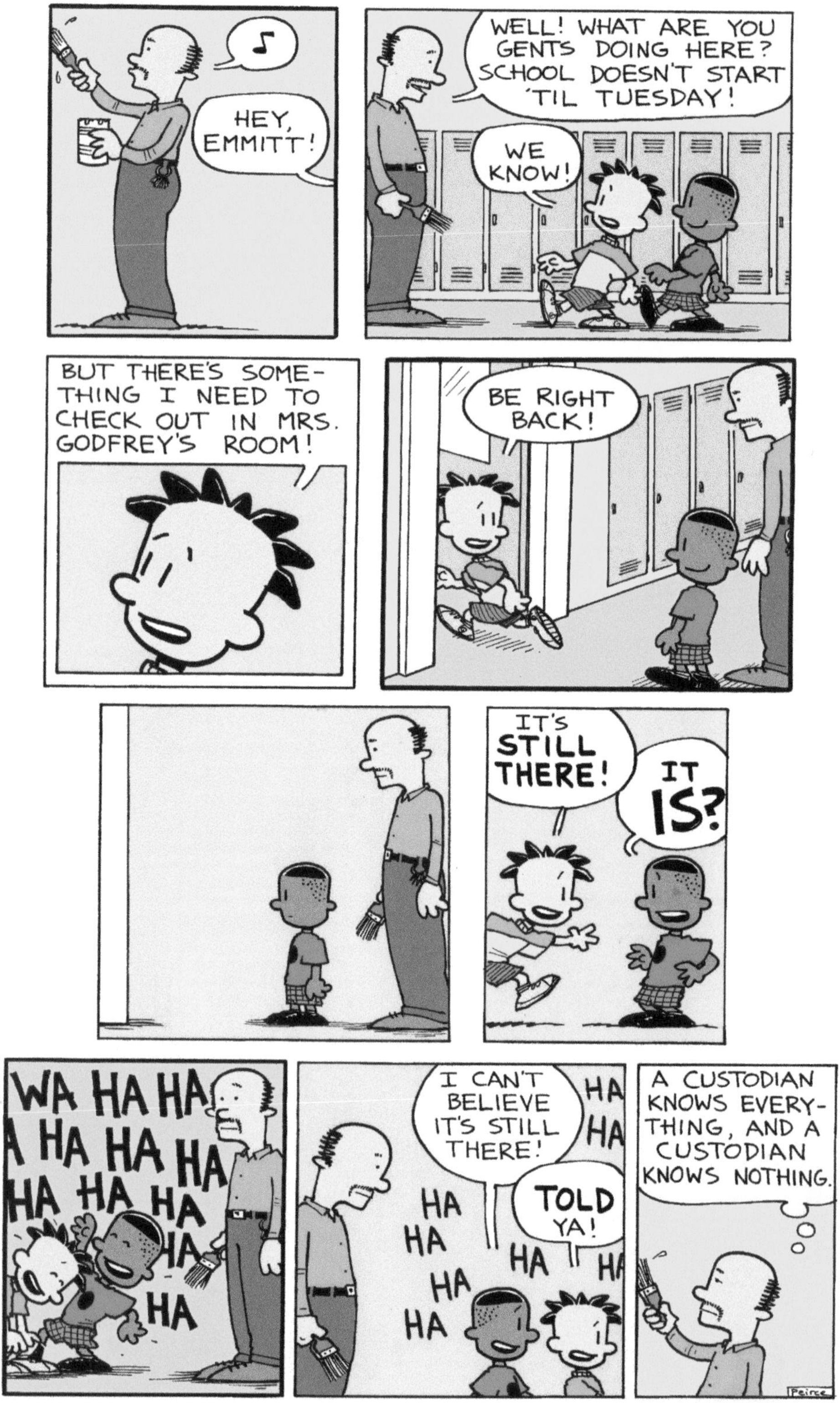
♪
HEY, EMMITT!
WELL! WHAT ARE YOU GENTS DOING HERE? SCHOOL DOESN'T START 'TIL TUESDAY!
WE KNOW!
BUT THERE'S SOMETHING I NEED TO CHECK OUT IN MRS. GODFREY'S ROOM!
BE RIGHT BACK!
IT'S STILL THERE!
IT IS?
WA HA HA HA HA HA HA HA HA HA HA HA HA HA
I CAN'T BELIEVE IT'S STILL THERE!
HA HA HA HA HA HA HA HA
TOLD YA!
A CUSTODIAN KNOWS EVERYTHING, AND A CUSTODIAN KNOWS NOTHING.
Peirce

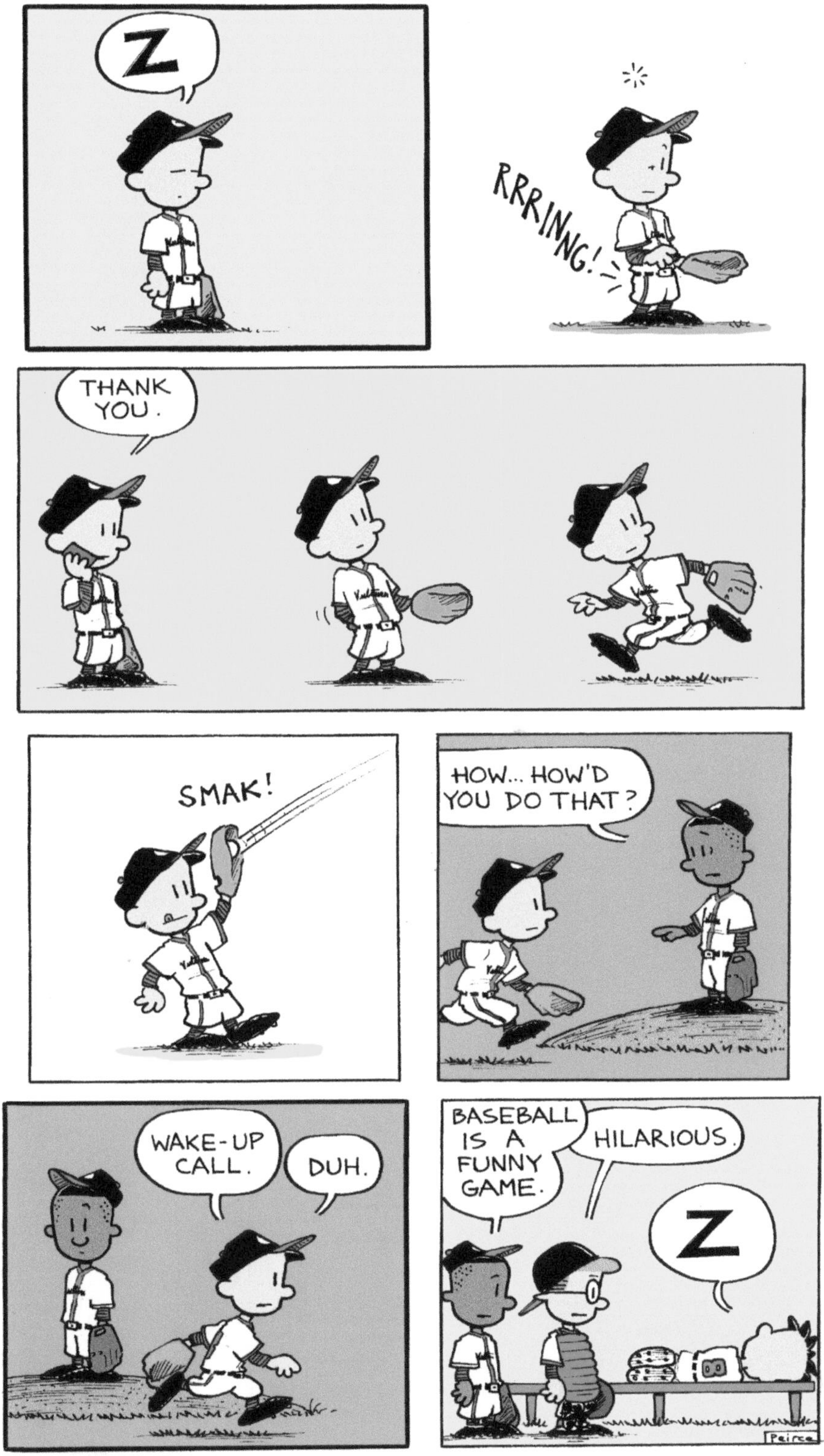

Z
RRRINNG!
THANK YOU.
SMAK!
HOW... HOW'D YOU DO THAT?
WAKE-UP CALL.
DUH.
BASEBALL IS A FUNNY GAME.
HILARIOUS.
Z
Peirce

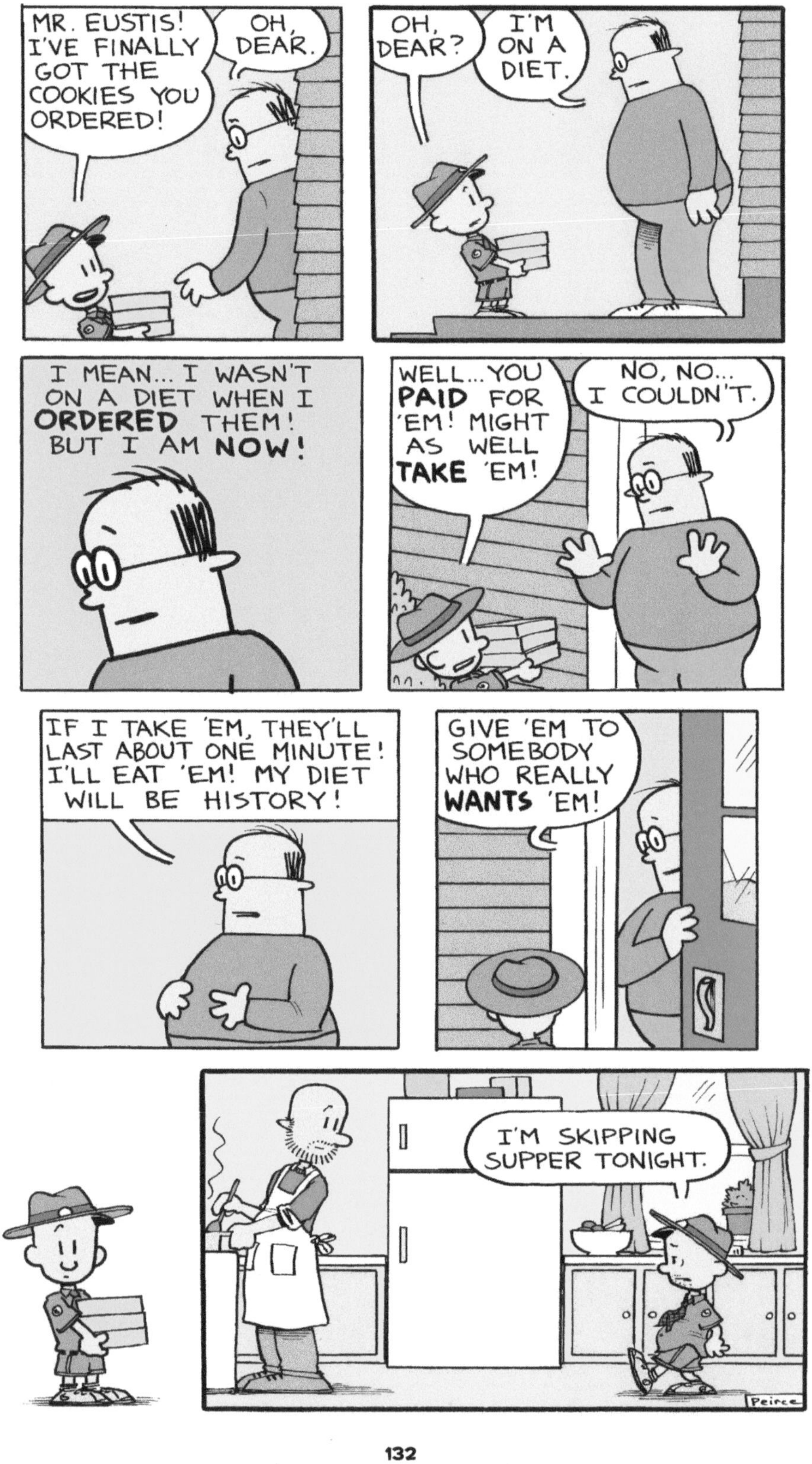
MR. EUSTIS! I'VE FINALLY GOT THE COOKIES YOU ORDERED!
OH, DEAR.
OH, DEAR?
I'M ON A DIET.
I MEAN... I WASN'T ON A DIET WHEN I **ORDERED** THEM! BUT I AM **NOW**!
WELL... YOU **PAID** FOR 'EM! MIGHT AS WELL **TAKE** 'EM!
NO, NO... I COULDN'T.
IF I TAKE 'EM, THEY'LL LAST ABOUT ONE MINUTE! I'LL EAT 'EM! MY DIET WILL BE HISTORY!
GIVE 'EM TO SOMEBODY WHO REALLY **WANTS** 'EM!
I'M SKIPPING SUPPER TONIGHT.
Peirce

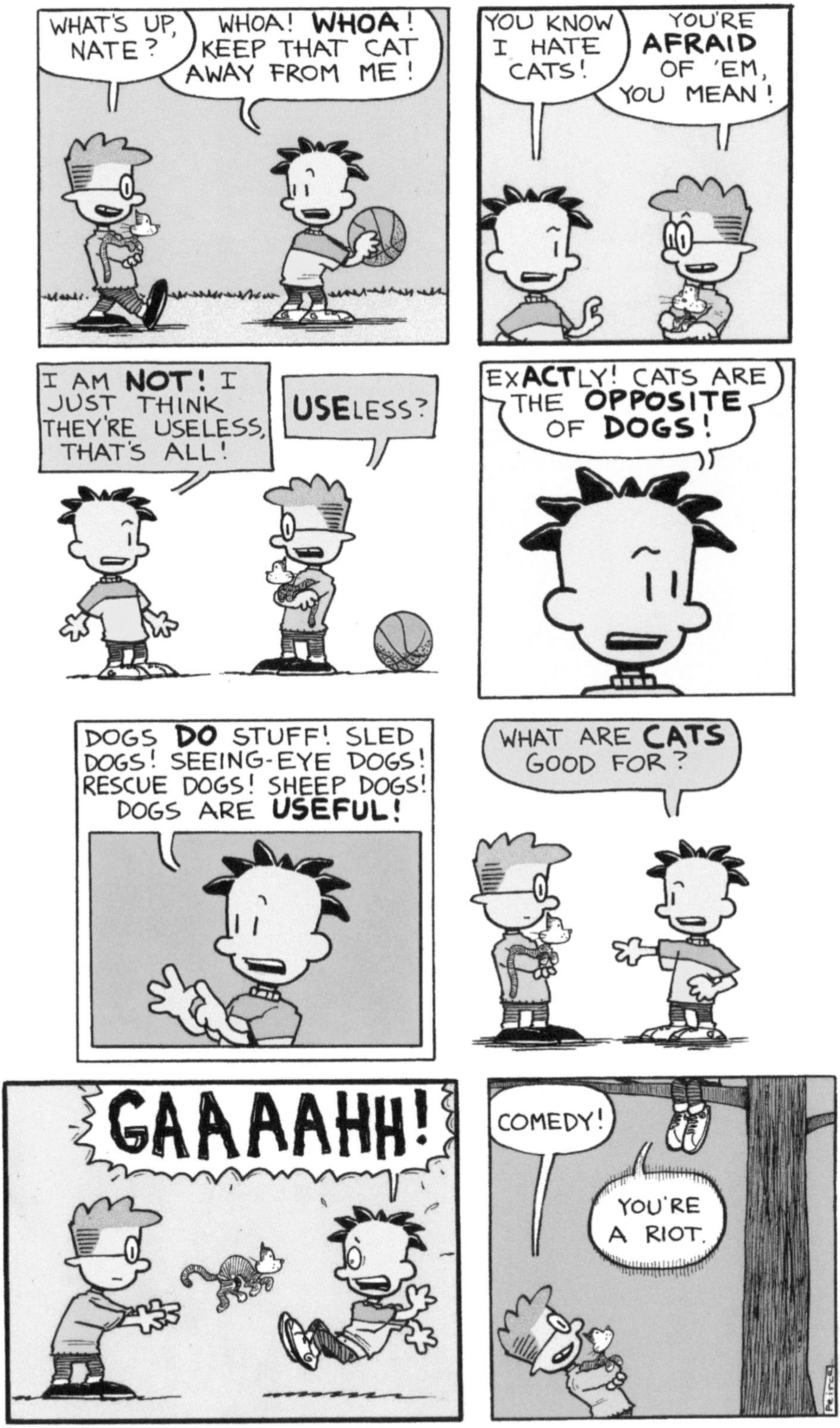
WHAT'S UP, NATE?
WHOA! WHOA! KEEP THAT CAT AWAY FROM ME!
YOU KNOW I HATE CATS!
YOU'RE AFRAID OF 'EM, YOU MEAN!
I AM NOT! I JUST THINK THEY'RE USELESS, THAT'S ALL!
USELESS?
EXACTLY! CATS ARE THE OPPOSITE OF DOGS!
DOGS DO STUFF! SLED DOGS! SEEING-EYE DOGS! RESCUE DOGS! SHEEP DOGS! DOGS ARE USEFUL!
WHAT ARE CATS GOOD FOR?
GAAAAHH!
COMEDY!
YOU'RE A RIOT.
Peirce

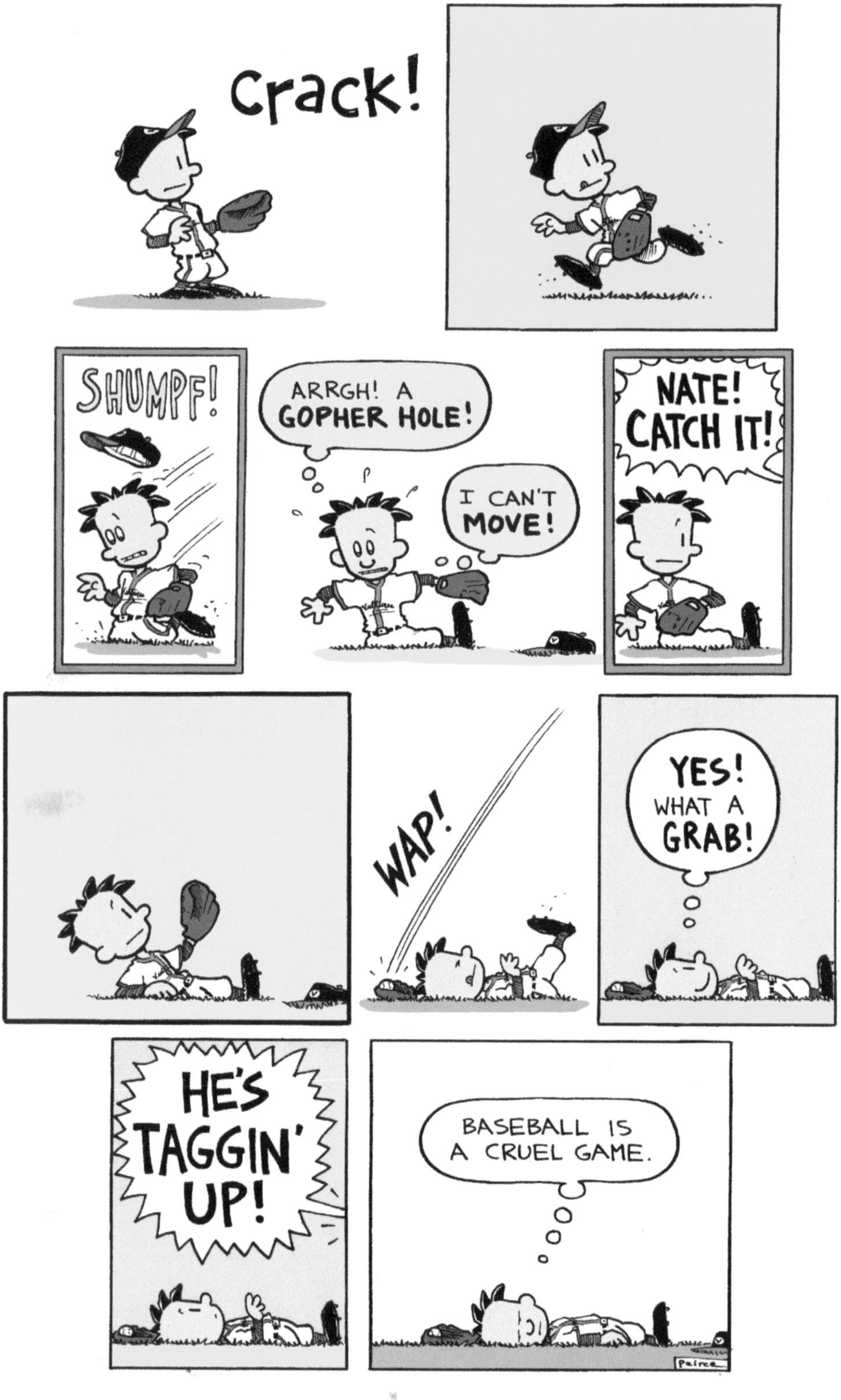
Crack!
SHUMPF!
ARRGH! A GOPHER HOLE!
I CAN'T MOVE!
NATE! CATCH IT!
WAP!
YES! WHAT A GRAB!
HE'S TAGGIN' UP!
BASEBALL IS A CRUEL GAME.
Peirce

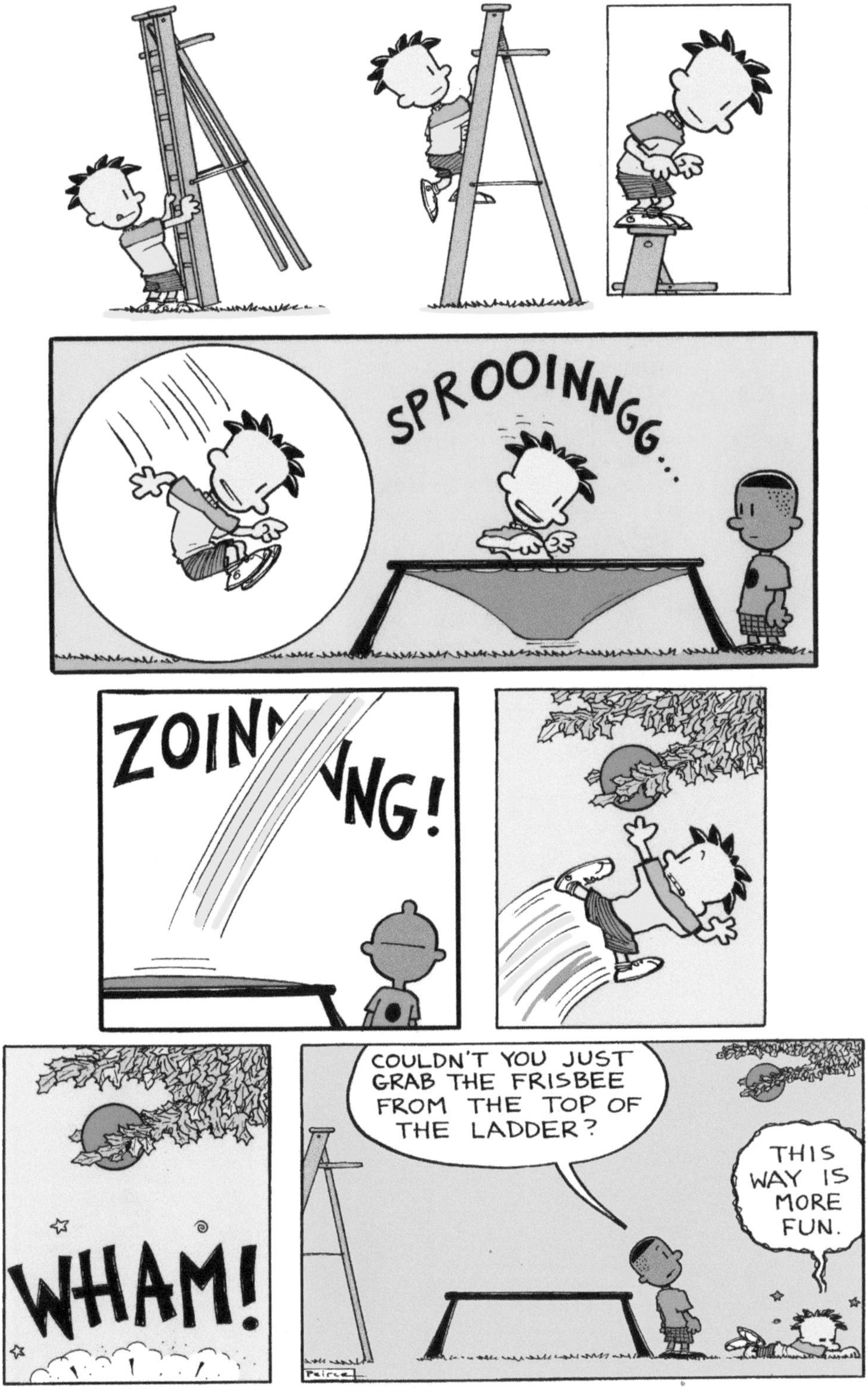
SPROOINNGG...
ZOINNNNG!
WHAM!
COULDN'T YOU JUST GRAB THE FRISBEE FROM THE TOP OF THE LADDER?
THIS WAY IS MORE FUN.
Peirce

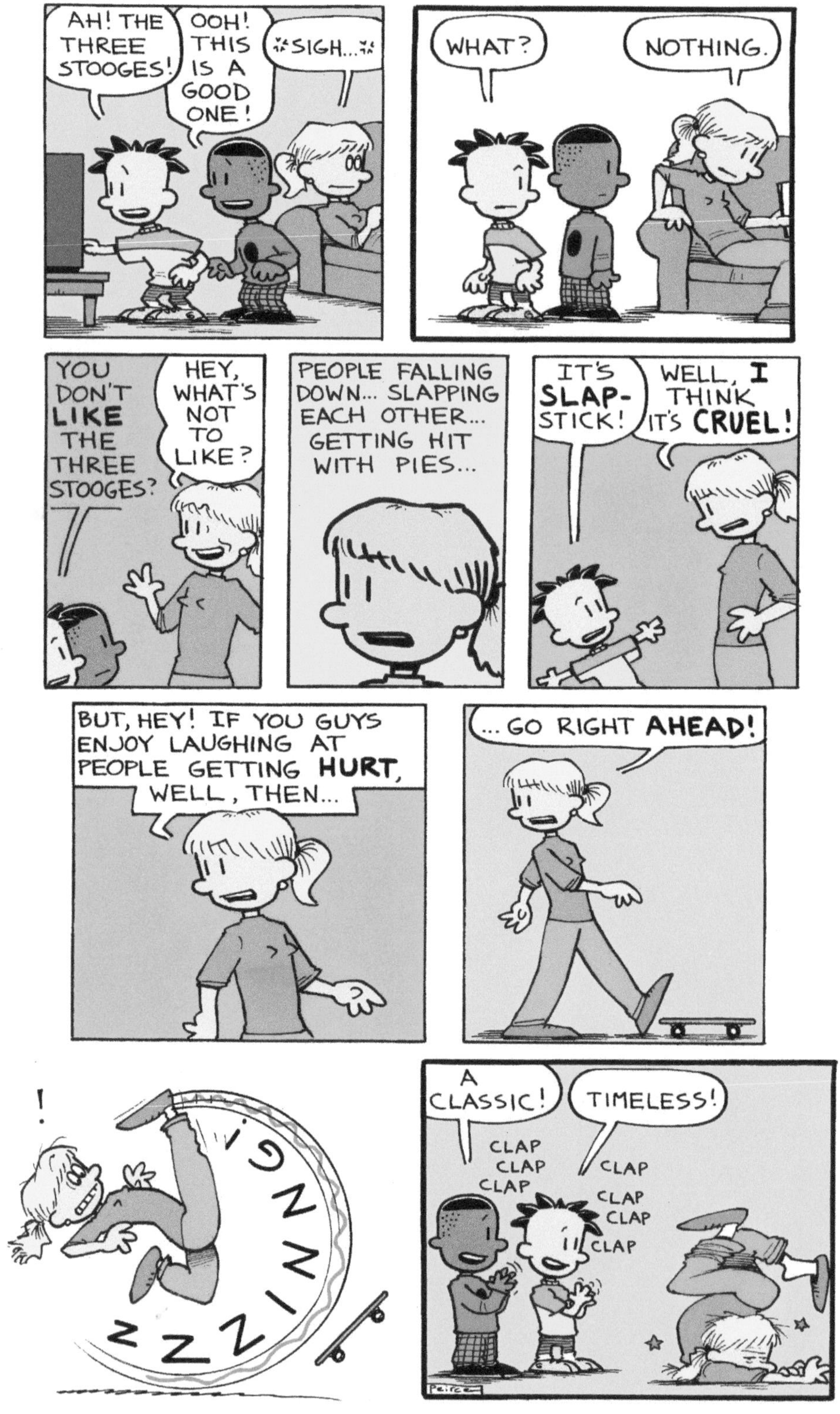
AH! THE THREE STOOGES!
OOH! THIS IS A GOOD ONE!
SIGH...
WHAT?
NOTHING.
YOU DON'T LIKE THE THREE STOOGES?
HEY, WHAT'S NOT TO LIKE?
PEOPLE FALLING DOWN... SLAPPING EACH OTHER... GETTING HIT WITH PIES...
IT'S SLAP-STICK!
WELL, I THINK IT'S CRUEL!
BUT, HEY! IF YOU GUYS ENJOY LAUGHING AT PEOPLE GETTING HURT, WELL, THEN...
... GO RIGHT AHEAD!
!
ZZZINNG!
A CLASSIC!
TIMELESS!
CLAP CLAP CLAP
CLAP
CLAP CLAP
CLAP
Peirce

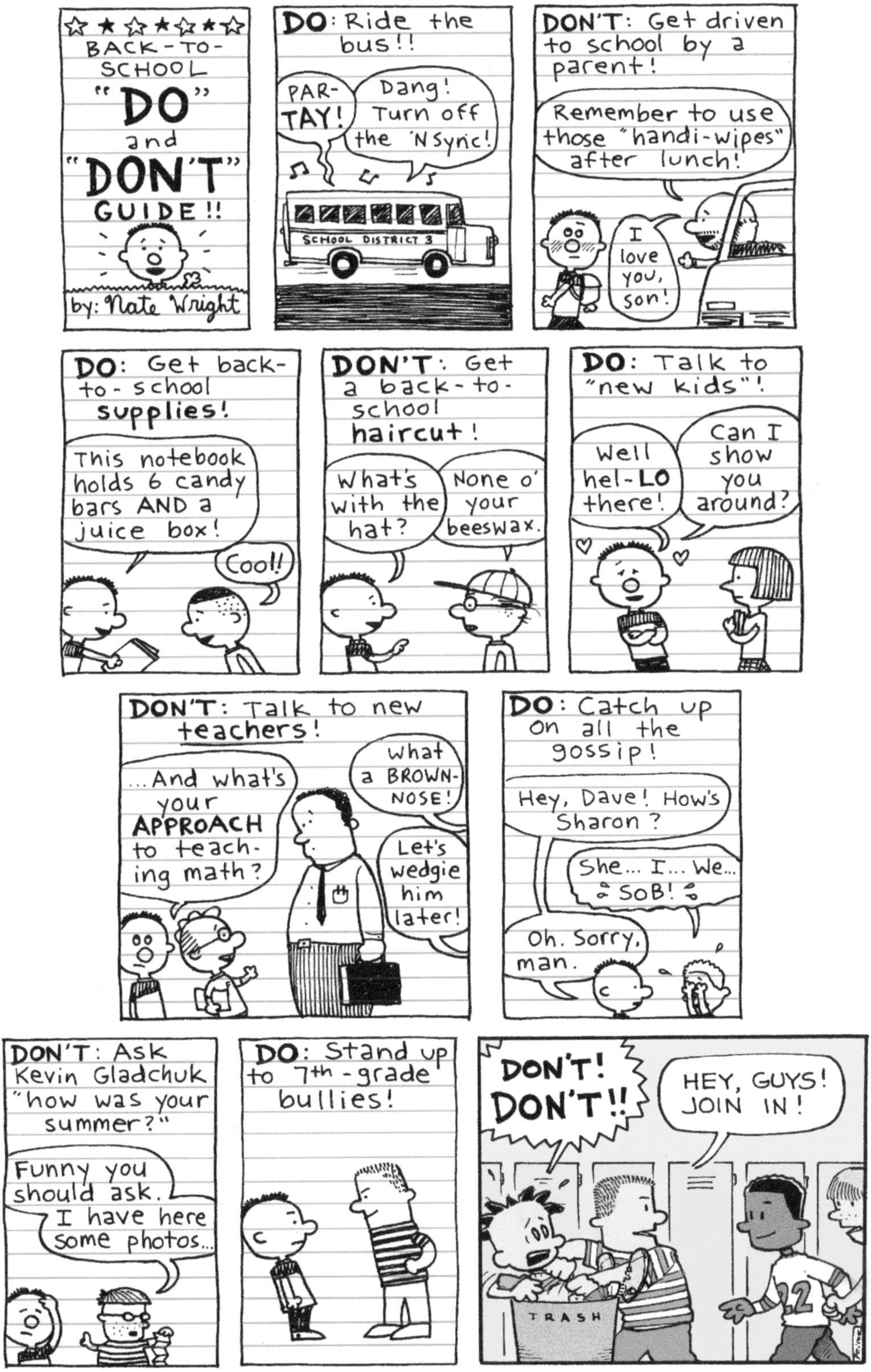

BACK-TO-SCHOOL "DO" and "DON'T" GUIDE!!
by: Nate Wright
DO: Ride the bus!!
PAR-TAY!
Dang! Turn off the 'NSync!
SCHOOL DISTRICT 3
DON'T: Get driven to school by a parent!
Remember to use those "handi-wipes" after lunch!
I love you, son!
DO: Get back-to-school supplies!
This notebook holds 6 candy bars AND a juice box!
Cool!
DON'T: Get a back-to-school haircut!
What's with the hat?
None o' your beeswax.
DO: Talk to "new kids"!
Well hel-LO there!
Can I show you around?
DON'T: Talk to new teachers!
...And what's your APPROACH to teach-ing math?
What a BROWN-NOSE!
Let's wedgie him later!
DO: Catch up on all the gossip!
Hey, Dave! How's Sharon?
She... I... We... SOB!
Oh. Sorry, man.
DON'T: Ask Kevin Gladchuk "how was your summer?"
Funny you should ask.
I have here some photos...
DO: Stand up to 7th-grade bullies!
DON'T! DON'T!!
HEY, GUYS! JOIN IN!
TRASH

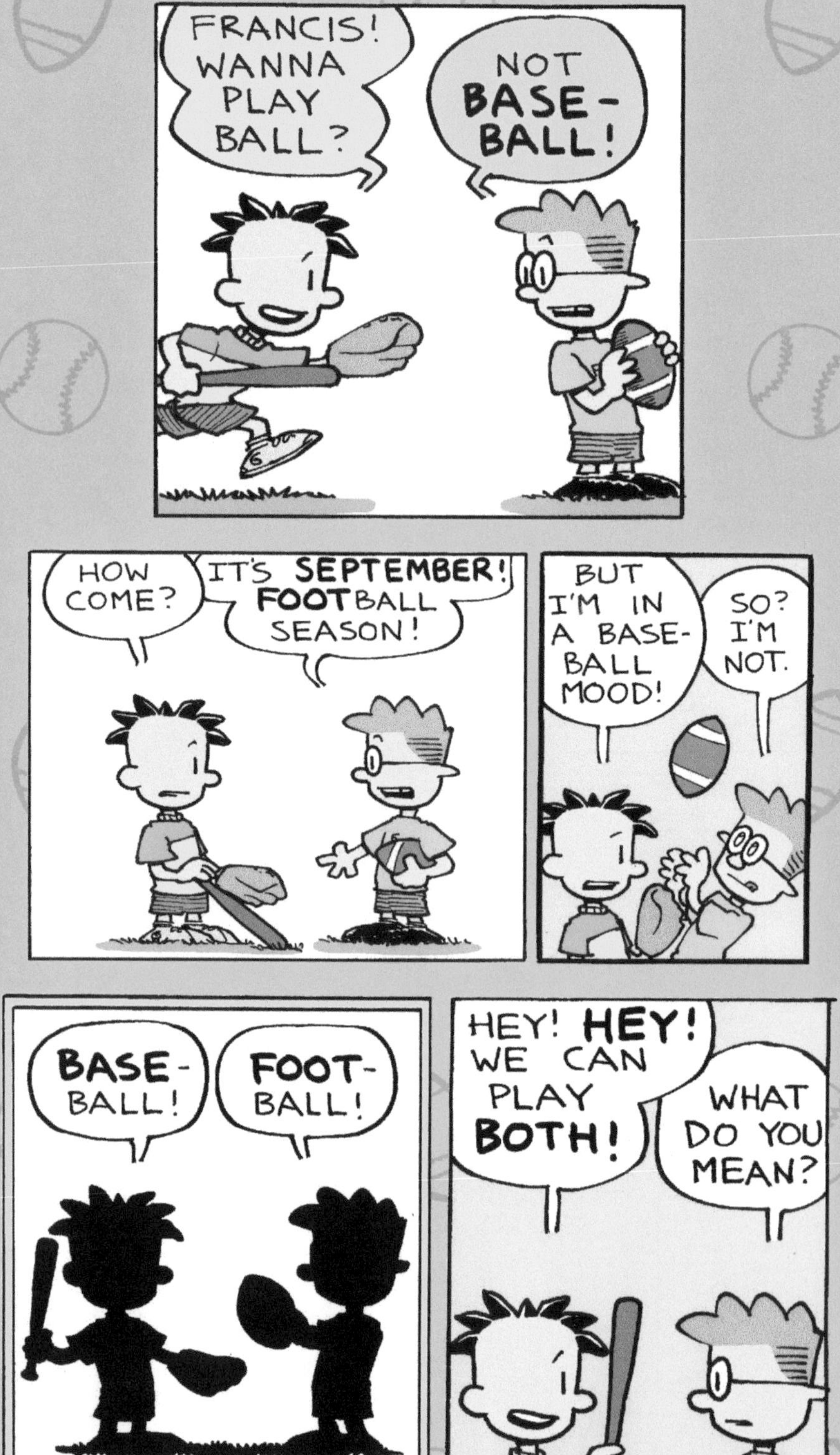
FRANCIS! WANNA PLAY BALL?
NOT **BASE-BALL!**
HOW COME?
IT'S **SEPTEMBER! FOOT**BALL SEASON!
BUT I'M IN A BASE-BALL MOOD!
SO? I'M NOT.
BASE-BALL!
FOOT-BALL!
HEY! **HEY!** WE CAN PLAY **BOTH!**
WHAT DO YOU MEAN?

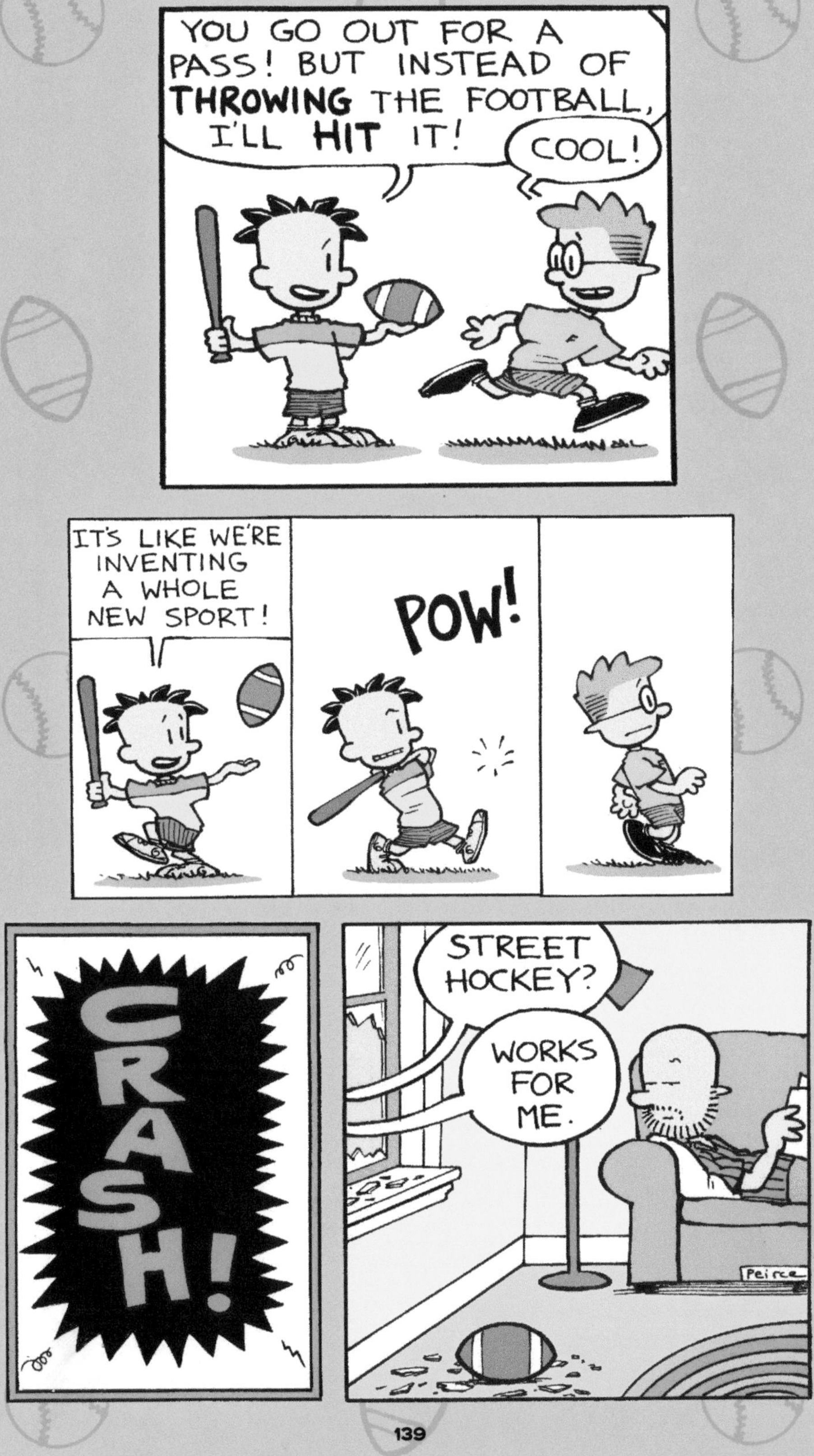
YOU GO OUT FOR A PASS! BUT INSTEAD OF THROWING THE FOOTBALL, I'LL HIT IT!
COOL!
IT'S LIKE WE'RE INVENTING A WHOLE NEW SPORT!
POW!
CRASH!
STREET HOCKEY?
WORKS FOR ME.
Peirce

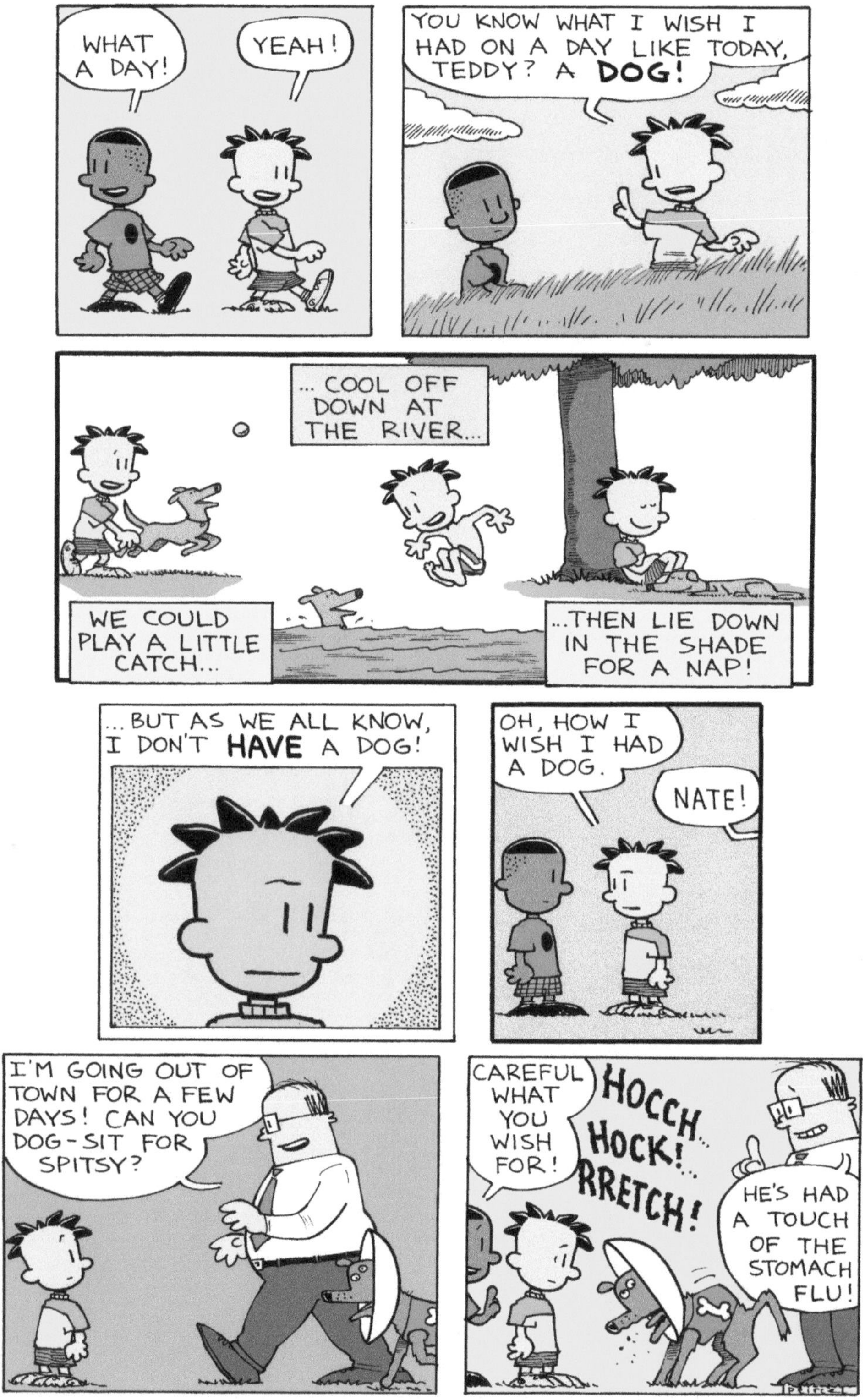
WHAT A DAY!
YEAH!
YOU KNOW WHAT I WISH I HAD ON A DAY LIKE TODAY, TEDDY? A DOG!
WE COULD PLAY A LITTLE CATCH...
... COOL OFF DOWN AT THE RIVER...
...THEN LIE DOWN IN THE SHADE FOR A NAP!
... BUT AS WE ALL KNOW, I DON'T HAVE A DOG!
OH, HOW I WISH I HAD A DOG.
NATE!
I'M GOING OUT OF TOWN FOR A FEW DAYS! CAN YOU DOG-SIT FOR SPITSY?
CAREFUL WHAT YOU WISH FOR!
HOCCH... HOCK!... RRETCH!
HE'S HAD A TOUCH OF THE STOMACH FLU!

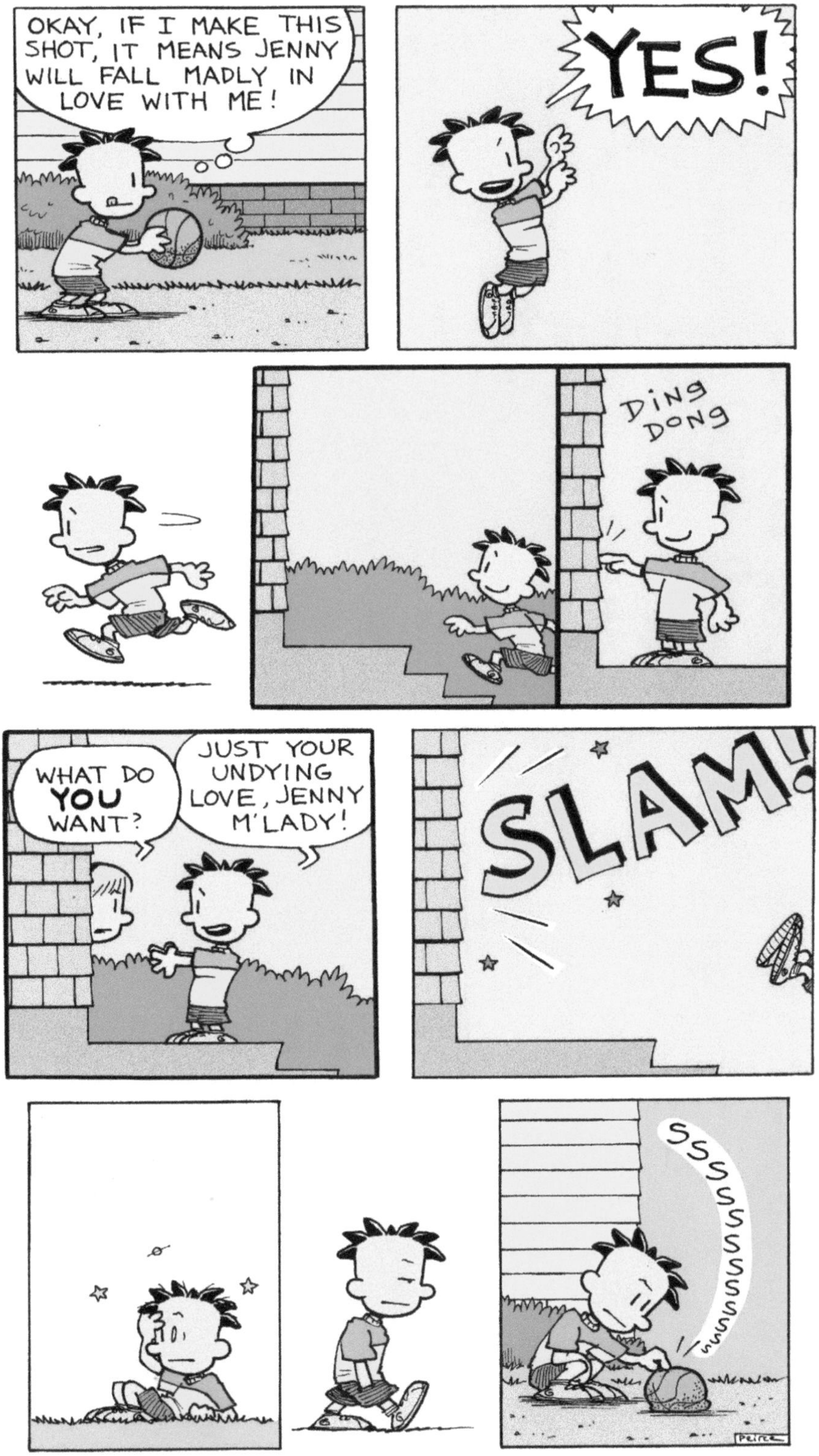
OKAY, IF I MAKE THIS SHOT, IT MEANS JENNY WILL FALL MADLY IN LOVE WITH ME!
YES!
DING DONG
WHAT DO YOU WANT?
JUST YOUR UNDYING LOVE, JENNY M'LADY!
SLAM!
SSSSSSSSSSSSsssssss
PEIRCE

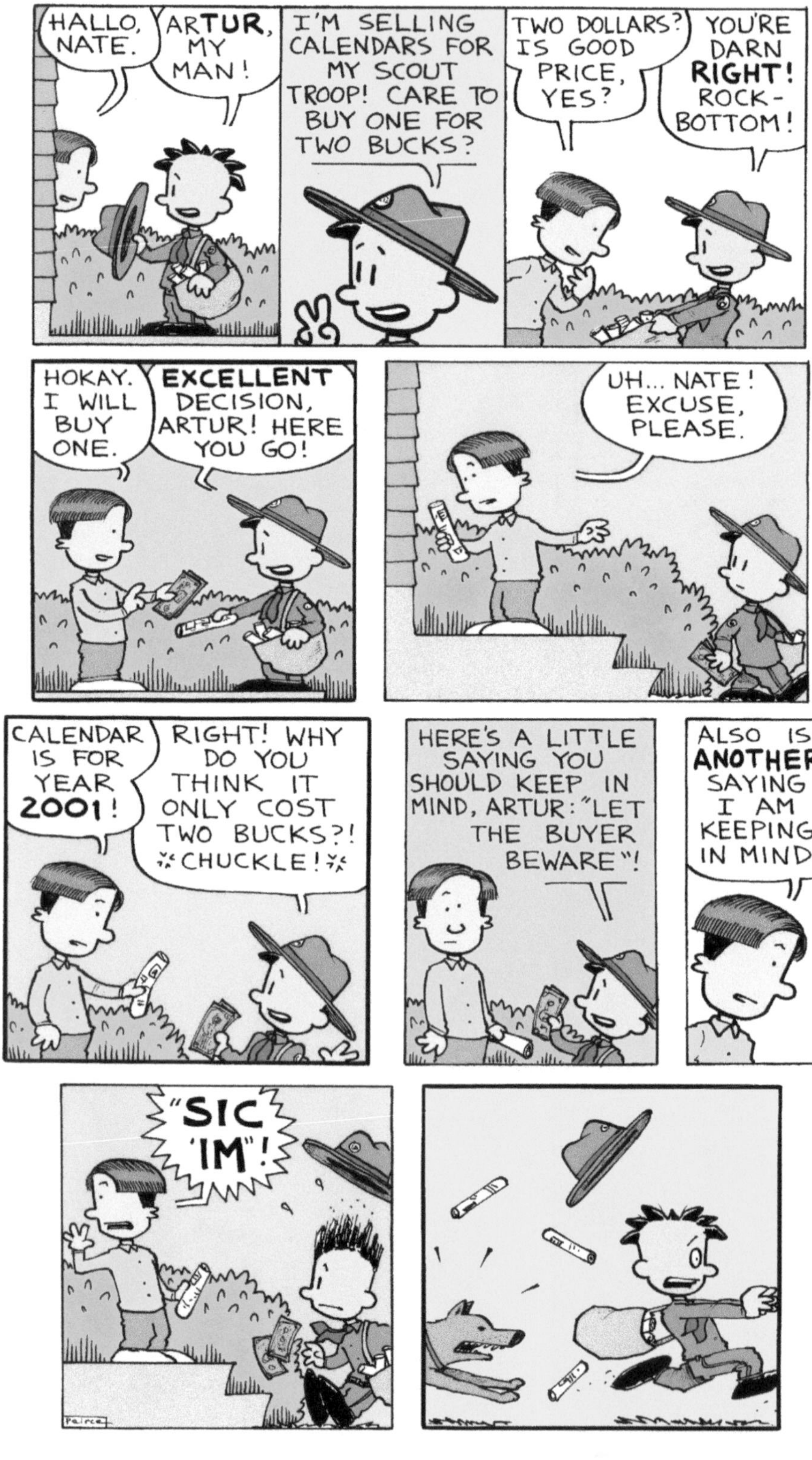
HALLO, NATE.
ARTUR, MY MAN!
I'M SELLING CALENDARS FOR MY SCOUT TROOP! CARE TO BUY ONE FOR TWO BUCKS?
TWO DOLLARS? IS GOOD PRICE, YES?
YOU'RE DARN RIGHT! ROCK-BOTTOM!
HOKAY. I WILL BUY ONE.
EXCELLENT DECISION, ARTUR! HERE YOU GO!
UH... NATE! EXCUSE, PLEASE.
CALENDAR IS FOR YEAR 2001!
RIGHT! WHY DO YOU THINK IT ONLY COST TWO BUCKS?! *CHUCKLE!*
HERE'S A LITTLE SAYING YOU SHOULD KEEP IN MIND, ARTUR: "LET THE BUYER BEWARE"!
ALSO IS ANOTHER SAYING I AM KEEPING IN MIND:
"SIC 'IM"!
PEIRCE

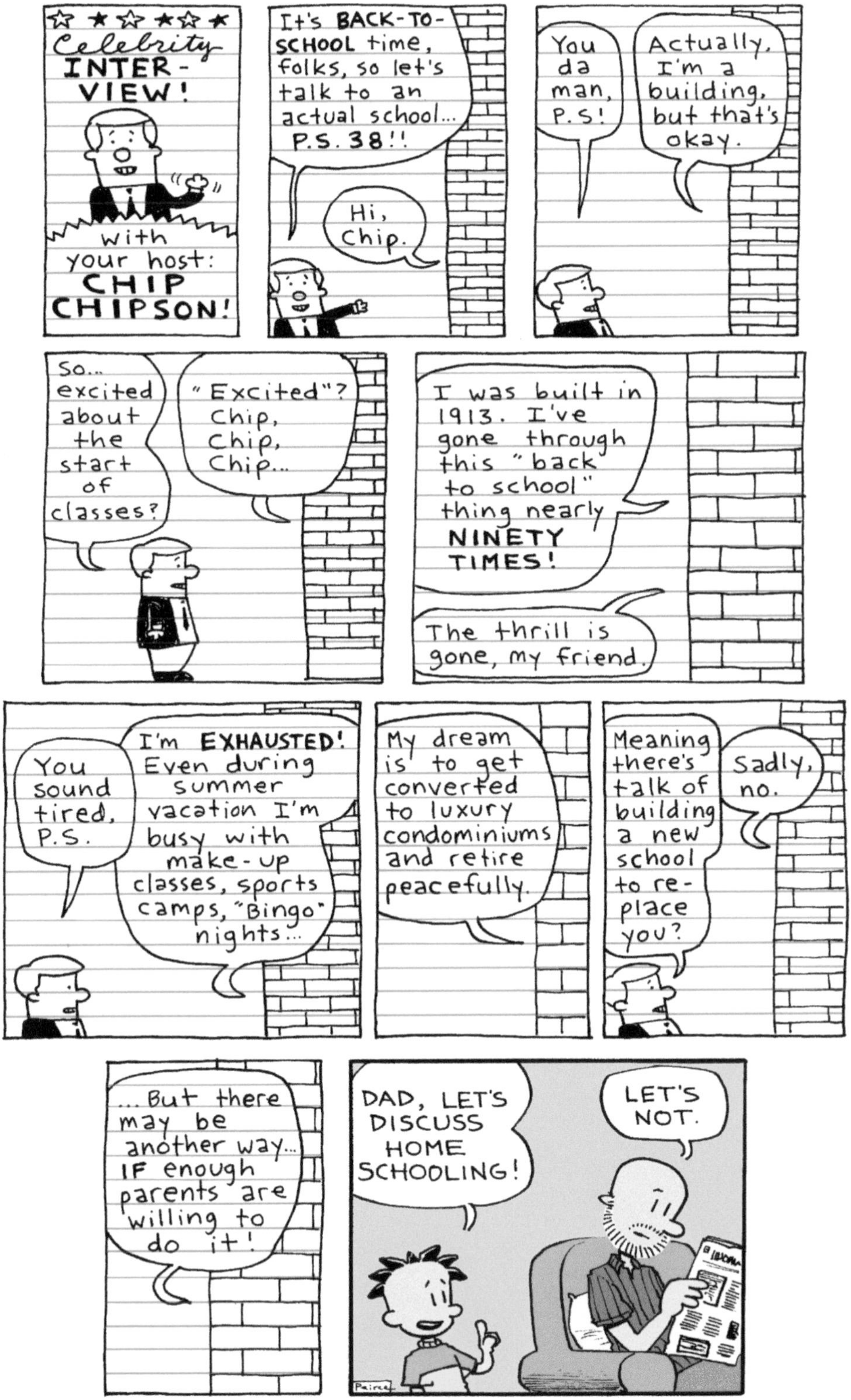
Celebrity INTER-VIEW! with your host: CHIP CHIPSON!
It's BACK-TO-SCHOOL time, folks, so let's talk to an actual school... P.S. 38!!
Hi, Chip.
You da man, P.S!
Actually, I'm a building, but that's okay.
So... excited about the start of classes?
"Excited"? Chip, Chip, Chip...
I was built in 1913. I've gone through this "back to school" thing nearly NINETY TIMES!
The thrill is gone, my friend.
You sound tired, P.S.
I'm EXHAUSTED! Even during summer vacation I'm busy with make-up classes, sports camps, "Bingo" nights...
My dream is to get converted to luxury condominiums and retire peacefully.
Meaning there's talk of building a new school to re-place you?
Sadly, no.
...But there may be another way... IF enough parents are willing to do it!
DAD, LET'S DISCUSS HOME SCHOOLING!
LET'S NOT.
Peirce

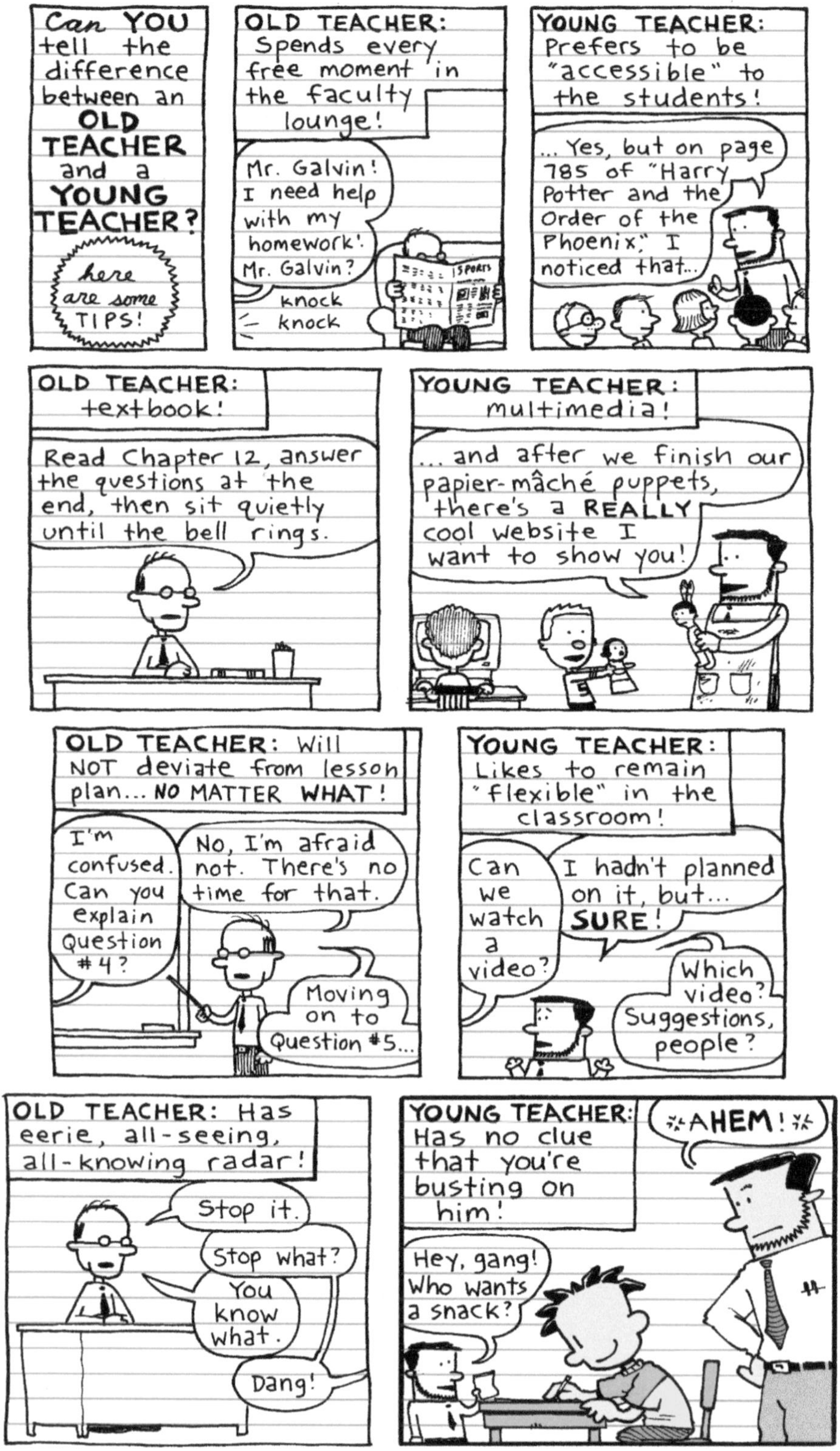
Can YOU tell the difference between an OLD TEACHER and a YOUNG TEACHER?
here are some TIPS!
OLD TEACHER: Spends every free moment in the faculty lounge!
Mr. Galvin! I need help with my homework! Mr. Galvin?
knock knock
SPORTS
YOUNG TEACHER: Prefers to be "accessible" to the students!
... Yes, but on page 785 of "Harry Potter and the Order of the Phoenix," I noticed that...
OLD TEACHER: textbook!
Read Chapter 12, answer the questions at the end, then sit quietly until the bell rings.
YOUNG TEACHER: multimedia!
... and after we finish our papier-mâché puppets, there's a REALLY cool website I want to show you!
OLD TEACHER: Will NOT deviate from lesson plan... NO MATTER WHAT!
I'm confused. Can you explain Question #4?
No, I'm afraid not. There's no time for that.
Moving on to Question #5...
YOUNG TEACHER: Likes to remain "flexible" in the classroom!
Can we watch a video?
I hadn't planned on it, but... SURE!
Which video? Suggestions, people?
OLD TEACHER: Has eerie, all-seeing, all-knowing radar!
Stop it.
Stop what?
You know what.
Dang!
YOUNG TEACHER: Has no clue that you're busting on him!
AHEM!
Hey, gang! Who wants a snack?

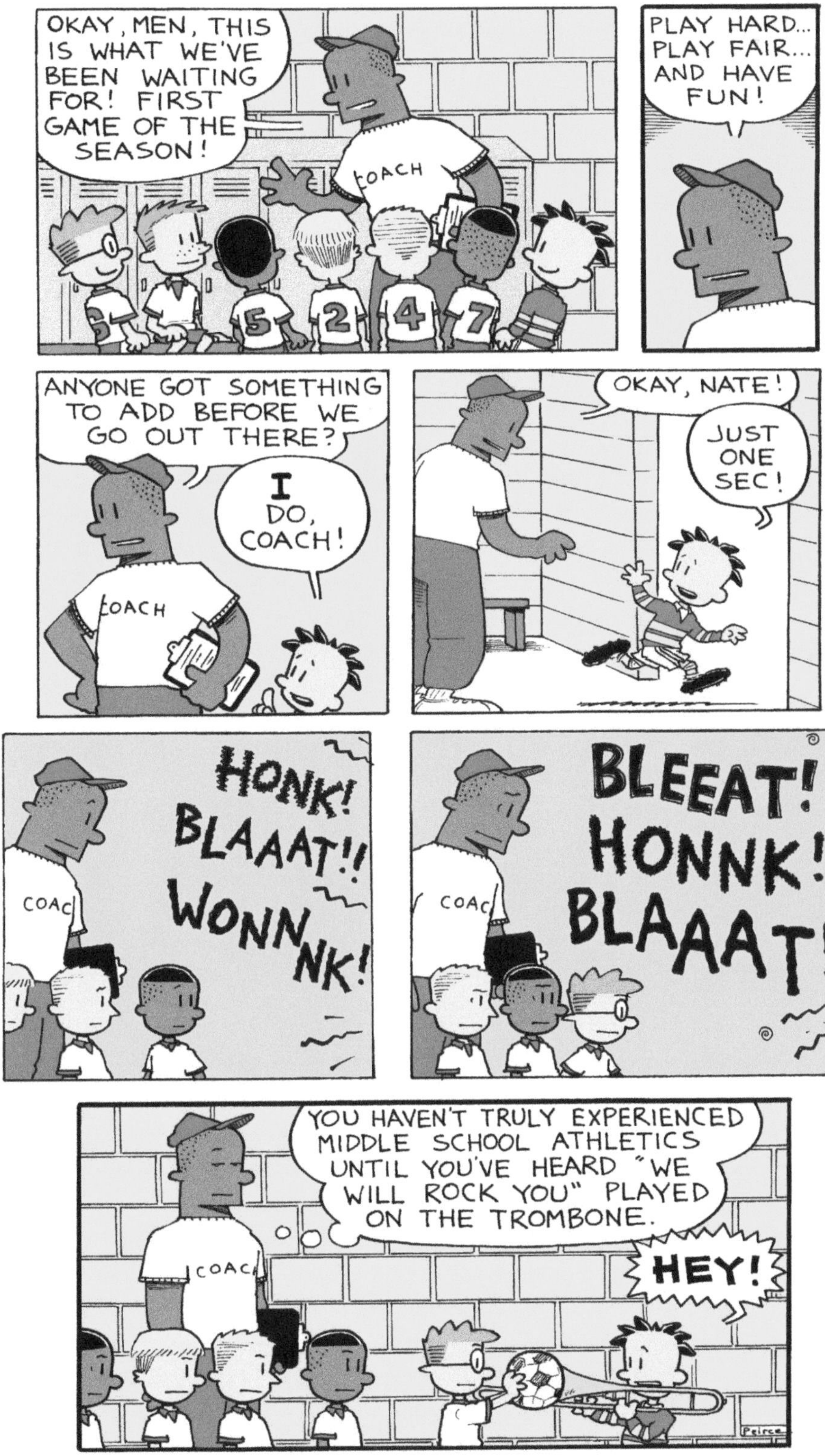
OKAY, MEN, THIS IS WHAT WE'VE BEEN WAITING FOR! FIRST GAME OF THE SEASON!
COACH
PLAY HARD... PLAY FAIR... AND HAVE FUN!
ANYONE GOT SOMETHING TO ADD BEFORE WE GO OUT THERE?
I DO, COACH!
COACH
OKAY, NATE!
JUST ONE SEC!
HONK! BLAAAT!! WONNNK!
COAC
BLEEAT! HONNK! BLAAAT!
COAC
YOU HAVEN'T TRULY EXPERIENCED MIDDLE SCHOOL ATHLETICS UNTIL YOU'VE HEARD "WE WILL ROCK YOU" PLAYED ON THE TROMBONE.
COAC
HEY!
Peirce

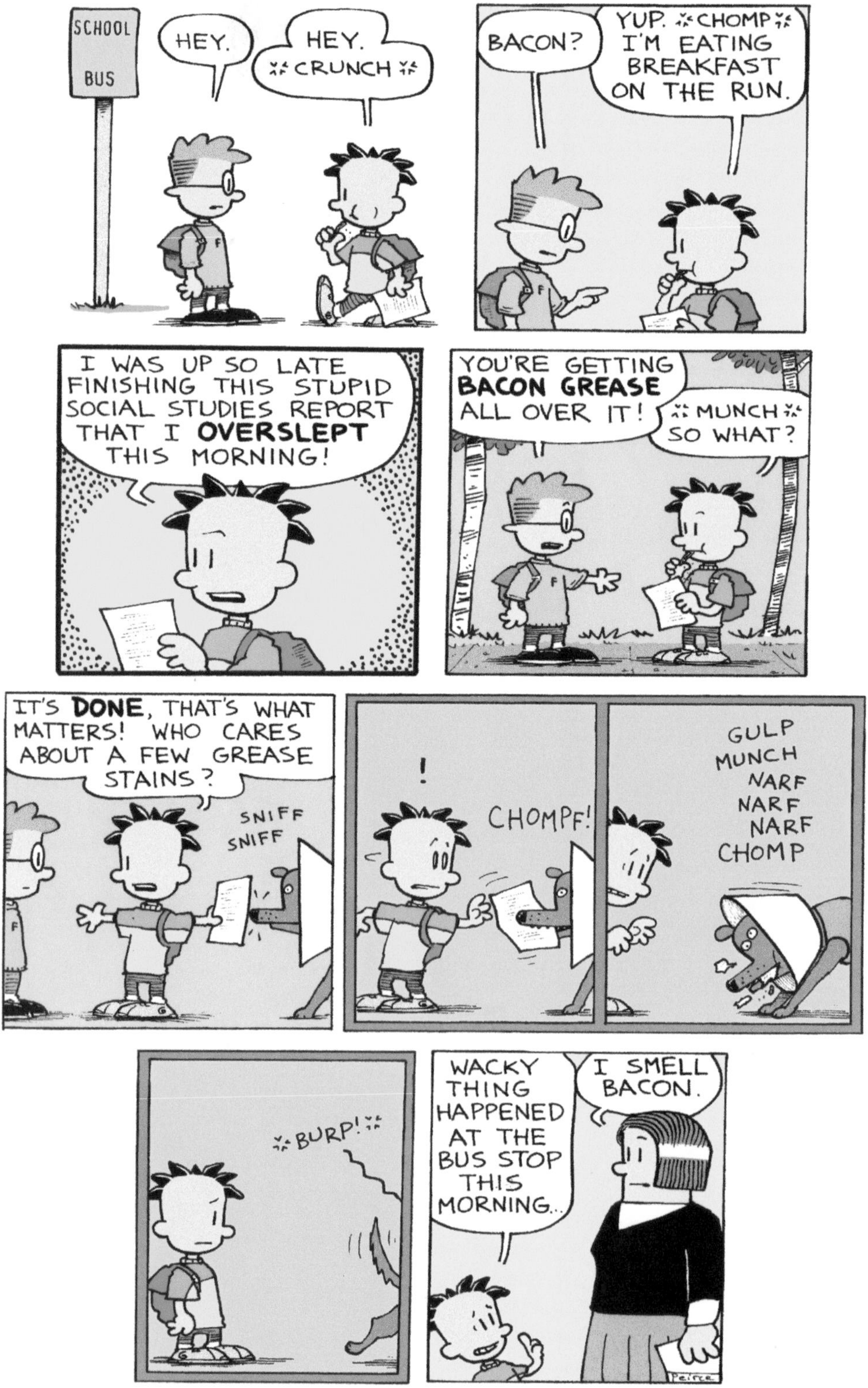
SCHOOL BUS
HEY.
HEY. ✲CRUNCH✲
BACON?
YUP. ✲CHOMP✲ I'M EATING BREAKFAST ON THE RUN.
I WAS UP SO LATE FINISHING THIS STUPID SOCIAL STUDIES REPORT THAT I **OVERSLEPT** THIS MORNING!
YOU'RE GETTING **BACON GREASE** ALL OVER IT!
✲MUNCH✲ SO WHAT?
IT'S **DONE**, THAT'S WHAT MATTERS! WHO CARES ABOUT A FEW GREASE STAINS?
SNIFF SNIFF
!
CHOMPF!
GULP MUNCH NARF NARF NARF CHOMP
✲BURP!✲
WACKY THING HAPPENED AT THE BUS STOP THIS MORNING...
I SMELL BACON.
PEIRCE

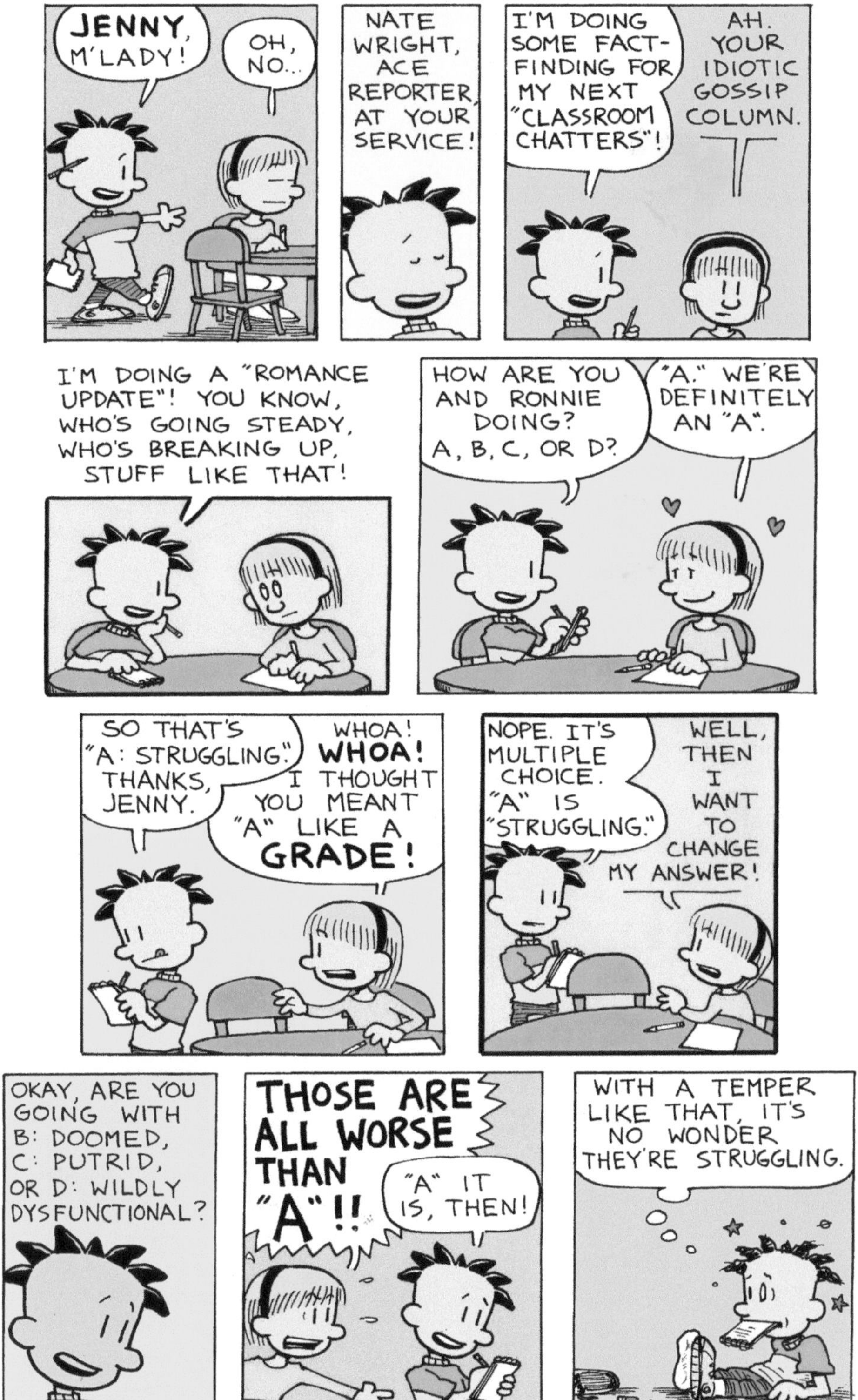
JENNY, M'LADY!
OH, NO...
NATE WRIGHT, ACE REPORTER, AT YOUR SERVICE!
I'M DOING SOME FACT-FINDING FOR MY NEXT "CLASSROOM CHATTERS"!
AH. YOUR IDIOTIC GOSSIP COLUMN.
I'M DOING A "ROMANCE UPDATE"! YOU KNOW, WHO'S GOING STEADY, WHO'S BREAKING UP, STUFF LIKE THAT!
HOW ARE YOU AND RONNIE DOING? A, B, C, OR D?
"A." WE'RE DEFINITELY AN "A".
SO THAT'S "A: STRUGGLING." THANKS, JENNY.
WHOA! WHOA! I THOUGHT YOU MEANT "A" LIKE A GRADE!
NOPE. IT'S MULTIPLE CHOICE. "A" IS "STRUGGLING."
WELL, THEN I WANT TO CHANGE MY ANSWER!
OKAY, ARE YOU GOING WITH B: DOOMED, C: PUTRID, OR D: WILDLY DYSFUNCTIONAL?
THOSE ARE ALL WORSE THAN "A"!!
"A" IT IS, THEN!
WITH A TEMPER LIKE THAT, IT'S NO WONDER THEY'RE STRUGGLING.
Peirce

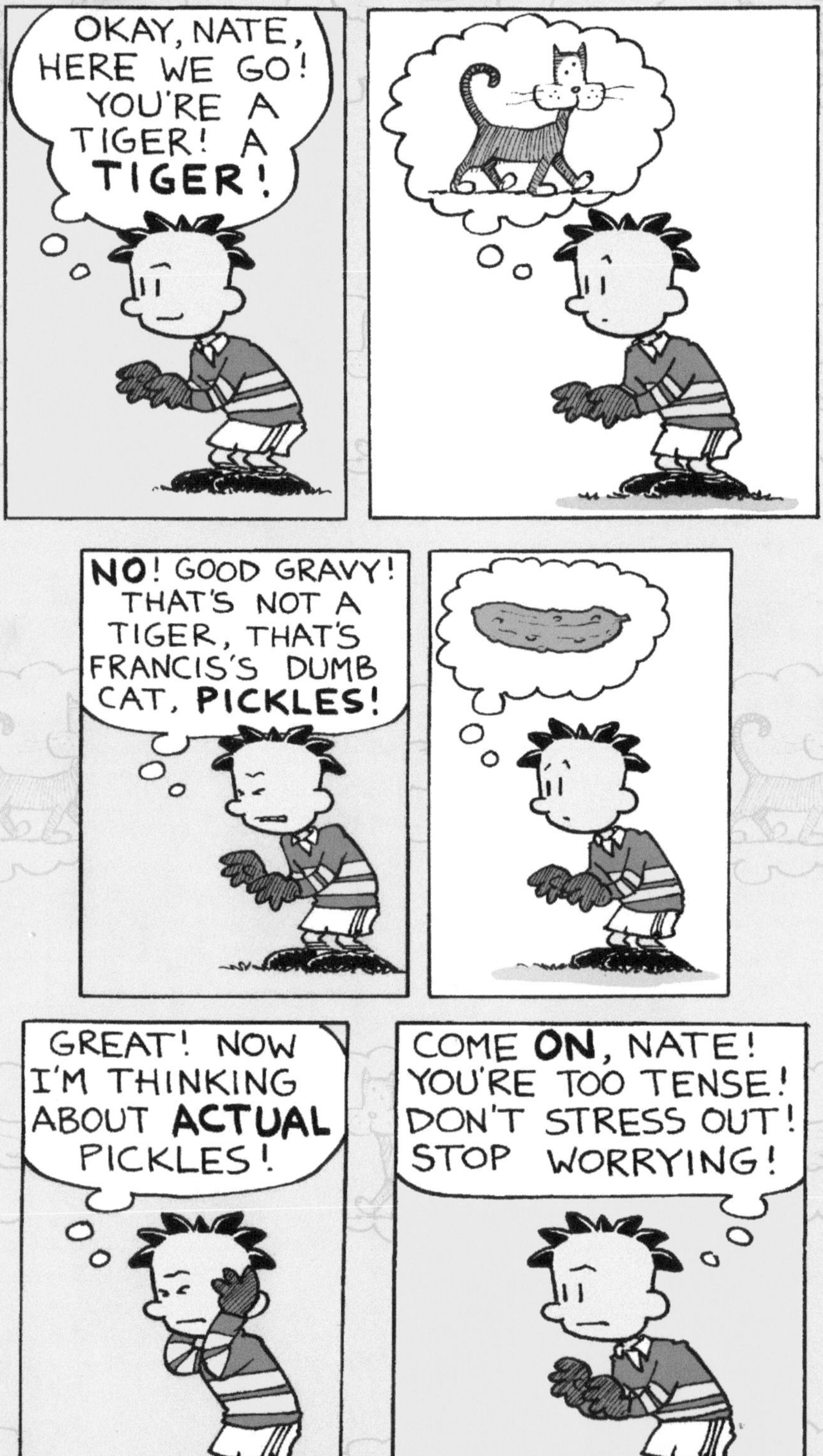
OKAY, NATE, HERE WE GO! YOU'RE A TIGER! A TIGER!
NO! GOOD GRAVY! THAT'S NOT A TIGER, THAT'S FRANCIS'S DUMB CAT, PICKLES!
GREAT! NOW I'M THINKING ABOUT ACTUAL PICKLES!
COME ON, NATE! YOU'RE TOO TENSE! DON'T STRESS OUT! STOP WORRYING!

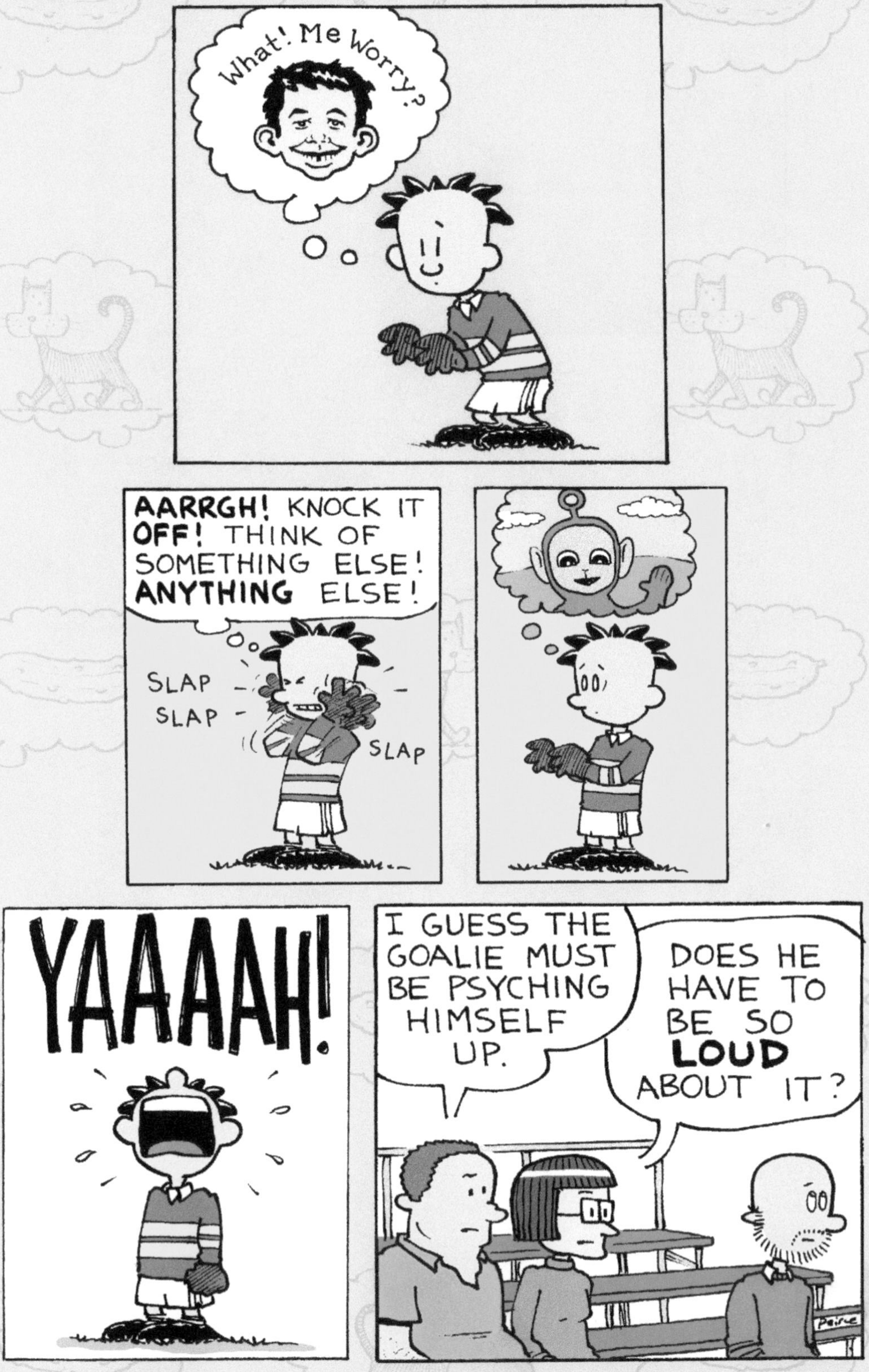
What!, Me Worry?
AARRGH! KNOCK IT OFF! THINK OF SOMETHING ELSE! ANYTHING ELSE!
SLAP
SLAP
SLAP
YAAAAH!
I GUESS THE GOALIE MUST BE PSYCHING HIMSELF UP.
DOES HE HAVE TO BE SO LOUD ABOUT IT?
Peirce

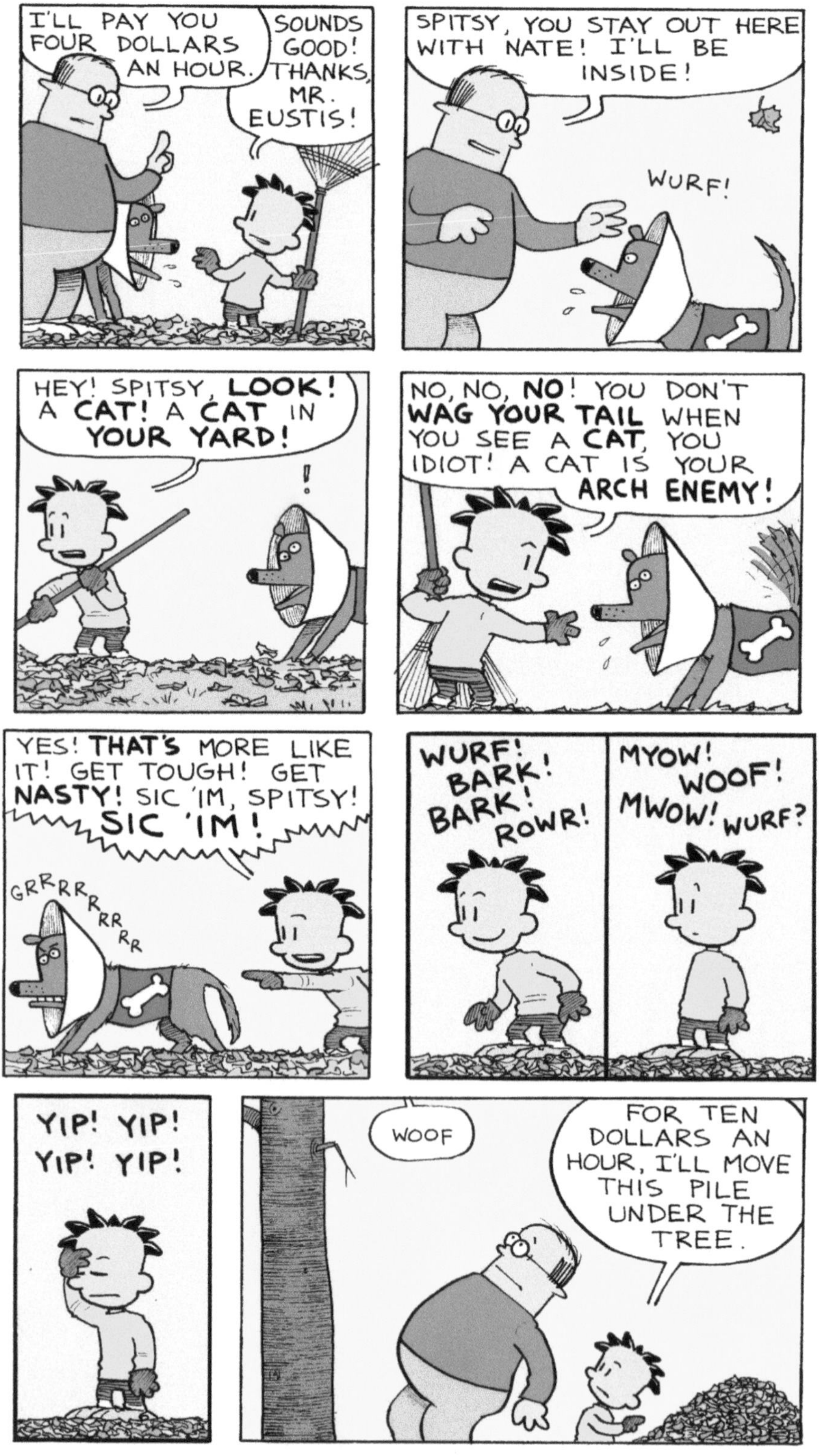

I'LL PAY YOU FOUR DOLLARS AN HOUR.
SOUNDS GOOD! THANKS, MR. EUSTIS!
SPITSY, YOU STAY OUT HERE WITH NATE! I'LL BE INSIDE!
WURF!
HEY! SPITSY, **LOOK!** A **CAT!** A **CAT** IN **YOUR YARD!**
!
NO, NO, **NO**! YOU DON'T **WAG YOUR TAIL** WHEN YOU SEE A **CAT**, YOU IDIOT! A CAT IS YOUR **ARCH ENEMY!**
YES! **THAT'S** MORE LIKE IT! GET TOUGH! GET **NASTY!** SIC 'IM, SPITSY! **SIC 'IM!**
GRRRRRRRRRR
WURF! BARK! BARK! ROWR!
MYOW! WOOF! MWOW! WURF?
YIP! YIP! YIP! YIP!
WOOF
FOR TEN DOLLARS AN HOUR, I'LL MOVE THIS PILE UNDER THE TREE.

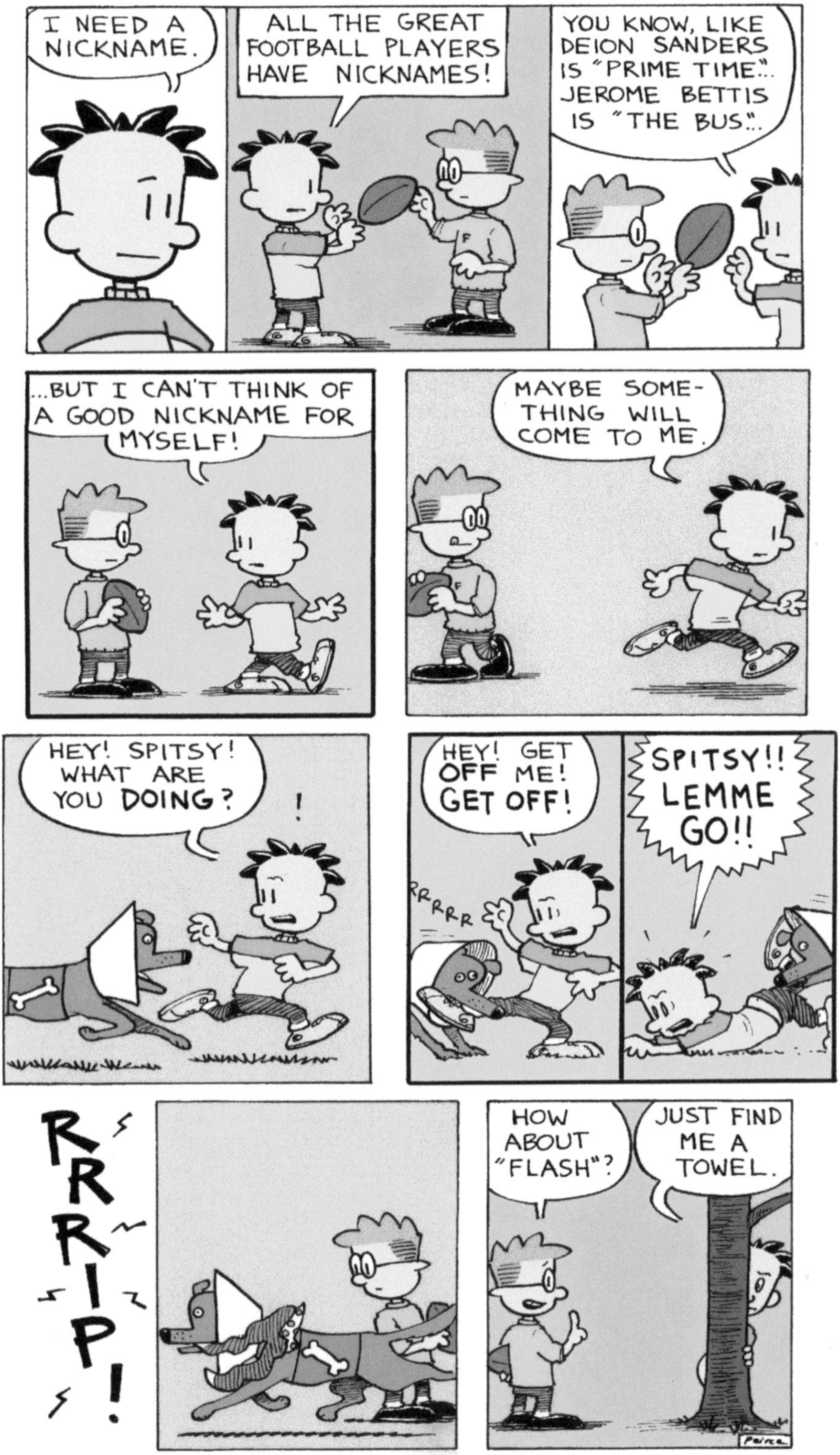

I NEED A NICKNAME.
ALL THE GREAT FOOTBALL PLAYERS HAVE NICKNAMES!
YOU KNOW, LIKE DEION SANDERS IS "PRIME TIME"... JEROME BETTIS IS "THE BUS"...
...BUT I CAN'T THINK OF A GOOD NICKNAME FOR MYSELF!
MAYBE SOMETHING WILL COME TO ME.
HEY! SPITSY! WHAT ARE YOU DOING?
!
HEY! GET OFF ME! GET OFF!
RRRRR
SPITSY!! LEMME GO!!
RRRIP!
HOW ABOUT "FLASH"?
JUST FIND ME A TOWEL.

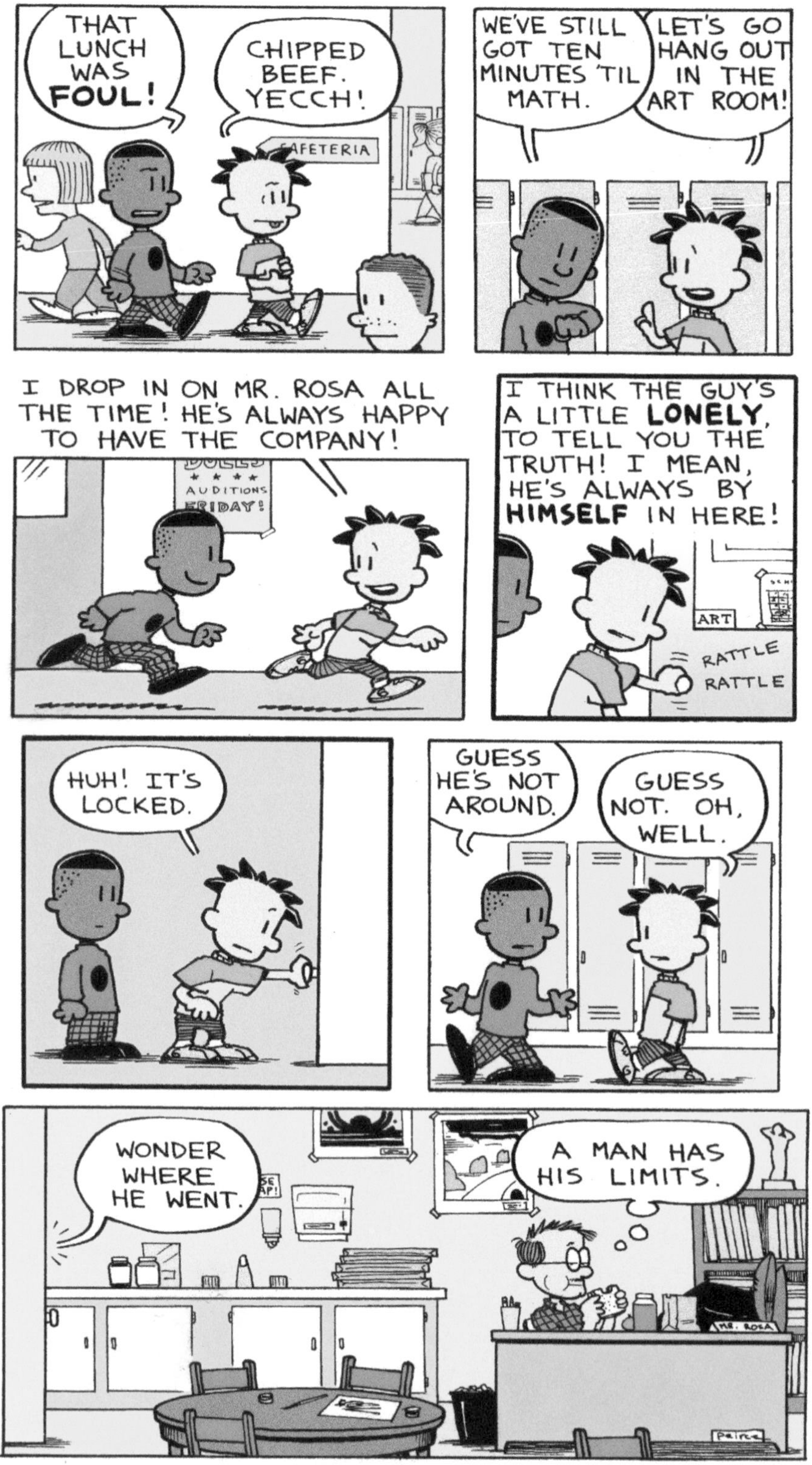
THAT LUNCH WAS **FOUL**!
CHIPPED BEEF. YECCH!
CAFETERIA
WE'VE STILL GOT TEN MINUTES 'TIL MATH.
LET'S GO HANG OUT IN THE ART ROOM!
I DROP IN ON MR. ROSA ALL THE TIME! HE'S ALWAYS HAPPY TO HAVE THE COMPANY!
AUDITIONS FRIDAY!
I THINK THE GUY'S A LITTLE **LONELY**, TO TELL YOU THE TRUTH! I MEAN, HE'S ALWAYS BY **HIMSELF** IN HERE!
ART
RATTLE RATTLE
HUH! IT'S LOCKED.
GUESS HE'S NOT AROUND.
GUESS NOT. OH, WELL.
WONDER WHERE HE WENT.
A MAN HAS HIS LIMITS.
MR. ROSA

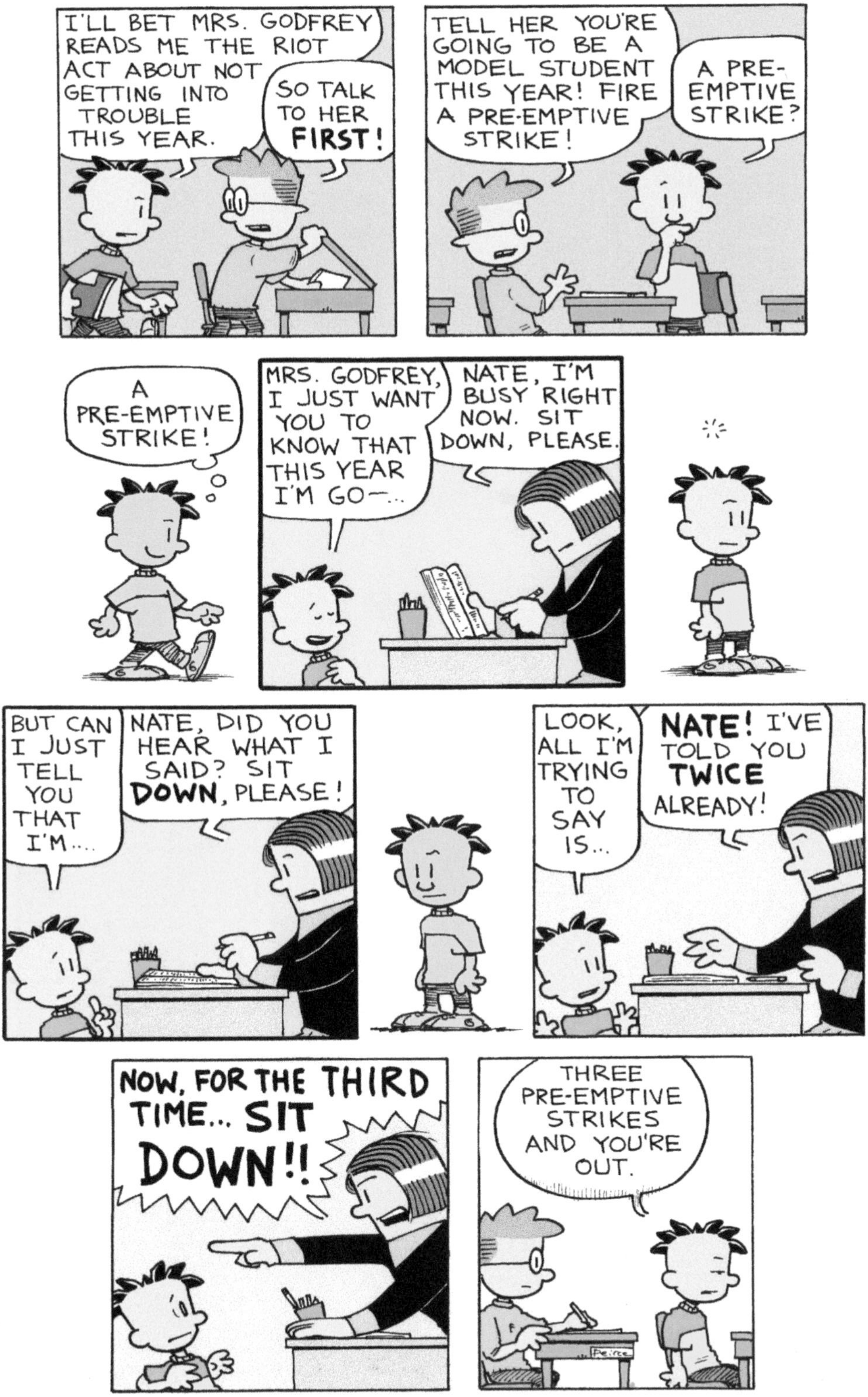
I'LL BET MRS. GODFREY READS ME THE RIOT ACT ABOUT NOT GETTING INTO TROUBLE THIS YEAR.
SO TALK TO HER FIRST!
TELL HER YOU'RE GOING TO BE A MODEL STUDENT THIS YEAR! FIRE A PRE-EMPTIVE STRIKE!
A PRE-EMPTIVE STRIKE?
A PRE-EMPTIVE STRIKE!
MRS. GODFREY, I JUST WANT YOU TO KNOW THAT THIS YEAR I'M GO—...
NATE, I'M BUSY RIGHT NOW. SIT DOWN, PLEASE.
BUT CAN I JUST TELL YOU THAT I'M...
NATE, DID YOU HEAR WHAT I SAID? SIT DOWN, PLEASE!
LOOK, ALL I'M TRYING TO SAY IS...
NATE! I'VE TOLD YOU TWICE ALREADY!
NOW, FOR THE THIRD TIME... SIT DOWN!!
THREE PRE-EMPTIVE STRIKES AND YOU'RE OUT.

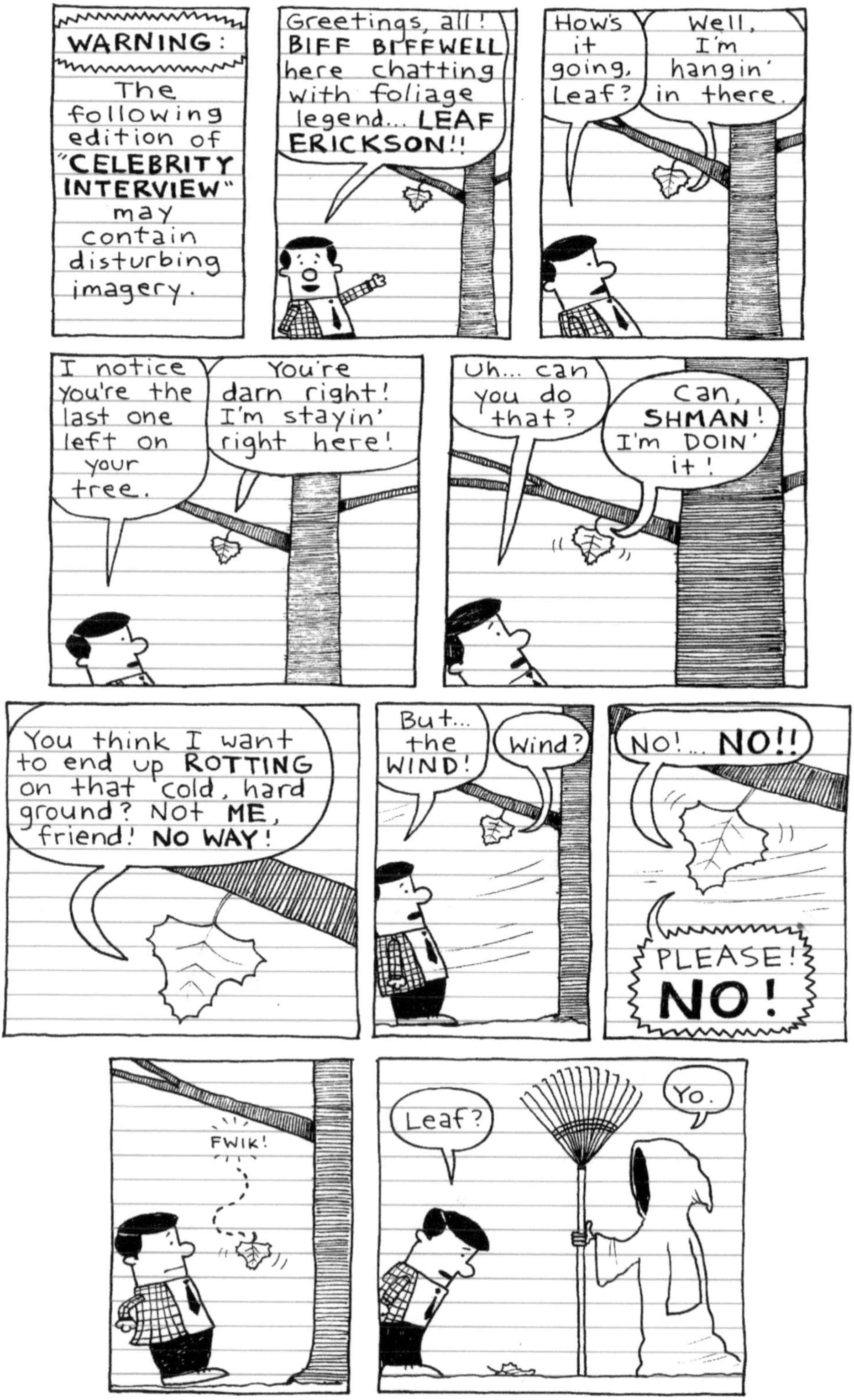
WARNING:
The following edition of "CELEBRITY INTERVIEW" may contain disturbing imagery.
Greetings, all! BIFF BIFFWELL here chatting with foliage legend... LEAF ERICKSON!!
How's it going, Leaf?
Well, I'm hangin' in there.
I notice you're the last one left on your tree.
You're darn right! I'm stayin' right here!
Uh... can you do that?
Can, SHMAN! I'm DOIN' it!
You think I want to end up ROTTING on that cold, hard ground? Not ME, friend! NO WAY!
But... the WIND!
Wind?
No!... NO!!
PLEASE! NO!
FWIK!
Leaf?
Yo.

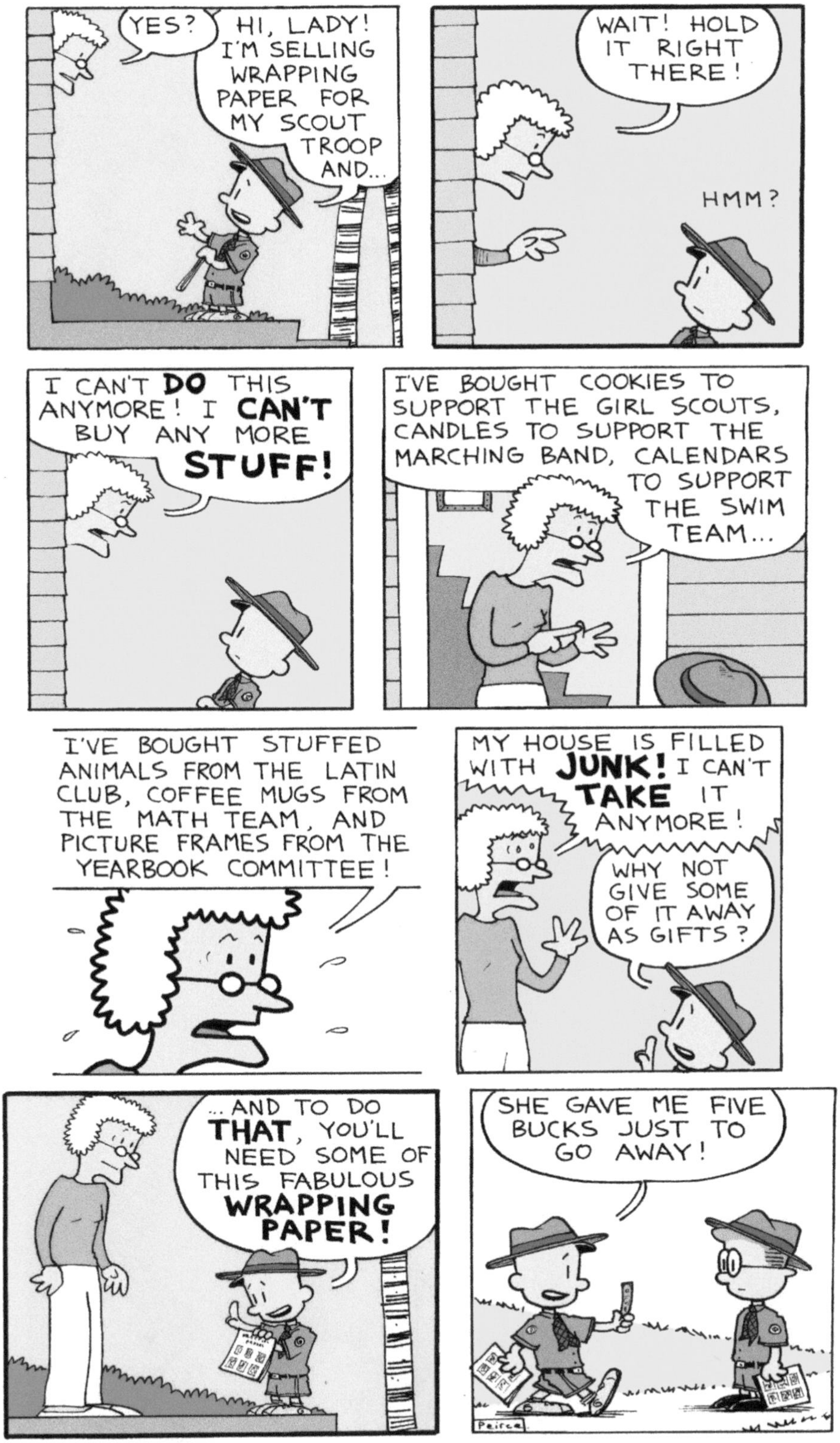
YES?
HI, LADY! I'M SELLING WRAPPING PAPER FOR MY SCOUT TROOP AND...
WAIT! HOLD IT RIGHT THERE!
HMM?
I CAN'T **DO** THIS ANYMORE! I **CAN'T** BUY ANY MORE **STUFF!**
I'VE BOUGHT COOKIES TO SUPPORT THE GIRL SCOUTS, CANDLES TO SUPPORT THE MARCHING BAND, CALENDARS TO SUPPORT THE SWIM TEAM...
I'VE BOUGHT STUFFED ANIMALS FROM THE LATIN CLUB, COFFEE MUGS FROM THE MATH TEAM, AND PICTURE FRAMES FROM THE YEARBOOK COMMITTEE!
MY HOUSE IS FILLED WITH **JUNK!** I CAN'T **TAKE** IT ANYMORE!
WHY NOT GIVE SOME OF IT AWAY AS GIFTS?
...AND TO DO **THAT**, YOU'LL NEED SOME OF THIS FABULOUS **WRAPPING PAPER!**
SHE GAVE ME FIVE BUCKS JUST TO GO AWAY!
Peirce

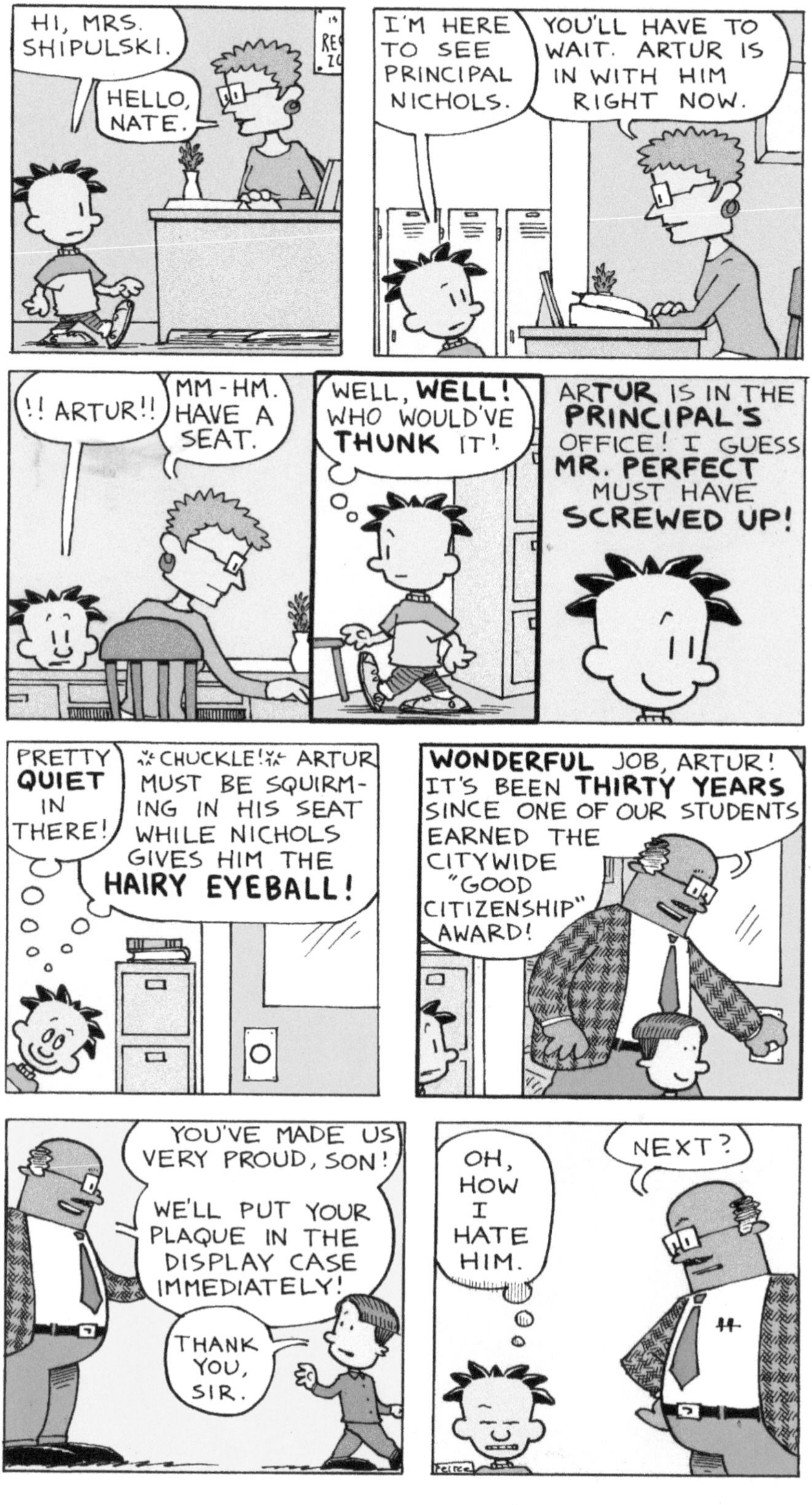
HI, MRS. SHIPULSKI.
HELLO, NATE.
I'M HERE TO SEE PRINCIPAL NICHOLS.
YOU'LL HAVE TO WAIT. ARTUR IS IN WITH HIM RIGHT NOW.
!! ARTUR!!
MM-HM. HAVE A SEAT.
WELL, WELL! WHO WOULD'VE THUNK IT!
ARTUR IS IN THE PRINCIPAL'S OFFICE! I GUESS MR. PERFECT MUST HAVE SCREWED UP!
PRETTY QUIET IN THERE!
CHUCKLE! ARTUR MUST BE SQUIRMING IN HIS SEAT WHILE NICHOLS GIVES HIM THE HAIRY EYEBALL!
WONDERFUL JOB, ARTUR! IT'S BEEN THIRTY YEARS SINCE ONE OF OUR STUDENTS EARNED THE CITYWIDE "GOOD CITIZENSHIP" AWARD!
YOU'VE MADE US VERY PROUD, SON!
WE'LL PUT YOUR PLAQUE IN THE DISPLAY CASE IMMEDIATELY!
THANK YOU, SIR.
OH, HOW I HATE HIM.
NEXT?

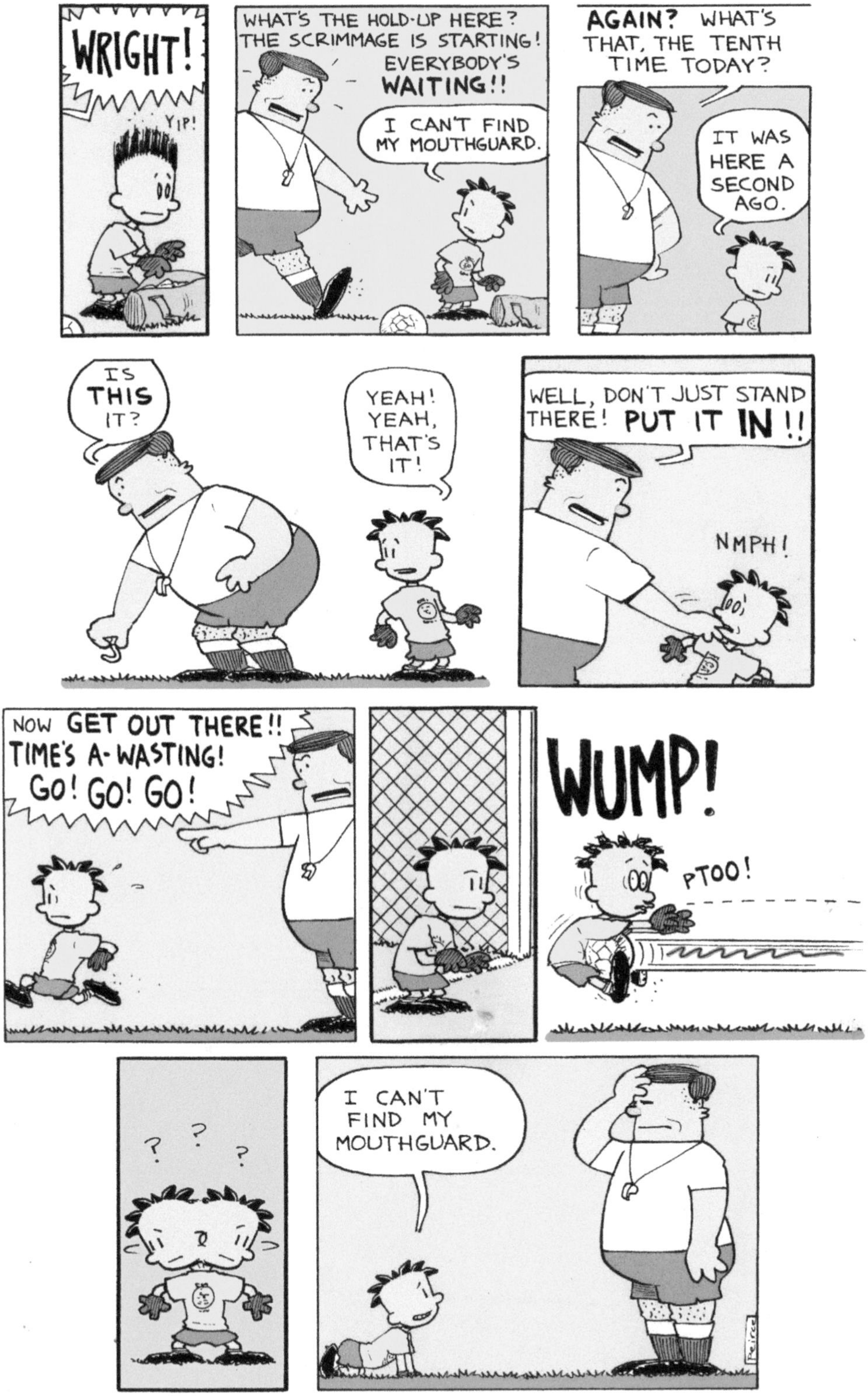
WRIGHT!
YIP!
WHAT'S THE HOLD-UP HERE? THE SCRIMMAGE IS STARTING! EVERYBODY'S WAITING!!
I CAN'T FIND MY MOUTHGUARD.
AGAIN? WHAT'S THAT, THE TENTH TIME TODAY?
IT WAS HERE A SECOND AGO.
IS THIS IT?
YEAH! YEAH, THAT'S IT!
WELL, DON'T JUST STAND THERE! PUT IT IN!!
NMPH!
NOW GET OUT THERE!! TIME'S A-WASTING! GO! GO! GO!
WUMP!
PTOO!
? ? ?
I CAN'T FIND MY MOUTHGUARD.
Peirce

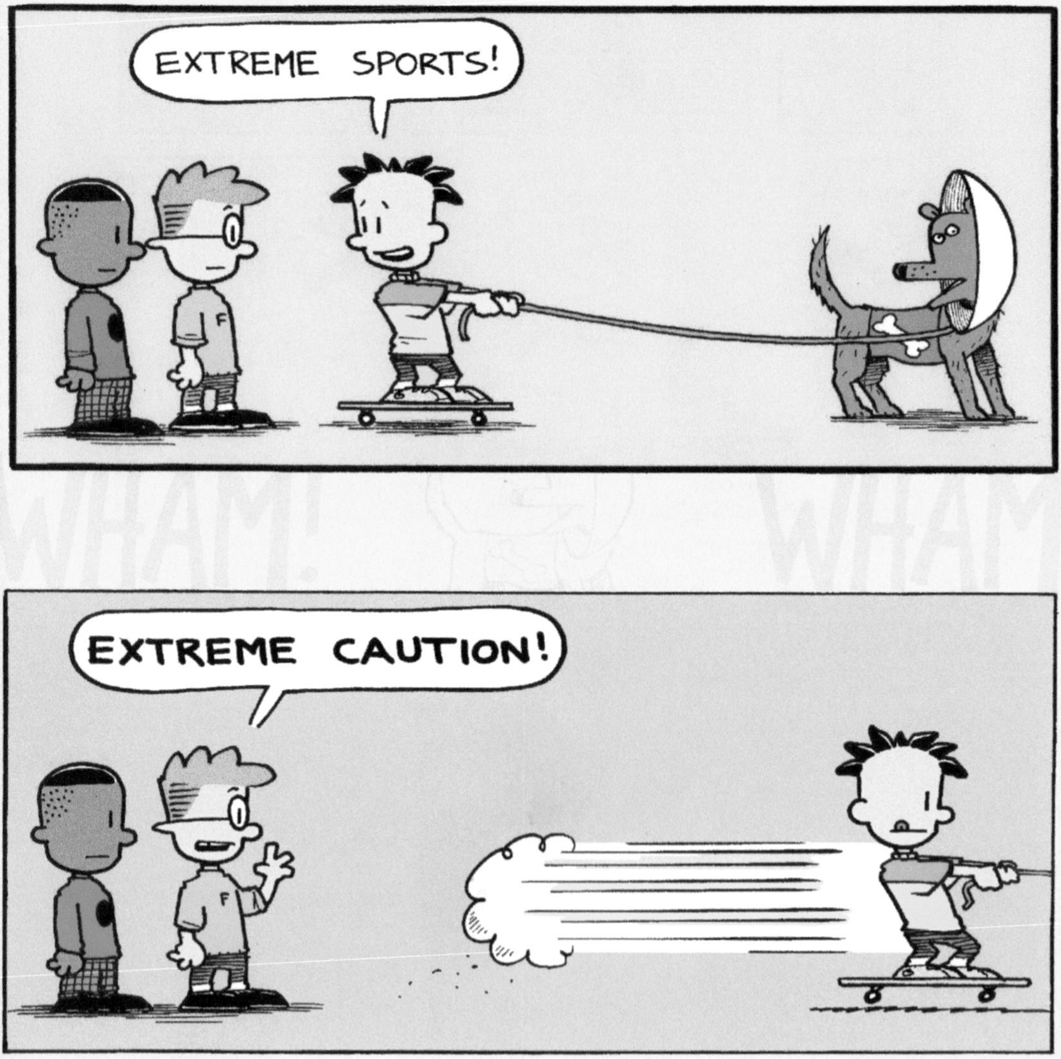
EXTREME SPORTS!
EXTREME CAUTION!

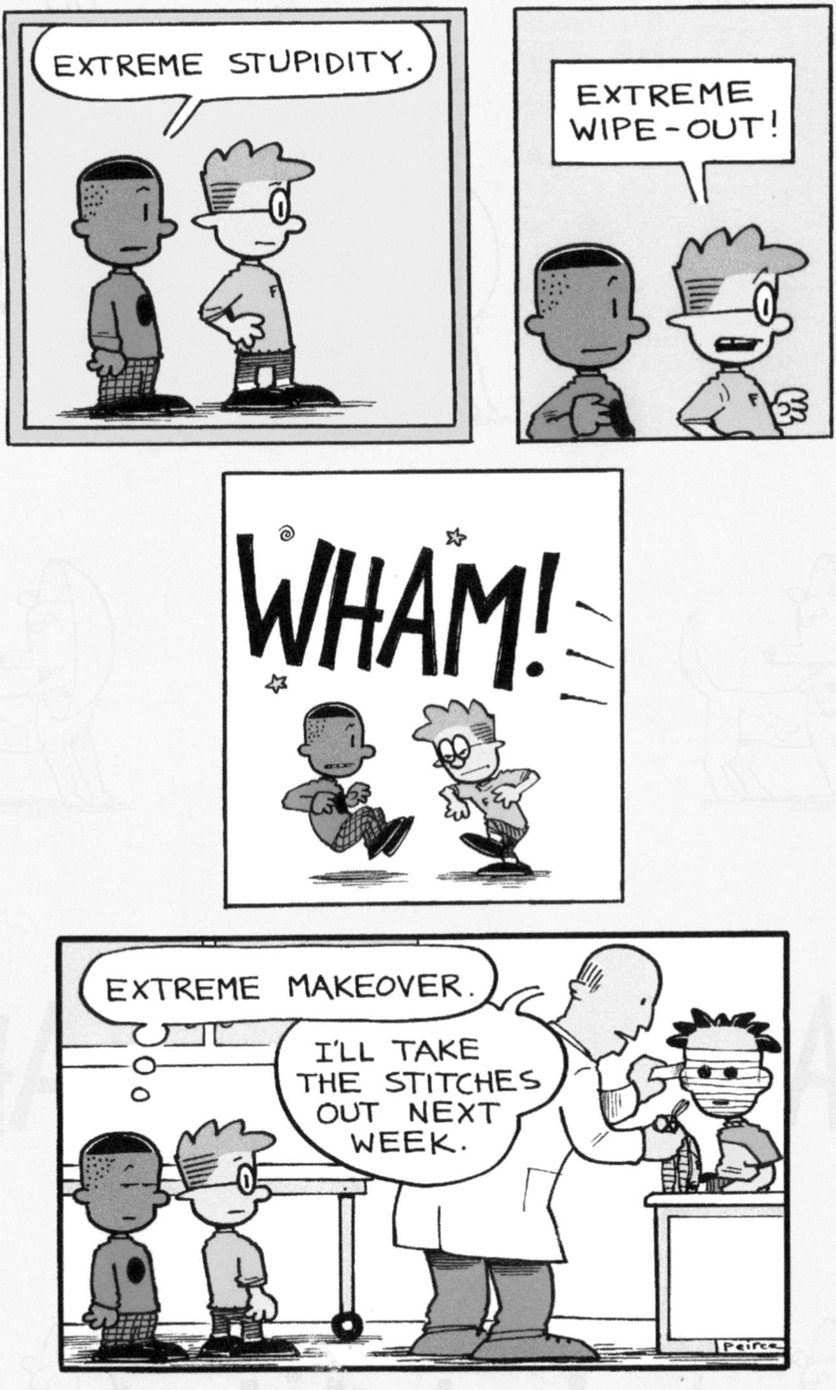
EXTREME STUPIDITY.
EXTREME WIPE-OUT!
WHAM!
EXTREME MAKEOVER.
I'LL TAKE THE STITCHES OUT NEXT WEEK.
Peirce

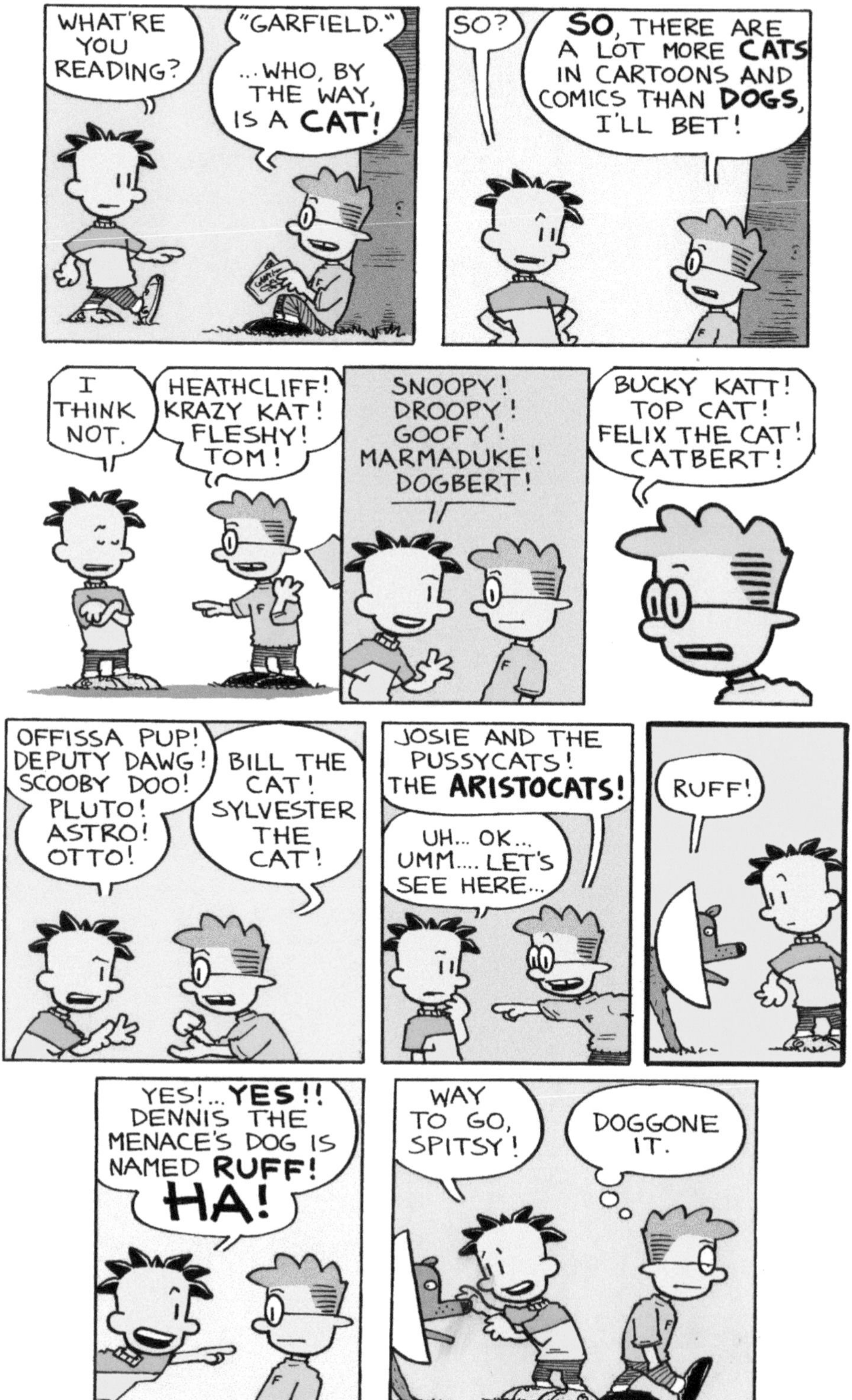
WHAT'RE YOU READING?
"GARFIELD." ...WHO, BY THE WAY, IS A CAT!
SO?
SO, THERE ARE A LOT MORE CATS IN CARTOONS AND COMICS THAN DOGS, I'LL BET!
I THINK NOT.
HEATHCLIFF! KRAZY KAT! FLESHY! TOM!
SNOOPY! DROOPY! GOOFY! MARMADUKE! DOGBERT!
BUCKY KATT! TOP CAT! FELIX THE CAT! CATBERT!
OFFISSA PUP! DEPUTY DAWG! SCOOBY DOO! PLUTO! ASTRO! OTTO!
BILL THE CAT! SYLVESTER THE CAT!
JOSIE AND THE PUSSYCATS! THE ARISTOCATS!
UH... OK... UMM.... LET'S SEE HERE...
RUFF!
YES!...YES!! DENNIS THE MENACE'S DOG IS NAMED RUFF! HA!
WAY TO GO, SPITSY!
DOGGONE IT.
Peirce

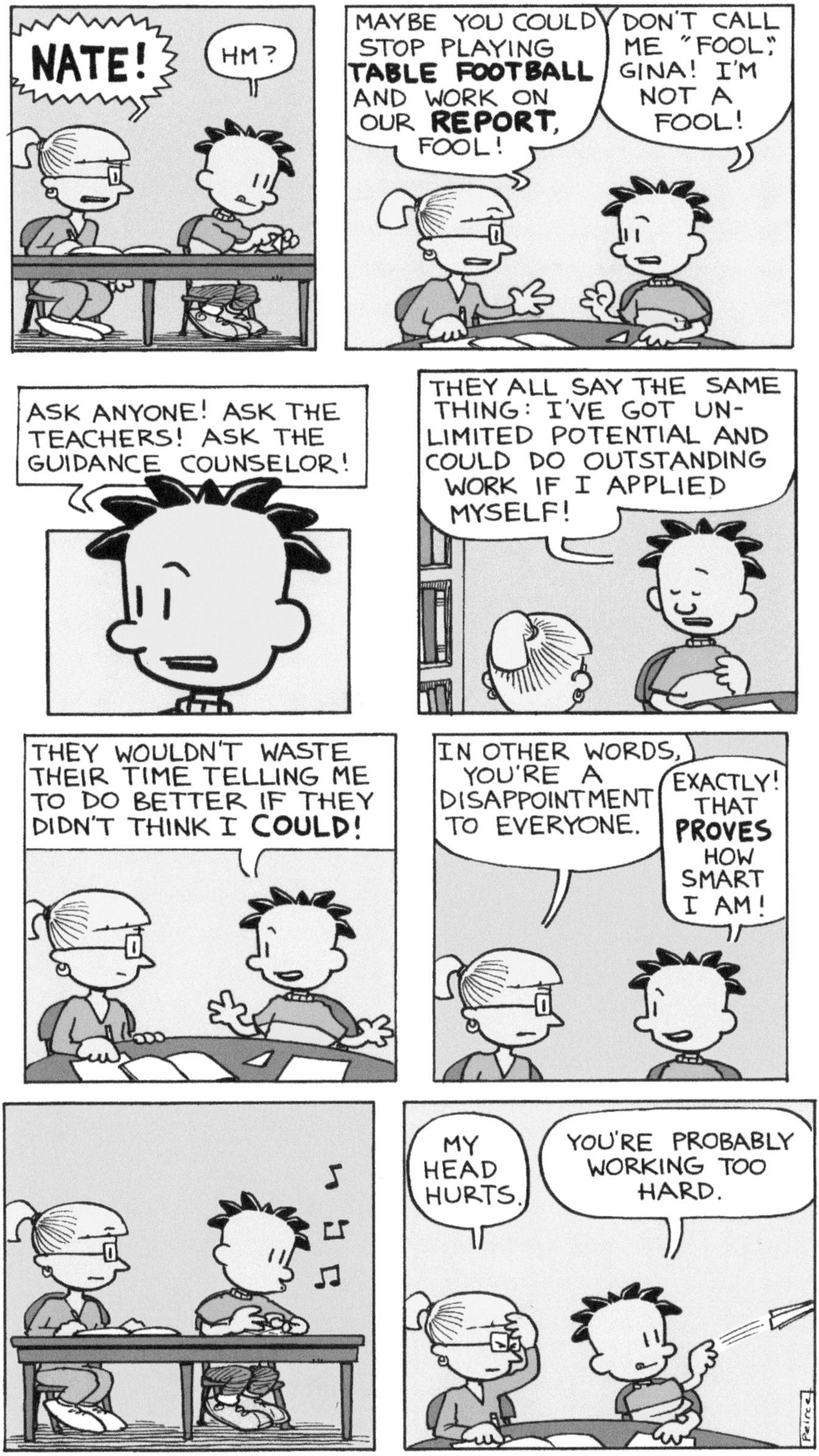
NATE!
HM?
MAYBE YOU COULD STOP PLAYING TABLE FOOTBALL AND WORK ON OUR REPORT, FOOL!
DON'T CALL ME "FOOL," GINA! I'M NOT A FOOL!
ASK ANYONE! ASK THE TEACHERS! ASK THE GUIDANCE COUNSELOR!
THEY ALL SAY THE SAME THING: I'VE GOT UN-LIMITED POTENTIAL AND COULD DO OUTSTANDING WORK IF I APPLIED MYSELF!
THEY WOULDN'T WASTE THEIR TIME TELLING ME TO DO BETTER IF THEY DIDN'T THINK I COULD!
IN OTHER WORDS, YOU'RE A DISAPPOINTMENT TO EVERYONE.
EXACTLY! THAT PROVES HOW SMART I AM!
MY HEAD HURTS.
YOU'RE PROBABLY WORKING TOO HARD.
Peirce

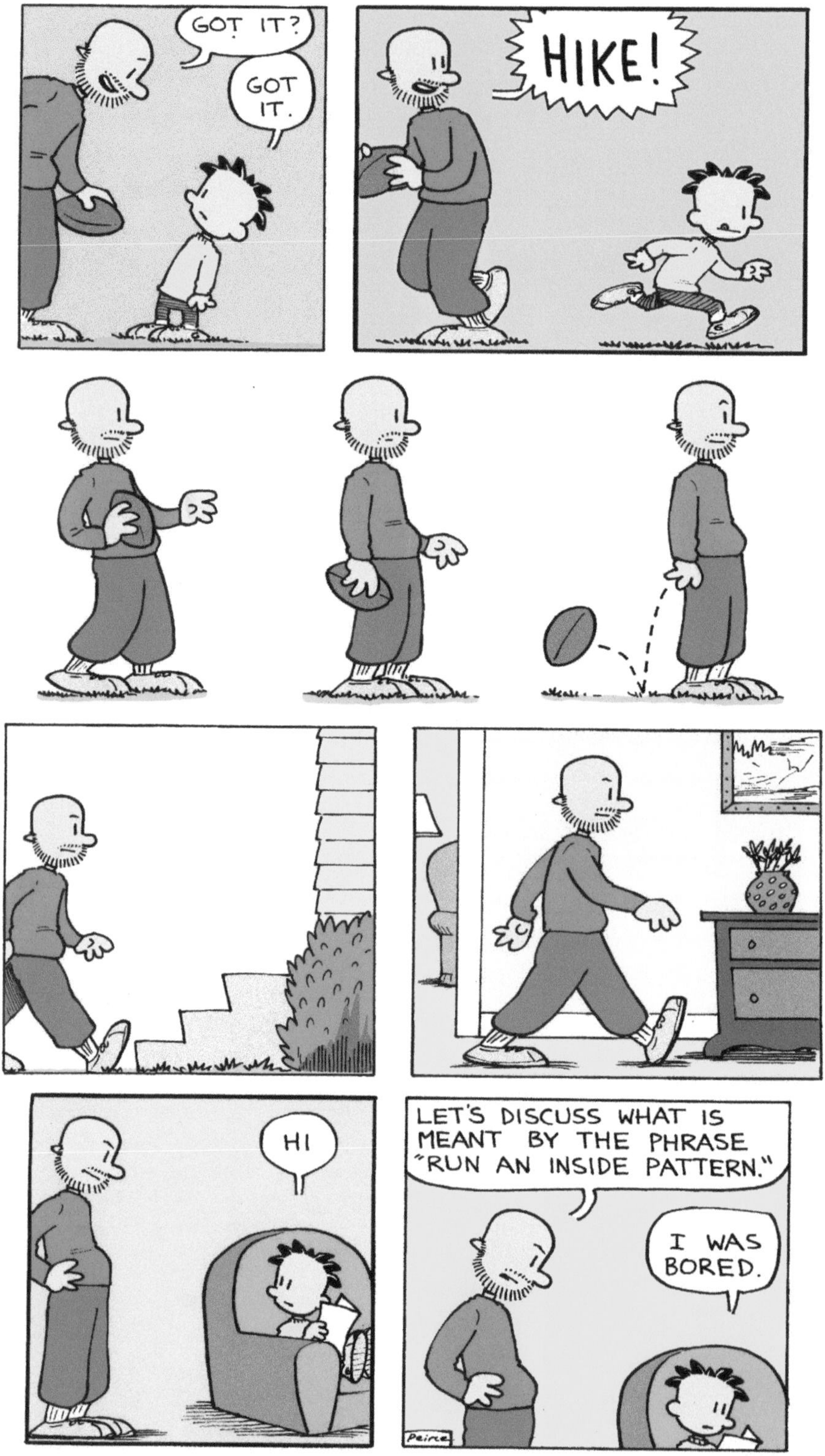
GOT IT?
GOT IT.
HIKE!
HI
LET'S DISCUSS WHAT IS MEANT BY THE PHRASE "RUN AN INSIDE PATTERN."
I WAS BORED.
Peirce

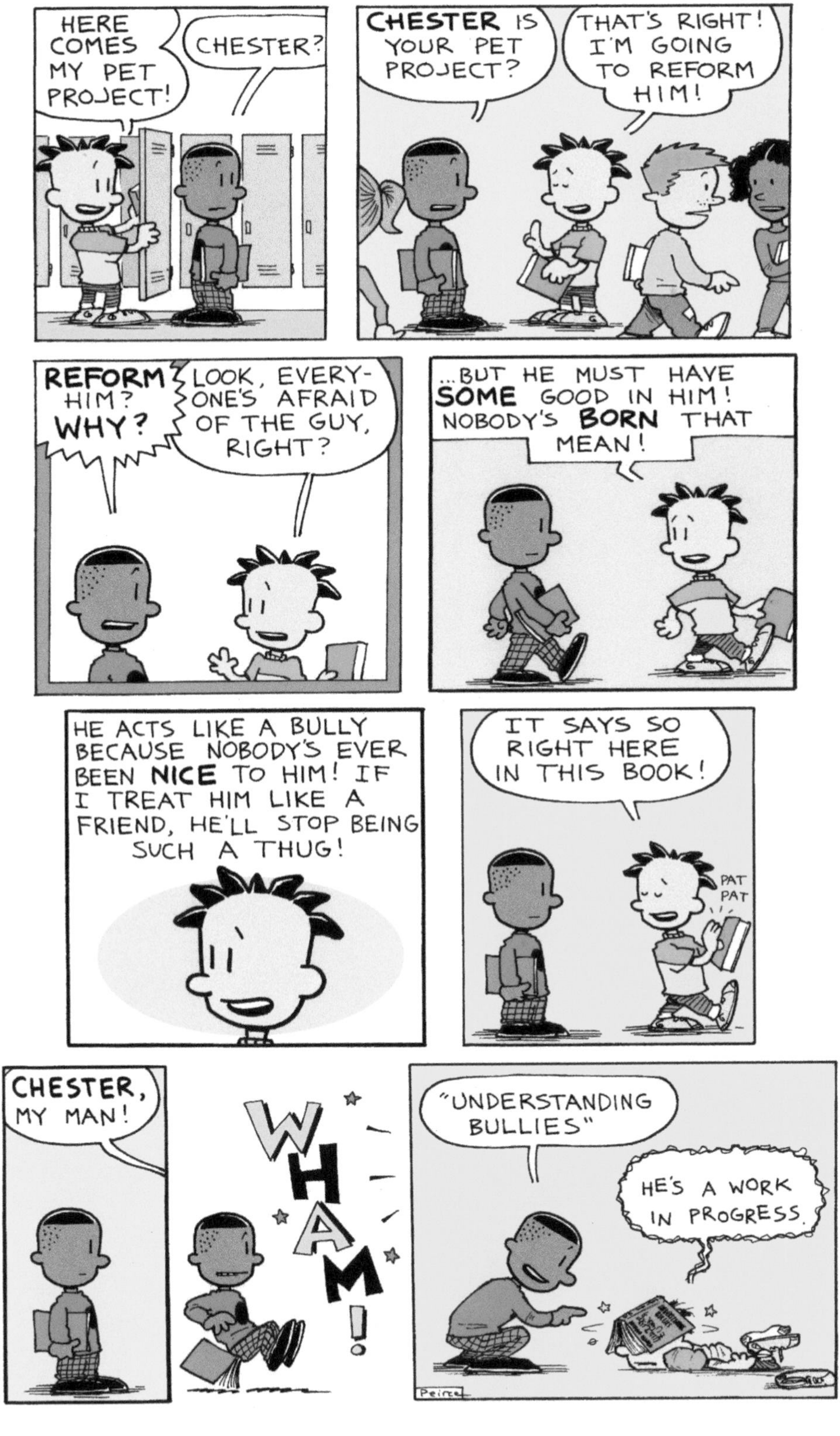
HERE COMES MY PET PROJECT!
CHESTER?
CHESTER IS YOUR PET PROJECT?
THAT'S RIGHT! I'M GOING TO REFORM HIM!
REFORM HIM? WHY?
LOOK, EVERYONE'S AFRAID OF THE GUY, RIGHT?
...BUT HE MUST HAVE SOME GOOD IN HIM! NOBODY'S BORN THAT MEAN!
HE ACTS LIKE A BULLY BECAUSE NOBODY'S EVER BEEN NICE TO HIM! IF I TREAT HIM LIKE A FRIEND, HE'LL STOP BEING SUCH A THUG!
IT SAYS SO RIGHT HERE IN THIS BOOK!
PAT PAT
CHESTER, MY MAN!
WHAM!
"UNDERSTANDING BULLIES"
HE'S A WORK IN PROGRESS.
Peirce

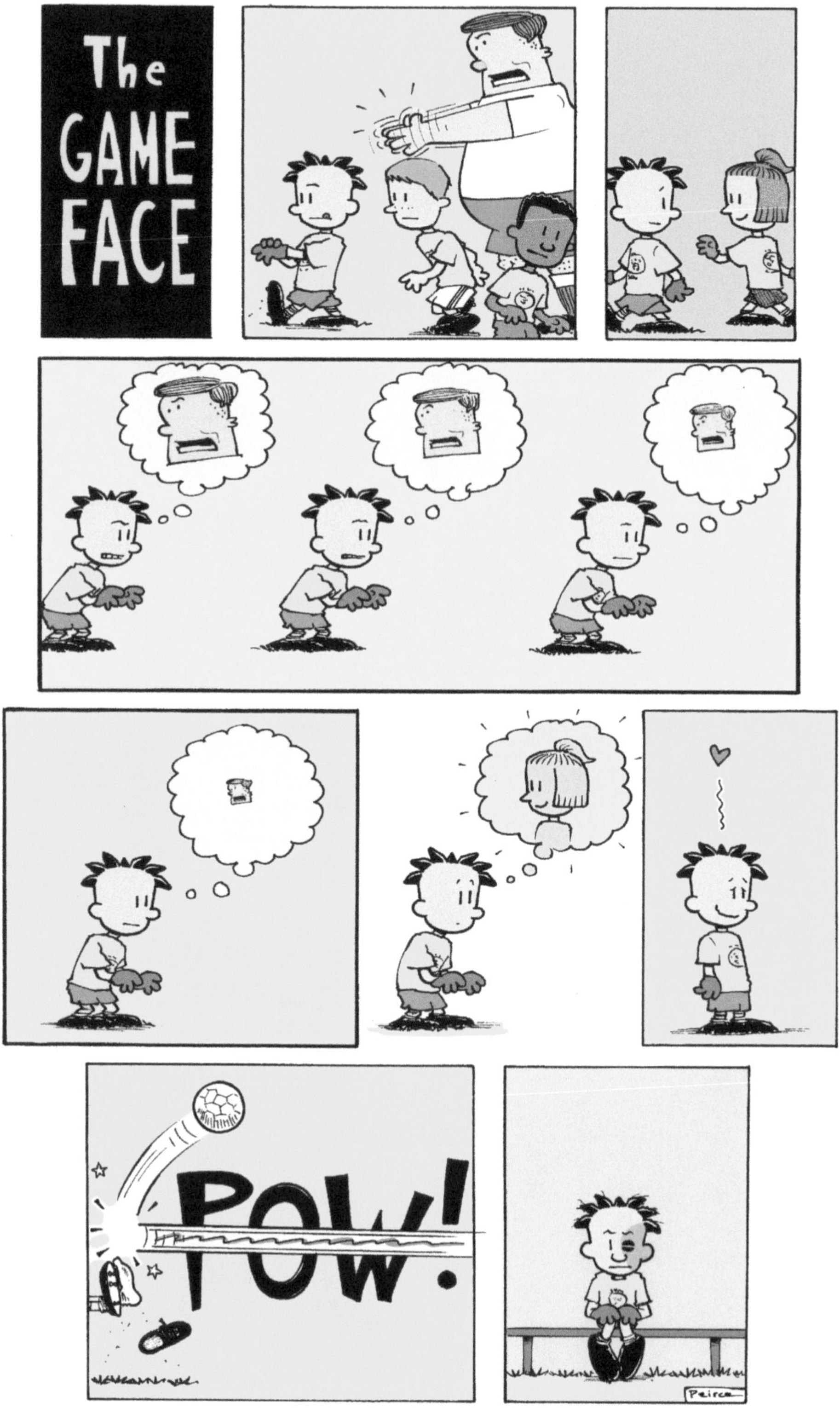
The GAME FACE
POW!
Peirce

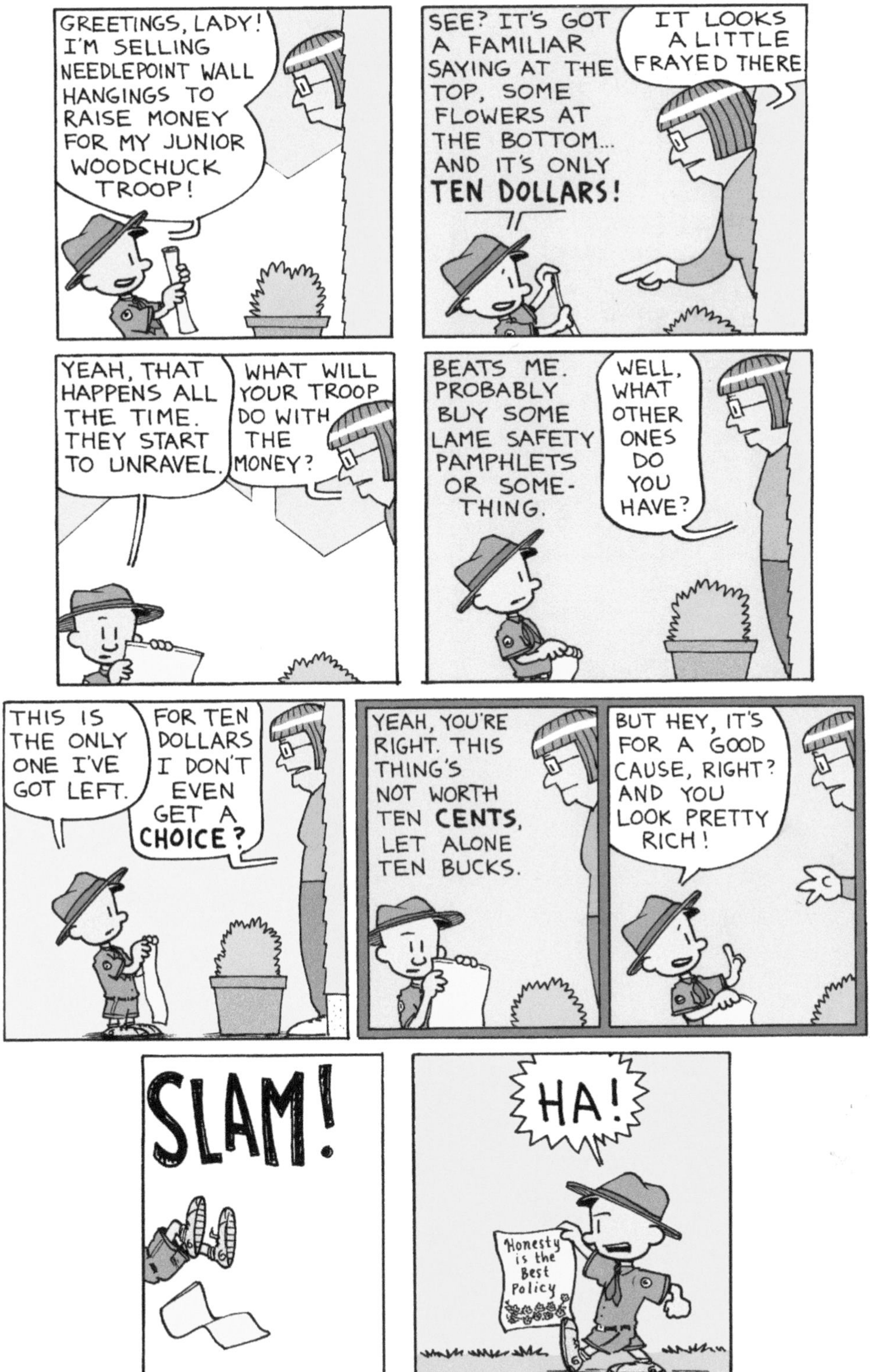
GREETINGS, LADY! I'M SELLING NEEDLEPOINT WALL HANGINGS TO RAISE MONEY FOR MY JUNIOR WOODCHUCK TROOP!
SEE? IT'S GOT A FAMILIAR SAYING AT THE TOP, SOME FLOWERS AT THE BOTTOM... AND IT'S ONLY TEN DOLLARS!
IT LOOKS A LITTLE FRAYED THERE.
YEAH, THAT HAPPENS ALL THE TIME. THEY START TO UNRAVEL.
WHAT WILL YOUR TROOP DO WITH THE MONEY?
BEATS ME. PROBABLY BUY SOME LAME SAFETY PAMPHLETS OR SOME-THING.
WELL, WHAT OTHER ONES DO YOU HAVE?
THIS IS THE ONLY ONE I'VE GOT LEFT.
FOR TEN DOLLARS I DON'T EVEN GET A CHOICE?
YEAH, YOU'RE RIGHT. THIS THING'S NOT WORTH TEN CENTS, LET ALONE TEN BUCKS.
BUT HEY, IT'S FOR A GOOD CAUSE, RIGHT? AND YOU LOOK PRETTY RICH!
SLAM!
HA!
Honesty is the Best Policy
Peirce

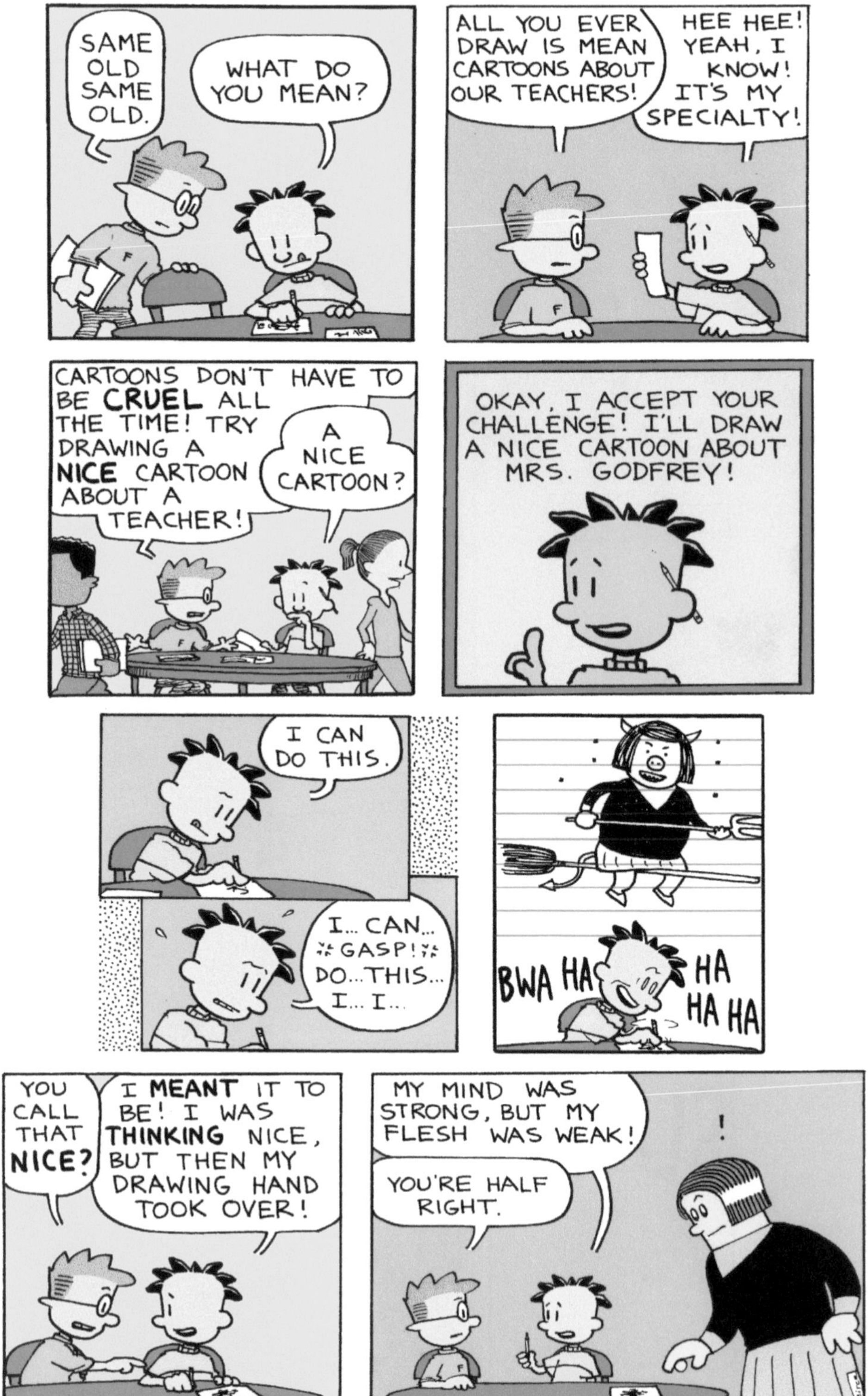
SAME OLD SAME OLD.
WHAT DO YOU MEAN?
ALL YOU EVER DRAW IS MEAN CARTOONS ABOUT OUR TEACHERS!
HEE HEE! YEAH, I KNOW! IT'S MY SPECIALTY!
CARTOONS DON'T HAVE TO BE CRUEL ALL THE TIME! TRY DRAWING A NICE CARTOON ABOUT A TEACHER!
A NICE CARTOON?
OKAY, I ACCEPT YOUR CHALLENGE! I'LL DRAW A NICE CARTOON ABOUT MRS. GODFREY!
I CAN DO THIS.
I... CAN... GASP! DO... THIS... I... I...
BWA HA HA HA HA HA
YOU CALL THAT NICE?
I MEANT IT TO BE! I WAS THINKING NICE, BUT THEN MY DRAWING HAND TOOK OVER!
MY MIND WAS STRONG, BUT MY FLESH WAS WEAK!
YOU'RE HALF RIGHT.
!

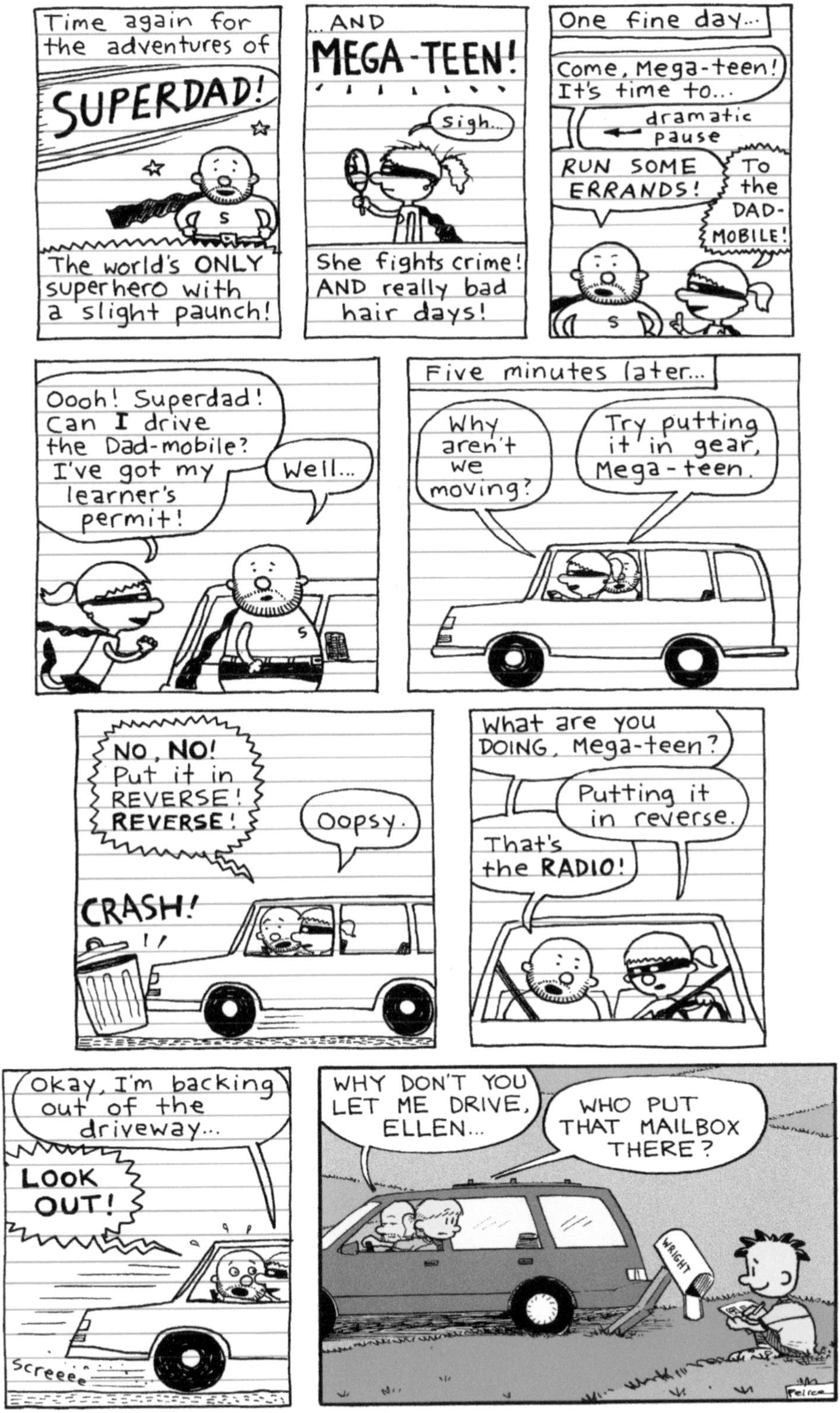
Time again for the adventures of
SUPERDAD!
The world's ONLY superhero with a slight paunch!
...AND
MEGA-TEEN!
sigh...
She fights crime! AND really bad hair days!
One fine day...
Come, Mega-teen! It's time to...
dramatic pause
RUN SOME ERRANDS!
To the DAD-MOBILE!
Oooh! Superdad! Can I drive the Dad-mobile? I've got my learner's permit!
Well...
Five minutes later...
Why aren't we moving?
Try putting it in gear, Mega-teen.
NO, NO! Put it in REVERSE! REVERSE!
Oopsy.
CRASH!
What are you DOING, Mega-teen?
Putting it in reverse.
That's the RADIO!
Okay, I'm backing out of the driveway...
LOOK OUT!
Screeee
WHY DON'T YOU LET ME DRIVE, ELLEN...
WHO PUT THAT MAILBOX THERE?
WRIGHT

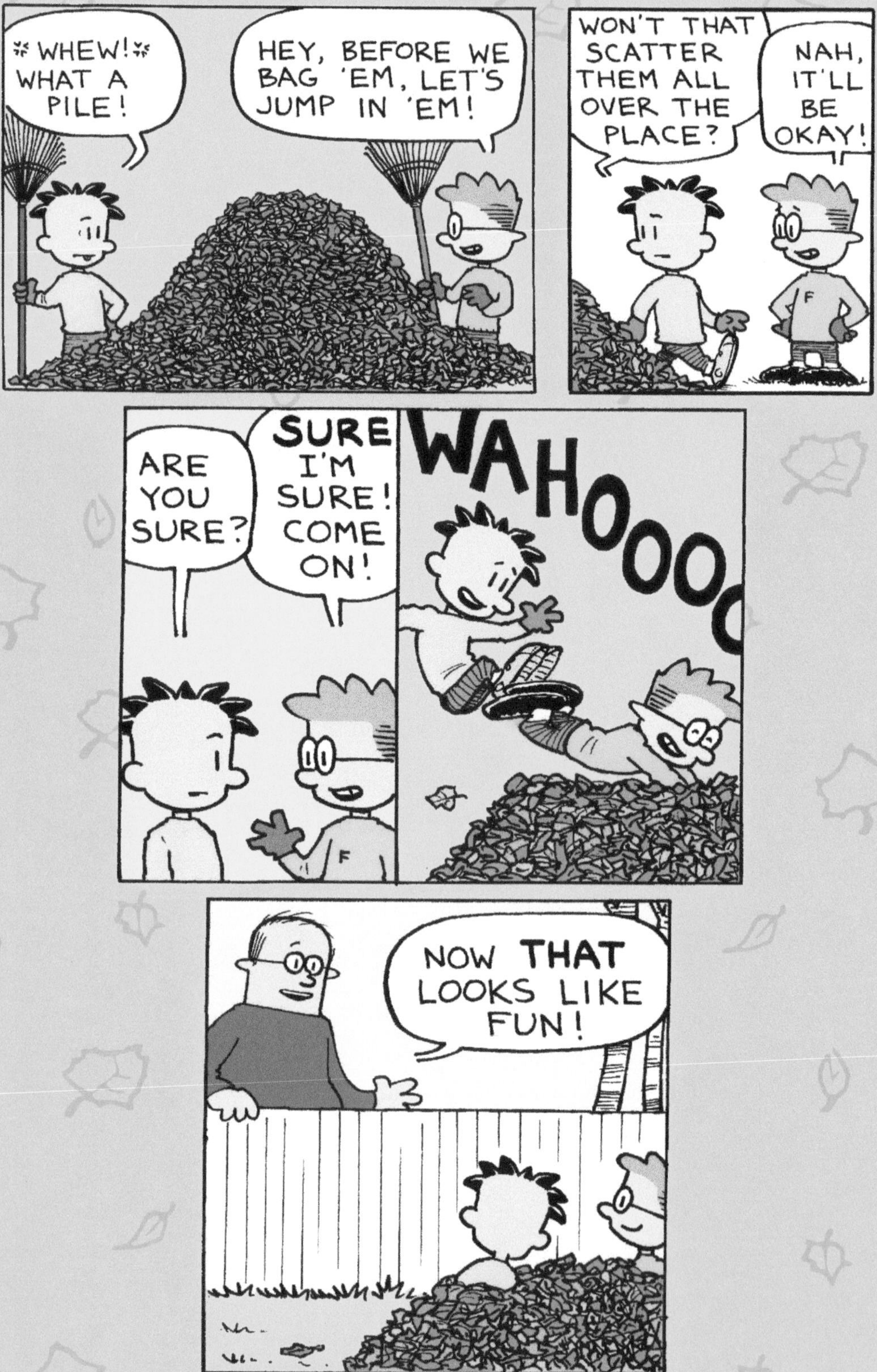
WHEW! WHAT A PILE!
HEY, BEFORE WE BAG 'EM, LET'S JUMP IN 'EM!
WON'T THAT SCATTER THEM ALL OVER THE PLACE?
NAH, IT'LL BE OKAY!
ARE YOU SURE?
SURE I'M SURE! COME ON!
WAHOOOO
NOW THAT LOOKS LIKE FUN!

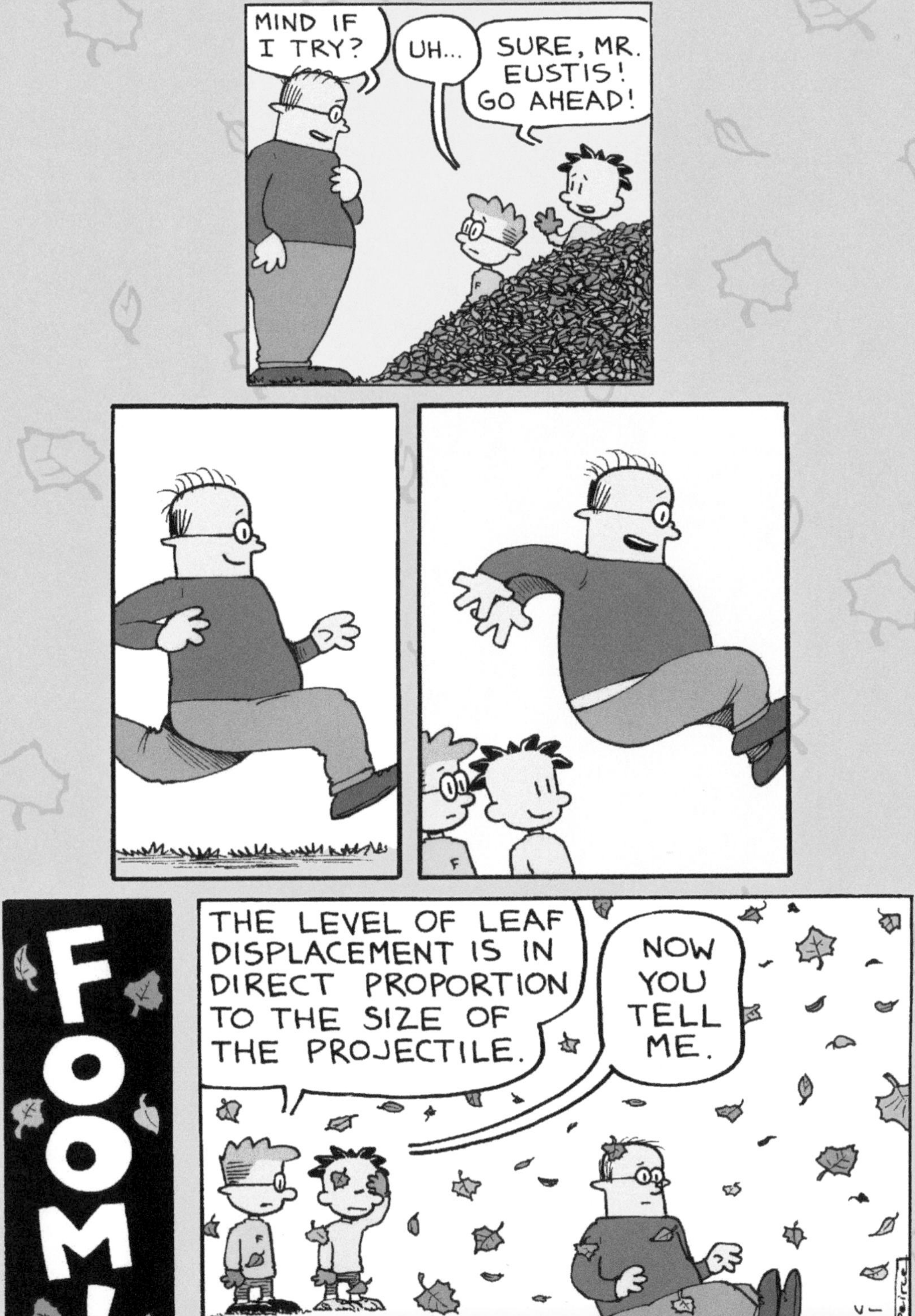
MIND IF I TRY?
UH...
SURE, MR. EUSTIS! GO AHEAD!
FOOM!
THE LEVEL OF LEAF DISPLACEMENT IS IN DIRECT PROPORTION TO THE SIZE OF THE PROJECTILE.
NOW YOU TELL ME.
Peirce

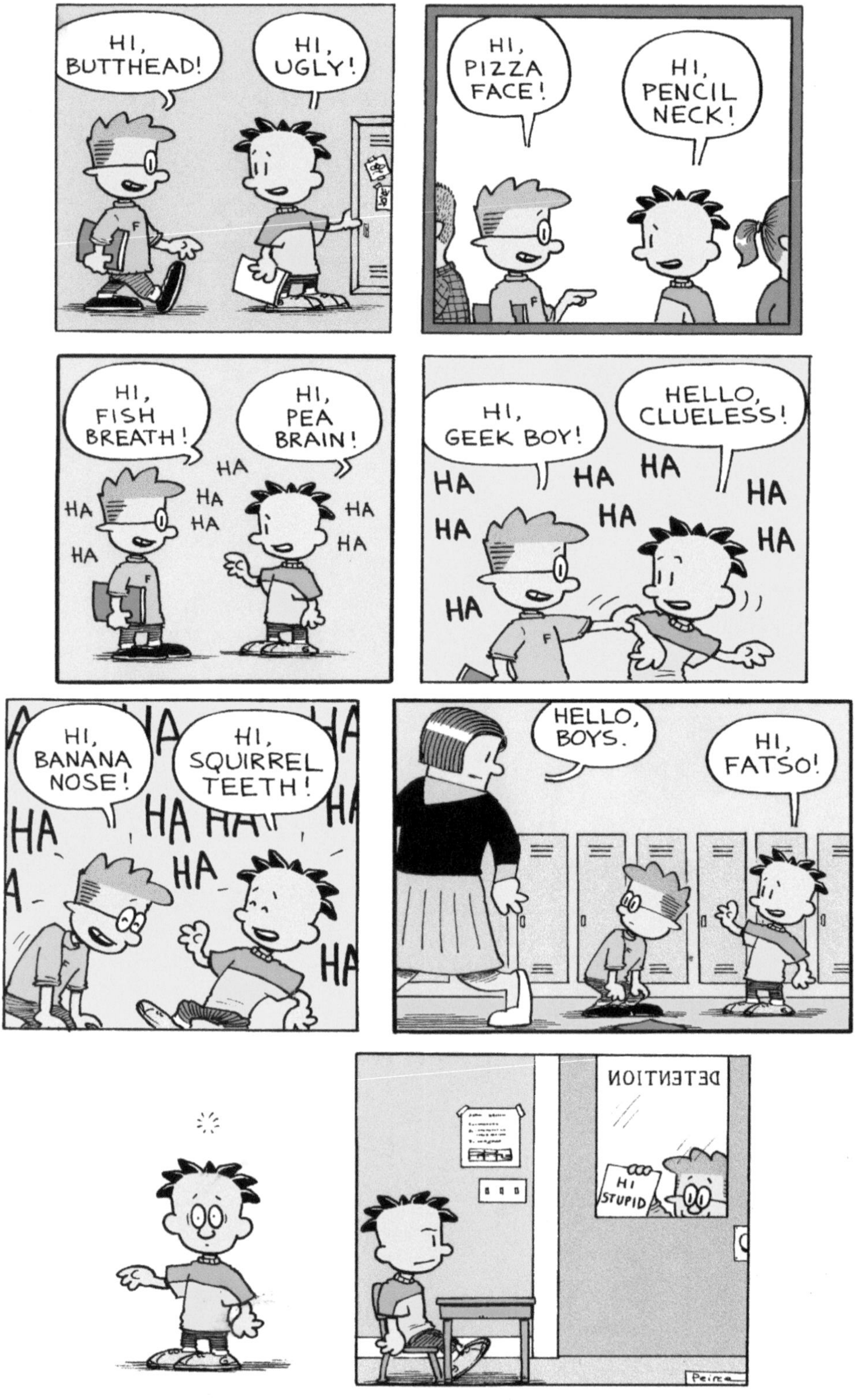
HI, BUTTHEAD!
HI, UGLY!
HI, PIZZA FACE!
HI, PENCIL NECK!
HI, FISH BREATH!
HI, PEA BRAIN!
HA HA HA HA HA HA HA
HI, GEEK BOY!
HELLO, CLUELESS!
HA HA HA HA HA HA HA HA HA
HI, BANANA NOSE!
HI, SQUIRREL TEETH!
HA HA HA HA HA
HELLO, BOYS.
HI, FATSO!
DETENTION
HI STUPID
Peirce

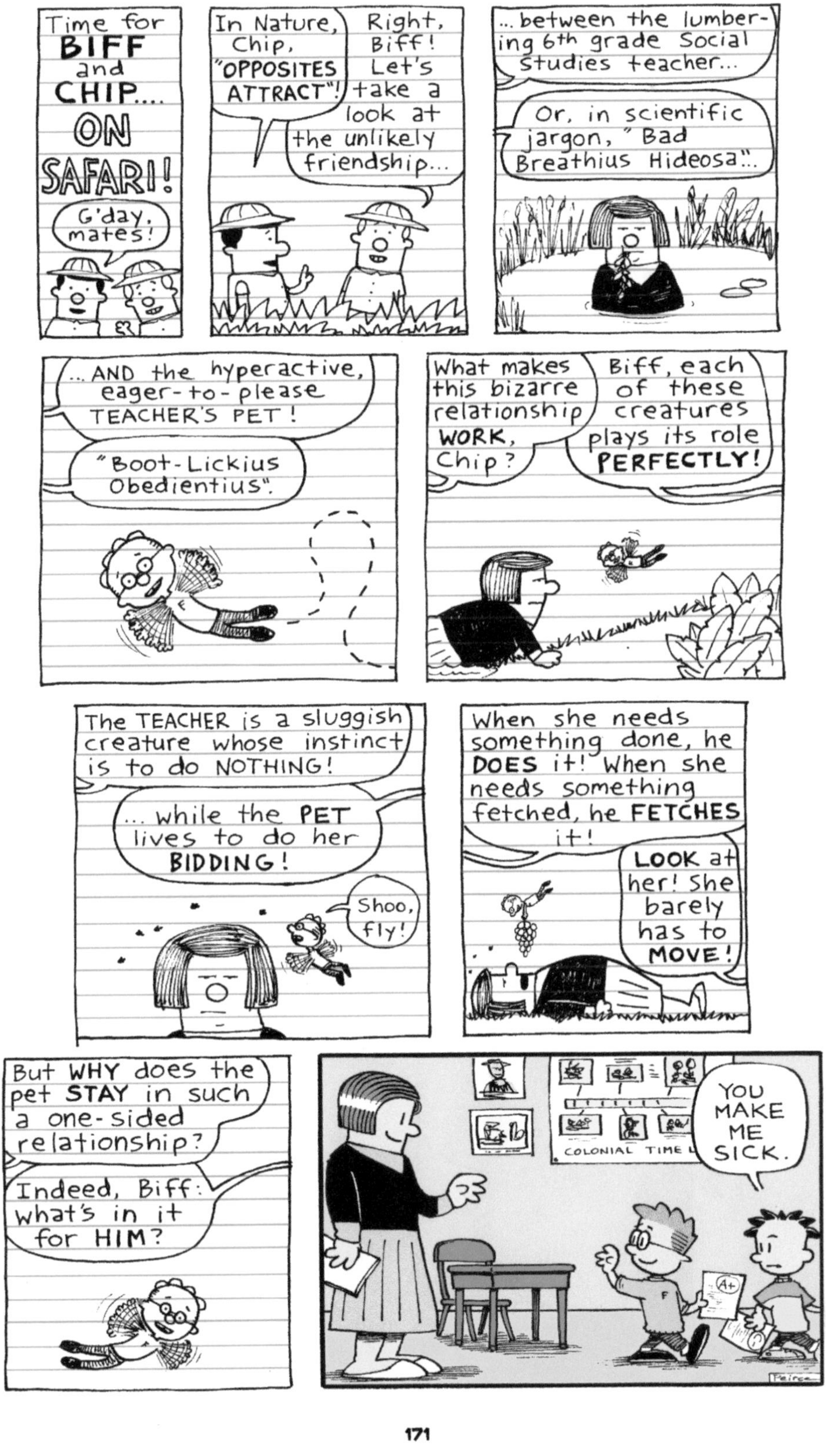

Time for BIFF and CHIP.... ON SAFARI!
G'day, mates!
In Nature, Chip, "OPPOSITES ATTRACT"!
Right, Biff! Let's take a look at the unlikely friendship...
...between the lumbering 6th grade Social Studies teacher...
Or, in scientific jargon, "Bad Breathius Hideosa"...
...AND the hyperactive, eager-to-please TEACHER'S PET!
"Boot-Lickius Obedientius".
What makes this bizarre relationship WORK, Chip?
Biff, each of these creatures plays its role PERFECTLY!
The TEACHER is a sluggish creature whose instinct is to do NOTHING!
...while the PET lives to do her BIDDING!
Shoo, fly!
When she needs something done, he DOES it! When she needs something fetched, he FETCHES it!
LOOK at her! She barely has to MOVE!
But WHY does the pet STAY in such a one-sided relationship?
Indeed, Biff: what's in it for HIM?
COLONIAL TIME L
YOU MAKE ME SICK.
A+

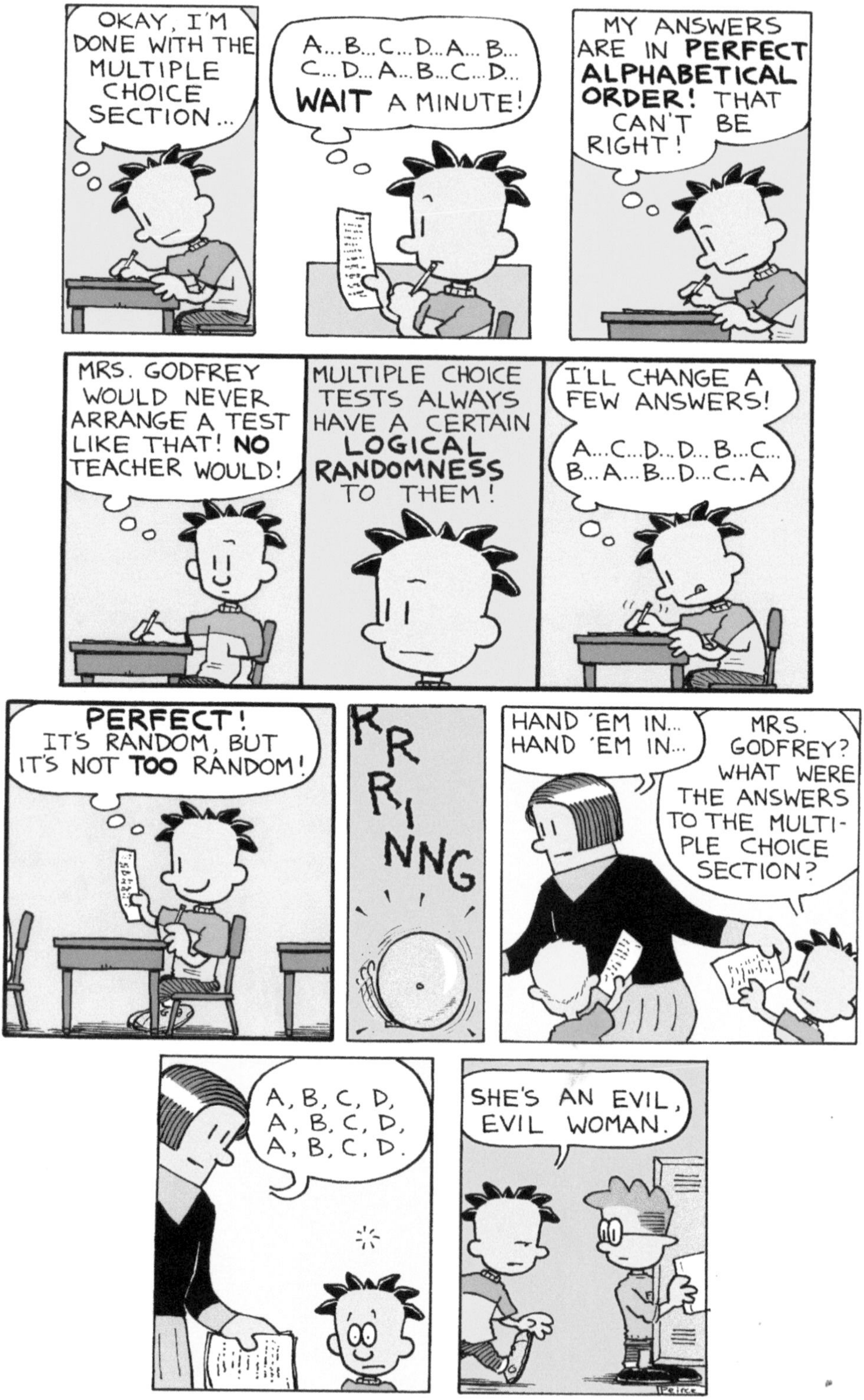
OKAY, I'M DONE WITH THE MULTIPLE CHOICE SECTION...
A...B...C...D...A...B... C...D...A...B...C...D... WAIT A MINUTE!
MY ANSWERS ARE IN PERFECT ALPHABETICAL ORDER! THAT CAN'T BE RIGHT!
MRS. GODFREY WOULD NEVER ARRANGE A TEST LIKE THAT! NO TEACHER WOULD!
MULTIPLE CHOICE TESTS ALWAYS HAVE A CERTAIN LOGICAL RANDOMNESS TO THEM!
I'LL CHANGE A FEW ANSWERS!
A...C...D...D...B...C... B...A...B...D...C..A
PERFECT! IT'S RANDOM, BUT IT'S NOT TOO RANDOM!
RRRINNG
HAND 'EM IN... HAND 'EM IN...
MRS. GODFREY? WHAT WERE THE ANSWERS TO THE MULTI-PLE CHOICE SECTION?
A, B, C, D, A, B, C, D, A, B, C, D.
SHE'S AN EVIL, EVIL WOMAN.
Peirce

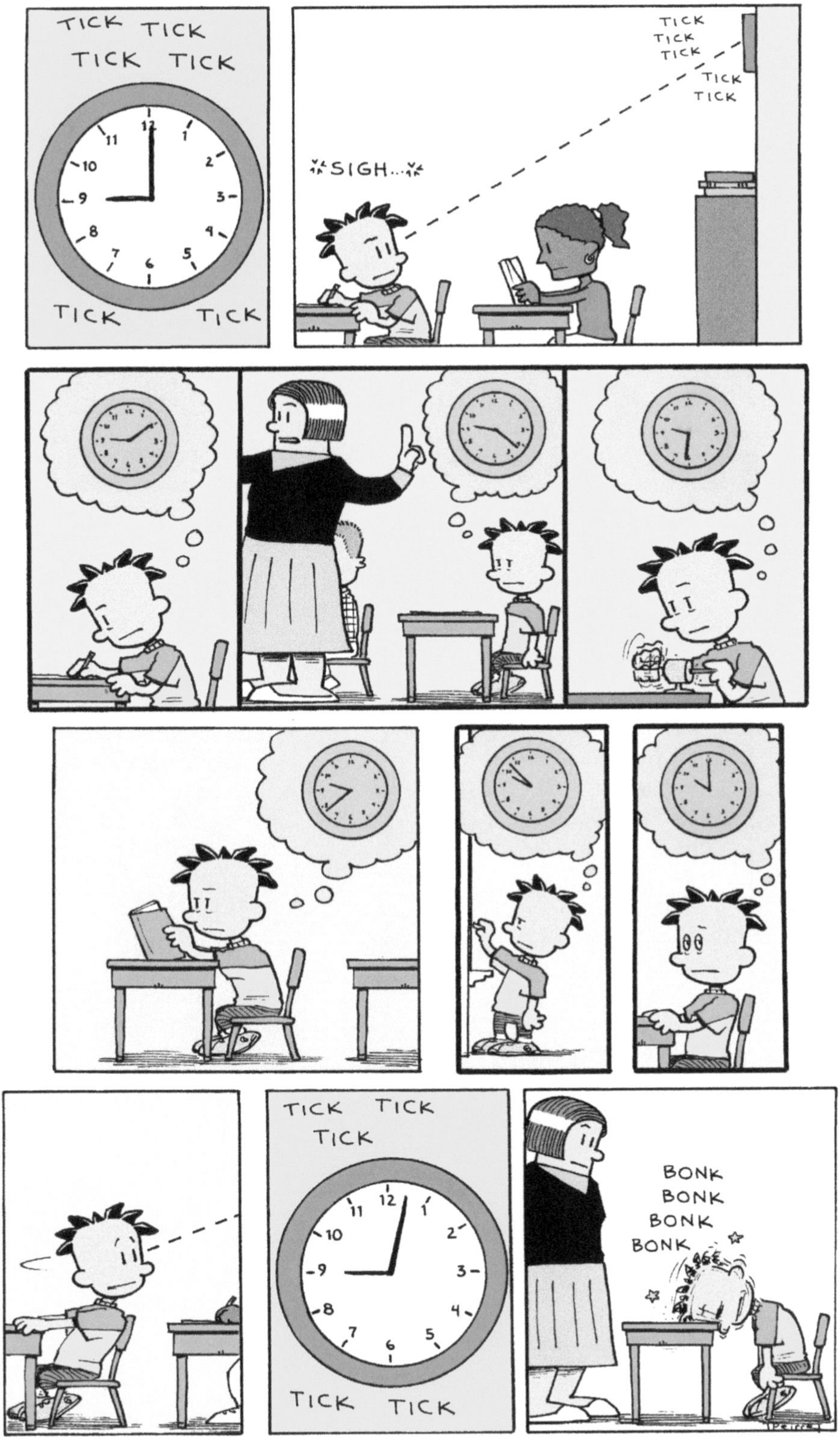
TICK TICK
TICK TICK
TICK TICK
TICK
TICK
TICK
TICK
TICK
SIGH...
TICK TICK
TICK
TICK TICK
BONK
BONK
BONK
BONK

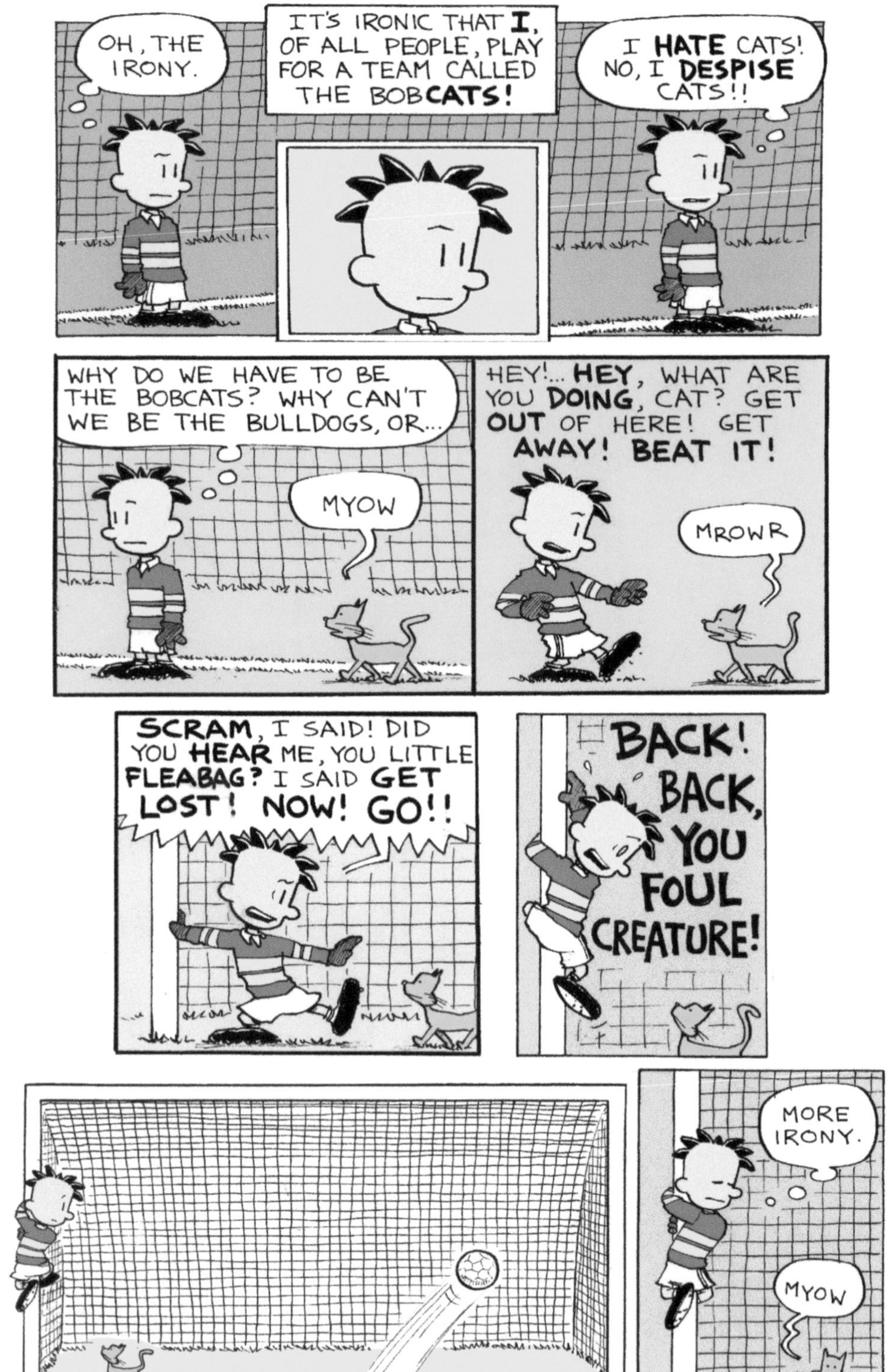

OH, THE IRONY.
IT'S IRONIC THAT I, OF ALL PEOPLE, PLAY FOR A TEAM CALLED THE BOBCATS!
I HATE CATS! NO, I DESPISE CATS!!
WHY DO WE HAVE TO BE THE BOBCATS? WHY CAN'T WE BE THE BULLDOGS, OR...
MYOW
HEY!... HEY, WHAT ARE YOU DOING, CAT? GET OUT OF HERE! GET AWAY! BEAT IT!
MROWR
SCRAM, I SAID! DID YOU HEAR ME, YOU LITTLE FLEABAG? I SAID GET LOST! NOW! GO!!
BACK! BACK, YOU FOUL CREATURE!
MORE IRONY.
MYOW

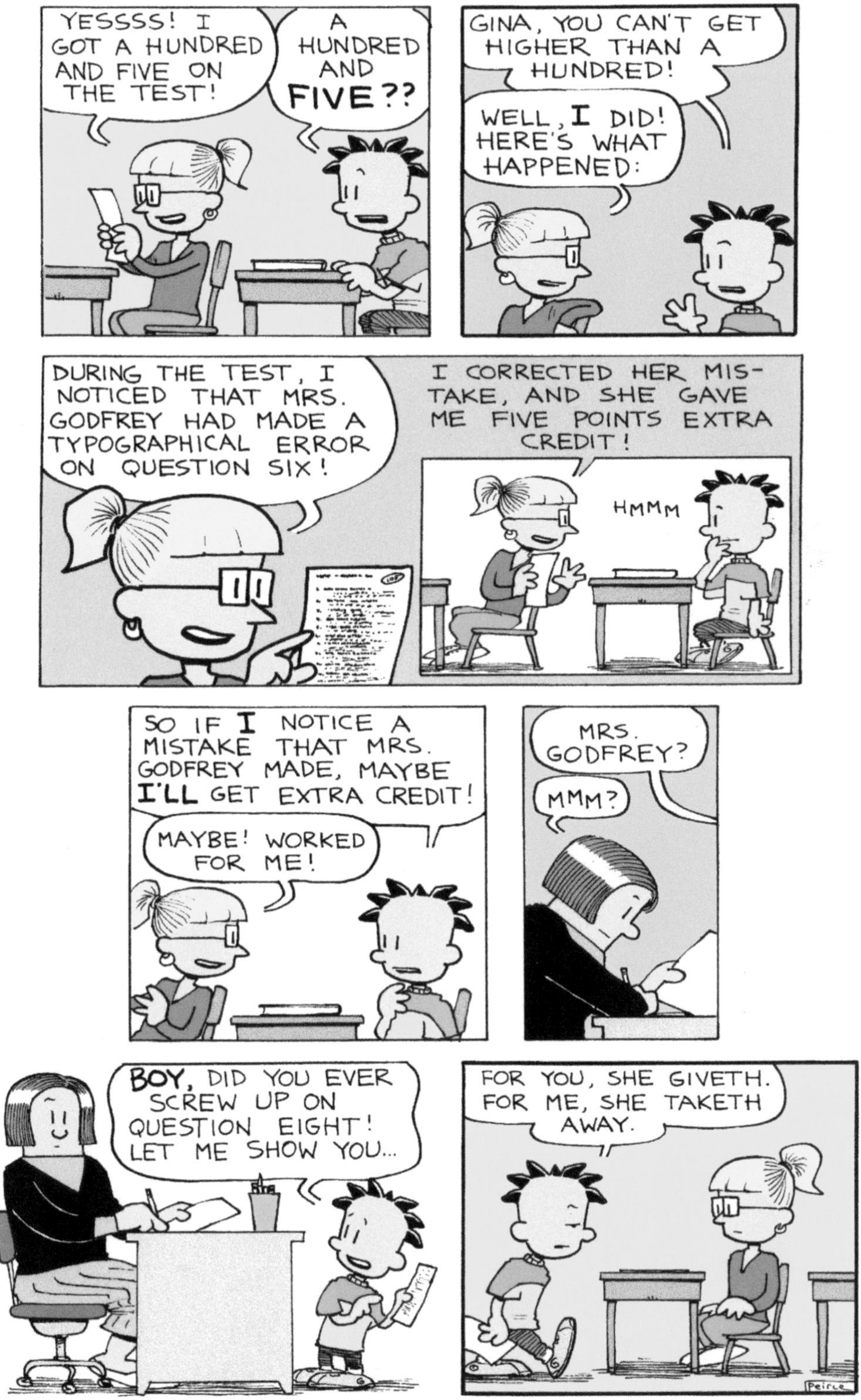
YESSSS! I GOT A HUNDRED AND FIVE ON THE TEST!
A HUNDRED AND FIVE??
GINA, YOU CAN'T GET HIGHER THAN A HUNDRED!
WELL, I DID! HERE'S WHAT HAPPENED:
DURING THE TEST, I NOTICED THAT MRS. GODFREY HAD MADE A TYPOGRAPHICAL ERROR ON QUESTION SIX!
I CORRECTED HER MISTAKE, AND SHE GAVE ME FIVE POINTS EXTRA CREDIT!
HMMM
SO IF I NOTICE A MISTAKE THAT MRS. GODFREY MADE, MAYBE I'LL GET EXTRA CREDIT!
MAYBE! WORKED FOR ME!
MRS. GODFREY?
MMM?
BOY, DID YOU EVER SCREW UP ON QUESTION EIGHT! LET ME SHOW YOU...
FOR YOU, SHE GIVETH. FOR ME, SHE TAKETH AWAY.
Peirce

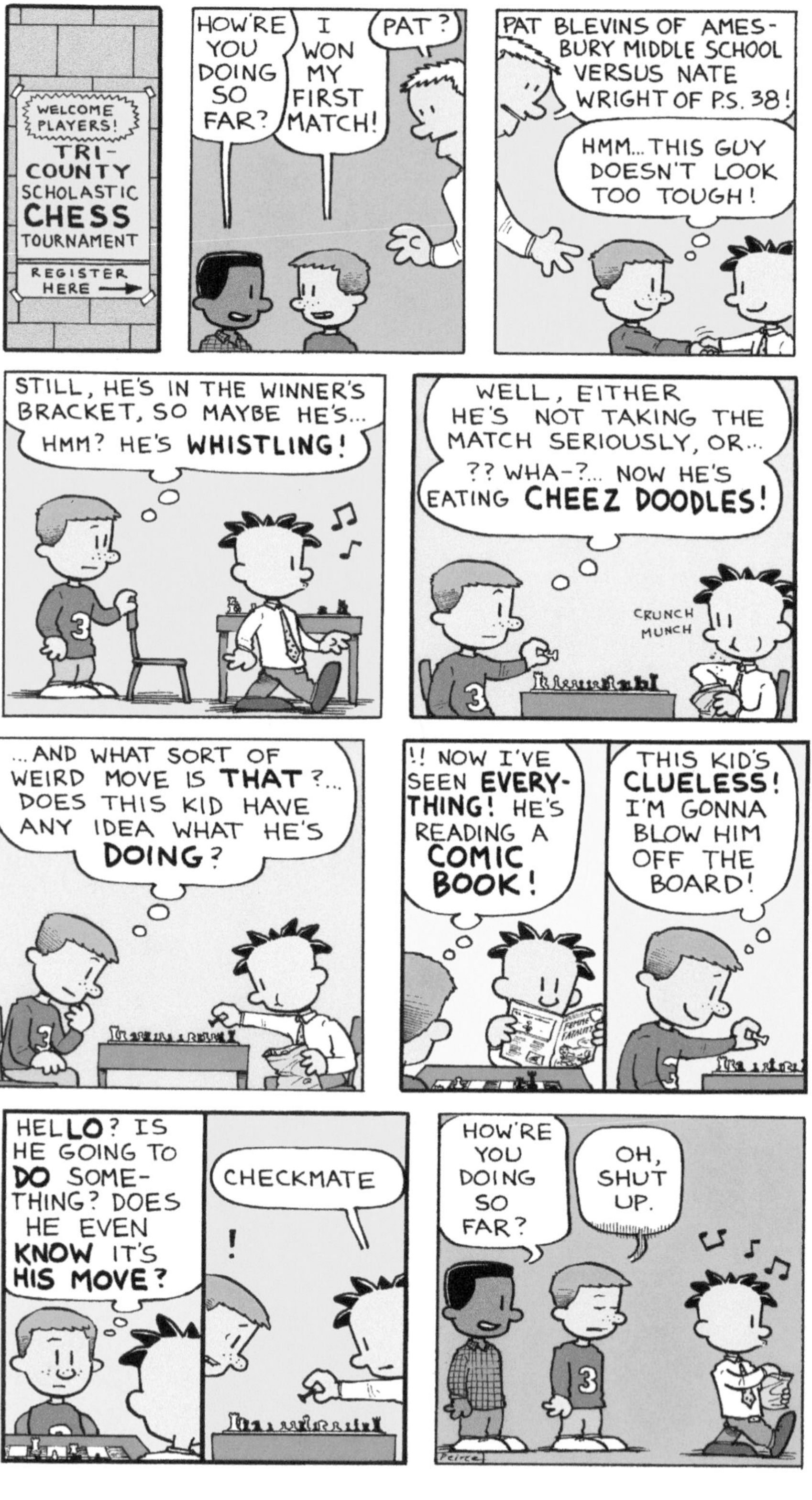
WELCOME PLAYERS!
TRI-COUNTY SCHOLASTIC CHESS TOURNAMENT
REGISTER HERE →
HOW'RE YOU DOING SO FAR?
I WON MY FIRST MATCH!
PAT?
PAT BLEVINS OF AMESBURY MIDDLE SCHOOL VERSUS NATE WRIGHT OF P.S. 38!
HMM... THIS GUY DOESN'T LOOK TOO TOUGH!
STILL, HE'S IN THE WINNER'S BRACKET, SO MAYBE HE'S... HMM? HE'S WHISTLING!
WELL, EITHER HE'S NOT TAKING THE MATCH SERIOUSLY, OR... ?? WHA-?... NOW HE'S EATING CHEEZ DOODLES!
CRUNCH MUNCH
...AND WHAT SORT OF WEIRD MOVE IS THAT?... DOES THIS KID HAVE ANY IDEA WHAT HE'S DOING?
!! NOW I'VE SEEN EVERYTHING! HE'S READING A COMIC BOOK!
THIS KID'S CLUELESS! I'M GONNA BLOW HIM OFF THE BOARD!
HELLO? IS HE GOING TO DO SOMETHING? DOES HE EVEN KNOW IT'S HIS MOVE?
CHECKMATE
!
HOW'RE YOU DOING SO FAR?
OH, SHUT UP.

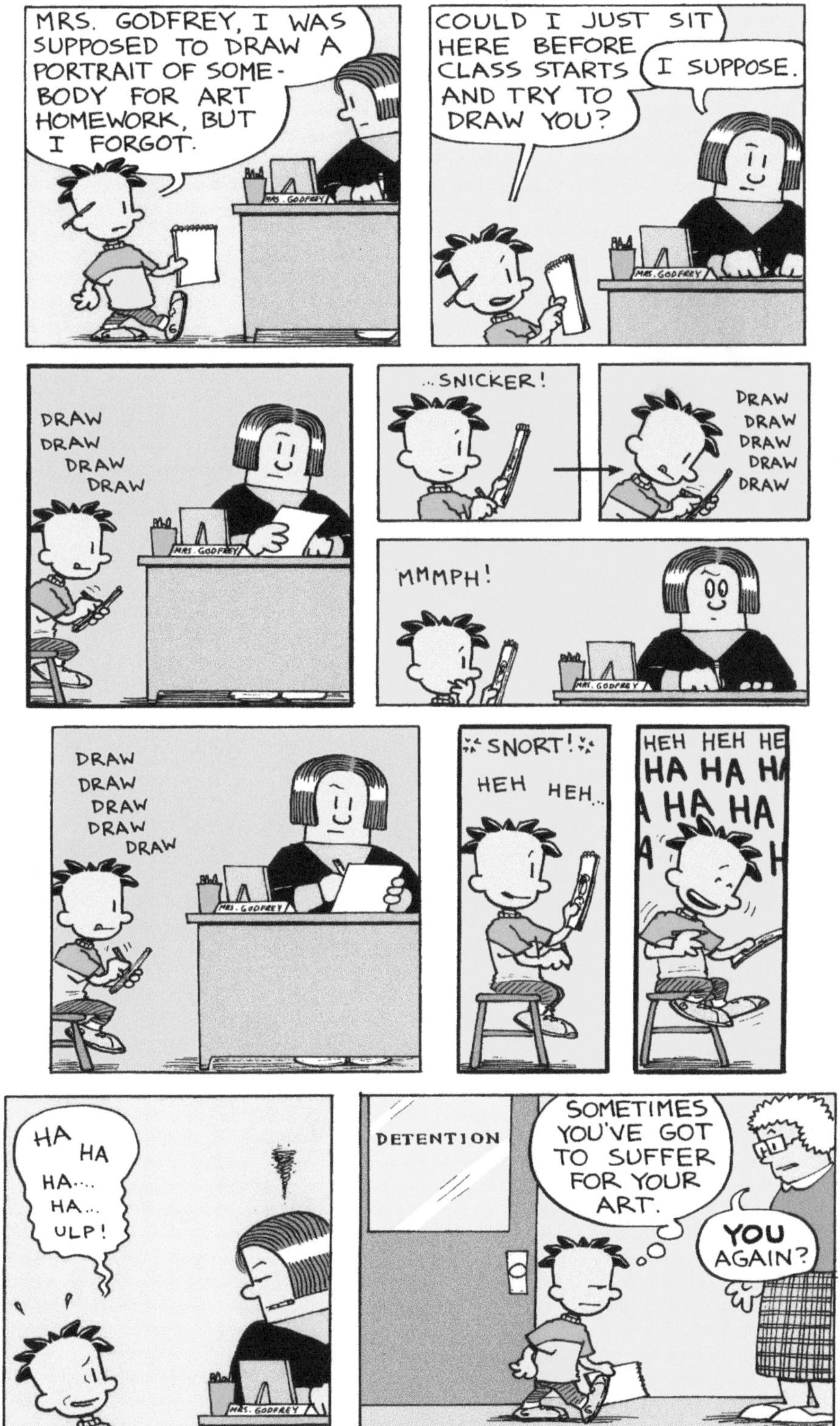
MRS. GODFREY, I WAS SUPPOSED TO DRAW A PORTRAIT OF SOME-BODY FOR ART HOMEWORK, BUT I FORGOT.
MRS. GODFREY
COULD I JUST SIT HERE BEFORE CLASS STARTS AND TRY TO DRAW YOU?
I SUPPOSE.
MRS. GODFREY
DRAW DRAW DRAW DRAW
MRS. GODFREY
...SNICKER!
DRAW DRAW DRAW DRAW DRAW
MMMPH!
MRS. GODFREY
DRAW DRAW DRAW DRAW DRAW
MRS. GODFREY
SNORT!
HEH HEH...
HEH HEH HE
HA HA HA
HA HA HA
HA HA
ULP!
MRS. GODFREY
DETENTION
SOMETIMES YOU'VE GOT TO SUFFER FOR YOUR ART.
YOU AGAIN?
Peirce

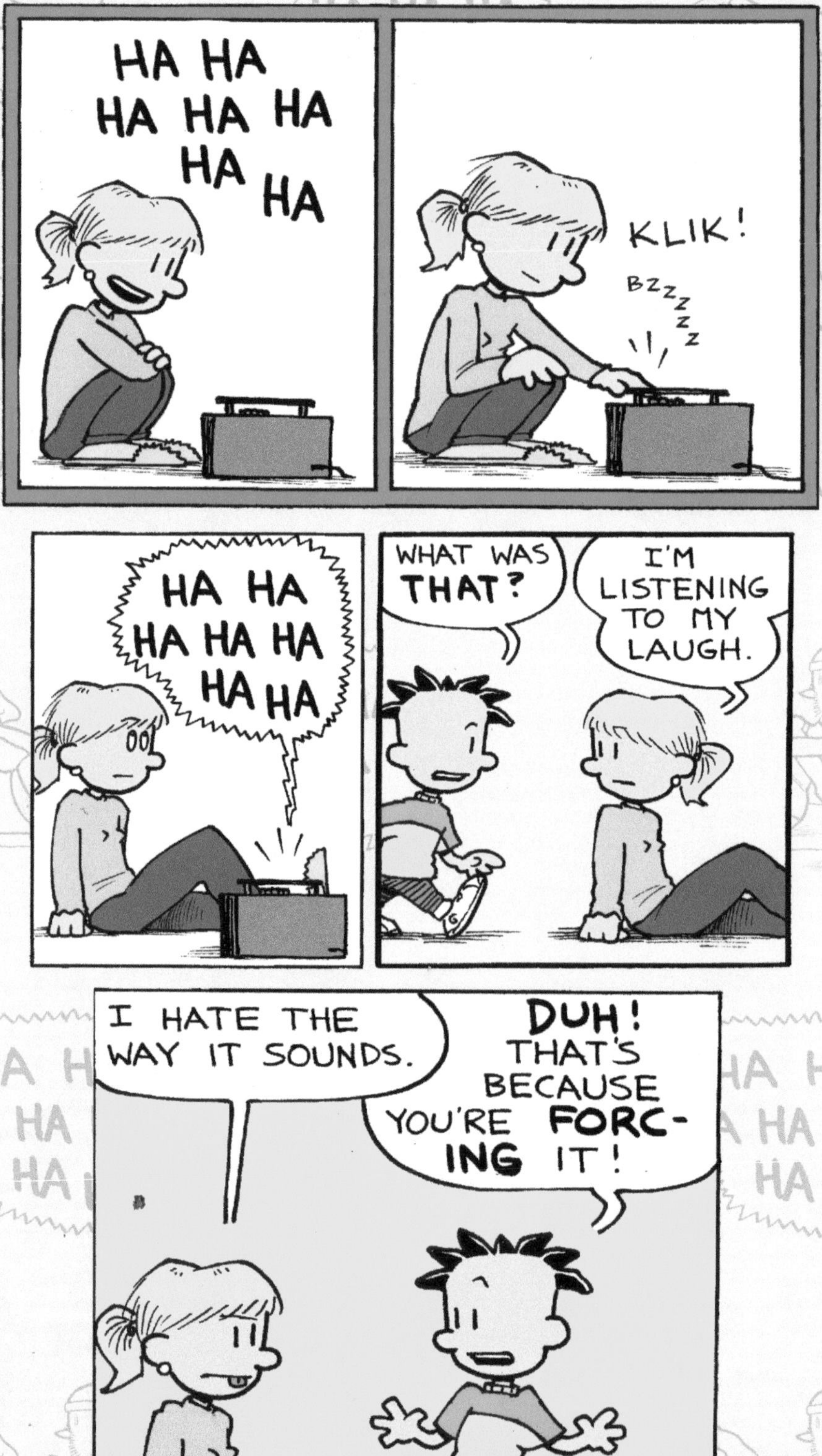
HA HA
HA HA HA
HA
HA
KLIK!
BZZZZZ
HA HA
HA HA HA
HA HA
WHAT WAS THAT?
I'M LISTENING TO MY LAUGH.
I HATE THE WAY IT SOUNDS.
DUH! THAT'S BECAUSE YOU'RE FORCING IT!

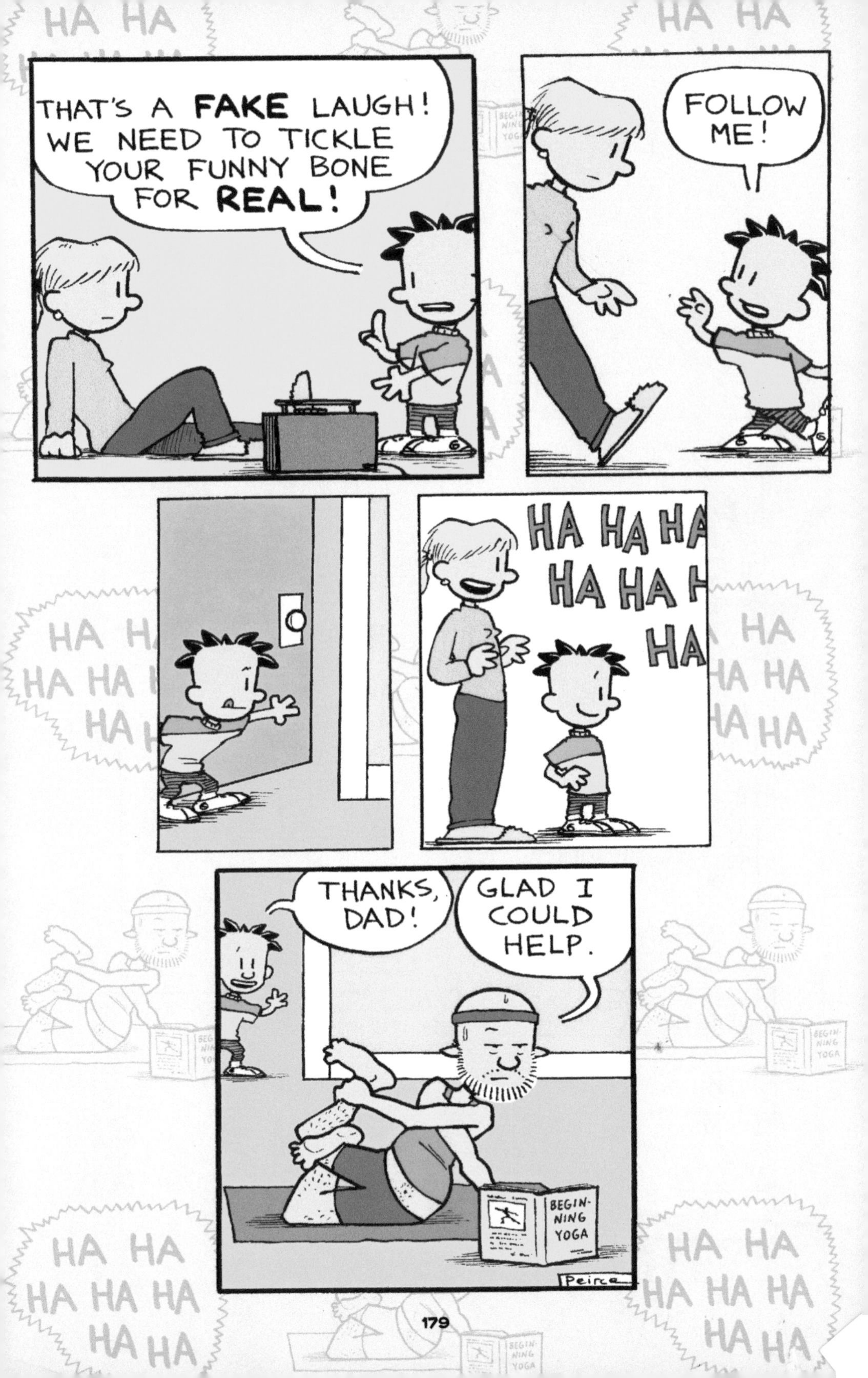

THAT'S A **FAKE** LAUGH! WE NEED TO TICKLE YOUR FUNNY BONE FOR **REAL**!
FOLLOW ME!
HA HA HA HA HA HA
THANKS, DAD!
GLAD I COULD HELP.
BEGIN-NING YOGA
Peirce

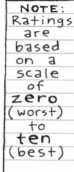

Nate Wright's

TEACHER RATINGS!

Where Do **YOUR** Teachers Rate in the HALL OF SHAME?

NOTE: Ratings are based on a scale of **zero** (worst) to **ten** (best)

MR. STAPLES (Math)

"< fun"

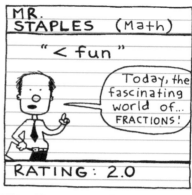

Today, the fascinating world of... FRACTIONS!

RATING: 2.0

MRS. BRINDLE (LIFE SKILLS)

"A recipe for disaster"

...and after 20 minutes, our "johnny-cake" is done!

RATING: 1.3

MS. LA CHANCE (French)

"Ooh La Loser"

Let the words RRRRROLL off your tongue!

RATING: 0.8

MR. GALVIN (Science)

"Boredom = mc^2"

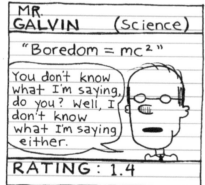

You don't know what I'm saying, do you? Well, I don't know what I'm saying either.

RATING: 1.4

MR. ALDRIDGE (Computer Lab)

Press "escape"

Wait. Wait. That wasn't supposed to... Okay, wait. Wait.

tik tak tik tak tik tak

RATING: 1.1

MRS. GODFREY (Social Studies)

"Oh, the humanity."

I summon thee, hounds of Satan!

RATING: −3,000,000

DO YOU ACTUALLY EXPECT ME TO PUT THIS IN THE DISPLAY CASE?

THINK OF IT AS A PUBLIC SERVICE!

OH, NO...

HEY, GUYS! CAN I PLAY?

SAY NO. SAY NO.

SIGH...

HOLD IT! STOP RIGHT THERE!

TURN AROUND! GO LONG!

I'LL HIT YOU IN THE END ZONE!

GO LONGER! LONGER!!

KEEP GOING!

LET'S GO OVER TO YOUR HOUSE.

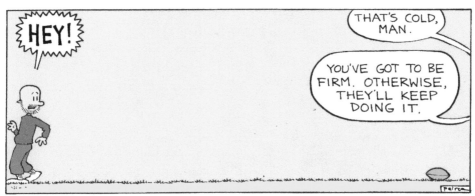

HEY!

THAT'S COLD, MAN.

YOU'VE GOT TO BE FIRM. OTHERWISE, THEY'LL KEEP DOING IT.

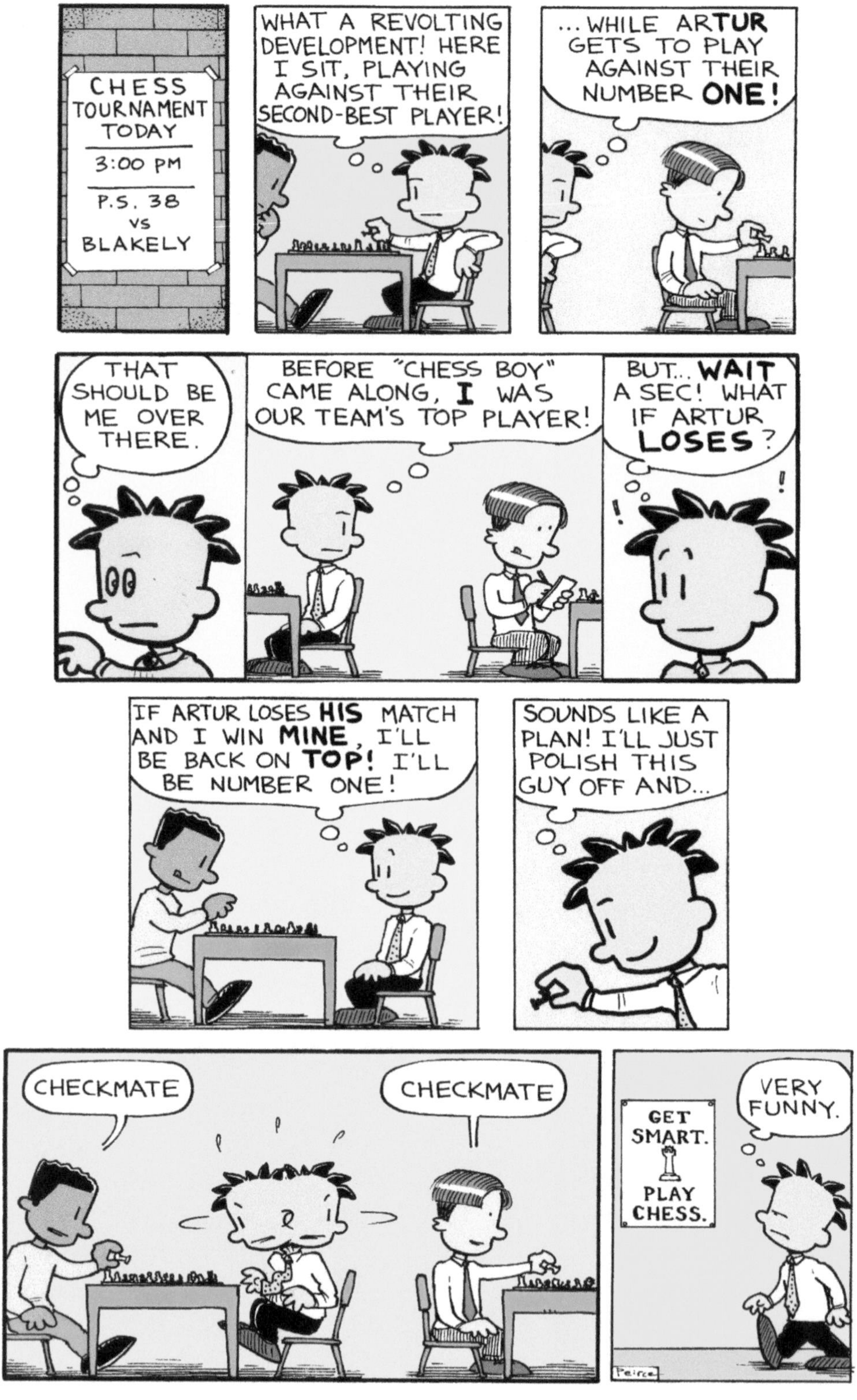
CHESS TOURNAMENT TODAY
3:00 PM
P.S. 38 VS BLAKELY
WHAT A REVOLTING DEVELOPMENT! HERE I SIT, PLAYING AGAINST THEIR SECOND-BEST PLAYER!
...WHILE ARTUR GETS TO PLAY AGAINST THEIR NUMBER ONE!
THAT SHOULD BE ME OVER THERE.
BEFORE "CHESS BOY" CAME ALONG, I WAS OUR TEAM'S TOP PLAYER!
BUT... WAIT A SEC! WHAT IF ARTUR LOSES?
!
!
IF ARTUR LOSES HIS MATCH AND I WIN MINE, I'LL BE BACK ON TOP! I'LL BE NUMBER ONE!
SOUNDS LIKE A PLAN! I'LL JUST POLISH THIS GUY OFF AND...
CHECKMATE
CHECKMATE
GET SMART.
PLAY CHESS.
VERY FUNNY.
Peirce

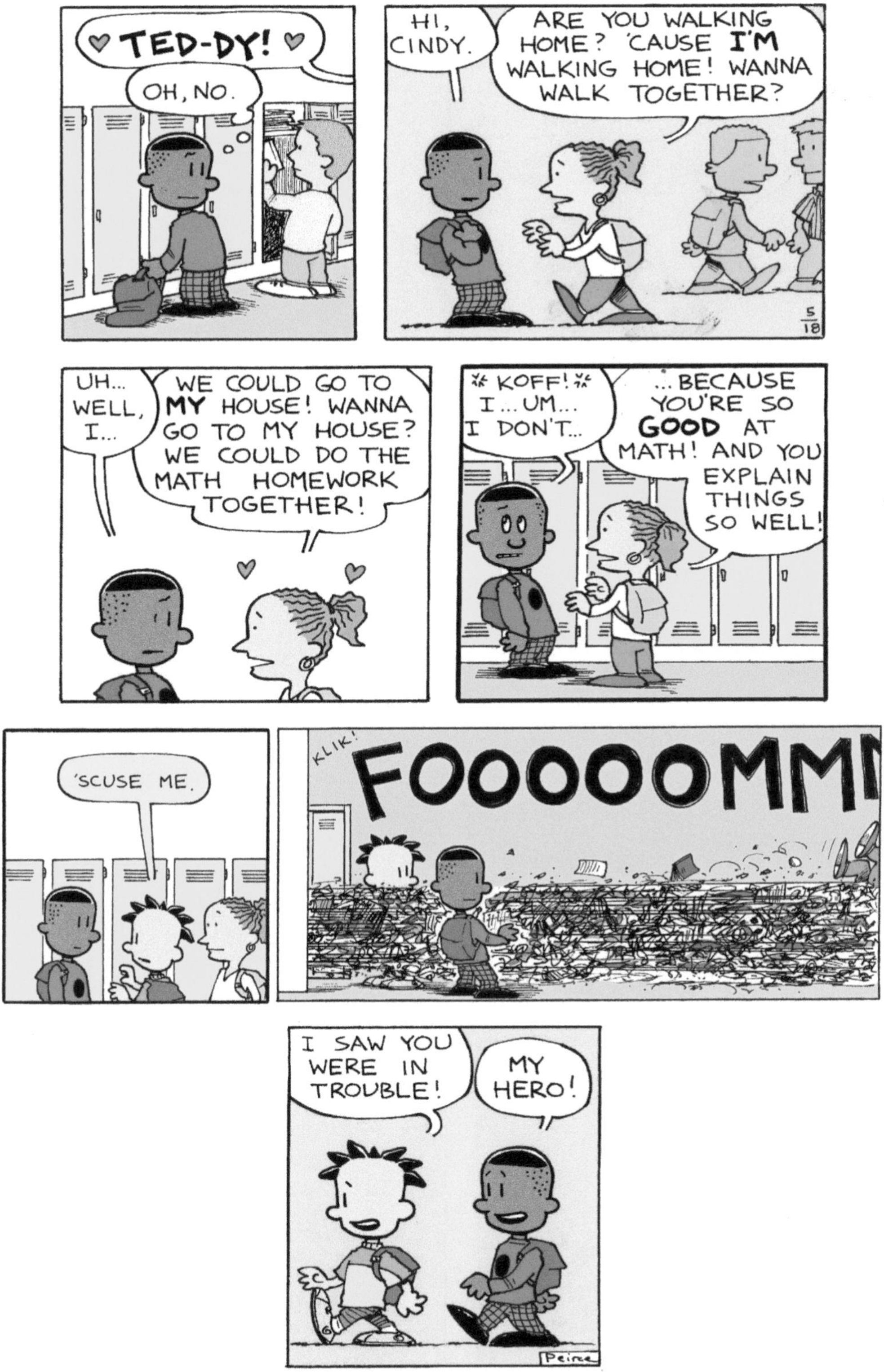
TED-DY!
OH, NO.
HI, CINDY.
ARE YOU WALKING HOME? 'CAUSE I'M WALKING HOME! WANNA WALK TOGETHER?
5/18
UH... WELL, I...
WE COULD GO TO MY HOUSE! WANNA GO TO MY HOUSE? WE COULD DO THE MATH HOMEWORK TOGETHER!
KOFF! I... UM... I DON'T...
...BECAUSE YOU'RE SO GOOD AT MATH! AND YOU EXPLAIN THINGS SO WELL!
'SCUSE ME.
KLIK!
FOOOOOMMM
I SAW YOU WERE IN TROUBLE!
MY HERO!
Peirce

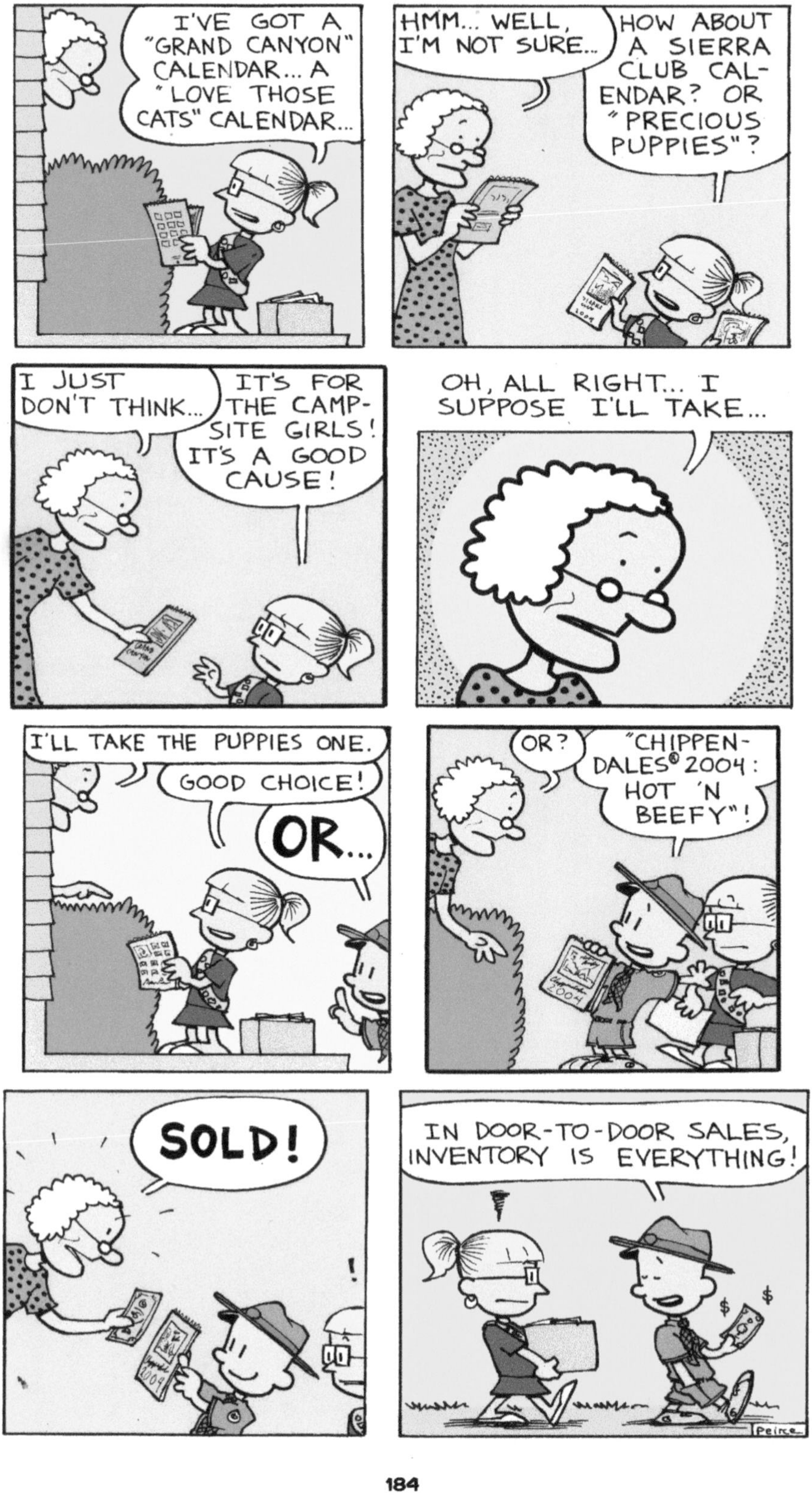
I'VE GOT A "GRAND CANYON" CALENDAR... A "LOVE THOSE CATS" CALENDAR...
HMM... WELL, I'M NOT SURE...
HOW ABOUT A SIERRA CLUB CAL-ENDAR? OR "PRECIOUS PUPPIES"?
I JUST DON'T THINK...
IT'S FOR THE CAMP-SITE GIRLS! IT'S A GOOD CAUSE!
OH, ALL RIGHT... I SUPPOSE I'LL TAKE...
I'LL TAKE THE PUPPIES ONE.
GOOD CHOICE!
OR...
OR?
"CHIPPEN-DALES® 2004: HOT 'N BEEFY"!
SOLD!
!
IN DOOR-TO-DOOR SALES, INVENTORY IS EVERYTHING!
Peirce

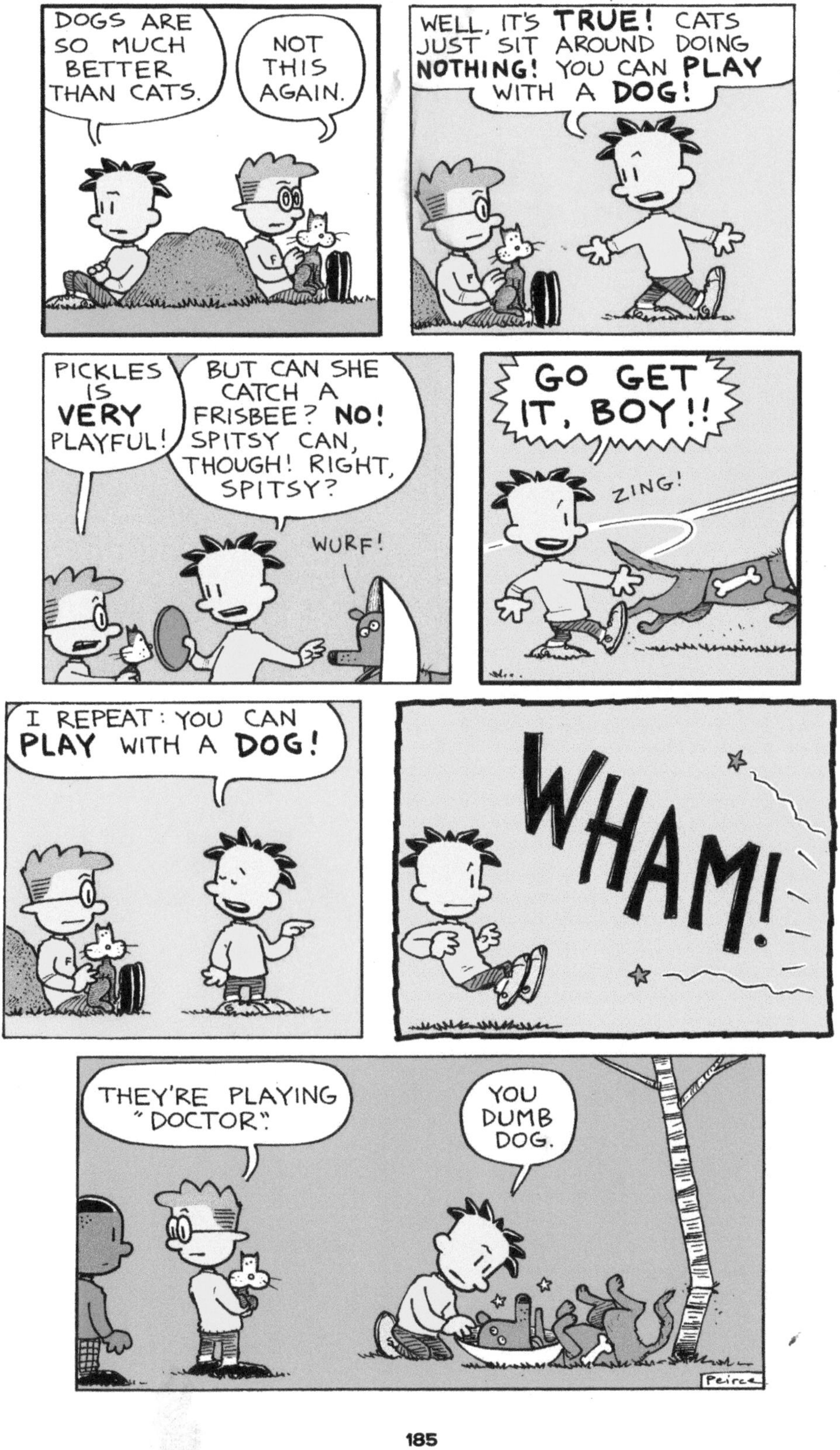
DOGS ARE SO MUCH BETTER THAN CATS.
NOT THIS AGAIN.
WELL, IT'S **TRUE!** CATS JUST SIT AROUND DOING **NOTHING!** YOU CAN **PLAY** WITH A **DOG!**
PICKLES IS **VERY** PLAYFUL!
BUT CAN SHE CATCH A FRISBEE? **NO!** SPITSY CAN, THOUGH! RIGHT, SPITSY?
WURF!
GO GET IT, BOY!!
ZING!
I REPEAT: YOU CAN **PLAY** WITH A **DOG!**
WHAM!
THEY'RE PLAYING "DOCTOR".
YOU DUMB DOG.
Peirce

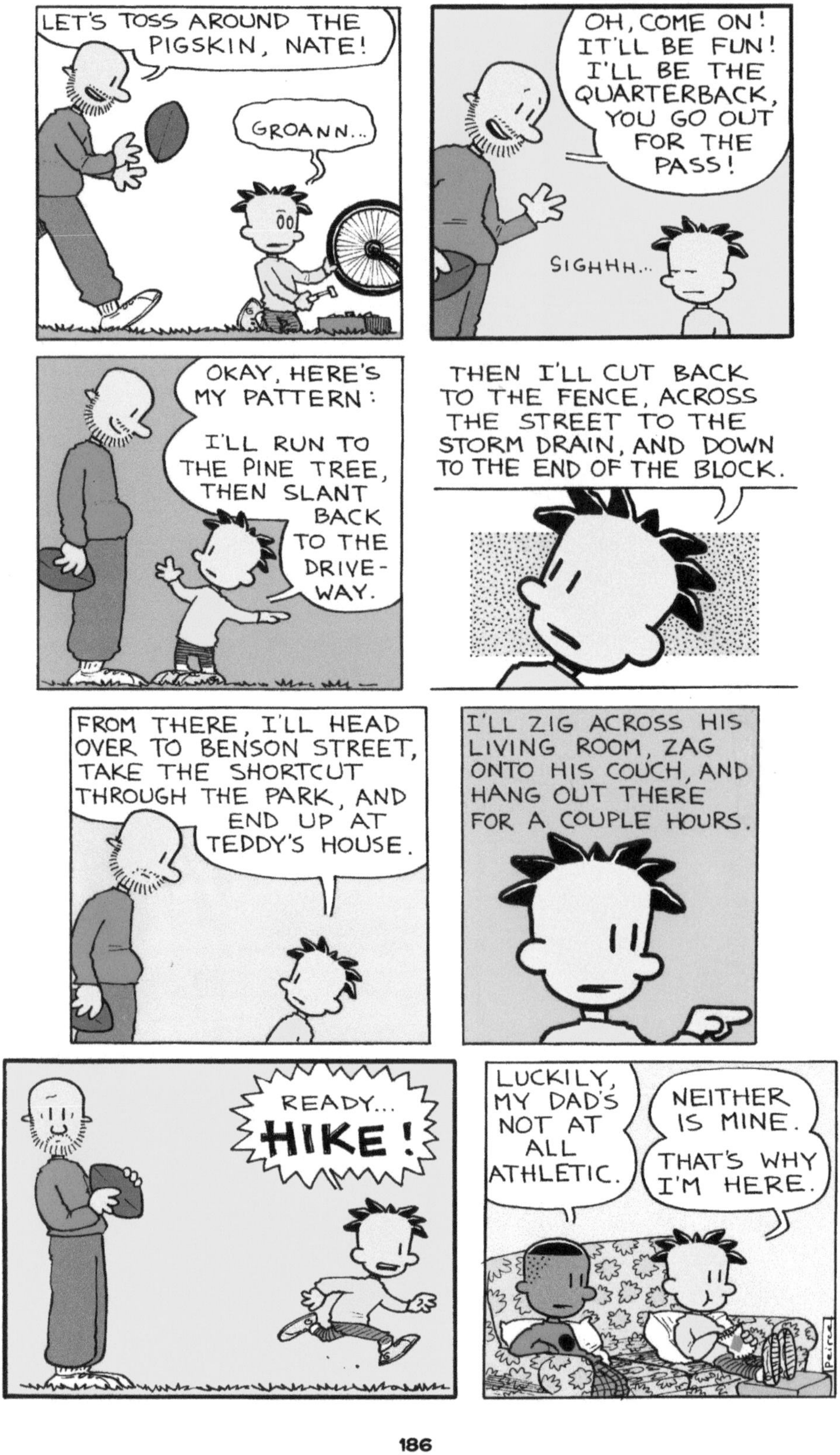

LET'S TOSS AROUND THE PIGSKIN, NATE!
GROANN...
OH, COME ON! IT'LL BE FUN! I'LL BE THE QUARTERBACK, YOU GO OUT FOR THE PASS!
SIGHHH...
OKAY, HERE'S MY PATTERN: I'LL RUN TO THE PINE TREE, THEN SLANT BACK TO THE DRIVE-WAY.
THEN I'LL CUT BACK TO THE FENCE, ACROSS THE STREET TO THE STORM DRAIN, AND DOWN TO THE END OF THE BLOCK.
FROM THERE, I'LL HEAD OVER TO BENSON STREET, TAKE THE SHORTCUT THROUGH THE PARK, AND END UP AT TEDDY'S HOUSE.
I'LL ZIG ACROSS HIS LIVING ROOM, ZAG ONTO HIS COUCH, AND HANG OUT THERE FOR A COUPLE HOURS.
READY... HIKE!
LUCKILY, MY DAD'S NOT AT ALL ATHLETIC.
NEITHER IS MINE. THAT'S WHY I'M HERE.
Peirce

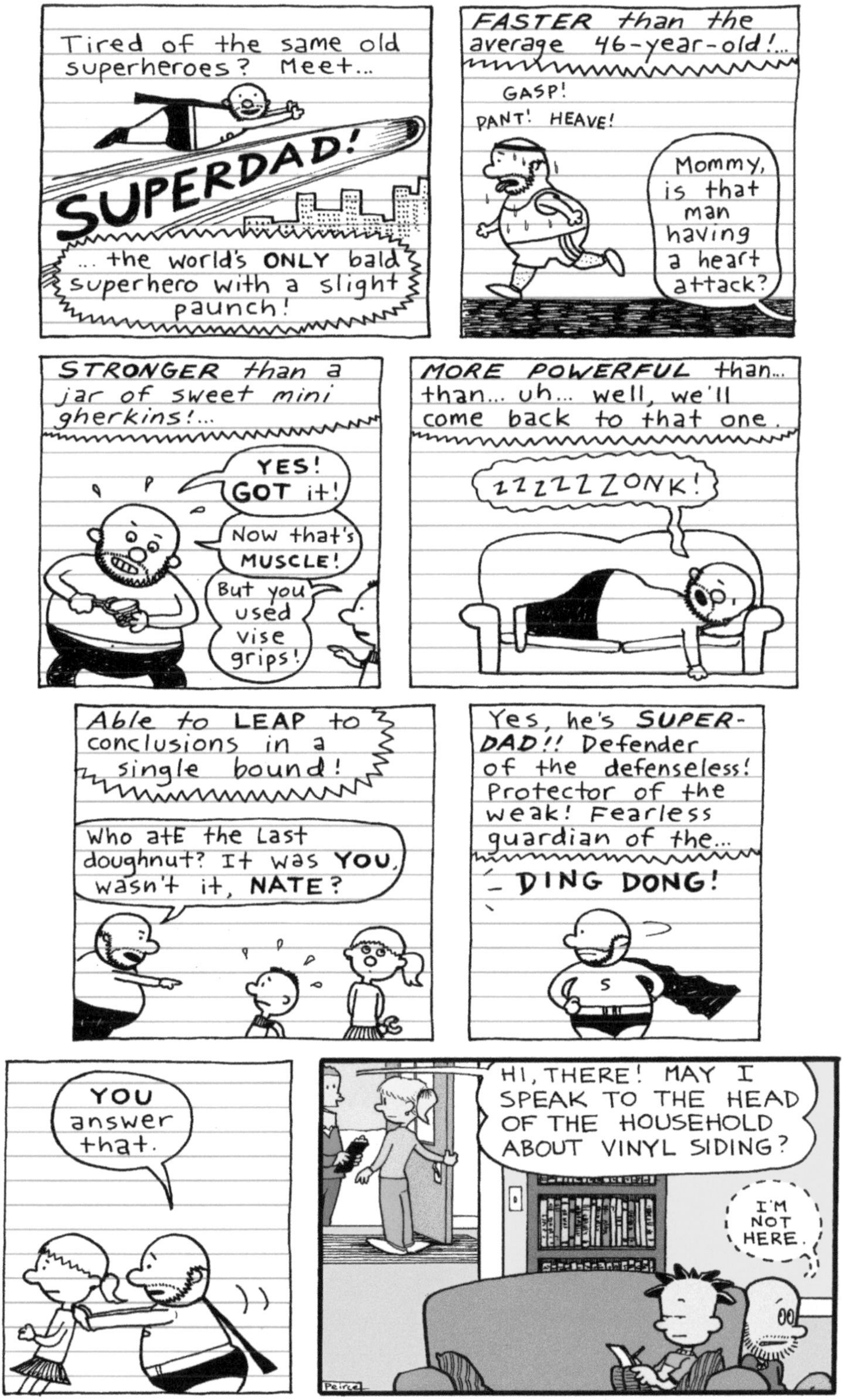

Tired of the same old superheroes? Meet...
SUPERDAD!
... the world's ONLY bald superhero with a slight paunch!
FASTER than the average 46-year-old!...
GASP!
PANT! HEAVE!
Mommy, is that man having a heart attack?
STRONGER than a jar of sweet mini gherkins!...
YES! GOT it!
Now that's MUSCLE!
But you used vise grips!
MORE POWERFUL than... than... uh... well, we'll come back to that one.
ZZZZZZONK!
Able to LEAP to conclusions in a single bound!
Who atE the Last doughnut? It was YOU, wasn't it, NATE?
Yes, he's SUPER-DAD!! Defender of the defenseless! Protector of the weak! Fearless guardian of the...
DING DONG!
S
YOU answer that.
HI, THERE! MAY I SPEAK TO THE HEAD OF THE HOUSEHOLD ABOUT VINYL SIDING?
I'M NOT HERE.
Peirce

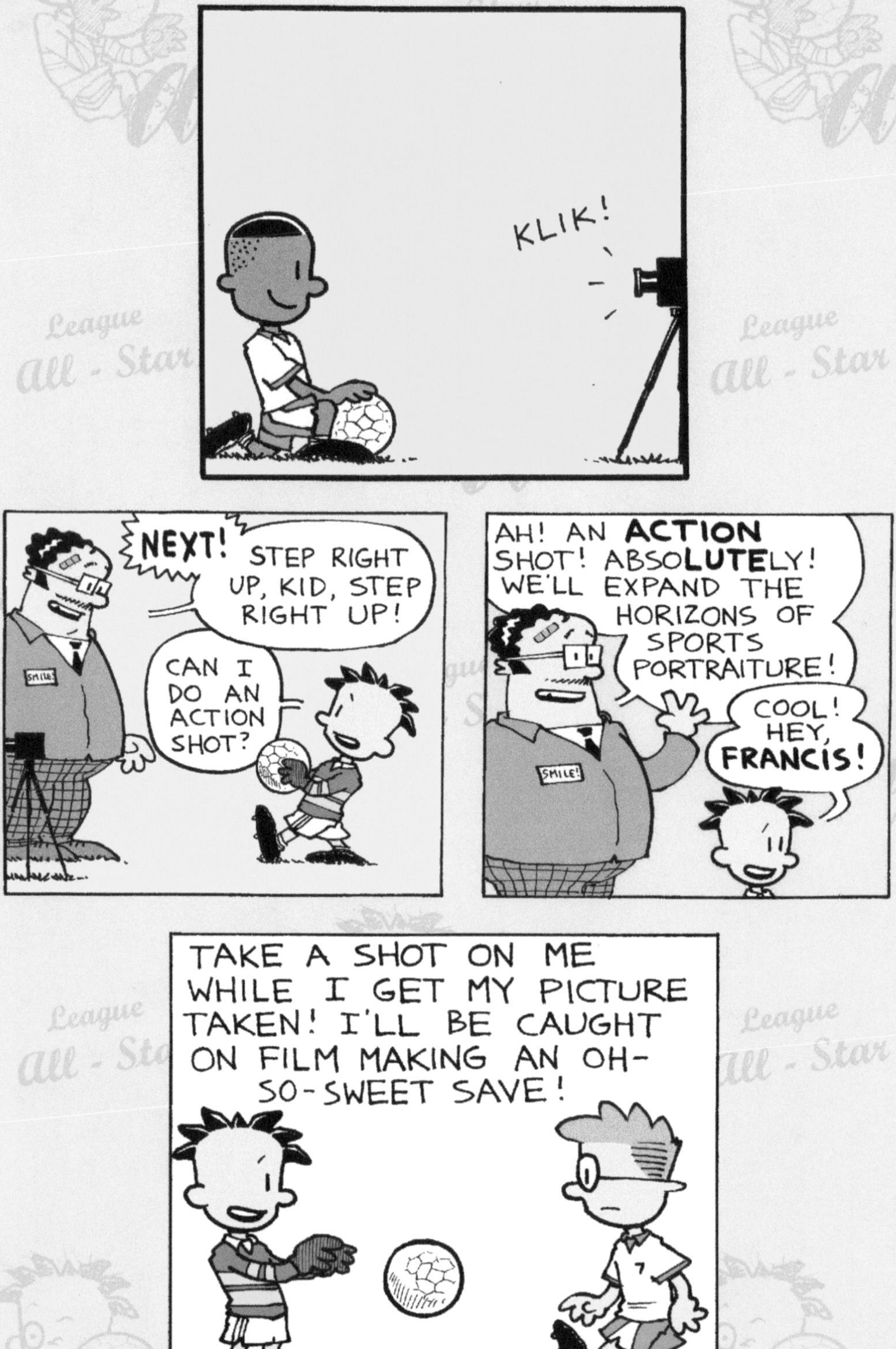
KLIK!
NEXT! STEP RIGHT UP, KID, STEP RIGHT UP!
CAN I DO AN ACTION SHOT?
SMILE!
AH! AN ACTION SHOT! ABSOLUTELY! WE'LL EXPAND THE HORIZONS OF SPORTS PORTRAITURE!
COOL! HEY, FRANCIS!
SMILE!
TAKE A SHOT ON ME WHILE I GET MY PICTURE TAKEN! I'LL BE CAUGHT ON FILM MAKING AN OH-SO-SWEET SAVE!
7

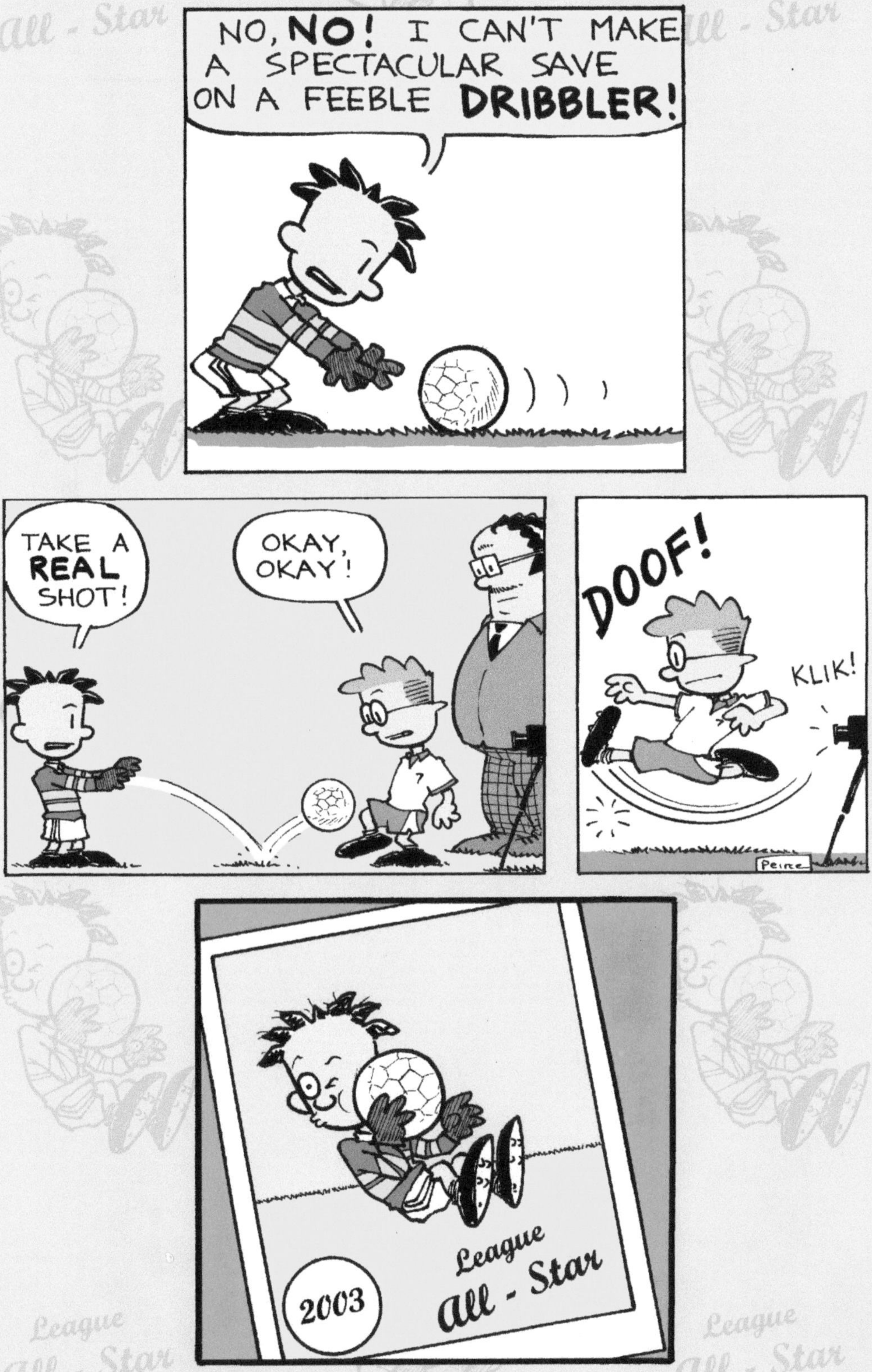
NO, **NO!** I CAN'T MAKE A SPECTACULAR SAVE ON A FEEBLE **DRIBBLER!**
TAKE A **REAL** SHOT!
OKAY, OKAY!
DOOF!
KLIK!
Peirce
2003
League All - Star

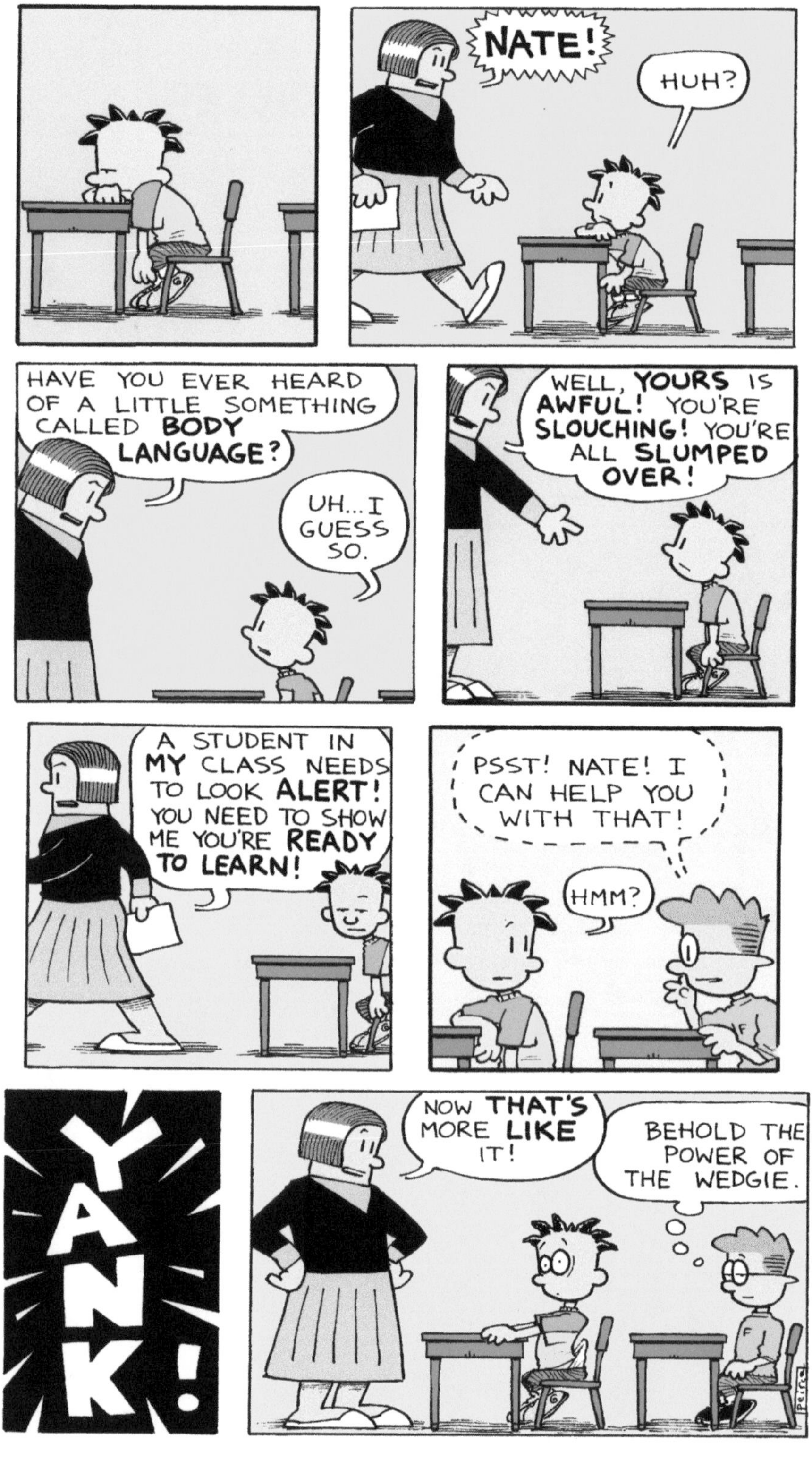
NATE!
HUH?
HAVE YOU EVER HEARD OF A LITTLE SOMETHING CALLED BODY LANGUAGE?
UH...I GUESS SO.
WELL, YOURS IS AWFUL! YOU'RE SLOUCHING! YOU'RE ALL SLUMPED OVER!
A STUDENT IN MY CLASS NEEDS TO LOOK ALERT! YOU NEED TO SHOW ME YOU'RE READY TO LEARN!
PSST! NATE! I CAN HELP YOU WITH THAT!
HMM?
YANK!
NOW THAT'S MORE LIKE IT!
BEHOLD THE POWER OF THE WEDGIE.

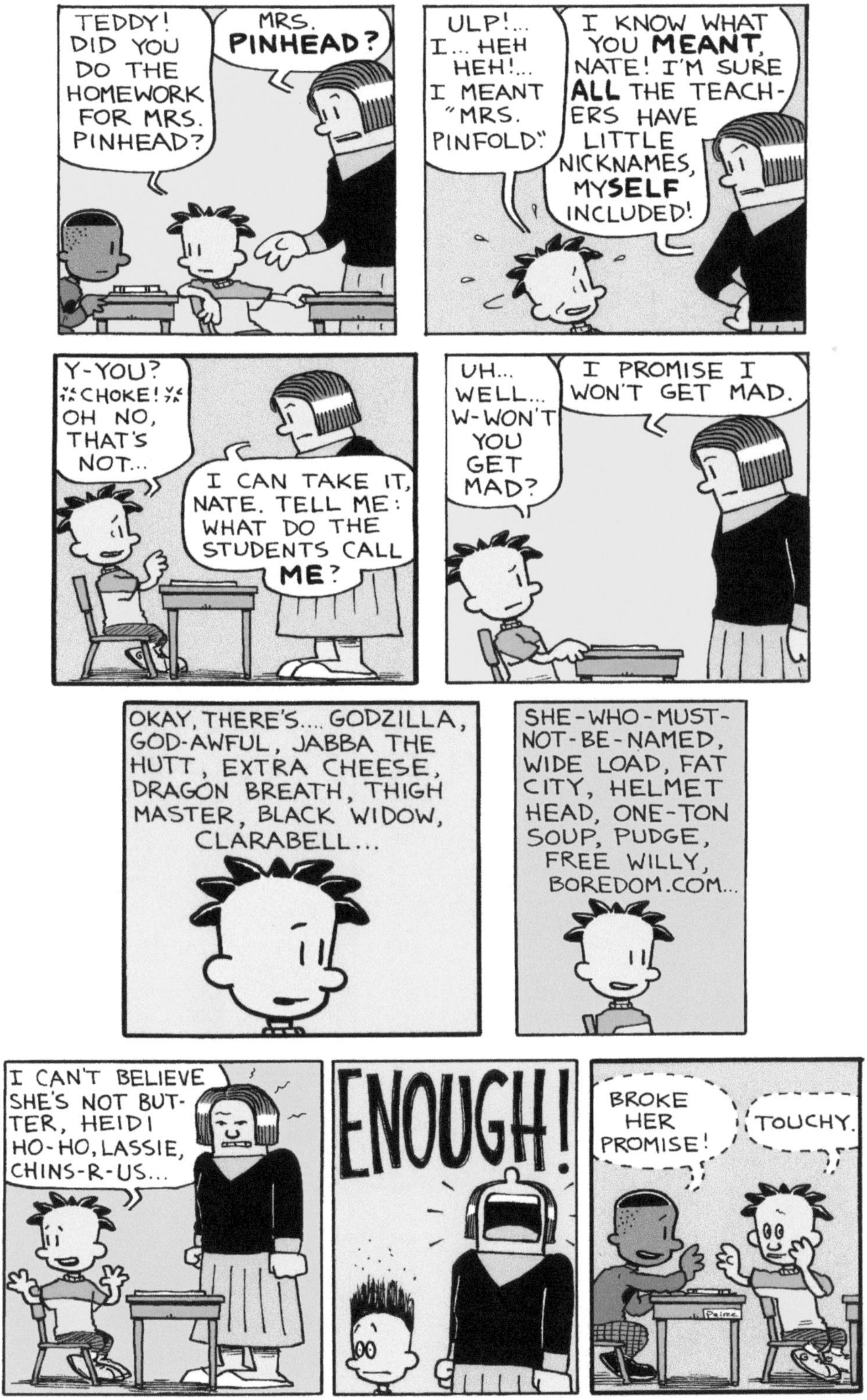
TEDDY! DID YOU DO THE HOMEWORK FOR MRS. PINHEAD?
MRS. **PINHEAD?**
ULP!... I... HEH HEH!... I MEANT "MRS. PINFOLD."
I KNOW WHAT YOU **MEANT**, NATE! I'M SURE **ALL** THE TEACHERS HAVE LITTLE NICKNAMES, MY**SELF** INCLUDED!
Y-YOU? CHOKE! OH NO, THAT'S NOT...
I CAN TAKE IT, NATE. TELL ME: WHAT DO THE STUDENTS CALL **ME**?
UH... WELL... W-WON'T YOU GET MAD?
I PROMISE I WON'T GET MAD.
OKAY, THERE'S.... GODZILLA, GOD-AWFUL, JABBA THE HUTT, EXTRA CHEESE, DRAGON BREATH, THIGH MASTER, BLACK WIDOW, CLARABELL...
SHE-WHO-MUST-NOT-BE-NAMED, WIDE LOAD, FAT CITY, HELMET HEAD, ONE-TON SOUP, PUDGE, FREE WILLY, BOREDOM.COM...
I CAN'T BELIEVE SHE'S NOT BUTTER, HEIDI HO-HO, LASSIE, CHINS-R-US...
ENOUGH!
BROKE HER PROMISE!
TOUCHY.

HERE, SHOOT SOME VIDEO OF MY HOME-WORK.
YOUR HOME-WORK?
I CAN NEVER GET MY HOMEWORK TO SCHOOL WITHOUT IT GETTING RUINED SOMEHOW!
THIS WAY I'LL HAVE PHOTO DOCUMENTATION THAT I DID THE ASSIGNMENT, NO MATTER WHAT HAPPENS!
ZOOM IN! GET A CLOSE-UP!
BZZZZZZZZ
OW!
BZZZAP!
SPLOOSH!
NO!
SHLOOOOOP!
NOT TO WORRY! I GOT IT ALL ON TAPE!
BOBO! COME BACK!
BOBO!
GRAB!
STOMP! STOMP! STOMP! STOMP! STOMP!
BAD BOBO! BAD!
... SO THEN Ⓑ CHIMPANZEE STOMPED ON Ⓒ VIDEOTAPE...
SIGH...

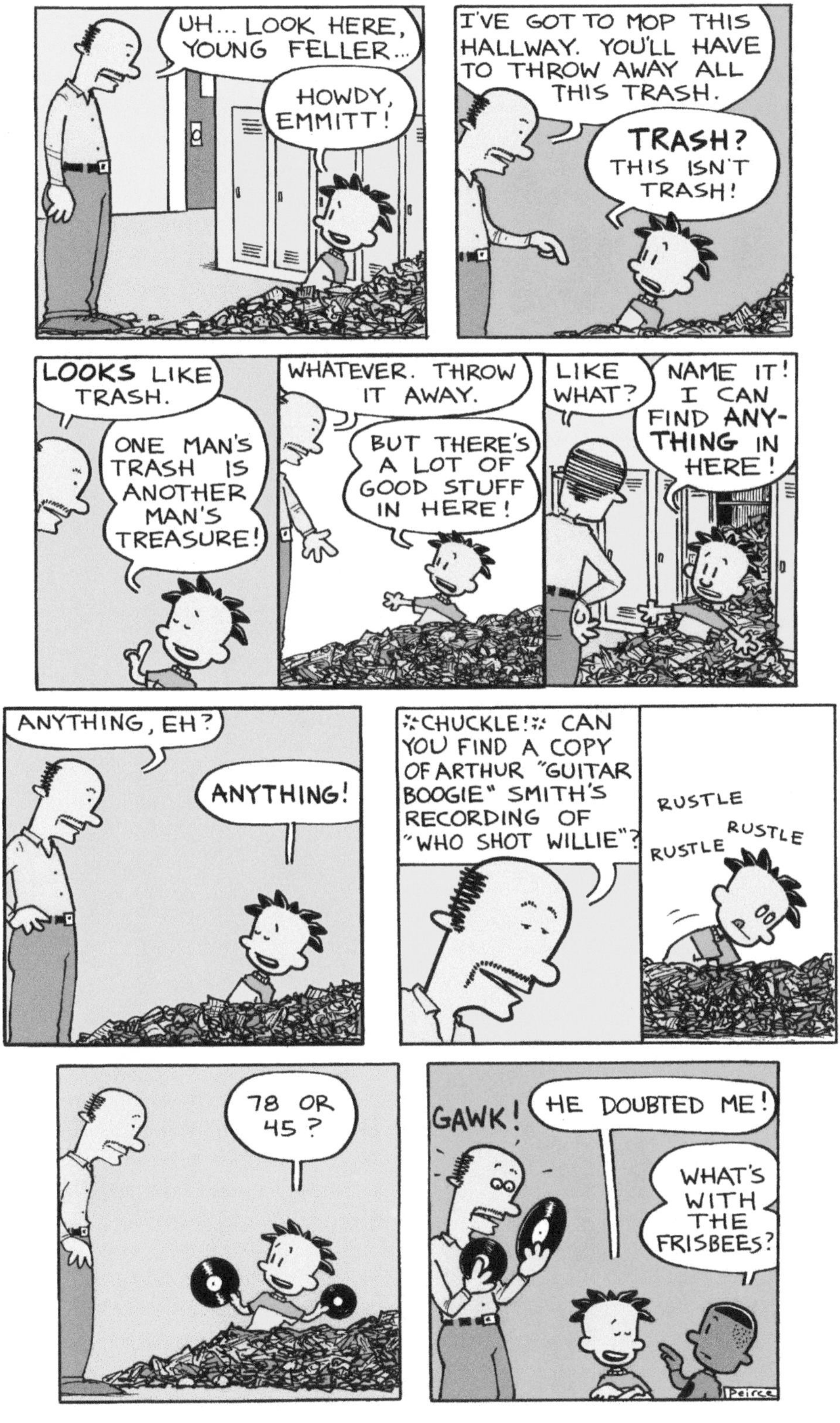
UH... LOOK HERE, YOUNG FELLER...
HOWDY, EMMITT!
I'VE GOT TO MOP THIS HALLWAY. YOU'LL HAVE TO THROW AWAY ALL THIS TRASH.
TRASH? THIS ISN'T TRASH!
LOOKS LIKE TRASH.
ONE MAN'S TRASH IS ANOTHER MAN'S TREASURE!
WHATEVER. THROW IT AWAY.
BUT THERE'S A LOT OF GOOD STUFF IN HERE!
LIKE WHAT?
NAME IT! I CAN FIND ANYTHING IN HERE!
ANYTHING, EH?
ANYTHING!
CHUCKLE! CAN YOU FIND A COPY OF ARTHUR "GUITAR BOOGIE" SMITH'S RECORDING OF "WHO SHOT WILLIE"?
RUSTLE
RUSTLE
RUSTLE
78 OR 45?
GAWK!
HE DOUBTED ME!
WHAT'S WITH THE FRISBEES?
Peirce

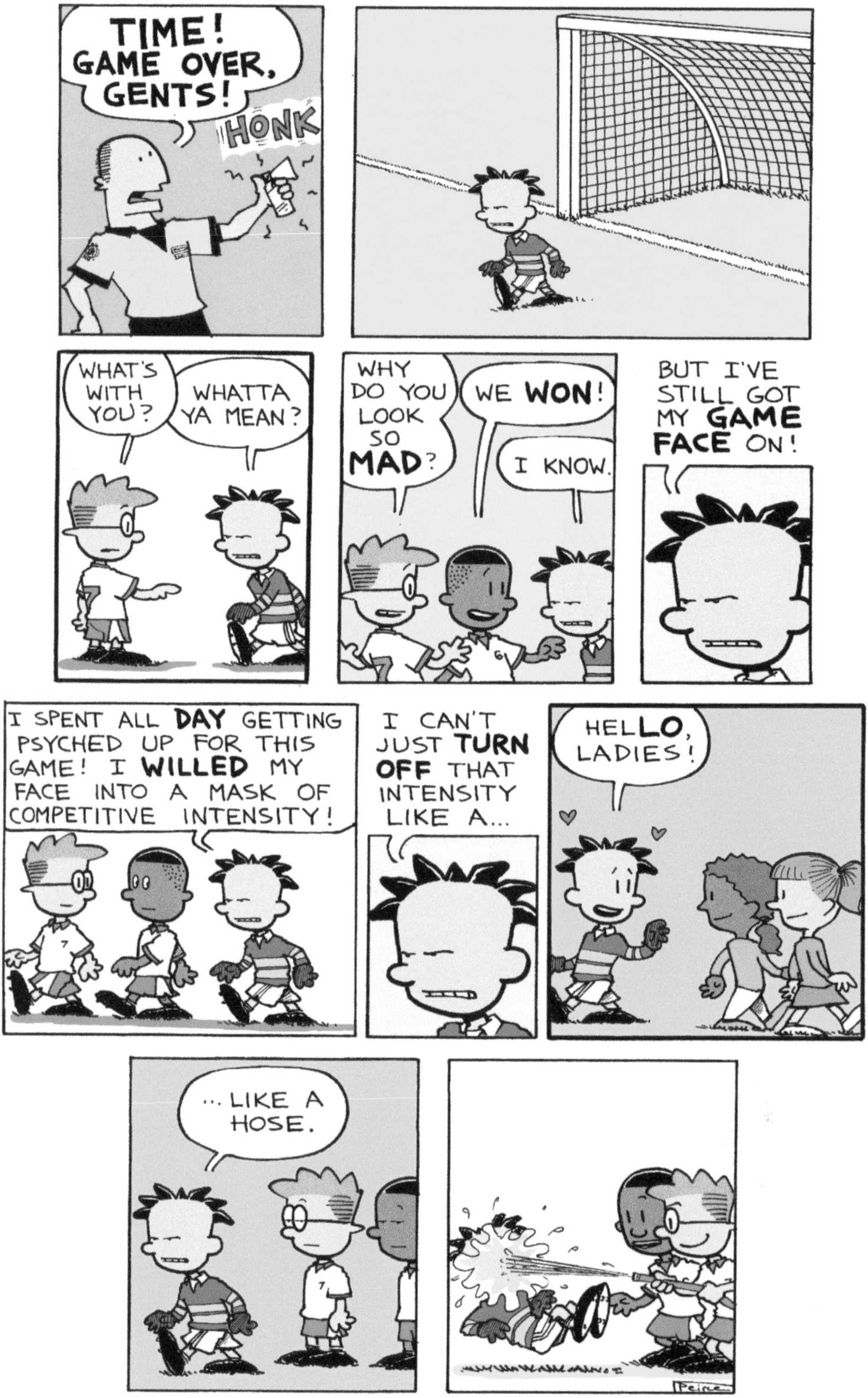
TIME! GAME OVER, GENTS!
HONK
WHAT'S WITH YOU?
WHATTA YA MEAN?
WHY DO YOU LOOK SO MAD?
WE WON!
I KNOW.
BUT I'VE STILL GOT MY GAME FACE ON!
I SPENT ALL DAY GETTING PSYCHED UP FOR THIS GAME! I WILLED MY FACE INTO A MASK OF COMPETITIVE INTENSITY!
I CAN'T JUST TURN OFF THAT INTENSITY LIKE A...
HELLO, LADIES!
...LIKE A HOSE.
Peirce

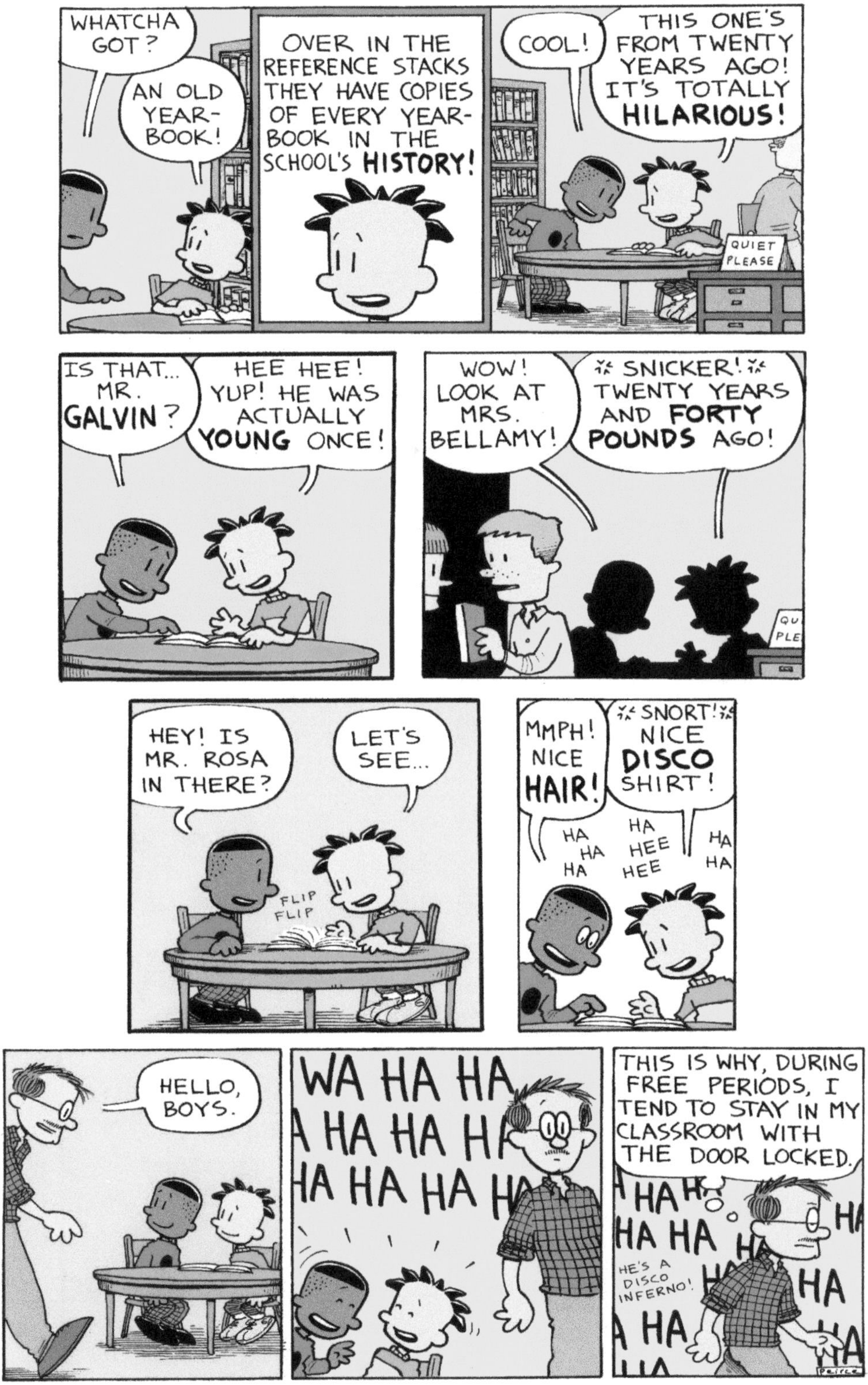
WHATCHA GOT?
AN OLD YEAR-BOOK!
OVER IN THE REFERENCE STACKS THEY HAVE COPIES OF EVERY YEAR-BOOK IN THE SCHOOL'S HISTORY!
COOL!
THIS ONE'S FROM TWENTY YEARS AGO! IT'S TOTALLY HILARIOUS!
QUIET PLEASE
IS THAT... MR. GALVIN?
HEE HEE! YUP! HE WAS ACTUALLY YOUNG ONCE!
WOW! LOOK AT MRS. BELLAMY!
SNICKER! TWENTY YEARS AND FORTY POUNDS AGO!
HEY! IS MR. ROSA IN THERE?
LET'S SEE...
FLIP FLIP
MMPH! NICE HAIR!
SNORT! NICE DISCO SHIRT!
HA HA HA
HA HEE HEE
HA HA
HELLO, BOYS.
WA HA HA
HA HA HA
HA HA HA HA
THIS IS WHY, DURING FREE PERIODS, I TEND TO STAY IN MY CLASSROOM WITH THE DOOR LOCKED.
HA HA HA HA HA
HE'S A DISCO INFERNO!

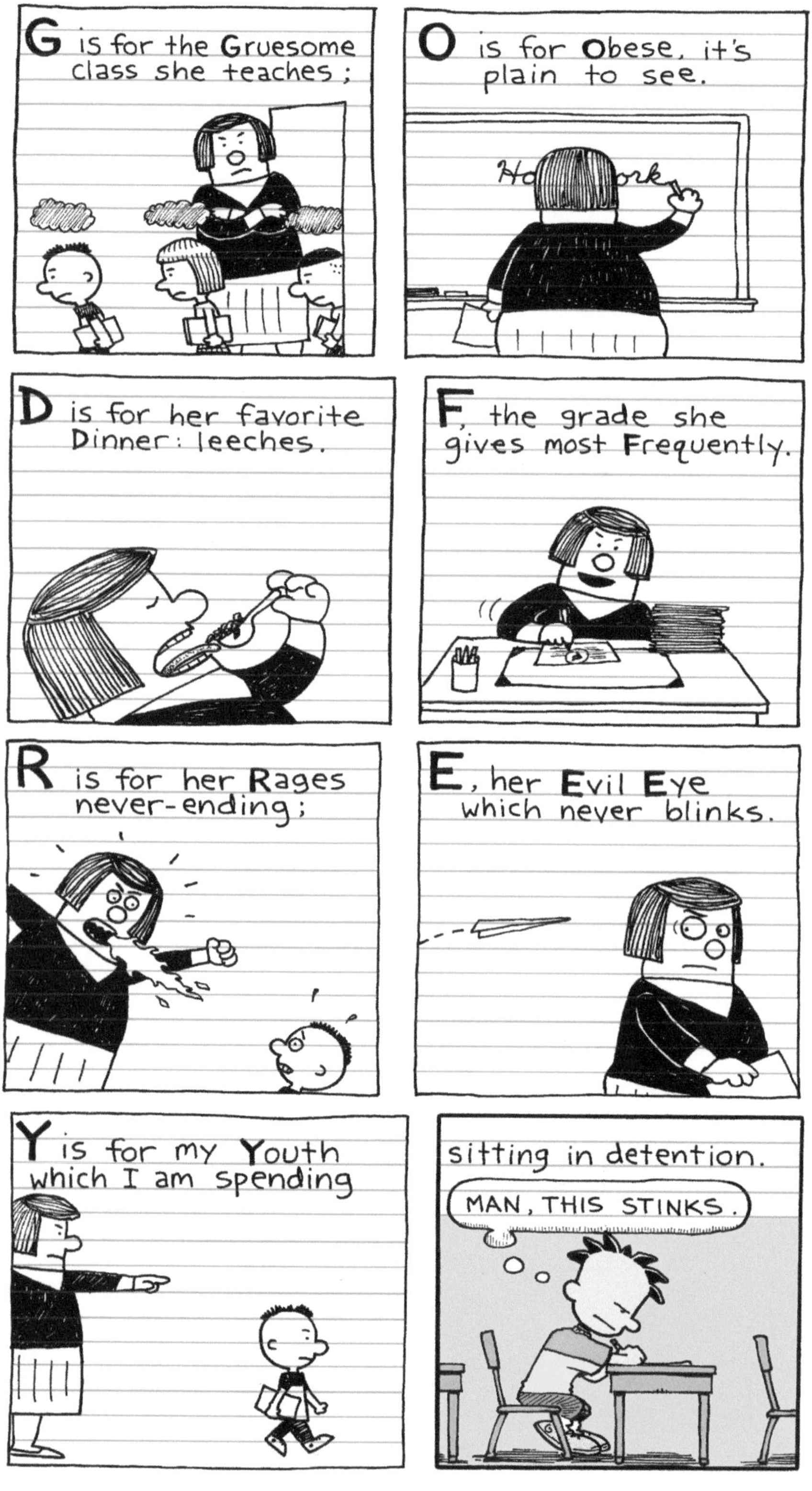
G is for the Gruesome class she teaches;
O is for Obese, it's plain to see.
Ho   ork
D is for her favorite Dinner: leeches.
F, the grade she gives most Frequently.
R is for her Rages never-ending;
E, her Evil Eye which never blinks.
Y is for my Youth which I am spending
sitting in detention.
MAN, THIS STINKS.

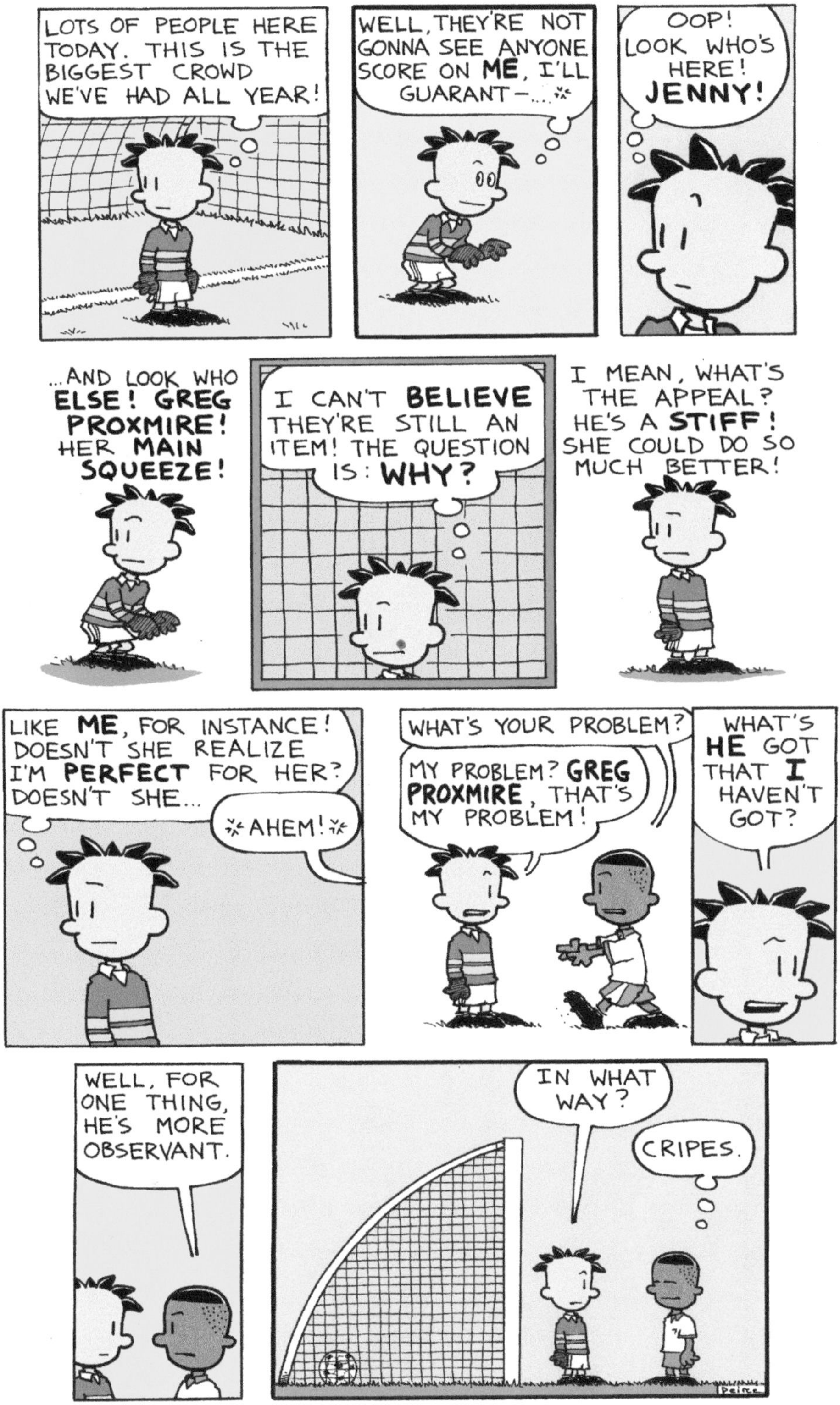
LOTS OF PEOPLE HERE TODAY. THIS IS THE BIGGEST CROWD WE'VE HAD ALL YEAR!
WELL, THEY'RE NOT GONNA SEE ANYONE SCORE ON ME, I'LL GUARANT–...
OOP! LOOK WHO'S HERE! JENNY!
...AND LOOK WHO ELSE! GREG PROXMIRE! HER MAIN SQUEEZE!
I CAN'T BELIEVE THEY'RE STILL AN ITEM! THE QUESTION IS: WHY?
I MEAN, WHAT'S THE APPEAL? HE'S A STIFF! SHE COULD DO SO MUCH BETTER!
LIKE ME, FOR INSTANCE! DOESN'T SHE REALIZE I'M PERFECT FOR HER? DOESN'T SHE...
AHEM!
WHAT'S YOUR PROBLEM?
MY PROBLEM? GREG PROXMIRE, THAT'S MY PROBLEM!
WHAT'S HE GOT THAT I HAVEN'T GOT?
WELL, FOR ONE THING, HE'S MORE OBSERVANT.
IN WHAT WAY?
CRIPES.
Peirce

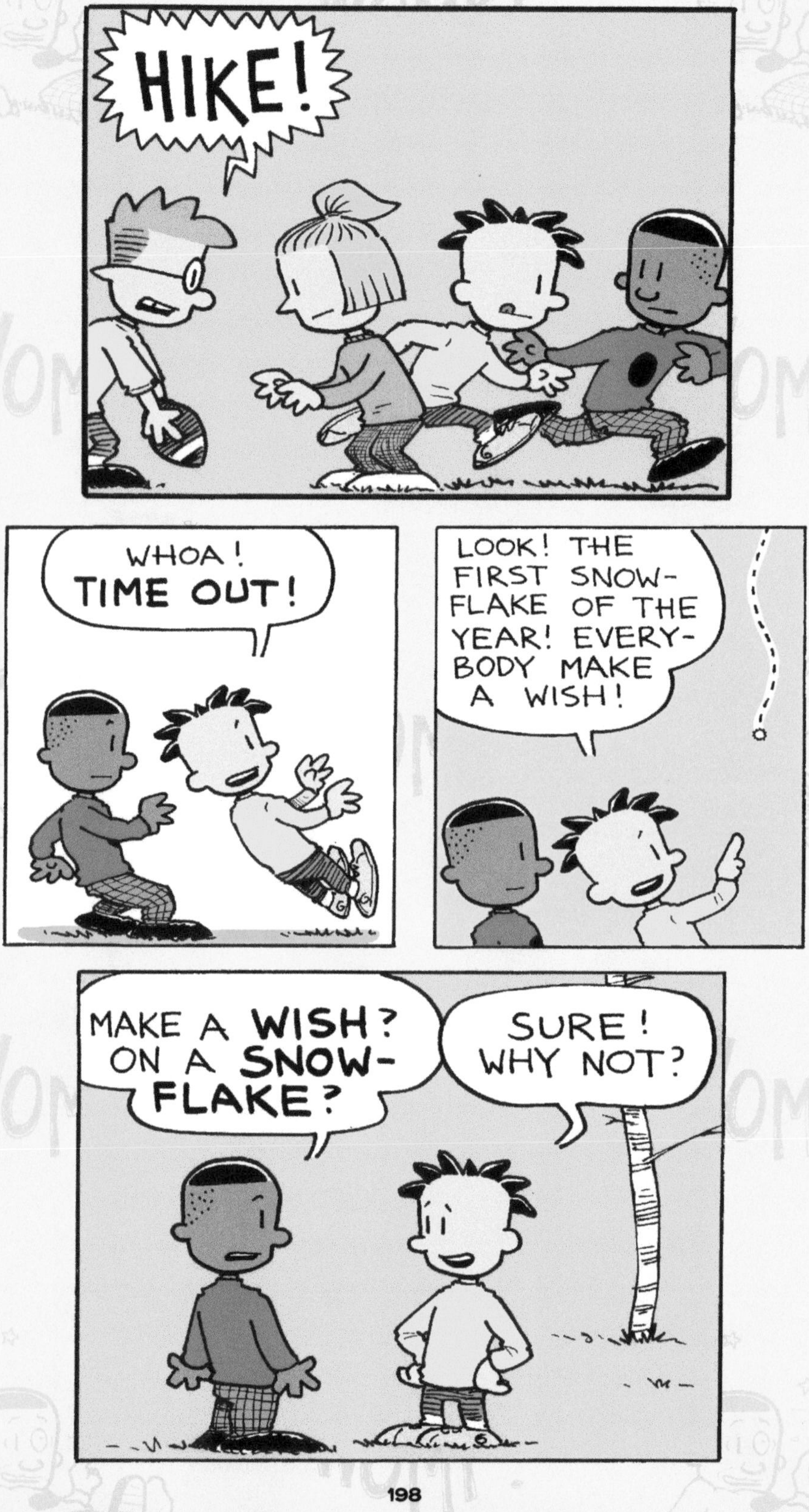
HIKE!
WHOA! TIME OUT!
LOOK! THE FIRST SNOW-FLAKE OF THE YEAR! EVERY-BODY MAKE A WISH!
MAKE A WISH? ON A SNOW-FLAKE?
SURE! WHY NOT?

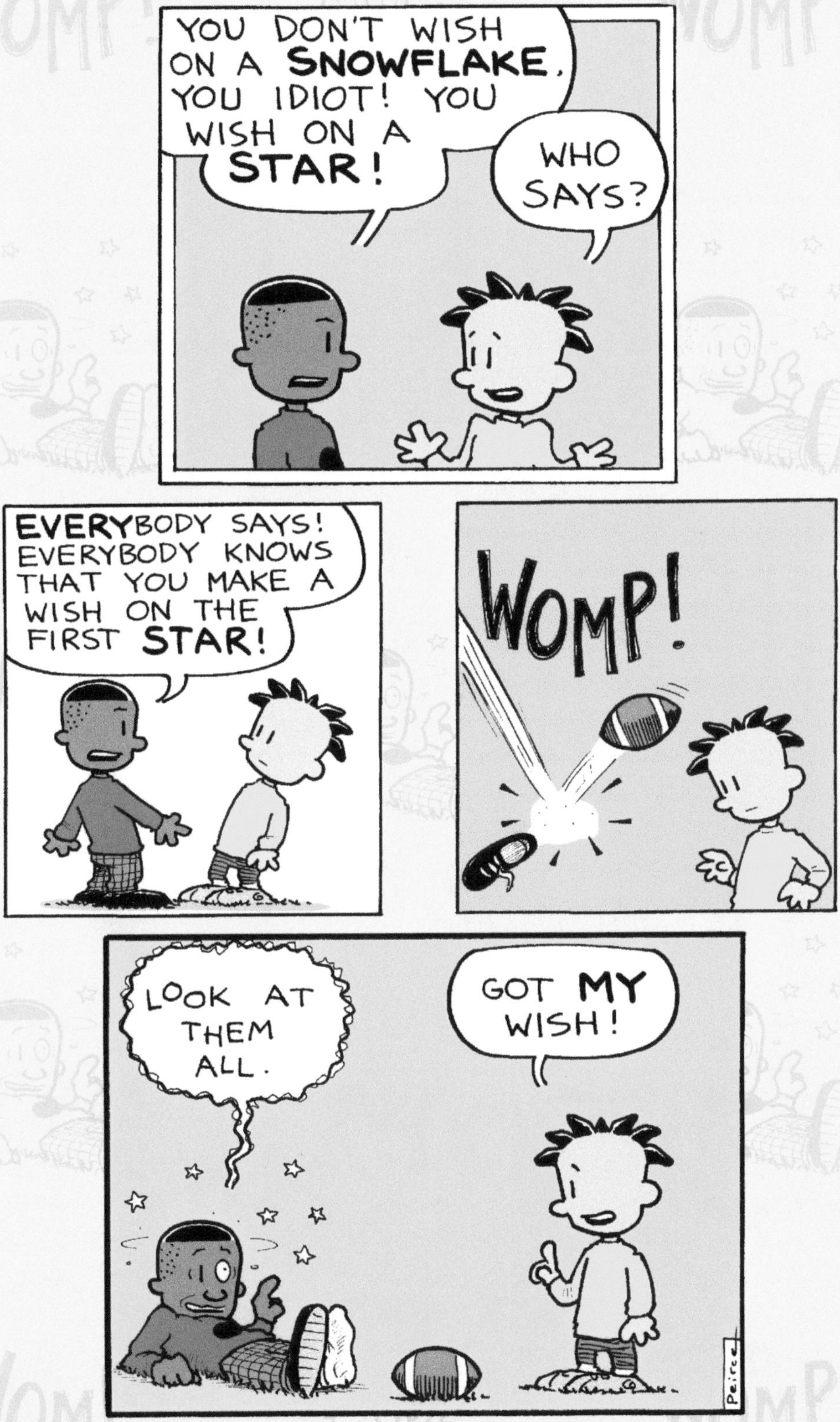
YOU DON'T WISH ON A SNOWFLAKE, YOU IDIOT! YOU WISH ON A STAR!
WHO SAYS?
EVERYBODY SAYS! EVERYBODY KNOWS THAT YOU MAKE A WISH ON THE FIRST STAR!
WOMP!
LOOK AT THEM ALL.
GOT MY WISH!
Peirce

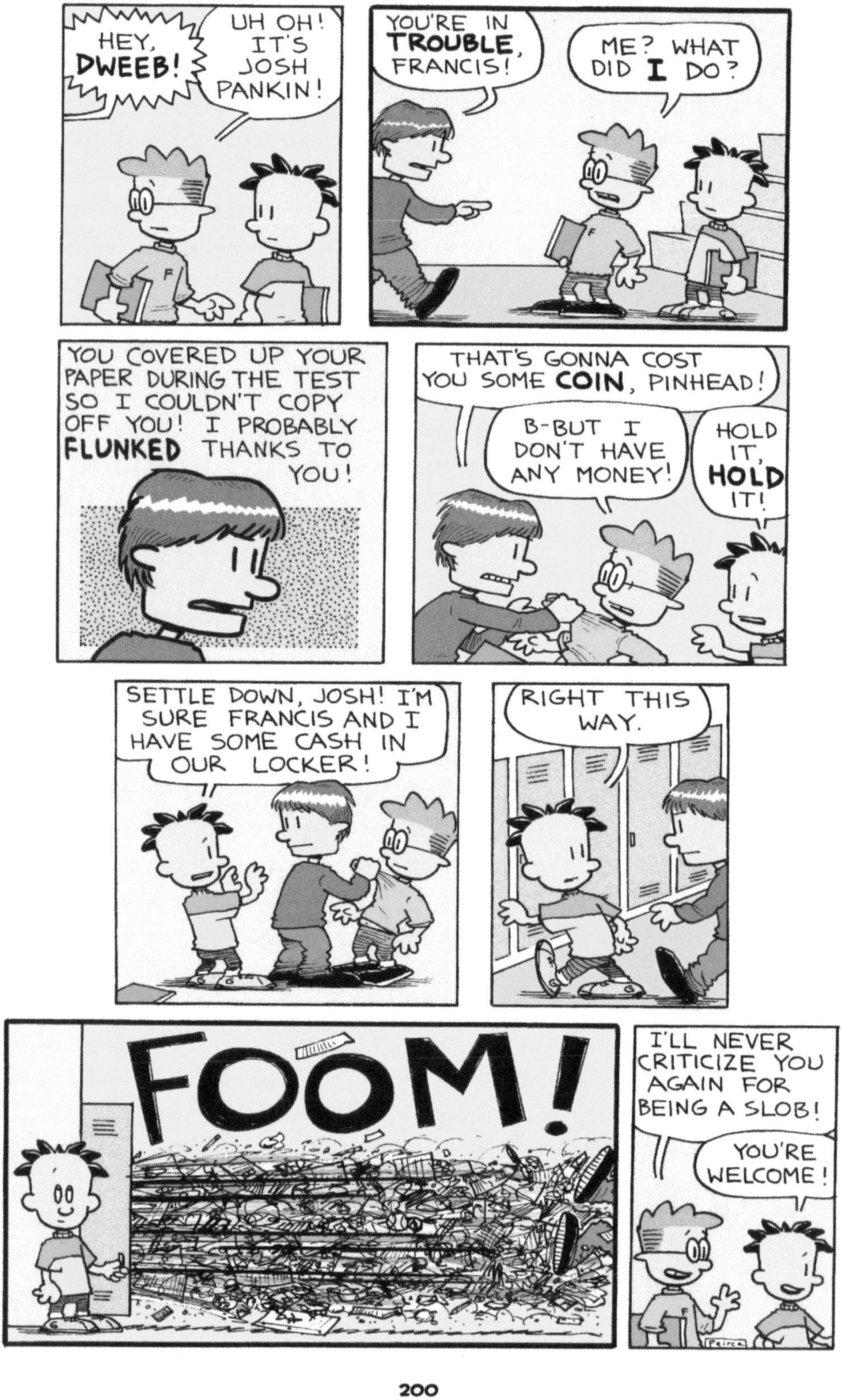
HEY, DWEEB!
UH OH! IT'S JOSH PANKIN!
YOU'RE IN TROUBLE, FRANCIS!
ME? WHAT DID I DO?
YOU COVERED UP YOUR PAPER DURING THE TEST SO I COULDN'T COPY OFF YOU! I PROBABLY FLUNKED THANKS TO YOU!
THAT'S GONNA COST YOU SOME COIN, PINHEAD!
B-BUT I DON'T HAVE ANY MONEY!
HOLD IT, HOLD IT!
SETTLE DOWN, JOSH! I'M SURE FRANCIS AND I HAVE SOME CASH IN OUR LOCKER!
RIGHT THIS WAY.
FOOM!
I'LL NEVER CRITICIZE YOU AGAIN FOR BEING A SLOB!
YOU'RE WELCOME!
Peirce

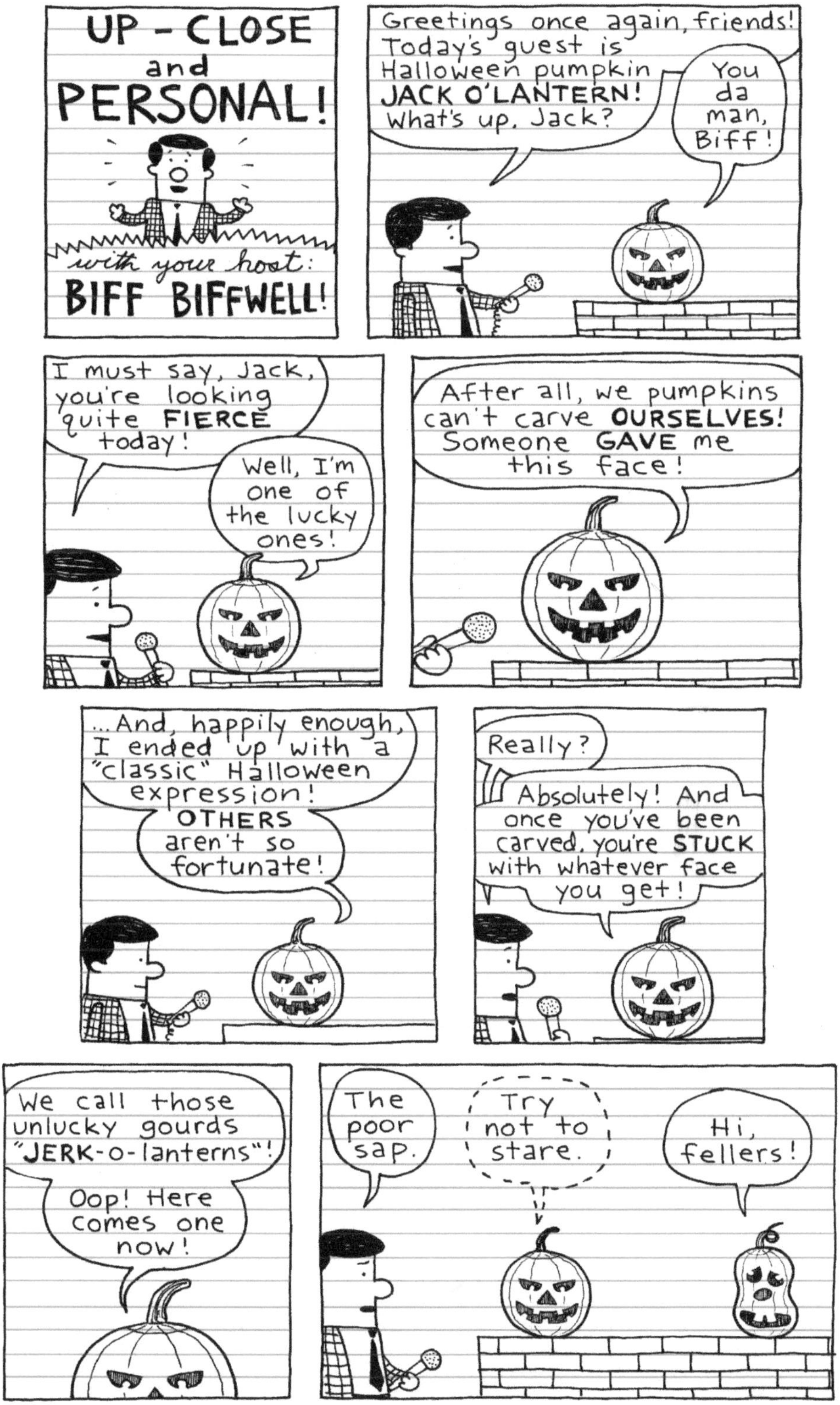
UP-CLOSE and PERSONAL!
with your host: BIFF BIFFWELL!
Greetings once again, friends! Today's guest is Halloween pumpkin **JACK O'LANTERN!** What's up, Jack?
You da man, Biff!
I must say, Jack, you're looking quite **FIERCE** today!
Well, I'm one of the lucky ones!
After all, we pumpkins can't carve **OURSELVES!** Someone **GAVE** me this face!
...And, happily enough, I ended up with a "classic" Halloween expression!
OTHERS aren't so fortunate!
Really?
Absolutely! And once you've been carved, you're **STUCK** with whatever face you get!
We call those unlucky gourds "**JERK**-o-lanterns"!
Oop! Here comes one now!
The poor sap.
Try not to stare.
Hi, fellers!

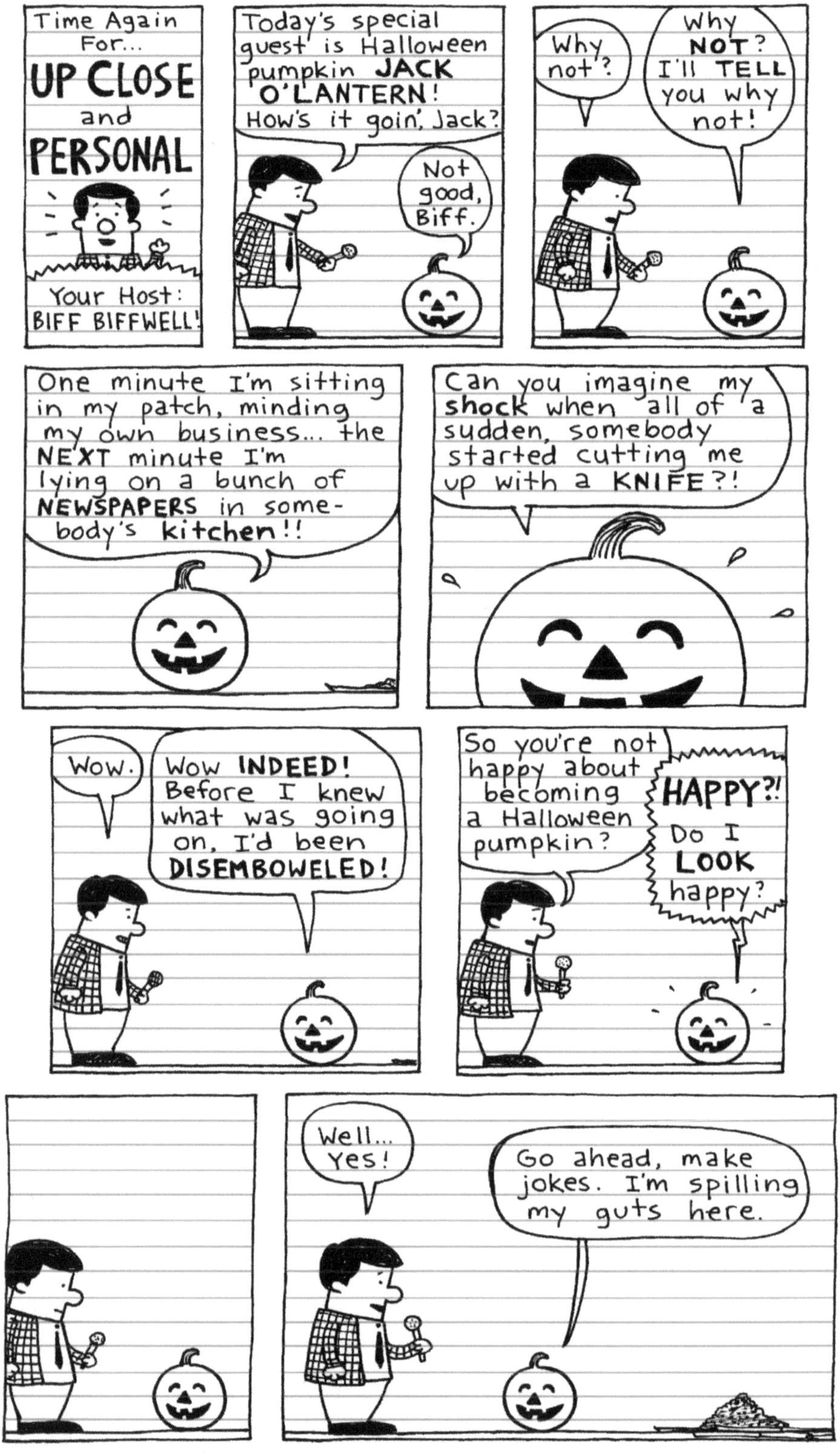
Time Again For...
UP CLOSE and PERSONAL
Your Host: BIFF BIFFWELL!
Today's special guest is Halloween pumpkin JACK O'LANTERN! How's it goin', Jack?
Not good, Biff.
Why not?
Why NOT? I'll TELL you why not!
One minute I'm sitting in my patch, minding my own business... the NEXT minute I'm lying on a bunch of NEWSPAPERS in some-body's kitchen!!
Can you imagine my shock when all of a sudden, somebody started cutting me up with a KNIFE?!
Wow.
Wow INDEED! Before I knew what was going on, I'd been DISEMBOWELED!
So you're not happy about becoming a Halloween pumpkin?
HAPPY?! Do I LOOK happy?
Well... Yes!
Go ahead, make jokes. I'm spilling my guts here.

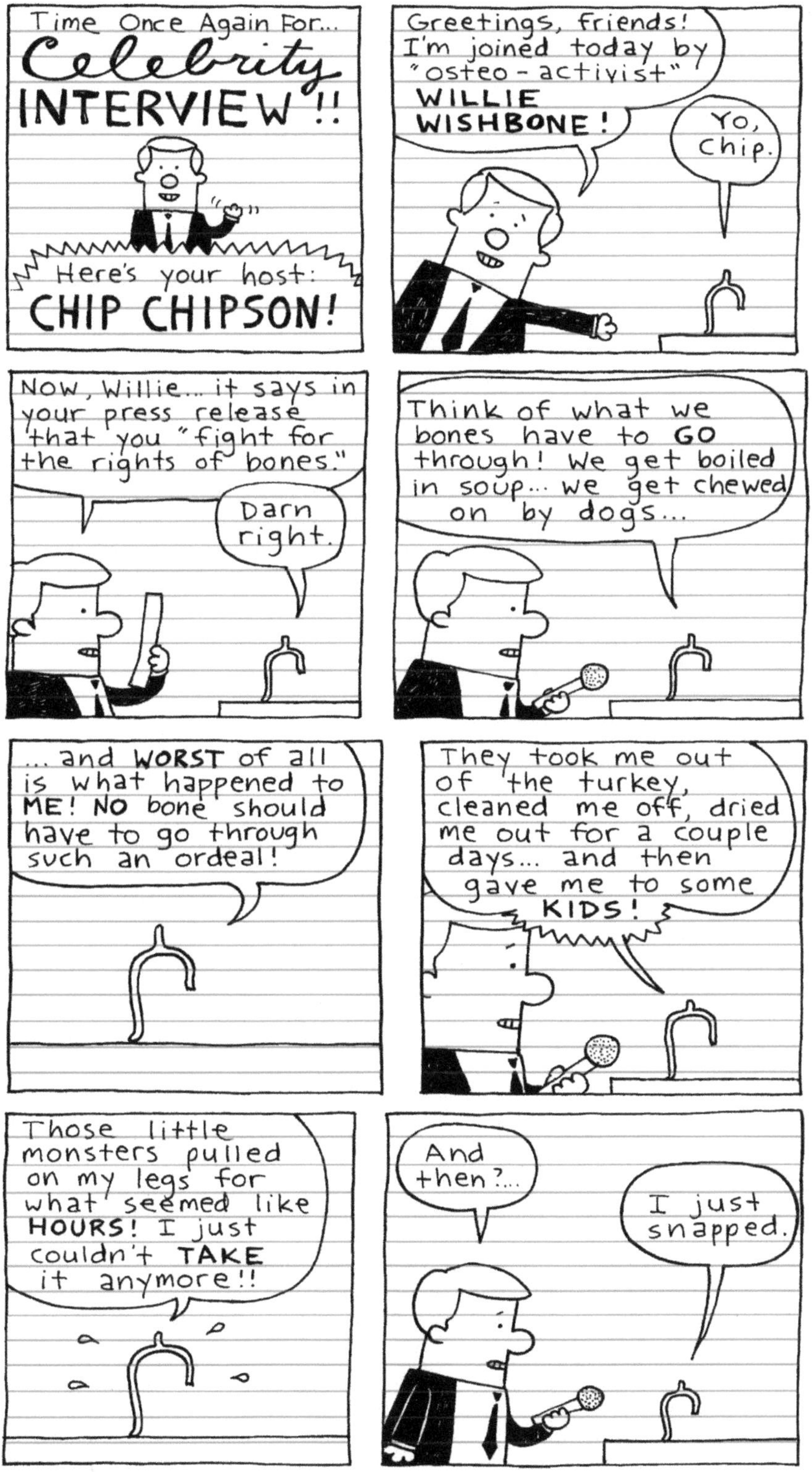
Time Once Again For...
Celebrity
INTERVIEW!!
Here's your host:
CHIP CHIPSON!
Greetings, friends! I'm joined today by "osteo-activist" WILLIE WISHBONE!
Yo, Chip.
Now, Willie... it says in your press release that you "fight for the rights of bones."
Darn right.
Think of what we bones have to GO through! We get boiled in soup... we get chewed on by dogs...
... and WORST of all is what happened to ME! NO bone should have to go through such an ordeal!
They took me out of the turkey, cleaned me off, dried me out for a couple days... and then gave me to some KIDS!
Those little monsters pulled on my legs for what seemed like HOURS! I just couldn't TAKE it anymore!!
And then?...
I just snapped.

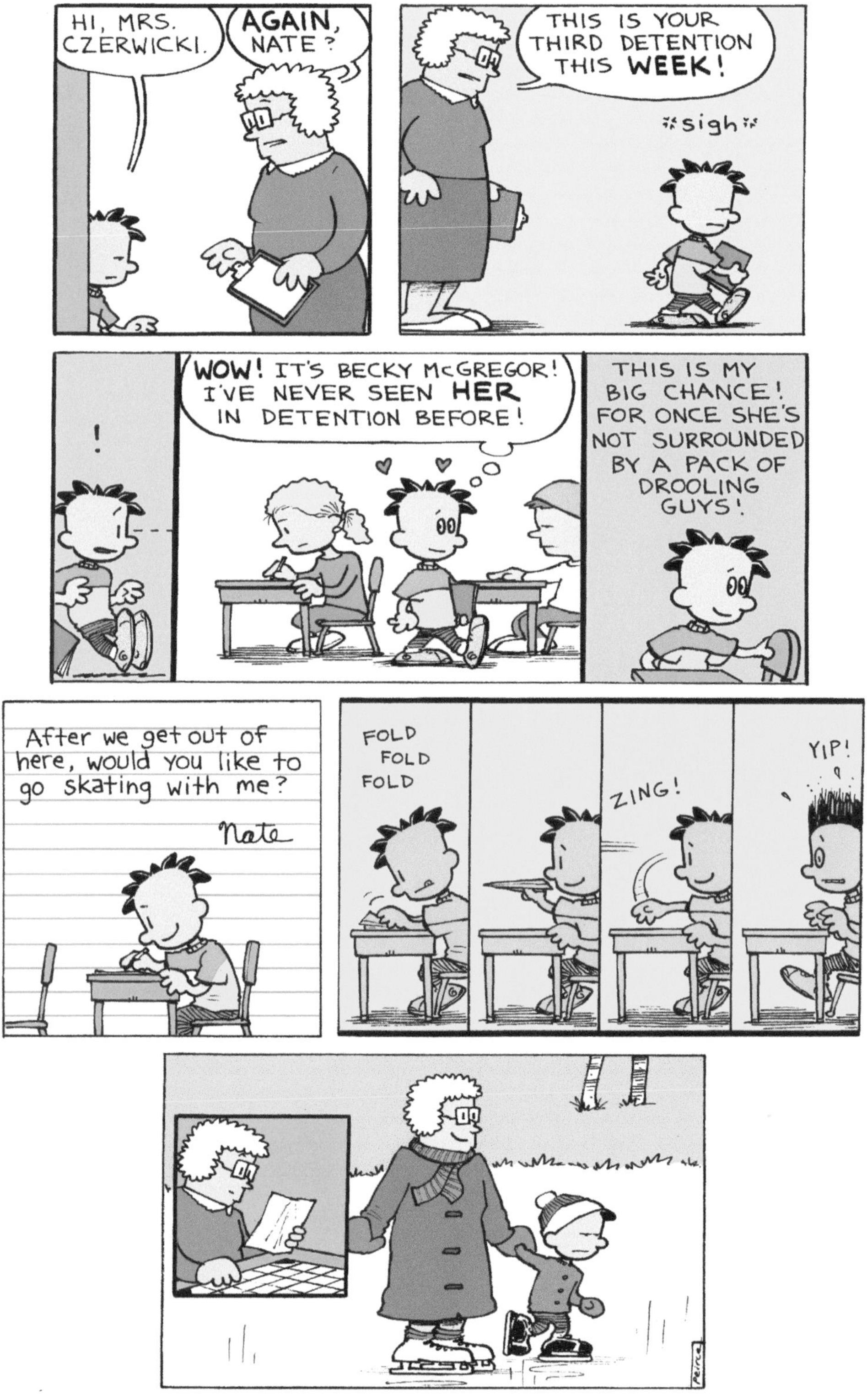
HI, MRS. CZERWICKI.
AGAIN, NATE?
THIS IS YOUR THIRD DETENTION THIS WEEK!
sigh
!
WOW! IT'S BECKY McGREGOR! I'VE NEVER SEEN HER IN DETENTION BEFORE!
THIS IS MY BIG CHANCE! FOR ONCE SHE'S NOT SURROUNDED BY A PACK OF DROOLING GUYS!
After we get out of here, would you like to go skating with me?
Nate
FOLD FOLD FOLD
ZING!
YIP!
Peirce

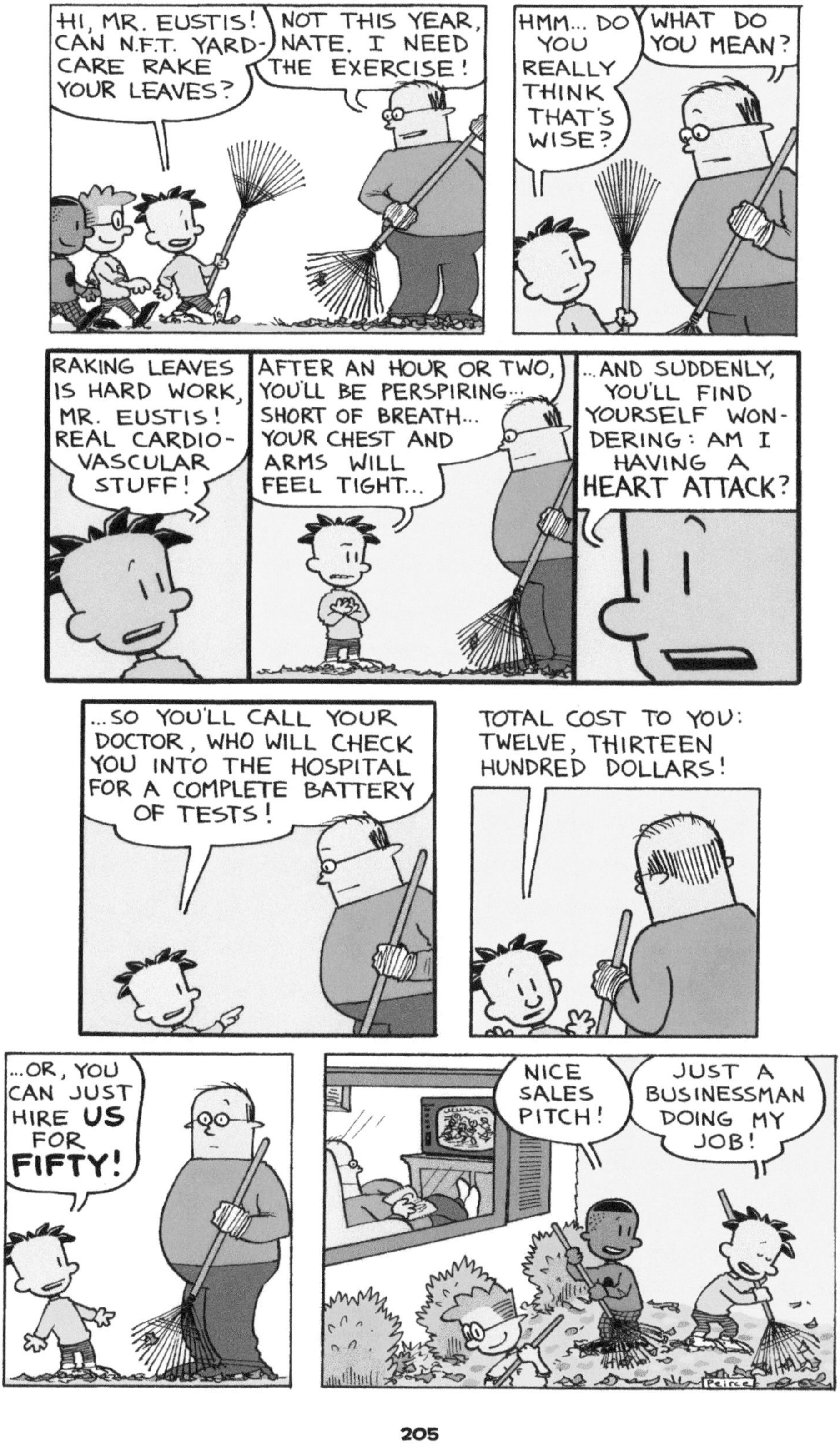

HI, MR. EUSTIS! CAN N.F.T. YARD-CARE RAKE YOUR LEAVES?
NOT THIS YEAR, NATE. I NEED THE EXERCISE!
HMM... DO YOU REALLY THINK THAT'S WISE?
WHAT DO YOU MEAN?
RAKING LEAVES IS HARD WORK, MR. EUSTIS! REAL CARDIO-VASCULAR STUFF!
AFTER AN HOUR OR TWO, YOU'LL BE PERSPIRING... SHORT OF BREATH... YOUR CHEST AND ARMS WILL FEEL TIGHT...
...AND SUDDENLY, YOU'LL FIND YOURSELF WONDERING: AM I HAVING A HEART ATTACK?
...SO YOU'LL CALL YOUR DOCTOR, WHO WILL CHECK YOU INTO THE HOSPITAL FOR A COMPLETE BATTERY OF TESTS!
TOTAL COST TO YOU: TWELVE, THIRTEEN HUNDRED DOLLARS!
...OR, YOU CAN JUST HIRE US FOR FIFTY!
NICE SALES PITCH!
JUST A BUSINESSMAN DOING MY JOB!
Peirce

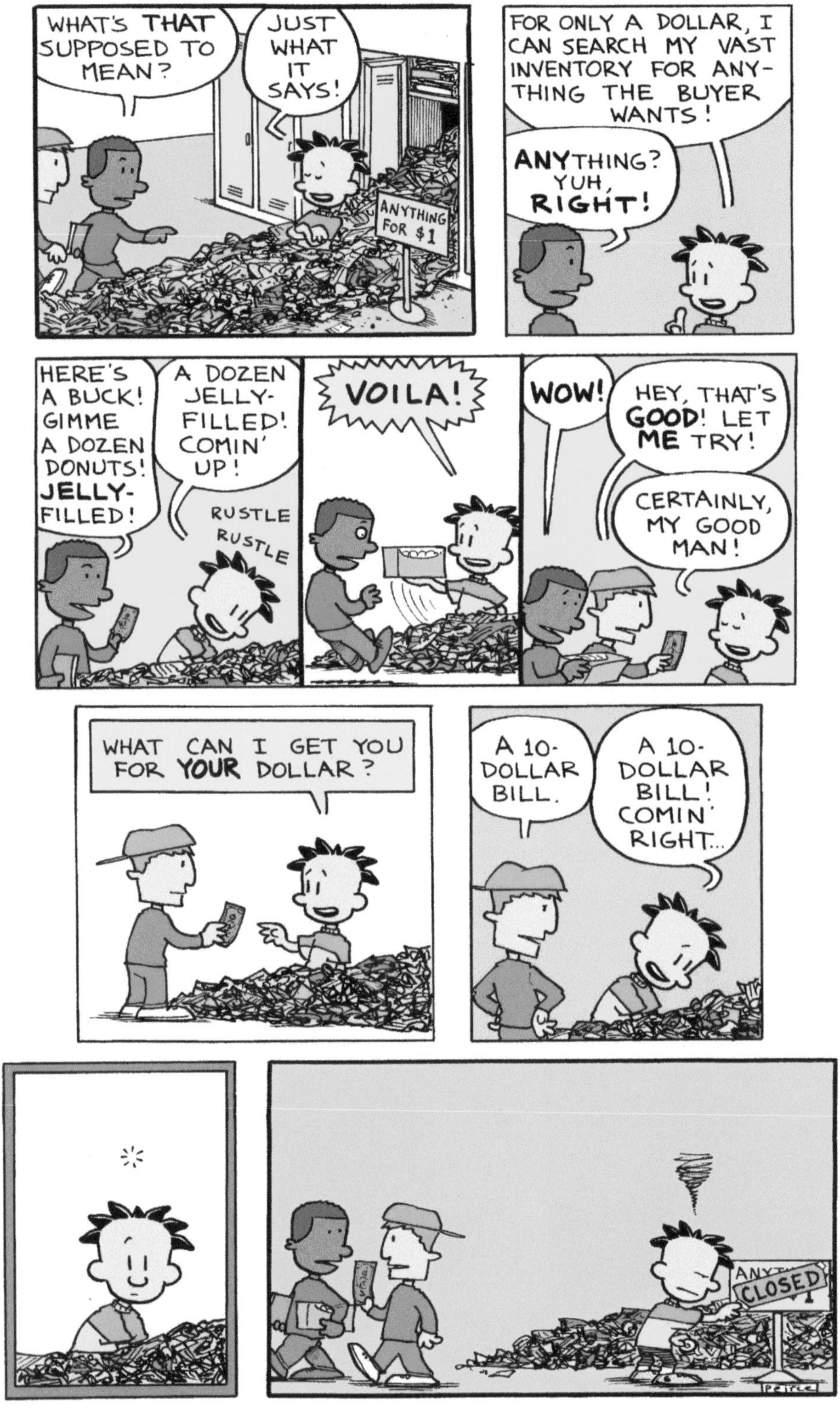
WHAT'S THAT SUPPOSED TO MEAN?
JUST WHAT IT SAYS!
ANYTHING FOR $1
FOR ONLY A DOLLAR, I CAN SEARCH MY VAST INVENTORY FOR ANYTHING THE BUYER WANTS!
ANYTHING? YUH, RIGHT!
HERE'S A BUCK! GIMME A DOZEN DONUTS! JELLY-FILLED!
A DOZEN JELLY-FILLED! COMIN' UP!
RUSTLE RUSTLE
VOILA!
WOW!
HEY, THAT'S GOOD! LET ME TRY!
CERTAINLY, MY GOOD MAN!
WHAT CAN I GET YOU FOR YOUR DOLLAR?
A 10-DOLLAR BILL.
A 10-DOLLAR BILL! COMIN' RIGHT...
CLOSED
PEIRCE

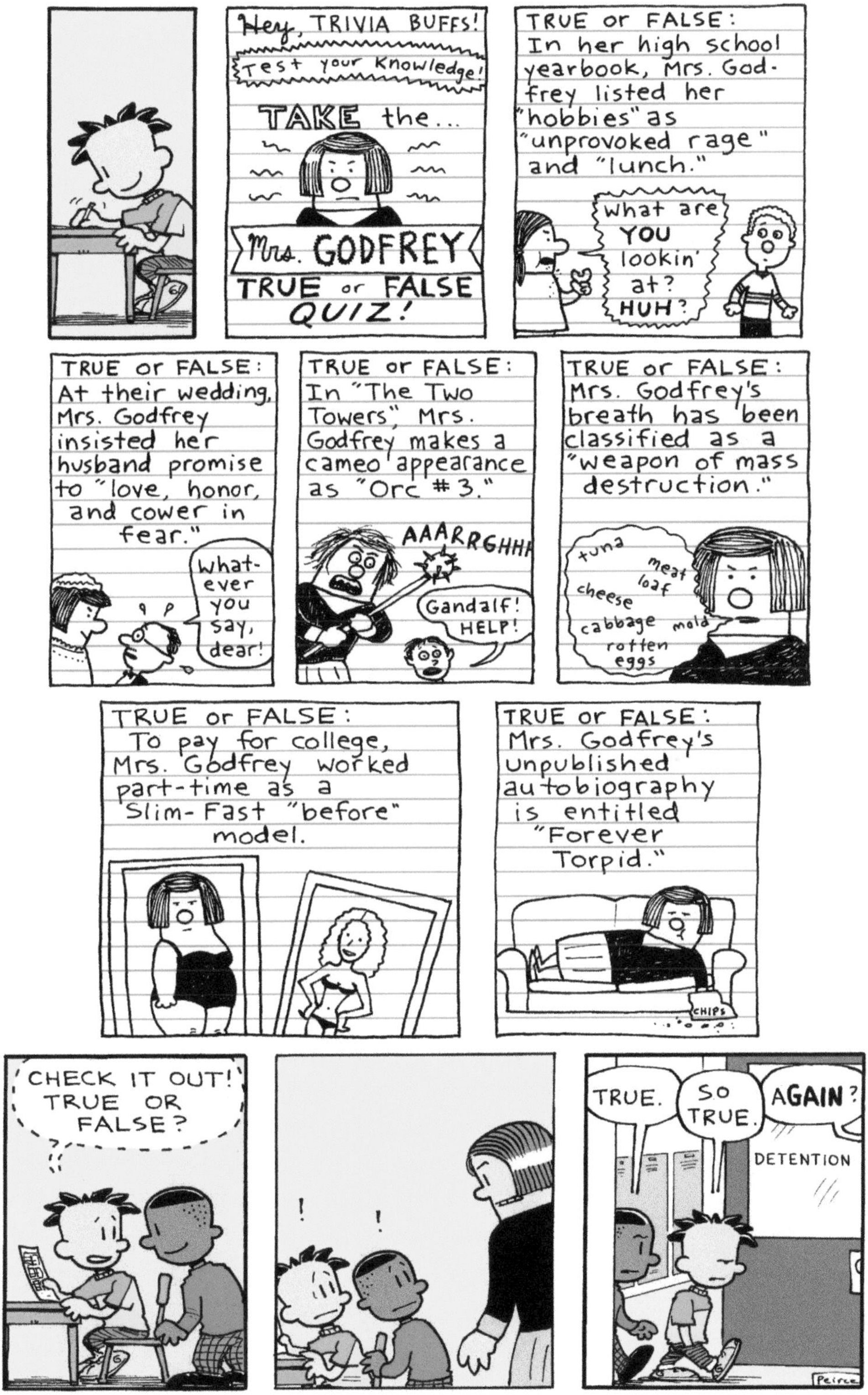
Hey, TRIVIA BUFFS!
Test your Knowledge!
TAKE the...
Mrs. GODFREY
TRUE or FALSE QUIZ!
TRUE or FALSE: In her high school yearbook, Mrs. Godfrey listed her "hobbies" as "unprovoked rage" and "lunch."
What are YOU lookin' at? HUH?
TRUE or FALSE: At their wedding, Mrs. Godfrey insisted her husband promise to "love, honor, and cower in fear."
What-ever you say, dear!
TRUE or FALSE: In "The Two Towers," Mrs. Godfrey makes a cameo appearance as "Orc #3."
AAARRGHHH
Gandalf! HELP!
TRUE or FALSE: Mrs. Godfrey's breath has been classified as a "weapon of mass destruction."
tuna
meat loaf
cheese
cabbage
mold
rotten eggs
TRUE or FALSE: To pay for college, Mrs. Godfrey worked part-time as a "Slim-Fast "before" model.
TRUE or FALSE: Mrs. Godfrey's unpublished autobiography is entitled "Forever Torpid."
CHIPS
CHECK IT OUT! TRUE OR FALSE?
TRUE.
SO TRUE.
AGAIN?
DETENTION
Peirce

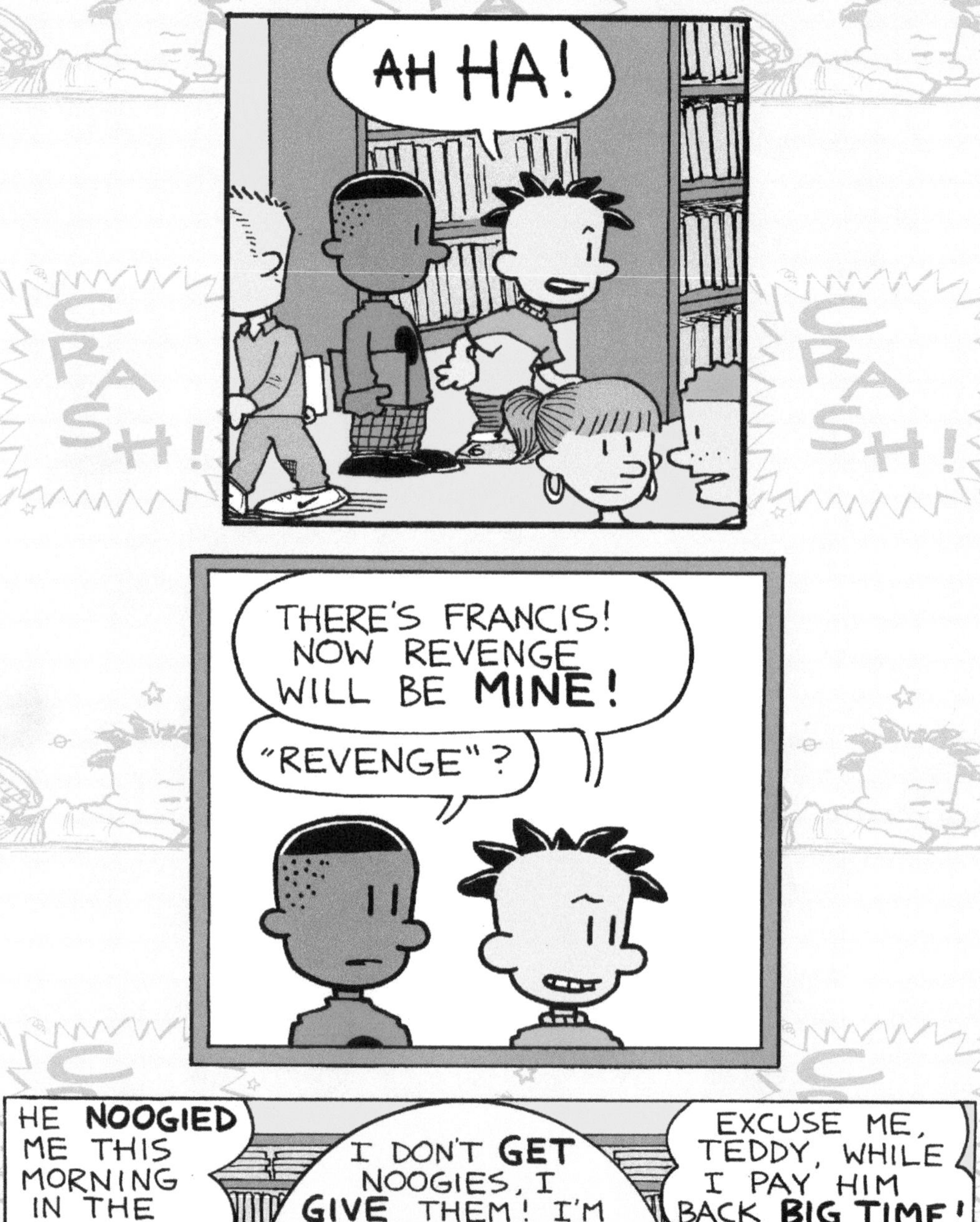
AH HA!
THERE'S FRANCIS! NOW REVENGE WILL BE MINE!
"REVENGE"?
HE NOOGIED ME THIS MORNING IN THE CAFETERIA!
I DON'T GET NOOGIES, I GIVE THEM! I'M THE NOOGIE KING!
EXCUSE ME, TEDDY, WHILE I PAY HIM BACK BIG TIME!

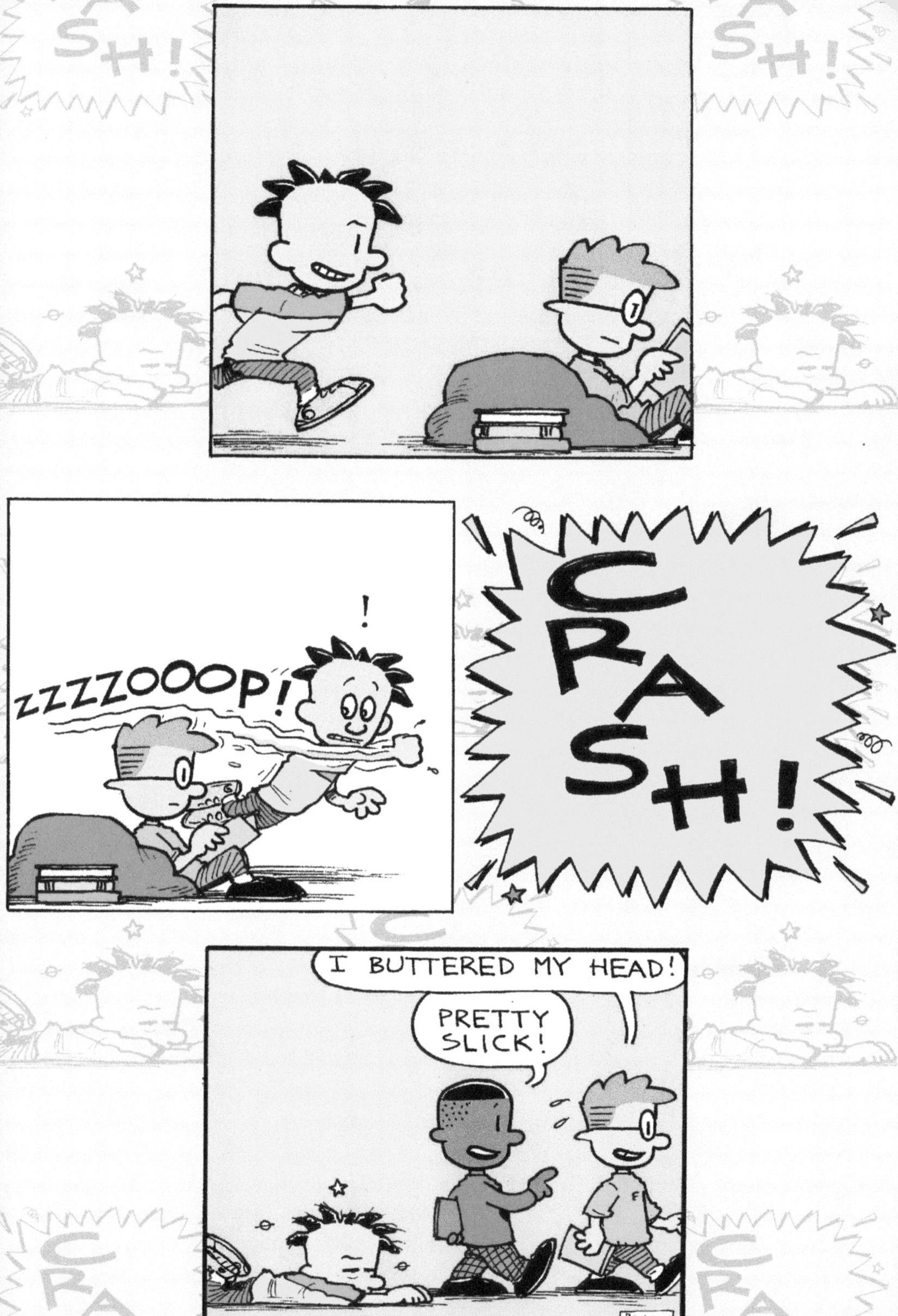
!
ZZZZOOOP!
CRASH!
I BUTTERED MY HEAD!
PRETTY SLICK!
Peirce

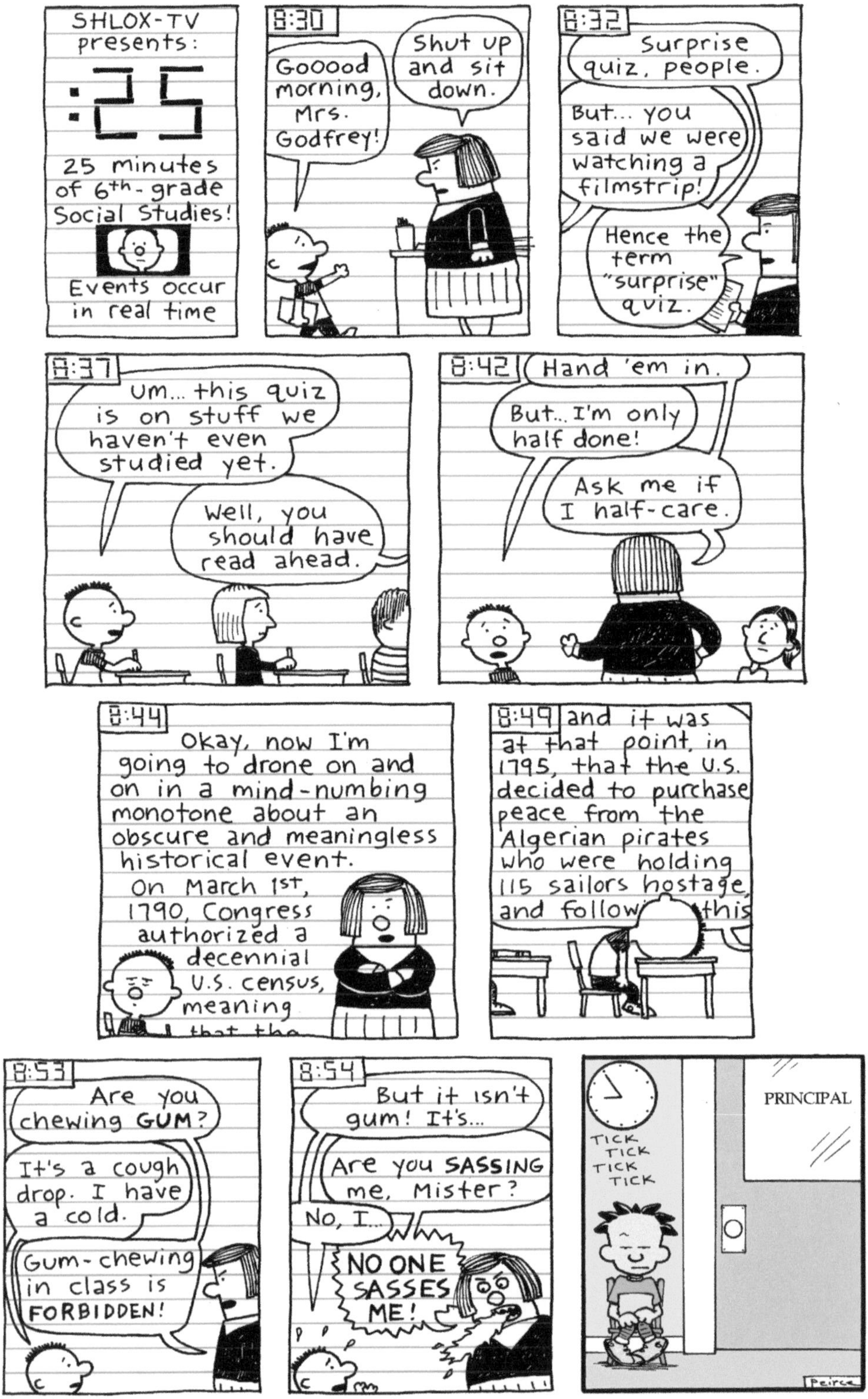
SHLOX-TV presents:
:25
25 minutes of 6th-grade Social Studies!
Events occur in real time
8:30
Gooood morning, Mrs. Godfrey!
Shut up and sit down.
8:32
Surprise quiz, people.
But... you said we were watching a filmstrip!
Hence the term "surprise" quiz.
8:37
Um... this quiz is on stuff we haven't even studied yet.
Well, you should have read ahead.
8:42
Hand 'em in.
But... I'm only half done!
Ask me if I half-care.
8:44
Okay, now I'm going to drone on and on in a mind-numbing monotone about an obscure and meaningless historical event.
On March 1st, 1790, Congress authorized a decennial U.S. census, meaning
8:49
and it was at that point, in 1795, that the U.S. decided to purchase peace from the Algerian pirates who were holding 115 sailors hostage, and follow this
8:53
Are you chewing GUM?
It's a cough drop. I have a cold.
Gum-chewing in class is FORBIDDEN!
8:54
But it isn't gum! It's...
Are you SASSING me, Mister?
No, I...
NO ONE SASSES ME!
TICK TICK TICK TICK
PRINCIPAL
Peirce

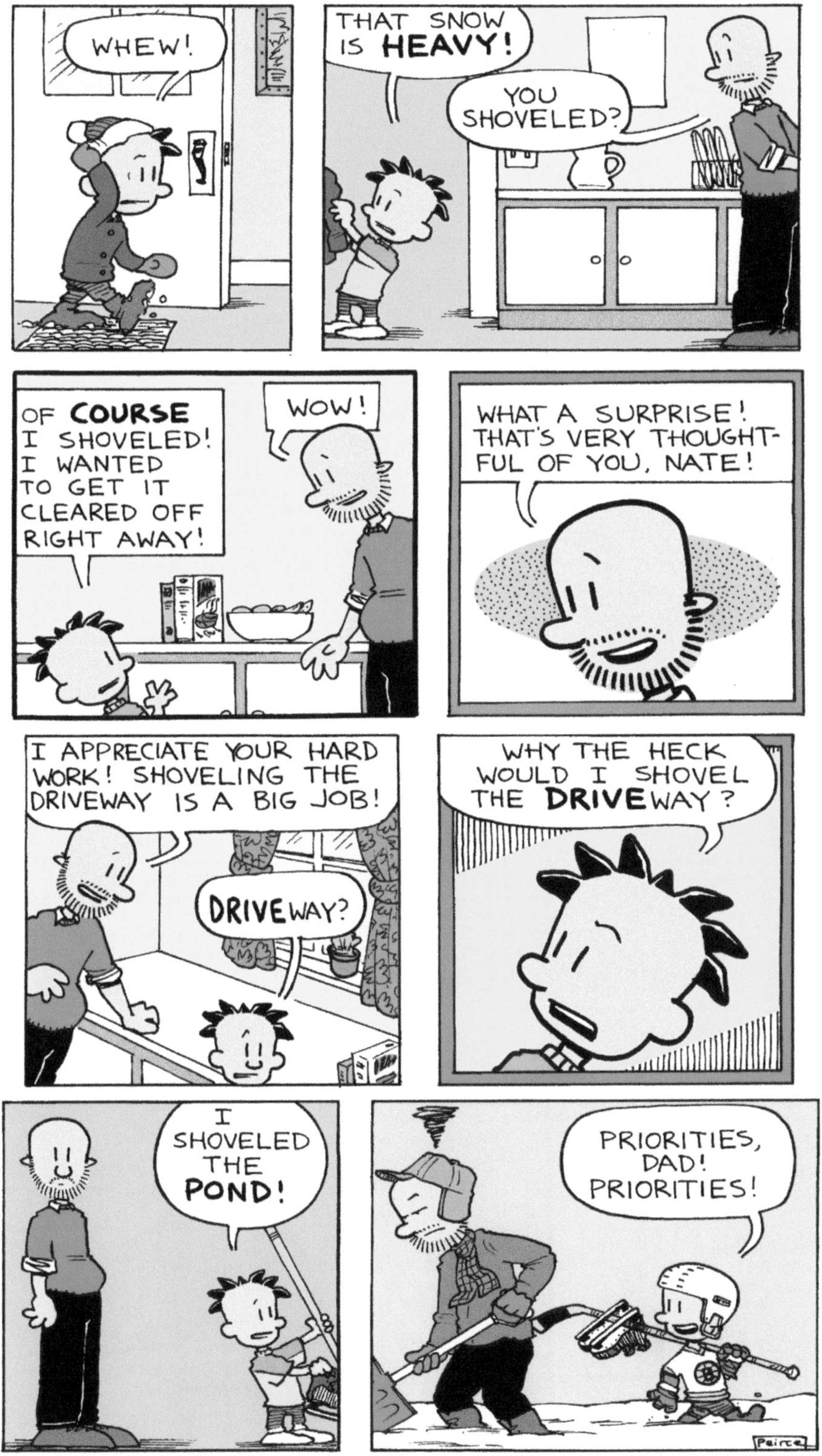
WHEW!
THAT SNOW IS HEAVY!
YOU SHOVELED?
OF COURSE I SHOVELED! I WANTED TO GET IT CLEARED OFF RIGHT AWAY!
WOW!
WHAT A SURPRISE! THAT'S VERY THOUGHTFUL OF YOU, NATE!
I APPRECIATE YOUR HARD WORK! SHOVELING THE DRIVEWAY IS A BIG JOB!
DRIVEWAY?
WHY THE HECK WOULD I SHOVEL THE DRIVEWAY?
I SHOVELED THE POND!
PRIORITIES, DAD! PRIORITIES!
Peirce

Welcome once again to... "MILD WORLD of SPORTS"
with BIFF BIFFWELL!
Hello, friends! Today we'll be treated to a gala FIGURE SKATING exhibition! Here to provide commentary is TODD ZAMBONI!
HI Biff!
Todd, who's our first skater?
It's ELLEN WRIGHT, unveiling a new program!
CLAP!
CLAP! CLAP!
CLAP! CLAP!
...And here comes her first jump!
She INVENTED that move! It's called the "ugly duckling"!
And now... a combination jump!
Yes, it's a combination of CLUMSINESS and INEPTITUDE!
WOW, Todd! What choreography!
I agree, Biff! WHAT choreography??
Like all good routines, this one tells a story!
Right, Biff! It's the story of an awkward girl who can't skate very well!
I must say, Todd, Ellen has some UNUSUAL moves!
She sure does! There's no telling what she'll do NEXT!
!
THAT'S A MOVE I'VE NEVER SEEN BEFORE
Peirce

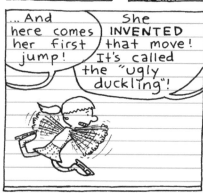

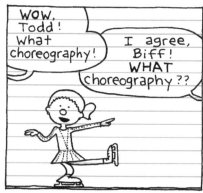

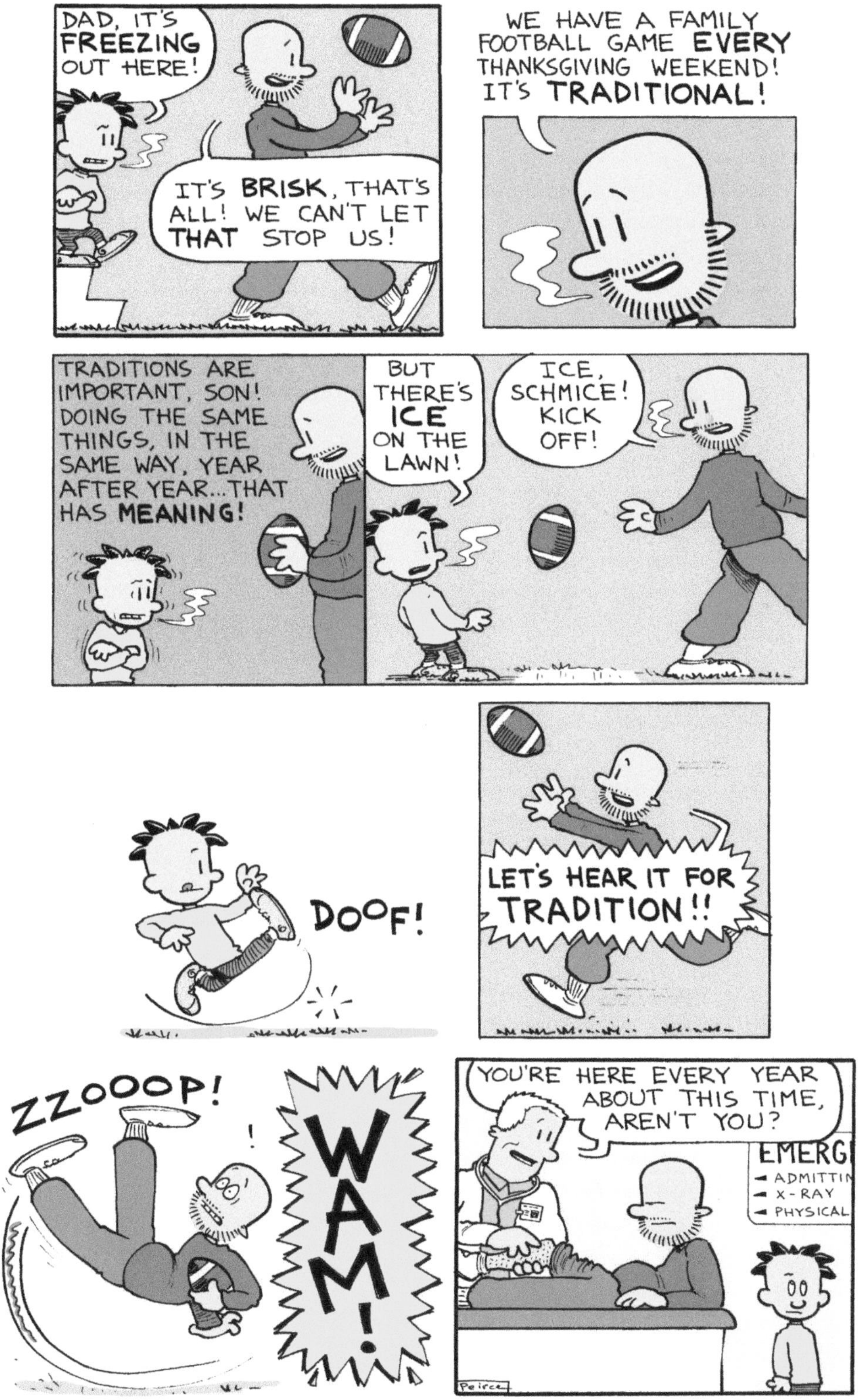
DAD, IT'S FREEZING OUT HERE!
IT'S BRISK, THAT'S ALL! WE CAN'T LET THAT STOP US!
WE HAVE A FAMILY FOOTBALL GAME EVERY THANKSGIVING WEEKEND! IT'S TRADITIONAL!
TRADITIONS ARE IMPORTANT, SON! DOING THE SAME THINGS, IN THE SAME WAY, YEAR AFTER YEAR...THAT HAS MEANING!
BUT THERE'S ICE ON THE LAWN!
ICE, SCHMICE! KICK OFF!
DOOF!
LET'S HEAR IT FOR TRADITION!!
ZZOOOP!
!
WAM!
YOU'RE HERE EVERY YEAR ABOUT THIS TIME, AREN'T YOU?
EMERG
ADMITTIN
X-RAY
PHYSICAL
Peirce

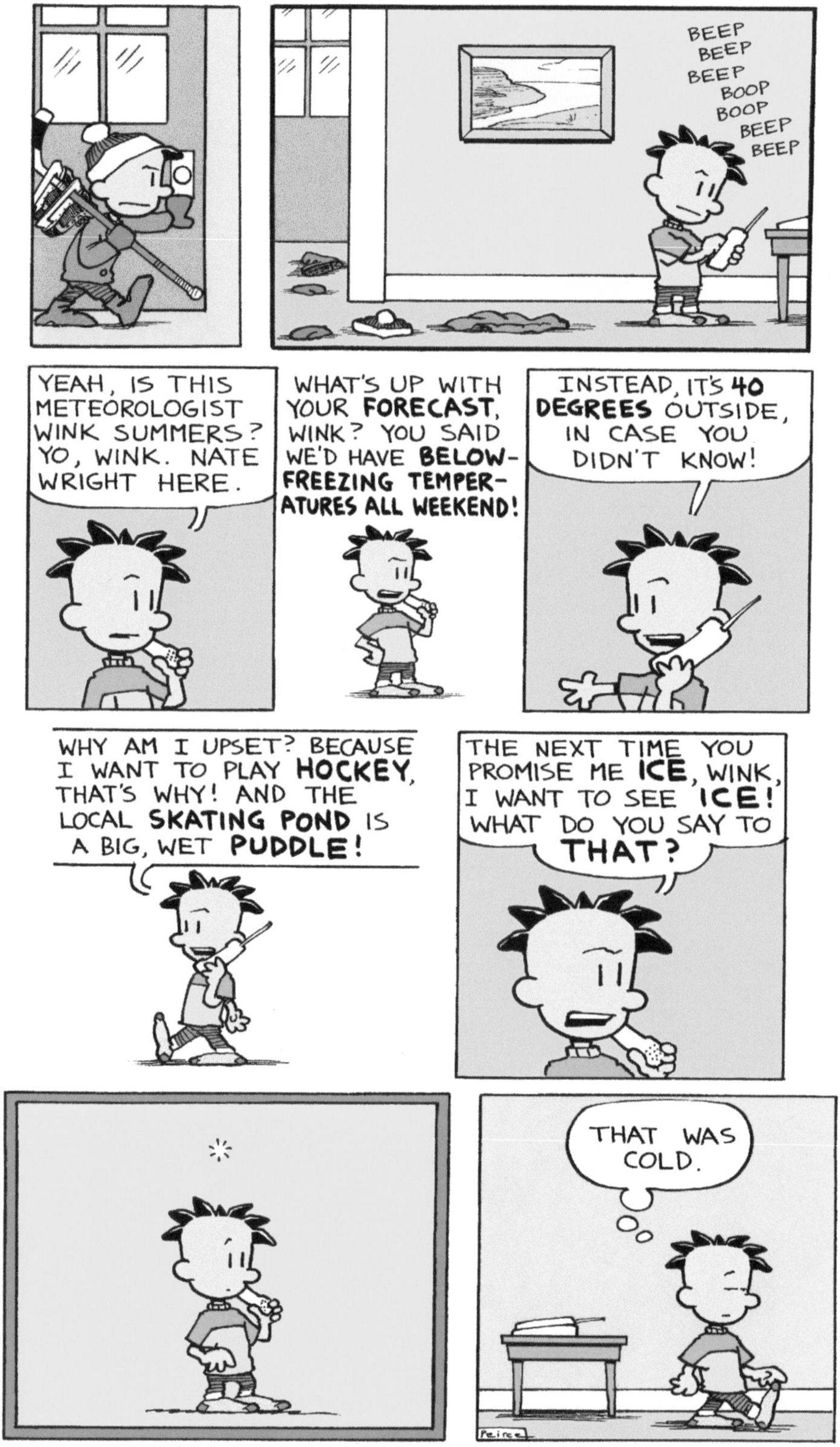
BEEP BEEP BEEP BOOP BOOP BEEP BEEP
YEAH, IS THIS METEOROLOGIST WINK SUMMERS? YO, WINK. NATE WRIGHT HERE.
WHAT'S UP WITH YOUR FORECAST, WINK? YOU SAID WE'D HAVE BELOW-FREEZING TEMPER-ATURES ALL WEEKEND!
INSTEAD, IT'S 40 DEGREES OUTSIDE, IN CASE YOU DIDN'T KNOW!
WHY AM I UPSET? BECAUSE I WANT TO PLAY HOCKEY, THAT'S WHY! AND THE LOCAL SKATING POND IS A BIG, WET PUDDLE!
THE NEXT TIME YOU PROMISE ME ICE, WINK, I WANT TO SEE ICE! WHAT DO YOU SAY TO THAT?
THAT WAS COLD.
Peirce

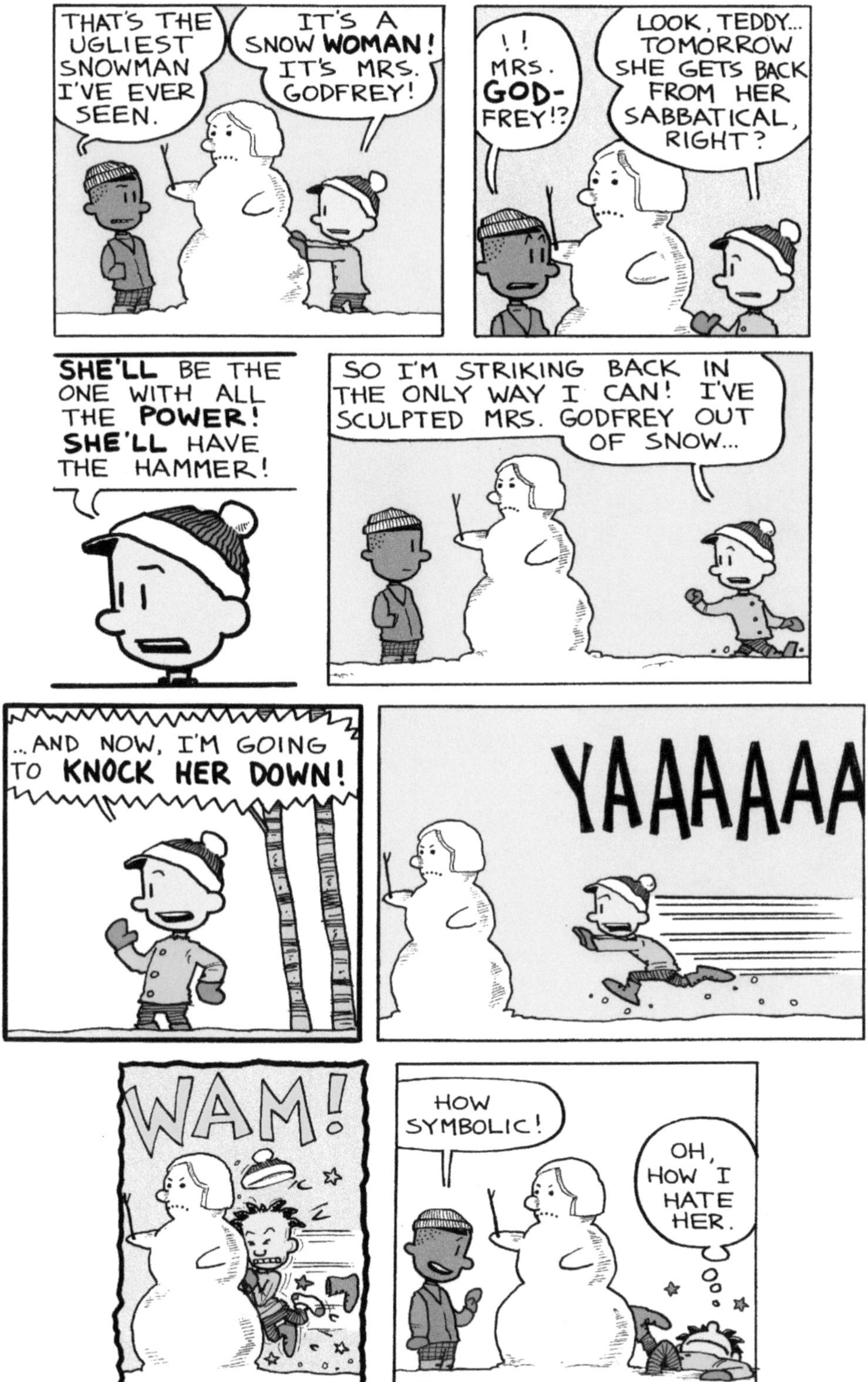
THAT'S THE UGLIEST SNOWMAN I'VE EVER SEEN.
IT'S A SNOW WOMAN! IT'S MRS. GODFREY!
! ! MRS. GOD-FREY!?
LOOK, TEDDY... TOMORROW SHE GETS BACK FROM HER SABBATICAL, RIGHT?
SHE'LL BE THE ONE WITH ALL THE POWER! SHE'LL HAVE THE HAMMER!
SO I'M STRIKING BACK IN THE ONLY WAY I CAN! I'VE SCULPTED MRS. GODFREY OUT OF SNOW...
...AND NOW, I'M GOING TO KNOCK HER DOWN!
YAAAAAA
WAM!
HOW SYMBOLIC!
OH, HOW I HATE HER.
Peirce

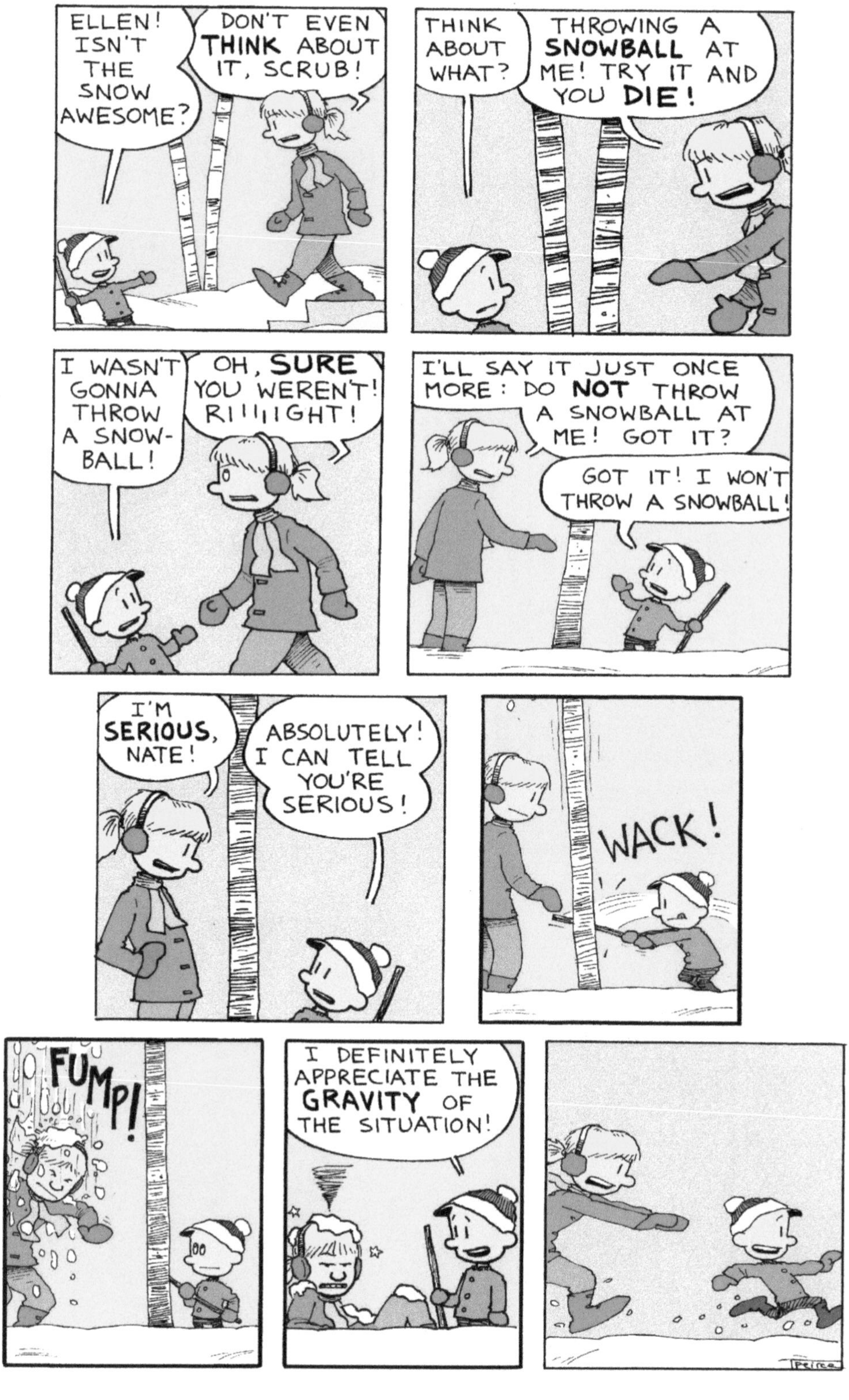
ELLEN! ISN'T THE SNOW AWESOME?
DON'T EVEN THINK ABOUT IT, SCRUB!
THINK ABOUT WHAT?
THROWING A SNOWBALL AT ME! TRY IT AND YOU DIE!
I WASN'T GONNA THROW A SNOW-BALL!
OH, SURE YOU WEREN'T! RIIIIIGHT!
I'LL SAY IT JUST ONCE MORE: DO NOT THROW A SNOWBALL AT ME! GOT IT?
GOT IT! I WON'T THROW A SNOWBALL!
I'M SERIOUS, NATE!
ABSOLUTELY! I CAN TELL YOU'RE SERIOUS!
WACK!
FUMP!
I DEFINITELY APPRECIATE THE GRAVITY OF THE SITUATION!
peirce

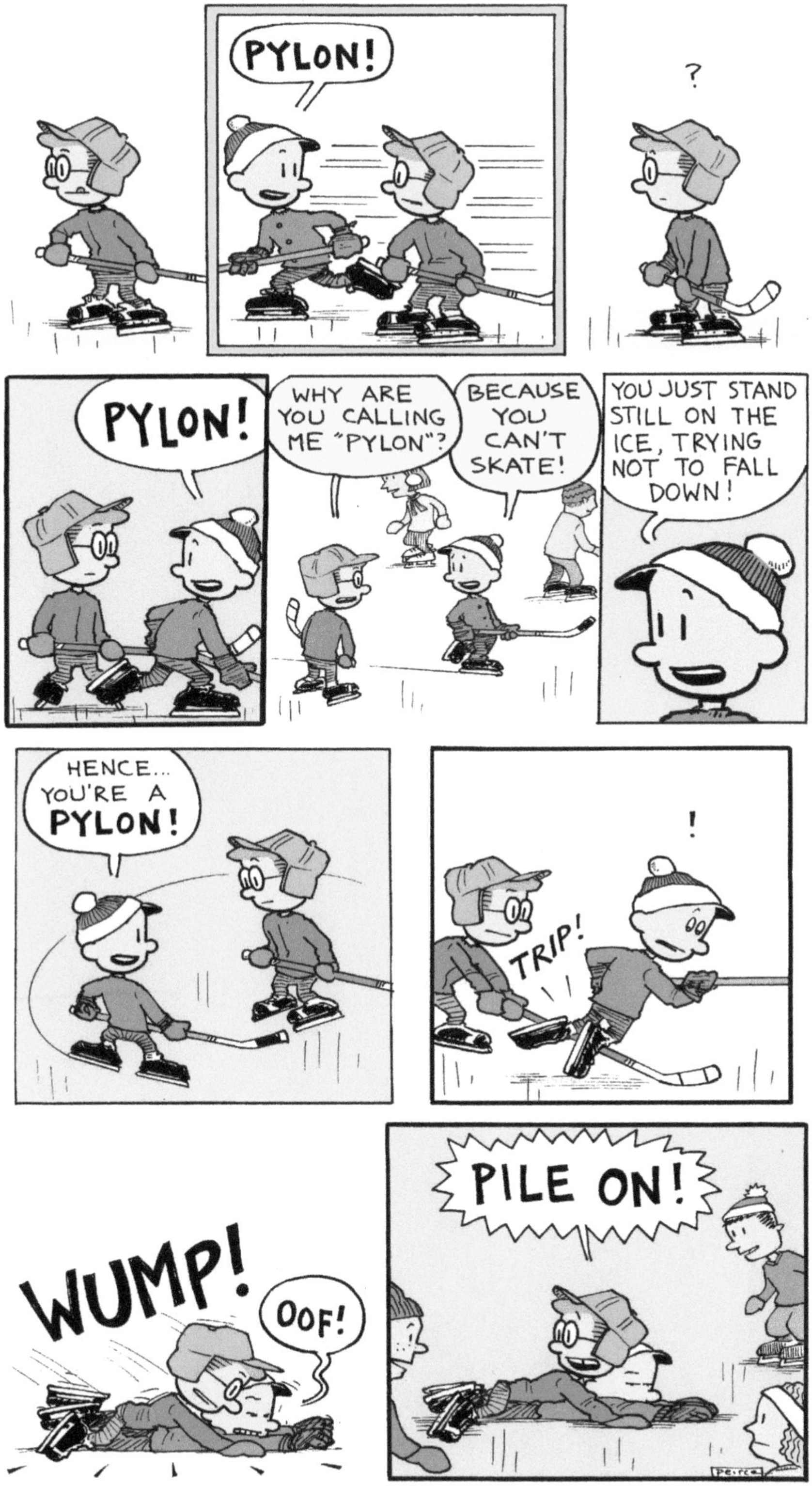
PYLON!
?
PYLON!
WHY ARE YOU CALLING ME "PYLON"?
BECAUSE YOU CAN'T SKATE!
YOU JUST STAND STILL ON THE ICE, TRYING NOT TO FALL DOWN!
HENCE... YOU'RE A PYLON!
!
TRIP!
WUMP!
OOF!
PILE ON!
peirce

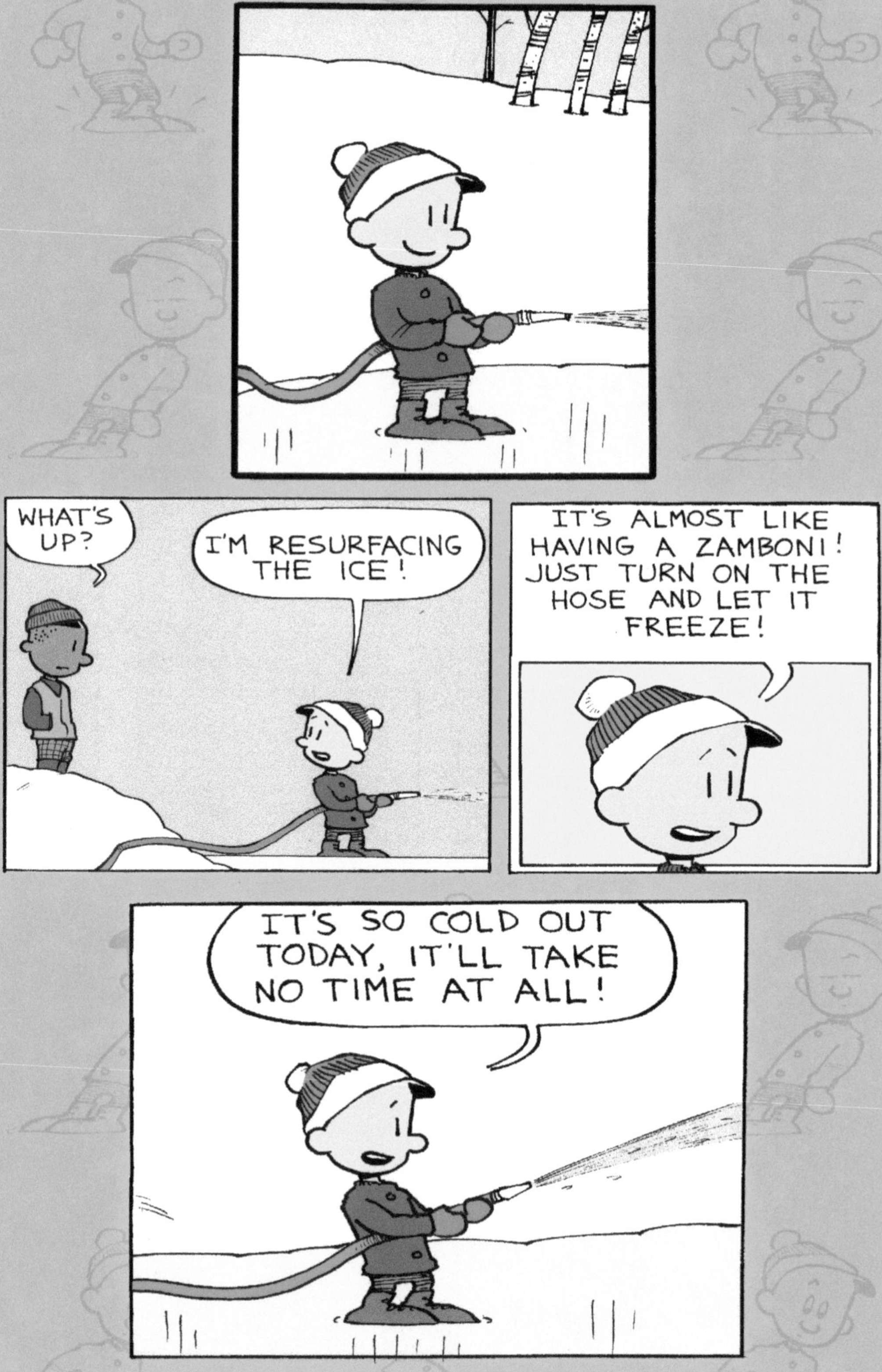
WHAT'S UP?
I'M RESURFACING THE ICE!
IT'S ALMOST LIKE HAVING A ZAMBONI! JUST TURN ON THE HOSE AND LET IT FREEZE!
IT'S SO COLD OUT TODAY, IT'LL TAKE NO TIME AT ALL!

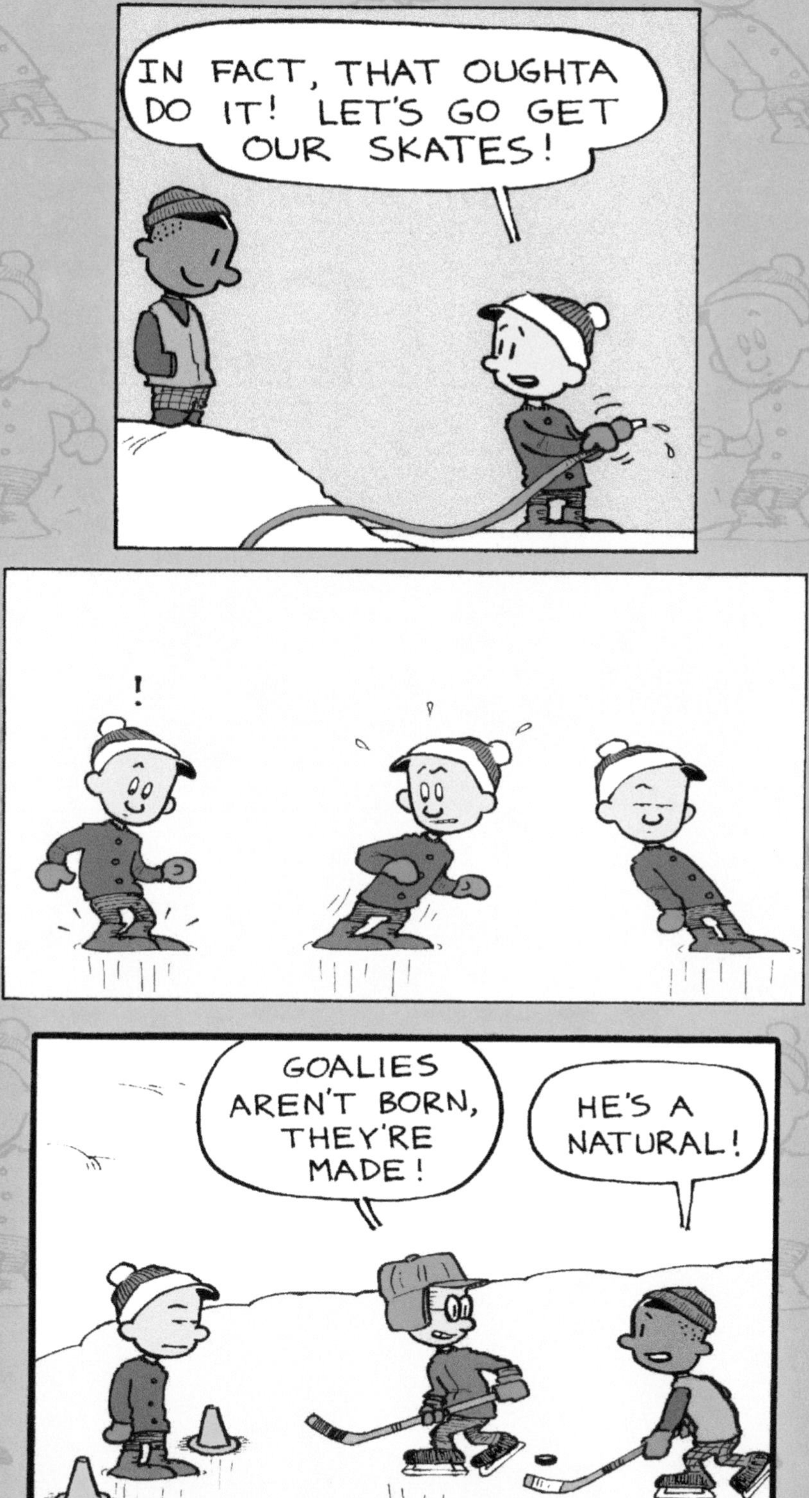
IN FACT, THAT OUGHTA DO IT! LET'S GO GET OUR SKATES!
!
GOALIES AREN'T BORN, THEY'RE MADE!
HE'S A NATURAL!

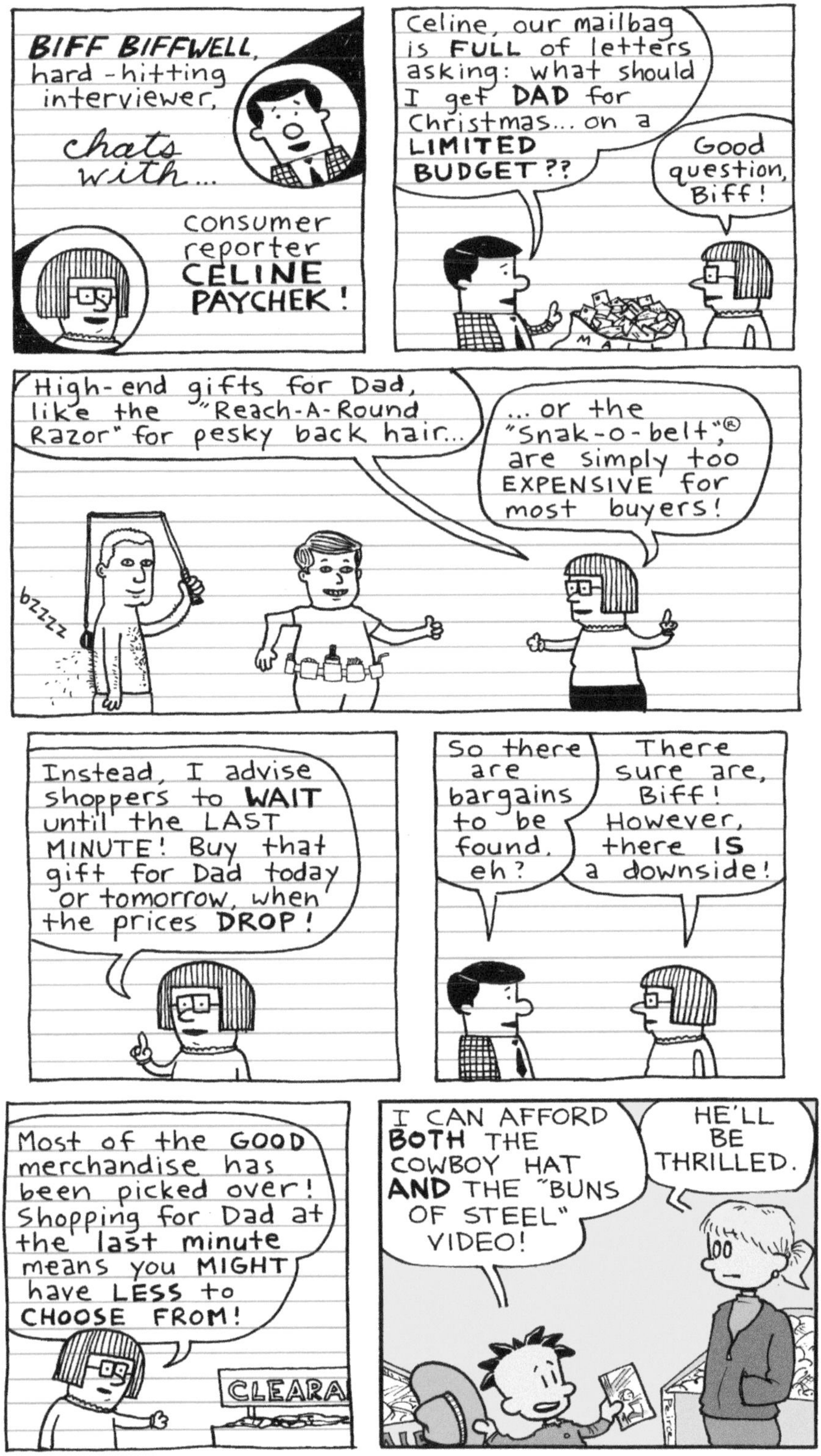
BIFF BIFFWELL, hard-hitting interviewer,
chats with...
consumer reporter CELINE PAYCHEK!
Celine, our mailbag is FULL of letters asking: what should I get DAD for Christmas... on a LIMITED BUDGET??
Good question, Biff!
MAIL
High-end gifts for Dad, like the "Reach-A-Round Razor" for pesky back hair...
...or the "Snak-o-belt"® are simply too EXPENSIVE for most buyers!
bzzzz
Instead, I advise shoppers to WAIT until the LAST MINUTE! Buy that gift for Dad today or tomorrow, when the prices DROP!
So there are bargains to be found, eh?
There sure are, Biff! However, there IS a downside!
Most of the GOOD merchandise has been picked over! Shopping for Dad at the last minute means you MIGHT have LESS to CHOOSE FROM!
CLEARA
I CAN AFFORD BOTH THE COWBOY HAT AND THE "BUNS OF STEEL" VIDEO!
HE'LL BE THRILLED.

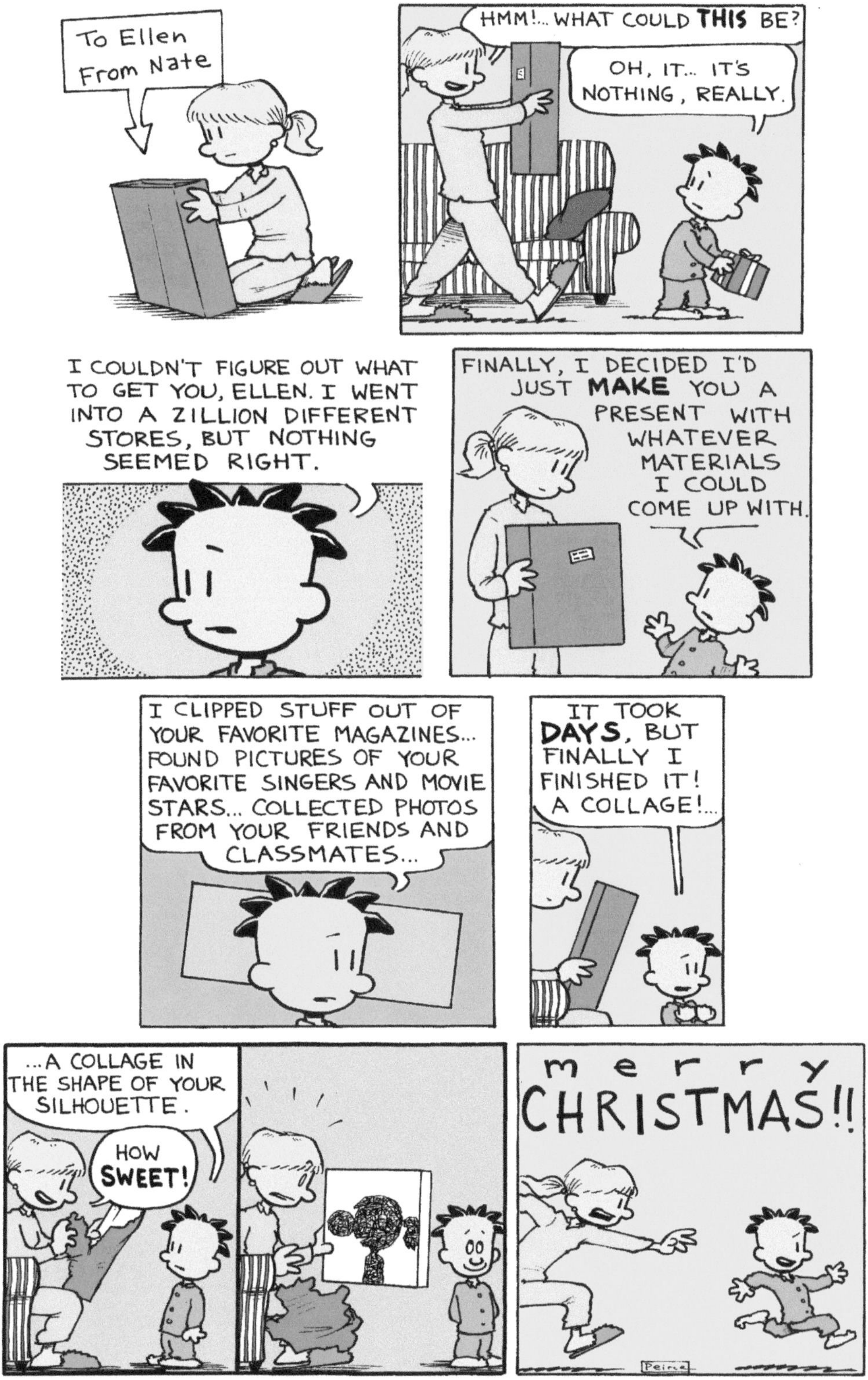

To Ellen
From Nate
HMM!... WHAT COULD **THIS** BE?
OH, IT... IT'S NOTHING, REALLY.
I COULDN'T FIGURE OUT WHAT TO GET YOU, ELLEN. I WENT INTO A ZILLION DIFFERENT STORES, BUT NOTHING SEEMED RIGHT.
FINALLY, I DECIDED I'D JUST **MAKE** YOU A PRESENT WITH WHATEVER MATERIALS I COULD COME UP WITH.
I CLIPPED STUFF OUT OF YOUR FAVORITE MAGAZINES... FOUND PICTURES OF YOUR FAVORITE SINGERS AND MOVIE STARS... COLLECTED PHOTOS FROM YOUR FRIENDS AND CLASSMATES...
IT TOOK **DAYS**, BUT FINALLY I FINISHED IT! A COLLAGE!...
...A COLLAGE IN THE SHAPE OF YOUR SILHOUETTE.
HOW **SWEET**!
merry CHRISTMAS!!
Peirce

Celebrity INTERVIEW!

with: BIFF BIFFWELL!

Friends, I'm chatting today with the big fella himself... SANTA CLAUS!

Season's greetings, Biff!

Santa, I've often wondered... what's the most FRUSTRATING part of your job?

These LETTERS, Biff!

Take THIS one, for example: a boy named NATE WRIGHT has asked me to bring him a DOG!

Sounds simple enough!

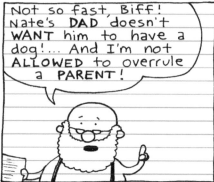

Not so fast, Biff! Nate's DAD doesn't WANT him to have a dog!... And I'm not ALLOWED to overrule a PARENT!

That DOES sound frustrating!

And UNFAIR! Just another case of a parent being SELFISH!

So what do you do? Punish Nate's Dad?

Hey, I'm Santa Claus! It's not in my job description to punish parents!

So instead, I pick up the phone and call my friend MOTHER NATURE!

Mother Nature? What can SHE do?

222

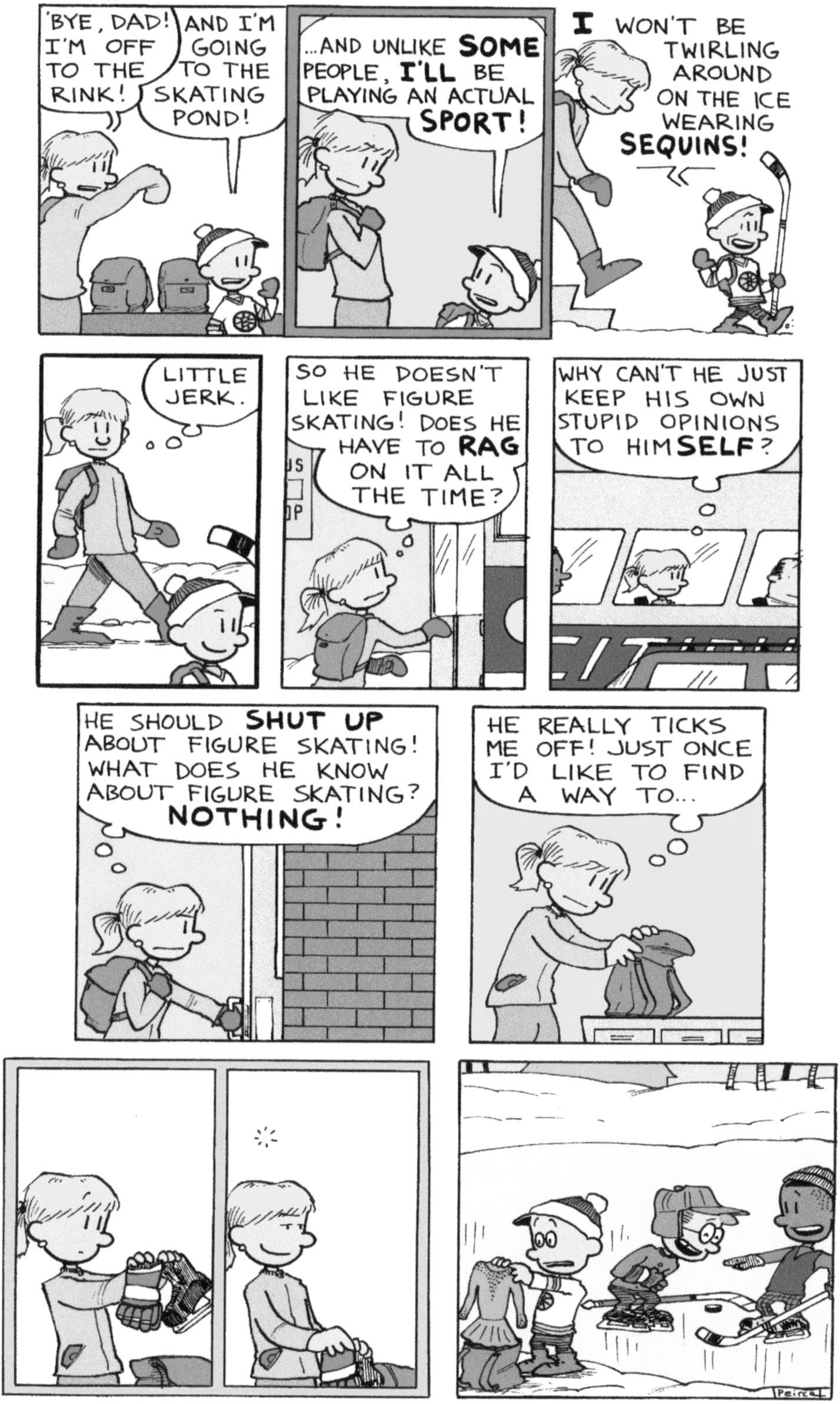
'BYE, DAD! I'M OFF TO THE RINK!
AND I'M GOING TO THE SKATING POND!
...AND UNLIKE SOME PEOPLE, I'LL BE PLAYING AN ACTUAL SPORT!
I WON'T BE TWIRLING AROUND ON THE ICE WEARING SEQUINS!
LITTLE JERK.
SO HE DOESN'T LIKE FIGURE SKATING! DOES HE HAVE TO RAG ON IT ALL THE TIME?
WHY CAN'T HE JUST KEEP HIS OWN STUPID OPINIONS TO HIMSELF?
HE SHOULD SHUT UP ABOUT FIGURE SKATING! WHAT DOES HE KNOW ABOUT FIGURE SKATING? NOTHING!
HE REALLY TICKS ME OFF! JUST ONCE I'D LIKE TO FIND A WAY TO...
Peirce

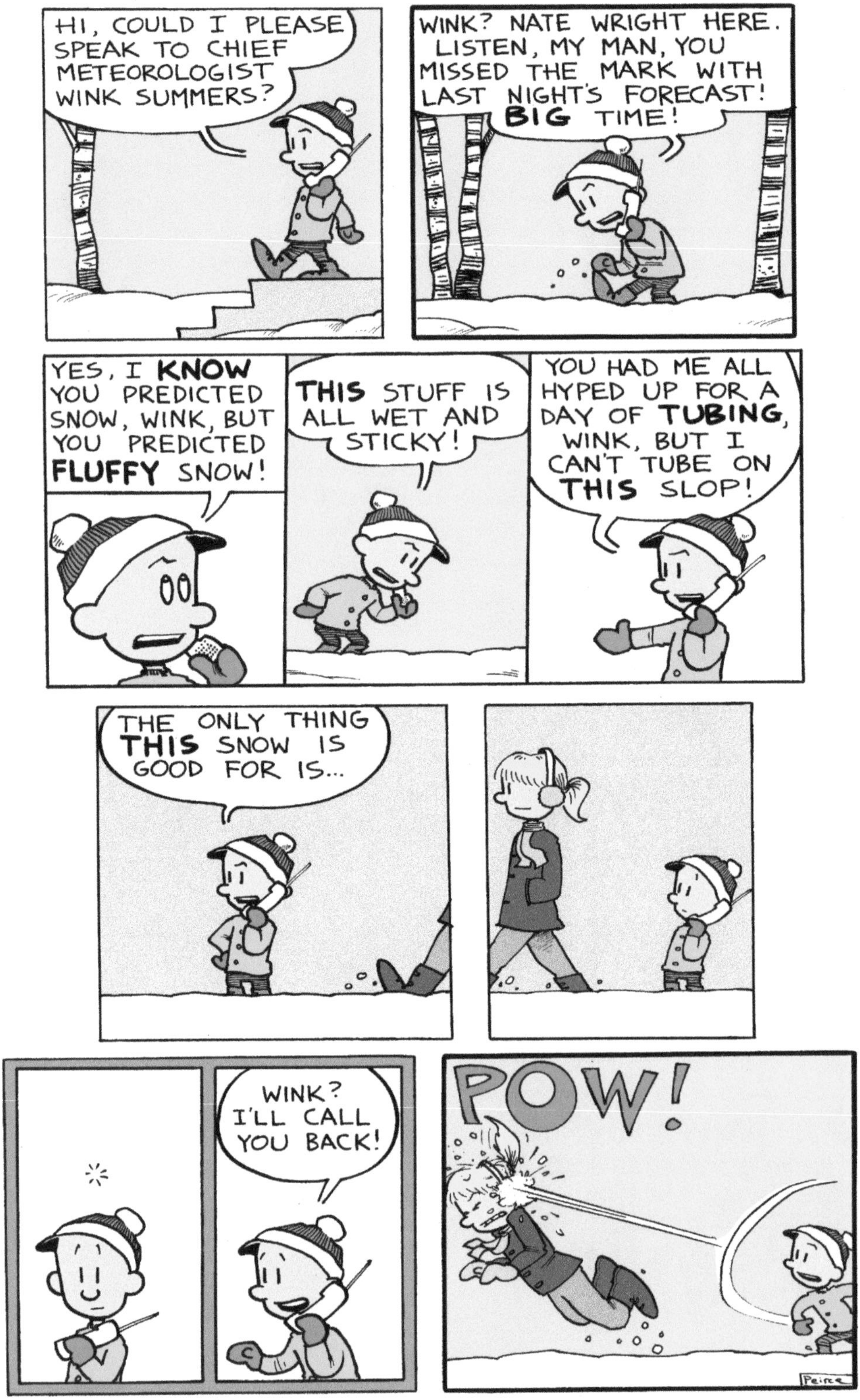
HI, COULD I PLEASE SPEAK TO CHIEF METEOROLOGIST WINK SUMMERS?
WINK? NATE WRIGHT HERE. LISTEN, MY MAN, YOU MISSED THE MARK WITH LAST NIGHT'S FORECAST! BIG TIME!
YES, I KNOW YOU PREDICTED SNOW, WINK, BUT YOU PREDICTED FLUFFY SNOW!
THIS STUFF IS ALL WET AND STICKY!
YOU HAD ME ALL HYPED UP FOR A DAY OF TUBING, WINK, BUT I CAN'T TUBE ON THIS SLOP!
THE ONLY THING THIS SNOW IS GOOD FOR IS...
WINK? I'LL CALL YOU BACK!
POW!
Peirce

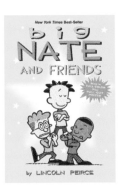

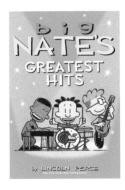

CPSIA information can be obtained
at www.ICGtesting.com
Printed in the USA
LVHW071820090622
720871LV00007B/272